Emma Blair was bo[...] Devon. She is the au[...] novels including *Scarlet Ribbons* and *Flower of Scotland*, both of which were shortlisted for the Romantic Novel of the Year Award.

For information about the author, visit
www.emmablair.com

Also by Emma Blair

HESTER DARK
NELLIE WILDCHILD
THIS SIDE OF HEAVEN
JESSIE GRAY
THE PRINCESS OF POOR STREET
WHEN DREAMS COME TRUE
A MOST DETERMINED WOMAN
THE BLACKBIRD'S TALE
MAGGIE JORDAN
SCARLET RIBBONS
THE WATER MEADOWS
THE SWEETEST THING
THE DAFFODIL SEA
PASSIONATE TIMES
HALF HIDDEN
FLOWER OF SCOTLAND
AN APPLE FROM EDEN
WILD STRAWBERRIES
GOODNIGHT, SWEET PRINCE
FORGET-ME-NOT
MOONLIT EYES
FINDING HAPPINESS
TWILIGHT TIME
LITTLE WHITE LIES
THREE BITES OF THE CHERRY
SWEETHEARTS

EMMA BLAIR OMNIBUS

Where No Man Cries

Street Song

sphere

SPHERE

This omnibus edition first published in Great Britain by
Sphere in 2007
Emma Blair Omnibus Copyright © Emma Blair 2007

Previously published separately:
Where No Man Cries first published in Great Britain
in 1982 by Arrow Books
Published by Warner Books 1997
Reprinted 1997, 1998, 2000
Reprinted by Time Warner Paperbacks in 2003
Copyright © 1982 Emma Blair

Street Song first published in Great Britain in 1986 by
Sphere Books Ltd
Reprinted 1988, 1989 (twice), 1990, 1991, 1992 (twice)
Reprinted by Warner Books in 1993
Reprinted by Time Warner Paperbacks in 2003
Reprinted by Time Warner Books in 2005
Reprinted by Sphere in 2007
Copyright © 1986 Emma Blair

A CIP catalogue record for this book is available from the British Library.

Papers used by Sphere are natural, recyclable products made from
wood grown in sustainable forests and certified in accordance with
the rules of the Forest Stewardship Council.

ISBN 978-0-7515-4007-9

Printed and bound in Great Britain by Mackays of Chatham Ltd
Paper supplied by Hellefoss AS, Norway

Sphere
An imprint of
Little, Brown Book Group
Brettenham House
Lancaster Place
London WC2E 7EN

A Member of the Hachette Livre Group of Companies

www.littlebrown.co.uk

Where No Man Cries

For Ina

Part I

The Dear Green Place

1921–22

1

With a final rub of the cloth Carrie McBain finished work on the grate. Sighing with contentment she sat back on her haunches and studied her handiwork. Black-leading the fireplace had always been one of her jobs until she got married and moved out of the house. Occasionally when she was back visiting, she still did it for her mother.

The windows were open and a strong shaft of warm August sunlight was beaming into the room. There were dust motes in the air which was filled with the sweet smell of grass and the perfume given off by the wild plants growing down by the river.

Carrie ran a hand over her distended stomach. It wouldn't be long now till the baby came – a fortnight, according to the doctor.

Carefully she wiped her hands on a rag before laboriously climbing to her feet. She had a pain in her back that had been with her for several months now, but it only really gripped her if she moved suddenly.

Crossing to a window she stared out at a man fishing in the River Cart. The man's long rod flicked lazily as he waded in close to the bank.

The river had once been well known for its salmon fishing, but that had been in the days before Armstrong's had been built. Now, in 1921, the ever-growing amount of effluence pouring out from the engineering firm was slowly but inexorably choking the life out of the river.

9

The salmon that survived were few.

Still, Carrie thought grimly, rather a poisoned river and families with food in their bellies than fat fish and starving folk.

She sighed and massaged her stomach. The wean was kicking again. There were times when it kicked so hard a limb would protrude quite plainly.

'Are you all right in there?' Winnie, a bustling, stout woman shouted from the kitchen.

'Aye, I'm fine, Ma!' Carrie called back. It wouldn't be long now till they stopped for a cup of tea. She was looking forward to that.

Carrie was always pleased to be back in the house in Tallon Street where she'd been brought up. Not that it was a house in the proper sense, being a three-bedroomed flat three-flights up. The word 'house' was a euphemism. In Glasgow everyone lives in a house whether it's a mansion in Kelvinside or a rat-infested single end in the Gorbals.

There had been a time when the Chisholms were tenement dwellers, but Big Donald, Carrie's father, was an industrious man with an eye always open to bettering the family lot. Thanks to his efforts they had been one of the first to move into Tallon Street, superior accommodation with every apartment boasting an inside toilet and bath, when it had been built by the Corporation.

Big Donald enjoyed his drink and tobacco. The difference between him and many of his workmates was that he knew when to call a halt. Never once had Winnie gone without money for the rent or food for the table because Donald's wages had been blown in the pub. That was something of which very few working-class women in Glasgow could boast. Donald Chisholm was a formidable man. A strict disciplinarian who believed that children should be seen and not heard.

When the children were young, God help any of them foolish enough to cheek Winnie in his hearing. Retribution, in the form of his leather belt across their backsides, was swift and painful.

Yet it was this same Donald who nearly always slipped his children sweeties and other goodies along with their Saturday pennies, for he dearly loved his wife and family although it would never have entered his head to actually say so to them. Amongst Glasgow folk that just wasn't the done thing. Any man foolish enough to do so, unless totally drunk and maudlin with it, would be considered soft and a jessie.

For Donald, love was a practical thing. Something to be practised rather than talked about. When Harriet, his eldest daughter, had had the croup as a baby he had thought it the natural thing to stay up night after night helping Winnie nurse her, while continuing to go to work each morning. He belonged to a hardy breed who believed in action rather than words.

Carrie's man, John, was another out of the same mould. In the Armstrong foundry, where he worked under Donald, he was well liked and had a name as a grafter.

Carrie thought of her husband now as she watched the fisherman wade amongst the rhubarb-type plants which grew in profusion along the river bank and in the shallows. They'd been married two years and this child was their first. She was desperately hoping for a boy, sure that a male child was what John wanted. But her husband wasn't to be drawn on the subject. He would only say that if the child was born healthy then he'd be pleased well enough.

Warmth flooded through Carrie as she thought of that. Like her mother she'd been lucky enough to find herself a good man. It was a fact she well appreciated.

She was about to turn and make for the bathroom to wash her hands when she heard a key scrape in the outside lock. When the front door closed it was done gently as though the person who'd entered was a stranger to the house.

Carrie frowned when she heard her father's voice speaking in low undertones. A swift glance at the clock on the mantelpiece confirmed that it was far too early for him to be home for his dinner. It was only ten thirty, a full hour and a half before the works' hooter was due to sound the break.

Besides, if it had been dinner time, then John and her younger brother, Hugh, would have been with him. John always came to the house in Tallon Street for his midday meal on the days when she was visiting.

Something was wrong. It had to be. Fear clutched her insides as she waddled to the door. It opened and Donald entered. Winnie, looking completely stunned, was behind him.

Carrie came up short when she saw her father's grim expression.

'There's been an accident at the foundry, lass,' he said.

'Hugh?'

'No, John.'

The breath caught in her throat and the baby fluttered in her belly. She'd automatically assumed that any accident must involve Hugh. He was such a daft lad at times, and at seventeen just at an age to do something silly and get himself hurt.

But John was always so careful. It had never entered her mind that something might happen to him. 'Is he bad?' she demanded.

For a moment Donald baulked at what he had to say. Then the words came, slowly, evenly and without emphasis. 'John's dead,' he said.

Carrie felt as though she'd been punched squarely on the forehead. She staggered back, her hands coming up to clutch at the life moving within her. It was some sort of horrible joke. It had to be.

'There, there lass,' said Donald coming quickly forward and taking her in his arms. His large, work-worn hands patted her hair.

'Dead?' The word slipped from her mouth to hang suspended in the air.

'Aye,' Donald replied softly.

Winnie sobbed and stuck a fist in her mouth. Her large

bosom heaved in sympathy.

'Oh, my God!' Carrie cried, her face crumpling into a concertina of pain and tears. Her whole body shook as she clung desperately to her father.

'Let it come. Just let it all come out,' Donald soothed, wishing he'd had the presence of mind to bring a drink home with him. If anyone ever needed one it was Carrie at this moment.

'I've got to go to him,' Carrie said suddenly. She wrenched herself from her father's embrace and staggered towards the door.

'Not yet! Not until they've had a chance to sort him out a wee bit,' Donald called after her.

Carrie whirled, her eyes filled with horror. 'What happened?' she demanded harshly.

Donald was suddenly reticent. 'Never you mind for the moment,' he replied. 'There's time enough to go into that.'

'I want to know! I want to know!' she screamed. Then she flew back to her father and thumped him on the chest. 'Tell me! Tell me!'

For once in his life Donald was at a complete loss. He glanced beseechingly across at his wife.

Winnie hurried over to take Carrie by the arm. 'Get a hold of yourself now!' she said sternly. 'This is no way to carry on.'

Carrie was hysterical as she continued pounding on her father's chest with her free hand. It seemed to her that a great chasm was threatening to engulf her.

'Tell me! Tell me! Tell me!' she screeched over and over again.

Donald knew his younger daughter only too well. Having worked herself up into this state only the truth would now suffice. 'John was crushed,' he said.

Carrie froze. 'Crushed?' Then the enormity of what that meant, in a foundry context, hit her. Her eyes rolled upwards and she dropped to the floor in a dead faint.

Winnie bent to attend to her daughter, at the same time telling Donald to hurry through to the kitchen and get some water. He left the room at a run, surprisingly nimble on his feet for such a big man.

Carrie's face was clammy to touch and there were large drops of sweat on her forehead. Her skin was a dirty white with a greenish tinge to it.

Winnie was using the hem of her dress to wipe away the sweat when Carrie's eyes blinked open. 'The pain!' she groaned.

Carrie's back arched and her body convulsed.

Winnie knew immediately what was happening. Taking a deep breath, she told herself to keep calm. When Donald returned, she took the cup from him and held it to Carrie's mouth. While Carrie drank she said, 'Go downstairs and see if Mrs Cooper is at home. If she is, then ask her to come up right away. When you've done that, run for the doctor. Tell him Carrie's started having her wean.'

Donald didn't bother asking his wife if she was sure. A man used to issuing orders, he also knew how to obey them. He rose at once from his kneeling position and tore from the room.

'Do you think you can make your bed?' Winnie asked.

Carrie gritted her teeth as another violent pain wracked her insides. Her breath came in pants as she waited for the pain to subside. When it was on the retreat she nodded.

One flight down, Big Donald was hammering on Mrs Cooper's door. She was a widow who lived directly below the Chisholms along with her teenage son, Robert. Although she had a name for sticking her nose into other people's affairs, she was also considered to be a reliable, trustworthy and good neighbour when needed.

When Mrs Cooper finally answered Donald, he hurriedly explained to her why she was wanted upstairs. Before he'd finished speaking she was undoing her pinny.

With a backward shout over his shoulder that he was off for the doctor, he clattered on his way. His heavy, tackety workboots struck sparks from the stone stairs as he ran.

By this time Winnie had managed to get Carrie into bed and stripped of some of her clothes. When Mrs Cooper arrived the two of them worked Carrie's dress up over her head and slipped it off that way.

Carrie stared up at the whitewashed ceiling. There was a far-away, glazed look in her eyes indicating she was in a state of shock.

Winnie and Mrs Cooper both knew from the frequency of the contractions that the birth was imminent and were praying the doctor would arrive in time. Still, if he didn't then they'd just have to deliver the baby themselves. It wouldn't be the first time either of them had done that.

'Poor lamb,' Mrs Cooper crooned, stroking the side of Carrie's cheek.

'Crushed,' Carrie said hollowly. Tears welled in her eyes and streamed down the sides of her face on to the pillow.

Mrs Cooper was left with Carrie while Winnie boiled some water and then ransacked her linen drawer for old sheets and towels.

Carrie threw back her head and screamed, not aware that her fingers, hooked like talons, were digging into Mrs Cooper's arm.

Between contractions Carrie mumbled her dead husband's name.

Mrs Cooper's heart went out to Carrie. She knew only too well what it was like to lose your man. It was six long, lonely years since she'd lost hers.

Donald burst into the surgery and demanded to see the doctor right away. The receptionist took one look at his frantic face and scurried off down a passageway to the consulting room.

Donald gulped in air. His chest was on fire, and he felt as though he'd swallowed a mouthful of molten metal. The thought of metal brought him back to the accident and those last few seconds before the five-ton casting crushed the life out of John McBain.

He'd been at the other end of the foundry and hadn't witnessed what had happened. What he did know was that the casting, being moved by crane, had veered and yawed out of control to slam into John who had been walking along a gantry.

Death had been instantaneous.

The question was why John was up in that particular gantry in the first place. The gantry had been declared unsafe the previous week and out of bounds until it was made secure.

Donald's thoughts were interrupted by the receptionist telling him to go through to the consulting room where the doctor would see him.

Donald was slightly in awe of Dr Robertson for no other reason than the fact the man spoke with a pronounced southern English accent.

Donald stood deferentially with cap in hand while he explained what had happened at the foundry and the effect the news of this had had on Carrie.

Before Donald had finished his story Robertson had already begun packing his black bag.

Hurrying through to the waiting room, Robertson issued a stream of instructions to the receptionist and then, with Donald hard behind him, he rushed out into the street to his car.

'Get in, man!' Robertson barked as Donald hesitated, unsure of whether or not he was to accompany the doctor.

Robertson cranked the car and it immediately burst into life. Seconds later they were chugging in the direction of Tallon Street.

In Carrie's old bedroom Winnie was holding one hand and Mrs Cooper the other while Carrie screamed, her legs jerking upwards and in towards her swollen torso. Dilation was already well advanced.

Winnie heard the rattle of a key in the outside lock and breathed a sigh of relief when, seconds later, she heard Robertson's cultured tones.

'It's yourself then, doctor,' Winnie said gratefully as

Robertson breezed into the room.

Behind Robertson's back, Winnie and Mrs Cooper exchanged glances. Although unspoken between them, they both knew something was wrong with Carrie's labour.

Donald had hung back in the hallway where he now lit a cigarette. This would be his station until it was all over. Here he would be on hand should they need him to do anything.

Robertson washed his hands in a steaming bowl of water provided for that purpose. Above the well-trimmed military moustache the keen, darting eyes were taking everything in. He had already noted that although trying to appear to the contrary, both Winnie and Mrs Cooper were uneasy about something.

'Now then, Carrie,' he said in his best bedside manner, 'let's just see what's what.' He sat on the edge of the bed and began to probe carefully with his fingers.

Carrie lay with her eyes closed. In her mind what she was seeing was a day not long before she and John had been married when he'd taken part in the all Glasgow tug-of-war championships. She'd been there cheering him on as his team, representing Armstrong's, had fought a valiant final contest with the City of Glasgow Police.

In the end the Armstrong team, amidst much shouting and general hullabalooing, had finally managed to pull their opponents over the line to win the match and championship.

The winners had received medals, silver inlaid with red and white enamel and topped by a scroll, which had later been inscribed with each of their names on the back.

John's medal was in the top drawer of the sideboard in McLellan Street: it was taken out every so often and polished. John was fond of saying it was the only thing he'd ever won. Now he'd never win anything else.

Carrie sobbed and a lump rose in her throat. Then the pain was back and there was no time to think of medals or anything else except the terrible, searing agony doing its damndest to split her in two.

Robertson was a worried man. His probing had confirmed that there were complications with the impending birth, a fact that had not been evident when he'd last examined Carrie a few weeks previously.

The baby's head, upon entering the pelvis, had failed to rotate through the required 180 degress, resulting in it now being in what was known as a persistent posterior position. He knew that if the birth went ahead this way he'd lose the baby for sure and probably Carrie as well.

As he wiped his hands on a towel, he was only too aware of the older women's eyes on him. He smiled and nodded reassuringly. Then, bending again over Carrie, he desperately cudgelled his brains for a way to remedy or at least help the situation.

Miracles do still happen, and that day one happened for Carrie McBain. Minutes before the baby started to emerge, its head suddenly rotated into the right position.

The first Robertson knew of his was when the head had appeared sufficiently for him to see that the forehead was facing downwards. He was suddenly bathed in warm, sticky sweat as he awaited further developments.

'Oh, Christ!' Carrie moaned. A trickle of bright red blood spilled from a corner of her mouth, the result of her having bitten her tongue during a particularly violent contraction.

'You're doing fine,' Winnie said.

'Just keep pushing,' Mrs Cooper added.

The baby's face slid fully into view and, as it did so, it turned sideways so that it was facing to the left.

Robertson heaved a sigh of relief. Everything was now normal.

The baby's face was a bright blue colour which, together with the black hair lying plastered to its head, was smeared with a white cheesy substance known as vernix. The face, screwed up in an angry grimace, also bore streaks of blood.

Carrie's body suddenly relaxed and she sucked in breath after breath. 'Is it over?' she asked in a thin, strained voice.

'Not quite,' Robertson replied. But you're half way there.'

The contractions started again almost immediately. Carrie's body seemed to explode from the inside as first one and then the other of the baby's shoulders emerged.

Her fingernails raked the bedsheet. The pain was now almost unbearable, and she felt that at any moment she was going to slip into the blessed relief of unconsciousness.

Not yet. Not yet, she told herself, over and over again. She wanted the baby fully born before she allowed herself the luxury of oblivion.

It crossed her mind then she might be dying. It seemed to her there was a warm blackness beckoning, and if she only allowed herself to be embraced by this all-enveloping calm she would never again waken in the world she knew. It would be so easy to slip over. John was waiting for her after all. They would be together again, this time for eternity.

The baby, a voice seemed to whisper in her ear, don't forget about the wee one. It'll need someone to look after it. Don't leave it all alone like John once was. He'd be furious to think you even contemplated the idea.

'Push Carrie! Push!' Robertson thundered.

Carrie grunted and did her best to obey, but the message being sent so urgently by her brain didn't seem to be getting through to her body.

Winnie wiped a fresh trickle of blood from the side of Carrie's mouth, while in her mind she relived the four births she'd undergone herself.

In the hallway Donald turned to face the outside door when it opened to admit Hugh. The boy's face was haggard underneath the dirt from the foundry. His brother-in-law was the first man he'd ever seen killed.

'Well?' Donald demanded quietly.

'The undertakers came and took him away. They want

to know whether he's to stay at their place or go up in a coffin to McLellan Street.'

Donald ran a hand over his face. This decision wasn't his to make. Only Carrie should decide what was to be done. That was her right.

Hugh jerked a thumb towards the bedroom. 'What's going on in there?'

In a low voice Donald told his son about the shock of John's death bringing on the baby. Hugh paled when a fresh bout of screaming rent the air.

Gratefully Hugh accepted a Willy Woodbine from his father and lit up. As he smoked he thought of the mangled mess which only that morning had been John McBain. In a macabre way it had fascinated him to discover the human body contained so much blood. The area round the gantry where the accident had taken place had been awash with the stuff. The body itself bore no resemblance to what it had once been.

The shock of seeing John's remains had been over-whelming, and for a few terrible minutes he'd thought he was going to throw up. Not that anyone would have blamed him if he had.

It amazed him to realize he was hungry. Death and birth might be all around him, but it certainly hadn't affected his stomach any. He wondered if he should sneak into the kitchen and make himself a jam piece. One thing was certain: there wasn't going to be any dinner that day.

'Do you think I should go and get Harriet?' he asked. His elder sister worked as a machinist in a clothing factory about half a mile away. Carrie had also worked there before having to leave because of her advancing pregnancy.

Big Donald shook his head. There was no point in taking the lassie away from her work when there were already enough people on hand. Besides, Harriet was naturally squeamish about certain things and would probably have ended up being more of a hindrance than a help.

In the bedroom Carrie gave a long drawn-out sigh as her body completed the ejection. The baby, large and raw-looking, slid neatly into Robertson's waiting hands.

Winnie craned forward. 'It's a wee boy!' she breathed.

'A wee boy,' Carrie repeated.

Mrs Cooper stuck her head round the door and called the news to Donald and Hugh.

Donald beamed and smacked his meaty hands together. 'That's rare!' he said.

Winnie and Mrs Cooper both laughed when the baby opened his mouth and gave a lusty cry.

'Is he . . . all right?' Carrie asked. It was the one question every newly delivered mother feels compelled to ask, and the one they dread to have answered in the negative.

Robertson thoroughly checked the baby's fingers, toes and external organs. 'He's a smasher,' he replied eventually. 'There's absolutely nothing wrong with him.'

Carrie nodded gratefully, the ghost of a smile hovering round her bloodless lips.

Robertson tied off the baby's umbilical cord and then handed him over to his grandmother.

Winnie swathed the baby, first in a torn-off piece of clean cotton sheet and then in a shawl that had been in the family for generations. Every one of her family had worn that shawl. It was part of Chisholm tradition.

Mrs Cooper washed Carrie down and then, with Robertson's help, changed the bedding. When Carrie had been made decent, Donald and Hugh were allowed into the room.

Donald stared in wonderment at the baby cradled in his wife's arms. The miracle of birth never ceased to amaze him.

The baby's eyelids flickered and jerked open. Eyes of the palest blue stared out at the world for the first time.

The mouth twisted and seemed to be preparing to cry again, so Winnie started humming a lullaby that had long been a great favourite of her. The mouth immediately slackened and settled back into repose.

Carrie felt more tired than she'd ever done before in her life. It was as though every particle of energy in her body had been carefully and methodically drained away.

The blackness was behind her now. She no longer felt drawn to what it had to offer. Her time for dying hadn't come yet.

Hugh was bursting with pride. He would have liked to hold the baby but didn't think that the manly thing to do. Instead he stuck his chest out and nodded knowingly as though he'd been through this sort of thing many times before.

'Please?' Carrie asked, holding out her hands.

Staring down at her newborn son, it seemed to her that his blue eyes were drinking her in, studying her every feature for future reference. But of course she knew that to be pure imagination on her part.

'He's to be called Angus,' she said. 'That was the name John and I had agreed on.'

Donald and Winnie nodded their approval. They knew that Angus had been the name of John's father who'd died before John was born.

History tragically repeating itself, Donald thought, somehow managing to retain the smile on his face.

'Angus,' Carrie said again. Laying her head back on the pillow, she closed her eyes.

A few seconds later both mother and son were fast asleep.

Mrs Cooper tiptoed from the room to put the kettle on for a cup of tea.

2

The day of the funeral dawned a scorcher. From horizon to horizon the sky was unmarred by even the vaguest wisp of cloud. The sun hung heavy and fat, looking like the centre of a perfectly fried egg.

Head bowed and supported on either side by Donald and Hugh, Carrie stepped aboard the hired black carriage which would take them to the cemetery.

All the curtains and blinds in Tallon Street had been drawn as a mark of respect. A neighbour from across the way stood with his cap in his hand. He wouldn't move until the carriage had gone past him.

It was the first time Carrie had been out since Angus's birth, and she felt a little light-headed. Anxiously she gazed up at the Coopers' window, fancying she could hear the wee fellow crying. Mrs Cooper was looking after Angus while she was at the funeral.

Winnie squeezed Carrie's arm, knowing what was running through her daughter's mind. Carrie's anxiety subsided and she shot her mother the briefest of smiles. Mrs Cooper was a dab hand with children. Angus would be all right in her more than capable hands.

The carriage moved forward at a dignified pace as they made their way up Tallon Street. Carrie had decided John was to remain at the undertakers until the time of the funeral. They were headed there now to pick up the coffin.

Harriet Chisholm stared stonily out the carriage

window as they clip-clopped up the cobbled street. She hated funerals. In fact, she loathed them so much the very thought of having to go to one was enough to make her feel sick for days beforehand. Harriet was only too well aware that one day she, too, would die and the thought terrified her.

As a wee lassie she'd had terrible nightmares about dying. Nightmares that would bring her out of her sleep whimpering with terror. With small fist stuck in her mouth and a cold sweat literally dripping from her, she'd lie staring into the darkness. Her nightmares about death were always the same: flesh-eating worms slowly devouring her body, the claustrophobia of the grave; and the awful, awful loneliness which was undoubtedly the worst thing of all.

Loneliness was a word Harriet was well acquainted with. For as long as she could remember she had been alone, with the sort of loneliness that's there even when you're surrounded by others.

Perhaps things would have been different if she'd been born pretty, or at least attractive. But she hadn't been. There had been no magical transformation for this ugly duckling. The ugly duckling had grown up into just as ugly a duck.

With bitter shame she remembered it had been a great dare at one time amongst the boys of her class to corner and kiss her. For a long time she'd wondered why she was in such demand till at a birthday party that beautiful blonde bitch, Aileen Summers, had whispered the answer in her ear during a game of postie postie.

She'd fled the room and the house, running down the road with a face awash with hot tears and Aileen's words still ringing in her ears.

The boys had been kissing her as the worst dare they could think of to test their manhood. 'Kiss Harriet Chisholm and not be sick' was how they put it. Laughing and wiping their mouths afterwards, saying it wasn't as bad as all that, as long as you kept your eyes shut so you didn't see her face.

Tall, angular and bony she'd been at school. And despite her many prayers she'd grown up exactly the same – a fact that burned resentfully in her breast, causing her to view the world through a cold and jaundiced eye.

Harriet's gaze flickered sideways to where Carrie was sitting with Winnie. Although hardly a raving beauty, Carrie was none the less far more attractive than she was. And how she'd always envied Carrie that.

If only men could see inside her, she thought. If only they would take the trouble to see the real her inside this hated shell which housed her being. But in her experience men didn't have that sort of insight when it came to women. All they were interested in were the externals.

She glanced across again at Carrie. It saddened her to see her sister so obviously suffering, but there was a side of her that was jealous of Carrie even now.

Hadn't Carrie had a man of her own? A good, loving husband who'd worshipped the very ground she'd walked on. And didn't she now have a gorgeous baby as a legacy of that marriage?

It was certainly a lot more than Harriet was ever likely to get.

Her eyes glittered as she stared out at the passing scene. She would have given anything to have landed a man like John McBain. And as for Angus, she would have sold her soul for a wean like him.

What was to become of her? she wondered bitterly. Was her fate to end up a dry old spinster? She was sure it was. Angus and any other nephews and nieces she might have would pay a duty call to Aunty Harriet on those Sunday afternoons when their parents forced them to come and see her.

'You're looking well, Aunty Harriet. And how are you today?'

Bitterness welled up inside her as she imagined how pitifully grateful she'd probably be for the visits while knowing that to them she would undoubtedly be a figure of fun, someone they laughed and sniggered about when they were on their own.

Her hands twitched towards her bag and the cigarettes it contained. But she daren't light up, even though she was desperate for a smoke. Her father would have a fit had she tried. And even though she was a grown woman she was still as scared of him as she'd always been.

She recalled the leatherings and beltings he'd given them all when they were young. Hugh and Carrie had taken their punishments in silence. As indeed had Alex. She, on the other hand, had howled the place down at the very threat of his hand or belt.

A physical coward, Donald had called her. And he was right. She couldn't stand pain and was convinced her sensitivity to it was far greater than other people's.

But Donald didn't agree. He just said she was a big feartie. Always had been and always would be.

God how she hated herself. If only she'd been born beautiful, or at least attractive. If only she hadn't been so damned clever, which seemed to put off so many men.

If only. . . . If only. . . .

Big Donald eyed Carrie closely. The loss of John had been a terrible blow to her, as indeed it had to them all. She was taking it badly but that was only to be expected. The pair of them had been so much in love.

At least she had the bairn to keep her occupied and help take her mind off matters. The wee chap would be a big solace to her in the difficult times ahead.

When they arrived at the undertakers, Donald and Hugh got out of the carriage and went inside. The hearse was already in place. The four black horses, each with a magnificent black plume flowing backwards from its head, were hooked up and waiting patiently to go.

After the coffin had been loaded aboard, the wreaths that had arrived at the undertakers were strewn decorously around it.

When all was ready, Donald and Hugh climbed back aboard the carriage, and followed the hearse to the cemetery.

Carrie felt as though she was only the shell of what she'd been before. She was learning to cope with the days, but the nights were something again. It was the early morning hours that were hardest, when she was up giving Angus his feed. Then she was all alone and, while the baby suckled, her mind filled itself with memories.

She'd lie in bed with her thoughts whirling after Angus had gone back to sleep. Once or twice it had been so bad she'd woken Harriet and kept her sister talking until the dawn came creeping over the chimney tops. She knew that was grossly unfair of her as Harriet had her work to go to, but Harriet had never complained.

The pair of them would lie there talking about anything and everything. It didn't matter what they spoke about. The important thing was they did. To her credit, Harriet understood that.

Hugh was sweating and uncomfortable because of the rigid shirt collar jabbing into his throat. He was dressed in his one and only suit with a black armband stitched round the right sleeve. He felt lost and rather lonely sitting there amongst his family. He would be glad when all this was over.

It was hard to believe that a man as full of life as John McBain had been was now dead, and that within the hour they'd be burying him in the cold, dank earth.

Gooseflesh prickled on Hugh's neck as it came home to him for the first time that he, too, was only mortal.

On the way to the cemetery men doffed their hats and caps while the few they passed in uniform saluted.

During the drive, Winnie's mind was filled with thoughts of her son, Alex, who'd been killed just outside Sherman, Texas, in 1911. Alex had been sixteen when he left home, saying in the time-honoured way that he wanted to see the world and maybe find his fortune.

He'd been gone a little over six months when word arrived back to say he'd been hurt badly in an accident. Three days later, further word came saying he was dead.

The people in the American hospital had been

extremely kind. A doctor had written them a letter which had come in the parcel containing Alex's effects. Some months later the same doctor sent them a photo of the grave.

Winnie kept that photo in her handbag so she could have it with her at all times. Never a day went by that she didn't take it out and look at it.

Occasionally on the anniversary of Alex's death Donald would go down to the pub and drink a lot more than was good for him. Those were the only times Winnie ever saw her husband the worse for wear because of alcohol.

Robert Smith and his wife, Meg, were waiting for them at the cemetery gates. The Smiths were the nearest thing John had to a family as they had taken him in when he was a bare-arsed lad after his mother died. No formal adoption had ever taken place, so John had always maintained his own family name of McBain.

After being greeted by the Smiths, Carrie had a few words with the other pallbearers. Two of these were foundrymen who had been particular friends of John and the third was a chap called Archie Marjoribanks, an old school chum with whom John had run the streets as a boy and who had kept in touch ever since.

Donald, Hugh and old man Smith comprised one line of pallbearers, the two foundrymen and Marjoribanks the other.

Once the coffin was shouldered, the six men moved slowly forward while the women followed.

A large gang from Armstrong's stood grouped round the graveside, a few of whom were in their work clothes as they would be going straight on to weekend caretaking duties after the ceremony.

The Reverend Duncan Forbes stood at the top end of the grave with a large, well-thumbed Bible open in his hand. Looking rather like an Old Testament prophet with his longish white hair and hawk-like, yet ascetic, features, he was a gentle man who genuinely cared.

Friends and neighbours from Tallon Street and

McLellan Street had turned up as well as various relatives of the Chisholm family. Chief amongst the latter was Donald's brother, Sandy, who was a merchant seaman.

The coffin was carefully laid by the graveside and the ceremony began with a prayer.

Old man Smith was heartbroken as he stared down at the coffin. John had been everything to him and his wife, the focal point of their waning lives. They had never had any children themselves, a fact to which he and Meg had never become reconciled.

It had always upset them both that John had never wanted to follow them into the newsagent and confectioner's shop they owned, which was a good, well-established business with an ever-increasing turnover.

Robert Smith sighed. If John had come into the shop, this would never have happened.

He glanced across to where Carrie was standing. He'd not altogether approved of that marriage, albeit it was obvious to anyone with half an eye in his head that John and the lassie had been daft on one another.

What had worried him at the time was the fact that the Chisholms and the Smiths – and since taking John in he'd considered John a Smith – although both working-class families, occupied different rungs on the social ladder. The Smiths were *rough*, whereas the Chisholms had bettered themselves by escaping into a *good* area. Cathcart was a far cry from Scotland Street where the Smiths lived and where John had been brought up. The Smiths were considerably well off, while the Chisholms lived from week to week on what was brought into the house.

Robert Smith greatly admired Big Donald, although the man's overpowering masculinity both awed and frightened him a little. Robert was a shy, retiring person, who, outside of business, had very little to say for himself. However, people who mistook his shyness for weakness soon learned better. In his own quiet way Robert was as ruthless as any self-made tycoon who's fought his way to the top.

What worried him now was the fact that Angus had

been left without a father, and he knew the harsh economic realities, both now and in the future. He knew Carrie would do her best by the child, and furthermore he trusted Big Donald to play his part in supporting the wee fellow, but Carrie would certainly find a capital sum handy. That was why he'd brought £200 along with him today.

The money hadn't come from a bank, but out of the safe he had bolted to the kitchen floor at home. A lot of people would have been surprised to know what was in that safe. Certainly the tax man would.

The Reverend Forbes spoke about John and the terrible tragedy that had befallen the McBain family. Then he called for them all to join him in singing 'Abide with Me'.

Carrie watched, dry-eyed, as the coffin was lowered into the grave. At a signal from the minister she stepped forward to pick up a handful of earth which she threw on to the coffin lid. One by one the chief mourners came forward and followed suit.

When the ceremony was over Carrie spoke to the men from Armstrong's who'd come along to pay their last respects. Some she knew, others she didn't.

Donald stood staring at the great mound of wreaths and flowers piled high beside the grave.

'They did him proud,' Robert Smith said, coming up to Donald from behind.

'Aye, they did that,' Donald agreed, lifting his eyes and staring out over the rolling green countryside.

Donald loved being in the country. He found it soothing after the racket and clatter of the foundry. The sky was clear now, but on weekdays when the Glasgow smokestacks and chimneys were belching soot and fug into the air, it was a different matter entirely. Then the sky was stained with a great grey cloud which hung, lowering, over the city.

It always amused Donald to think that the word Glasgow came from the Gaelic meaning 'Dear Green Place'. What a joke when you considered the filthy industrial hell that 'Green Place' had now become.

Winnie and Harriet waited patiently while the Reverend Forbes quietly spoke to Carrie. Judging from the expression on her face she seemed to be finding some comfort in what he was saying.

Winnie finally caught Donald's attention and signalled to him that they really must be away if they were to get back in time to receive those who were coming to tea.

Carrie had one last look at the grave. As she turned away the gravediggers moved into position and soon their spades were flying rhythmically.

When they had all arrived back at Tallon Street, Carrie stopped off at Mrs Cooper's for Angus.

Bella Millar, who lived in one of the ground floor apartments, and Mrs McElvey from across the street, had laid out the tea while the Chisholms were at the funeral. Both of these women were close friends of Winnie and the girls.

A few people had already arrived, the Smiths amongst them, and these had been ushered into the big room where they now stood talking and trying to be at ease.

Winnie said hello and then fled to the kitchen, leaving Harriet to play hostess, a task she performed easily.

Drinks were dispensed and then shortly afterwards everyone was asked to go through to the front room where an assortment of borrowed tables and chairs had been arranged so that the entire company could sit down in one sitting.

After the meal Big Donald asked them all to go back through to the big room where there would be more drinks for those who wished them.

Winnie, Harriet and a few of the women – Meg Smith insisted on being one of them – stayed behind to clear things away and do the washing up. They would have their own blether while they were getting on with it, and then go back to the big room.

In the big room Archie Marjoribanks found himself standing close to Carrie who was talking to the young

Robert Cooper. Marjoribanks had already consumed a large number of whiskies, some of which had come from the half bottle he was carrying in his inside jacket pocket, enough to make him half cut and querulous. Accepting another large one from Donald, he literally threw it down his throat. Turning to Carrie he said, 'I only hope Armstrong's are going to pay you a fair bit of compensation. They must be liable, surely to God, as John was killed on the premises.'

A sudden feel of unease settled on the room at these words and those who worked at Amrstrong's glanced from one to the other.

'It's not quite as black and white as that,' Donald said. He then tried to change the subject but Marjoribanks would have none of it.

Marjoribanks was a man of medium height with a stocky build and auburn hair. He would have been reasonably handsome if it hadn't been for his eyes which gave him a foxy look.

'I don't understand,' Marjoribanks persisted, his attention now centred on Donald. 'John was killed in the foundry, therefore compensation must be due. Surely that's the way it is nowadays?'

'Sir Alan might not see it that way,' Donald replied softly.'

'Sir Alan?'

'Him that owns the place. John was on a gantry that had been declared unsafe and put out of bounds when the accident occurred. You can bet Sir Alan's going to make an awful lot of that.'

'I see,' said Marjoribanks, frowning.

'The union will be meeting Sir Alan first thing Monday morning,' Donald continued. 'We should know what's what then.'

Wishing to put an end to the conversation, Donald moved to the bottles to pour out more drinks. He was furious with Marjoribanks, thinking the man crass and insensitive. Talk of compensation was completely out of order at a time like this.

Unaware of the offence he'd caused, Marjoribanks turned his attention back to Carrie. Although he'd met her several times in the past he'd never bothered to have a really good look at her. He saw now that she was a rather attractive woman and one very much to his taste.

Carrie decided to check up on Angus. She gave Marjoribanks a brief smile in passing because he was staring so intently at her.

Marjoribanks quickly returned the smile, convinced that Carrie had taken a shine to him. Later, the memory of that smile started him thinking.

Carrie was coming out of the bedroom where Angus was sleeping when she found Robert Smith waiting for her. She genuinely liked the old man, having always found him sympathetic. She didn't know about his early objection to her marriage as John had never seen fit to mention it to her.

Robert Smith pressed a buff-coloured envelope into her hand. 'A little something to help you and the wean out,' he said.

'Oh, but I couldn't!'

'Don't be daft, woman. Of course you can,' he said and folded her fingers round the envelope.

Carrie took a deep breath. This was most unexpected. 'Well, if you're sure . . . ?'

'Of course I'm sure. I wouldn't have given it to you otherwise.'

Carrie wondered whether the thing to do was to open the envelope there and then or wait till later. When she saw he was staring expectantly at her she presumed he wanted her to open it in front of him.

Using her finger she slit the envelope. She gasped when she saw the thickness of the wad of fivers that were inside.

Robert Smith wasn't a man who gave much away, but when he did he enjoyed the experience. The thunderstruck expression on Carrie's face delighted him. He would derive enormous pleasure in describing that expression to his wife, Meg, whose voice he could now hear coming from behind the closed kitchen door.

'We just ask that you bring the wee fellow to see us once in a while,' he said. Leaning across he kissed Carrie on the cheek. Then he was swiftly making his way back to the big room where he intended having a large glass of Donald's whisky.

Carrie slipped back into the bedroom where Angus was sleeping and stood with her back pressed hard against the door. Her hands were trembling as she slowly counted the wad of fivers.

'Two hundred pounds,' she breathed. Her heart was thudding and her legs felt weak at the knees. The hand holding the money was sticky and hot.

Closing her eyes, she offered up a silent prayer of gratitude. There was a halfpenny policy on John's life, but when that was realized it would hardly be enough to bury him, much less anything else.

The £200 windfall was a fortune to her and she swore there and then to put every farthing of it to good use. Now it wouldn't be necessary for her to find a job right away which was an enormous weight off her mind as jobs were so few and far between.

When she rejoined the assembled company she felt a sense of optimism for the future that she hadn't known before.

3

Early on the Monday evening Winnie was sitting at the big room window. From this vantage point she could see the bend beyond which lay the sombre-looking cluster of buildings comprising Armstrong's. The hooter had just blown and at any moment the men would come streaming round the bend, hurrying home for their tea.

Normally, Winnie would have been in the kitchen getting the evening meal ready, but that night they were having salad and the rest of the boiled ham left over from the funeral. Everything was already prepared and laid out on the front room table, waiting for Donald and Hugh to arrive.

Carrie was in the bedroom feeding the wee one while Harriet was talking to her.

Winnie gently massaged her left temple. She had a bit of a headache which had been brought on by the day's heat. It had been another scorcher. Every window in the house was wide open to any breeze that might be about to waft through.

Winnie had spoken to Carrie that afternoon about the house in McLellan Street, wanting to know what Carrie's plans were. The one thing Carrie was certain about was that she didn't want to go back there to live. The place held too many memories for her.

She had said they'd speak to Donald that night to see if he'd be agreeable to Carrie and Angus staying on permanently in Carrie's old room. As Harriet would have to share the room with the two of them, she too would have to be consulted.

The first of the men had started coming round the bend which meant that it would only be a matter of minutes before Donald and Hugh were home.

She often thought that Donald expected too much from Hugh, and consequently was far too hard on him. The trouble was that Donald couldn't seem to understand that Hugh was going through a stage he himself had never been allowed, for Donald's youth had ended abruptly when he was ten years old on the day he went to graft in the bakery.

According to Donald there had been fourteen of them, slaving away in a room little bigger than the one she was in now, and at least one-third of that space had been taken up by the two ovens.

On a number of occasions Donald had described to her what it had been like to walk into that room when the ovens were going full blast. Like being thrust into the very maw of hell itself, was one way he'd put it.

It hadn't been uncommon for grown men to suddenly keel over in a dead faint, and once a man called Barton had thrown himself to the floor where he'd cried and drummed his fists like a baby.

In those days Donald hadn't known what it was to own a pair of shoes, but he had known what hard work was. By Christ he had.

The Chisholms were a Highland family, as were her own, who'd made the long trek south to the big city because they'd been slowly starving to death on their croft outside a village called Invershuie.

Donald's father knew a lot about sheep and precious little else. But work was to be had in Glasgow, and not long after his arrival, he had landed himself a job as a labourer down at the Broomielaw, working for a well-to-do tobacco merchant called Gordon.

Alastair Chisholm was thirty-two years old the day he dropped down dead, so completely and utterly exhausted that his worn-out body had no other recourse but to up and quit on him. When he'd died, Donald had just turned ten and Sandy was thirteen. There was another brother, Willy, who was seven, and Nettie, the only girl in the family, who was three.

A week after his father died, Donald started at the bakery. Sandy had already been grafting for just over a year at a rope works.

The young Donald had worked his fingers to the bone helping to keep the family alive, and later when the chance of an apprenticeship came up in a city foundry he'd jumped at it.

By that time Willie was older and able to bring in some money, and Nettie wasn't such a tie on their mother who was able to get to do scrubbing and general housework.

By the time Donald was twelve, the hard, punishing

work he'd been forced to endure had long since knocked any vestiges of his youth clean out of him. He'd become a man in every sense of the word.

Winnie sighed and patted the greying hair piled up on her head in two side rolls. Before they went to sleep that night she'd have another quiet word with Donald, asking him to try and be more understanding with Hugh.

Winnie started, realizing she'd drifted off into a world of her own. Crowds of men were hurrying past now, while just up ahead she could make out Hugh's tall, slim figure.

Hugh looked up at the window and saw his mother's face peering down at him. He gave her a cheery wave before turning into their close and bounding up the stairs three at a time.

Winnie was waiting for him at the door.

'Papa's stayed behind to have a word with the union official. He said to tell you he won't be long .'

Winnie read Hugh's face correctly. 'The meeting didn't go well, then, I take it?'

Hugh pushed past her into the house, wanting for once to be the first at the sink. Normally that was Donald's privilege. 'No, it didn't,' he called back over his shoulder. 'But I think you'd better wait and hear the story from Papa. You know what he's like about that sort of thing.'

Harriet emerged from her bedroom to glance questioningly at Winnie who in a few terse sentences explained the situation. Harriet made a sort of harrumphing sound, a vocal mannerism of hers which could make her appear very formidable indeed, and disappeared back into the bedroom to relay the information to Carrie.

Carrie had been in a depressed state of mind ever since that morning when she'd been back to McLellan Street to pick up some more clothes for herself and the baby.

There had been the terrible moment when she'd come across some dirty clothes of John's which had been pushed into a corner. His own distinctive smell still clung to them and that had hit her like a body blow.

Then there had been his pipe; his spare collar studs lying on the mantelpiece above the fireplace, his favourite chair which he'd been threatening to repair for over a year, and the brass poker he'd made in the foundry when an apprentice.

The sight of each of these articles which she so closely associated with him had torn afresh at her still raw grief.

'Are you all right?' Harriet asked.

Carrie somehow managed a smile. 'Just thinking. Remembering.' Then suddenly, 'I saw that Archie Marjoribanks giving you the eye the other day. If you ask me, I think he took a fancy to you.'

Harriet snorted and looked away. 'Don't be soft. That sort of man wouldn't be interested in the likes of me.'

'Why not, for heaven's sake?'

Harriet smiled grimly and didn't reply. Instead she started buffing her nails. She would have liked to grow them long and talonlike, but of course that was impossible when she spent five and a half days every week knocking her pan out over an industrial sewing machine.

God, how she hated the factory! With her brain she should have been able to do a lot better for herself than that. The trouble was there were so few opportunities for women and virtually none where something more than hard physical slog or a beautiful body was demanded of one.

Harriet ground her teeth in frustration, thinking that the entire world had conspired to thwart her ambitions.

Well, one day the work situation would have to ease, and when it did she wouldn't be slow in putting herself forward. Unless, of course, there were other ways to skin this particular cat?

That sudden electrifying thought was something completely new, and she wondered why it hadn't occurred to her before.

Her eyes half closed and a look of muted excitement settled on her face as she began to brood on the idea of a possible alternative.

In the bathroom Hugh finished his wash and vigorously dried himself off. It had been a terrible day in the foundry with everyone being acutely aware that young John McBain, who'd been laughing and joking with them only a few days previously, was now dead and buried.

The entire work force had paused when the casting, still with traces of blood on its side, had been hauled away by a gang of labourers to be loaded on to a wagon and dispatched to the people who'd placed the order for it. Armstrong's wasn't the sort of firm to destroy a perfectly good casting just because some poor bugger had the misfortune to be killed by it.

Going through to the living room, Hugh threw himself into one of the fireside chairs. He was ravenously hungry but knew only too well that no one would be allowed to start on their tea until Big Donald arrived home and was ready to sit down. That was one of the house rules.

It was over an hour later when the front door clicked to announce Big Donald's return.

When he entered the living room he found Winnie, Carrie and Harriet waiting expectantly for him. Hugh, head fallen to one side, was fast asleep and snoring.

Donald wasn't a man who believed in mincing words so he came straight to the point. 'There's no hope for a penny piece of compensation, lass,' he said to Carrie. 'Sir Alan just won't entertain the idea.'

Carrie hadn't believed it would be much, but she had expected something. She'd thought that Armstrong would have felt obliged at least to make a token gesture. It seemed that wasn't to be the case. She thanked God yet again for Robert Smith's £200, without which she would have been destitute.

'The mean, miserable bastard!' Harriet hissed.

'Did you speak to Sir Alan yourself?' Winnie asked.

'I did,' Donald replied. 'The trouble is that John was up on that gantry without authority. Sir Alan argues that it doesn't matter that the casting was out of control. If

John hadn't been where he was he wouldn't have been killed. Sir Alan says that as John's death was John's own fault, he daren't make even an *ex gratia* payment to Carrie in case it sets a precedent.'

'What do you think, Papa?' Carrie asked in a tight voice.

Donald's face contorted into a mask of suppressed fury. He clenched and unclenched his massive fists. A terrible injustice had been done that day and what angered him was that he'd been totally powerless to do anything about it.

'I did think of telling Armstrong what to do with my job.'

Winnie paled, and a vein in her neck began to throb.

'But, of course, there wouldn't have been any sense in that. There isn't a snowball's hope in hell of me or anyone else in the works getting another job in Glasgow at the moment, and that's why that man can treat us any way he bloody well pleases.'

'You did right, Papa,' Carrie said. 'John wouldn't have expected you to do otherwise.'

Harriet said, 'I was talking to a girl at work the other day whose husband was recently out at the Gareloch. According to him, it's chock-a-block with laid-up ships.'

'She told the truth,' Donald growled. 'That's why there are no orders on the books. There's a glut of merchant tonnage left over from the war, far more than is now needed. If things go on the way they are I can see at least half the men on Clydeside being idle before the year's out.'

'Oh, don't say that!' Winnie exclaimed, her eyes wide with fear.

Donald stalked to the sideboard where he knew there to be some whisky left over from the funeral. He poured himself a large one and gulped it down. Then he poured himself another.

He was worried sick that he might end up in the position of not being able to provide for his family. To Donald that was a horrifying prospect, and the worst sin a man like him could commit. The entire strength of his male ego was centred round two things: his virility, and his ability to be the family bread-winner.

Crossing to the open window, he gazed down on to the back green. His overriding fear was that they'd lose this house and be forced to move back to the slums from which he and Winnie had struggled so hard and so long to escape.

Winnie sighed and ran a hand wearily over her hair. The possibility of Donald being made idle was some- thing she was going to have to face. Somehow she was going to have to find a way of cutting back so that she could put a wee bit by against that black day, should it ever arrive. Still, looking on the bright side, no matter how bad things got, there was bound to come a time when they'd get better again. That thought lightened her heart and, combined with the love she had for her family and they for her, gave her the courage to face whatever the future held in store for them.

Thinking of the slums had led to Donald remembering his mother. She'd been a beauty in her day, with long, flowing, lustrous hair and a peerless complexion. But her looks had soon withered as a result of producing four children and then struggling to cope when Alastair died. When she was thirty-five her face was heavily lined and she had grey hair which turned snow white a decade later.

Many's the time they'd all huddled together for warmth in the one bed while she regaled them with tales of Invershuie. She'd speak of her young days and the adventures she'd had in the wild glens and mountains surrounding the village.

Once she'd confided to them that she'd known their father all her life and there had never been anyone else whom she'd ever wanted to marry. Young Nettie had cried at that, saying she hated Glasgow and wanted her daddy back. Fiona Chisholm had held her only daughter tight then and in a cracked voice confessed that she too wanted their daddy back.

Donald finally emerged from his dream to remember that he still had John's last wage packet in his trouser pocket.

Crossing to Carrie, he laid the small brown envelope in her lap. 'That was what John had coming,' he said, unable to keep the bitterness out of his voice.

Winnie startled everyone by rising and declaring, 'I hope that man Armstrong rots in hell for what he did today.'

She stared defiantly round the room: it was almost unknown for her to swear.

'Amen to that,' said Donald, agreeing with his wife's sentiments. 'Now let's eat before our stomachs begin to think our throats have been cut.'

Hugh needed no further telling. He was the first one to sit at the table.

4

Summer gave way to autumn and that, in turn, to winter. Early one Saturday evening in February, Hugh answered a knock on the front door to find Archie Marjoribanks standing there with a bunch of flowers in one hand and a brown paper bag full of clinking bottles in the other.

For a moment Hugh was taken aback. Then, grinning, he ushered Marjoribanks through to the living room where the family was assembled.

When Carrie heard Marjoribanks's voice in the hall-way, she shot Harriet a look which clearly said, 'See I was right. He *is* interested in you!'

Harriet frowned, an action she normally tried to avoid as it caused a deep cleft of unattractive flesh to appear above her nose.

As Marjoribanks entered the room, Donald carefully folded his evening paper and laid it by the side of his chair. Rising slowly and ponderously, he shook Marjoribanks by the hand.

The flowers were for Winnie. They were terribly expensive at this time of year, but although she protested, she was obviously delighted and touched.

The bottles were beer and lemonade.

Hugh hurried to the sideboard where the glasses were kept while Marjoribanks was urged to sit down.

Marjoribanks cleared his throat and said he hoped they didn't mind him visiting, but being an old china of John's he was naturally concerned as to how Carrie and the baby were managing.

He was hastily assured by Winnie that mother and son were doing just fine. Carrie smiled and confirmed that this was so.

Hugh poured the beers and shandies while Carrie handed them round. He hesitated over whether or not to pour himself one. Empty glass in hand, he turned to gaze inquiringly at Donald, who after only the briefest of hestitations gave him the nod to go ahead.

For a while Donald and Marjoribanks discussed the state of the country which they both agreed had deteriorated since the previous summer. Then they talked about the pay-offs which had taken place at Armstrong's just before Christmas when 180 men had been sent home at the end of the week with the words ringing in their ears that they weren't to bother reporting back the following Monday.

Amrstrong's was a marine engineering firm, manufacturing and servicing pumps for the ships built on Clydeside. It had taken time but now the general slump in the yards was feeding back to the ancillary firms depending on them of which Armstrong's was one.

Normally a person of definite opinion, Donald now

found himself in the unusual position of not being sure what he thought of Marjoribanks. The man *had* spoken out of line at the funeral tea, but perhaps that wasn't such a bad thing after all. He had been concerned for Carrie's rights. But there was something elusive about the man, some aspect of his personality which defied Donald's analysis.

He had a great deal of charm, there was no denying that. He smiled a lot. Maybe too much. And he certainly knew how to flatter, as had been demonstrated in the little speech he'd made to Winnie when handing her the flowers.

Perhaps it was the flattery which had triggered his unease, Donald thought. He distrusted people who used flattery to their own advantage.

The conversation veered on to Marjoribanks's job, and much to Hugh's delight it transpired that he worked on the railways.

Hugh was something of a railway buff, having become mad keen on them when he was only a tiny lad. He now spoke eagerly with Marjoribanks about the far-reaching changes taking place at that time amongst the many railway companies up and down the length and breadth of Britain.

Marjoribanks was a shunter with the Caledonian Railway which was soon to integrate with a new company to form what was to be known as the London, Midland and Scottish Railway, LMS for short.

A light came into Marjoribanks's eyes as he talked about the engines currently in use with Caledonian, such as the old Dugald Drummonds whose designer was renowned for experimenting with 200lb pressure – a fearsome figure at the time.

Hugh wanted to know about the new Cardean Class 4-6-0 and the Pickersgill's two cylinder 4-6-0 express due to go into general service later that year.

Donald's unease melted as Hugh and Marjoribanks delved deeper into the facts and figures of the Caledonian and its rolling stock.

It was soon apparent from Marjoribanks's enthusiastic comments that he both loved and was good at his job. This put him several notches higher in Big Donald's estimation.

After more discussion Marjoribanks extended Hugh an invitation to come along to the Central Station one weekend, promising to show him around and, if possible, give him a short ride in an engine cab.

Needless to say, Hugh was ecstatic and immediately asked if the following Saturday would be suitable. The date was fixed, and to the accompaniment of a delighted laugh from Hugh they shook hands on it.

After that Winnie rose to say she was going to make a cup of tea. She had just baked some fresh scones that afternoon and wanted to impress Marjoribanks with them. Both Carrie and Harriet offered to help, but she told them to sit down again as she could manage on her own.

Winnie had guessed correctly that there was more to Marjoribanks's visit than a mere social call. What was yet unclear to her was which of her two daughters he was interested in. Carrie with Angus to look after needed another man, of course, but in a way she rather hoped it was Harriet he had his eye on.

Harriet worried her at times. She was too introspective and given to brooding for her own good. The real trouble with Harriet was that she was extremely intelligent and refused to hide the fact. Obvious intelligence tended to put men off as she'd once tried explaining to her, but Harriet had merely glowered and thrust her chin forward.

Look at her now! Winnie thought. Sitting there staring daggers at poor Mr Marjoribanks, who so far hadn't spoken one word out of place and had, in fact, been civility itself. No wonder she couldn't land herself a man if that was the way she treated them!

Harriet was surprised by her reaction towards Archie Marjoribanks. Coldly dissecting that reaction, she came to the conclusion he both attracted and repelled her at the same time.

He was a smoothie, all right – glib and surprisingly articulate. But his accent was dreadfully common. Far more so than John's had been, who had been brought up in the same district as he.

She wondered if it was the way his eyes bent in towards one another that put her off. To her mind they made him look like a crook.

Harriet had just lit her umpteenth cigarette since Marjoribanks's arrival when she suddenly became aware that he was staring at her. Her gaze flickered towards him and their eyes locked.

The embarrassed burning sensation started in the pit of her stomach and then swiftly radiated outwards. She wanted to squirm under that gaze, knowing he was mentally stripping her with a clinical objectivity that was both exciting and disgusting. There was a wealth of sexual knowledge in those eyes so dispassionately viewing her. That and a glint of humour as though he was inwardly laughing at the pitiful object she saw herself to be.

Fury exploded within her. How dare he look at her as if she were some common tart parading on the street corner! She wanted to pick something up and throw it at him. She wanted to grind her cigarette into his leering face. She wanted Donald to thrash him within an inch of his life and then throw him down the stairs. She wanted
. . .

When the full realization of what she really *did* want burst in her, she was filled with both horror and shame.

Marjoribanks's mocking eyes once more trapped hers, this time for only the briefest of seconds – just long enough for him to let her know he was aware of what was running through her mind. Then he deliberately turned his back on her and struck up a new line of conversation with Donald who at that moment had just stopped speaking.

Harriet had an overwhelming urge to leap to her feet and flee the room, but she fought it down. This is ridiculous, she told herself. She was a mature woman of twenty-eight and not some silly wee lassie to be reduced to a jelly just because a man had looked at her *that* way. Of course it wasn't the look that was really bothering her, but rather what it sparked off within her. For the first time in her life she found herself scared of a man, not merely because he was bigger and stronger than she was, but due to something that went far deeper and whose roots were lodged in the very essence of her femininity.

A few minutes later Winnie bustled in, pushing a trolley loaded down with goodies. Carrie broke off speaking to help her mother by handing out the plates while Winnie poured the tea.

Marjoribanks was highly amused at Harriet's reaction to him. It was a long long time since he'd come across a girl at that age whom he could immediately sense was a virgin. In a way she reminded him of his dead wife, Libby, who'd also had that supercilious quality which he'd found so attractive.

For a moment or two he considered changing his mind about which sister to go after, but in the end decided it had to be Carrie. At least he wouldn't mind waking up in the morning and seeing her face next to his, which was a lot more than he could say for Harriet. Jesus, she was plain! But there *was* sex there. A vast untapped reservoir desperate to burst its banks. He could have relished being the one to do the bursting.

Sipping his tea he turned his attention to Carrie. Her pins were good which was important. He appreciated good legs. The backside, belly and breasts were overweight, but that would be because she was still feeding. She had an excellent profile, and her facial skin was flawless, unlike Harriet's which was marked from childhood spots.

But what was most in Carrie's favour was that she had an extremely pleasant personality as well as being easy to get on with and always eager to please. He knew all this for fact as John had mentioned it to him more than once.

The conversation died abruptly when they heard Angus yelling in his bedroom. Carrie hurried away to attend to him. She returned minutes later to report that the wee fellow must have been having a nightmare which luckily hadn't woken him.

At first Marjoribanks had viewed Angus as a liability, but thinking the matter through he'd come to realize how the child could be used to his advantage. If he did get married to Carrie, then Angus would be an enormous lever he'd have over her.

Half an hour later he decided it was time to go. Having reconfirmed Hugh's visit to the Central Station on the following Saturday – that had been a stroke of luck as it gave him the perfect opportunity to wangle another social call – he said his good-byes.

'Well, well, well,' said Donald after Marjoribanks had gone. Thoughtfully he rubbed his chin.

'I'll do the washing up,' said Harriet and started to gather the dirty dishes together. The trolley rattled as she vigorously pushed it from the room.

Hugh excused himself and went through to the big room where he slept on a bed settee. He wanted to go over his books on railways and dream about the coming Saturday.

Carrie had another look at Angus before taking herself through to the kitchen to help Harriet. 'What do you make of that, then?' she queried.

Harriet harrumphed. 'Make of what?' she snapped in reply.

Carrie was well used to her sister's moods and rudeness. Harriet just wouldn't have been Harriet without the tartness and caustic replies. Both in looks and temperament, they were as different as the proverbial chalk and cheese.

'I'm talking about Archie Marjoribanks paying a call,' Carrie said drily.

Harriet shrugged.

'You must have made some impression!'

'If you really want to know, I think he's got an awful

big tip for himself. He's arrogant, conceited and probably in the long run a bore to boot.'

Carrie turned her back to hide the smile which crept across her face. 'I can see he impressed you,' she said, her voice crackling at the edges with laughter.

Harriet glowered into the sink. The emotions Marjoribanks had aroused frightened her. There had been a few terrible moments back there in the living room when she'd fantasized about him using her. Degrading her. Even now the thought made her shiver.

'Are you all right? You've gone all pale suddenly,' Carrie said anxiously.

Harriet shrugged dismissively. 'I'm fine. Just tired, I think. We've been busy at the factory.'

'Well, that's something to be thankful for. Being busy, I mean. There are plenty who'd give their eye teeth to be in your shoes.'

'I'm only too aware of that,' Harriet said wearily.

'He was married, you know.'

'Who?

'Archie Marjoribanks. His wife died of cancer. I remember John telling me. He knew her, of course, but I never met the woman. I hardly know him, come to that.' She paused to stare thoughtfully before adding, 'I'm pretty sure there's a daughter, but I can't remember what her name is.'

Harriet sighed. 'For the last time, I'm not interested in him nor he in me,' she lied.

'Then why did he bother visiting?'

This was another of those times when Harriet wasn't sure whether Carrie was being naïvely ingenuous or downright dense. 'Well, there *are* two eligible females in this house now you know.'

'What?'

Harriet dried her hands on a spare tea towel before taking herself through to the living room for a last cigarette before bed. She left a stunned Carrie staring after her.

Carrie's thoughts were whirling. It had just never

entered her head that she might be the one who interested Marjoribanks.

Her first impulse was to dismiss the notion of a relationship out of hand as John was only six months dead and still very much in her heart.

Taking a deep breath, she told herself to hold on a minute and give the matter some thought. If what Harriet said was true, then this wasn't an opportunity to be lightly tossed aside.

For the moment, anyway, she had no feelings for Archie Marjoribanks, but he seemed personable enough and had a good sense of humour – an important point for Carrie.

Although still only twenty-one, she was well aware of how difficult it was going to be for her to land another husband with Angus in tow. She appreciated only too well the reluctance of Glasgow men to take on someone else's family. But Marjoribanks was a widower with a wee lassie of his own which rather put him in the same boat she herself was in.

Of course no one could replace John. There was no question of that. What she had to do was consider the practicality of this possible new situation.

She could go on living here in Tallon Street – Donald had told her she and the baby were welcome as long as they wanted to stay – but with things as bad as they were and steadily getting worse it would certainly be helpful to the family if she was to get out and re-establish a home of her own.

She still had most of the £200 Robert Smith had given her, which meant she was economically independent for some time yet. But that money wouldn't last forever, and when it finally did run out, where was she going to get a job when there were virtually none to be had? She'd already been back several times to the factory trying for her old place and each time had been turned down flat.

Biting her lip, she wondered if John would have approved of her remarrying. Of course he would, she told herself. John had been a practical man who would have appreciated that life had to go on. He wouldn't have expected her to remain static. Especially not when an opportunity like this presented itself. John and Archie had been close friends when they were running the streets together. If she was going to remarry then it seemed the sensible thing to choose a man of whom John had so obviously been fond. Then there was the fact that Archie worked for the railways in a job that was known not only to be highly paid but also secure. Both these factors counted for an awful lot in these desperate times.

She decided her best policy for the moment was to go to bed and sleep on all this. If she could sleep, that is, with her mind in such a turmoil.

But Carrie did sleep and it was Harriet that the early hours of the morning found wide awake and staring at the ceiling. She was smoking a cigarette and thinking about Australia and the correspondence she'd had recently with the Australian authorities in London. It seemed her chances were high of being accepted for immigration; this was an alternative to her present life which attracted her. There was still an interview to come which meant she had to travel to London in about a month's time and, all being well with the outcome, there was no reason why she shouldn't set sail before the end of the year.

The thought of travelling to the other side of the world excited her immensely. The long sea voyage, the exotic sights, the new people she would meet. She'd already made up her mind to go to Sydney first because that seemed to be the centre of things down there.

It amazed her that she was so unafraid of leaving everyone and everything behind. Perhaps the fear and possible misgivings would come later when things were fixed and it was time for her to leave.

It was going to be so good to get away to a new life and the many things she would be experiencing for the first time. Not that her mother and father hadn't done their best by her, they had. It was just that she felt so confined and constricted by life in Glasgow. Also she felt ashamed that she was twenty-eight years old and still not married. Occasionally at work she'd catch girls looking at her in a funny way and she'd know they'd been talking about her. Pitying her.

Well, she didn't need anyone's pity. Not now or ever.

There would be a man in Australia for her. There just had to be!

She drew on the cigarette and gradually calmed down. What she was dreading most was telling Winnie and Donald she was going abroad. That was going to be sheer bloody murder.

Casting her mind back she remembered what it had been like when Alex left home. There had been an atmosphere in the house for weeks beforehand that you could've cut with a knife. Winnie's face had been continually tripping her while Donald had been like a rumbling volcano threatening to explode at any moment.

Alex had been fresh-faced and bright-eyed that morning he'd set off on his great adventure. Carrie, Hugh, Winnie and she had crowded the big room window as Alex and Donald, her father carrying Alex's suitcase, walked down the street to the tram stop.

Several of the neighbours had thrown their windows open and shouted good luck. Alex had responded with a cheery wave and in one instance with a kiss blown to an old wifey who'd been especially fond of him and he of her.

On reaching the top of the street, he'd turned and stood for a few seconds, drinking it all in: absorbing and memorizing every little detail to take with him on his journey.

Then he was gone and that was the last they ever saw of him.

Now she was going to have to tell her parents that she, too, was going to leave them by going overseas. It would break their hearts.

Sighing, she reached for yet another cigarette. The night had been a long one.

5

Nobody was surprised when Archie Marjoribanks turned up with Hugh after the lad's visit to the Central Station. The idea of being invited to tea had of course been craftily planted by Marjoribanks himself who'd accepted immediately Hugh made the proposal.

Arriving at the Chisholm house, Marjoribanks announced he'd just had a marvellous idea. He'd noticed a fish and chip shop round the corner and why didn't he take them all there for their tea, his treat? He beamed Carrie a winning smile which left no doubt that it was definitely Carrie he'd set his sights on.

Harriet said she was sorry but she had to wash her hair while Winnie came up with the excuse she was a wee bit chesty and going out in the cold might aggravate it. Donald said he would bide at home with his wife.

That left Hugh and Carrie with Hugh mad keen on the idea. Carrie swithered for a moment or two, saying that it wasn't all that long till Angus's feed. She finally agreed after Marjoribanks promised to get her there and back again within the hour.

As this was to be Carrie's first time out with Marjoribanks, Winnie didn't think it a bad thing at all for Hugh to be going along with them. That way things didn't look too obvious for either party and it would also take the pressure off a little bit.

The fish and chip shop was almost deserted, which meant they had no trouble getting seats at one of the marble-topped tables. Having helped Carrie sit down, Marjoribanks slipped Hugh a ten bob note and asked him to go up to the counter and do the ordering.

Carrie was suddenly shy and self-conscious as it had been a long time since she'd been out with a man other than John. She was grateful when Marjoribanks offered her a cigarette as it gave her hands something to do.

While Hugh waited patiently to be served Marjoribanks reminisced about the days when he and John had been youngsters together. Because he had a marvellous way with a story he soon had Carrie laughing so much she had to fumble in her handbag for a hanky with which to dab her streaming eyes.

Marjoribanks had enormous charm and he knew how to use it to best advantage. He now set to work on Carrie, breaking her down, reaching out to her with his personality, enveloping her with warmth and good feelings. By the time Hugh brought over their fish teas he'd sold himself to her lock, stock and winning smile.

While they ate Carrie inquired about his daughter. She nodded sympathetically when in hushed tones he told her how dreadfully the wee lass – who was six and called Sheena – was missing her mum. No matter how hard he tried to compensate for this loss, it just wasn't good enough by a long chalk.

Carrie commiserated about how difficult things must be for the pair of them and he, pulling a wry face, agreed.

Suddenly it dawned on Hugh that there was a lot more going on around this table than at first met the eye. Carefully he listened and watched till, with a shock, he realized Carrie and Marjoribanks were actually making up to one another.

Self-righteous anger blazed in him. John was hardly dead and buried and here was Carrie all set to get off with the man's supposed china!

But Hugh wasn't a fool and he had reached the stage

where he was learning to think twice about things before opening his mouth and making comment.

He recalled the funny look his mother had given his father just before they'd left the house and which he'd momentarily puzzled about at the time. Now the meaning of that look became clear to him. It had been one of connivance, which could only mean that not only were his parents aware of what was going on but that they actually approved!

Now he knew why Marjoribanks had wanted him to do the ordering. It was so these two could have time to chat on their own.

He was inordinately pleased with himself at having figured all this out and decided the best thing he could do would be to remove himself for a little while longer.

Hastily he finished what was left on his plate. Then with a cough he announced he was just going to pop out for an evening paper.

When Carrie said she needed some cigarettes it was Marjoribanks who insisted on handing him the money for them.

He rose and excused himself saying he wouldn't be long but already he'd made up his mind to spend a good fifteen or twenty minutes in the snooker room round the corner. When he strutted out into the drizzle that had started to fall he felt very grown up and wise in the ways of the world.

After Hugh had gone, Carrie told Marjoribanks about her trying to no avail to get her job back at Ballogie Clothing where she'd worked alongside Harriet before having to leave on account of her pregnancy.

This time it was Marjoribanks's turn to make sympathetic noises. When he asked her how she was managing, she told him about the money Robert Smith had given her.

'A good man, old Robert. One of the best,' Marjoribanks stated. His face suddenly creased into a dark scowl as he added, 'but you should have had some compensation from Armstrong's. It was criminal right enough that you didn't.'

There was black bitterness inside Carrie whenever she thought about Armstrong's and Sir Alan in particular. It wasn't an act of charity she was after. The very suggestion would have horrified her. But when a man had worked as hard and diligently as her John had done for Armstrong's then surely his life was worth something!

The flowers and wreaths at the funeral from Armstrong's had all been from John's mates. There hadn't been one solitary bloom from the management. And you would have thought that inquiries would have been made. A word to Donald or someone sent down to chap the door. But no. Nothing at all. Only silence. As far as Sir Alan Armstrong was concerned she and Angus might just as well never have existed.

Dragging herself back from her thoughts she discovered Marjoribanks was talking about where he lived.

His house was in Laidlaw Street which ran off Scotland Street where the Smiths had their shop. What he had was a room and kitchen one flight up. A good house, he assured her, with a range and cavity bed in the kitchen. This latter Sheena slept in while he was through in the front room.

'Tell me about your wife?' Carrie asked. 'I'd like to know.'

A sad, pained expression clouded Marjoribanks's face. She'd been a local girl whom he'd first met when he was Hugh's age. They'd taken an immediate liking to one another and started winching right away. A year after they'd met they got married and a few years later Sheena came along.

It had been a happy marriage. Although mind you they'd had their ups and downs, but then what couple didn't?

With a laugh Carrie agreed. She and John had been known to have had a few right old barneys in their time.

The laughter between them suddenly died as Marjoribanks's face became hard and his cheeks seemed to sink in upon themselves.

In a flat voice he said Sheena had been three when Libby's pain started. Excruciating pain that had caused her to shriek and scream in agony.

Various doctors had been consulted, all of whom agreed on the diagnosis and also on the fact there was nothing they could do for her other than try to alleviate the pain.

At twenty-two years of age Libby had advanced stomach cancer. Her torture had lasted just under a year until a few days before Sheena's fourth birthday when she'd passed away one night in her sleep. As far as he was concerned that final release was a blessing.

Carrie's heart went out to Marjoribanks and the wee lassie whom she hadn't yet met as she listened to all this. Finally after a long silence she said, 'I'd like to meet Sheena sometime.'

Marjoribanks immediately brightened and asked if she'd like to bring Angus over to Laidlaw Street the following Saturday when they could all have tea together?

Carrie replied she'd enjoy that. The arrangement was that she'd take the tram to Scotland Street where Marjoribanks would be waiting to meet her. He did offer to come to Tallon Street and collect her but she laughed that off saying she was perfectly capable of making the journey on her own.

Shortly after that her breasts began to ache and she felt the tell-tale wet which told it was time to feed the bairn. Luckily, Hugh arrived back with his paper and her cigarettes, having been gone almost a full half-hour.

Once outside, Marjoribanks took hold of her by the arm and together the three of them dashed down Tallon Street while above them the heavens opened and heavy rain fell in thundering sheets.

Later, when Carrie emerged from feeding Angus she found Marjoribanks had gone, having taken advantage of a break in the rain.

When she told Winnie and Donald about the arrangement that had been made in the fish and chip shop, Donald's reply was a non-committal grunt while

Winnie's only comment was that it wouldn't do her any harm to get out and about a wee bit more.

Sitting by the fire reading a book, Harriet looked up but didn't speak. She was convinced Carrie was making the biggest mistake of her life but refrained from saying so in case it was misinterpreted as jealousy on her part.

When the following Saturday arrived and it was time to embark on her visit, Carrie wrapped Angus up warmly and bound him to her by means of a tartan shawl. Donald himself saw her to the tramstop.

The journey was a familiar one for Carrie; she'd done it a number of times in the past with John but also on several occasions since the funeral when, true to her word, she'd taken Angus with her over to see the Smiths.

Marjoribanks was waiting for her as arranged and side by side they set off down Scotland Street.

With a new eye, Carrie viewed the area, for if things worked out between her and Marjoribanks this would be where she'd be coming to live.

She had to admit she didn't view the prospect with any great enthusiasm. The streets were manky and in parts choked with litter and refuse. The air smelled strongly of sewage and toilets. Many of the people they passed looked as though they hadn't seen a wash flannel in weeks, while others were so filthy they stank to high heaven.

Faces were pale and thin, features pinched, and although it was February nearly all the children were barefoot.

A couple of tough looking young boys clattered by propelling an iron hoop from a beer barrel by whacking it with a length of wooden stick.

A little girl sat with her feet dangling in the gutter and nursed a dolly made from rags. The doll was tattered and falling apart. She was singing a haunting lullaby about poverty and deprivation she'd learned at her mother's knee, and she sang it with feeling.

Carrie couldn't help comparing Scotland Street with

Tallon Street, something she hadn't actually consciously done before. And on this same conscious level she began to appreciate just how far her father's strivings had brought the Chisholm family.

She told herself that if Donald and John had been able to escape with squalor then so could she and Archie Marjoribanks. All it needed was incentive and determination and she had plenty of both.

Her heart plummeted when they turned into Laidlaw Street. Several of the houses were lying empty with their windows smashed in. They looked like eyeless and toothless monsters who'd succumbed to a combination of internal rot and old age.

Women sat by open windows chatting to their neighbours on either side and occasionally calling to one another across the street, even though it was raw and bitter out.

Carrie gulped as she turned into Marjoribanks's close. There was water running down the walls while from the back of the close came the distinctive stomach-churning smell of an overflowing outside lavatory.

'We're nearly there,' Marjoribanks said quickly ushering her up the stairs. 'I can't tell you how much Sheena is looking forward to meeting you.'

Pulling a large brass key from his pocket he opened the door to his first landing room and kitchen.

Expecting the worst by now Carrie was surprised to find the hallway immaculate, the linoleum on the floor dazzling in its brightness.

Sheena was waiting for them in the kitchen. She was standing in front of a blazing range on which a blackened kettle busily boiled its head off.

The first thing Carrie noted about the lassie was how scared she looked. No doubt it was at the prospect of meeting her. The second thing she saw were the scrapes and bruises on the girl's face.

Archie introduced them and very shyly Sheena extended her hand for it to be shaken. Although the room was warm the hand in Carrie's was as cold as ice. It was also limp as though Sheena wasn't used to shaking hands or else was frightened to put any expression into the gesture.

Carrie beamed Sheena a smile which seemed to put the girl at ease a little. Then Archie mentioned that the kettle was boiling and immediately Sheena scuttled to make some tea.

The kitchen gleamed just like the hallway and on mentioning this Carrie was informed by Archie that Sheena did all the cleaning round the house. Carrie was most impressed by this and said so. This earned her a grateful look from Sheena who was busy spooning tea from the caddy into the pot.

At the back of the range a soot-blackened crock hung on a hook and from this a tantalizing smell wafted forth. Carrie asked what was cooking. Sheen responded that it was an Irish stew.

Carrie was amazed at Sheena's capabilities. Not only was this chit of a girl running the entire household but she was making a damn good job ot if to boot!

Having been instructed to sit in what was obviously the best chair Carrie was then handed a cup of tea by Sheena. Before the girl could draw away Carrie clasped her chin and turned her head to one side. The scrapes and bruises were worse than Carrie had first thought; one bruise in particular was very angry and inflamed.

Prompted by Carrie the girl explained she'd missed her footing on the landing one night and tumbled down an entire flight of stairs.

Having said that, Sheena broke away from Carrie and hurried over to the range where she made herself busy.

Since their arrival the light had faded rapidly leaving the kitchen dark and filled with dancing shadows from the glow from the range.

Marjoribanks lit a spill which he used to light the two gas points jutting out above the brass rail running along the mantelpiece. The kitchen was instantly saturated with warm yellow light.

Carrie asked Sheena if she'd like to hold Angus and

wasn't at all surprised at the enthusiastic reply she received. After all, what little girl doesn't like to fuss with a baby.

Sheena very sensibly said she'd better sit down first before she held Angus. This she did in an old mothering chair which it seemed she'd long since claimed as her own.

Sheena had long, dark hair which fell rather limply in loose waves. Her eyes were two enormous blackcurrants far older and wiser than normal for girls of that age. Her nose had a slight droop at the end giving her something of a witchy appearance. Strangely sensual and provocative mulberry coloured lips added to the effect.

As though she'd been handling babies all her short life Sheena snuggled Angus deep into the crook of her arm and began to hum a popular tune of the day.

For a few seconds Angus showed concern at being deprived of his mother. Then his face burst into a smile and he frothed bubbles. He'd found a new friend.

Carrie rose and crossed to the sideboard on which stood a picture in a frame. As she'd guessed, it was of Archie and Libby's wedding.

Libby was small, dark and looked just like a grown up version of Sheena.

Carrie was suddenly aware of Marjoribanks standing beside her and that he to was gazing down at the picture. His lips were pursed and the sadness she'd seen in the fish and chip shop was back in his eyes.

'She looks nice,' Carrie said.

'I thought so and so did John. He always maintained I got the better bargain by far.'

Carrie couldn't think of a reply to that so she returned to her chair. Staring into the fire's flickering flames, she was aware of being closely studied by Sheena.

She liked the girl and was certain she was liked in return. All that was needed was a little time for the pair of them to get used to one another. If all went well it shouldn't be too long before they were great friends.

Carrie turned and indicated Angus. 'He's certainly

taken to you,' she said.

Sheena smiled, suddenly wide open and vulnerable. 'I like him too. I could sit here cuddling him all night.'

Angus cooed and stuck a chubby fist in the air. From the look on his face it was an idea he heartily approved of.

'Libby and I had hoped to have more children,' Marjoribanks said softly, then shrugged philosophically, 'But of course that wasn't to be.'

'Who knows how these things finally turn out?' Carried said enigmatically. A brief glance in his direction told her he'd got the point.

A little later she took Angus back to let Sheena get on with the business of setting out the meal. She thought the best thing to do was sit back and not interfere. Sheena might be young but for the time being, anyway, this kitchen was her preserve.

When everything was ready Carrie laid the now fast asleep Angus on his rug in front of the fire, close enough to benefit from the warmth but far enough away to escape any flying sparks.

She knew he wouldn't sleep too long as it was his feed time soon and he was notoriously prompt in his demands when it came to that.

The stew was excellent, certainly as good as anything she could have turned out and she didn't hesitate in saying so.

Besides the stew there were jacket potatoes and thick slices of bread and butter – navvies' doorstops, Winnie would have called the latter – all of which went down a treat.

It transpired that Libby had been teaching Sheena to cook ever since the lassie was old enough to take things in, which was just as well, Archie joked. His cooking was so abominable as to be completely inedible.

As soon as the meal was finished Sheena cleared the table and started the washing up.

Having asked Archie to remove himself to the front room Carrie lifted the now grizzling Angus and started feeding him.

While Angus sucked lustily Carrie sat watching Sheena working at the sink. With her sleeves drawn back, the girl was standing on a chair humming to herself as she attacked the pile of dirty dishes in front of her.

Carrie shook her head in wonderment. The girl was so grown up. It was hard to remember that Sheena was six and not sixty, for that was how she continually came across. A wee old wifey who'd seen and done it all and consequently would stand no nonsense from anyone.

Carrie winced as Angus nipped her nipple, his way of telling her that that breast was empty and would she please change him over. 'Beast!' she grinned.

For a while she tried to engage Sheena in conversation about school but the girl was vague and unforthcoming on the subject.

When Angus had been fed she called Marjoribanks back through and told him it was time she was going.

She changed the baby's nappy and then wrapped him up warmly. After shrugging herself into her coat Archie helped bind the baby to her by means of the tartan shawl.

When she was ready she solemnly thanked Sheena for the meal and said she hoped she would be seeing her again soon. Sheena seemed pleased by that prospect.

As they walked down the stairs Marjoribanks said the people on the ground floor had been on to the factor about the overflowing cludge and the factor had promised to have it seen to within the next few days. He didn't refer to the water running down the close walls.

Carrie had hoped to call in on the Smiths but there was no time for that now.

On the previous occasion she'd been up to see them, Robert had let drop several times that she'd be surprised if she knew what was in the black metal safe he kept bolted to the kitchen floor. There had been sly references to pearls and other extremely expensive items. When she'd obviously looked doubting he'd hurried from the room to return with a gorgeous piece of scrimshaw which she'd duly admired.

Thinking about it afterwards she'd come to the conclusion the fly old devil must be acting as a receiver for illegal merchandise brought in from abroad. The docks weren't all that far away and as a consequence the area was well frequented by merchant seamen.

She hoped old man Smith wasn't going to land himself in trouble, for his wife Meg's sake as much as his own.

When they reached the tramstop Archie asked to see her again and suggested the following Friday. He said he would like to take her dancing or if she wasn't up to that yet how about the pictures?

Carrie replied the pictures would be the best idea and a time was agreed when he would pick her up at Tallon Street.

Carrie immediately made a mental note that she was going to have to wean Angus onto a bottle so she wouldn't be as tied as she was now. She decided to buy the necessary paraphernalia first thing on Monday morning and try him on it.

During her journey home she thought about her meeting with Sheena. She'd been worried in case the girl turned out to be a problem but her fears had proved groundless. She and Sheena were going to be the very best of pals. She was sure of it.

As soon as Carrie let herself into the house she knew something had happened. Through the open doorway to the living room she saw her mother sitting at the table with a face like fizz.

She settled Angus in his bed before taking her coat off and going on through.

Donald sat hunched in his chair, pipe clamped between his teeth, glowering into the fire. Underneath the glower he looked angry and hurt.

Harriet was sitting on the pouffe by the window. Her face was pale, her expression one of defiance.

'Have you heard the latest?' Winnie demanded.

Carrie shook her head.

'Harriet is emigrating to Australia.'

It was a bombshell which left Carrie literally stunned.
It was so unexpected, so completely out of the blue.
'When?' she finally managed to get out.

'I'll have to go to London in three weeks for an interview. If I'm successful I'll know sometime after that,'
Harriet replied.

Winnie rose and, looking to be on the verge of tears,
left the room.

After the door had closed behind her mother Harriet
said, 'It's my life. Surely I'm allowed to decide what I
want to do with it?'

Donald didn't reply but savagely poked the fire instead.

'Well?' The word cracked between Harriet and her
father like a rifle shot. But there was no disrespect in her
tone. Rather a plea to be understood.

'You're within your rights, lass,' Donald said reluctantly. Then as an afterthought, 'It's Alex, you see. She
can't forget what happened to him.'

'I don't want to hurt anybody, Papa. I just want to do
what I think is right for me.'

Carrie wasn't sure whether or not it was her imagination but it seemed to her that Donald had aged since
she'd seen him last earlier in the day.

Donald took a deep breath and knocked out his pipe.
He saw a lot of himself in Harriet. Good points as well as
bad. Losing her this way would be like losing an arm. Of
his children she was the one he'd always most closely
identified with.

'I'd better see to your mother,' he said, adding, 'we
won't stand in your way, lass. As you say, it's your life.
Best do with it as you see fit. Tonight was . . . well, let's
just say tonight was a wee bit of a shock, that's all. No
doubt we'll have grown to accept it by the morning.'

'Thanks Papa.'

He followed Winnie through to their bedroom where,
as he'd known he would, he found her lying crying in the
dark.

'I knew it wasn't going to be easy and it wasn't,'

Harriet said.

'Want to talk about it?'

'No. Tomorrow maybe but not now.'

Carrie understood. She stayed long enough to smoke a last cigarette and then she left Harriet alone and gazing into the fire.

In times like these great comfort and solace could be found in a fire.

This would be first time Harriet had ever been out of Scotland and naturally enough she was excited at the prospect.

It was bitterly cold in the train compartment due to the heating not working so she was grateful for the woolly rug Winnie had insisted she bring with her, and for the flask of hot tea Carrie had made and packed.

It hadn't been easy getting time off from Ballogie Clothing but luckily she was chums with Jakey Sanderson, the supervisor. He'd managed to wangle it for her after she'd explained the position to him, having first of all sworn him to secrecy.

What Harriet didn't know was that Jakey had a cousin who'd been pestering him for months to get her a job which he'd promised to do the moment one of his girls left. That was why he'd been so obliging in helping Harriet get a few days off so she could travel to London.

As the train thundered through the night Harriet reflected that the days following her telling Winnie and Donald about her plans to emigrate hadn't been nearly so bad as she'd expected. There had been a weary, resigned quality about Winnie but there were no further words of either argument or recrimination. Regardless of hurt, acceptance had been total.

She'd gone into the big room one night to find Winnie sitting quietly by the window staring at the photo of Alex she always carried in her handbag. With guilt lying in her stomach like a lump of lead she'd turned and left the room.

Hugh's reactions to her news had been different to

anyone else's in the family. He'd been so excited you'd have thought it was him who was going rather than her.

The rhythmic clickety clack of the wheels finally lulled Harriet into a fitful sleep. When she woke the train was pulling into Euston Station.

Punctual to the minute, she presented herself at the address in the Strand where she'd been instructed to go.

For half an hour she sat on a hard wooden bench and then an official came out to see her. Gravely he told her the person she'd been due to see was off sick and could she possibly stay overnight at their expense and come back the following morning.

She was delighted as she'd been dreading the long return journey. Quickly she agreed and a taxi took her to a small hotel in Euston Square.

The room she was shown into was far grander than she could have afforded, so this little touch of luxury was an added bonus. She had a cup of tea and a token rest. Then she took herself out onto the streets of London.

Midday found her in Soho standing outside a little restaurant. Thinking herself terribly daring, she went inside and ordered something to eat.

Filled with all sorts of exquisite things and, as a consequence, feeling extraordinarily happy and alive, she strolled to Regent Street where she spent a long time window shopping.

Eventually, exhausted and foot sore she made her way back to the hotel in Euston Square where she slept for several hours like the proverbial log.

In the hotel the evening meal was called dinner and served a lot later than the tea she was used to.

At the appropriate time she made her way down to the dining room where she found a number of guests already gathered. Spying a small table set to one side she decided that was for her and sat down. She was unfolding her napkin when a deep voice said, 'Excuse me ma'am but I think you've made a mistake. This table is reserved for me.'

Harriet looked up, flushing as she did so. The man had

no sooner spoken than she'd seen the 'reserved' sign set out quite plainly in front of her. 'I'm terribly sorry,' she said and started to rise.

The man was short, paunchy and balding with a round, jovial face and laughing eyes. 'No please!' he said laying a restraining hand on her arm. 'Now that rights have been established it would be my pleasure if you would join me.'

Harriet was at a loss to know what to do. Her mind was made up for her when the man said, 'That's settled then,' and sat down facing her.

He was a lot older than she was. Nearly fifty she guessed. With a voice that came out as a lazy drawl and had a rather hypnotic quality about it.

'My name's Lou Dansie,' he said sticking out his hand.

'I'm Harriet Chisholm,' she replied as they shook.

'Scots?'

She nodded.

'Aaah! I thought so. Unmistakable, that brogue. I knew a lot of Jocks during the war.' He leaned across and whispered confidentially. 'I was sure as heck pleased those guys were on my side. Yes siree!'

She had to laugh. 'You must be an American.'

'From Los Angeles. And you?'

'Glasgow.'

'I've heard about there,' Dansie said. 'I think it would be too heavily industrial for my taste. Too dirty.'

Thinking that Dansie was being disparaging about her city, Harriet's temper flared. Then she realized from the look on his face that he'd merely been passing comment. Instantly she relaxed again, contrite at her hot-headedness.

'Aye well a place is *who* you know. If you're ever in Glasgow come and see my family and me. We'll try and see to it that you go away with a favourable impression.'

'I might just take you up on that,' Dansie replied, thinking that Harriet's spontaneous offer of hospitality was just like the Jocks he'd known in France. Those guys would share their last grain of food with you rather than let you go without.

Because he was easy to talk to Dansie soon had Harriet chattering on about her family and their life in Cathcart.

'Now, how about some claret?' he finally interrupted.

Harriet was taken aback. The fact of the matter was she'd never tasted wine in her life, it being viewed with the utmost suspicion north of the border.

Dansie saw her hesitation. 'Perhaps you'd prefer a burgundy or a beaujolais?' he asked.

Harriet decided frankness was always the best policy. She admitted that wine was totally unknown to her but as he seemed so keen on the idea she wasn't averse to trying some.

Dansie was aghast, declaring this to be a situation that would have to be remedied. He immediately summoned the wine waiter.

Harriet could hardly believe her ears when he ordered champagne. 'But that must be so expensive!' she gasped.

Dansie chuckled, enjoying the gesture he was making. The women he normally mixed with wouldn't have shown as much enthusiasm or delight had he been showering them with fistfuls of diamonds. 'Nothing less will do to mark the occasion!' he stated firmly and dispatched the wine waiter with a flourish.

Harriet had already decided she liked this little, stout man from America. Despite the differences in their ages and backgrounds there was an empathy between them.

Dansie was an expert at getting people to unburden themselves and this talent he now exercised on Harriet, who began to speak at length about her plans for emigration.

When the champagne came Dansie proposed a toast to Harriet wishing her success and happiness in her new life. Harriet declared she would drink to that and did so with a laugh.

She liked the champagne. It was light and tickly like cider only a lot more so. But it didn't seem to have a kick to it.

Dansie smiled enigmatically when she said that.

There was a bloom in Harriet's cheeks and a sparkle in her eyes that had nothing whatever to do with the wine. The dry spinster was being transformed into a desirable woman, desirable because she knew the man sitting opposite saw her as such.

After a while it dawned on Harriet she'd been doing all the talking. So telling Dansie it was his turn she shut up.

'Do you ever go to the motion pictures?' he asked.

The unexpectedness of the question and its seeming irrelevance caught her off guard. She nodded. She and Carrie often went, enjoying the sheer escapism the cinema had to offer.

With a smile Dansie informed her he was a contract writer with United Artists, the company formed two years previously by Mary Pickford, Douglas Fairbanks, Charlie Chaplin and D.W. Griffith.

Harriet was rocked. She was with someone who actually knew the fabled stars of the silver screen! Men and women who were like gods to her.

She listened eagerly to Dansie's account of life in Hollywood. The parties. The swimming pools. What a cut-throat business the movie industry was. The ambitions of the young hopefuls who flocked there. The bitter disappointment that lay in store for so many of them.

The razzle-dazzle of an opening night; what it was like to discover you'd been involved in a success, a failure.

Personalities who worked for Metro, Universal, Cosmopolitan, Vitagraph, First National, Paramount, Selznick. The names rolled off Dansie's tongue as naturally as Glasgow districts would have rolled off hers.

Films of the previous year he'd personally seen being made: 'The Four Horsemen of the Apocalypse', 'The Queen of Sheba', 'The Square Shooter', 'The Lotus Eater', 'Camille', 'A Virgin Paradise'.

Harriet was completely entranced by the spell of words that Dansie wove. She'd been transported to a world a million miles away from Tallon Street and

Ballogie Clothing. Here was glamour, excitement, all the things she so desperately craved in life. Dansie went on to describe how he'd been irresistibly drawn towards movies having seen Florence Lawrence in 'The Biograph Girl' and a one-reel version of Tolstoy's 'Redemption' in 1909.

To start with he'd worked as an actor, it seeming the obvious way to get into the industry. But as time went by he'd grown more and more frustrated by the actor's role until one morning it had come to him like a bolt from the blue that writing was his true vocation. He had realized his destiny in life was to be a motion picture script writer.

He laid his right hand on the table and pointed to a heavy gold ring he wore. 'Mary herself gave me that,' he stated proudly.

'Pickford?'

He nodded.

Harriet gingerly reached out and touched the ring. She might have been touching the Holy Grail so reverential was her gesture.

The courses came and went while Dansie explained he'd been sent to Britain to gather background material for a new picture he was to write for Fairbanks and Pickford.

The previous year Fairbanks had starred in 'The Three Musketeers' and the production had been so successful that he was to star in another costume drama. The subject chosen had been Bonnie Prince Charlie. Fairbanks would play the Prince, of course, while Pickford would be Flora McDonald.

So far Dansie had been in London for a fortnight and during that time he'd been researching Charles Edward Stuart at the British Museum. This would take him at least another week and then he was travelling north by motor car to Scotland where he would tour round all the places known to be associated with the Young Pretender's uprising.

Harriet put up no resistance when Dansie ordered brandies. She'd have drunk turpentine by now had he suggested it. Anything so long as this conversation continued.

Over coffee Dansie suggested they go on to a night club where they could talk further and perhaps dance. Harriet accepted instantly.

Sheena Marjoribanks lay in her cavity bed in the darkness listening to the sound of her father snoring through the wall. She shivered at the memory of the thrashing he'd given her a few nights previously with the thick leather belt he wore round his work trousers.

He'd been drinking. Not too much but still enough to spark off one of his terrible rages.

She could remember the many times he'd used that same belt on her mother and her mother screaming and pleading in the front room while she lay huddled here in her bed listening to it all.

'Oh, mummy!' she whispered stuffing her hand into her mouth. Tears burst from the corners of her eyes. Her mother's face danced before her. Those sad, forlorn features crammed full of misery and despair.

Some day she was going to escape from all this, she promised herself. As soon as she was old enough she was going to walk out through that front door and never come back.

In the meantime it would be good to have an ally about the place. She saw Carrie could be an ally and she would bring a baby to hug when the nights were long and cold and it was lonely to be on your own.

Thinking of Angus made her smile, and with him still in her thoughts, she drifted off to sleep.

Beside Harriet, Lou Dansie lay sleeping with his arm thrown over the top part of his face. His mouth puckered every time he exhaled, which he did often and noisily.

Harriet was glowing inside. The aftermath of love-making had left her for the first time in her life feeling fulfilled. She'd waited long enough for this moment but the wait had been worthwhile.

She ran her hands over her breasts and down her long, lean flanks, the flesh tingling to her touch. It might have been slumbering through the years until this small, paunchy American had come along and with a wave of his magic wand (she smiled at that) brought it ecstatically alive.

Dansie groaned and turned on to his side so that his back was towards her. She stared in fascination at the thick matting of black hair which started at the nape of his neck and grew downwards. Reaching out she stroked the hair on his shoulders, causing him to quiver.

'What are you thinking about?' he asked without turning round.

'You.'

'What about me?'

'You've told me nearly everything about yourself except the most important thing. Are you married?'

Dansie thought of his wife, Bess, and their daughter, Bonnie Sue who were 6000 miles away in Hollywood. It had been years since things were good between him and Bess but they'd stuck it out together because of the kid.

Hollywood was filled with children whose parents were divorced. Both he and Bess knew only too well what the majority of these kids turned out like. Lost souls. Neurotic messes. Bums. And in some extreme cases all three combined.

Neither he nor Bess could bear the thought of their daughter ending up like that, so they'd clung on to the few tattered remnants of their relationship.

'Well?' Harriet prompted.

'I'm married.'

He'd had to be, of course. It would have been too easy otherwise.

'Harriet?'

She drew him to her while placing a hand over his mouth. 'There are only a few hours left before you have to go back to your own room. Use them to love me,' she whispered.

6

Sitting by the window watching the men from Armstrong's trudge home from their work, Winnie's heart sank within her. The spring had gone out of their step, and without exception they walked with eyes downcast. Instead of the usual hum punctuated by the occasional laugh or piece of horse play, there was an air about them that was dark and sombre.

Winnie knew the signs. There had been a big lay-off. The only question remaining was how many had been made idle?

Closing her eyes and clasping her hands in her lap, she offered up a brief prayer. Luckily Donald was a gaffer and as such would be among the last to go. Hugh was still an apprentice which was an advantage at a time like this. Apprentices were always kept on to the end because they were cheap labour.

It was a strange night out, the sky peculiarly overcast and everything very still. The only sound to disturb the brooding silence was the tramp of the men's tackety boots on pavement and road.

There was Mrs McElvey's man, Bill, looking as though he'd lost a pound and found a tanner. Dazed and bewildered, he turned into his close and vanished from view.

Wee Tommy Taylor who always whistled to and from his work turned into Tallon Street. He wasn't whistling now.

Behind Tommy Taylor came Davey Beattie who

every Hogmanay came out onto the street directly after the bells to play his pipes. The expression on his face was the one he'd worn for weeks after receiving word that his two boys had fallen at Ypres.

Winnie rose and went through to the kitchen to make sure the tea was ready to go onto the table. That's where she was when the front door opened.

Wiping her hands on her pinny she hurried into the hall where she found Donald staring at the yellow distempered wall as though some profound truth was being unfolded to him there.

'Donald?'

When she got no reply or even a flicker of recognition she tried again. 'Donald?'

Coming out of the deep trance, he shook himself.

'How many?' Winnie asked, trepidation large within her. She'd never seen Donald in this sort of state before.

It took him a full minute, but finally he got that one terrible word out. 'Everyone,' he rasped.

She slumped and had to hold on to the wall for support. It was the nightmare come true. '*Everyone?*'

He nodded. 'Every last man jack of us laid off until further notice.'

Somehow she found the strength to stagger back to the kitchen where she sat on the edge of the opened coal bin.

Big Donald ran his wife a glass of water and then called through to Hugh that he wanted him.

Hugh was handed money by his father and told to run down the road and get a bottle of whisky.

'God knows but we all need a dram,' Donald said, adding, 'And if we don't get one the night who knows when we'll get the chance again?'

'This means we'll have to get by on Harriet's money and whatever Carrie can put into the kitty from what's left of old man Smith's two hundred,' Winnie said.

Donald and Winnie looked at one another, each with the same thought in mind. When Harriet went to Australia there wouldn't even be her money coming in.

Winnie buried her head in her hands, her mind numb at the prospect of what lay ahead of them.

Donald sat on the coal bunker beside his wife and, in a gesture that was both rough and gentle, put his arm round her shoulders. 'We'll get by somehow, lass. You just wait and see. After all, we've never died a winter yet!'

His voice was jocular and full of hope. Exactly the opposite to what he was feeling.

Sitting there, he noted that the linoleum under the sink was beginning to go. Well, it would be a long time now before that was replaced.

He clasped and unclasped his fist in frustration. There had to be work somewhere! And even as he was trying to reassure himself he knew in his heart of hearts the position was hopeless. There were tens of thousands out of work on Clydeside and now he and the rest of the men from Armstrong's had joined their ever swelling ranks.

Sneeringly he thought of Lloyd George and the coalition government. What a fiasco! What a shambles! It was long overdue for the working man to take power into his own hands in order to shape both his and his country's future. Only with the Labour Party in control would the ordinary man in the street get a fair crack of the whip. That was something Donald believed fervently and with total commitment.

Donald and Winnie were still sitting on the edge of the bunker when Hugh arrived back with the whisky. Carrie was with Hugh, having met up with him at the bottom of the stairs. She'd already heard the news on the street and had come straight home from her shopping.

Standing now just inside the kitchen door, Carrie watched Donald pour out four very large glasses of whisky.

Holding his glass, Hugh opened his mouth to make a flippant toast, but clamped it shut again when he saw the brooding volcanic expression on his father's face.

Sipping her whisky Carrie thought about Archie Marjoribanks. He'd already hinted at marriage, but she'd contrived to let him know that out of respect for John she wanted to wait a little while yet. Now it seemed she was going to have to think again due to this sudden alteration in circumstances.

She'd arranged to meet Archie in two nights' time when they planned to go to the jigging. She would sort it out with him then.

Hugh felt strangely lightheaded, a state which had nothing whatsoever to do with the drink but rather because it was gradually sinking into him that he'd been laid off and was now without a job.

Long, boring days stretched endlessly before him. The prospect was depressing. He'd seen what enforced idleness had done to other men, turning them into cabbages with no hope. No future. No nothing! It terrified him that he, too, in time would become like them.

He remembered then what Aly Paterson had said to him when he'd given up running with the milk to start in at Armstrong's. 'You're the best lad we've ever had and it breaks my heart to see you go,' Aly had said. Well, Aly still had the dairy up at Muirend and still did morning deliveries. It was certainly worth a try.

Harriet arrived home several hours later, having taken the midday train from Euston. Harriet thought it's an ill-wind which blows no one any good when she was told the calamitous news about Armstrong's. This was precisely the excuse she needed on which to hang her change of plans. She announced she had no intention of going to Australia now as it was essential she stayed at home and kept on her job at Ballogie Clothing.

Both Donald and Winnie were most humble at what they thought to be their daugher's· enormous self-sacrifice.

What neither of them knew was that Harriet had already decided not to emigrate and hadn't even bothered to attend the interview for which she'd gone down to London especially.

Lou Dansie had paid the hotel bill. The arrangement between her and Dansie was that he would come to

Glasgow and see her before motoring through to Edinburgh where he intended making his base of operations while in Scotland.

She would be travelling through to stay with him at weekends.

Shortly after Harriet's return, Hugh slipped down to the wash-house where he kept his bike. He'd decided there was no time like the present to find out what the current situation was at Aly Paterson's dairy.

It was several miles from Tallon Street to Muirend and all of it uphill.

As Hugh strained at the pedals he recalled that a lot of the enjoyment of running with the milk had been the horses whom he'd liked enormously and who'd liked him in return.

There had been one which had been his favourite, an old black beast named Squinty whose eyes were so crossed as to almost disappear into one another.

He thought now of Squinty with affection and wondered whether the old horse was still going strong or if it had finally got past it and been put down.

He turned the bike off the hill and into Aly Paterson's driveway. The house situated at the end of the long run up was an imposing edifice of grey stone which Aly had built many years previously to replace the very old and tiny one already on the site.

In front and to one side of the house stood the dairy building; facing that across the yard were the stables.

Besides this small complex Aly also owned a farm on the road to East Kilbride from where he supplied the dairy with milk.

Aly himself answered Hugh's ring and after shaking hands and being pounded on the back Hugh was ushered straight into the parlour where several logs were crackling away cheerily in the large stone fireplace.

Aly's wife, Greta, greeted Hugh as a long lost son. Kissing him on the cheek, she announced she would away through and put the kettle on and see if she could find a nice wee bit of shortie.

Aly pooh-poohed this idea saying that as Hugh was a man now and doing a man's job – Hugh winced at that – he should be given a man's drink. The whisky decanter was then duly taken from the sideboard and a large one poured.

Acting on doctor's orders Aly didn't drink any more, what with a weak heart and high blood pressure. Thinking it unfair to indulge when her husband couldn't, Greta had also forsworn alcohol.

'To Stewart!' Hugh toasted bringing grins of delight to the Paterson's faces. Stewart was their only child and the apple of their eye.

Hugh had first met Stewart when he'd come to work at the dairy and the pair of them had taken an instant liking to one another. After a few weeks the two of them had become almost inseparable.

Now Stewart was at agricultural college in Dumfriesshire where he was learning the very latest in farming methods. On leaving college he would take over the farming side of the business.

Greta confided in Hugh that Stewart had met a lassie and it seemed an engagement was in the offing. But before Hugh could offer his congratulations, Greta went on to say in a sepulchral tone that, nice as the lassie was, she had one terrible drawback. She was, horror of horrors, *English!*'

Hugh was astounded by this disclosure. He wondered what had come over his old pal. Stewart married to an Englishwoman! It was unthinkable.

'Dear me,' he said, shaking his head.

Greta sniffed.

'It's enough to drive a man to drink,' said Aly, looking longingly at the decanter. But a sharp glance from Greta was enough to dispel the notion. When it came down to it he enjoyed living more than he did the booze.

Quickly changing the conversation Greta asked Hugh to what they owed the honour of his visit? In a few terse sentences he told them about the closure of Armstrong's which meant he was now out of a job.

Both the Patersons were shocked by this news and Greta immediately rose and refilled his glass.

'There have already been marches out in Rutherglen,' Aly said, grim faced. 'Thousands of men protesting that there's no work for them and demanding something be done about it. There's nearly two million unemployed in the country now, you know.'

'Two million?' Hugh repeated. He found the figure staggering.

'Thing are as bad as they've ever been,' said Aly. His own particular business hadn't yet felt the squeeze but if the present downward spiral continued then it was only a matter of time.

The white collar workers who comprised the majority of his customers had so far escaped the ravishes of being thrown out of work. But they were far from immune.

Hugh then bluntly asked if he could have his old job back and was told he could start first thing Monday morning. The going rate was three shillings a day which added up to twenty-one shillings a week. Only a shilling less than he'd been earning at Armstrong's!

Hugh was jubilant and profuse in his thanks, but Aly would have none of it, saying what were friends for if they couldn't do you a good turn when it was needed.

Hugh said his good-byes. Outside the house he whistled as he mounted his bike. He couldn't wait to get home and tell Donald and Winnie.

After Hugh had gone Greta said gently, 'You didn't really need another boy, did you?'

Aly shrugged and stuck his hands in his trouser pockets. 'What else could I do?'

Smiling, Greta crossed to her husband and hooked her arm round his. 'You're a big softie and I love you for it,' she said.

Clutching one another like teenagers they made their way upstairs.

Hugh arrived home just as Winnie was making a last cup

of tea before going to bed. Unable to contain himself he burst into the kitchen and blurted out his news to her.

Winnie's eyes were decidedly dewy as she folded him in her arms and hugged him tight. She then called out to Donald to come away through and hear what his big son had to tell him.

Donald listened in silence while Hugh reported the outcome of his visit to the Patersons. When Hugh had finished Donald cleared his throat and said gruffly they had a big son right enough.

Winnie knew how hard Donald was taking all this. It was going to tear him apart inside for the family to be dependent on what Hugh and Harriet brought in. But better that than them all slowly starving to death on the pittance the broo* would allot them, she thought grimly.

That night Harriet tossed and turned. Her newly awakened body was afire while her mind churned with thoughts about the man who'd started the blaze.

What had really changed her mind about emigration was finding out that as well as researching the Bonnie Prince Charlie film in Scotland, Lou intended remaining on there while he wrote the first drafts of the script – at least six months' work. That and the fact that his marriage was on the rocks.

A lot could happen in six months. And she would see that it did.

Early next morning Donald's eyes flickered open at their usual time. With the customary grunt at Winnie he climbed out of bed and stretched himself by the window. He was about to pull on his work trousers when Winnie quietly said, 'You've forgotten, Donald.'

It all came flooding back to him in a wash of resentment and sour bile. He was laid off. Useless.

His shoulders sagged and something of his masculinity seeped out of him. He was no longer the provider. Instead he would have to go down and join the dole

* Unemployment exchange.

queue, making himself in his own eyes no better than a common beggar. It was a galling thought and made him feel bitterly ashamed.

He sat on the edge of the bed and started to speak. Out came many ideas and theories that had been percolating in his mind since the end of the war.

'They've got it all wrong,' he said slowly. Choosing his words with care. 'There are all these capitalists like Sir Alan Armstrong who've got the wind up and instead of spending their money they're hoarding it away in banks where it isn't doing anyone any good. If they keep on like that then the damn money will eventually become worthless. Not even worth the paper it's printed on. What they should be doing is spending and expanding trade. It's as obvious as the nose on your face but none of them has the sense to see it.

'Trade! If we don't do that then we stagnate, which is exactly what's happening to the country today. The capitalists are running scared and all they can think to do is hide away in their big houses assuring one another it'll all blow over. Well I've got news for them. This time things could get so bad that none of us will come out of it.'

With eyes blazing he continued, 'They must find the courage to take their money out of the banks and spend great chunks of it. It's the only way. Our only possible salvation!

'They have to recognize that for the truth before it's too late because if they don't it'll be the end of Britain as a country, far less a world power. God help us!'

Folding his pants, he laid them over the arm of the chair and then crawled back into bed where he lay with his arms by his side, staring at the ceiling.

Eventually he fell into a fitful sleep to dream of the first Labour government putting the country to rights and sorting out all social injustices.

Like everyone else who worked at Ballogie Clothing Jakey Sanderson had long since got used to the continual roar of more than 200 heavy industrial sewing machines clattering away flat out.

He strode down the back row of machines till he came to Harriet's where he stopped and waited till she realized he was there. When she looked up, he nodded in the direction of the cubicle that served him as an office. She gesticulated back she'd be right with him as soon as she'd finished off her present seam.

Jakey and Harriet were old pals, having known one another for many years, ever since Jakey had moved to Cathcart from Govan, in fact.

For a while they'd seen each other regularly at dances, and he had always come across and asked her up. The pair of them were excellent dancers and were rated highly amongst the Glasgow crowd. This was praise indeed as dancing was and always has been a sort of second religion in the city, the first of course being football.

As he let himself into his office, Jakey thought longingly of the cup of tea due to be served him soon. He had a terrible hangover from the night before, having run into his cousin Isa's man, Matt. It was to Isa that he'd promised the next available job.

The first thing Matt had asked about was the job, and it had been to Jakey's great delight that he'd been able to say one was coming up soon.

Matt had insisted they celebrate the news on him. Repairing to the nearest pub, pint after pint had been called for till they were both nearly awash. Then again at Matt's insistence they'd changed to big whiskies which had flowed in a seemingly never-ending stream.

Not once had Jakey been called on to put his hand in his pocket.

There was a knock on the cubicle door and Harriet entered to find Jakey sitting behind his desk beaming up at her.

'Well?' he demanded.

She couldn't think what he was talking about. 'Well, what?'

'How did the interview go?'

Of course he would want to know. He had gone to the trouble of arranging time off for her, after all. Normally she would have thought, but since meeting Lou Dansie her mind had become preoccupied with the American to the exclusion of all else.

'I'm afraid I got turned down,' she lied smoothly. Then with a wry smile, added, 'So it looks like you'll have to keep putting up with me.'

Jakey had to turn away so she didn't see the brief flash of combined anger and panic which contorted his face. This was terrible. More than that it was disastrous! He'd assured Matt the job was in the bag and as a consequence eagerly accepted all those drinks bought him by Isa's grateful husband. He'd committed himself, damn it to hell!

Things wouldn't have been quite so bad if it hadn't been Matt he'd promised, for Matt was a notorious hardman who carried a razor and had the reputation of breaking people's limbs just for fun. In local parlance Matt was a right heidcase.

He mopped sweat from his brow and then leaned back in his chair to stare up at Harriet. He liked the woman. Always had done. And she was a great partner at the jigging, unlike his wife who danced as though wearing clogs and two left ones at that. But now she'd landed him in a proper pickle and no mistake!

One way or another Isa was going to have to be found a job, and soon, because if she wasn't Matt would be round wanting his pound of flesh. And like Shylock, Matt had a nasty habit of putting a literal interpretation on things.

'Are you all right? You're looking awful funny,' Harriet asked.

Jakey forced a laugh and replied he was suffering from a wee touch of indigestion which he was sure would soon pass.

He then muttered a few words of sympathy to Harriet about not being accepted for emigration and she played along by pretending to be disappointed.

After she'd gone he hunched forward and stared morosely at his desk. There wasn't a hope that any of the other girls would hand in her notice in the near or even distant future. They would all be hanging on to their jobs like grim death. Even more so now that Armstrong's had closed down, throwing many of their relatives and boy-friends out of work.

But a solution to his dilemma would have to be found, and even now he knew what that solution was going to be.

Sighing, he reached for a cigarette and lit up. Much as he liked Harriet he feared Matt Walker even more.

At five am on the Monday morning Hugh presented himself at Paterson's dairy. As he was the first to arrive he went into the stables to have a look round for Squinty, and it was with a whoop of delight that he found his old friend munching away on some feed. A welcoming neigh told him he hadn't been forgotten.

He made a big thing of the horse, rubbing and scratch-ing its head while in response it nuzzled him under the armpit.

'Who the hell are you?' the voice demanded roughly.

Hugh turned to find himself staring at a squat, middle-aged man of less than normal height. Normally an easy-going, affable chap who rarely took exception to any-one, Hugh did so now. The moment he set eyes on Ronnie Sproat he knew he'd met an enemy.

He explained who he was and why he was there and then waited while Sproat considered this news.

What Hugh saw filled him with apprehension. Sproat was a walking powerhouse, his chest thick and burly, his thighs and biceps chunky with muscle. His face was concave, the nose no more than a button. His neck was short and sat atop his shoulders rather like a main branch sprouting from an oak. His eyes were dark and in this particular light like two empty holes punched on either side of his nose.

Hugh, on the other hand, was tall and willowy slim. It

would be a number of years yet before he came into his full strength.

Hugh knew that Sproat could beat the living daylights out of him without even half trying.

'I've heard of you,' Sproat sneered, showing badly decayed teeth, several of which were green with infection.

'Oh aye?' said Hugh, a little scared and not quite sure what was going to happen next. What he couldn't understand was why a discerning man like Aly Paterson had taken on a brute like this.

'You were a pal of Stewart's, were you no'?' Sproat demanded, picking his nose.

Hugh nodded, wary, waiting for anything to happen.

Sproat cogitated again and from the heavy frown on his face it was obvious his thinking processes were somewhat on the slow side.

Hugh found himself twitching and desperately wishing Sproat would say something. These long silences were unnerving.

'Did you know Stewart, then?' he asked finally, more to break the silence than because he was curious.

'I knew him all right,' Sproat replied, his eyes glittering ominously. 'I took over from him as head boy when he went away to college.'

Squinty snorted and tried to poke his nose back into Hugh's armpit.

Sproat's eyes narrowed as he watched this interchange between Squinty and Hugh, nodding to himself as though he found this of great significance. Then turning abruptly on his heel he strode from the stable.

Hugh breathed a sigh of relief and sank back against a wooden wall support. He didn't know what all that had been about, but one thing was sure – Stewart and Sproat were enemies and somehow the emnity between these two had reached out to include him. He just prayed Sproat wouldn't assign him to the lead cart which would, of course, be driven by Sproat personally.

He could hear Aly's voice now out in the yard so he

walked to the stable door. He saw that Aly was deep in conversation with Sproat.

Sproat was completely transformed from the brute who'd confronted him. The man's face was wreathed in smiles as he bowed and scraped obsequiously to Aly Paterson. Ronnie Sproat looked as though butter wouldn't melt in his mouth.

Glancing up, Aly caught sight of Hugh and beckoned him over. Hugh was introduced to Sproat who, with a grin, said they'd already met.

The other lads were arriving. Several of them had started to drag the gaudily painted carts from the back of the stables where they were kept. A shout went up from one of them to announce the arrival of the milk from the farm.

Hugh had just finished helping to load the last of the churns when he witnessed an incident which confirmed for him the sort of man Ronnie Sproat was.

A youngster of about twelve had arrived late, and Sproat, having manoeuvred him into a quiet corner, was now chiselling him about it.

Abruptly and savagely Sproat's hand swung to connect with the side of the boy's head, which knocked him off his feet and against a wall.

Just about to put the boot in, Sproat hesitated when he saw Hugh staring at him. Turning, he strolled slowly away, leaving the boy coughing and gasping on the ground.

Hugh ran forward and helped the boy to his feet. There was an angry weal on his face but no real damage had been done.

The lad thanked Hugh profusely, saying in a small scared voice that Sproat was a holy terror and God help anyone who crossed him.

It was obvious to Hugh that Aly Paterson couldn't know what was going on and the lad verified this by telling him Sproat had Aly eating out of his hand.

The lad then scampered off to his cart and climbed aboard. He and another young boy bent their heads together to discuss what had just taken place. They glanced fearfully across to the centre of the yard where Sproat stood with chest thrown out and thumbs hooked into his wide leather belt.

Judging from the expression on Sproat's face he thought himself the cock of the walk.

With a flash of insight Hugh realized that Sproat was mentally unbalanced. The man was a nutter and as such to be feared all the more.

Minutes later Sproat shouted Hugh across. Pointing to the stables he told Hugh to go in and get Squinty plus another horse to make up a pair.

When Hugh had led the two beasts out Sproat told him to couple them up to the lead cart. Having done that Sproat gestured him to find a seat amongst the churns.

Hugh's heart sank as he swung himself up over the tailboard. He was wondering just what he'd let himself in for.

7

Once the decision was taken, Carrie and Archie didn't waste any time. He took out a special licence and arranged for the ceremony to take place that Saturday at the old registry office in the Candleriggs. A quiet affair was planned with only the immediate family plus a few select friends.

Big Donald offered to have everyone back to Tallon Street after the marriage had taken place but Archie discreetly suggested it might be better if the gathering was held at what would be his bride's new home. Big Donald was only too happy to comply as it meant he wouldn't have to pick up the tab.

Things were extremely tight in the Chisholm household, the budget being literally managed on halfpennies and farthings.

Early on the big day, Harriet casually announced to the rest of the family that a friend of hers from London would be dropping by and furthermore he was coming to Laidlaw Street with her. She had, of course, first spoken to Carrie about this to obtain Carrie's permission.

This shock announcement was further compounded when at a few minutes past ten o'clock a magnificent 1920 Sunbeam 16 Tourer drew up outside the close.

Children playing in the street abandoned their games to come and gawp while all around curtains twitched as the neighbours peeked out, trying to see what all the commotion was about.

Never a shy woman at the best of times, Mrs McElvey threw her window right up and leaned out across the sill so she could get the best possible view.

The Sunbeam was a dull silver colour with a hood that folded back. It was Lou Dansie's pride and joy and the only one of its kind in California.

He'd ordered the car originally as a bit of one-upmanship but had soon come to love it for itself. He had brought it to Britain – the land where it had been built – for the simple reason he hadn't been able to bear leaving it behind.

Dansie was still shaken from his drive through Glasgow. He'd seen slums in America but nothing to compare with what he'd just witnessed:

It was a relief to find the street Harriet lived in a paragon of working-class respectability. He wouldn't have to worry about getting his throat cut here.

Carrying various packages containing presents he mounted the stairs to the top landing where the Chisholms lived. Harriet met him at the door and kissed him on the cheek. Then she ushered him inside to where the family were waiting in the living room.

Hands were shaken all round and the packages handed over to Winnie, who was momentarily flummoxed: this was the last thing she'd been expecting.

Carrie excused herself saying she had a lot yet still to do and Dansie replied he fully understood.

When Winnie discovered one of the packages contained a bottle of best malt whisky she handed it to Donald who went to the sideboard for glasses.

It was customary for drink brought into a house to be at least started on, if not finished, in the presence of the giver.

Big Donald was stumped for a second when Dansie said two ounces of liquor would do for him but in the end resolved his quandary by pouring out a large one which seemed to meet with Dansie's approval.

In the kitchen Winnie was unpacking large bars of chocolate and all sorts of strange and exotic foods.

Besides the food there were three beautiful silk headsquares, one for each of the women.

Donald was naturally curious about how Dansie and Harriet had met in London. Bluntly he asked how the meeting had come about?

Dansie's reply was near enough the truth. He said he and Harriet had been staying at the same hotel and had been forced through circumstances to share a table at dinner. Learning he was coming north to Scotland, she had extended an invitation for him to come and meet her family, an invitation he had been delighted to accept.

For over an hour the two men talked about the terrible unemployment ravaging the western world until Winnie interrupted them by announcing it was time she, Harriet and the baby left for Laidlaw Street where a meal was waiting to be prepared and laid out.

Dansie said it would be his pleasure to run them over there providing someone navigated for him.

Winnie was thrilled at the prospect of riding in the Sunbeam. It would be her first time in a motor vehicle.

Dansie was delighted and promised her she would sit

up front with him.

With Angus wrapped up tight against the cold they trooped downstairs where Dansie made a bit of a fuss ensuring Harriet and her mother were seated comfortably.

The neighbours were back at their windows as the Sunbeam moved sedately off down the street with children running screaming behind it.

During the drive Winnie asked Dansie if he'd ever been to the town of Sherman in Texas? When he said he had, she sighed and sank further back into the car's ample upholstery. In a small voice she requested he tell her what sort of place it was and what its inhabitants were like?

The request puzzled Dansie who knew nothing about Alex. But it was obviously important to Winnie so he did his best to comply.

All the time he spoke of Sherman, Winnie listened intently, drinking in every word.

When he had finally exhausted his knowledge of the subject she thanked him courteously and for the remainder of the journey sat tight-lipped and introspective.

By the time they reached Laidlaw Street they'd passed through some of the worst slum areas and it was an extremely humble Lou Dansie who parked the Sunbeam outside Marjoribanks's close.

His own problems which had seemed so enormous were really of little consequence when compared to all this. For the first time he began to view his life and the job he did in perspective. It was a sobering thought.

After seeing the women and baby upstairs he returned to the Sunbeam, worried that the rough looking crowd surrounding it might damage it in some way. For a few minutes he dithered, not sure how to tackle the situation. Then he had a brainwave. Approaching two of the toughest looking men there he politely asked if they'd be willing to do a job for him.

Both men were gaunt from hunger. They glanced at each other and then one growled they might be interested providing Dansie made it worth their while.

In actual fact they were desperate for work and would have done nearly anything to earn a few bob but their pride demanded they didn't appear too eager, especially as it was a foreigner they were dealing with.

Dansie handed them five shillings each and told them to sit in his car and see no damage came to it. When it was time for him to leave he would give them a further ten shillings each providing the car was just as he'd left it.

The two men couldn't believe their luck. This was a Godsend. And money for old rope, to boot! They climbed into the Sunbeam from where the larger of the two announced in a very loud, gravelly voice that if any so and so as much as breathed on the gentleman's motor then he and his good friend Sammy here would personally mollicate the unfortunate.

Dansie went back up the stairs with a lighter heart, convinced his car was in good hands, as indeed it was.

In the house he was introduced to Archie and Sheena who were both in a fluster trying to get dressed. He was grateful for the huge fire stoked up in the kitchen range. The Chisholm place had been terribly cold, he'd thought. And he'd no sooner seated himself close to the roaring flames than Winnie plonked Angus on his lap telling him to mind the wean.

He liked children so it was no hardship for him to entertain Angus while Winnie and Harriet got on with the business of preparing the meal.

As Archie and Sheena finally left for the registry office Archie called out that they shouldn't be too long and that there was drink in the sideboard. Everyone was to help themselves.

After Archie and Sheena had noisily clattered their way downstairs Harriet opened a screwtop of beer and handed it to Dansie. When their hands accidentally touched she smiled as did he.

In a surprisingly short time those who'd attended the ceremony were streaming in through the front door. Carrie and Archie were covered in confetti and laughing like excited children.

Dansie was introduced round while Archie got out the drink.

Big Donald and old man Smith found themselves together and for a few minutes chatted about Carrie and Archie. Then Robert brought up the subject of Donald having been laid off.

There was a hollowness where his belly should have been as Donald described what it was like signing on the dole. The queues that stretched seemingly for miles. The ranks of men shuffling forward inches at a time for the indignity of being given a few miserable shillings' charity.

The air of degradation and hopelessness that hung over these men like a pall. The lined faces twisted with worry and fear.

The collective sigh that seemed to go up from time to time as though the men had just realized anew that they were of no further use to society and had been discarded on the Corporation midden.

Donald threw whisky down his throat and followed that with the remains of his beer. He shuddered and exhaled slowly.

There was no self pity in him. He knew what he was and that he was as good at his job as the next man. Better probably. He had a reputation as a grafter and a perfectionist who took pride in his work which was why he'd been the youngest foreman Armstrong's had ever appointed.

Robert Smith wanted to express his sympathy with the situation but wasn't quite sure how to do so. Words seemed so inadequate. In the end he offered to get Donald another drink.

Standing by himself in a corner Hugh was already a little tiddly as he brooded about Ronnie Sproat. Life had been hell for him since he'd started back at the dairy, Sproat making him do the work of two, if not three. Every time there was a full churn to be moved or lifted Sproat saw to it that he did it on his own. On top of that he'd been forbidden to ride on the cart which meant he had to run alongside all the time.

He'd made a few discreet inquiries amongst the other lads but none of them knew what the trouble had been between Sproat and Stewart. Or if they did they were keeping stum.

He'd considered going to see Aly Paterson to tell him what was going on but that was before he'd realized how much Aly relied on the odious Sproat, who toadied up to Aly at every occasion.

Aly wasn't a well man. The trouble with his heart had slowed him down a lot and as a result he'd sloughed off more and more of the dairy's running onto Sproat's shoulders. Sproat was only too pleased to accept the additional responsibility as, apart from increasing his pay packet, it also gave him more power. And power was something Sproat liked very much.

Hugh knew now that, albeit he and the Patersons were close, should it come to a showdown, he was far more likely to be shown the door than Sproat. Aly had come to rely on his head boy.

There had been the incident at the stables just the other day when things had nearly flared into an all out confrontation. He'd been gathering some feed to place in Squinty's stall when suddenly a pitchfork had come plunging down from the hayloft to miss him by inches.

Sproat had been full of apologies, a combined sneer and half laugh in his voice as he spoke them. He'd said that his hands must be greasy for the pitchfork to have slipped out of them like that.

Completely drained by shock, Hugh had stood there for a few moments while anger alternated hot and cold within him. Pulling himself together, he bent down and picked up the pitchfork. Its prongs were bent at their tips from the impact with the stone floor.

Monkey-like Sproat leapt onto a dangling rope and descended. When he faced Hugh his eyes were mocking and full of malicious glee.

Hugh desperately wanted to lash out, to have a go at

this horrible man whom he detested so much. But somehow he managed to keep his fury under control, reminding himself that a blow up on his part was precisely what Sproat was after as it would merit Sproat giving him the sack.

Knowing Hugh was dying to hit him Sproat smiled and thought perhaps one more turn of the screw might do it.

Sproat was convinced Hugh was after his job as head boy. After all, wasn't Hugh a great china of the high and mighty Stewart? The same Stewart who'd once threatened him with dismissal should he ever be caught bullying any of the boys again.

Fear grabbed at Sproat's stomach as he thought of Hugh being made up to head boy: if that was ever to happen his little secret would be out with dire consequences for him.

Still smiling Sproat took the pitchfork from Hugh and on turning away pretended to slip. With a yell he fell over while bringing the pitchfork sharply down so that it cruelly raked Squinty's left flank.

Squinty squealed as blood spurted. Hunching his head, he frantically drummed his rear hooves and then lashed out with them.

Hugh was well aware that this had been a deliberate act on Sproat's part. The bastard had definitely had it in for Squinty ever since his first day back at the dairy when he'd said he and Squinty were old pals.

'Whooaa there boy!' Hugh shouted, running round to the side of the stall and clambering up its side so that Squinty could see him.

As soon as the horse's hooves had started flashing Sproat had rolled to safety. He frowned now as he lay on the floor. His plan wasn't going to work. Instead of coming at him Hugh had gone to the horse.

'It's all right! It's all right!' Hugh soothed, stroking the side of Squinty's head. The beast's eyes were rolling with fright and pain. Every few seconds a fresh wave of tremors rippled through its body.

Hugh looked at Sproat now standing well back from

the stall. 'It seems to be your day for accidents,' he said, not even bothering to hide the sarcasm and contempt in his voice.

Sproat didn't like that and for a moment it seemed he might made an issue of it. Instead, he shrugged and threw the pitchfork clattering onto the floor which caused Squinty to whinny and lash out again.

'That animal should have gone to the knacker's yard long before now,' Sproat said. 'It hardly does enough work to earn its keep.'

Hugh bit back the angry words crowding his mouth. Squinty might be old, but he grafted damned hard and what's more Sproat knew it. The thing was Aly would believe what Sproat told him and it could well be that out of sheer spite and maliciousness Sproat would arrange for the horse to be done away with.

As casually as he could Hugh said, 'I know a farmer who's on the lookout for an old cuddy. He'll pay reasonably for one too. Certainly more than the knacker's yard would. I'll mention it to Aly as it would mean a few more quid in his pocket should he decide to replace Squinty here.'

It was a complete fabrication which he'd made up on the spur of the moment and judging from the sour look on Sproat's face it would seem his bluff was going to work. Squinty was safe for a while yet.

After Sproat had left he washed Squinty's flank down and painted the wounds with antiseptic. Luckily for the horse they weren't nearly as bad as they looked. The scores were long but shallow, and, providing infection didn't set in, should heal quickly.

While Hugh continued to brood about Ronnie Sproat his uncle Sandy had at last managed to get Winnie on her own, something he'd been trying to do since they'd arrived back from the registry office.

Nodding in the direction of the hallway he whispered for her to follow him as he wanted a quiet word.

Out in the hallway he drew the living room door to

before turning to a puzzled Winnie. Slipping some crumpled white paper into her hand he said that was a wee something to help her and the family get by.

The crumpled white paper was two fivers which expanded from the ball they'd been crushed into when she unclenched her hand. 'Och Sandy,' she said gratefully. He and his wife Mary had their own family to keep which couldn't have left them with all that much to spare at the end of the week.

'I had some good overtime on my last voyage,' Sandy said, 'And I'm away again within the next fortnight so we'll be sitting pretty for a while at least.' Slightly embarrassed now he added. 'There's no need to say anything about this to that soft brother of mine. He'd probably make you hand it back.'

Winnie knew that Sandy was right. This was best kept quiet between her and her brother-in-law.

'It's just a loan, mind!' she insisted, coming to terms with accepting the money that way.

'Aye of course. If that's how you want it.'

'I do,' she replied, knowing in her heart of hearts there was a certain futility about her promise to pay it back as Donald could well be idle for years.

Standing on her tiptoes she pecked Sandy on the cheek. 'I won't forget you and Mary for this,' she said, a catch in her voice.

Poor Mary who was so fat that a trip down to her local shops and back again was the best she could manage. Hence the reason why Sandy had attended all the official family functions on his own for the past few years. 'Once round aunt Mary, twice round the block' had at one time been a saying that would always raise a laugh. But that had been in the days when a joke could still be made out of Mary's fatness.

Opening the front door Winnie rushed down the stairs to the toilet on the half landing. Having bolted herself in she stuffed the fivers down her bra. Then she sat down and had a right good bubble to herself.

*   *   *

Early the next afternoon Jakey Sanderson used his keys to let himself into Ballogie Clothing. There was nothing unusual in this as he often worked an hour or two on a Sunday in an effort to try and keep pace with the ever increasing amount of paperwork expected of him.

The machine room floor was a different place without the constant roar that filled it during the week. His footsteps echoed hollowly as he made his way to the back row where Harriet's machine stood.

Sitting, he thumbed the switch which caused the gun metal grey machine to surge with power.

There were three bundles of finished trousers lying beside the machine. Each tied with string and bearing Harriet's personal marker. Every machinist had her own personal marker so that it was always known who had done what and that way any item could be referred back to the person responsible for it.

Jakey untied the first bundle and lifting the top pair of trousers onto the machine set to work.

In a little under an hour he had altered various seams on half a dozen pairs of trousers in such a way as to make it look like faulty workmanship on Harriet's part.

When he was finished he switched off the machine and retied the bundles. Having checked that everything was just as he'd found it he left the factory and headed for home.

On the Monday afternoon Winnie was down on her hands and knees waxing the hallway linoleum when the front door opened and Harriet appeared.

'What brings you home at this time?' Winnie demanded, thinking Harriet must have been taken ill.

Harriet stood staring numbly down at her mother and looking as though the question hadn't got through to her. Her face was strained and there was a puzzled expression in her eyes.

Donald entered the hallway from the living room where he'd been idly carving Angus a wooden boat for when the lad was older.

'What's going on then?' he asked.

'I've been given the sack,' Harriet stated bluntly.

Winnie sucked in her breath and her hand came up to her mouth.

'What happened, lass?' Donald asked quietly, not betraying by the merest flicker just how shaken he was by this latest calamity.

They all went through to the living room. Harriet told them how Jakey Sanderson had come storming up to her with several bundles of trousers saying her work on these was a bloody disgrace.

The entire factory had come to a halt as hot words were bandied between herself and Jakey who'd proceeded to humiliate her by waving the offending articles in the air and shouting in a voice loud enough for everyone to hear that an apprentice could do better work than she could.

At that, her temper had boiled over – as Jakey had known it would – and she'd traded insult for insult till in the end he'd trumped her acid retorts by declaring she was fired.

Stunned, she'd collected her few things together and gone through to the accounts office where she'd had to wait half an hour while they made up her time.

Some of the girls had made a few voluble remarks about the sacking but they weren't in a position to do anything about it. Not one of them would stick her neck out in case she, too, lost her job.

After hearing all this Winnie groaned and sat back in her chair. Closing her eyes she gently massaged her forehead with workworn hands. With Harriet's money now gone it meant they were reduced to having to live off Donald's broo money and what Hugh brought in from the milk.

Harriet shook her head. She was at a complete loss to understand how she had turned out seams like the ones Jakey had confronted her with. And yet they were undeniably hers. The bundles they'd come from had all borne her personal marker.

Donald asked if there was any chance Jakey would change his mind. Harriet's reply was that he wouldn't.

If the sacking had been done in the privacy of his office then she would have gone back to him and pleaded for another chance. But as it had occurred with the entire factory listening on – and bearing in mind some of the things she'd called him which everyone had heard – there was no likelihood whatsoever of him reversing his decision. Too much face was involved.

'I'm sorry, Papa,' Harriet ended up saying.

Donald rose and crossed to her. He tried to smile but didn't quite manage to pull it off as he patted her on the shoulder.

He desperately wanted to be out of the house. He felt hemmed in. Claustrophobic. He would walk down to the river and watch the water swirl by. There was a certain therapeutic effect to be gained from watching running water, he'd always thought.

'It seems you've sacrificed the Australian idea for nothing,' Winnie said. Dejectedly she headed for the kitchen to put the kettle on.

Donald left Harriet sitting staring into space. As he made his way down to the front close he patted the one remaining Willy Woodbine in his pocket. All that remained of the five packet Carrie had slipped him earlier on in the week. He would smoke that as he watched the water. He had nothing better to do.

Harriet and Lou Dansie sat in the Bluebird Cafe. He listening while she recounted what had happened at Ballogie Clothing.

Dansie was secretly pleased at this turn of events. He'd managed to secure a rented house for himself in Edinburgh and all that week had been puzzling about how to get Harriet to come and share it with him. Now he knew.

When he put his suggestion to her she sat back and stared at him as though he'd just pulled a rabbit out of a hat, which, in a way, he had.

Naturally she didn't want Donald and Winnie to know they were living together. Dansie's reply to that was she would take digs, which he would pay for. And as far as anyone in Glasgow was concerned that would be where she was staying. In reality, however, she would be living with him in St Stephen's Place.

Harriet was a realist who was never slow to grasp an opportunity when it presented itself. Dansie's plan solved both her major problems in that it meant she would not only be working again but would also be with him.

After they'd finished their ice creams they walked to the nearby Queen's Park where they hammered out the details. Harriet was elated after the week's depression. Everything was going to be all right after all, thanks to Lou.

On an impulse she stopped and throwing her arms round him kissed him deeply. Several passers by stopped to stare but that didn't bother her. She was truly happy which was all that mattered.

When they arrived back at Tallon Street she announced straight off that Lou had engaged her as a researcher for his film about Bonnie Prince Charlie at the marvellous wage of three pounds ten shillings per week.

Winnie gasped when she heard. It was as much as Donald in a good week with lots of overtime had ever earned at Armstrong's.

Harriet hurried on to say she would also be taking typing lessons and when she was proficient would be helping Lou type out his script.

Of course all this meant she would have to stay in Edinburgh where the job was and she had decided that digs were the most suitable thing.

When Harriet mentioned she'd be sending home two pounds per week Winnie was so relieved she collapsed into a chair and for a moment it seemed she might even burst into tears.

Dansie then suggested Harriet return with him to

Edinburgh where he would put her up in a good hotel until she found suitable digs. He stressed the fact he was desperate for her to start as soon as possible.

Harriet hid the elation bursting within her. The idea of the hotel was merely a sop for her parents. That night she'd be ensconced in St Stephen's Place. In bed with Lou Dansie where she belonged.

With everything now neatly arranged Harriet hurried through to the bedroom to pack. While she was doing this Dansie reflected on the great changes wrought in his life since meeting her. The long stale years with Bess had been blown away, leaving him gloriously alive again. He and Harriet were no two ships passing in the night. He'd known that instinctively as had she. Theirs was a relationship with a long term stamp on it.

And hadn't Harriet pointed out to him that Bonnie Sue was now at an age where she wouldn't be nearly as affected by a divorce as she would've in the past?

That thought had certainly given him a lot to chew on, just as Harriet had intended.

8

It was early in the summer when things finally came to a head between Hugh and Ronnie Sproat. So far Hugh had been able to ride everything Sproat had thrown at him; in fact the more he'd done so, the more desperate Sproat had become.

Enormous changes had taken place in Hugh since he'd come back on the milk. His experiences with Sproat had toughened him both mentally and physically, transforming him from a boy/man into a fully fledged male.

He'd also broadened out a lot and the constant exercise of running miles per day plus hauling and humping heavy churns had increased his strength to the point where he thought he could at least give Sproat a good go of it should they ever square up to one another, a situation Sproat seemed determined to bring about.

Having just returned from the morning round Hugh led Squinty to his stall where he left him standing just in front of the opening into it. First he would rub Squinty down and then when that was done to his satisfaction he'd feed the old horse. Humming to himself, Hugh reached for the hand brush hanging from a beam.

Hidden in dense shadow Sproat stood at the back of the stables watching every move Hugh made. He had a brown feed sack clutched in one hand which every so often twitched as something stirred inside.

A few days before Sproat had noticed that Hugh was terrified of rats. He wasn't too keen on them himself, come to that, but they certainly didn't frighten him the way they did Hugh.

There are always rats around stables although there weren't many in this one thanks to the big ginger tom Aly kept who was a notorious and fearless ratter.

The previous evening Sproat had returned to the stables where it had taken him several hours of patient waiting in order to trap the long sleek beast now held prisoner in the sack.

Grinning in anticipation, he thought of the terror and blind panic Hugh would experience when the rat landed on him. He was going to enjoy this. He was going to enjoy it a lot.

He flexed the thick, corded muscles running the length of his shoulders and down his arms. If only Hugh would lose control and take a swing at him then his day would really be made. Given the slightest provocation he would beat Hugh to a pulp and relish every second of it.

But Hugh had to make the first move. That was a prerequisite. When the story came to be told to Aly Paterson he must be able to protest that he'd only been defending himself.

Stealthily he crept forward, watching out that he didn't tread on anything that would make a noise.

He froze when the rat squeaked and scratched its claws on the inside of the sack. But Hugh, completely engrossed in what he was doing, heard nothing.

Sproat continued his advance only to freeze a second time when he heard the voices of several of the lads outside. For a moment it seemed the lads would come into the stables, but having paused by the doorway they continued on past.

Sproat breathed relief. He would have been furious had the lads intruded to spoil his fun, the more so as he'd specifically detailed all of them to be working across at the dairy for the next half hour. It was no accident he and Hugh were the only ones in the stables.

Masking himself behind a partition belonging to one of the horse stalls, he felt for the thick leather glove tucked into his belt. Once the glove was on he laid the sack down on the floor in such a way that its opening was spread out in a taut line. Hurriedly he placed his feet so that most of the opening was blocked off, leaving only a narrow passage for the rat to get through.

Minutes later he was cursing inwardly. Although the rat was running around inside the sack it seemed too stupid to be able to work out what it had to do to escape.

'Come on, damn you!' he breathed. He was crouched over the sack, his gloved hand poised to swoop once the beast began to emerge.

Suddenly the rat found the passage and wriggled through so quickly he almost lost it. Three times he grabbed before he managed to get his fingers round its neck.

With vicious looking claws tearing the air the rat was hoisted up off the ground. Its black beady eyes glared malevolently as it looked for someone, something, on which to vent its fury.

Sweat was coursing down Sproat's face and back as he held the rat at arm's length. Raising himself up on his tiptoes he peered over the partition to see what position Hugh was in.

Hugh pulled the brush in long even strokes along Squinty's pelt. The horse was still steaming a little from its morning's exertions and the warm animal smell it gave off was one Hugh found extremely pleasant.

When Squinty snickered he didn't pay any attention thinking the old horse was telling him to hurry up so he could get his nose into the feed which was next on the agenda.

This time Squinty whinnied with a note which caused Hugh to pause in mid-stroke and look round.

The scream was torn from him when he saw the rat, claws extended and eyes ablaze, hurtling through the air straight towards him. His right hand with the brush still banded to it struck out and with good luck more than good judgement he connected with the rat, knocking it squealing to one side.

Sproat stood with hands on hips silently roaring with laughter. The look on Hugh's face as the rat had come hurtling towards him had been absolutely priceless.

The rat twisted in mid-air and as it dropped towards the floor its flailing claws managed to catch onto and sink into soft, warm flesh. Its teeth guillotined down to bury themselves in Squinty's leg.

Squinty reared up and shrieked, an almost human sound that raised the hair on the back of Hugh's neck.

Again and again the rat's claws cruelly raked Squinty's leg. Freeing its teeth it took its time about selecting a fresh target. This time when it bit a jet of darkly coloured blood shot out from a severed artery.

Numb with fright Hugh stood watching Squinty rear and plunge. He desperately wanted to help but the only thing he could think of was to grab hold of the rat and tear it free. But with the best will in the world there was just no way he could bring himself to do that.

Sproat's silent laughter stilled when he heard the distinct sound of Aly Paterson's voice at the stable door. It wouldn't do for him to be found standing by watching while one of their horses was in obvious trouble. With a shout he rushed forward to try and knock the rat off Squinty's leg with a piece of harness.

Eyes rolling and frothing at the mouth, Squinty thought this was some new enemy come to attack him. Wheeling suddenly round he lashed out with his rear hooves, catching Sproat full in the chest.

Surprise was written all over Sproat's face as he flew backwards to land with a sickening thud on the stone floor.

'What in the name of the wee man is going on here?' Aly demanded, Greta by his side.

The rat tore itself free and jumped to the floor where it went scampering away to disappear behind a bale of straw.

Hugh ran forward to try and grab hold of Squinty but the horse would have none of it. Iron hooves stamped savagely down, causing sparks to fly from the stone floor as it backed away.

Sproat saw his danger and tried to roll to safety but the excruciating pain tearing his chest apart forced him to stop and gasp for breath. As Squinty's flicking tail and backside reared over him he just had time to cover his face with his arm before the animal's hooves came pile-driving down.

Sproat yelled in agony as his legs broke under the impact. He fainted clean away when a sliver of white bone came jabbing through his trouser leg.

Squinty staggered and then sank to his knees in a pool of arterial blood. His eyes were already glazing in death when Hugh took hold of his head and began stroking it.

'There, there old boy,' Hugh whispered, letting Aly and Greta attend to the stricken Sproat.

'I'll send for the doctor!' Greta yelled to no one in particular as she ran from the stables.

'And a vet!' Hugh called after her, knowing full well

that long before a vet could arrive it would be all over for his old pal.

Sproat was still out cold, blood trickling from a corner of his mouth.

Squinty's exhaling breath rasped out causing his nose to flutter. His flanks heaved while all around him the pool of blood grew wider.

At the end of a mighty convulsion it was all over. What light was left in his dulled eyes winked out as death claimed him for her own.

'What happened?' Aly Paterson asked. He could see how moved Hugh was by the old horse's death.

Hugh shook his head, still shocked by the speed with which events had taken place.

Of one thing he was certain, however: Sproat was behind all this. The only trouble was he had no way of proving it.

In a voice husky with emotion he told Aly the literal truth of what had happened. Concluding his story, he was aware that Sproat had come to and was watching him from behind half closed lids.

Any lingering doubts about Sproat's involvement were blown away. The bastard was guilty as hell!

Greta returned to say one of the boys had been dispatched for the doctor.

Sproat was in terrible pain which, to give him his due, he bore remarkably well. Both his legs were broken and several of his ribs.

In a croaking voice he said he wasn't to be moved till after the doctor had examined him. He was scared that if he was, one of his broken ribs might puncture a lung.

A number of the lads came crowding round the stable door to see what had happened, a few of them not bothering to hide the triumphant glint in their eyes when they saw Sproat lying there in obvious agony.

Hugh pulled himself together and took command. He ordered two of the horses brought from their stalls and hitched to a delivery cart. When it was time for Sproat to be removed to hospital this would be as good a way as any to do it.

The boys accepted Hugh's commands willingly and set about their appointed tasks with a lightness in their step that hadn't been there before.

Sproat asked for a cigarette and got one. He coughed a little as he smoked and there was a strange, resigned look in his eyes. Occasionally he smiled in a lopsided, cynical way as though amused at some private joke.

The doctor arrived a quarter of an hour later and got on with his examination.

Greta was sent into the house for an old sheet which was torn into strips and used for bandages. After Sproat's chest had been strapped up rough splints were fashioned and bound tightly to his legs.

That done, all the available lads were called in to help as Sproat was manhandled onto a plank which was lifted and slid onto the waiting delivery cart. Two of the boys were designated to drive the cart to the hospital while the doctor followed on behind in his car.

There was nothing left for Hugh to do now but organize Squinty's burial. This he did in a piece of ground at the back of the dairy building which was nicely secluded with lupins and other wild flowers growing in profusion.

Insisting on digging the grave alone, he sweated over it for what seemed an eternity. When it was finally ready he got those boys still remaining to help him load the carcass onto a bogey which they trundled to the graveside.

When Squinty was deposited at the bottom of the grave he sent the lads away again while he filled it in.

When the burial was completed Aly Paterson brought him over a screwtop of beer and together they stood looking down at the mound of freshly turned earth.

It was then Aly asked him to take over as head boy. He immediately accepted. Both of them were aware it would be a long time before Sproat was fit to work again. Those legs alone would take months to heal. The job paid two pounds a week.

He was invited over to the house where he once more

went over his version of what had happened in the stables. As he spoke Greta tut-tutted and shook her head. She wasn't particularly partial to rats either.

On the first Friday after the incident Hugh did a money collection of all the rounds. It didn't take him long to work out that what he'd taken was in excess of Sproat's figures. Furthermore, no matter how hard he tried, he couldn't make this discrepancy resolve itself.

Armed with both money and books he went straight to Aly Paterson and the pair of them sat down to work out just what was what.

It became clear that Sproat had been on the fiddle to the tune of five pounds a week, a sum he'd gradually built up to and thereafter maintained.

Aly was shocked and heartbroken by this revelation, so much so he broke his rule and had a drink. Over their dram he sought Hugh's advice. Should he prosecute or merely cut his losses and let things go at that?

Hugh took his time in replying. He wasn't a vindictive person but not only was Sproat a bully and a thief, the villain was also responsible for Squinty's death and that was something he could neither forgive nor forget.

'Prosecute,' he advised.

When Ronnie Sproat finally did appear in court he was found guilty of embezzlement and sentenced to three years in Barlinne Prison. Hugh was there to hear sentence passed and it was with a grim smile that he watched Sproat being led away.

Squinty was revenged.

Harriet had never been happier in her life. She and Lou Dansie had long since settled into St Stephen's Place where they spent long hours working, he on his script which was coming along famously and she either researching or typing up his pages for him.

She'd discovered she had a natural aptitude for typing and had consequently picked it up easily and quickly. She was studying shorthand which she found more difficult to assimilate but was none the less becoming proficient at.

She adored the researching side of her job, taking great delight in visiting museums and other such places to pore over ancient and usually musty tomes, ferreting out snippets of information which she then fed to Dansie as though they were rare treats.

Nor was her research confined solely to the academic. Several times Dansie sent her off to various parts of the country where her brief was to quizz the locals and write down stories that had been handed down by word of mouth from generation to generation about the Prince and the Jacobite rebellion.

Harriet thrived on all this. Her new life seemed as far removed from Cathcart and Ballogie Clothing as St Stephen's Place was from the far side of the moon.

A bloom had appeared in her cheeks. The sort that love, happiness and a full sex life brings.

They often ate out, frequenting the best restaurants the capital had to offer. Other times they stayed cosily at home while Harriet cooked. She was a good cook who'd got a lot better since being encouraged to experiment, something Donald would have viewed with horror.

They drank a lot of wine. Dansie bought it by the case and had it delivered to the door.

They attended many concerts and plays – a whole new world for Harriet.

It was after just such an excursion to the theatre that they returned home one night to find a telegram lying on their front door mat.

Neither were particularly perturbed by this as telegrams were commonplace to their household, United Artists often cabling Dansie and he replying by the same method.

This one was different, however, as it came from Bess.

Dansie sat and read the telegram several times before looking up. When he did so it was obvious the wire contained bad news.

Crossing to the brandy decanter, he poured himself a stiff one.

With narrowed eyes Harriet sat patiently by waiting for the worst. She knew instinctively something momentous had occurred.

'It's Bonnie Sue,' Dansie said, his eyes filling with sudden tears. 'She's been taken into hospital. The doctors don't know what's wrong yet but whatever it is, it's serious.'

Harriet had never seen a grown man cry before and for a moment was quite mesmerized by it. Where she came from a man would rather die than be seen in such a state. Only women and weans cried. A man was above such a blatant show of emotion.

Finally she roused herself to ask if this mightn't be a ruse on Bess's part to lure him back to Los Angeles?

Dansie's brow creased as he considered this possibility. There was no reason why Bess should know about him and Harriet. Certainly he had never mentioned it in any of his letters home. But these things do have a way of leaking out and it wasn't impossible that news of their liaison had somehow travelled 6000 miles.

When he spoke it was to say Bess was capable of many things but not of using Bonnie Sue in that particular way. As far as he was concerned the telegram was genuine and he would treat it as such. Anyway he couldn't afford not to.

It was too late for him to do anything that night other than draft a reply. In the morning he would go straight to Waverley Station and catch a train for London from where he'd embark on the first available New York bound ship.

Harriet was shaking inwardly as she went upstairs to pack Lou's things, while he drank more brandy and pencilled out his reply.

There was to be no sleep for either of them that night. Instead they lay in bed and talked in whispers about what was to happen while he was away.

It was agreed between them that she would stay on at St Stephen's Place doing what research she thought might be beneficial and getting on with her shorthand studies.

He would give her a cheque before he left in the morning and once back in Los Angeles he would make the necessary arrangements for her and the house's upkeep through his bank.

The Sunbeam he would leave behind for his return.

They made love after that until it was time to rise and get ready to go to the station.

Harriet was desolate as she climbed into the cab Dansie had hailed in the street. Everything had happened so quickly she still couldn't believe that within the hour he would be on his way back to America.

There was an air of unreality encompassing her as she gazed through the cab's window at the cobbled streets and passing grey stone tenement buildings. She imagined this must be something like how Carrie had felt when told about John McBain's death.

Her left hand was opened and something cold slipped onto her wedding finger. When she looked down she saw she was now wearing Dansie's heavy gold ring, the one given him by Mary Pickford.

'Keep that for me till I get back,' he said, closing her hand into a fist again.

There was so much she wanted to say but the only words that would come seemed trite and meaningless. Looking into his eyes she could see it was the same with him so she snuggled close and they stayed that way till they arrived at the station.

It was cool inside the station with sudden gusts of wind that caused men to hold onto their hats and women to clutch at their skirts.

She went to purchase newspapers and a few magazines while he stood in line to buy his ticket. As they walked the length of the platform Harriet felt as though someone was hacking at her insides with a blunt knife. She wanted to shout, scream, throw her arms round Lou.

Instead they kissed one last time and then he said he thought she should go, that way would be better for both of them.

For a few seconds more they remained clutched to one

another, and then tearing herself free she turned and walked back the way they'd come.

Time passed.

There was a letter from New York, another from Los Angeles, and after that silence.

The long weeks became a month and the month became two, then stretched to three. During this time Harriet busied herself as best she could and tried to delude herself that everything was all right.

Then one day while she was busy round the house and for once had neglected to go down to see what the mailman had delivered, the long awaited explanation came.

With trembling fingers she ripped open the envelope and sat down to read what Lou had to say.

Bonnie Sue had been stricken with a brain tumour which had come within an ace of killing her. A surgeon called Krantze had developed a brand new technique for dealing with this most horrible ailment and as a last resort had been instructed to operate.

The result had been only partially successful. Bonnie Sue's life had been saved but a terrible price had been paid. From now on the girl would be little better than a vegetable, her mind permanently that of a six-year-old.

An ice cold wind blew through Harriet when she read that. She knew then that Lou Dansie would never be coming back to her nor would she be going to him.

In that instant her whole life crumbled and fell apart. Her lips thinned to become a bloodless slash and her face sank in upon itself to become pinched and shrewish. She'd become the epitomy of an ageing spinster.

She continued reading: Bess knew nothing at all about their affair nor was he going to tell her now. There would be no divorce. As Bonnie Sue desperately needed both her parents from now on there was no way he could bring himself to break up his marriage, inflicting further pain and anguish on his mentally crippled daughter.

He was truly sorry. He still loved Harriet as much as

he had on the day they'd parted. But their affair was ended.

Harriet stopped reading to light a cigarette. She stared at her hands, wondering why she'd never noticed before how close her veins were to the surface? What a peculiar observation for a time like this, she thought.

Gazing round the room it seemed to her everything was just that little bit more so than it normally was. Colours more vivid. The ticking of the clock more resonant. Her senses of smell and touch more acute than usual.

It crossed her mind that she might be in a state of shock or on the verge of a nervous breakdown.

She returned again to the letter.

United Artists had cancelled the film about Bonnie Prince Charlie and a new project on the life and times of Robin Hood with Fairbanks again scheduled for the title role, was being set up.

This was a further blow to Lou who had invested a great deal of time and effort in his Bonnie Prince Charlie script.

He didn't elaborate on why the film had been cancelled but as he was working on a new assignment for United Artists she assumed it wasn't because of any fault on his part.

The latter pages of the letter consisted of instructions for winding up the let on the house and the disposal of the Sunbeam. She was to keep the money realized from the sale of the car. The various bits and pieces he'd bought she was to do with as she wished.

He ended the letter by repeating his love for her, adding that he wanted her to keep his Mary Pickford ring as a memento in the hope she would never forget him. He was never going to forget her till his dying day.

She laid the letter down and lit another cigarette from the butt of the first. Crossing to the whisky decanter she poured herself an extra large one.

Memories of the happy times they'd spent together came flooding back to her. Large, fat tears welled from the corners of her eyes to meander slowly down her cheeks. The dream was gone, the illusion burst. Hollywood and her love had somehow blown away, leaving only the reality of impending spinsterhood behind.

Finishing her drink she poured herself another. She wished Carrie had been there for her to talk to. Of all the people she knew her sister was the one most likely to understand just how she felt.

Picking up the letter and decanter she started for the bedroom. Tomorrow would be soon enough to begin what had to be done.

For the rest of the day she would lie womblike in the bed they'd shared together. She'd drink a lot and cry even more. Tears might be futile but they did bring some sort of relief.

The thick gold ring weighed down her wedding finger. Sometime soon she'd buy a gold chain on which to hang it round her neck. Bringing the ring to her lips she kissed it. 'Oh my darling!' she whispered.

Part II

Rosemary for Remembrance
1931–1938

9

Angus was ten years old when the Marjoribanks moved to Holmlea Road just round the corner from Tallon Street. The new house had three bedrooms, a kitchen, a living room, and an inside toilet cum bathroom. Carrie had never got used to either the stairhead closet or the zinc tub in front of the fire, so she appreciated the bathroom most of all.

Angus had a bedroom all to himself which he thought a grand thing, although at night he missed Sheena's heavy breathing, which had always been a great comfort to him, and the long whispering sessions they'd often secretly indulged in.

Now Sheena had left school and was employed as a conductress on the trams.

The work situation had eased over the past few years. Armstrong's had re-opened and one of the first people to be re-employed had been Donald, taken back in his old capacity as foreman moulder.

Although asked, Hugh hadn't returned to Armstrong's. He preferred staying on at Paterson's Dairy.

Aly was dead. His heart had finally given out and he'd passed away peacefully in his sleep three years previously. Stewart had married his English sweetheart and was now boss at Muirend and the farm just off the East Kilbride Road.

Hugh was still called head boy although he was really more of a manager as Stewart spent nearly all his time out at the farm where he and his wife lived.

Hugh had no regrets whatsoever about his decision. He enjoyed his work and loved being with the horses. The offer of a few pounds more per week wouldn't have enticed him back to the bedlam of the foundry.

On Angus's first day at Holmlea Primary he was taken along to a Mr Barr's class where he was told to sit beside a boy called Robin Kirkpatrick. The lesson at the time was spelling and during it the two boys stole surreptitious glances at one another, each trying to size the other up.

When the bell rang for playtime Angus followed the rest of the class downstairs and out into the playground where he found a quiet corner by some palings to eat the jelly pieces Carrie had packed for him.

He was in the middle of his second piece and watching some lassies playing peerie when Robin Kirkpatrick and several other boys came strolling across. Inside Angus was tense but, trying to appear nonchalant, he wiped jelly from his chin. He knew whatever happened next would decide whether or not he was accepted.

Robin Kirkpatrick was roughly the same height as Angus but a lot broader in the chest and shoulders. He had a rather ruddy face inclined towards pudginess. His hair was a deep auburn and hung limply in long and somewhat greasy strands.

Thinking it might be interpreted as a sign of weakness Angus decided not to speak first so he continued trying to look nonchalant as he switched his gaze from the peerie-playing lassies to a game of footer taking place further up the playground.

Robin Kirkpatrick noted Angus's interest in the footer and that gave him inspiration for his first question. 'Which team do you support?'

Angus turned to stare at Kirkpatrick, acting surprised at being addressed.

'What?'

The aggressiveness in Angus's voice threw Kirkpatrick a little. He was used to other boys being wary of his size.

'I said, who do you support?' This time he matched Angus's aggressive tone.

'The 'Gers are the boys,' Angus stated, as though it were Holy Catechism.

'Aye. That's right enough!' Kirkpatrick replied with grudging approval. Angus's answer had been the correct one.

By this time Angus had come to the conclusion that with the possible exception of Kirkpatrick none of the boys surrounding him were nearly as tough as some he'd known in his old school. There had been a number of real hardmen in his class there, all right.

'Where do you stay then?' Kirkpatrick continued doggedly.

When Angus replied he was living in Holmlea Road he was asked which number. It transpired he and Kirkpatrick were neighbours, living next close to one another.

The next question was what did his father do?

Angus replied that his father was dead – that caused several blank stares and shuffling of feet – but that his step-father was an engine driver. He added the last bit not out of deference to Archie but because flyly he knew the effect it would have.

Several of the boys gaped and even Kirkpatrick was taken aback. An engine driver! Probably the ambition of half the lads in that crowded playground.

'For LMS,' Angus threw in for good measure, smiling inwardly at the effect his words had produced.

'Gosh!' exclaimed one of the boys, his face full of awe.

Kirkpatrick broke the spell by stepping forward and slapping Angus on the back. He and the others were about to play a game of Cowies and Indians and would Angus care to join them?

Angus groped in his jacket pocket for the rubber dagger he had there and announced he would be only too happy to take part.

When it came to choosing up it seemed everyone

wanted to be on his side. Having an engine driver in the family did have its advantages.

After that Angus and Kitty – Robin hated the name but it was what everyone insisted on calling him – became the best of pals and through his new found friend Angus soon learned his way round Cathcart and all the best play places.

As summer gave way to autumn the pair were often down at the Cart, a place called Sandybank being their favourite spot, where they fished with string and jam jars for baggy minnows and the red bellied tiddlers known, for some obscure reason, as 'doctors' or 'docs'.

Snow came early that year and with it Hugh to Holmlea Road humping a present for Angus.

When Angus arrived home from school that day he found Hugh sitting in front of the fire chatting to Carrie. The present, wrapped in canvas bagging, took pride of place in the centre of the kitchen floor.

Hugh was extremely fond of his nephew and now that Carrie and Archie were living in the neighbourhood he was hoping to see a lot more of the lad than he'd done in the past. The present was by way of an overture to Angus who he hoped would soon find time to visit him at the dairy.

Angus ripped the canvas bagging away and whooped with delight at the newly made sledge, smartly painted in dark green with a red and black lightning flash running its entire length.

For Hugh, the beam on Angus's face was ample reward for the couple of hours it had taken him to make the sledge. He'd got the idea of knocking it together when he'd come across the runners stuck in a corner at the back of the hay loft. They'd been pretty rusty but with a bit of elbow grease he'd soon had them gleaming like new. The wood had come from an ancient cart in the process of being cannibalized.

Thanking Hugh profusely, Angus bolted down his tea, dying to get out in the snow and try out his new sledge. It was a brammer and far better than any the boys round about possessed.

He would call on Kitty and together they'd away up to the Queen's Park Reccy Ground, the most popular sledging site in the district.

After Angus had gone Hugh asked Carrie if everything was all right? She was dreadfully pale with dark heavy rings under her eyes. He'd also noticed some bruises on her arms and suspected Marjoribanks was knocking her about. This wasn't the first time he'd spotted black and blue marks on her.

Carrie knew precisely what her brother was driving at but shrugged it off, saying she wasn't sleeping too well with Archie working so many lates and nights.

When Hugh stared pointedly at the bruising she added casually she'd slipped the other day and banged her arm against the coal bunker. Having told the lie, she promptly changed the subject by putting a fresh kettle on for Sheena's tea and announcing the lassie would be arriving in from her work at any minute.

Carrie's attitude to Archie was complex. Over the years he'd worn her down to the point where she now dully accepted her lot.

It wasn't as though Archie was all bad, she'd often told herself. He did have his good points. He'd never been a day out of or off work since they'd got married and every Friday he came straight home and paid her the housekeeping money without fail.

He was also a generous man. All she had to do was ask and if it was possible he'd get it for her. Occasionally he would even surprise her by bringing home a gift which he'd hand over, saying gruffly it was a wee minding he thought she might like.

She'd long since come to the conclusion there was something wrong inside Archie's head. He could be pleasant and charming one minute, a raging animal the next, capable of almost anything.

Sexually there was a perverted side to him which he often indulged in. At such times all she could do was grit her teeth and pray the ordeal would soon be over.

Why she didn't leave Archie? In the beginning she had often considered it. But her options were strictly limited: getting a job – which still wasn't all that easy to come by – and finding a place where she and Angus could live together or, failing that, returning to Tallon Street.

There was no question of her finding another man. She wouldn't have wanted to even had it been possible.

What it boiled down to was she had reconciled herself to making the best of a bad job. Archie might be a sadistic bastard but he wasn't entirely unlivable with.

What she had made crystal clear to him was that if he ever beat up Angus the way he beat her up that would be the end of it. She would pack what few things she and the lad had and go.

Running a hand through greying hair she took a deep breath and wished she could find more energy. She was always so tired nowadays, drained to the point where she found it a terrible struggle just to get through the daily grind.

She had developed a permanent stoop and her skin had a washed out look about it.

At thirty-one she looked in her mid forties.

On arriving at Queen's Park Reccy Ground Angus and Kitty immediately joined in the fun, taking alternating shots to zoom over the hard packed snow, lying face down on the sledge or else sharing the same ride together by sitting one in front of the other.

It was Angus who first noticed the two lassies in trouble. The girls were about the same age as himself and Kitty, maybe just a little younger, and both dressed in extremely smart uniforms. They were surrounded by a gang of toughs intent on mischief.

'Yeh toffee-nosed Parkies!' one tough jeered, spitting at the taller of the two girls who recoiled in disgust as the gob landed on her coat.

Angus had never heard the expression 'Parkies' before. Kitty informed him Park School was up the town somewhere and catered for the daughters of the very rich.

Angus had no sympathy with rich girls. Or rich anyone come to that. But he did think it a bit thick that ten boys had ganged up on two puny lassies.

The tough who'd spat darted in and, catching the taller girl's scarf, yanked it from round her neck. The girl showed a lot of spunk in lashing out at him but missed and would have gone toppling over if it hadn't been for her companion catching and steadying her.

The second girl was close to tears which she was desperately trying to hold back. The taller girl stood proud and defiant with a look of utter contempt for their tormentors written across her face.

The tough with the scarf tied it round his waist and, wiggling his hips provocatively, taunted the taller girl by proposing she come and take the scarf back off him.

Hoots of strident laughter and obscene suggestions made both girls blush with embarrassment.

Angus knew the sensible thing would be to ignore what was happening but there was something about the taller girl which struck a sympathetic chord in him, making him want to go to her defence. When she caught his eye and silently pleaded with him he knew he was going to have to get involved.

At that moment one of the toughs ran at the taller girl and catching her by the shoulders sent her spinning to the ground. The tough immediately sat on her back and proceeded to rub her face with a handful of slush.

The girl spluttered and choked as the slush was driven into her mouth and up her nostrils. Her hat had been picked up by a tough who was now sporting it on his head.

'That's enough. Let her go now,' Angus said quietly, his fists balled by his side ready for action.

The tough sitting astride the taller girl stared incredulously up at Angus. 'What did you say, Jimmy?' he demanded.

'Let the lassie go,' Angus repeated.

Slowly the tough rose from his sitting position till he was fully upright on his rather bandy legs. With a nod to his mates he started moving in on Angus and Kitty who were now standing back to back. With a sudden roar all ten toughs simultaneously launched their attack.

For a few minutes Angus and Kitty held their own with hard blows given and taken by either side.

The beginning of the end came when Angus's feet were kicked from under him and with a strangled yell he went crashing to the ground. With no one to guard his back, Kitty was soon overpowered and when he fell, he landed heavily on Angus.

Kitty grunted with pain as a boot came thudding into his side. What he couldn't understand was why Angus had got them into this fight in the first place, over two lassies who undoubtedly had more money than sense. It was beyond him.

Angus and Kitty would have been onto a right doing but for the sudden intervention of Robert Cooper, Winnie's downstairs neighbour's son, who was now a houseman in the nearby Victoria Infirmary.

Robert and a few of his friends had been out for a breath of fresh air when they'd caught the sound of the fight. Seconds before he fell Angus had been recognized by Robert who immediately strode into action.

Tough after tough was hauled of the still struggling Kitty and Angus and thrown unceremoniously to one side. When the toughs realized they were facing new adversaries, and grown up ones at that, they lost heart and took to their heels.

The only injuries Angus and Kitty had were a few scratches plus a cut lip on Angus's part. They were both extremely lucky and knew it. The toughs could just as well have been carrying weapons which they wouldn't have hesitated in using.

A shaken Angus blurted out to Robert Cooper what had happened but when he came to look round for the Park School girls they'd both vanished. He was hurt, feeling the least the lassies could have done was to say thank you.

It was Kitty who pointed they'd probably run off when

they'd seen he and Angus were getting the worst of the punch up.

Robert and his pals insisted Angus and Kitty accompany them back to the hospital so that their cuts could be attended to. Despite protestations that they were both all right, the pair of them were taken back to the infirmary's casualty department to have iodine painted on their faces.

Several nurses came in to see the heroes – the nurses' words, not theirs – who'd been so gallant in going to the assistance of the put upon wee lassies. Angus and Kitty squirmed with embarrassment and couldn't wait to flee the building. But first they were taken along to a side room where tea and fancy cakes had been put out, a treat from these self same nurses whom Angus and Kitty now concluded weren't so bad after all.

Finally they did escape out into a night filled with swirling snow. Deciding it was getting late, they agreed to go home. As the pair of them trailed along the road Angus's mind was filled with images of the taller girl who'd had her face rubbed with slush. It was the queerest thing but in that moment when their eyes met and she had silently pleaded with him it was as though he'd known her all his life.

Arriving home he found Sheena sitting by the fire engrossed in a romantic novel. She looked up to tell him word had come for Carrie to go to Tallon Street as Winnie had taken ill.

Angus was immediately concerned as he was very fond of his granny. From what little Sheena knew he gathered Winnie had come down with a bad cold which had suddenly turned into something else.

Carrie's instructions were for him to go to bed when he got in and if she wasn't back by morning Sheena was to get the breakfast.

He then had to explain the iodine marks on his face. Not wanting to mention the Park School girls in case Sheena thought him soft he told a version of the story that excluded the two lassies.

Then he hurried through to his bedroom where he dried down the sledge before changing into his pyjamas.

Having changed and pulled the bedclothes back he decided on a last trip to the bathroom.

His feet pattered on the linoleum as he made his way along the hallway. The bathroom door swung open to his touch to reveal his step sister in all her naked glory.

Angus gawped. This was the first time he'd seen Sheena with no clothes on since she'd reached puberty. His eyes travelling from the generous swell of her breasts down to the furry clout protruding from between her legs. His mouth was suddenly dry and his heart palpitating fit to burst.

Sheena stared at Angus, as surprised as he was at his barging in on her. She was sure she'd locked the door! When she saw the transfixed expression on his face, her mouth slowly curved into a smile.

Angus wanted to turn and run but his feet were rooted to the spot. There was a terrible compulsion in him to reach out and touch his step-sister's naked flesh.

Sheena realized what was going through his mind and that excited her. 'Come here,' she said crooking a finger at him.

Like an automaton Angus moved towards her.

He stopped when he was only inches away, his eyes riveted on one of her nipples.

The hand that took his sweaty one was cool. 'Oh Sheena,' he mumbled as his fingers enclosed a breast.

At the back of his mind he was terrified the outside door would open to admit either Carrie or Archie. He daren't even think of what would happen should he and Sheena be found like this.

Sheena knew what she was doing was unforgivable but she couldn't help herself. There was a lot more of Archie in her than either he or she knew.

Angus started to tremble as his hand was guided down the length of his step-sister's body to come to rest on the woolly clout between her legs. The hair was a lot more wiry than he'd expected and it was damp which surprised him as he'd walked in on her before she'd had her uppey and downey.

The bathroom was warm. Heated by a small stove standing by the wc, the paraffin aroma mingled with the sweet and distinctive smell given off by Sheena's naked body.

'Are you scared?' she asked softly.

He lyingly shook his head.

Sheena's face was glistening with sweat and her lips parted in a way that made her look catlike. There was a burning sensation in her throat and between her legs where Angus's hand was. At that moment she would have given anything for him to have been a few years older.

Letting his hand go she said, 'You'd better run along to bed now and leave me to get washed.'

Angus nodded, not trusting himself to speak. His thoughts were whirling and confused, part of him wanting to run away from there as fast as his legs could carry him while another part wanted to stay.

It came to him consciously then that the Sheena he'd known these past ten years had changed beyond all recognition and in doing so had left him behind. She was no longer the same She-she who'd mothered him and held him tight in bed while strange things were happening between Archie and Carrie through the wall.

'Go Angus!' she commanded, turning her back on him and fumbling with the taps.

This time he wanted to reach out and touch her for quite different reasons than before. He couldn't bear the thought that the She-she he'd known was now lost to him. It was like losing an arm or leg.

'Go!' she repeated.

And he did.

When he was in his bed he hid under the covers and cried softly to himself, not because of what had happened but because he knew it marked the end of an era in his life.

That night he dreamt of the taller of the two Park School girls standing stark naked in the centre of the Reccy Ground.

Only it wasn't her own but rather Sheena's body she was flaunting beneath the falling snow.

Winnie was hot, sweaty and bordering on delirium. Although Carrie had changed the bedclothes not half an hour since, again they were saturated.

With hands clasped and shoulders hunched Donald sat by Winnie's bedside where he'd been since she'd taken a turn for the worse not long after he'd arrived in from his work.

He looked lost and very scared, for once not bothering to mask his emotions with manly indifference.

Dr Robertson had already been and gone and would return later. Solemn on arrival, he'd been downright grave on leaving.

Winnie blinked as globules of sweat rolled down her forehead and into her eyes. Instantly Carrie was there with a wrung out cloth to dab away the sweat and cool down her flushed cheeks.

Winnie turned her head to one side so she could look at Donald. She hadn't noticed before, probably because it had been a gradual thing. But she could see now just how much he'd aged during his six years of being idle.

There was skin hanging where his jowls had been and the neck below had gone thin and scrawny. Those magnificent broad shoulders which had been his pride and joy were now bent and bony, their muscles having withered with the onset of old age.

Closing her eyes she allowed herself to drift, seeing Donald as he'd been when they'd first met. He'd been tall and straight then and she the envy of every woman who saw them walking out together. She could remember thinking him a braw but serious young man whose one line of conversation consisted of what he was going to make of himself in life.

Whenever she could arrange to have a Sunday off he'd come and collect her and together they'd go walking down by the River Kelvin or in the Botanical Gardens, both of which were just across the way from the house in Bellhaven Terrace where she'd worked.

It wasn't long before they'd discovered they had a lot in common, coming from the same Highland stock: in her case from the clachan of Fanagmore on the banks of Loch Laxford in the wilds of Sutherlandshire.

For eighteen months Donald courted her. Then one summer's evening down by the Kelvin he'd asked her to marry him. She'd been so excited that for a full minute she hadn't been able to speak while he, poor man, died the death thinking she was going to turn him down.

But of course she hadn't, and the wedding, conducted by the young Reverend Duncan Forbes, had been one to remember.

Sandy Chisholm had been there with his wife Mary, as well as his other brother, Willy, his sister, Nettie and her man.

And Donald's mother, Fiona – looking grim and forbidding and every inch the Chisholm matriarch – had come, softening a little as the night wore on and more than just a few drams vanished down her throat.

From her own side two of her sisters had made the journey from Fanagmore. Her father and mother wouldn't dream of leaving the croft while the third sister didn't come because they only had enough money to send two.

Both Kathy and May had arrived looking prim and proper at the Orange Hall, intent on showing that anyone from Fanagmore was just as good, if indeed not better, than anyone from the heathenish Glasgow where it was well known all sorts of unspeakable things happened to a body if she wasn't careful. But time and whisky had loosened their reserve as well till in the end they'd been wheeching it up with the best of them.

Then it had been home for Donald and Winnie to their

own wee hoose in the Calton where after three years of
marriage their firstborn came into the world. Alex had a
wild look in his eye even as a baby. He grew up to be
smaller than his father but just as broad-shouldered.
Alex with the silvery laugh, which always made Winnie's
insides jump just to hear it. And so clever with his hands
he even won grudging praise from Donald. Grudging
only inasmuch as Donald didn't want the lad to get
swollen headed. Privately Donald was delighted,
although he'd never dream of saying so to anyone other
than her.

Winnie's eyes blinked open and she realized she must
have fallen asleep and been dreaming. Everything had
been so real – as though she'd somehow managed to step
back in time.

'Oh Donald!' she husked, her throat parched from
fever.

'I'm here lass. I'm here,' he said, taking her hands in
his. Putting a strained smile on his face he told her to rest
easy and she would soon be better.

He didn't believe that and neither did she. But they
were both wrong.

For three days Winnie was at death's door and then, as
suddenly as its onset, the fever broke and she started to
mend.

During this time she'd been nursed by Carrie and
Harriet taking it in shifts while Donald had remained
steadfastly by her bedside only leaving the room when
nature demanded it.

Learning that his mother wasn't going to die after all,
Hugh was so relieved he decided to lash out and buy her
something really special to cheer her up.

He took a tram into town where, because the capital
outlay was beyond him for the moment, he bought her a
wireless set on the newly introduced idea of hire purchase.

Winnie was delighted with the gift, though scanda-
lized by its extravagance.

He left her listening avidly to a discussion about house

plants on the Home Service.

It was during tea that night that Harriet quizzed him about the wireless and he let slip he'd bought it on the never never.

The moment the words were out of his mouth he realized he'd made a terrible mistake. He should have known Donald would view with horror buying anything on hire purchase.

'What did you say?' Donald demanded, his voice tight with suppressed fury.

Hugh carefully laid his knife and fork on the plate before him. Taking a deep breath he sat back in his chair.

Before replying, he re-examined his motives for using the hire purchase agreement and came to the conclusion they were good ones.

He'd wanted to buy his mother a present and what he'd known she'd appreciate most had been for the moment outwith his pocket. The hire purchase scheme was merely a device allowing him to get round this temporary shortage of funds and enabling Winnie to have the set when she could most use it.

Speaking slowly and carefully he repeated his earlier statement.

The thick hairs protruding from Donald's nose quivered, the nostrils dilating and the nose itself flattening. He was appalled. What Hugh had done was unforgivable!

Fierce Highland pride welled up inside him. The creed was simple. If you couldn't afford to buy something then you went without until you could. The last thing you did was to enter into some sort of Shylock arrangement. Hands once renowned for their strength knotted into fists. He wanted to reach over and slap Hugh, to knock some sense into his son's head. Where was Hugh's pride? His self respect?

It didn't matter that Hugh's motives were laudable. If he hadn't been able to pay cash for the present then no present should have been made. Winnie could well do without. She'd survived fifty-seven years without a wireless so a wee while longer wasn't going to make all that much difference.

It was a matter of principle. He had his standards which were his father's and his father's father before him. He expected his family to live the same way. Donald's chair scraped back as he rose to his feet. Silently he strode from the room and a few seconds later the wireless playing by Winnie's bedside was switched off.

Hugh sighed and looked from Carrie to Harriet. What upset him most was that Winnie was going to lose her wee bit of comfort because he hadn't the sense to keep his mouth shut.

The living room door banged against the wall as Donald entered carrying the wireless. Crockery and cutlery jumped as the set was dumped on the table.

'Take the wireless back and we'll forget all about it. And you've your mother to thank for that. I was all for throwing you out of the house for doing such a damned stupid thing.'

Normally Donald wouldn't have over-reacted the way he was doing now but he was bone tired and not thinking straight. Nearly losing Winnie had exacted a terrible toll from him: it was affecting his judgement and sense of perspective.

'You would've thrown me out for that?' Hugh said, completely stunned.

'Oh Papa!' Carrie breathed.

All eyes turned as Angus entered the room. The happy expression on his face died as he realized something was going on. When Carrie beckoned him to her side he ran there to stand wide eyed and silent.

Driven by an inner demon Donald rattled on. Alex would never have passed up the chance of going back to Armstrong's. Alex would never have dreamt of playing milkie when there were men's jobs to be had. And most pertinent of all Alex would never have shamed his mother by buying her a present on hire purchase!

Harriet sucked in her breath.

Carrie bit her lip,

Awed and frightened by what was going on Angus clung tightly to Carrie's skirt. He didn't want his grandpa and Uncle Hugh to be like this. He wanted them to be friends.

Hugh had never realized how bitterly Donald had resented the fact he'd never resumed his job at the foundry. Nor had he realized his father had found him so much wanting compared to his dead brother.

'So there,' said Donald glowering. And coming forward he reached out with the intention of poking Hugh in the chest.

In the space of a few seconds Hugh's whole life had altered dramatically and would never be the same again. With a snarl he pushed his father's hand away and taking a step backwards said, 'Lay a finger on me and so help me God I'll flatten you.'

Donald laughed cruelly. 'Do you think you're man enough then?'

'Aye. I think I am,' Hugh retorted.

'This is ridiculous,' said Harriet. But before she could continue she was interrupted by a voice from the doorway.

'What's going on here?' Winnie said, the words little more than a whisper. She was in her nightdress with a shawl slung over her shoulders. She clung to the door frame for support.

'Winnie! You shouldn't be out of your bed, lass!' Donald exclaimed and hurried over to her.

'I could hear the shouting,' she said.

He ignored that and, turning her round, led her back towards their bedroom.

'You stay here,' Carrie instructed Angus before dashing after her parents and Harriet who'd gone ahead to straighten out the bed.

Suddenly Hugh was trembling and like a jelly inside. Not wanting Angus to see the emotions playing over his face he walked swiftly to the window and stared out over the backgreen and the River Cart beyond.

Donald had been right about one thing. The time had come for a break to be made. After what had been said it was impossible for him to remain in his father's house.

'Have you ever considered running with the milk in the mornings?' he asked.

Angus was taken aback at this coming straight out of the blue and for a moment or two was at a loss for words. It had been an ambition of his for some time now to go out with his Uncle Hugh on the milk rounds. Finding his voice again, he blurted this out, adding he had a pal who was just as keen as he was.

Pleased by the lad's reply, Hugh said that when Carrie pronounced Angus old enough he was to come out to the dairy where he and his china would be fixed up with jobs.

Going through to the big room Hugh packed his few possessions. He couldn't bring himself to walk out without saying goodbye to his mopther so tapping on her door he went in to tell her he was going.

'Oh son!' was all Winnie could say.

'Where will you stay?' Harriet asked.

Hugh shook his head. He hadn't got that far yet. With a lump in his throat he kissed his mother and turned to go.

'Don't forget to take the wireless with you,' Donald said uncompromisingly.

When Carrie let her brother out the front door he had his suitcase in one hand and the offending wireless on his shoulder. He walked up the street to the tramstop without once looking back.

Donald was a lot more shaken by what had happened than he let on. He hadn't meant to say some of those things to Hugh but somehow in the heat of the moment they'd come thundering out.

'I think I could sleep for a wee while,' Winnie lied. She wanted to be alone.

Harriet left the room to join Carrie and Angus through in the kitchen where the two women set about washing and drying the dishes while Angus sat watching.

Donald entered the kitchen carrying a bottle of whisky a little over half full plus two screwtops. 'Out,' he said, signing towards the door.

When Angus made to leave Donald restrained him. 'The men stay,' Donald growled, closing the door behind the bewildered females.

Donald poured two drams, one large, one small. The latter he topped up with water.

'Slainte!' man and boy chorused in unison.

The rawness of the alcohol caused Angus to scrunch up his face and cough. Donald chuckled. There were times when Angus reminded him of Alex as a boy. The eyes were the same, as was the way they both had in certain moods of thrusting out their lower lip.

But if Angus had Chisholm characteristics there was also a lot of John McBain in him. The same stubbornness. The same ability to withdraw into himself and view the world as though from a great distance. The same basic common sense which had made John McBain admired and respected by so many of his workmates and pals.

Donald poured himself another dram and added a beer as a chaser. He could see Angus was struggling with his drink but obviously determined to get it down.

'What do you want to be when you grow up?' he asked abruptly.

There was no hesitation about Angus's reply. He'd known the answer to that question for a long time. 'To start with I'd like to work at Armstrong's like my Da,' he said.

Donald grunted his approval, moved by the light shining in the boy's eyes, a light that was always there when Angus spoke of John McBain.

You could do a lot worse than Armstrong's,' Donald said. 'A lot of good men have learned their trade there.'

For a while both of them were silent, Angus imagining

what Armstrong's was like, Donald thinking of the reality.

'After I'm time served I'd like to go to sea. Do you think my Da would have approved?' Angus asked.

Donald considered that. 'I don't see why not,' he replied. 'It's a good life at sea if you enjoy that sort of thing and if you find it doesn't suit you or get tired of it there's nothing to stop you coming ashore again. There's lots hereabouts have done that.'

Angus stared into the pale amber of his drink and, as though it were a crystal ball, imagined some of the exciting and exotic places he would visit with the Merchant Navy. The prospect sent shivers up and down his spine and goose bumps on his arms.

'To Armstrong's and the sea, then!' Donald toasted.

'To Armstrong's and the sea!' Angus responded.

'What are you two up to in there?' Carrie demanded anxiously from behind the closed door.

'Men's talk!' Angus replied, at which he and Donald burst out laughing.

10

Angus had to wait until the following autumn before he was given permission by Carrie to run with the milk. In just under a year he'd grown nearly a foot which had changed him from a compact, chunky lad into a tall, gangling one.

Carrie knew it was just the age he was but nonetheless it worried her to see how drawn and haggard he'd become. It was only after a long talk with Hugh that she agreed for Angus to go to work for the dairy, the theory being fresh air and exercise couldn't help but do him good.

It was still dark that first morning when Angus dragged himself out of bed at four thirty to stand hopping on the cold linoleum floor while he struggled into his warmest clothing. He was bleary-eyed, with a sour, bilious feeling in the pit of his stomach as he made his way through to the kitchen where Carrie was waiting for him with a cup of tea and a hot bacon roll.

Spirits revived, he rushed downstairs and out to the backgreen where his bike was kept chained to a railing, the same bike that had once belonged to Hugh and which he'd fallen heir to when big enough to reach the pedals.

Kitty, sitting astride his machine, was waiting for him outside the front close and together they headed for Muirend.

Kitty had also grown during the past year but with him there had been none of the runaway stretching that had so elongated Angus's body. Whilst steadily inching upwards Kitty had managed to retain his powerful physique, which was, if anything, even more burly than before.

The friendship between the pair of them had gone from strength to strength till now it was hard to imagine them apart. They practically lived in one another's pockets.

When they arrived at the dairy Hugh was already busy about the yard. The day he'd left his father's house he'd taken himself to the dairy where he'd explained his plight to Greta Paterson. Greta's response had been immediate. He was to stay with her in the big house where she was fed up and sometimes a little scared of living on her own. He would be her lodger paying a nominal rent.

It hadn't taken him long to settle in and soon he'd come to regard the house as a home away from home.

The dairy with Hugh in charge boomed and before long he began to think of expanding.

After considering Hugh's plans – for if the outlet side of the business expanded then the production side would have to as well – Stewart Paterson came to the conclusion that what Hugh had in mind was viable and immediately set to work organizing his end of things.

The first thing Hugh did was to order four new delivery carts and a few weeks before taking delivery, he travelled down to a farm he knew of in Selkirkshire where he bought eight young horses to add to the dairy's complement.

New rounds meant more staff, which had made him think of the promise he'd made Angus the previous year. He and Carrie had talked the matter through and it was finally agreed Angus could make a start. They would see how the lad got on.

Apart from his health, Carrie's main worry was, at eleven, Angus was still a little young to run with the milk. After all, for five days a week he would still have a full day's schooling to get through after he'd done his round. But Hugh had been able to put her mind at rest with a few well chosen arguments, plus the promise that if Angus's schoolwork suffered in any way then the lad would be made to give the job up.

The first thing Hugh showed Angus and Kitty how to do was harness the horses and after that the correct procedure in loading churns and stacking the crates of bottles.

Hugh had timed the boys' start to coincide with the first day of the new rounds and, much to their delight, they discovered he would be in charge of the cart they were to be on.

When it was time to set off Hugh shouted to them to climb aboard and the moment they'd done so he flicked the reins and the cart jolted forward.

As they went, Hugh explained he'd already solicited the area they were to service and as a result they had a considerable number of orders to start off with.

Over a bridge across the River Cart they went, the air filled with the thunderous noise from a nearby weir, and then on towards the Old Castle Road.

This was new territory for both Angus and Kitty who gazed about with unbridled curiosity.

Although still dark, they could make out many large houses of the type favoured by the rich and well to do. There was a rural, village-like atmosphere about the place which they took to right away, it being such a contrast to Holmlea Road.

Soon they were sweating profusely as they raced from door to door filling the orders while Hugh moved the cart slowly along and kept an eye on them to see no mistakes were made.

Hugh was inordinately proud of Angus and secretly wished that Angus was his son.

During the past few years it had become a fetish with Hugh to have a son of his own but, try as he might, he just couldn't seem to find a woman whom he wanted to marry.

There were girl friends in plenty, and even a few affairs. But although he enjoyed the company of all these girls there wasn't one of them he was interested enough in to marry.

There were times when he was convinced he was destined never to meet a girl with whom he could fall in love and his fate was to remain a bachelor to the end of his days. When that mood was on him he would become depressed and take to the bottle, often sitting in his room drinking alone and sinking deeper and deeper into melancholia.

Dawn was breaking when they stopped at Young's Bakery, where Hugh treated Angus and Kitty to a bag of freshly baked rolls and a pint of milk each to wash them down. He had brought a flask of tea for himself which he now drank while smoking a cigarette.

It was Kitty who spotted the apple orchard behind a high stone wall completely encircling a house far bigger and grander than any of its neighbours. Nudging Angus he gestured towards the orchard, muttering in a low voice that the apples looked ripe and ready for plucking.

Casually the pair of them sauntered round to a better vantage point and after a whispered discussion came to the conclusion the wall wasn't as formidable as it had first appeared and that a couple of bright sparks like themselves shouldn't have too much difficulty in getting over it. They decided Saturday night would be the best time for a raid and that they would come back and try their luck then.

When the round was over they returned to the dairy, where Hugh showed them how to brush down and feed the horses. Having completed both these tasks to Hugh's satisfaction, they climbed onto their bikes and headed for home, where they would have a proper breakfast before going to school.

Carrie was waiting anxiously for Angus but her fears were allayed somewhat when she saw the sparkle in his eye and the colour the fresh morning air had brought to his cheeks. Nonetheless she would watch him closely for the next couple of weeks to make sure he wasn't over-taxing himself.

As the week passed Angus and Kitty came to know their milk round inside out. Every morning they'd stop at Young's the bakers for rolls and every morning they'd eye the apple orchard and discuss their plans for the forthcoming raid.

Finally Saturday arrived and after tea that evening they cycled over to the Old Castle Road and the tall imposing grey stone house with the orchard in its grounds.

It was that curious Scottish phenomenon, the gloaming, when they made their move.

Angus stood with his hands pressed against the wall while Kitty climbed onto his shoulders and from there leapt up to catch hold of the top of the wall. Once atop the wall Kitty lay along it and dangled an arm which Angus was able to grab hold of. Kitty then hauled Angus up beside him.

For the space of a few seconds they straddled the wall and then having made sure the coast was clear dropped down the other side to land in thick, luscious grass.

Angus's heart was thudding as he snaked towards the nearest tree, nearly jumping out of his skin when a large hoodie crow cawed shrilly overhead and went flapping past to disappear round the side of the house.

Reaching the tree, Angus grasped hold of the lowest branch and hauled himself up.

The trees, like most cultivated ones, were ridiculously easy to climb and soon the pair of them were pulling apples from the branches and stuffing them into their many and voluminous pockets, the garments they wore being chosen for this particular asset.

'You there! Boy! Come down this instant!'

The voice was female and rang with authority, its owner standing with hands on hips beneath Angus's tree, glowering furiously up into the foliage.

'If you don't come down right away I'll set the dogs loose in here while I ring for the police.'

Angus peered down but all he could see was a pair of legs beneath a crumpled skirt. Feeling sick, he decided the only thing to do was as he was bid. The thought of the police being called in terrified him for if they reported to Archie what he'd been up to then Archie would undoubtedly leather the backside off him.

'I'm coming missus!' he called out and started to descend, thinking he mustn't give Kitty away as, so far anyway, it seemed he was the only one to be spotted.

When he jumped from the lowest branch, he landed badly, causing him to topple over and go crashing to the ground. Ruefully he picked himself up and turned to face the female who'd caught him.

With a shock, he realized it wasn't a woman confronting him, but a girl, and furthermore one whose face was vaguely familiar.

'You!' the girl exclaimed and frowned.

Suddenly Angus placed her. The girl was the taller of the two from Park School whom he and Kitty had rescued from the toughs.

'I didn't know it was your house,' he mumbled and immediately felt a right fool as that seemed such a daft thing to say in the circumstances. Then accusingly, 'Why did you run off that night?'

Thrown onto the defensive, the girl sniffed, 'Well, if you must know, my friend and I could see you weren't going to win against those awful boys so we decided to run and fetch a policeman, only by the time we returned with one everyone had gone.'

'Oh!' said Angus, quite deflated.

'Were you badly hurt?'

Angus stuck out his thin, bony chest, an action which made him look ridiculous. He had one sock up and one down. His knees were covered in dirt and there was a jagged tear in his short grey pants from scrambling down the tree.

'We did win,' he tried to say casually, but instead it came out somewhat pompously.

The girl smiled and fractionally raised an eyebrow.

'We did!' Then in a smaller voice because he could see written all over her face she thought him a liar, 'A man I know and some of his friends happened by and they helped us out.'

Suddenly they were grinning at one another, he remembering how at their previous meeting he'd got the impression he'd known this girl all his life.

'My name's Rosemary,' she said, tilting her head to one side and studying him.

'Mine's Angus.'

'Angus,' she repeated, tasting the word as though it were something strange which had found its way into her mouth.

'And I'm Kitty and is it safe for me to come down now?' Kitty called from the tree in which he was hiding.

Rosemary thought that very funny and asked with a giggle if there were any more of them?

Kitty replied there weren't and dropped out of his tree, landing amidst an explosion of apples which seemed to burst from every part of his person.

Rosemary beckoned them into the shadow cast by the wall, explaining as they moved quickly through the grass that her father would be furious if he caught them and would certainly prosecute.

They left the orchard by the front gate, Rosemary having first checked they weren't being overlooked from the house. And once outside the three of them made their way to the bikes parked round the corner.

As they walked Rosemary questioned Angus about where he lived and how he and Kitty had come to know of her father's orchard.

Angus explained about his Uncle Hugh and the dairy and that he and Kitty came past her house every morning on their milk run. The fact that a milk run had been started up in the area interested her and she told Angus to call at the house next morning. She would see an order was waiting for him.

She said her mother had mentioned only a few weeks previously that the house could do with having its milk delivered so this was her opportunity to see her mother's wishes were carried out. At least so she told Angus.

Bidding Rosemary goodbye, Angus and Kitty slowly cycled in the direction of Holmlea Road, munching as they went.

They hadn't gone very far when Kitty started to tease Angus, saying Angus had a fancy for the Parkie girl and was she now to be regarded as Angus's girlfriend?

Angus's reply was a well aimed apple which caught the jeering Kitty on the side of the head causing him to momentarily lose control of his bike and very nearly come off.

The next morning Angus informed Hugh that the occupants of Arnprior House – the name of the mansion where Rosemary and her parents lived – wanted to place an order for a daily delivery.

Hugh was curious as to how Angus knew this but Angus just shrugged and said it was so.

With Angus in tow Hugh personally went up to

Arnprior House where at the rear entrance a servant girl answered their ring and placed a sizeable order.

Angus had been hoping for a glimpse of Rosemary but when he failed to see her he told himself it was ridiculous even to think she might be up and about at that time of morning.

When he got home after the round Carrie informed him she was going over to Scotland Street later in the day to see Robert and Meg Smith, and she wanted him to come with her. She'd never stopped being grateful to Robert for his generosity to her after John died.

Carrie knew the Smiths had fallen on hard times of late. Several business deals of Robert's had gone awry and he'd had to sell the shop to cover his losses.

That afternoon Carrie and Angus took a tram, getting of at the stop closest to the tenement where the Smiths lived. They hurried up the close to chap at the Smiths' door. It was opened by Meg looking a lot older than either of them remembered.

Meg was delighted to see them and ushered them straight through to the kitchen where Robert was sitting hunched in front of a mean fire.

If Carrie had been shocked by the change in Meg then she was positively stunned by Robert's transformation. Countless stitches laced one side of his face with the surrounding flesh yellowy purple and angry looking. The really big change in him, however, was in the eyes, which had a vacuous, glassy stare about them. When he tried to greet her and Angus all he could manage was to mutter incoherently in heavily impedimented speech.

Meg explained what had happened as she went about putting on the kettle for a cup of tea.

Robert had been over the Clyde on business when he'd run foul of a gang called the Conks currently terrorizing the Bridgeton area.

'The Norman Street Conquerors', to give them their full title, were a product of the times, a bunch of violent although not always stupid men who derived pleasure from terrorizing other people. Usually they'd gang up on their victim at night, invariably razoring him before getting him down on the ground where they would then either stab or kick him to death.

Robert had been lucky. Two patrolling policemen had whistled up reinforcements, forcing the Conks to give him the boot and flee.

He'd been taken to Duke Street Hospital where his slashes had been attended to. He'd then been examined by a consultant who'd confirmed the Casualty doctor's suspicion that brain damage had been sustained.

Meg tried to keep a brave face as she recounted this tale of woe but there was a catch in her voice and several times she had to turn away in order to restrain the tears threatening to engulf her.

No matter how hard she tried for it not to be, Carrie's gaze kept being drawn back to Robert, whose mouth hung slack and whose chin was covered in running streaks of spittle.

She noted the black safe had gone from its place on the floor, the safe Robert had been so fond of boasting about and around whose contents he'd always woven such a shroud of mystery.

Meg went on to tell Carrie that what little money she and Robert had left would soon be gone and then heaven alone knew what would become of them.

Carrie felt guilty thinking about the two hundred pounds Robert had given her but there was just no way she could return so large a gesture. Archie might well be in regular work but at the end of most weeks what he'd earned had gone.

Totting it up in her head she estimated she had just under fourteen pounds rainy day money hidden away at the bottom of an old tea caddy in her kitchen press, hardly a fortune but at least something to give Meg Smith.

Robert grunted and squirmed in his seat and a few seconds later a terrible smell began to permeate the room.

Meg sighed, a defeated almost at the end of her tether

look settling on her face. Smiling wryly at Carrie, she crossed to Robert and helped him to his feet.

Carrie offered to help but Meg said it wouldn't be necessary. The tea was now masked and if Carrie would pour herself and Angus out a cup she would take Robert through to the other room and do what had to be done.

Angus knew by hearsay a great deal about the Conks and over tea proceeded to tell his mother about the big battle they'd had recently with a rival gang called the 'Savoy Indians'.

Angus was still chuntering on about gang warfare when Meg arrived back to tell them Robert had started to doze off so she'd bundled him into bed where he'd stay for a good couple of hours at least.

Carrie, profoundly moved by the succession of tragedies that had befallen the old couple, commiserated with Meg.

In her anguish Meg let slip that the dealings Robert had been involved in for some years outside the shop and which had finally ruined him hadn't been entirely above board. This was, of course, what Carrie and her family had suspected for a long time. Well, Robert had more than repaid the penalty for his avarice and no man would ever reproach him now.

When it was time to go, Meg kissed Carrie on the cheek and then insisted on doing the same to Angus.

During the journey home both Carrie and Angus were silent. Once Angus shivered but his mother didn't notice. She was too wrapped up in her own thoughts about the old couple they'd left behind in Scotland Street.

Sir Alan Armstrong was a small, blunt-faced man with broad powerful shoulders and piercing blue eyes. He looked more like a man used to hard physical labour than the executive he was.

He sat now in his wood-panelled office overlooking the River Cart with a frown on his face and a cup of coffee in his hand.

His desk was neat and tidy, everything squared away

in its place. And that was the trouble! He would have preferred the desk to be littered with papers and plans: that would have meant there were orders coming in.

There were still a few orders waiting to be filled but once those were gone there none to take their place.

Sir Alan grunted with annoyance and swallowed the remains of his coffee. Laying down the cup and saucer he rose and strode to the window where he stood with feet slightly apart and hands clasped behind his back.

He was an angry man, but angry with himself more than anything else. Years ago he'd been advised to diversify his interests, to partially retool and turn out new products as a back up to the traditional Armstrong marine pumps.

There had been that desalination idea which he'd finally rejected because it meant investing a considerable amount of venture capital of which he'd had more than enough at the time, profits for the preceding few years having been exceptionally high.

Well, one thing was certain, he swore to himself. If he did somehow manage to survive this crisis then there would be no need to urge him to diversify in future. He'd learned his lesson and he'd learned it the hard way.

On a sudden impulse he strode through to his secretary's office and instructed her to book him on that night's London sleeper. Then he gave her the names of various London bankers and told her to make appointments with them for the following day.

He'd already been to London several times trying to secure a sizeable loan or second mortgage – his house already had a second mortgage on it – the buildings, plant and machinery that made up his firm. The trouble was that London banks had no confidence in Glasgow any more; to them the Clyde was dying a slow lingering death and any investments made by them would only prolong the agony.

Naturally this was a belief he contested and tomorrow he would once again try to argue them round to his way of thinking.

What was needed was for something cataclysmic to happen, not only to Glasgow but the country as a whole. It was a dreadful thought but he couldn't help thinking another war would be the answer.

He stood by the window watching the gulls fly overhead. The last war had been a terrible affair but how private enterprise had prospered while it lasted! The Clyde had never been so busy, every yard bustling like a beehive as ship after ship was built and launched.

He smiled grimly remembering what Armstrong's had been like in those days: everyone working as many hours as he was able and the order books filled to overflowing.

Sir Alan sighed. Great days! Great days! But would their like ever come again?

He and Cordelia had been married during the war and, my God, but they'd been in love! His heart swelled now just thinking about it. He'd taken her on honeymoon to Dunoon where they'd had the most glorious week before returning to the house he'd bought and had done throughout in the Old Castle Road.

Anxiety fluttered within him at the thought he might lose that house along with the firm. Virtually every ha'penny he owned plus a lot more he'd borrowed was sunk into making Armstrong's once more a viable proposition.

For the umpteenth time he told himself there had to be a way out of his present financial predicament. There just had to!

Taking out a clean white hanky he dabbed hands suddenly clammy with sweat. If the worst came to the worst he knew he wouldn't be able to face Cordelia and the girls. He would kill himself first.

That was why there was a small automatic pistol locked away in one of his desk drawers which he wouldn't hesitate to use if there was no other recourse left open.

He glanced sideways at the painting of his father hanging above the fireplace. That craggy, battle-scarred face had never know either defeat or failure. Or if it had, they'd been only little ones and nothing like the unholy mess he was now neck deep in.

His father would have known the right thing to do in the circumstances because his father had always known the right thing to do: that had been his father's particular genius.

He hadn't exactly liked his father but he had admired him. Sir William Armstrong had been a man you might hate. And plenty had. But at the end of the day you just had to admire him for the clever conniving double deal-ing devious bastard he'd been.

Still thinking about his father, Sir Alan strode from his office and down stairs that would take him to the yard below. It was a long-standing policy of his to try and make a surprise visit once a day to a part of the works and that day he decided on the foundry.

Big Donald wiped sweat from his brow as he watched white hot molten metal being poured in a sizzling, eye blinding stream into a mould that was the last of a batch of three. Beside him stood Gemmill, the chief pattern maker, who was waiting to discuss a mould that had been ordered and which Gemmill had run into difficulty with because of the peculiar dimensions involved.

Big Donald made a waving sign which was the signal for a foundryman to tap off the streaming metal. Sitting securely atop a brace of joined bogeys, the mould was then wheeled away by another two foundrymen who steered it by means of long iron poles with hooks on the end fitted into rings projecting from the mould's side.

'Now then,' shouted Gemmill – it being necesary to shout because of the constant roar that was part and parcel of foundry life – and immediately launched into a technical explanation of his problem.

As Donald listened his eyes were continually roving over every part of the foundry visible from where he stood; he kept a continual watch over his domain. Con-sequently he was the first one to see Sir Alan enter the foundry through a side door from a back part of the yard.

His eyes flicked again, rechecking that every man was

hard at work and everything was as it should be. Then he interrupted Gemmill to shout instructions to a crane operator working overhead.

'Morning Chisholm. Morning Gemmill,' Sir Alan said.

Gemmill jumped as though stung. He'd been totally unaware of Sir Alan's approach.

'How is everything going then, Chisholm?' Sir Alan demanded.

Donald said everything was fine and went on to explain the current stages of the various jobs in hand. While he was doing this, Gemmill shifted uneasily from foot to foot and every few seconds shot an ingratiating smile at Sir Alan.

Donald knew Gemmill to be a crawler and detested him for it, not that Gemmill was alone in his arse-licking attitude towards the management. There were many who were just as bad, if not worse, than him. With a few of them it was because that was the way they naturally were but with the vast majority it was because they were continually terrified of putting a foot wrong and losing their previous jobs.

Donald sympathized with these men but at the same time found it difficult to stomach what they did. The whining subservient tone they invariably adopted when talking to the management made him want to puke with disgust.

Gemmill was speaking now, taking up a point Donald had made and needlessly elaborating on it.

'You there!' Sir Alan shouted and strode away, leaving Gemmill in mid-sentence.

Donald quickly glanced round at the man Sir Alan had called out to and noted with relief that it wasn't a foundryman but one of the electricians who serviced the works. The electrician who'd been with Armstrong's for many years doffed his hooker doon as Sir Alan crossed to speak to him.

What Sir Alan wanted to know was why the electrician had put a sixty watt bulb in as a replacement for one that had blown in his private cloakroom when he had specifically asked for a hundred watt to be used?

The electrician bobbed his head in acknowledgement of Sir Alan's question. In a subservient voice he explained a hundred watts were too much for the tiny cloakroom and that sixty were more than sufficient.

To Sir Alan the electrician's reply was no less than sheer insolence. He had personally issued the instructions and no matter that the man may well be right he expected all his instructions to be carried out without question.

A frown furrowed Donald's brow as he listened to the exchange between Sir Alan and the leckie, who was cringing with a terrified expression stamped across his face.

'I beg your pardon, sir?' the electrician queried. Sure he'd heard incorrectly.

'You're fired,' Sir Alan repeated, adding with a snarl, 'Collect your time from the office and then get out.'

Donald opened his mouth to intervene. Then caution warned him if he wasn't careful he'd be the next to get his marching orders. He slowly shut it again, promising himself never to have the temerity to despise Gemmill and the like again for, by keeping quiet now, wasn't he just as bad as they?

Feeling sick, he turned away, unable to stand the sight of the grovelling electrician clutching at Sir Alan's trouser bottoms. He noted that Gemmill was watching with bulging eyes.

Sir Alan snorted and tore himself free from the leckie's frantic grasp, his eyes narrowing when he saw the way Gemmill was staring at him.

With a gulp Gemmill turned to Donald and started talking absolute nonsense about the job they'd been discussing before Sir Alan's arrival.

Donald knew the electrician vaguely. The man was married with a large family to support. Donald didn't envy the poor bugger having to tell his wife he'd been sacked and that from now on they were going to have to exist on the dole.

One thing was certain: having been sacked from one job it would be many a long day before the leckie found another, if indeed he ever would.

Crossing back to Donald and the chief pattern maker, Sir Alan said, 'Now then Gemmill. You were saying?'

Gemmill's voice quavered as he spoke but somehow he managed to pull himself together enough to make sense out of his reply.

No one looked at the electrician who, with head bowed, dragged himself from the foundry floor.

Angus was jolted from his sound sleep by a howl of anguish reverberating round the house. For several moments his mind remained fuzzy and then he snapped wide awake with the realization that it was his mother's voice he'd heard.

Carrie lay sprawled across the bed with Archie towering over her. She was sobbing and desperately trying to protect herself from the blows raining down.

She cried out in agony as a fist thudded deeply into her stomach. Half out of his mind with drink Archie grabbed hold of her nightdress and savagely jerked it down to expose her breasts. Laughing, he fell across her and began to suck.

Archie lifted his head as the door flew open and Angus burst into the room. 'Get out!' he slurred.

Angus was horrified at what he saw. Apart from the fact Carrie was near naked her face was horribly puffed and swollen, the flesh round one fast-closing eye rapidly assuming a greeny-purple colour.

'Angus!' Carrie croaked and thrusting Marjoribanks from her hastily yanked her nightdress back into place.

Angus started towards the bed but he'd only gone a few paces when arms restrained him and Sheena's voice whispered in his ear, 'Don't!'

Marjoribanks glowered at his daughter and stepson. 'Go back to bed!' he rumbled. Beside him, Carrie grimaced as his hand tightened on her thigh.

'You leave my Ma alone!' Angus screamed and

desperately tried to break away from Sheena who, luckily for him, was able to retain her hold.

Carrie swung her legs over the side of the bed and started to stand up only to be knocked back again by a sudden swipe from Archie who grunted she was to lie as she was.

Sheena stared in contempt at Archie. Her mind filled with memories of similar scenes from her early childhood when it had been *her* Ma he'd been abusing.

The breath caught in her throat and she drew back, dragging Angus with her, when she saw the look on Archie's face as he stared hard at her body. She, like Carrie, was clad only in a nightdress. It was the sort of look a girl should never experience from her father.

'You're obscene!' Sheena spat, drawing Angus even closer to her so he effectively covered her front.

For a man who'd consumed so much alcohol Marjoribanks moved astonishingly fast. One moment he was squatting atop his bed. The next he'd streaked across the room to backhand Sheena across the face.

Sheena screamed as she tumbled to the floor. Angus's anger gave way to fright as he was spun to one side where he stood gawking at Marjoribanks and wondering where all his courage had suddenly disappeared to.

Archie stood over his daughter staring down at her. 'You're a whore just like your mother was,' he breathed. 'I've seen it in you for years.'

'My Ma was no such thing. You're a fucking liar!' the girl retorted.

His hand flashed again to crack against her mouth, the force of the blow causing her head to bounce off the floor and her lower lip to split.

'Mind your tongue!' he roared.

Carrie slid from the bed. She had to get Angus and Sheena out of here. Better she take what he had to dish out than either of them. When he was in this sort of mood there was only one thing would calm him down. The sooner she got it over with the sooner he'd be snoring like a pig.

'Come away back to bed, Archie,' she pleaded, at the same time signalling to Angus to get out of the room.

'My Ma was not a whore,' Sheena insisted, her voice quiet and filled with dignity.

Marjoribanks stared hungrily at his daughter's voluptuous body lying spreadeagled before him and strove to remind himself that she was his own flesh and blood and as such untouchable. But by God she was beautiful!

His pulse quickened and there was a stirring in his groin which Sheena couldn't help but notice as he was stripped down to his long johns.

She averted her gaze and momentarily closed her eyes. There was a great pain inside her which had nothing to do with physical hurt. She felt lost. That and alone and terribly afraid.

Ignoring Carrie's signalling Angus ran to his mother and threw his arms round her waist, wishing fervently he was a grown man able to tackle Marjoribanks.

As he clung there an idea was born to him. He had to start making money, lots of it, so that one day he would be in a position to rescue Carrie from this brute she was married to.

Resolve hardened within him. He would buy her a nice wee house where the pair of them could live happily together. Sheena, too, if she wanted to join them.

Sheena slid herself away from Archie and cautiously stood up. Blood from her split lip dripped onto her nightdress.

'Run away through now. There's a good boy,' Carrie whispered to Angus.

'Everything is going to be all right, Ma. I'll see to it,' he whispered in reply.

Carrie frowned, realizing from his tone there was far more to his words than their apparent surface value.

Letting Carrie go, Angus crossed to his step-sister and took her by the hand. 'Goodnight Ma,' he said. Pulling Sheena so that she followed him, the pair of them left the room.

Less than a minute later Carrie was sprawled across

the bed with Archie heaving on top of her.

Big Donald was no fool and had known for a long time that Archie was beating Carrie. But according to the unwritten laws of the society they lived in it wasn't his place to interfere unless approached directly by her.

He was so angry the night Carrie appeared with a black eye and badly bruised face he had to go for a walk down by the river in order to bring under control the fury boiling within him.

During that walk Donald decided that although it wasn't his place to interfere, there was nothing to stop him conniving to find out just how bad the situation was. He would do this by arranging for one of the women to sound Carrie out on the subject.

After much cogitation he came to the conclusion Harriet was best suited for the task as Carrie was far more likely to open up to her sister than she would be to Winnie.

It was well known in the family that Marjoribanks invariably worked late on a Wednesday so Harriet chose that night to present herself at the house in Holmlea Road.

Physically, the past ten years hadn't been at all kind to Harriet. Her face had sharpened while her body had become sticklike. She smoked incessantly and drank cup after cup of black coffee. These two items to a large extent formed her staple diet.

Businesswise Harriet had prospered greatly since her affair with Lou Dansie. She'd sold the Sunbeam and used the money to buy her own small house in Wilton Street in Glasgow's fashionable West End area.

Having completed her typing and shorthand courses, she'd returned from Edinburgh with a wardrobe of smart business clothes to set about finding herself a job suited to her new skills.

The Scottish Amalgamated Insurance Company was situated in Hope Street where in a large gothic building it had both its Head Office and Glasgow Branch.

Harriet's position had been in the communal typing pool serving the Head Office's Accident Department and the Glasgow Branch but after a few years she'd landed the plum post of personal secretary to the manager of Glasgow Branch. This position was the second highest post open to a female within the company, the highest being personal secretary to the general manager himself.

During this time Harriet received several wistful letters from Lou Dansie asking after her and also informing her he and his wife Bess were succeeding in making something of a go of it for Bonnie Sue's sake.

Ruthlessly she'd never replied to any of these letters. A finish had been made that was neat and clean which was how she wanted it to stay.

After a while the letters had stopped coming and now her only reminders of Lou Dansie were Mary Pickford's ring which she wore on a gold chain round her neck and his name when it flashed up on the cinema screen credits as it did from time to time.

There had been no more men after Lou, partly because for a long time after he'd gone she hadn't wanted another relationship, but also because she hadn't been given another opportunity.

So Harriet had thrown herself into her work, so much so that within the company she'd soon gained enormous respect for her ability and dedication.

Carrie was less than delighted to see Harriet as she'd been trying to avoid as many people as possible until her face was more or less back to normal. However she made her sister welcome, ushering her through to the kitchen where she put the kettle on for tea.

The first thing Harriet did was to light the inevitable cigarette. She had a dreadful smoker's cough and as a result of this was forever clearing her throat. The second thing was to inquire after Angus whom she was told was out playing with one of his pals. That pleased Harriet as with Sheena also out of the house it meant she'd managed to catch Carrie on her own. At first Carrie was reluctant to be drawn, but, with a little bit of coaxing, the words were soon tumbling forth.

Even before Carrie had started telling her about how Marjoribanks carried on Harriet worried about her sister. She found Carrie terribly pale and drawn with skin the colour of fresh putty and ribs that jutted where once they had been encased in firm flesh.

Harriet roughly estimated Carrie had lost a stone in weight since the pair of them had last been together a little over six months previously.

Carrie was philosophical about Archie, considering his tempers and violence something that had to be endured. According to her, the beatings weren't as frequent as they'd once been nor were they as severe. The incident of the black eye was a particularly harsh one.

As Carrie spoke, a tale of sleepless nights, headaches, abdominal pains and a more or less general loss of interest made Harriet even more convinced her sister was seriously ill. Whether or not this illness had anything to do with the beatings she could only speculate on.

Completely caught up now, Carrie began to describe some of the sexually perverted practices Archie was so fond of indulging in and which she found totally repugnant.

Harriet swallowed hard, her insides fluttering as her imagination ran riot. Despite herself she couldn't help but picture Archie doing to her some of the things he did to Carrie.

Ten years was an eternity to go without a man, especially for someone like her who was a passionate woman. Besides there was a dark side to her nature she'd long been aware of which secretly hungered after the sort of treatment Archie was so fond of dishing out.

In the end it was established Carrie would stay on with Archie – unless he attacked Angus in which case she would leave – intent on making the best of it.

Harriet's advice to her sister was to go and see Dr Robertson for a thorough check up as it seemed obvious to her there was something physically wrong with Carrie which needed attention.

Shortly after that Sheena arrived home and Harriet took her leave to pay Tallon Street a quick visit in order to give Donald an edited version of what she'd learned.

That night Harriet had great difficulty in getting to sleep.

11

Weeks passed and Angus didn't see Rosemary again until the Christmas holidays which meant a fortnight's glorious release from school.

On the third day of the holiday he went personally as usual to deliver the milk to Arnprior House where he found a note addressed to him stuck in one of the empties. It was from Rosemary asking him to meet her at one-thirty inside the castle.

Foolishly he mentioned the note to Kitty and for the rest of the morning had to endure taunts and innuendoes which, no matter how much he threatened Kitty, laughingly persisted.

The castle was situated just up the hill from Arnprior House and was now a mere shell of its former glory. It went back at least to Mary, Queen of Scots but beyond that Angus knew nothing of its history.

After his dinner, Angus cycled to the castle. Then, leaving his bike, he climbed the stone wall surrounding the ruin on three sides.

Rosemary was waiting for him, sitting in a downstairs

window opening staring across at the heavily wooded area on the other side of the Cart.

'Hello. I'm glad you could come,' she said and smiled.

Angus was so overcome that what was supposed to be an accomplished lighting of a cigarette turned into a ham-fisted fumble. He succeeded in getting the cigarette alight only after two matches had blown out and he'd very nearly burned himself.

Rosemary had changed considerably since their first meeting the previous year. Her face was well on its way to losing its childish lines while her figure now boasted small firm breasts.

'I thought I might have seen you before this,' Angus said, immediately wishing he hadn't as it tipped her off he'd been thinking about her.

Before replying Rosemary asked for a cigarette, and using a lighter produced from her pocket, proceeded to light up in precisely the sort of expert manner he'd intended impressing her with.

There was a teasing note in Rosemary's voice when she informed him he might not have seen her but she'd seen him when he was delivering the milk.

Part of him was gratified to know she'd also been looking out for him but another part was mortified because of the many times he'd stood unashamedly goggling up at Arnprior House wondering which window was hers.

My God, but he must have looked glaikit standing there with his mouth hanging wide open! Quickly he turned away so she couldn't see the sudden flush which flooded his face.

Rosemary puffed on her cigarette and wondered what it was about this tall, gangly boy which intrigued and attracted her so much? Certainly there was an affinity there which she hadn't encountered in any other man and that puzzled her, as she couldn't think why it should be.

'Come and sit here and tell me about yourself. I'd like to know,' she said, sounding strangely grown up.

Angus sat on the spot indicated and instantly became aware of the warm, soapy smell emanating from her. It had the effect of making him feel all sort of jumpy and peculiar inside.

He couldn't bring himself to stare directly into her eyes so he pretended great interest in his cigarette.

'Well?' she prompted.

Slowly and hesitatingly he began telling her about life in Holmlea Road. How he hated his step-father. And how someday when he'd saved enough money he would buy a small house where he and his mother and step-sister could live in peace away from Archie Marjoribanks.

The more he spoke the more confidence he gained and soon he was telling her all about his real father who'd been killed the day he was born in an accident at Armstrong's. As he talked about John McBain his voice filled with pride and his eyes shone with a combination of admiration and love for his dead parent.

His tone became bitter as he recounted to Rosemary how Sir Alan Armstrong had refused his mother compensation for his father's death and because of this Carrie had been more or less forced into remarrying a brute who bashed her about.

Having finally found enough courage to look directly into Rosemary's eyes, he glanced up to find her shrunk back against the side of the window staring at him as though he'd turned into some sort of horrible monster.

'What's wrong?' he asked.?

'Don't let me hear you speak about Sir Alan that way ever again,' she replied coldly.

In that instant it clicked with Angus the name on the milk book for Arnprior House was Armstrong but he'd never made the connection as there had to be hundreds with that name in Glasgow.

'An uncle?' he queried.

'My *father*,' she stated.

How could Angus speak about her father like that! Why, everyone knew daddy was the most warm hearted, generous man you could ever hope to meet.

'How was Mr McBain killed?' she asked eventually, her voice dripping ice.

'He was crushed to a pulp by a casting that got out of control,' adding as though an afterthought, 'strawberry jam.'

The colour fled Rosemary's cheeks.

Angus went on. 'The union tried to get Sir Alan to give my Ma compensation but your father wouldn't entertain the idea. He maintained my Da was responsible for getting himself killed which meant he wasn't liable.'

'And was it your father's fault?' Rosemary asked quietly.

Angus thought of the snapshots he'd seen of his dad. A man of medium height. Broad-shouldered. With an open smiling face. Hair cut short. Greased and swept back from the forehead.

Apart from the snapshots the only mementoes Carrie retained were the medal John McBain had won in the tug-of-war championships when he'd been a member of the Armstrong team, and an old black leather wallet, ripped on one side, with the initials J.McB. in faded gold lettering on its front.

Angus had always found it difficult to broach the subject of his father's death with Carrie, partly because he found it acutely embarrassing to do so and partly because of the pain and anguish it caused her to be reminded of that day. Consequently it was his uncle Hugh he'd turned to for the details of what had happened in Armstrong's foundry on the morning of 12 August, 1921 when John McBain was killed.

'Well?' Rosemary prompted.

'My father was on a gantry that had been declared out of bounds because it was unsafe. We don't know why he was there, only that he was. The casting was being moved when the craneman lost control, allowing it to smash into the gantry. That was the end of my dad.'

Angus paused before continuing. 'My father was in

the wrong but then so was the craneman. Also what Sir Alan might have taken into consideration were the number of years my dad had worked for him. And my grandfather. But he didn't. Despite union pressure he disclaimed all liability and that was that.'

While Angus spoke Rosemary was fiddling with her charm bracelet, hooking a finger under it and tugging outwards. Her anger had dissipated, the last vestiges of it blown away by the sad and hurt expression on Angus's face as he told her about his father.

She desperately wanted to reach out and touch Angus. To draw him to her. To mother him. At that moment she felt as old as Eve.

'I'm going to marry you when we're grown up,' she stated abruptly and in a matter of fact tone of voice.

Angus blinked, not quite sure he'd heard correctly. 'Eh?' he queried.

'I'm going to marry you when we're grown up,' Rosemary repeated. 'I knew it that day at the reccy ground when you saved me from those roughs.'

Laughing when she saw the stunned expression on his face, she went on, 'Don't ask me how I knew. I just did.'

Angus tried to digest that. There was an inevitability about the pair of them he had felt that first day same as she had. But marriage! He hadn't quite got round to projecting their relationship that far ahead.

'Aren't you going to kiss me?' she asked, dropping her head fractionally to one side and looking at him quizzically.

'If you like.'

'Well, if you'd rather not!' she said mercurially and made to move. Her huffiness was replaced by a smile the moment he reached out to restrain her.

Angus knew he was being awkward and clumsy but somehow it didn't matter. All thoughts of denied compensation and Sir Alan Armstrong fled his mind as he took her in his arms.

He started when her tongue licked out to probe the

inside of his mouth. He'd heard about french kissing but this was his first experience of it.

Her hands worked up and down his back and as they did so her bracelet caught in his coat. Snapping open, it flew from her wrist.

'Oh no!' she cried as she saw the bracelet bounce and slide down the rockface to land in a crevice about twenty feet below the window.

The pair of them leaned out of the window to stare at the bracelet so plainly and tantalizingly in view below them.

Rosemary was distraught. Not only was the bracelet an expensive one it was also her favourite piece of jewellery.

Angus knew he was going to have to make an effort to retrieve the bracelet. He studied the sheer rockface falling away beneath them to the Cart below.

Section by section, hold by hold, he worked out a route that would take him down to the crevice where the bracelet was lodged. It wasn't too difficult a descent, he told himself. The trick would be to go slowly and whatever happened not to panic.

Taking off his coat he folded it and placed it on the castle floor. He was nervous. His stomach turned over and his heart thudded in his chest.

He wiped sweaty hands on his trousers before taking off his jacket and placing it neatly on top of his coat.

'Don't be daft!' Rosemary said, placing a hand on his arm.

'Did you really mean what you said?' he asked.

'About what?'

'Us getting married when we're old enough?'

Her mouth creased into a grin. 'Of course.'

Angus took a deep breath. 'It'll be all right,' he said moving to the window and swinging himself up on the sill. 'You'll see.'

He dropped his legs over the side and carefully groped with his right foot for the toe hold he'd picked out. There was a stiff breeze blowing which caused his hair to flap and the back of his shirt to fill out like a sail.

Adrenalin pumped through him as he crabbed his body down. Sliding his left hand across the rockface in search of the grip he knew to be there. From the safety of the window twenty feet hadn't looked very far but once out on the rockface that twenty feet was more like twenty miles.

Rosemary was leaning out of the window staring down. She thought Angus a crazy, impetuous fool and she loved him for it. Without taking her eyes from him she offered up a silent prayer on his behalf.

Angus paused to catch his breath. Already his arms and legs were aching with strain. What really worried him, however, was the possibility of a paralysing cramp setting in, the outcome of which didn't bear thinking about.

A sudden picture flashed through his mind of himself and Rosemary dressed in wedding clothes coming out of a church together. Hand in hand they climbed into a car and then he was throwing handful after handful of coppers out the window, while on the pavement a horde of children dived and swooped, grabbing what they could from the scramble.

With a shake of his head he chided himself to concentrate or it wouldn't be an imaginary wedding he'd be playing a chief role in but rather a very realistic funeral. Glancing up he saw Rosemary staring anxiously down at him.

'Are you all right?' she called.

He nodded and then brought his attention back to the rockface. He was more than halfway to the bracelet and coming up to a traverse which would be the most difficult part of the descent.

Inch by inch he edged his way down and then across. Crying out once in pain when his hand slipped, tearing a patch of skin from his palm.

The wind was worrying him a lot now. It had changed direction in the last few minutes and seemed to be both trying to pry him off and suck him from the rockface at the same time. Gritting his teeth he pressed his body hard against the rock and continued on into the traverse.

He was well aware he was being foolhardy if not downright stupid in trying to retrieve the bracelet. But after what Rosemary had said to him it was important to him to do this thing in order to prove what he felt for her – tangible proof of what he truly felt and believed.

Coming out of the traverse he descended a few more feet which brought him to the crevice where the bracelet was. Carefully bending down, he picked it up and dropped it into his pocket.

He took a few moments to catch his breath and then he started retracing his steps.

Rosemary wanted to shout words of encouragement but wisely decided not to in case she distracted him.

Angus was tiring fast now. His shoulders ached abominably and his legs threatened to buckle under him at any moment.

He wondered what the sensation would be like if he was to fall? Would he be conscious all the way down or would he know very little about it, having been knocked senseless on the first bounce? Was there life after death, or nothing at all?

Rosemary knew something was wrong. Three times he'd reached up to grasp the next hold and three times his hand had fallen away again.

Angus laid his cheek against the cool rock and sucked lungful after lungful of air down the raw barbed tunnel of his throat. He could go no further. He was buggered.

Far below he could hear the fast flowing Cart while in the distance there were voices calling to one another. Off to the left a number of herring gulls were crying as they wheeled towards some unknown destination.

A muffled sob escaped him. He didn't want to die. He didn't want to die at all!

'Angus?'

The word was a whisper in his ear. A vocal caress that might have been an angel beckoning him.

'Are you ok?'

Of course he wasn't bloody ok! Any second now he

was going to fall backwards off this bloody rockface to be smashed to smithereens.

Suddenly he started to chuckle and that eased the tension which had seized his body. He was desperate for a pee! Of all the times and places for that to happen! His chuckle became a giggle with a hysterical ring to it.

He nearly jumped out of his skin when a hand touched his. 'Jesus!' he exclaimed and twisted his head round to find Rosemary right there beside him.

'I'll help you the rest of the way,' she said.

Her hand on his was the contact through which strength poured from her to him. He could feel his body recharging, coming alive again.

And he knew then he was going to make it. With Rosemary beside him there was nothing he couldn't do.

'Careful now!' he warned as she broke the grip and started to make her way back up to the window.

When she reached the window she swung herself onto the sill. Dropping her legs into the room and then screwing round to grasp hold of Angus's extended arm.

She pulled him up till his head and shoulders were framed in the window and then, grabbing his braces, hauled on them so he came tumbling headlong into the room where they both landed in a heap on the floor.

For what must have been been a full five minutes Angus didn't attempt to speak, happy just to lie there revelling in the fact he was still alive.

Finally he produced the charm bracelet from his pocket and laid it in her hand.

Rosemary's eyes were shining as she snapped the bracelet round her wrist. 'Thank you,' she said.

'It was nothing,' he replied and they both burst out laughing at how silly and masculinely vain that sounded.

'I'll never forget today as long as I live,' Rosemary said.

This time he put his tongue into her mouth causing her to squirm and rub up against him.

When they eventually broke apart he had to excuse

himself as the desperate need to relieve himself had returned.

Going to another part of the castle he did it against a lichen spattered wall.

He was fastening his buttons when he became aware of being watched from the doorway.

'I've never seen a man doing it before,' Rosemary said, no hint of awkwardness in her voice.

Angus was acutely embarrassed and quickly did up the remainder of his buttons. 'You gave me a fright sneaking up like that,' he said, forcing out a laugh.

Rosemary stared at the long ribbon flowing along the floor and said men must have far bigger bladders than women to be able to pass as much water as Angus had just done.

The streaming pee reminded Angus of an old Scots custom which he now told her about. He felt he had to say something this was the first thing that came to mind.

According to tradition if a couple were to join hands, jump over a stream and on landing proclaim themselves man and wife then this was as binding in the eyes of God and the community as if they'd been legally married in church.

Hearing this, Rosemary came straight to his side and took one of his hands in hers. Nodding towards the still flowing pee she said if that didn't constitute a stream then she didn't know what did and would he marry her here and now, please?

They had to run to catch up with the pee. Jumping over it they declared they took one another for spouse.

Rosemary was suddenly shy then, giggling a little till Angus sealed their oath with another kiss.

Once over the outside wall and back on the road they crossed over and squeezed through a hedge which brought them out onto a cleared part of the hill. Climbing to the memorial to the ill-fated Mary, Queen of Scots, they stood looking out over Glasgow lying before them.

Anxious to cement over their previous rift as well as being genuinely curious, Angus asked Rosemary what sort of man Sir Alan was?

As Rosemary spoke a lifestyle completely outwith Angus's experience gradually unfolded. He heard of Balls. Dinner parties. Holidays abroad in France and Italy. Of huntin' shootin' and fishin'. Of fast cars and expensive ones. Of clever conversation where wit was the commodity prized above all else. In fact all the glamorous things money and position can provide.

The thought of being a rich businessman fascinated Angus. Not for him the total renunciation of the capitalist class as propagated by Big Donald. And the more he thought about it the more he was attracted to himself in that image.

Intense excitement gripped Angus with the realization that he'd arrived at a major juncture in his life. Suddenly the way ahead was crystal clear and he knew precisely the direction he wanted the rest of his life to take.

There would be no apprenticeship and going to sea after it was completed. Instead he would stay on at school to take his Highers, after which he'd enter the business world. That was where his destiny lay. He was convinced of it.

In a halting voice he told Rosemary of his revelation and as he spoke she too was caught up in the mesmeric dream now holding him fast in its spell.

Of course, all this was a long way ahead, an eternity it seemed at the moment. But all would come to fruition with the passage of time.

Just how he was going to make his fortune wasn't clear to him yet but he had no doubt the details would come with more thought on the subject. The important thing for the moment was the overall concept which lay dazzling and glittering with promise in his brain.

Not for him the anonymity of the proletariat. He was going to be a *somebody*.

In mock anger he shook his fist at the dirty industrial metropolis that was his birthplace and where his roots ran deep. 'I'm going to beat you! I'll have you dancing to my tune before I'm finished! Just you wait and see!' he roared defiantly.

Radiantly happy Rosemary put her arms round his waist. The world was truly a marvellous place. Angus had found his dream and they'd both found one another.

Her cup was running over as hand in hand they ran back down the hill towards the hedge.

When Rosemary eventually returned to Arnprior House she found her father back from the latest of his many recent London trips. There were also several guests being entertained, Sir Hamilton McLaren, a wealthy landowner and friend of her father, and his two sons, Iain and Peter.

Although she'd met Sir Hamilton before she'd never met his boys so when introductions were made they all trooped through for tea.

Iain was the elder son, being several years older than she was. While Peter was a year younger than she.

Iain, several years older than Rosemary, was dark and brooding with thick, heavy eyebrows and a face that had a saturnine quality about it. His skin was sallow and shone as though polished. His eyes black introspective and inclined to flash from time to time. He was an extraordinarily handsome young man in the blazer and tie of the Glasgow Academy.

Peter, a year younger than she, was the complete antithesis of his brother. Chunky in build, with yellow hair, he had a marvellously outgoing personality.

Cordelia Armstrong was the perfect hostess as she presided over tea, happy because for the first time in a long while her husband was too.

Before Hamilton's surprise arrival he'd had time to tell her the good news. The money he'd been so desperately in need of to keep the works afloat had been found. Armstrong's had been saved, or its fate postponed for some time anyway – literally at the eleventh hour, for if the money hadn't been forthcoming within the next few days then final notice would have had to have been served on all employees.

Sir Alan was jubilant as he sipped his tea. Later when the girls were in bed he would crack a bottle of their favourite champagne and together he and Cordelia would toast this last minute reprieve.

My God, but it had been hard graft convincing the board of the merchant bank he'd been conferring with to part with the capital he needed. But by dint of perseverance and hard fought argument he'd eventually won them round.

Mind you, he was paying a terrifically high rate of interest on the loan but what else could he expect? If he could only survive the next couple of years he was sure the works could establish itself in the black once more. His reason for thinking this was based on the disturbing rumours that were beginning to reach Britain from the continent. Mutterings of discontent with the threat of more than words to come.

Over in Spain the new republic wasn't proving at all popular while the Fascists under a certain General Franco were growing in strength daily. Those in the know were convinced an armed conflict between the two parties was inevitable.

Then, of course, there was this fellow Herr Hitler and his National Socialists over in Germany. Now if that man attained power then Germany would be bound to initiate an expansionist programme to try and win back some of the territories she'd lost as a result of the Great War.

It didn't matter if Britain was directly involved or not. Any hostilities in Europe were bound to stimulate the British shipbuilding industry. In fact this stimulation had already begun if he was reading the signs correctly. Weren't many of the ships that had been lying in mothballs for years being dusted off and sold to a suddenly demanding market in secondhand tonnage.? Something was afoot all right. Every instinct he possessed told him so.

Perhaps he hadn't been so persuasive in his arguments to the merchant bank after all. It might just be they knew even more than he did about the current European situation.

He was musing on that when his eye lit on Rosemary. How grown up she'd become recently. When she left Park it would be a finishing school for her. In Edinburgh perhaps or else one down in England. The continent was, of course, now ruled out.

His ruminations were interrupted by Sir Hamilton McLaren suggesting the entire Armstrong family come over to the McLaren house in Carmunnock for dinner sometime in the near future.

Hearing Cordelia accept, a date was set there and then.

This invitation secretly pleased him as he'd been cultivating McLaren for a number of years now and this family get together heralded a breakthrough in their relationship.

It was some hours after the McLarens had departed before Rosemary was able to get her father alone, finally cornering him in his study where he was attending to a pile of personal correspondence.

What Angus had told her about John McBain had been preying on her mind so she'd decided to ask her father for his side of the story.

Sir Alan was astonished when she put the question to him and asked how she'd come to hear of the case after so many years. She shrugged her shoulders and made some vague reply.

Sir Alan took time to collect his thoughts by pouring himself a stiff brandy and soda. He remembered the details of the John McBain affair quite clearly. At the time it had been a stroke of luck that he'd managed to wriggle out of paying the then Mrs McBain compensation, as money had been tight.

What no one knew apart from him was that McBain had been up on that gantry on his express orders to deal with a small matter that had needed attending to.

After the accident he'd naturally kept stum. To have

done otherwise would have been to admit liability. He'd felt sorry for Mrs McBain. But it was a hard world they lived in. Then and now.

Putting a smile on his face he recounted what had happened to Rosemary. The only detail he omitted was the one that mattered most.

When the interview with her father was finally concluded Rosemary was in no doubt that he'd been in the right.

When Angus arrived home after being with Rosemary he was bursting with good humour. The good humour and the whistling died when he discovered Archie to be the only one in.

With a glass of neat whisky in his hand and a half bottle at his feet Archie sat gazing into the kitchen fire. The ruddy glow from the flickering flames giving him a demonic look that accentuated the closeness of his eyes.

Archie had been at times viciously cruel to Carrie but in his own twisted way he'd come to love her. So it was with a sense of shock he'd taken a telephone call in the station manager's office that afternoon to be informed by Dr Robertson that Carrie had collapsed while out shopping and had been taken to the Emergency Department of the Victoria Hospital where she'd been found to be suffering from advanced TB. Tuberculosis. The very mention of the word was enough to still conversation and cause the heart to grow chill with fear. How many poor souls had died from that dread killer in Glasgow alone? The answer was incalculable.

Archie gulped back his drink and then poured himself another. He knew Angus hated him but it wasn't an emotion he returned. If anything, he rather respected the boy for the obvious guts the lad had. He would have liked to get close to Angus but somehow had never been able to.

Archie sighed. He was still in his dungarees with hands and face black and ingrained with oil. He knew he should get up and wash himself but he couldn't find the energy.

Sheena would be back from work soon and he'd get washed then while she made the tea. If there was anything in the house to make that was. Carrie had been out shopping when she'd collapsed.

He'd wanted to go round to the Victoria right away but had been dissuaded from doing so. He was told that Carrie would have already been dispatched by ambulance for Bellfield Sanatorium near Lanark where a bed was waiting for her.

It had been agreed he'd go to the sanatorium first thing in the morning, taking along a number of articles Dr Robertson had suggested Carrie would need.

He could hear Angus through in the boy's bedroom and knew the lad would stay there until teatime, it being Angus's habit to stay well clear of him whenever possible.

He hawked into the fire and watched while the thick phlegm sputtered and hissed on a burning coal, offering up a silent prayer of gratitude that it wasn't he who'd come down with TB. He certainly wasn't a coward but there were things he was deathly afraid of and illness was one of them.

He would go to the sanatorium but hate every second he was there. The smell common to all hospitals always succeeded in putting the fear of God into him.

The outside door opened and banged closed again which meant Sheena was home. He'd been waiting her arrival before breaking the news to Angus.

'Angus! Sheena!' he called out. 'Come away ben. I want to talk to the pair of you!'

Sheena came first, taking the long pearl-tipped pin out of her hat and allowing her hair to fall free to her shoulders. Somehow she contrived to remain voluptuous and seductive looking in spite of the severe green uniform encasing her from neck to mid-calf.

Angus entered the room, annoyance at being disturbed written all over his face. He'd been cutting up a length of red inner tubing which was going to form part of his new catapult.

Archie stared Angus straight in the eye. 'I've got some bad news for you lad,' he said. 'Your Ma collapsed in the street this afternoon and has been taken into hospital. The doctors say she's got TB.'

Angus's mouth fell open and he stared blankly at his step-father. It was some sort of cruel joke. It had to be! Archie was having him on. Taking the mickey.

'Jesus Christ!' Sheena said and sat down.

'You're kidding me?' Angus husked, wilting when Archie shook his head.

'She's been taken to a place out by Lanark. I'm going to see her in the morning. You can come with me if you like,' Archie said.

Angus looked down, seeing nothing. He wanted to run away. To hide. In fact to be anywhere except where he was. Turning abruptly, he fled the room.

Sheena was about to go after him when she was brought up short by Archie telling her to look in the press and see if there was anything there they could have for tea. When she replied there was only a loaf in he said he would go over to Tallon Street and break the news to the Chisholms. He'd pick up some fish suppers on his way back.

He had another dram before going through to the bathroom for a wash. Ten minutes later when he quietly let himself out the front door Sheena's voice could be heard coming from Angus's bedroom where she was doing her best to comfort her distraught step-brother.

The next morning Angus didn't run with the milk nor did Archie go to work.

Angus went down to the front close at his usual time to find Kitty waiting for him. He explained to his pal why he couldn't manage that day and Kitty promised to relay what had happened to Hugh.

Sheena made them a cup of tea and a slice of toast each for breakfast and then he and Archie, both dressed in their Sunday best, left the house to catch a tram.

During the entire journey Angus sat rigidly beside Archie staring out at the passing scenery. His eyes were red and puffy from being awake most of the night.

Arriving in Lanark, they inquired the way to Bellfield Sanatorium from a passer-by who informed them they had a mile and a half hike in front of them. It was either that or wait nearly two hours for the next local bus. They elected to walk.

The sanatorium was a large, imposing early Victorian building surrounded by well-tended lawns and a sprinkling of trees. It sparkled in the weak sunlight, giving the impression it was regularly scrubbed outside as well as in.

Loathing all institutions, Archie hated the place on sight. He shuddered as he and Angus walked through the heavy wooden doors opening into the marbled reception hall.

For half an hour they waited and then a young nurse arrived to escort them to the ward where Carrie was. The nurse's eyes opened fractionally when she saw Angus but she didn't pass any comment.

With the nurse leading the way they tramped along a seemingly endless maze of wood and marble corridors.

The thing that struck Angus most about the sanatorium was how cold it was. Despite the time of year every window was open wide so that the temperature inside the building was the same as it was out.

At the entrance to Carrie's ward they were again instructed to wait and this time they had to stand as there were no chairs or benches available where they might sit.

Within minutes a hatchet-faced woman approached them and announced herself to be Sister McMillan in charge of the ward.

The sister's next words caused Angus great consternation when she declared it was against the hospital's rules for children under the age of fifteen to be allowed into the wards.

Angus shot Archie a beseeching look which he transferred to the sister who stared back at him pityingly but resolutely.

Archie Marjoribanks may have done some terrible

things in his life but he did something then which went a long way to absolving many of them. Putting a winning smile on his face, he asked Sister if he might speak with her in private and together they moved off to a nearby alcove where Archie began exercising his not inconsiderable charm.

Angus never did find out what Archie said to Sister McMillan but, whatever it was, it secured for him the rare privilege of breaking the hospital rule.

Visitors were only allowed in one at a time and it was Archie's suggestion that Angus go first. Before going behind the screens masking the entrance to the ward Angus was handed a bagful of grapes and a box of chocolates by Archie and told to give them to Carrie, saying they came from him.

'Ach away and don't be daft!' said Archie when Angus tried to thank him.

Angus found Carrie near the end of a long row of beds. She was lying flat out with her eyes closed and the blankets pulled up to her chin.

She looked terrible. Her face was the colour of curds and her cheeks so sunken it gave her a skeletal appearance.

For a few moments he stared at his mother while she dozed. His chest heaved and he had to swallow repeatedly to hold back the tears.

'Ma?' he whispered, a catch in his voice.

Carrie's eyelids flickered and then slowly opened. Pain and suffering stared out. 'Hello, son,' she smiled.

He couldn't help what happened next. With a sob he threw himself beside her and, as his warm cheek touched her cold one, a dam seemed to burst inside him. The tears he'd been desperately holding back since Archie broke the news to him came flooding out.

Carrie stroked his hair while he cried and cried, his face buried in her pillow to try and stifle the racking sobs bursting from him.

'Just let yourself go, son,' she said quietly, thinking how much like his father he was becoming now his face had started to mature. Her guess was he'd end up a far taller, slimmer version of his father. She was still worried by the fact he was painfully thin but she'd reconciled herself to the idea that only time would alter that. It would be another year or two before he started to fill out and lose the gazelle quality he now had.

When his crying had finally run its course he used the corner of her top sheet to dry his eyes. He glanced round to see if any of the other patients were staring at him but they were all busy pretending they'd neither seen nor heard anything. The two ladies on either side of Carrie kept their noses buried deep in newspapers.

He wanted to know how long Carrie would be in the sanatorium but all she could tell him was she'd be there until better which could be anything from nine months to a year. Then she'd be back on her feet and singing like a lintie, she said, which brought a smile to Angus's face and even wrung the faint beginnings of a laugh from him.

A tremendous will to live was born in Carrie at that moment. She had to hang on. Her son needed her.

Angus had reached that terribly difficult stage of puberty and adolescence and if, during this time, the additional burden of being orphaned was thrust on him the consequences could well be disastrous. As the doctors would come to tell her again and again. They could do only so much to affect her cure. The real key to her getting better lay in her wanting to do so. For her, Angus became the key. The prime motivation.

They talked a little while longer and then it was time for Angus to go if Archie was to see Carrie as well.

At the screens he turned back and waved, knowing this would be the last look he'd have of her till she came back home again.

'Oh Ma!' he muttered. His heart felt it must surely snap in two. Swinging round he vanished from the ward.

As things turned out, Carrie's prediction of nine months to a year was somewhat optimistic. It was to be over two years before Angus saw his mother again.

When Archie arrived to sit by her bedside he was told

she'd come to a decision: Angus was to go and stay at Tallon Street until she was better.

Thinking it was him and his temper Carrie was worried about Archie wisely agreed. What he didn't realize was he was only part of the problem.

Carrie had often said she wasn't as green as she was cabbage looking. She knew there was a bond between Sheena and Angus that transcended normal step-sister/brother relationships. She would have trusted the young woman that Sheena had become with her life but she did not want her to be constantly alone with her son.

Archie promised faithfully that Angus would be packed over to Tallon Street that very day. Then and only then did Carrie begin to truly relax.

After a few minutes stilted conversation, Archie cleared his throat and in a whisper said he was going to try and control himself a lot more in future. Picking at his fingers he said he was going to miss her terribly and hadn't realized until this happened just how lucky he was to have a wife like her.

Carrie was astounded by this. These were the first intimate words she'd heard from Archie since their courting days. Furthermore, she could tell by his tone of voice and the expression on his face he meant what he said.

'Is it too late for us to start again?' he asked.

There was something boyish and appealing about Archie when he was like this that made you almost forget the cruel, roaring bully he could be.

Carrie lay back and watched a nurse making a bed on the other side of the ward. The nurse was young and fairly pretty with a face full of hope and expectation. Just like she'd once been so long long ago.

She wondered what she'd ever done to lose John McBain. Get saddled with Archie Marjoribanks. And now contract tuberculosis.

Archie was incorrigible. She knew no matter how hard he tried to reform he'd always revert back to type. The man was sick, not in the body like she was but in the mind where it lay darkly hidden. A malignancy that could be truly awesome when it manifested itself.

She was so tired she felt she could close her eyes and sleep for a hundred years. It was as though her very substance had nearly all melted away, leaving her a pale imitation of the woman she'd once been.

Looking a picture of melancholy, Archie sat staring at Carrie. He might have been a cur who'd been temporarily whipped into submission.

'We'll try again,' Carrie replied, knowing it was a futile gesture but feeling this reaffirmation of commitment was the best thing in the circumstances.

Archie nodded his gratitude, genuinely intending to keep his side of the bargain.

A few minutes later when he started to speak again he discovered she'd drifted off into what looked like a very heavy sleep.

With a rough tenderness he tucked her arms under the bedclothes and kissed her on the forehead. Then with a flashing smile to a hovering nurse he walked swiftly from the ward.

Hugh hadn't been back to Tallon Street since the day he'd left with the wireless on his shoulder. He came now knowing as it was the afternoon Donald would be at work. He didn't want to see his father. It was Winnie he wanted to speak to.

His mother answered the door wearing her pinny, her hands and arms covered in flour.

Exclaiming in delight, Winnie threw her arms round Hugh and hugged him tight. He didn't care that flour was deposited in streaks all over the good tweed jacket he'd bought only a few weeks ago.

When they finally disentangled themselves he was taken through to the kitchen where Winnie put the kettle on.

Hugh hardly recognized the kitchen. To begin with, electricity had been installed in the house which meant the old gas lighting outlets were gone. On one side a brand new cooker stood proudly. The small copper had been replaced by a washing machine. The kitchen had also been repainted as indeed had the hall and living room.

Winnie washed her hands at the sink and then, having masked the tea, buttered some piping hot scones fresh from the oven.

As they were going through to the living room Hugh broached the subject of his quarrel with Donald and was sad to hear his father was still angry with him. If there was to be a reconciliation it obviously wasn't going to be for some time yet.

They talked about Carrie and the shock it had been to hear of her being taken to Bellfield Sanatorium. It was unspoken between them but each blamed Archie for Carrie's present state. By now the entire family had come to know Archie Marjoribanks for what he was and if Carrie found understanding and perhaps pity for her husband she was the only one to do so.

Winnie went on to say Angus was sleeping in the room his mother had once shared with Harriet and seemed to be settling down well although at fifty-eight she was finding him quite a handful to have around the house.

This was just as Hugh had suspected and was the principle reason for his visit. He had come to ask Winnie if Angus might not be better off at the Paterson house with him? His idea was that when he eventually married – as he presumed he would someday – he would adopt Angus as his son.

Winnie could see that although Hugh's intentions were admirable he hadn't quite thought this proposal through. Tactfully she explained it was doubtful if Carrie would be willing to part with Angus or Angus with her.

If Angus had been a babe in arms and Hugh married to someone Carrie knew and approved of then that might have been a different kettle of fish. But it was her opinion, as she was certain it would be Carrie's, it was best for things to remain as they were.

Winnie added she was sure Carrie would be pleased to

know Angus had another place to go where he would be welcome. After all, she and Donald weren't getting any younger and who knew what the next day would bring?

Winnie was pleased Hugh had brought up the subject of marriage. At twenty-eight she thought it high time he settled down and raised a family of his own.

Hugh was in full agreement with this and in fact would have liked nothing better but as he hesitatingly explained he just couldn't seem to meet the right woman.

Somewhat embarrassed he said he'd chaffed enough personable lassies at the dancing but none of them had ever struck the right chord in him. He didn't want to get married just for getting married's sake. He wanted to marry someone he genuinely felt something for, someone he could see himself spending the rest of his life with.

There was very little Winnie could say to that except she was sure it would come out all right in the end.

The last thing she wanted was for Hugh to turn into some sort of eternal bachelor, knowing that would be totally wrong for him.

'I'll know her when I meet her,' Hugh said, eyes clouding with introspection.

Winnie sighed. 'I hope you do, son,' she replied in a voice full of sympathy.

While Winnie washed the tea things and saw to a pineapple upside down cake she had in the oven Hugh went through to the big room where he stood by the window looking up the road to the bend round which Armstrong's lay.

It was a bitter cold day and there was ice on the Cart. The air was heavy with grey chimney smoke while from beyond the bend came the thick black fug which proclaimed the Armstrong furnaces to be going full blast.

He lit a Willy Woodbine and wondered if there was something wrong with him that he couldn't meet a lassie he liked well enough to settle down with? He found it difficult to put into words just what he was looking for. Decent looks certainly. He couldn't see himself being drawn to somebody who was ugly. But the looks were only part of it. There was a lot more to what he was after than that.

He stood at the window pondering till the light faded into late afternoon darkness. Finally he shrugged and dismissed all thoughts of women from his mind.

One thing was certain though whomever he married he'd expect her to deliver him a son in time. Lassies round the house were fine and dandy but a boy was the thing. That was what he wanted.

He said goodbye to Winnie through in the kitchen, slipping a pound note into her pinny pocket and telling her to buy a wee extravagance for herself.

All the way up the road to the tramstop he dreamed of being a father with a son by his side.

Aye, boys were the ticket right enough. They made a man immortal.

12

During the next few years Angus and Rosemary saw as much of each other as was possible and all the while their relationship strengthened and developed.

Angus had moved back to Holmlea Road the same day Carrie returned from Bellfield Sanatorium. The reunion had been a joyous one but it had nearly broken his heart to see how gaunt and pitifully thin his mother had become. She was so changed it had taken him a moment or two to recognize her when she and Archie walked through the front door.

True to his word Archie tried to mend his ways, never

drinking and not once losing his temper, forever fussing round Carrie and even bringing her treats such as flowers and sweets.

At first it was thought amongst the family that Carrie would soon recover her former strength but as the months passed it became evident she would never be the same again.

As Donald remarked, all the sap had been drained out of her leaving only a shell of the woman who'd married John McBain and given birth to Angus.

Sheena had gone from the house and no one knew where. Not long after Carrie had been taken into Bellfield Archie had come home from work one night to discover a note which baldly stated she was leaving for good. Inquiring at the tram depot at the top of Holmlea Road he'd been told she'd handed in her notice with the intention of going south. Several clippies said she'd mentioned London while one was adamant it was Birmingham she was headed for.

From that day on not another word was heard from Sheena. Angus sorely missed her.

Angus was now at Queen's Park Secondary School where he was doing extremely well. An incident occurred in his first year which became legendary and marked him out as something of a wit and character. When asked in music class what a violin concerto was he'd blithely replied it was a small violin.

Perhaps it was the way he said it or the extremely serious expression he wore that convinced the rest of the class he was taking the mickey for, with a sort of combined hoot, they all dissolved into helpless laughter.

That reply earned him four of the belt and for a long time the nickname of Concerto McBain.

Physically Angus had grown even taller so that now he topped six feet, still skinny but wiry with it. He walked with a permanent stoop which made him look rather like a coat hanger on legs.

He'd been staying at Tallon Street only a short while when he'd secretly taken on an evening paper round which had been something Carrie had been completely against in case he overtaxed himself.

When Donald eventually found out he'd summoned Angus through to the front room where the pair of them thrashed the matter out. The upshot was that Angus would be allowed to continue running with the milk in the mornings and papers in the evenings just as long as it didn't interfere with either his health or school work, which it never did.

Week after week Angus put money by and soon his savings began to mount up. He bought a metal box with a padlock on the front and it was in this he kept the pound and ten shilling notes which began to accumulate.

His business ambitions remained as strong as ever and often he and Rosemary would discuss what it would be like when they grew up and were able to marry.

In this particular vision of the future Rosemary had replaced Sheena and the house the new triumvirate lived in was considerably more grand than the simple room and kitchen that had been his first conception.

The one fly in the ointment so far was he hadn't been able to decide what line of business he should go into. But he had no doubts whatsoever this would be revealed to him in time.

So far he'd been most secretive about his ambitions, not even disclosing them to Carrie when she came out of the sanatorium. Only Rosemary knew of his plans and the motivation behind them.

As the spring of 1936 gave way to summer Rosemary became much preoccupied with trying to think up something unusual to give Angus for his birthday. Birthdays were a big thing between them due to the fact they'd both been born on the same day, he the twelfth of August, 1921, she exactly one year later.

One of their favourite haunts was Paterson's Dairy, where Hugh always made them welcome no matter what the time of day or how busy he was. Although Hugh knew Rosemary lived in the big house in Old Castle Road he still wasn't aware she was Sir Alan

Armstrong's daughter.

It was there one Saturday afternoon when she and Angus were helping to muck out the stables that the idea came to her.

Hugh had recently bought a stallion called Royal Standard with the intention of breeding, which would add another string to the dairy's bow.

Angus had been called out of the stables for a few minutes, leaving Rosemary at work on her own. What happened next caused her to catch her breath: Royal Standard having got out of his own stall, reared onto his hind legs and mounted a mare called Gypsy.

The enormous penis sunk to its hilt to be drawn out and sunk again and again. With a most unhorsy low grunt Royal Standard pulled himself free and, as he did so, a gush of sperm exploded from Gypsy's rear.

The most marvellous sensations invaded Rosemary's stomach, making her flesh go all prickly. All she could think about was having that done to her.

She and Angus had petted of course but she'd limited this to her breasts and not beyond. Now she felt she wanted to go further and in that instant it dawned on her what the perfect birthday present for Angus would be.

When Angus returned to the stables he found her flushed and with a peculiar glint in her eye as she wielded her pitchfork with gusto. Asking her what was up he was told to mind his own business and all would be revealed, she giggled, in good time.

Mystified, Angus set to work beside Rosemary and falling into the rhythm of the job the incident passed from his mind.

Sir Alan Armstrong was a happy man as he sat in his office sipping his morning sherry.

Like some great beast, the works rumbled below and around him proclaiming Armstrong's to be in full production once again.

The books lying open in front of him were healthier than they'd been in years with more orders flooding in every day.

As he sat staring out of his window, Sir Alan mused on the fear and trepidation that was abroad in the land and had been ever since 7th March when the German Chancellor Herr Hitler's armed columns had streamed into the Rhineland where they'd reoccupied the main German towns.

All Europe was in a furore over this, especially the French government under M. Sarraut.

France was now looking to Great Britain as the British had guaranteed the French frontier against German aggression. Earlier, they'd put a great deal of pressure on France for the evacuation of the Rhineland.

At one fell swoop Hitler had not only violated the Peace Treaty but also the Treaty of Locarno, throwing into great consternation those powers ranged against him.

Lloyd George's response to this flagrant breach of faith had been placatory: 'In my judgement Herr Hitler's greatest crime was not the breach of a treaty because there was provocation.'

Lloyd George's statement was interpreted to mean Hitler's provocation was the failure of the Allies to disarm themselves more than they had done.

Now massive fortifications were being built in the Rhineland which, according to Winston Churchill, meant a great barrier of concrete was being raised which would effectively alter the whole aspect of Middle Europe.

Sir Alan smiled as he sat back in his chair to light up one of his favourite Cuban cigars. War was now inevitable. There could be no doubt about it. Those appeasers in Whitehall would eventually have to stop playing the ostrich and face reality. Herr Hitler was intent on expanding Germany's diminished colonial power and like Napoleon before him his ultimate aim was the conquest of Europe.

A frown flitted across Sir Alan's face. War meant work, which in turn meant Armstrong's was bound to make money hand over fist. If properly handled, the works would never again be in danger of closure. The other side of the coin was that many good men were bound to die, which genuinely saddened him.

Guilt niggled his insides as he thought of how much he'd hoped and prayed for this coming conflict. He'd been thinking of himself, his family and the works, not the poor sods who were going to get chopped or maimed and the loved ones they'd leave behind.

'Damnit to hell!' he exclaimed and poured himself another sherry. It was a rare occasion when he indulged in more than one at this time of the morning.

He pondered for a little while, desperately trying to salve his conscience and dispel the terrible guilt feelings growing in him with every passing second.

His face lit up in a smile as the idea came to him. When war finally did erupt those working in Armstrong's would find themselves in reserve occupations. Well, the least he could do was take on as much staff as possible thereby assuring a few more local men the chance of escaping the front line.

His conscience now assuaged, he picked up the small brass bell standing on one side of his desk and gave it two sharp rings.

He would dictate a memo immediately and see it was posted on the works noticeboard without delay. Slitting his eyes, he worked out just how many additional time served men he could take on and for good measure tacked on a number of apprentices.

Sir Alan's memo duly appeared on the noticeboard that afternoon: Donald read it en route to the pattern makers' offices. He forgot about it until the evening when the hooter had blown and he was on his way home. He recalled then how Angus had once confided in him he wanted to work for Armstrong's just like his Da before him.

Donald made a mental note to go over to Holmlea Road and speak to Carrie and the lad after tea.

Carrie was sitting knitting while Archie sprawled in the

chair facing her reading the evening paper.

Angus was through in his room counting his money. It was a Friday and he'd been paid for both his jobs.

When Carrie called him to come away ben the kitchen he carefully padlocked his metal box which he then placed in its hiding place behind some odds and ends on a shelf in the cupboard.

Satisfied everything was in order, he went through to see his grandfather whom he'd heard arrive while he was in the middle of his weekly count.

Donald disliked intensely being in Archie Marjoribanks's company nowadays. He always had the overpowering urge to backhand the man for the way he'd treated Carrie and still did as far as he knew, although according to Winnie things were a lot better between them of late.

Fancying he could still take Archie in a fight, Donald didn't appreciate just how much he'd deteriorated during the past few years. He'd shrunk several inches while his chest was now a parody of its former burly and muscular self. The fact was Donald had become an old man without realizing it. In a stand up fight he wouldn't have stood an earthly against Archie.

Carrie told Angus to sit and when he'd done so went on to tell him of the marvellous opportunity that had come his way.

With Donald being a senior gaffer it was certain anyone he put up for a job – and certainly John McBain's son – would be accepted.

Angus was thunderstruck. It had just never crossed his mind this sort of thing might happen. In a great rush of words he told them he didn't want to go to work for Armstrong's any more but wanted to go into business instead.

His confession was greeted by surprise – none of them had even the faintest inkling of Angus's change of heart. When Archie asked Angus what sort of business he would like to go into all Angus could do was blush and reply he didn't know yet. Archie snorted and muttered something about delusions of grandeur.

Donald was filled with consternation as he lit up his pipe. What had happened to the common sense he'd always credited the lad with having? Business wasn't something people of their class got mixed up in. That was strictly for those who went to fancy schools and spoke with a plum in their mouths.

Besides being in business meant you became one of *them*. A capitalist! It was the very nature of the beast.

Carefully Donald unscrewed the bowl of his pipe and knocked dottle into his hanky. As he cleaned the mucky inside of the bowl he thought that it was common for lads of Angus's age to have flights of fancy. Well there was nothing wrong with that as long as they were eventually made to realize the difference between those and the reality of their situation.

He sucked his pipe back into life and then began to speak in the calm, reassuring voice he employed when faced with a difficult situation on the foundry floor. He said Angus wanting to go into business was all very well and good but did Angus appreciate just what he'd be up against?

Angus replied rather stiffly he wasn't quite sure what his grandfather was getting at, wincing as Donald then went on to make pertinent point after point.

Angus hung his head under the gentle but penetrating and most disconcerting onslaught. He didn't have the answers to any of this. All he did have was a dream and enormous faith in his own ability to accomplish what he set out to do.

The more questions thrown at him the more frantic Angus became. He desperately wanted to try and explain his dream but found no matter how hard he groped for the words they just wouldn't come. It all seemed so clear when he was discussing it with Rosemary but here talking to adults it was a different matter altogether.

What he did manage to get out was he considered it imperative to get his Highers for without those behind him he would be at a definite disadvantage for getting on.

As the words jerked from his quivering mouth it suddenly dawned on him with resounding clarity that to men like Donald and Archie formal education beyond being able to read, write and count meant very little. To them a trade was the thing, the be-all and end-all.

Archie was in an irritable mood. The rheumatism which had suddenly started bothering him lately was giving him gyp. He thought if only he could have a wee half gill it might ease the terrible nagging pain.

Archie considered what Angus was saying to be a right load of nonsense. The lad didn't realize just how lucky he was, being handed an opportunity like this on a plate. Times might have eased but there still weren't that many jobs going you could afford to pick and choose. Silly bugger with his high-faluting notions. Secretive, too, the way he hoarded the money Carrie allowed him to keep in that metal box through in his room.

The boy was becoming miserly and that was something he detested. Money was for spending, not for hiding away in the back of a cupboard. It was high time Angus was taught a lesson regarding money (in the hope it would bring him to his senses).

Archie grimaced and rubbed his arm. Bloody rheumatism! He would get Carrie to make him a hot bread poultice after Donald was gone.

Carrie appreciated Angus was highly thought of scholastically at school and that his teachers were keen for him to stay on and take his Highers. The trouble was she'd never thought all that much about it, her assumption being he'd still want to leave Queen's Park when old enough to go up by.

At the end of a further half hour's argument Donald was still maintaining Angus should forget this daft business notion and sign apprenticeship papers with Armstrong's where he would learn a useful trade.

Folding her arms across her chest Carrie declared her mind was made up. Angus would not be going back to school at the end of the summer holidays but would be starting with Armstrong's.

'It's for the best son. I know you'll agree with us in a few years time when you come to see things in perspective,' Donald said slightly pompously.

Angus jumped to his feet. He couldn't bear to stay in this room a second longer. He had to get out. It didn't matter where as long as it was a quiet spot where he could sit and nurse his anguish.

'Angus!' Carrie yelled. But it was no use. He was gone. The front door banged behind him.

'Delusions of grandeur,' repeated Archie, shaking his head and kneading his arm.

Carrie stared at the doorway through which Angus had vanished. She knew she was right in insisting he get settled into a good job, especially now her health was giving her cause for concern again.

Angus leaned into the wind and forced his legs to pump harder and harder. His chest was heaving while his short hair spiked out behind him as he sped along the road on his bike.

It wasn't fair. It just wasn't fair! he raged. His knuckles turned white as he strained at the handlebars as though they were a length of steel he was trying to bend in half.

He would never marry Rosemary now. How could he! She was the boss's daughter while he would never be anything more than an employee. A journeyman. A nothing!

His long legs whirled faster and faster till he and his bike were a blur flashing through the night.

Suddenly as though a stopcock had been opened, his anger was gone leaving him feeling washed out and taut as a thinly stretched wire. His hands were trembling as he stopped pedalling to stare round and see where he was.

Instinctively he'd taken the road he travelled every morning to Paterson's Dairy and even now was coasting into Muirend. That pleased him for if there was anyone he could speak to at a time like this it was his uncle Hugh.

Hugh was humming merrily to himself as he put a Windsor knot in his tie. He was off to the jigging and looking forward to it. Outside the house stood a brand new Wolseley Hornet he'd bought for £175 and which had been delivered from the saleroom that very afternoon.

Moving to the window he twitched back the curtain and gazed down at the bright red car. It was a beauty all right and in his estimation well worth every penny.

For months now he'd been coveting the saleroom models and wondering where he could get £175 from. Then he remembered the wireless set he'd bought for Winnie and which now stood on top of his dressing table.

The Wolseley people had been only too happy to enter into a hire purchase agreement and as a result the shining wee beauty now standing outside was his.

He was still at the window, reluctant to take his eyes off the Hornet, when Angus appeared cycling towards the house.

He frowned when he saw the look on Angus's face. Moments later he was hurrying down to the front door where the bell was already clanging.

'You'd better come away up and tell me all about it,' he said. He gestured towards the stairs leading to his bedroom.

There was a packet of Pasha lying beside the wireless and without asking permission Angus helped himself to one.

Hugh closed the bedroom door and stood with his back to it. 'Your mother?' he queried, for his first thought had been something had happened to Carrie.

'No,' Angus said huskily, smoke rising from him as though he was a newly stoked chimney. He declined when Hugh suggested he sit. Instead, striding up and down the room, the words poured from him.

While Angus ranted Hugh crossed to the press from which he produced a screwtop whose contents he poured equally into a brace of tumblers. Angus accepted his on the move and greedily drank it down.

All the words that had steadfastly refused to come earlier now poured from him as he told Hugh about Rosemary and the plans they'd had for their future.

One of the main reasons for the words not coming in Holmlea Road was because he hadn't wanted to bring Rosemary into it, knowing only too well the derisory reaction he would have had from Donald had he announced that he planned to marry Sir Alan Armstrong's elder daughter. But here with Hugh he had no such inhibitions.

Hugh sipped his beer and listened in silence, thinking about something his mother had once said about still waters running deep. He'd thought he knew Angus and yet here was a completely new side to the boy he hadn't even suspected existed.

It amused him greatly to learn Rosemary was Sir Alan's daughter. Jesus, but Angus aimed high!

When Angus spoke about his ambitions in the business field his eyes glowed, only becoming dull again when he remembered these ambitions would probably never be fulfilled.

Finally he stopped talking and turned to Hugh with an expectant look on his face, waiting for his uncle's comments and advice.

Hugh was well aware of the responsibility now resting on his shoulders. What he said next could well affect Angus for the rest of the lad's life.

The damnable thing was he could see Donald's point of view only too clearly. Angus came from a working-class background and people from there just didn't aspire to the heady levels inhabited by Armstrong and his family.

It was obvious there was a great deal of love between Angus and Rosemary but how was she going to feel in the future when able to look beyond the bounds of passion? And if she and Angus did get married how would he be affected in the years to come?

A man like Sir Alan would denigrate the lad and treat

him as both an inferior and a lackey, to say nothing about how Angus could expect to be treated by the Armstrongs' friends.

Angus would be a misfit, the proverbial round peg in a square hole. And no matter how strong his relationship with Rosemary this could only lead to friction and eventual unhappiness between the pair of them.

Hugh knew that when Donald spoke of *us* and *them* his father had the rights of it. Maybe someday things would be different. He wasn't a prophet and couldn't say. But certainly in the year 1936 that was how it was.

'Well?' Angus prompted.

Hugh took a deep breath and then proceeded to speak for a good ten minutes. When he finally finished Angus looked the most miserable young man there had ever been.

Hugh's words were a death knell to Angus, each one another brick in the wall that had suddenly sprung up between himself and Rosemary. He'd come to Hugh looking for hope and all he was getting were reasons why he should give up all idea of marrying Rosemary Armstrong.

Hugh could see Angus thought he'd let him down so he apologized saying that was how he saw the position and surely Angus wouldn't want him to lie or pretend otherwise?

For Angus two things were crystal clear. The first was that he loved Rosemary and no matter what happened to him in life she would remain his rightful partner.

The other thing was that he wasn't cut out any longer to work at Armstrong's. There had been a time when he would have slotted neatly into that niche but that was before he'd met Rosemary and the candle of ambition had been lit within him.

They sat and talked for a while longer and then Hugh took Angus down to the front of the house to admire the Wolseley.

Hugh had the idea then of forgetting all about going to the jigging and taking Angus out for a run in the car. But

Angus declined, saying he just wasn't in the mood and perhaps they could go another time.

Angus clambered onto his bike. Hugh reached out and shook him by the hand. Angus appreciated the gesture as it signified that Hugh now accepted him as a man.

After Angus had gone Hugh went through and sat with Greta Paterson for a while. She listened sympathetically as he told her about Angus's problems. When he asked her opinion she said he'd done all he could and to have advised the lad otherwise would have been the sheerest folly.

The Plaza Dance Hall had the name of being a right toffee-nosed place where anyone bearing even the faintest resemblance to scruff was definitely not welcome. Dressed in his good suit with a brand new shirt and tie on Hugh didn't anticipate any difficulty in being admitted.

Having parked his car he made his way to the Star Bar directly facing the dance hall.

The interior of the pub was blue with smoke and there were the usual raucous Friday night voices everywhere. He ordered a pint of heavy and a half of whisky. Knocking the whisky back, in a single gulp, he washed it down with a gulp of beer.

He was deep in thought about Angus when he heard himself being hailed from the other side of the bar. Looking up, he saw a chap called Kenny White whom he'd been friendly with at school edging through the crowd towards him.

The two men shook hands, genuinely pleased to see one another. Kenny offered to buy Hugh a refill which Hugh readily accepted. They toasted each other and drank. Kenny informed Hugh he was waiting for a china who was going to make up a foursome with his girlfriend's pal.

They were deep in speculation about the forthcoming football season and how the 'Gers would do when Hugh saw the two girls enter the pub to stand rather self-consciously while they stared round.

One girl's face lit up when she spied Kenny and after a hurried whisper to her companion the pair of them began making their way over.

'Your bird and her pal I think,' Hugh said out the side of his mouth, thinking Kenny had acquired a bit of taste in his old age as both women were classy looking.

Introductions were made, Kenny's girl being Mary Maude and her pal Janey McIver. Hugh shook hands with both of them and then asked what they were having to drink as it was his round.

Once the drinks were in Hugh found himself standing beside Janey and as Kenny and Mary were deep in conversation on their own he felt duty bound to chat with the lassie, not that talking to her was all that much of a hardship. Besides being pretty like many Glasgow women, she had an incisive wit which could make you laugh one minute and cut you to the bone the next.

Janey informed Hugh they were also off to the Plaza that night. Usually she and Mary went to Barrowland but had decided on a change because she had recently broken off with a boyfriend of long standing and didn't want to run into him in case he caused trouble.

While Janey talked Hugh wondered how Kenny had come to get mixed up with a couple of left-footers like these. For it was obvious to him that was what they were, each having the map of Ireland written clearly across her face.

Half an hour later Kenny glanced at his watch and looked anxiously at the door. Fifteen minutes after that he was downright embarrassed as it was now obvious his china wasn't going to show which meant Janey had been given a dissy.

He went up to the bar and got yet another round. Then, surreptitiously, he gestured to Hugh to follow him to the cludgie.

Kenny was frantic and straightaway pleaded with Hugh to fill in for his missing friend.

With the thought that Janey was a fenian uppermost in his mind, Hugh tried to decline but Kenny wouldn't take no for an answer. Kenny confessed he was loopy about Mary and had been trying to get her to go out with him for weeks. Mary wasn't his girlfriend at all, although he desperately wanted her to be. This was their first date together.

Having made his impassioned plea, he produced a small silver flask from his pocket which he thrust into Hugh's hands, urging him to have a dram.

Under the circumstances Hugh felt he had no option other than to agree to be Janey's partner, leaving Kenny free all evening to dance with Mary rather than having to share himself between the two women.

Kenny was delighted and much relieved by Hugh's capitulation and they each had a large swallow from the flask before heading back to the bar where they found both girls looking miserable as sin.

They chatted for a few minutes and then Hugh suggested that as he was also going to the Plaza why didn't he join them to round off the numbers?

Janey flashed him a grateful smile. Finishing their drinks, they left the pub and crossed over the road.

The decor of the dancehall was very genteel with acres of plush and a great many potted plants. The ages of the clientele varied from teenagers to couples in their late forties and early fifties. A number of the older men were wearing tails.

Janey fitted snugly against Hugh when they took to the floor and soon they were enjoying themselves, having a 'rer ter', as the expression goes.

Much later they were cooling themselves with soft drinks when Kenny materialized to announce with a sideways wink to Hugh that he and Mary were off. Without actually saying so, he made it quite clear he and Mary wanted to leave alone.

Having gone this far Hugh decided he might as well go the whole hog and lumber Janey. During the last waltz he put it to her and she rather shyly agreed.

Reaching the Wolseley, he proudly showed it to her, having first made a quick tour of inspection to ensure it hadn't been vandalized in his absence. Janey was most impressed by the fact he had a car and said it was the first time she'd ever been driven home in one. Hugh replied she was the first Catholic he'd ever taken home. He'd meant it as a joke but somehow it didn't quite come out as one. Janey's eyes flashed as she bit back the retort that had sprung so readily to her mouth.

There it was, out in the open at last, the unspoken barrier that had existed between them all night. Religion.

'Aye, well,' said Hugh sadly, helping Janey into the car.

Janey knew exactly what he meant. There was an enormous gulf of bitterness and hatred between their two sides, a gulf that was rarely successfully crossed. Conditions, environment and prejudice bred at the breast saw to that.

As they drove into the festering area that was the Gorbals, Janey mumbled she wanted to thank him for coming to her rescue earlier on and he mumbled back it had been his pleasure.

Thistle Street was a grey canyon whose floor was strewn with garbage and with walls looking as though they were suffering from an advanced case of leprosy. It was a miracle of human will that such an immaculately turned out lassie as Janey could have come from a slum like this.

Hugh killed the engine and for a moment or two they sat in silence. Hugh finally cleared his throat to say he'd better get on back home as he had to be up at the crack of dawn.

In a flash Janey was out of the car, a wry smile on her face as she reached back in again to shake him by the hand. 'Perhaps we'll bump into one another some other night,' she said.

Then turning on her heel she was gone, clattering up her close.

'Aw to hell with it!' Hugh said savagely, angry and

upset and not wanting to admit to himself the reason why.

The Wolseley roared into life, peeling so fast down the street it left a long strip of rubber behind as a souvenir.

As he glared through the windscreen he told himself Kenny White was a mug. There was no future in getting involved with a left footer. That road could only lead to the worst sort of trouble.

The car had already turned out of sight when a wan face appeared high up in one of the tenement windows to stare out onto a street now empty apart from a drunk clinging for dear life onto a lamp standard while he spewed his guts into the gutter.

Sadly, Janey left the window and started to undress. When she crawled into bed it was to lie beside three of her sisters, two of whom slept up the way while she and the fourth slept down.

There were ten McIver children and all of them slept in that one tenement room.

It was a long time before she fell asleep but when she did it was to dream she was back amongst the plush and potted plants of the Plaza dancing with Hugh Chisholm.

'Property,' Sir Hamilton McLaren boomed, 'That's the thing. You can't go far wrong with property. Mark my words.'

There were four of them round the wrought iron lawn table, Sir Hamilton and his wife Elizabeth – Lize as she was known to her friends – plus Sir Alan and Cordelia.

This was the third time the Armstrongs had visited the McLarens and, as Sir Alan had wanted, a strong bond of friendship was growing up between the two families.

Sir Alan mused on Sir Hamilton's word as he sipped a cold glass of Sauterne and watched his daughters, Rosemary and Diane, riding with Iain and Peter McLaren in the far distance. He thought speculatively and not for the first time how well his girls got on with the McLaren boys, a fact he might well be able to exploit at a later date.

'Take industry like you're in,' Sir Hamilton went on, warming to his favourite subject. 'That comes and goes according to the state of the country's and the world's economy, but with property you don't have to worry because it's a permanent fixture. Well, almost permanent anyway. And as long as there are people needing a roof over their heads you're in business. Recession or boom, it's all one to the property owner.'

Sir Alan wondered if this was the diversification he'd long been looking for. Another two or three years the way things were going and he'd be in a position where he could afford to hive off a substantial amount of venture capital. Property might well be the sort of secondary investment which would suit him down to the ground and ensure he'd never again have to think of using that small automatic pistol lying in the dark recesses of his desk.

A little later Cordelia caught her husband intently eyeing Iain McLaren, sizing the lad up. Then she saw his gaze move from Iain to Rosemary and back again. The hint of a smile blossomed at the corners of her mouth as she correctly guessed what was running through his mind.

Well, why not? she thought. The boy was handsome, intelligent, and one day would be worth a fortune. She doubted there was a better prospect in all Scotland.

With a gracious nod to the attendant butler she accepted more wine. It was turning out to be a most interesting and enjoyable afternoon. Giving a brittle laugh, she turned her attention back to Hamilton who'd just delivered the tag line to some absurd joke he'd been telling.

While her parents and the McLarens laughed Rosemary attacked the plate of salmon set before her. She munched hungrily and as she ate she wondered for the umpteenth time why it was so long since she'd heard from Angus.

Twice she'd been up early enough to look out on the milk cart doing its rounds and neither time had he been with it. Could it be he was ill or had been involved in an accident?

She came to the decision she would rise early again next morning and if he still wasn't on the cart she'd go down and have a word with Kitty to find out just what was what.

With her mind now partially at rest she glanced across to where Diane was deep in conversation with Peter. Those two certainly got on like a house on fire, but then everyone got on with Peter. He was such a laugh and always tremendous fun to be with. Not at all like Iain who was quiet and intense with the loner's habit of often retreating within himself.

She watched Iain carefully wipe his mouth, every gesture neat and precious.

Her thoughts were interrupted by Diane shrieking with laughter as she tumbled down a grassy bank while Peter, who was obviously the culprit, stood grinning from ear to ear.

'Come on!' Diane yelled to Rosemary, as she got to her feet, her face red from heat and exertion. 'Let's give him some of his own medicine!'

Rosemary smiled and jumped up. As she did so, she stretched out her hands and waggled her fingers, knowing Peter was hypersensitively ticklish. Even the threat of it was enough to send him into paroxysms of laughter.

Peter yelped as both girls advanced on him. He'd gone too far and would now have to pay the penalty. 'That's not fair!' he protested and turned to run.

Iain smiled thinly at the goings on, rather enjoying them although horseplay wasn't something he personally liked getting involved in. He invariably found it undignified and degrading but only in himself and not in others.

As Peter ran off with Diane and Rosemary in pursuit a white vapour trail suddenly appeared in the sky above them.

Iain shielded his eyes as he followed the aeroplane from whose fuselage the vapour was streaming. The plane roared closer and then banked to come winging directly overhead.

He held his breath. For a split second every detail of the plane's underbelly was visible to him. Then it was gone, disappearing fast towards the horizon while behind it the vapour trail very slowly began to break up and disintegrate.

His mind filled with the excitement the plane had generated in him. He began to think what it must be like to be high in the air flying like a bird. What a glorious sense of freedom that must be!

Staring up at the sky he pictured the plane zooming overhead with himself at the controls. He found the image almost unbearably exciting.

It was mid-afternoon when Carrie and Winnie alighted from the tram into Scotland Street. It was quite some time since Carrie's last visit to the Smiths so another was well overdue.

Mounting the close stairs they rapped on the Smiths' door. They were about to turn away thinking no one was home when the door opened a few inches and an eye peered out.

'Robert?' Carrie queried. The sudden and bizarre appearance of the eye had given her a fright.

There was a pause during which the eye studied her curiously and then the door swung open to reveal old man Smith.

Both Carrie and Winnie were shocked at the sight of him. His face was ingrained with what looked like coal dirt while his hair was long, matted and tangled.

His shirt was open and collarless and, judging from its state, hadn't been changed in weeks. His trousers were tied round the middle with a piece of manky string below which his flies were completely undone. When he moved his flies opened wide revealing the fact he wasn't wearing any underpants.

His face broke into a sudden grin and extending a gnarled bony hand he invited them inside.

The poor man's completely off his chump, Winnie thought, wondering what Meg was thinking of to allow him to get into such a state. She gestured Carrie to go in first and then followed closely at her daughter's heels.

Both women gagged as the overpowering stench filling the house hit them. Winnie gulped and held a hanky to her nose as she followed Carrie and Robert through to the kitchen.

Despite the fact it was high summer and exremely warm out, there was a fire blazing in the grate but the fire wasn't a coal one. Broken pieces of furniture which had evidently been chopped by the hatchet lying just inside the fender, burnt away.

'Where's Meg?' Carrie asked, trying to act as though everything was normal and just as it should be.

Robert's eyes took on a faraway look and his mouth twisted into a secret smile.

Snapping out of his dwam, Robert started humming to himself, a strange discordant tune of his own composition. And crossing to where the hatchet was lying he picked it up and hefted it in his skeletal hand. Without warning the hatchet hissed through the air causing Winnie to give an involuntary little scream and hastily step backwards.

The hatchet crashed into the remains of a wooden chair, breaking the seat part jaggedly in two. Again and again Robert swung the hatchet till the chair was reduced to an untidy pile of kindling.

With dribble running over and through the growth on his chin he piled every last sliver of this kindling onto an already stacked and roaring fire.

Sweat dripped from Carrie as she squatted beside Robert Smith and forced herself to look into those demented eyes. 'Where's Meg?' she asked again, her voice soothing and coaxing.

The scars from the stitches lining Robert's face appeared angry in the reflected firelight. His mouth opened and he tried to speak but all that came out was more spit and animal grunts.

Then for a brief second his eyes cleared and once more he tried to speak. But it was no use. What emerged had no meaning, at least none Carrie could decipher.

Reaching out, he laid a begrimed hand on Carrie's arm and as he did so several large tears burst from the corners of his eyes. The sanity vanished as swiftly as it had appeared. He snatched his hand away and, hunkering on his feet like a dog, began to snigger.

'I think we'd better look around,' Winnie said.

Carrie nodded agreement and came to her feet while Robert ceased sniggering to gaze in fascination into the roaring blaze.

Side by side Carrie and Winnie ventured out of the kitchen and back into the hallway where the terrible stench seemed stronger. When they entered the bedroom they found it pitch dark and the stench stronger still.

'Oh my God!' exclaimed Carrie when she'd swept the curtains back.

Encased in a thick flannelette nightgown, Meg's decomposing body lay stretched out under the bedclothes. Her white hair was fluffed out halo-like round her head while what remained of her eyes stared sightlessly at the ceiling.

For a minute, Winnie thought Robert might have done for his wife with the hatchet or some other such weapon but a cursory glance was enough to verify Meg had died in her sleep or from natural causes while in bed.

Catching hold of the window, Carrie jerked it open to allow some of the stink out and fresh air in. She then asked her mother what they should do and Winnie replied the best thing would be to inform the police.

The problem was solved for them when from the kitchen came a great whoofing sound, unmistakable to those who have ever had a chimney catch fire.

Carrie dashed back through to make sure Robert was all right to discover him capering in front of the flames, cackling like a banshee.

When the firemen arrived they came charging up the

close to be met at the door by Winnie who explained to them what the situation was.

Carrie and Winnie waited on till the fire had been extinguished and the police had taken Meg away for an autopsy and Robert to Gartnavel Hospital for the mentally disturbed.

Badly shaken by their ordeal, they returned home bearing the sad news of what had happened to the Smiths.

Robert died in Gartnavel before the year was out and was buried alongside his beloved Meg. Officially, the cause of death was heart failure but those who'd heard him keening and calling for his dead wife were convinced it was really a broken heart he'd died of.

But then one is merely a romantic version of the other.

Head bowed and hands sunk deep into his overall pockets Angus trudged homeward having just finished his daily stint at Armstrong's.

He'd been working there for several weeks and, as he'd known he would, he hated every minute of it.

Once he'd seen the big white chief himself stalking across the yard and had been filled with a combination of anger, resentment and shame to think he'd been literally forced to work for the man whose daughter he'd planned to marry.

He now thought of Rosemary in the past tense, convinced their relationship was at an end.

He'd also seen Donald a number of times and had avoided his grandfather, blaming Donald for the fact he'd been apprenticed when where he really wanted to be was back at school studying for his Highers and planning his entry into the business world.

He started out of his melancholic reverie on hearing himself hailed and, turning round, saw it was Kitty who'd shouted and was hurrying to catch him up.

Kitty had also applied for an apprenticeship at Armstrong's but had been turned down. There had been a host of applications but only the lucky and the well connected had received a letter of acceptance, enclosing indenture papers to be signed.

After talking it over with his parents, Kitty had decided he, too, would leave school: with the way things had generally picked up, surely it wouldn't be long before he could land himself a decent job?

In the meantime, he was still running with the milk and had taken over Angus's paper round. He'd just made his final delivery for the evening.

'I want a word with you,' Kitty said, falling in beside Angus.

'Oh, aye?'

'Rosemary came out to see me this morning, asking why she hadn't heard from you. And I may tell you the poor lassie was worried stiff. She thought you must have been ill or had an accident or something.'

The blush swept up Angus's neck to invade his face. Stopping he fumbled for his cigarettes. Somehow managing to keep his face averted, he offered one to Kitty and then struck a match which they both used.

The plain fact of the matter was that he'd been putting off and putting off contacting Rosemary to tell her what had happened. He just couldn't seem to summon up the courage to tell her all his plans for the future lay in ruins and there was now no way he could ever see the pair of them getting married.

His wretchedness showed clearly as he strode along the street, his long legs going at such a pace that Kitty several times had to break into a trot to keep up.

Kitty had been all set to jibe Angus but now wisely decided not to. As they hurried along, Kitty told Angus that Rosemary had sent the message she would meet him in 'their place' at three on the Saturday afternoon after their birthday which was the following week.

What Rosemary was referring to as 'their place' was a spot upstream on the Cart which she and Angus had stumbled onto by accident some years ago on an exploring trip.

It was a small cave halfway up a steep bank, screened by trees and a mass of foliage. They called it the bear cave – the pretence being that it had once been a bear's lair – whose existence they kept secret.

Kitty went on to say he'd told Rosemary the story of the apprenticeships coming vacant at her father's works and how Angus, at his mother's insistence, had been made to apply and that the application had been duly accepted. He'd added ruefully that his had been turned down.

'How was she looking?' Angus asked, his voice shaking a little.

Kitty grinned and replied she hadn't sprouted a moustache if that was what Angus was worried about. Angus laughed and snapped out of his mood.

'Three o'clock on the Saturday afternoon?' he queried.

Kitty nodded and then playfully punched his pal on the arm. 'Go on, you great big long streak of misery,' he said. 'Do yourself a favour. Go and see the lassie.'

Arriving home, Angus quickly washed and then went through to his room where he would wait until called for his tea. As he changed out of his working clothes all he could think of was his forthcoming rendezvous with Rosemary.

Now a move had been made, he couldn't wait to see her again.

The day had dawned a beautiful one – just what Rosemary had been praying for. She was carrying a picnic basket in one hand and an old mac slung over her shoulder as she made her way through the undergrowth towards the bear cave.

There was something primeval about this section of the riverbank, she'd always thought. It wouldn't have surprised her in the least had she suddenly come face to face with an ancient Celtic tribesman daubed with woad, or if a sabre-toothed tiger had suddenly appeared on a branch of one of the many trees surrounding her.

She was feeling nervous and rather tired, having had trouble sleeping the night before. Her mind had been racing with thoughts of today and what she planned to make happen.

In a pocket of her mac was a packet of contraceptives which she'd finally obtained from a school chum called Margie McIntyre who had a reputation for being wild and a great one for the boys.

In the picnic basket were all sorts of goodies she'd scrounged from cook plus a bottle of wine she'd managed to lift when everyone's back was turned.

She stopped when she heard voices and, from a vantage point behind a tree, watched four wee boys dressed as Red Indians making their way in the direction she'd just come from. Judging by the way they were creeping along they were in the middle of a game, so no doubt there would be another band of them somewhere around.

A little further on she had to climb the steep bank, working her way behind masses of foliage, to the spot where the bear cave lay hidden.

The first thing she did was to lay the mac on the ground and then she began setting out the picnic things.

She heard him coming before he actually appeared. Suddenly he was there, standing in the mouth of the cave grinning down at her.

It might have been years since they'd last spoken, both were that awkward and shy.

'Happy birthday!' Angus said and thrust a brown paper parcel into her hands. He sat on the mac beside her and watched while she undid the string.

Rosemary exclaimed with delight when she opened the box. Inside were a pair of matching tortoise shell combs which she knew would look marvellous in her hair.

Although Angus had developed a fetish about making and saving money he wasn't scared to spend it when the occasion arose and could be extremely generous at times. To him money was always the means to an end and never the be-all and end-all in itself.

'They're gorgeous,' Rosemary breathed, her face beaming. Leaning across she kissed him on the lips.

'I'll give you yours later,' she added, a mischievous twinkle in her eye.

Like a lot of people who consider themselves to be at fault, Angus couldn't wait to explain himself. In a great rush of words it all came tumbling out.

According to Angus, his life lay in ruins and their relationship in tatters but Rosemary knew this just wasn't so. His having to go to work for her father might appear a setback but who knew how time might transform this into a positive advantage?

A little perspective was needed, she told him sternly. After all, school certificates were never a guarantee for success. What really mattered was determination and a willingness to work longer and harder than anyone else. An astute mind – if you didn't have that no amount of school certificates were going to give it to you – a shrewd business sense and, above all, motivation.

There was a fierceness in Rosemary as she spoke these words – the mother hen cajoling her favourite chick.

She wanted to take Angus by the shoulders and shake all this ridiculous defeatist talk out of him. So what if he had to spend the next few years learning to be a fitter? With the right motivation spurring him on being a fitter need only be the first rung on the ladder.

Angus stared at Rosemary in amazement, a new shame growing in him at how ready he'd been to throw in his hand. As she was now making abundantly clear there were more ways than one to skin the proverbial cat.

In a moment of insight it came to him that their love was only on the threshold of its potential. There were depths he could plumb with Rosemary that would take them a lifetime to fulfil.

'Well?' she demanded.

He smiled wryly. 'With you beside me I doubt if there's anything I couldn't do. You're all the motivation I'll ever need.'

Her nostrils flared and her breathing became laboured. She'd suddenly started thinking about Royal Standard again and what she'd seen him do to the mare, Gypsy.

She poured wine into cups and having passed one to Angus offered up a toast. 'To us!' she murmured. Her eyelids drooped to give her a catlike appearance.

Lying back on the mac, she beckoned him to her. Mouth met mouth and as they did so she guided his hands to the swell of her breasts.

His hands slid under her blouse to stroke and knead her flesh. He fumbled with her bra, cursing himself for having a handful of thumbs, till she came to his assistance by deftly flicking open the hooks and eyes.

She could feel how ready he was, strong and hard pressing down through her skirt.

She ran her hands over his back and then down to clasp his bottom. When she looked into his eyes he was staring quizzically back.

Groping in the mac pocket she pulled out the packet of contraceptives. 'Happy birthday!' she smiled.

He was dumbfounded. 'You mean . . . ?'

She nodded and then shrugged herself free of her blouse and bra, throwing them to one side where they lay in an untidy heap.

Angus gulped and his face drained of colour. This was a moment he'd often thought and dreamt about and now, incredibly, it had arrived.

'Come on!' she urged, undoing her skirt.

Angus was trembling as he took off his jacket and shirt. He unbuttoned his flies, feeling embarrassed and strangely vulnerable.

'Don't forget your socks,' Rosemary said with a giggle.

The giggle relaxed him with the reminder that it was his Rosemary he was doing this with and not some strange girl who meant nothing to him. There was no need for fear or embarrassment. Not with Rosie.

'Angus?'

She was laying stark naked with her hands by her sides and a soft smile on her face.

His stomach muscles rippled and although it was warm in the cave goose bumps broke out on his back and along the length of his arms.

'Scared?'

'Of course not!' he replied indignantly and just that little bit too emphatically.

'I am.'

'There's nothing to worry about. I won't hurt you. I promise,' he said.

They kissed again and as they did so his hands slid down her body.

'Don't forget the johnnies,' she whispered throatily in his ear.

Somehow he managed to rip the packet open but his hands were shaking so much he would never have got it on if she hadn't helped him.

Theoretically he knew what to do next but faced with the reality it was a different matter altogether. It just wasn't as straightforward as he'd been led to believe. If only he could see what he should have been getting at but he couldn't bring himself to visually examine her there as that would have seemed so clinical.

He poked but didn't seem to be getting anywhere until she reached between them to grasp him. Then there was yielding flesh and he was sinking deep inside her.

Her face screwed up in pain and with a hiss she told him to stop, which he did with alacrity, thinking he'd done something wrong. But after a few seconds the pain passed away and she told him to continue.

'Oh Rosie!' he whispered, feeling he should be saying something and not quite knowing what.

The laughter suddenly filling the cave was like an ice cold douche to the pair of them. Each froze in mid-action, not willing to believe their ears.

Rosemary nearly died of shame when she turned her head to see a group of wee boys gawping at her and Angus from the cave entrance. There were five of them all dressed as cowboys. The other half of the group she'd seen stalking through the undergrowth earlier.

Angus knew he had to do something and fast. Pulling himself free he made a roaring noise and simultaneously contorted his face in simulated anger.

Screeching and laughing the boys turned and fled back down the bank as fast as they could go.

'And don't dare come back again!' Angus yelled, shaking his fist after them, not realizing how utterly ridiculous he looked standing there with a condom hanging from his dangling penis.

In a flurry of cowboy hats and brightly coloured chaps the wee boys were gone.

'It seems our secret place isn't so secret after all,' Rosemary said, and started to laugh hysterically.

Seeing the funny side of the situation Angus joined in and when he sat beside her tears were streaming down both their faces. When the laughter finally subsided he poured them both more wine.

'Are you *sure* they've gone?' Rosemary asked after she'd drained her cup.

He crossed to the cave entrance and peered but of the wee boys there was no sign.

Rosemary had that craving feeling back in her stomach. She stared hungrily at Angus who stared hungrily back.

This time there was no fumbling or uncertainty.

'Oh!' she gasped.

A little later he cried out and as he did so she wrapped her legs tightly round him and exhaled a long, satisfied sigh.

Angus lay limp in her arms. 'That was definitely the best birthday present I've ever had,' he said.

In the years to come, if he'd been asked to pick out the happiest moment in his life, he would have had no hesitation in picking that one.

13

By the winter of the following year Angus had grudgingly become reconciled to working at Armstrong's.
He'd also set himself up a rather lucrative sideline by
keeping book on the Scottish horse and dog races and
was to be found every race day taking bets during the
breaks in the toilet.

The idea of making book had come to him when he
noticed many men in the works were keen on having a
flutter. The nearest bookie operated nearly a mile away,
so here was a heaven sent opportunity to cash in on a
situation crying out to be exploited by some bright spark
like himself.

First of all he'd had to learn the intricacies of betting
and this he'd done by paying a fitter and dedicated
punter called George Edgar to teach him.

For finance he'd used his savings which at the incep-
tion of the book stood at an astonishing £235, most of
which he'd saved from his milk and paper rounds.

It appealed to Angus's sense of irony that, as time
passed, he was making far more from his book than the
pittance he was being paid in his position as apprentice.

He rarely took home less than a fiver a week from his
book and on several occasions it had been as much as a
tenner – more than double what the highest paid worker
at Armstrong's was getting.

He was seeing Rosemary as often as he could and
sleeping with her whenever possible.

By now Diane and Kitty had become friendly as it was always easier for Rosemary to get out at night with her sister. Kitty had been introduced to make up the foursome and luckily he and Diane had hit it off right away.

Rosemary and Diane always told their parents they were going somewhere locally – to the pictures or dancing – but invariably went further afield to lessen the risk of being seen with Angus and Kitty.

Their luck held out for a long time until one Saturday evening at a dance in the Croftfoot Boy Scout Hall Angus and Rosemary were spotted by a lad called Tod Gemmill. Tod was the son of Ronnie Gemmill, Armstrong's chief pattern maker and as big an arse-licker as his father.

Tod was an apprentice same as Angus although older and in the third year of his apprenticeship. And he recognized Rosemary, having seen her several times at the works with her father.

It was obvious to Tod that Angus and Rosemary were close and he judged from the easy way they had with one another they'd been winching for some time. That gave him food for thought. He made a mental note to mention it to his father.

Hugh was also at the dancing that night, only in his case he'd gone to the St Andrew's Halls in the centre of the city. It was the back of ten when he decided he'd had enough and would drive home to Muirend.

He was passing another dancehall called the Locarno when he noticed a girl struggling with a burly chap. The girl's face swung round into full profile and it was with a shock he recognized Janey McIver whom he hadn't seen since the night he'd dropped her off outside her house in Thistle Street.

He pulled the car into the kerb, rolled down the window and caled out, 'Everything all right, Janey?'

With a sob Janey succeeded in wrenching herself away from the man and, running across to the car, quickly climbed inside. 'Get the hell out of here quick,' she gasped, looking thoroughly frightened as the man she'd been struggling with started fumbling with the door handle.

Hugh let the clutch out and the Hornet leapt away. The man uttered a curse as he was sent spinning into a passer-by, causing the two of them to go crashing to the pavement.

It took a few minutes and a cigarette to calm Janey down. Once she was capable of speaking coherently she explained the chap had been her old boyfriend who was refusing to get the message and take no for an answer.

She'd been at the Locarno that night when suddenly Francey had appeared at her side, demanding she dance with him.

She'd agreed to have one dance to humour him but at the end of it when she'd tried to excuse herself he'd physically forced her to stay on the floor, at the same time declaring in a loud voice to all and sundry she was his girl and the sooner she learned to accept the fact the better.

She'd been scared stiff by then as she'd known from the smell of his breath and the glassy look in his eye he'd been drinking heavily and in that mood was capable of almost anything.

She'd danced the next half hour with him and then pleaded to be allowed to go to the toilet as she was bursting. It was a request Francey couldn't very well refuse so he'd reluctantly consented saying he'd be waiting for her when she came out again.

Knowing he'd be watching, she'd made a show of entering the Ladies. Chancing her luck, she sneaked out less than a minute later, hoping he'd be looking elsewhere and not expecting her to reappear so soon.

Her luck had held as far as the cloakroom. But as she was hurrying from there with her coat over her arm, Francey had spotted her. The ensuing argument had continued out into the street at which point Hugh had come driving by.

As Hugh listened to all this he couldn't help but think

what an attractive woman Janey was. Furthermore she had a certain something which made him feel relaxed and easy in her company.

When they reached St Enoch Square she thanked him again for coming to her rescue and suggested he drop her off on the corner where she could catch a tram.

Hugh wouldn't hear of it, insisting that as Thistle Street was en route to Muirend anyway, the least he could do was take her home.

Both of them were delighted at seeing one another although neither would have dreamt of saying so. Occasionally Janey glanced at him out the corner of her eye while he used the windscreen mirror to catch a glimpse of her.

When they arrived at Thistle Street there was an awkward pause between them which Janey finally broke by asking if he'd like to come up for a cup of tea and a biscuit?

Hugh agreed. Enjoying Janey's company so much he was reluctant to be parted from her.

They climbed the close stairs to arrive at a badly chipped green door.

The kitchen he was ushered into was warm and friendly. It was also crammed with children of all sizes, shapes and ages.

What caught and held his attention were the holy pictures on the walls. There was one of the Virgin Mary with the infant Jesus, another of Jesus wearing a crown of thorns. One of a kind-faced man surrounded by animals whom he guessed was St Francis. Plus a very large one in a gilt frame of Pope Pius XI. There were also two statues on either side of the mantelpiece – Mary and Joseph.

He gulped at this overpowering display of Popery. Here were all the things he and every other Protestant boy in the city like him had been brought up to hate and despise. Involuntarily he shrank within himself, rueing his folly in allowing himself to come into such close contact with the Roman Church.

Mrs McIver was a stout woman of his mother's age who came forward to shake him by the hand after Janey had recounted what had happened both inside and outside the Locarno and how his timely intervention had saved her from something which might well have ended up nastily.

McIver was furious, saying Francey was a bad lot and should he run into Francey he would give him what for. In the meantime would Hugh care for a wee drop of the cratur rather than the tea his good wife was offering? Before Hugh could reply glasses were out and a bottle was being opened.

Hugh's apprehension about his surroundings melted a little as the whisky warmed and soothed him. And soon he began to relax. It transpired that McIver was even more of a radical left winger than Big Donald and soon he and Hugh were arguing the toss about the pros and cons of the new Coalition Government led by Neville Chamberlain, and the attitude of that government in relation to Spain which was being torn apart by the most dreadful civil war.

After a while a small child of about three came and clambered onto Hugh's lap. Hugh stroked the wee lad's hair and then tickled him under the chin, causing him to snort with laughter.

'You like weans, then?' Mrs McIver asked.

Hugh smiled and admitted freely he did, adding that one day when he was married he was hoping to have lots of his own, especially boys whom he was particularly fond of.

Janey sat silent through all this watching Hugh as he talked with her mother and father, admiring his well-spoken manner and the way he held his own against her Da who was a notorious bully when it came to exchanging views, particularly political ones.

When Hugh finally rose to go he was told by Mrs McIver he'd be welcome any time he cared to call. They shook hands all round, then Janey showed him to the front door. The kitchen door was diplomatically shut behind them after they'd made their exit.

Hugh was in a terrible quandary. He liked Janey tremendously – there was no doubt in his mind about that, just as there was none about her liking him in return. But what use was it trying to start a relationship that was bound to founder on the rocks of religion? Words from the old song came leaping to mind.

T'was in County Tyrone in the town of Dungannon,
Where's many a rumption myself had a han' in.
Bob Williamson lived there a weaver to trade,
And all of us thought him a stout Orange blade.

On the twelfth of July as it yearly did come.
Bob played on his flute to the sound of the drum.
Well you can talk of your piano, your violin or lute,
But there's nothing to beat the old Orange flute.

But Bob the old bastard he took us all in,
He married a fenian named Brigid McGinn.
Turned Papish himself and forsook the old cause,
That gave us our freedom, religion and laws. . . .

'I enjoyed meeting your family,' Hugh said, hating what was coming next.

Janey smiled and nodded, waiting.

Outside a cat began to yowl while from a house some-where close by came the unmistakable sound of a couple having a barney.

'It wouldn't work Janey. You know that as well as I do,' he mumbled.

Her smile stretched and stretched till it seemed her face must surely be sliced in two. Her eyes had a dead, marbled look about them. She'd known he was going to say this but would have given anything to have had herself proved wrong. He was right of course. Trying to mix the green and orange was just asking for trouble, especially if children were to become involved.

'Goodbye,' she whispered, hesitating for a brief second before going to him and kissing him full on the mouth. Then she was gone. The badly chipped green door closed behind her with a click that had the ring of finality about it.

Hugh stuck his hands in his pockets and trudged downstairs. He felt as though he'd just lost both arms.

He was fumbling for his car keys as he came out of the close but when his gaze lit on the Hornet he stopped dead in his tracks. 'Oh no!' he exclaimed, fury bursting within him.

The Hornet's beautiful red paintwork had been viciously scratched and scraped from nose to boot while the upholstery had been ripped and slashed to shreds.

He felt sick, cursing himself for being so stupid as to leave the car parked in a Gorbals street.

The laugh was low and evil and came from directly behind him. Swinging round he found himself facing a grinning Francey.

'Like your fancy car now, Jim? Maybe that'll teach you to take off with my bird and make me look stupid,' Francey spat.

'You fucker!' Hugh hissed and stepped forward intent on smashing Francey in the face.

Laughing again, Francey brought his right hand from behind his back to reveal a rusty iron bar. The bar whistled through the air in an overhand arc that brought it smashing against the side of Hugh's head.

Hugh's legs were suddenly jelly, buckling under him to send him crashing to the filthy pavement.

Again and again Francey's foot thudded into his ribs and back.

He tried to wriggle out of the way but instead got it full on the chin. There was a splintering sound and blood everywhere as he flipped over onto his back.

He must have passed out, for the next thing he knew Francey was gone and he was staring up at a night sky filled with clouds and smoke from tenement chimneys.

He grunted with pain as he rolled onto his side and shuffled himself to the tenement wall which he used as a steadying post to bring himself to his feet.

He spat out gobs of congealed blood and gritty

fragments of teeth. Many of the teeth left were broken, jagged and excruciatingly sore, as indeed were his chest and back.

Coughing up more blood he staggered into the close and, like a drunken man, made his way upstairs to the McIvers' door which he hammered on with his fist.

Suddenly Mr and Mrs McIver were there and arms were being thrown round him.

'Francey,' he croaked.

There was so much pain wracking his mouth and body it was with relief he greeted the darkness.

Donald fidgeted as he and Winnie sat outside Ward 5 of the Victoria Infirmary. The staff nurse had been in to inform Hugh they were waiting and he'd sent back word his present visitor wouldn't be long.

A few minutes later the swing doors opened and an extremely pretty girl emerged from the ward, smiling to the staff nurse as she passed. The nurse then turned to the Chisholms and said they could go away in now.

Winnie and Donald turned to stare at one another, both of them having noted the Saint Christopher dangling from Janey's neck and wondering what business a Catholic girl could have with their Hugh?

Now the moment had arrived for Donald to go in and see Hugh he was reluctant to do so without first knowing he'd be welcome. Voicing his fears to Winnie she agreed to sound out the ground.

Hugh was a sight, his face puffed up like a balloon, from the combination of the kicking and having the remainder of his teeth extracted.

When Winnie confirmed the staff nurse's message that his father was also here, he fell silent for a few seconds before mumbling she'd best call him in.

'It was his own idea, I assure you. You two might have had your differences but that doesn't alter the fact he still loves and worries about you, son,' Winnie said before walking back to the swing doors and beckoning Donald to come away through.

The two men solemnly shook hands. Then Donald asked what the damage was and how it had come about?

According to Hugh, he'd been lucky. Apart from the loss of his teeth he was merely bruised, which looked a lot worse than it actually was.

He went on to tell them about rescuing Janey McIver and how her ex-boyfriend had been waiting for him after he'd said goodnight to her and her family.

Winnie sat quietly on the one chair provided, listening to the men talk about the violence that was an inter-woven part of the city's fabric. She would wait till Hugh was better and out of hospital before chiselling him about this McIver lassie.

She prayed to God there was nothing serious between him and the girl, because there would be the most almighty ructions if there were! Her gaze fastened on Donald emphatically making a point.

Sir Alan Armstrong's brow was deeply furrowed as he read the report presented to him that morning by the private detective he'd hired to find out exactly what was going on between Rosemary and young McBain.

It surprised him just how many times the pair con-trived to meet. Going alone with Diane to the local pictures and dancing indeed!

But what really upset him was the detective's state-ment they were having an affair.

According to the detective, friends of the family had been away on holiday during the past few weeks and Rosemary had somehow contrived to get hold of the key to a small guest flat at the back of the empty house where she and Angus had gone on a number of occasions to make love. Peering through a window, the detective had actually seen them in the act.

Laying down the report Sir Alan made a mental note to thank Gemmill for putting him onto this. A reward would come later.

He could forbid Rosemary ever to see McBain again but, knowing his daughter as he did, a face to face confrontation wasn't the way. What was needed here was something subtle, something devious to cause a break between the pair. And break there would have to be and soon if his plans for her future were to have any real hopes of success.

It came back to him she'd once asked him the ins and outs of John McBain's accident. She must have been seeing the lad even then.

A glance at the calendar confirmed there were only a few days left till Christmas. He would use the holiday to think up a plan to get young McBain out of Glasgow and away forever. For if they were as deeply committed to one another as the detective said it would have to be as drastic as that to ensure the affair was over and done with.

Dismissing the matter from his mind, he turned his attention to a sheaf of papers which had arrived in from his solicitor. Some property was about to come onto the market of the sort he'd been looking for as an investment. Within seconds he was totally absorbed by the details of the buildings under proposal.

On Christmas Day Iain and Peter McLaren arrived at Arnprior House with gifts for the girls.

Rosemary and Diane were delighted with what they'd received – perfume in both cases – and somewhat embarrassed by the fact they hadn't thought to buy the McLarens anything.

Iain shrugged that one off with a suitable comment and then changed the conversation by announcing he'd just passed his private pilot's licence a few days previously.

He'd been taking lessons for some time now and had acquired himself the reputation round the aerodrome as an excellent pupil and a potentially outstanding flyer.

Rosemary thought this news marvellous and immediately pressed him to take her up as soon as it could be arranged.

Iain replied he'd be only too happy to oblige providing

Sir Alan agreed, which Sir Alan did.

Watching Rosemary and Iain together started Sir Alan thinking about Angus McBain again and as he thought he played with one of his cuff links which had been a Christmas present from Cordelia. They were twenty-two carat gold inset with diamond chips.

Suddenly it was there, fully hatched in his mind, a plan to take care of young McBain – neat, simple and very thorough. McBain wouldn't have a leg to stand on.

Reaching for the decanter he poured a round of sherries and the toast he proposed was Iain and Rosemary's flight together.

He smiled as he drank because only he was aware of what he'd really meant by that.

Mid-morning of the first day back to work after the New Year Angus was summoned to Sir Alan's private office. He went convinced Sir Alan had at last found out about him and Rosemary and all hell was about to break loose because of it.

For fifteen minutes he was kept waiting in the secretary's outer office before being ushered through to the inner sanctum.

He tried not to wilt under the accusing gaze knifing into him, forcing himself to stand perfectly still.

'I hear you've been taking bets, making book as I believe it's called,' Sir Alan said abruptly.

Relief surged through Angus. It wasn't what he'd been expecting although this was certainly serious enough. 'Yes sir,' he replied.

Sir Alan made a pyramid with his hands and launched into a reprimand scathing in its severity.

There was no way Angus could defend what he'd been doing and knew it. He did point out to Sir Alan, however, that he'd never made book in the company's time.

Sir Alan took the point but countered by saying the important thing was that an illegal act had been taking place on his property which was something he couldn't countenance.

Angus sighed inwardly. Here was the best money-making scheme he'd had to date about to go down the plughole. But if Sir Alan would only overlook it this time Angus gave his word it would never happen again.

Sir Alan grunted and appeared to consider that. He reached for the humidor and took its top off, exclaiming with annoyance when he saw it was empty.

'Wait here,' he snapped and left the room, closing the door behind him.

For a full five minutes Angus was left in the office alone and then the door opened to re-admit Sir Alan puffing on a fat cigar.

In a few short sentences Sir Alan stated he was willing to overlook the matter this once, qualifying himself by adding he hadn't forgotten John McBain had died in his foundry nor that Donald Chisholm was a treasured employee.

With a wave of his cigar, he told Angus to get back to work and he would expect Angus to keep his side of the bargain.

Angus thanked the still glowering Sir Alan profusely and then hurriedly took his leave, thankful he'd been let off so lightly, as he could well have lost his job or even been reported to the police.

He was hurrying back across the yard when suddenly a figure seemed to fly out of nowhere and crash into him so violently both he and the figure went tumbling to the ground.

'I'm helluva sorry, Angus, my fault entirely. I just wasn't looking where I was going,' Tod Gemmill said, springing to his feet and helping Angus to his. 'No bones broken I hope,' Tod added, patting Angus down.

'I'm fine,' Angus replied and shrugged himself away from the questing hands.

Tod grinned wryly. 'No offence?'

'None taken,' Angus confirmed and hastily resumed his way back to the job.

It was just before the lunchtime hooter when another messenger arrived from Sir Alan to say Angus was wanted back again in his office. Thoroughly mystified, Angus trotted back across the yard and up the stairs to be told to go straight through as Sir Alan was waiting for him.

The moment Angus opened the door to the inner office he knew something was dreadfully amiss. Looking like the wrath of God, Big Donald, with cap in hand, stood at one end of the desk while at the opposite end was a constable and what was unmistakably a plain clothes man.

Sir Alan glanced up. 'Come in McBain and shut the door behind you,' he said.

Completely bewildered, Angus stepped forward to stand beside his grandfather.

In a tight, angry voice Sir Alan introduced Detective Inspector Hammill and Constable Forbes, neither of whom gave Angus any sign of acknowledgement. Then with a wave of his hand in the Detective Inspector's direction, Sir Alan sank back into his leather padded chair and proceeded to light a fresh cigar from the now full humidor.

The detective inspector came straight to the point. Earlier on Angus had been called into this office to speak with Sir Alan on a company matter and was it not true that while he was here Sir Alan had left him alone for a few minutes?

'Yes, that's correct,' Angus admitted. He looked at his grandfather hoping for some clue as to what all this was about but Donald refused to meet his glance.

'Would you mind turning out your pockets?'

The question came from the detective inspector and was delivered in such a way as to leave Angus in no doubt that to refuse would be admitting guilt to whatever it was he stood suspected of.

Angus declared he had nothing to hide but before he complied would they mind telling him what this was all about?

Hammill cleared his throat and then went on to say an extremely valuable pair of cuff links – twenty-two carat gold inset with diamond chips – had gone missing that morning from Sir Alan's desk and all those who'd been in the office were being asked to cooperate in trying to solve the matter.

Angus couldn't remember having seen any cuff links and said so, adding that he was only to happy too cooperate as he didn't want anyone thinking him a thief.

There were five pockets in his overalls and the cuff links were in the right leg one.

The moment he felt the unusual bulges he knew with a sickening certainty what they were. He paled and loked from Hammill to Sir Alan, whose eyes were hooded behind a cloud of smoke.

It was the constable who worked the cuff links up the length of the long pocket till they popped out into his hand. He set them carefully on the desk's well polished top for all to see.

They were gold inset with diamond chips.

Donald took a deep breath which he slowly exhaled.

'There's been some sort of mistake,' Angus said almost hysterically, realizing only too well how pitifully inadequate and clichéd that sounded.

'That'll be for the court to decide,' said Hammill, scooping up the cuff links which he informed Sir Alan would have to be taken along and used in evidence.

Sir Alan cupped his chin in his hand and looked thoughtful, a pose he held for over a minute while he stared hard at the squirming Angus.

Finally, with a sad shake of his head, he thanked the policemen for coming along and informed them he'd decided not to make any formal charges.

Hammill tried to argue but Sir Alan was resolute in that he intended dealing with the matter himself. With a disappointed shrug Hammill capitulated and returned the cuff links.

Hammill and the constable then took their leave, both shooting Angus filthy looks as they did so.

'Have you anything further to say?' Sir Alan asked.

'It wasn't me. I swear it!'

'Then how did the cuff links come to be in your overalls?'

Angus slumped. He had no answer to that one.

Sir Alan puffed on his cigar knowing he now had Angus exactly where he wanted him. In his victory, he allowed the triumph he felt to show in his eyes. Angus, who happened to glance directly into his face at that precise moment, noticed it.

Suddenly everything clicked into place and Angus knew without a shadow of a doubt it was Sir Alan himself who'd had him framed.

He remembered then Tod Gemmill careering into him in the yard and that part of the mystery was solved. So he'd been right to start with. Armstrong *had* found out about him and Rosemary and this was the bastard's way of putting the boot in.

Sir Alan busied himself trimming his cigar and said it was, of course, impossible for Angus to continue working for him. Furthermore he felt it his duty not to give Angus a reference as should there ever be a repeat of this type of incident it would only reflect on his good name.

For the second time within minutes Angus was stunned. Without a reference he was virtually unemployable, not only on Clydeside but everywhere.

Still busy with the end of his cigar, Sir Alan went on to say in view of what had happened to Angus's father and bearing in mind Donald was an employee of long standing he was prepared to give Angus a letter of introduction to an old friend of his who owned a firm similar to Armstrong's down in Newcastle.

The letter would set out the reasons for Angus's dismissal but would also plead he be given a second chance.

'You can go now,' Sir Alan said. 'I'll have the letter typed out this afternoon and taken to your home by hand.'

In a completely flat voice Donald said in all the years he'd worked at Armstrong's he'd never asked for time off but he would like some now if it was possible?

Sir Alan told Donald to go home and not come back

till the morning, saying the request was perfectly understandable in the circumstances.

Angus and Donald left the office and went down the stairs and into the yard where Donald told Angus to wait while he collected his coat from the foundry.

Angus was lighting a cigarette when he saw a group of lads hurry out of a door. Amongst them was the unmistakable figure of Tod Gemmill. The cigarette went spinning as Angus ran across the yard.

Gemmill saw Angus coming and froze. His eyes bulged and he went white with fright as Angus ground to a halt in front of him. Guilt was written clearly all over his face.

The other lads looked on curiously, wondering what was up.

Angus told himself this was neither the time nor place to settle with Gemmill. That would be when he could get Gemmill alone and there were no witnesses to see what happened.

Reaching out, Angus tapped Gemmill lightly on the shoulder. 'From now on your jacket's marked,' he said quietly. Rounding on his heel, he strode back to where Donald was now waiting for him.

Once out of the works Donald said they would go into the swing park just a little way down the street. Angus knew then there was going to be a confrontation between them.

In the middle of a grassy expanse Donald stopped and turned to face Angus. 'Now tell me the truth. Did you take those cuff links?' he demanded harshly.

There was no lying to Donald in this sort of mood and thankfully Angus didn't have to try. Starting at the beginning he told Donald about meeting Rosemary Armstrong all those years ago and how things had developed between them. The only fact he omitted was he and Rosie were actually sleeping together.

He went on to say Sir Alan must have found out about their relationship and this was his way of trying to break them up.

He then described the incident with Tod Gemmill: Tod had planted the cuff links either when they were on the ground together or when Tod had been supposedly checking to see he was all right. He added that was what he'd been chiselling Gemmill about while Donald was away getting his coat.

Donald's eyes never wavered from Angus's as he listened to this explanation. He knew it had to be the truth he was hearing for apart from having an honest ring about it the story was just too fantastic and elaborate to be otherwise.

When Angus finally finished he grunted and, gesturing towards a bench, said they should sit and have a smoke.

As he packed his pipe he asked what sort of girl Rosemary Armstrong was. Angus spoke of her in glowing and loving terms.

They sat in silence for a wee while after that. Donald's heart was heavy, knowing Angus was going to come out of all this an all-round loser. There was no way Angus could thwart a man as powerful and influential as Sir Alan Armstrong.

What Angus wanted more than anything else was to talk things over with Rosemary. She had a way of putting everything into perspective that he badly needed now.

He would go and see her as soon as he'd parted from his grandfather.

Rosemary's cheeks were still glowing with exhilaration as Iain turned his father's car into Old Castle Road.

As promised, Iain had collected her that morning and driven her out to the aerodrome where the Avro trainer was fuelled ready and waiting for them.

With a beautifully smooth take off they were airborne and she was revelling in the sheer gut-wrenching excitement of her first ever flight.

She'd hung on for grim death when Iain looped the loop and then threw the aircraft into a steep left hand bank that sent them corkscrewing towards the ground at an incredible rate.

With plenty of altitude to spare Iain had brought the Avro out of its spin to send it winging away from the city and out over the Campsie Hills where snow lay hard upon the ground. The air buffeting them in the face seemed to be composed of countless millions of tiny, stinging icicles.

All too soon the joy ride was over and they were motoring back to Arnprior House with Rosemary plaguing the life out of Iain every inch of the way. At last, as he was opening the door of the car, he relented and agreed to take her up again soon.

Impulsively Rosemary threw her arms round his neck and gave him a big smacker full on the lips.

Coming to try and contact her, Angus had seen the car draw up and had immediately recognized Rosemary in the front passenger seat. Handsome-looking bugger she was with, he'd thought, as he'd watched Iain walk round the car to open her door. He couldn't believe his eyes when he saw Rosemary throw her arms round Iain McLaren's neck and kiss him.

In his already tremulous state this was another body blow which stunned him even more than what had happened in Sir Alan's office.

He stood rooted, watching amazed as the pair of them ran hand in hand towards the front door.

At the door Rosemary paused to peck Iain on the cheek and then they had vanished inside with the door banging shut behind them.

Completely numb, Angus turned and started the walk back to Holmlea Road.

Rosemary. *His* Rosie, had somebody else!

The horrible suspicion dawned she was the one who'd told her father about their affair. After all, why should Sir Alan suddenly *now* discover their secret. Was this her way of getting rid of him so he could be replaced by the new chap?

There could be no denying what he'd witnessed back there in the street, nor that Sir Alan had sacked him in a way that ensured he had to leave the city if not for good then certainly for a long time to come.

Sweat broke on his brow at the thought of the saturnine-looking chap being Rosemary's lover. Nausea rumbled inside him and he had to stop and lean against a standard lamp where he threw up into the gutter.

'Oh, you bitch!' he whispered.

Outrage gave way to a bottomless chasm of despair. Closing his eyes he saw her face and heard her voice whispering the sort of love talk she'd been fond of using.

Was she saying the same things even now to her new bloke? Had she managed to sneak him up to her bedroom where they were . . . ?

Staggering like a drunken man, he made his way down the street. Seeing nothing. Hearing nothing. Thinking far too much.

He was still beside himself when he came to his close. There was a clattering on the stairs and suddenly Kitty was standing beside him saying he'd just been up chapping at his door wanting to tell him the most marvellous news.

Angus forced some sort of composure into his face as Kitty burbled on that at long last he'd landed himself a real job as a stoker aboard a ship called the *Almuria* which was at the moment tied up in the Govan Docks.

Eyes shining, Kitty said he was hoping Angus would go out with him that night for a celebration drink as it wasn't every day he landed a job or left home.

A good bucket was just what he needed Angus decided. He congratulated Kitty and then arranged for the pair of them to meet up directly after tea.

With a whoop of delight Kitty was gone, rushing down the street like some kid who'd just discovered Christmas.

Angus knew Archie wouldn't be home yet so he decided this was as good a time as any to tell Carrie what had happened. He found her in the kitchen standing over a simmering pot of leek and potato soup which he asked her to leave and come and sit down for a little while.

It wasn't easy but he hadn't expected it to be. Starting at the beginning he told her the entire story exactly as he'd related it to Donald.

'That man!' Carrie said when he was finally finished. Putting her head in her hands, she burst out crying. Angus took his mother in his arms and sat there rocking her back and forth the way she'd often rocked him when he was little.

Harriet had been into town to the pictures and was now on a tram swaying along Argyle Street taking her home. To pass the time, she started to read a magazine containing the latest film news she'd bought in the foyer of the picture hall.

The article on page three drew her eye the way a magnet does iron. In heavy type it stated veteran screenwriter Lou Dansie had recently died of a heart attack in his Hollywood home.

Her hands came up to touch the gold chain round her neck, tracing its length till her long fingers came into contact with the heavy ring dangling from its inverted apex.

Turning out of Argyle Street, the tram rattled northward to come eventually to Byres Road where Harriet got off.

She walked up the street, a tall, ugly-looking woman whose skin was a muddy grey colour and whose eyes burned with a strange intensity.

A wee boy in her way took one look at her face and hastily scuttled round her. The wee boy shivered as he hurried along.

He didn't like woman with faces like that. They gave him the willies.

Angus and Kitty were in a West Nile Street pub when Kitty came up with the suggestion they take a taxi down to the Govan Docks and have a look at the *Almuria*.

Half an hour later they were standing on the quayside staring up at a rusty old heap that should have been consigned to the breaker's yard years before. Both had screwtops in their hands.

Already a little maudlin from drink Angus kept maintaining the *Almuria* was as fine a ship as he'd seen and Kitty should be proud of sailing on her, adding he only wished he was, by God.

Kitty fell silent for a few seconds while his alcohol-soaked brain laboriously worked out the possibilities that had just come to him.

Finishing his screwtop, he threw it into the water. 'Want me to try and get you a job tomorrow when I report on board?' he asked in a slurred voice.

Angus blinked. Here was something that bore consideration.

'I don't know if there's anything going, but it wouldn't hurt to ask,' Kitty said, a huge, sloppy grin plastered all over his face.

'Why the hell not!' Angus exclaimed, thinking he'd rather do anything than be forced into going to Newcastle. It was just he hated the thought of having to comply totally with Sir Alan's manipulations.

'You serious?'

'Never more so.'

'Then I'll ask the morn.'

Angus put his arm round Kitty's shoulders. The idea of going to sea with his old china really appealed and he said so.

Laughing, the pair of them headed in the direction of the nearest boozer.

'Do either of you fellows have the time?'

Angus giggled and was about to make a negative reply when suddenly the tart's face was caught in a shaft of light from a nearby ship. He frowned, thinking she looked familiar, and then with a shock it dawned on him just who it was.

'Sheena?'

They stared at one another, then uttering a cry she flew into his arms.

'I'm sorry,' she whispered.'I didn't know it was you.'

With a sad shake of his head he told her it didn't matter. Then he suggested they go for a drink over which she could tell him everything that had happened to her. They were lucky enough to find an empty table at the back of the pub. Sheena told them she'd gone to London when she'd left Holmlea Road. Work had been almost as difficult to find there as it had been in Glasgow and for a while she'd lived pretty rough. Sally Ann hostels. Rowton Houses. And even Battersea Park.

From London she'd gone to Cardiff where one night in Tiger Bay she'd been forced – as a means of survival, she said emphatically – to cash in on her one asset.

Angus stared into his drink, shocked by this revelation and feeling somehow guilty as though he was partly to blame.

He then asked her the question that had been bothering him all this time. Why had she upped so suddenly and left Holmlea Road?

Her eyes clouded as she told him she'd known it was only a matter of time before Archie forgot himself and under the influence did something they'd both regret for the rest of their lives.

'Jesus!' said Kitty.

With a shrug Sheena added, 'He was always a randy sod as you well know Angus. And with Carrie in hospital and you over in Tallon Street that left just him and me. It would have been inevitable.'

Far too soon time was being called. Having found Sheena Angus didn't want to let her go again. At least not yet. So he suggested Kitty make his own way back to Holmlea Road while he went on to Sheena's place as he had a lot more to talk over with her.

The tenement Sheena took him to was tall, dirty and cankerous. There were three other females sharing the house with her and all of them were on the game plying the dockside trade.

The room itself was neat and tidy and smelled strongly of Sheena, a smell that brought a host of half forgotten memories flooding back into his mind.

Sheena had an almost full bottle which she produced from behind a fancy cushion bearing the legend 'A Present From Shangai' embroidered on its front.

For a while she spoke about herself and then in a quiet, sympathetic voice asked him what his problem was. She'd always been able to read his face like the proverbial book and had known since early on in the pub something was bothering him.

They talked and drank into the small hours and then when there was nothing left to be said or excuses to be made they went to the well-used bed jammed hard up against one wall. They stripped and made love.

He cried out once but it was Rosemary's name which burst from his lips and not Sheena's.

He came apart then, and mercifully screened by the all enveloping darkness, cried his heart out while she stroked and soothed him.

If he'd searched far and wide he wouldn't have found a better comforter than his step-sister who'd loved him since he was a baby.

Two days later Angus, with case in hand, opened his front door bound for the Govan Docks. Kitty had come up trumps in securing him a stoker's job.

He'd left his money box with Carrie, his instructions being she was to open a bank account in her name which she could draw on if she needed to, or if she decided to buy the house they'd so often talked about and which had long been his obsession.

Her parting present was his father's black leather wallet with the initials J.McB. in faded gold lettering on its front.

What Angus didn't know was the previous day Carrie had been to see Dr Robertson for the results of her latest tests. Her TB was active once more.

With a final kiss on the landing, he was running downstairs with Carrie calling after him, 'Look after yourself, son and mind the company you keep!'

'I will, Ma!' he yelled back. 'And you look after

yourself too!'

Carrie smiled grimly at that. Turning, she shuffled back into the house to make out a list of all the things she would need to take with her to the sanatorium.

Part III

The Digger's Dream

1942–1944

14

Physically Angus had changed considerably during the four years he'd been at sea. Long hours working with the shovel had filled him out and now iron hard muscles rippled where once there had been only boyish skin and bone.

There were three of them in the boiler room and they worked stripped to the waist. Lowest on the totem pole was a young lad called Sanderson whose job it was to trim the coal. Angus was stoker, Kitty steam boss.

The ancient *Almuria* was having to steam continually at full speed to keep up with the rest of convoy PQ 17, and consequently was threatening to shake herself apart in the process.

They'd set sail from Reykavik in Iceland heading north for Jan Mayen Island and Bear Island, beyond which they were scheduled to turn onto a southeast course that would bring them down through the Berens Sea into the White Sea and their destination, Archangel.

PQ 17 was carrying vital supplies to help save Stalingrad.

Angus and Kitty sat on a pile of coal and lit up. Both were too tired to indulge in unnecessary conversation so they savoured their cigarettes and thought fondly of their bunks.

The hatch to the boiler room burst open and a greaser called Hay came rushing in to relate breathlessly that a signal had been received on board – the convoy was to scatter. Furthermore, their Royal Navy escort was to withdraw westward at high speed.

Both Angus and Kitty exclaimed aloud on hearing this news. It could only mean the pocket battleship, *Tirpitz*, had set sail from her lair in Norway's Trondheim Fiord. For the convoy to be told to scatter as opposed to disperse must mean the *Tirpitz* was almost upon them.

But why had their escort been instructed to proceed westward when the *Tirpitz* would be approaching from the southeast?

The penny dropped simultaneously. The Admiralty didn't intend losing any more of its warships by sending them up against far superior firepower which could only result in their annihilation.

PQ 17 had been abandoned to face the full fury of the pride of the German Navy.

'My God!' whispered Angus.

Hay fled the boiler room, shouting over his shoulder he would keep them informed of any fresh developments.

Soon the coal was flying as the *Almuria* made its bid for survival by veering onto a fresh course that would take it to the Russian Islands of Novaya Zemla. The *Almuria's* captain had chosen this heading because he judged it to be in the completely opposite direction to the course the *Tirpitz* must be coming up on.

Shortly afterwards in the wireless room, the operator bent to his task as the stories started flooding in. The scattering convoy was already in deep trouble although the *Tirpitz* hadn't yet been sighted.

Aboard the *Bolton Castle* the ship's gunners were busy firing at circling Focke-Wulfs and Shads when suddenly a Stuka came seemingly from nowhere to straddle the ship from port to starboard, obtaining a direct hit.

To those watching from nearby ships it seemed the *Bolton Castle* virtually disintegrated, although, incredibly, the ammunition she was carrying didn't explode.

Aboard the *Paulus Potter* her British gunners kept

attacking planes at bay until for a third time a stick of bombs dropped close to the ship. Earlier misses had sprung her plates and shifted her engines but these latest bombs blew the ship's rudder off and damaged her propeller. The order was quickly given to abandon ship.

As the afternoon wore on a mist appeared and with it fresh waves of German planes.

The deadly U-boats had also put in an appearance, their torpedoes soon notching up an ever increasing toll.

But where was the *Tirpitz*? That was the question on everyone's lips as they anxiously watched the southeast.

Alarm bells suddenly clamoured throughout the *Almuria* and a lookout was frantically pointing at five torpedo planes flying in on the starboard bow. Oerlikons and Bofors started up as one of the planes peeled off to begin its run into attack.

The plane seemed to stagger in mid-air as direct hits were scored on it. But seconds before it broke in two it dropped a single torpedo which ran straight and true for the *Almuria*.

'Hard a starboard!' hissed the captain on the bridge. Moments later the old lady began to swing agonizingly slowly in that direction.

The same lookout who'd first spotted the plane stood watching goggle-eyed as only a few feet away the torpedo ran on a parallel course with the *Almuria*. But the ship had completed its successful evasive manoeuvre and the torpedo was gone.

Down in the boiler room Angus, Kitty and Sanderson were force feeding their complaining charge in an effort to try and wheedle a few more knots out of the old lady who was sorely resenting their exertions.

Hay reappeared with a bottle of whisky in his hand saying he'd been saving it for a special occasion. But he thought he'd better drink it now as he might never get another chance to do so.

Angus gulped down a belter and rifted. He passed on the bottle before crossing to his jacket. From his inside pocket he took his father's old black leather wallet.

The clipping was yellow and faded, the face staring back at him one he'd always see clearly in his mind till his dying day.

Below the blurred photograph of the happy bride and groom was an account of the wedding reception held in the groom's house in Carmunnock.

Less than a year after he'd gone to sea she'd married the chap he'd watched her kissing that day her father had contrived to fire him. Her married name was Mrs Iain McLaren.

It was Carrie who'd cut the photo and attendant story from the *Glasgow Herald* and sent it to him with a note saying she thought he should see this.

Carrie had been in Bellfield Sanatorium at the time, her second incarceration lasting eighteen months.

But Angus didn't know that. At Carrie's insistence the pretence had been kept up she was fit and well, and life in Holmlea Road was carrying on as normal.

Angus was still staring morosely at the newspaper clipping when there was an explosion aft which knocked everyone in the boiler room off their feet.

The whisky bottle went spinning from Hay's hand to crash against the bulkhead where it shattered.

'We're hit!' Kitty yelled, and came to his feet to discover the ship was listing badly.

Tottering, he staggered for the hatch with the rest of them close behind.

'Torpedo's blown the arse right off her!' a frantic seaman shouted.

There was a second explosion aft and the lights started to flicker and go out one by one. The air was filled with screams and curses as terrified men battled their way up from the lower decks. Kitty stumbled and would have fallen if Angus hadn't caught him by the shoulders. 'Thanks mate,' Kitty gasped.

Then the pair of them ran for another hatch beyond which was the sea deck.

The *Almuria* was heeled over at about a thirty degree angle. The great heartbeat of the engines suddenly stilled and in that moment the grand old lady died. All that remained now was the internment which would follow hard upon the death.

Angus blinked as he burst into bright daylight. Running to the guard rail, he peered over to see a lifeboat and raft filled to overflowing already about twenty yards away. Further down the ship men were leaping overboard.

Turning to tell Kitty there was nothing left for them to do but jump, he found himself alone.

Swearing volubly, he scrambled over the guard rail, and ran along the black painted hull. Reaching the point where it curved away to the sea below, he jumped as far out as he could.

His feet knifed into the water and he went down and down into an inky blackness. His last surprised thought was the water wasn't nearly as cold as he'd expected. He was wondering why that should be when unconsciousness claimed him.

When he came to he was coughing and spluttering into Kitty's lap. There was the most awful taste in his mouth and breathing was excruciating. Every inhalation seeming to fan the inferno blistering the inside of his ribcage.

He took in the fact he was in a lifeboat with Kitty and four others. All of them he recognized as lower deck members.

Kitty used his sleeve to wipe Angus's mouth and while doing so informed him he'd swallowed some fuel oil from another ship sunk in the area.

When he heard that, Angus stared up at the gun metal sky convinced he was going to die. He'd heard fuel oil burned the lungs out and the poor bastards who'd swallowed the stuff died screaming in agony unless lucky enough to be shot through with pain killer.

He asked Kitty if there was a medical kit aboard, knowing from the expression on Kitty's face before his friend could reply what the answer was.

'We'll be picked up soon. You just wait and see,' Kitty

said with a smile. But there was no conviction in his voice.

While Angus tried to rest Kitty explained what had happened during those last few minutes aboard ship.

He'd seen the lifeboat they were now in bobbing for'ard and, running to investigate, had got himself out of Angus's line of sight. At that point Angus had jumped overboard.

Guessing what had happened, he'd rowed the boat round to where Angus would have entered the water to find him floating face up.

After another racking coughing fit, Angus said as he was going down he'd imagined the water to be warm which couldn't be so. And yet if it wasn't, why hadn't he frozen to death before Kitty reached him?

Kitty's reply was the water hereabouts was indeed warm which he could only think must be due to some vagary of the Gulf Stream.

Angus closed his eyes and wondered how long it would be before his pain became intolerable? He was still speculating when a black conning-tower broke surface on the lifeboat's starboard side.

The U-boat surfaced fully and several of its crew emerged to bring machine guns to bear on the lifeboat.

'Oh Christ!' said Kitty quietly, convinced they were about to be riddled with bullets.

The U-boat closed in on the now pitching lifeboat and as it did so an officer cupped a hand to his mouth and, in perfect English, yelled, 'What ship were you? And where were you bound?'

Those aboard the lifeboat glanced from one to the other but no one replied.

The German officer tried again, 'Why do you want to go to Russia? Are you Bolsheviks?'

One of the British seamen shook his head in reply which was the only answer to that line of questioning any of them were prepared to give.

The officer leaning from the conning-tower realized this and, with a wry smile, inquired if they had a compass on board?

It was Kitty who replied they hadn't and it was to him the compass was thrown which, despite the lifeboat's pitching, he deftly caught.

The same officer informed them in which direction land lay. Then he apologized for not being able to take any prisoners on board as he was already full.

In an incredibly short time the U-boat was once more submerged leaving the lifeboat yawing on waves created by its disappearance.

Time passed and they lost sight of the other lifeboat and raft which according to their compass had gone off southwards.

They took it in turns – with the exception of Angus – to row in the direction the German officer had told them was landfall. But as there was only one set of oars and they were all verging on the point of exhaustion progress was pitifully slow.

Hope of survival was fading amongst them when, in the early hours of the following morning, a grey warship was spied heading in their direction.

At first they thought she was German. But when she drew nearer and they saw her markings and the flags she was flying a ragged cheer broke out.

The ship was a destroyer called the *Wahroonga* belonging to the Royal Australian Navy.

When the watching sailors saw the state they were in more than a dozen Aussies clambered down the scrambling nets to help.

'You just give him here, sport,' a rangy Aussie said, taking Angus from Kitty.

Angus groaned as he was draped over the Aussie's shoulder.

Halfway up the nets a sudden spasm seized him causing him to spew the most evil looking mess down the Australian's back from where it spattered onto the destroyer's side.

Dimly Angus heard the *Wahroonga's* engines surge with power and then something cold and sharp was pressing into his arm.

He knew no more.

Lazily and reluctantly Angus allowed himself to drift awake. Still with his eyes closed he listened to the rhythmic beat of the engines, thinking the *Almuria* was sounding very different to what she normally did.

Then in a rush it all came back to him, including the fact the *Almuria* was at the bottom of the sea.

There was an antiseptic smell in the air and on opening his eyes he found himself staring up at a white bulkhead. Putting two and two together wasn't hard. He was in the *Wahroonga's* sick bay.

'Orderly, he's awake!' a thickly Australian accented voice called out from close by.

Turning his head, Angus found himself staring at a man about his own age grinning at him from the next bed. He and the man were the only patients in the sick bay.

'G'day how do you feel?' the man asked.

Before Angus could reply the door opened and the orderly entered. The orderly promptly repeated the question. Angus replied he'd felt better but certainly wasn't complaining. He was pleased just to find himself alive.

After the orderly had gone Angus turned back to the patient in the next bed who informed him his name was Sean O'Rourke from Sydney.

Angus introduced himself and asked if his shipmate Robin Kirkpatrick was all right.

With a laugh O'Rourke said Kitty had spent hours by Angus's bedside until ordered to his quarters for much needed sleep.

Angus then learned he'd been unconscious for nearly seventy-two hours.

The doctor, a middle-aged man, was greeted by O'Rourke with the words, 'Hello there, Tom. You're looking a bit crook yourself today.'

Angus was amazed at the informality between officer

and hand and was later to discover this was very much an Australian characteristic.

While examining him, Dr Speke told Angus he'd been extraordinarily lucky as the fuel oil he'd swallowed appeared to have been greatly diluted by its passage through the sea. And spewing as Angus had done while being carried up the *Wahroonga's* side had emptied his stomach of what fuel oil hadn't yet been absorbed into his system.

The summation of all this was Angus was going to live, although it would be some time before he was back on his feet again.

Before taking his leave Speke warned Angus against smoking stating it would probably take his lungs years to recover and to smoke in the meantime would merely be to court disaster

The look on Speke's face left Angus in no doubt as to what the outcome would be should he refuse to give up cigarettes. With a mental shrug he acquiesced. It was a small price to pay for his life.

After Speke had taken his leave Kitty came roaring in to throw his arms round Angus.

News of PQ 17 was bad. In fact, it was downright disastrous.

It wasn't yet known exactly how many of the convoy had been sunk. But piecing together the reports the *Wahroonga* had picked up if more than a handful of the thirty-one merchantmen had escaped it would be a miracle.

As for the *Tirpitz* it seemed she and the pocket battleship, *Scheer* had been sighted by a reconnaissance plane. But the time and place of the sighting made it impossible for either battleship to have been near PQ 17 when the Admiralty sent out the order for the escort to head west and the convoy to scatter.

Angus was appalled. For it surely meant the convoy had been abandoned prematurely if not unnecessarily.

'There must be facts we don't know about,' Angus said, to which Kitty raised his eyebrows and shrugged.

Angus's next question was where was the *Wahroonga* bound? And what was she doing in these waters operating on her own so far from the British battle fleet?

Kitty's reply was quite simply he hadn't been able to find out. He'd been summoned to see the *Wahroonga's* captain to whom he'd given full details of the *Almuria's* sinking. But on inquiring where and when the survivors could be expected to be put ashore Captain Tolman had become evasive, saying somewhat obliquely the *Wahroonga's* course and destination couldn't be disclosed at the present time.

All Kitty could add was there were some Russian civilians aboard and he guessed the *Wahroonga's* mission was somehow tied up with them.

Angus and Kitty looked questioningly at O'Rourke who promptly said he didn't know where they were headed for, nor did he even know where they'd been except it had been bloody cold there.

Kitty went on to say he'd been quartered in with the cooks with whom he was getting on handsomely. So far he hadn't been allotted any duties so he was taking life easy.

Angus asked O'Rourke why he was in the sick bay, to be told the Australian's legs had been machine gunned during a recent action. But more O'Rourke wouldn't say.

The next day they put into Reykavik where the *Wahroonga* was swiftly refuelled. But there was no shore leave allowed nor were any civilians, including the Port Authorities, allowed aboard.

Angus assumed he and the other survivors would be off-loaded here but he was wrong. When the *Wahroonga* sailed again they were still on board.

Angus concluded the *Wahroonga* must be headed for a British port but when an entire week passed bringing them into latitudes unmistakably southerly to Britain he had to accept that wherever else the Australian warship was headed it certainly wasn't Blighty.

When they passed the equator Dr Speke informed

Angus he could try walking now, but to take it easy for a while and not overdo things.

Angus discovered the great majority of Aussies were compulsive gamblers so a new way was found of passing the time by playing brag and pontoon.

It didn't take him long to realize he was a far cleverer gambler than the rest of the school. And this he set out to capitalize on, which he did with enormous success.

A number of times Angus and Kitty saw the Russian civilians, heavy set, broody men who stuck together and rarely spoke to anyone other than themselves. But the *Almuria*'s survivors were never introduced and it became an unspoken agreement between the British and Australians that the Russians were never approached or even referred to in conversation.

It was while steaming in the direction of St Helena that Kitty started having trouble sleeping at nights. So much sweat dripped off him, he commented, it was just like lying in a shallow bath. It forced him to get up and prowl the ship, sometimes talking to the night watch, other times sitting for'ard staring out to sea and enjoying whatever breeze there was.

During one such occasion he decided to go below and have a natter to his friends, the cooks, who were preparing the morning meal.

He didn't stay long as the galleys were indescribably hot but while there was offered an ice cold can of beer which he gratefully accepted.

Halfway through the beer he noticed an opened can of dill pickles which he fell upon, having an enormous passion for this delicacy.

When he left the galleys a little later the pickle can was empty.

Angus and O'Rourke were in the middle of their breakfast when Kitty entered the sick bay to sit between them. O'Rourke noticed Kitty was looking pale under his tan and mentioned the fact. Kitty replied he'd been feeling a little nauseous and lightheaded for the last half hour although he couldn't imagine why.

Thinking he was suffering from heat exhaustion, Angus suggested Kitty go back to his bunk and lie down. Even a number of the heat-hardened Aussies had succumbed, so brutal was the weather.

After some coaxing, Kitty agreed and with a wry, apologetic smile got to his feet and lurched from the room.

Angus called after the departing Kitty he would drop by the cooks' quarters later on to see how Kitty was feeling.

Then he and O'Rourke, having finished their breakfast, got the cards out as the off duty members of the gambling school would shortly be dropping by. Soon the incident faded from both their minds.

Lunch came and went till finally the game was abruptly halted – Angus having made his usual killing – by the arrival of Dr Speke to change O'Rourke's dressings.

While Speke was attending to O'Rourke Angus slowly walked the length of the ship, then descended several decks to where the cooks' quarters were situated.

He found Kitty fast asleep, curled into an embryonic position facing the bulkhead.

Kitty's breathing seemed regular enough so Angus decided the best thing to do was leave him sleeping until he awoke of his own accord.

That evening he checked on Kitty again but this time it was difficult for him to see properly as most of the cooks were already in bed which stopped him from putting on the light.

However, from what he could hear, Kitty's breathing was strong and regular so he decided to leave well enough alone.

The heat broke that night with an electric storm. To the accompaniment of far-off thunder, great, jagged streaks ripped the heavens apart. Then the rain came pounding down to lash the *Wahroonga* from stern to prow.

The next morning dawned blissful and quiet with only

an unaccustomed freshness in the air to remind those aboard the *Wahroonga* of the previous night's storm.

After breakfast Angus waited for Kitty. When he didn't appear Angus decided to go below to see if he was still feeling ill.

The moment he placed his hand on Kitty's arm he knew something was dreadfully wrong. Grabbing Kitty by the shoulders, Angus heaved, causing him to flop over onto his back.

Angus stared down at the mottled face and glazed eyes. He knew his friend was dead. It was unbelievable. Yet there was the gruesome evidence before his eyes.

'Oh Kitty what happened, son?' he said, laying a hand on his friend's icy cheek.

For a while he sat thinking back over the many good times he and Kitty had shared together since meeting on his first day at Holmlea Road Primary. The fights where they'd fought side by side. The adventures they'd had. Running with the milk. Going out as a foursome with Rosemary and Diane. Secrets shared. Money loaned and borrowed. Laughter.

Kitty had been as close to him as a brother. Closer in some ways. And now he was gone. Blown away like so much chaff in the wind.

With tears in his eyes, Angus rose and went looking for Dr Speke.

Kitty was buried at sea that afternoon. His body was weighted and wrapped in canvas, draped with the Union Jack, and after Captain Tolman had spoken a few words from the Bible, dropped overboard.

When Angus got back to the sick bay after the funeral he found a double tot of grog and a sympathetic O'Rourke waiting for him. He drank off the rum and then sat silently on his bed waiting for Dr Speke to come and tell him the results of the autopsy carried out on Kitty's body before it had been committed.

Speke arrived to say his findings were that Kitty had

died from a severe dose of food poisoning in which there had been complications.

Just what these complications were exactly Speke didn't know. As he explained to Angus, he didn't have the equipment on board to carry out the tests for their analysis.

What had been established was the pickles Kitty had eaten were at fault. Samples taken from his stomach had shown them to be toxic in the extreme, probably due to a combination of the severe heat and their being left in the can.

Incredulity was stamped all over Angus's face as he slowly shook his head in disbelief. To think what Kitty had been through since the start of the war, including the PQ 17 debacle and the sinking of the *Almuria*. To end up dying because of some stupid pickles!

It was farcical. A grisly joke no one, least of all Kitty, was laughing at.

15

It was nine pm on a Friday night and Carrie knew she was going to be in for another bad time. Archie should have been home hours ago but as he hadn't yet appeared she could only assume he'd gone to the boozer.

Pay night was just another excuse for Archie who since having returned to the drink was now worse than he'd ever been.

He continually complained of pains in his arms and legs but refused to go and see Dr Robertson to find out what was wrong with him. Instead he consumed more and more alcohol, claiming only drink deadened the pain.

And of course the more bevy he put away the more impossible he was to live with, the beatings he constantly dished out more violent and brutal than they'd ever been in the past.

Sighing, Carrie rose and crossed to the oven to have yet another look at his tea which she was trying to keep warm.

Thinking she would make some fresh gravy to try and keep the meal moist she put on the kettle and then returned to her chair in front of the fire.

Carrie was a changed woman since Angus had left Glasgow to go to sea. Her hair was prematurely white while her face had become permanently gaunt and haggard. But the biggest change was in her body, which was skeletal.

The last incarceration in Bellfield Sanatorium had done the trick of completely curing her TB. But what a price had been exacted! It was as though all her bodily juices had been bled from her, leaving her a walking talking shadow of her former self.

She must have dozed off for suddenly she started awake to hear the kettle whistling and Archie's key scraping in the lock.

Her heart sank the moment he lurched into the room. He was so drunk he could hardly stand up.

Just inside the door he stood swaying for a few seconds before staggering to the table and collapsing onto a chair. In a slurred voice he demanded to know where in the hell his fucking tea was?

It was too late now to make gravy. So she switched off the kettle and placed the meal, dry as it was, before him.

Archie prodded it with his fork while muttering under his breath. With a snort he threw the fork onto the plate, then thrust it all to one side.

Taking the initiative – a ploy that sometimes worked – Carrie asked him what he expected when he came rolling in hours after he was supposed to get home? It was hardly her fault his meal was in such a state and why didn't he away through . . .

Her voice was drowned as, with a roar, Archie snatched up the plate and threw it at the wall where it smashed into smithereens leaving a gooey mess sliding floorward.

Carrie blinked and then hastily retreated. Turning, she ran, intending to pick up her coat in the hall and make for Tallon Street. But she never even reached the kitchen door as Archie was too quick for her.

She gasped as his hand grabbed her shoulder. Then she screamed as he threw her roughly against the wall.

'No Archie! Please!' she pleaded to no avail. His balled fist homed in on her shrunken right breast.

'Fuckin' no use bitch!' he spat. He hit her again, this time on the left breast.

What followed was a nightmare for Carrie as his fist thudded time and time again into her defenceless body.

With a cry she fell to the floor while he crouched above her.

Looking up she had difficulty in focusing and his leering face swam as though she was viewing hit through several feet of water. Both her eyes had been hit with solidly connecting punches.

Archie was suddenly limp inside, the anger momentarily burned out of him. He hurried to the bathroom where he was hideously sick.

Carrie whimpered as she rolled onto her knees and then struggled to her feet. In the hall she tugged her coat from its peg and, heaving it round her shoulders, somehow got herself through the doorway and down the stairs.

It was Mrs Kirkpatrick who found her slumped at the close mouth.

'Oh, hen!' Mrs Kirkpatrick whispered sympathetically when she saw the state Carrie was in.

Carrie rubbed her eyes but it didn't help. Her vision was still blurred and out of kilter. In a croaky voice she asked Mrs Kirkpatrick to help her to Tallon Street.

Taking one of Carrie's arms Mrs Kirkpatrick hooked it round her shoulders and that way the two of them staggered down the road.

Harriet was making her weekly visit to her parents' house and it was she who opened the front door to Mrs Kirkpatrick's frantic knocking. Exclaiming in horror, Harriet helped Mrs Kirkpatrick take Carrie through to the living room where Winnie and Big Donald were sitting by the fire.

Winnie's hand went to her mouth when she saw Carrie. Then she was on her feet helping Harriet and Mrs Kirkpatrick seat Carrie in the chair she'd just vacated.

Big Donald was frozen with shock, sickened by the dreadful state Carrie was in. Her two enormous black eyes puffed out even further as he watched.

'Archie?' he asked, his voice cracking with anger.

'Oh Papa!' Carrie mumbled. Turning to Winnie she buried her head in her mother's skirt.

Donald decided this had gone far enough. When his daughter came home in this condition it was high time for something drastic to be done.

He strode from the room to the kitchen where he groped in the coal bin for the heavy hammer kept there.

He was slipping it into his trouser pocket when Carrie supported by Harriet appeared beside him.

'No, Papa. He's not worth it,' Carrie said through a slash of bloodless lips. 'I'm leaving him anyway. Tonight was the finish.'

For a few moments Donald was undecided. Then he nodded. 'Away ben and I'll be through,' he said. But before Carrie could turn to leave the kitchen he swept her into his arms and hugged her close. It was a massive demonstration of emotion from a man rarely given to showing his feelings.

After Mrs Kirkpatrick had left Carrie was given a hot bath and helped into some clothes of Winnie's.

It worried her she'd left behind Angus's money box still containing most of what he'd left her – she never had got round to opening a bank account – behind in Holmlea Road.

If she was going to be on her own from here on she was going to need that money to support herself until she was able to sort things out and get a job.

Convinced Archie would be dead to the world by now in a drunken stupor she was all for returning to Holmlea Road, but when she told the others of her intention they ganged up on her saying she was in no fit state to make the journey there and back.

The last thing any of the women wanted was for Donald to go, so it was decided Harriet would get the money box.

Harriet's heart was in her mouth as she climbed the stairs her sister had fled down a little earlier.

She listened at the door before inserting Carrie's key in the lock. Quietly the door swung open.

Every light in the house was blazing while from the bathroom came the most terrible stench of sick. She put the door on the latch and tiptoed through to the bedroom where she found Archie sprawled across the bed snoring like the drunken pig he was.

Excitement tied Harriet's stomach up in knots as she took various items of clothing from the wardrobe and chest of drawers and packed them in a suitcase.

Archie moved once, suddenly rolling from one side to the other. But after a snort and cough his snoring became regular again.

Closing the suitcase Harriet stole from the room.

She laid the suitcase by the front door, then turning back went into the bedroom that had once been Angus's. The money box was hidden inside the cabinet of an old broken gramophone player.

Tiptoeing back to the front door, she reopened the suitcase and stuffed the money box inside.

Relieved at having successfully accomplished her mission she was just about to close the door behind her when she remembered seeing a framed picture of Angus in his bedroom and thought it was surely something her sister would want.

Leaving the suitcase outside on the landing she quietly made her way back to Angus's bedroom.

The moment she picked up the picture she knew she wasn't alone. Whirling around, she discovered Archie standing swaying in the doorway.

His face cracked into a grin as he grabbed hold of the door handle to steady himself. Without taking his eyes from her he shut the door behind him and stood with his back to it.

Harriet knew there was no use pleading to Archie's better side. In his present state he didn't have one.

'Shite but you're ugly!' he said, tilting his head to one side to watch her reaction.

He'd always wanted to hurt and humiliate Harriet for no other reason than she was the type of woman who provoked that sort of reaction in him.

Slowly and with great emphasis he began to unbuckle his belt.

'Don't be stupid!' Harriet snarled as Archie advanced on her. 'I'm your wife's sister, man!'

Archie took no heed as he contrived to steer her into a corner.

Suddenly he pounced and she was in his arms. Silently they struggled, landing on Angus's bed.

Even before they'd stopped bouncing his hand was up her skirt tugging at her knickers.

His breath was hot and smelly, his chin a strip of sandpaper threatening to rip the skin from her face. 'You bastard!' she spat.

Strong hands clamped themselves on her rear. Then before she'd realized what his intention was she'd been flipped over and a forearm was pushing her shoulders down into the mattress.

Penetration was quick, savage and incredibly painful.

Later that night feeling utterly defiled and degraded Harriet lay in bed staring wide-eyed at the ceiling.

When she'd returned to Tallon Street she'd been able

to carry it off saying Archie had been dead to the world just as Carrie had said he'd be.

She'd desperately wanted to confide what had happened to her. But that hadn't been possible.

One breath of it to Donald and he would kill Archie. She had no doubt whatever about that. Nor could she speak to her mother who would be bound to tell her father.

That left Carrie but how could she tell her own sister when Archie was Carrie's husband? Carrie's cross had been hard enough to bear without her adding to it.

Nor was there anyone else she could confide in about so intimate a matter.

'Oh Lou!' she whispered. Feeling more alone than she'd ever done in her life, she wept long and bitterly.

In the summer of 1943 Hugh came home on leave.

It was a beautiful day, fresh and clear with a hint of salt wind blowing in from the coast.

It was his first trip home since enlisting and he'd been looking forward to it for months now, ever since it had first been whispered in the mess that a leave was on the cards.

He was humming as he turned into the drive leading up to the Paterson house.

For a brief moment he stopped to stare fondly at the house which looked just grand and exactly as he remembered it. Then he was striding forward hoping Greta was home.

She was. With a great cry of delight she flew into his arms where he birled her round and round.

She took him away through to the kitchen where she put the kettle on and brought out the special home made shortie.

Pouring the tea, she suddenly stopped to stare proudly at him sitting in Aly's old chair. His various flashes and badges proclaiming him a sergeant in the Highland Light Infantry.

He was smiling and laughing a lot but there was something in his eyes which hadn't been there before. She'd seen a similar look in men's eyes after the Great War. Once acquired, the look was never lost.

Hugh was eager to be brought up to date on what was happening in the dairy and on the farm, which Stewart had won exemption to stay behind and run.

'And how is Stewart, the old sod?' he asked.

Greta opened her mouth to reply but no words came. She covered her face as great racking sobs were wrenched from her.

Instantly Hugh was by her side, cooing words of comfort and holding her close while she sobbed onto his shoulder.

Her body shook as she told him Stewart and his entire family – his wife and the three children – were all dead.

'How?' Hugh asked in a whisper.

Greta's hands twined and intertwined as she told the story. Just over a month earlier a German bomber had either got lost or funked the attack which had done so much damage to Clydebank that night. Or perhaps the plane had been damaged and unable to continue.

Anyway, the pilot had decided to jettison his load and return to base.

The house and everyone in it had gone up in one enormous, blinding flash seen for miles in all directions. No trace of any of the bodies had ever been recovered.

Hugh listened to all this in silence. Suddenly the day outside wasn't so bright any more.

Greta had another bubble and while she did he whispered various things he hoped might bring her a little consolation.

When Greta had got hold of herself again she washed her face. Then the pair of them went outside.

What was worrying Hugh was with Stewart gone Greta was having to manage the entire kit and caboodle on her own. But she put his mind at rest saying she had some excellent lads working for her. And then there was Mr KcKeand and Mr Farquharson, two retired farmhands who were proving to be a big help in looking after the cows.

In fact Greta was pleased she had the work to occupy her – she was going out in the lead cart herself every morning – it kept her from brooding too much on what had happened.

Inside the stables Hugh inhaled the well remembered smell he'd missed so much. It was the rarest perfume to him.

Returning to the house Greta took Hugh round the side to the make-shift garage where he found his Wolseley Hornet, resprayed black after the Francey affair. It was a little dusty but otherwise in excellent condition.

Petrol was rationed but Greta had managed to save quite a bit from the dairy's allocations. This she'd stored at the back of the garage in tins.

Showing Hugh where the cache was she told him to see he enjoyed himself while his leave lasted.

She hurried away in the direction of the back door.

The one o'clock hooter had just finished sounding as Donald slipped out of Armstrong's and headed in the direction of home.

He'd only gone a few yards when a motor drew up beside him and a voice said, 'Would you like a lift, Papa?'

Big Donald's gaze swept over Hugh, taking everything in. 'Aye. That would be grand right enough, son,' he replied.

When he was comfortably seated he and Hugh solemnly shook hands.

They found Winnie in the kitchen. She laid down the spoon she'd been using and carefully wiped her hands before taking Hugh in her arms and holding him to her.

'When are you going away again then, son?' she asked.

Hugh laughed. 'You might let me get my foot in the door before you ask me that,' he joked.

'Ach ye ken fine what I mean,' Winnie replied, wiping

her nose with her pinny. She was desperately trying not to cry.

Carrie would be home in a few minutes, Donald informed Hugh. He went on to tell him about the Archie Marjoribanks business and how Carrie, having returned to Tallon Street determined to make her own way, had landed a job back at Balogie Clothing as a supervisor, the same position Jakey Sanderson had once held. Jakey like all the other men who'd been employed at the factory was off fighting.

According to Donald, Carrie had been made supervisor because it had been recognized she wasn't up to handling a heavy sewing machine any more. This, coupled with the fact she had previous experience of the factory and was a lot older than the majority of girls currently employed there, had made her the ideal choice for the vacant position.

As things turned out, it had been an inspired placing as Carrie was one of the most popular and efficient supervisors the factory ever had.

While they ate Hugh told his parents about what had happened to Stewart Paterson and his family.

'Those poor weans,' Winnie said and sadly shook her head.

Donald said Sandy and Mary were also dead, Sandy having passed away in his sleep and Mary succumbing a few months after him from a heart attack.

The door opened and Carrie entered.

For a moment Hugh failed to recognize his sister; her new thick pebble glasses somehow completely altered her appearance.

Although she was drawn and haggard, there was a light-hearted expression on her face he couldn't recall seeing there since those far off days when John McBain had been alive.

Brother and sister embraced, both genuinely pleased to see one another.

For the rest of the dinnertime Carrie kept them in stitches recounting the trials and tribulations of working for Ballogie Clothing.

As the dishes were being cleared Winnie asked Hugh if he'd be wanting the front room while he was home on leave? A flash of pain flitted across her face when he replied he'd be staying out at Muirend.

Seeing her disappointment, he muttered he planned going out with the milk in the mornings, and as there was a great deal to be done round the dairy it was just as well for him to be there close at hand.

With dinnertime over Hugh elected to drive Carrie round to Balogie Clothing where he deposited her at the front door amidst a gaggle of giggling girls.

He then parked the Wolseley and went for a stroll round old familiar streets and places. As he walked he soaked up the Glasgow atmosphere he'd missed so much.

Presuming he came out of the war intact the last thing he wanted was to leave Glasgow. And yet if things turned out as he planned he might well have to.

For hours he walked the streets of Cathcart and Battlefield, biding his time till five o'clock when he returned to the Wolseley and drove to Thistle Street. He parked in front of Janey McIver's close.

He knew from their correspondence she was generally on her way home from work at this time so he lit a cigarette and sat back to wait.

It wasn't long before he saw her familiar shape walking up the street towards him.

She must have been preoccupied for she didn't notice the car and would have turned directly into her close had he not leaned out and said, 'Hello Janey.'

As recognition flooded her face, her mouth dropped open in astonishment. 'Hugh!' she exclaimed excitedly.

Immediately he was out of the car and at her side, and not giving a damn who was watching, he took her in his arms and kissed her.

They moved into the relative privacy of the close mouth where he asked how long it would take her to get ready to go out for a hurl in the car?

In a trembling voice, she said she would need ten

minutes to change. She was back in five.

Once she was seated beside him a feeling of completeness settled on Hugh, dispelling any doubts he might have had. Janey was the woman for him all right. Together they were a couple.

During the drive he told her where they were going and why. On reaching the farm, Hugh parked beside the barn. An old man appeared as though by magic and, remembering what Greta had told him earlier, he presumed this to be either Mr McKeand or Mr Farquharson. It turned out to be Mr McKeand.

Once he introduced himself Mr McKeand immediately relaxed, having heard all about him from Stewart and Greta in the past.

McKeand accompanied them over to where the house had stood. All that was left was a blackened pit filled with scorched bricks, pieces of burnt wood and some lumps of melted metal.

Hugh squatted and silently did what he'd come to do – pay his last respects.

Mr McKeand went off to attend to some matter concerning the cattle so Hugh showed Janey round the farm.

It was a fine evening and as the gloaming came upon them Janey told Hugh that sad as the circumstances were, she was enjoying this breath of fresh air.

With the wind blowing in her hair and bringing a flush to her cheeks Janey looked as though she might have been born to the country. Hugh's heart swelled at the thought of spending the rest of his days with her in an environment similar to this one. He envisioned the pair of them surrounded by an enormous family of boys, happy as two pigs in the proverbial muck.

He lit cigarettes and placed one between her lips. Then straight out he asked if she'd marry him?

Janey caught her breath, momentarily thrown by the abruptness of the proposal.

Collecting herself, she said she had no doubts at all

about what she felt for him. But what about the old brick wall that had always loomed between them in the past?

Hugh's eyes took on a faraway look. He began to talk about some of the things he'd experienced on active service.

He spoke of the men he'd known, all types, shapes, sizes and religions, including a Buddhist who had been a real eye opener for him.

Men with whom he'd shared life and death. Men of many background from all over the world whom he'd seen at their glorious best as well as their worst.

Hugh groped for words. He wasn't a particularly articulate person but he managed to put over to Janey what he'd come to realize.

When you were in a tight spot and a man braved his life to save yours it didn't matter if he was a Protestant or Catholic. What did matter was he'd laid his life on the line for you.

When a man lay dying with both legs blown away it didn't matter what religion he was. You gave him what relief and comfort you could.

When you hadn't tasted water for days it didn't matter what religion the man was who offered you a swallow from his canteen. You accepted and were grateful.

Catholic and Protestant. *The Sash My Father Wore.* *The Soldier's Song.* Rangers and Celtic. He had no time any more for that sort of bigoted nonsense. He'd finally come to see it in its true light.

Janey replied that might be so, but it didn't alter the fact this was Glasgow and here such things were given enormous importance.

For a Protestant to marry a Catholic was just asking for trouble and in a halting voice she said so.

Hugh sighed. He wanted Janey as his wife and was prepared to do almost anything to get her, even becoming a Catholic.

She came into his arms and they kissed. She said it wasn't necessary for him to turn his coat as long as he agreed she could continue as a practising Catholic and their children be brought up as such.

Hugh had already considered this alternative and rejected it. He thought it best in the long run for their children if the entire family belonged to the same religion.

He went on to say when the war was over, should they run into any unpleasantness, he was quite prepared to go abroad and start a new life where such things were of less significance.

'And how about your family? How are they going to take it?' Janey asked.

Hugh pulled a face and admitted he was expecting the worst, from his father in particular, but that was something he would have to face and live with.

As they walked back to the Wolseley Hugh wondered what God in His heaven thought of what the Protestants and Catholics and many other religions and branches thereof did in His name. If He had a sense of humour He must be laughing at the sheer hypocrisy of it all. When He wasn't weeping in despair, that was.

16

Sir Alan Armstrong lay back in the plush interior of his Rolls and drew with great satisfaction on a very large Cuban cigar.

He'd just concluded a deal which now made him the biggest single property owner in the Gorbals.

He smiled as the smoke blackened tenements flicked by. When the war was over there was bound to be a building boom. There certainly would be if he had anything to do with it.

He'd kick out the slummies, raze the tenements, and then build for the type of tenant who'd once lived there when the Gorbals had been a superior class of district.

The idea was his brainchild entirely, and one which was going to make him an enormous pile of money.

His enjoyment faded at the thought of the small family supper he was now on his way to attend – once he'd picked up Cordelia from Arnprior House – out at Bearsden where Iain and Rosemary lived.

They'd only been living at Bearsden a few weeks when Iain had announced he'd joined the RAF, a move everyone who knew him at all well had been expecting him to make.

Thinking of Rosemary's marriage brought Angus McBain back to Sir Alan's mind. Rosemary's initial pique at finding herself discarded had quickly given way to anger which in turn had been transplanted by the most awesome fury. In such a state she had been putty in his hands and it hadn't been long before she and Iain were engaged.

It hadn't been a long engagement. He'd seen to that. He'd wanted her wedded, bedded and with an offspring on the way before she regained her equilibrium.

Well he'd succeeded with two of his aims at least. The war and Iain's long partings from Rosemary had so far left the third unfulfilled.

The Battle of Britain had been a personal triumph for Iain: he'd emerged covered in glory and had been swiftly promoted to the rank of Squadron Leader.

After Spitfires he'd been transferred to Lancasters and from there he'd gone on to command a squadron of Mosquitoes. It was in one of these he'd very nearly been brought down by anti-aircraft fire over Caen.

From what Sir Alan had heard, the plane had been extensively hit but against all odds Iain had managed to bring it limping back across the Channel to crash land at his home aerodrome.

That had been a little over a year ago and since then

Iain had been hospitalized from the fearsome burns he'd sustained in the crash.

At first his life had been feared for, so bad were his injuries. But thanks to a great deal of dedicated nursing combined with superb work by the specialist involved he'd been able to pull through.

Iain was due home that evening. The small family supper was in his honour.

Rosemary sat staring into her vanity table mirror, scrutinizing her face which she'd stopped making up for the moment because her hands were shaking so badly.

She was wondering about Iain's face which she hadn't seen, except swathed in bandages, since the crash.

For the umpteenth time in the last hour she glanced at the bedside clock. His expected arrival was drawing inexorably closer. She'd wanted to go to the station to meet him but he'd vetoed that in his last letter saying he much preferred her waiting for him at home.

As she sat staring at herself she thought of the three times she'd been down to the nursing home in the Cotswolds – she'd have gone more often only Iain had been dead against it – where he'd been slowly nursed back to health. The last time the plastic surgeon had taken her aside for a little chat, as he'd called it.

According to him a great deal could be accomplished with plastic surgery but miracles were beyond them. They'd done their best and were pleased with the results. He hadn't elaborated further.

There was a crunching of gravel outside as a motor car arrived. Her mother and father's voices came wafting up. They'd hoped Diane would be able to accompany them but she'd phoned to say she couldn't make it as she had to be on duty. She was an ambulance driver with the ATS.

Hours after he should have done Iain still hadn't arrived and a sort of pregnant depression hung over those waiting as the minutes ticked relentlessly by.

Finally, with an exclamation of annoyance, Sir Hamilton rose to announce this was becoming ridiculous and he was going to ring the Central Station to find out the state of the trains.

Sir Alan poured more drinks in the hope of relaxing the tension holding them all as though they'd been collectively caught in a vice.

Sir Hamilton was frowning when he re-entered the room to say the person he'd spoken to had informed him that, although dreadfully late, Iain's train had arrived in an hour and a half ago. Rosemary began twisting her wedding ring.

'Listen!' said Sir Alan urgently when they caught the sound of a car pulling into the driveway.

All eyes swung to the door as footsteps echoed in the hall.

The door opened and Iain stood revealed. Rosemary's gaze was fixed on the buckle at his middle when she heard the involuntary gasp wrenched from Cordelia.

Slowly, reluctantly her eyes inched up his tunic to be arrested by his neck.

The flesh there was an angry red shot through with streaks of white giving it a sort of marbled effect. It took an almost superhuman effort to lift her gaze that little bit higher.

What caught and held her attention were his eyes. Cold and hard, they glittered like those of a snake. There was a chilling quality about them, so completely different from their previous liquidity.

There were no eyebrows above the eyes. Those had gone, leaving in their place twin lines of puckered scar tissue.

Large patches of skin were shiny yellow. Other areas glistened with the same red and white marbling effect as on his neck.

His cheeks had sunk right in leaving the bones above them jutting out.

He was mainly bald with only a few tufts of coarse hair sticking out here and there.

The overall impression was of a decomposing death's head.

Rosemary was only too aware that Iain was watching her, studying her reaction, waiting for her to say something.

She bludgeoned her numb brain to think of a few kind words. But nothing came. She was completely mesmerized by that death's head with its glittering snake's eyes.

As the silence began to lengthen Sir Alan realized something had to be done and quickly. Snatching up a glass, he poured a very large drink into it and walking swiftly across the room grasped Iain's hand which he vigorously pumped up and down, at the same time saying, 'It could have been worse, lad. At least you're alive. That's the main thing.' He then thrust the glass of whisky into the hand he'd been shaking.

The spell was broken. Lize was suddenly on her feet and rushing to Iain. Large, fat tears oozed from her eyes to run rolling down her face.

Striding across to his son, Sir Hamilton shook him by the hand but couldn't yet trust himself to speak.

Inwardly Rosemary was cursing the plastic surgeon for not giving her more of a warning. Burned and scarred, yes, that she'd been led to expect. But nothing like the horror now confronting her which was straight out of her most terrible nightmares.

She knew what she had to do next and the thought revolted her.

'Welcome home, Iain,' she said, and going up on her tiptoes, kissed the twin lines of scar tissue – identical to those where his eyebrows had been – that were all that remained of his lips.

Wryly Iain said, 'They tell me in time I'll get used to how I look but personally I doubt it.'

Sir Alan went round with the whisky bottle and no one even thought of refusing.

Now feeling in full possession of himself, Sir Hamilton asked Iain what had kept him as his train had arrived a considerable time before he'd shown up at the house.

Iain sipped his drink. Then in a peculiar unemotional voice he requested his mother and father sit as he had some rather bad news for them.

Staring into his glass, Iain went on to say he'd been informed by Sir Hamilton's chauffeur who'd met him off the train that shortly after Sir Hamilton and Lize had left for Bearsden a telegram had arrived in from the War Department. The chauffeur had learned of the telegram having rung Carmunnock on servants' business.

The reason for his further delay was that he'd taken it upon himself to go out to Carmunnock and open that telegram.

His voice remained completely unemotional when he said it was just as he'd feared. Peter who was also in the RAF had been shot down and killed.

Lize sobbed and bit her lower lip. Sir Hamilton's expression was one of complete devastation.

Rosemary thought of Diane who was in love with Peter and had been expecting to marry him when the war was over.

'There may be some mistake? Perhaps he was only shot down?' Lize said hopefully.

Iain shook his head. 'Peter's dead,' he said emphatically.

Collapsing, Lize sank sideways onto her husband's lap where her entire body convulsed with grief.

Sir Hamilton was so stricken by this new blow the best he could manage by way of attempted consolation were some half hearted pats on the back of Lize's head and a few mumbled words it was doubtful she even heard.

A little later their chauffeur took Sir Hamilton and Lize home. And shortly after their departure, the Armstrongs left also.

While Iain went upstairs with the remainder of the whisky bottle Rosemary stayed behind to tidy away a few odds and ends. Finally when she'd run out of excuses for remaining downstairs she took a deep breath and went up to her husband.

The bedroom was in darkness. Iain was sitting on a chair by the window which had its blackout curtains pulled fully back.

As she undressed he said it was perfect flying weather and round about now from all over Britain RAF bombers would be taking to the air and winging towards Germany.

Without changing tone and as though it was the same topic of conversation, he said he would understand perfectly should she want a divorce.

Rosemary's thoughts were whirling at this new turn of events. Here being handed to her on a platter was the perfect way out of what she considered to be their disastrous marriage.

She could remember only too well what had been going through her mind when Iain had proposed. By accepting, she'd imagined she was somehow getting back at Angus, hurting him the way he'd hurt her.

But the only person she'd hurt was herself – and Iain, should he ever find out the truth of why she'd married him.

Here was Iain proposing the divorce she so desperately wanted but with circumstances as they now stood she knew she wasn't going to be able to leave him.

Her original mistake was about to be compounded and there was nothing she could do about it, unless she was prepared to live the rest of her life with his blood on her hands.

That Iain was brave and courageous there could be no doubt. His exploits in the RAF spoke for themselves. But there are more more than one kind of bravery and courage.

If she was to falter now in what he believed to be her love for him she would be killing him as surely as if she'd presented him with a loaded pistol and told him to go ahead and use it.

Within days, perhaps even hours, of her leaving him he'd be dead. A suicide.

She was so certain of that she would have bet her own

life on it.

Here he was prattling on about divorce but in his heart of hearts he was praying she was going to say she would stay on with him.

She knew he didn't think she would. But optimist that he was he recognized there was a possibility she might and because of this had come home instead of killing himself in the nursing home.

She knew he wanted to be certain she was leaving him before he did the deed.

Goddamn you, Angus McBain! She raged inwardly. It's all your fault I'm in this impossible position. Why did you have to run off like you did? And where in hell's name are you now?

Her anger died as suddenly as it bloomed at the thought he, too, like Peter might be dead, a victim of the war.

Realizing Iain had stopped speaking she dragged her attention back to him.

Poor sod whose misfortune it was – apart from this latest tragedy of his face – to love a woman who didn't love him in return.

'Well?' he queried.

With that one word he was asking her whether he was to live or die.

'Come to bed,' she said, fixing a half smile on her face. Perhaps in time they both might get used to the way he now looked. But like him, she doubted it.

'Marry a Catholic!' Donald exploded.

Slowly he climbed to his feet from the chair he'd been slumped in. And as he did the years appeared to melt away from him till he was once more the awe inspiring figure Hugh remembered so vividly from his youth.

Winnie hovered nervously in the background, her eyes fastened on her husband as she waited to see what he was going to do. She was sick with worry for Hugh and terrified of what this might do to Donald who, despite his bravado and self-imposed heavy work schedule – and unknown to Hugh – hadn't been a well man of late.

Donald's nostrils flared, their thick projecting hairs thrilling like a flight of arrows.

'Marry a Catholic!' he said contemptuously. It was a preposterous idea and Hugh must be loony to even consider it. Mixed marriages never worked: they were doomed to failure from the very start.

Hugh's reply was the marriage wouldn't be a mixed one as he intended turning.

Donald caught his breath and for a split second it seemed he was going to stride forward and strike his son. But somehow – and the effort it took was both enormous and evident – he managed to restrain himself.

Picking up his pipe, he began packing it, a device he often employed when wanting time to think.

Hugh seized on this opportunity to try and explain to his father just how much the war had changed him.

Quietly he related to Donald the same experiences he'd told Janey about and how all these had combined to open his eyes about many things, not least of all the sheer ridiculousness and hypocrisy of the Glasgow religious situation.

When Hugh had finally finished there was a brooding silence in the room. It was broken by Winnie asking where he and Janey intended living?

Hugh replied Greta Paterson had insisted they stay with her as there was more than enough room in the big house for the three of them.

Being entirely practical, Winnie approved whole-heartedly of this arrangement.

Donald couldn't help but be impressed by the Hugh the war had moulded, seeing in his son many characteristics he'd always considered missing before. A lot of what Hugh said had struck home, making Donald think again about a lifetime's prejudice.

Donald also reminded himself that in these his twilight years, with Angus grown up, he wanted other grand-children to spoil and get close to.

But *Catholic* grandchildren! It was so completely against everything he'd always believed in and stood for. Winnie caught her man's eyes and silently pleaded with him to make his peace with Hugh – for her sake if nothing else.

It was probably the hardest decision Donald had ever made in his life.

It had hurt him deeply when he and Hugh had been estranged previously. And with a war on who knew what might happen?

He would never forgive himself, nor would Winnie forgive him, should Hugh be killed while sundered from his family. The very thought was unbearable.

They would talk about him at work, of course. That went without saying. See Big Donald Chisholm there. Did you know his son upped and married a fenian and went left footed himself? The bastard actually turned his coat! And they would spit in disgust to emphasize the point.

It would be bloody hard but somehow he'd find a way of living with it. He'd have to. For when it came right down to it he couldn't deny Winnie the only son she had left.

'So when do we get to meet this lassie of yours, then?' he asked.

Winnie's eyes shone when she heard that. Rising, she said she'd away through to the kitchen and put the kettle on. She managed to hold back the tears till she'd hurried from the room and shut the door behind her.

She couldn't remember when she'd been so happy.

When the time came for Hugh to return to his regiment his wife of ten days accompanied him to the station.

They held each other close to the very last minute. Hugh finally boarded the train. A whistle shrilled and the train jerked forward.

He hung out of the window, smiling, blowing kisses and feeling terrible.

Janey waved and waved till the train turned a bend

and disappeared from view.

Turning, she made her way back to the barrier, not yet aware her and Hugh's dearest wish had already been granted them.

She was carrying his child.

17

'Hot by name and hot by nature,' Angus said to the sweat slicked body of the woman he'd just been making love to.

Molly Hotblack laughed, a rumbling, sexual sound that came from deep within her magnificent chest.

Angus stared at her in open admiration. There was a wildness about her which fascinated and attracted him. She was fierce and dazzling like the landscape round the small Queensland township of Bundegai in which they now were. A sun woman who at the height of her passion literally blinded him.

He watched while she lit a cigarette and drew the smoke deep into her lungs. She didn't offer him: he'd given up that day aboard the *Wahroonga* when Dr Speke had told him either to finish with smoking or else it would finish with him.

The *Wahroonga* and Kitty, only a year ago and yet seemingly an eternity away. He never thought of Kitty but it brought a lump to his throat, as it did now.

Molly swung herself from the bed and ran her hands down her golden tanned thighs. Her long, auburn hair danced round her shoulders.

'A shower, I think, and then it's back to the slave mill,' she said.

'You don't have to go back to work again, do you?'

She shrugged. ''Fraid so, I promised to cover for Gilly who's down with a crook tum.'

Angus pulled a face. He'd been hoping they'd have a bite together before he headed back for the digging. Usually when he came into Bundegai it was an overnight stop but this time it was merely a flying visit to pick up some provisions.

He put his hands behind his head and watched as she moved towards the bathroom.

'Leave the door open so I can watch you,' he called out.

'Voyeur!' she shouted back.

'Too right!' he replied, and they laughed, both knowing as far as she was concerned it was true. He could've sat for hours just staring at her naked body.

While Molly enjoyed her shower Angus's mind drifted back to the *Wahroonga* and all that had happened to him since the Australian warship had put him ashore at Sydney. For this had been their destination. Once there, the mysterious Russians had been hurried ashore and whisked off in an official looking car.

Angus had been kept aboard until visited by an Australian army major who'd sworn him in under the Official Secrets Act. It had been made crystal clear to him that if he ever so much as mentioned the Russians and the fact they'd been brought to Australia he'd spend the rest of the war behind bars. And from the look on the major's face he knew that to be no idle threat.

After the swearing in bit had taken place he and O'Rourke had been carted off to an ambulance which had taken them to a military hospital in the suburb of Homebush.

A great many tests had been carried out on him. At the end of the first fortnight he'd been taken aside and the news broken to him. His war was over, nor would he ever be fit enough to go back to sea.

What it all boiled down to was that his lungs had taken one hell of a beating from the fuel oil he'd swallowed and would never be the same again. From now on he had to take it fairly easy. Hard graft such as he'd become used to as a stoker was out. Any job he took would have to consist of light duties only.

It had been an awful blow to him but in his heart of hearts he'd been expecting something like that. After all, he knew you couldn't expect to swallow fuel oil and get away scot free. If anything, he'd been damned lucky and could only thank his lucky stars he'd spewed his guts up while being carried aboard the *Wahroonga*. If that hadn't happened Kitty wouldn't have been the only one to have died aboard the warship.

For three months he'd been in the hospital before being declared fit enough to be discharged.

By that time he and O'Rourke had become even thicker than before. And he'd been only too happy to accept O'Rourke's mother's invitation, Mrs Boo as she was called, to come and stay at the O'Rourke home overlooking Manly Beach.

Mrs Boo was an ancient, gnarled old biddy, tough as an old roo skin, according to O'Rourke. Angus came to think very highly of her.

There was no Mr Boo. He'd died some years previously. So with O'Rourke's return there were three of them in the dilapidated wooden house.

By the time O'Rourke was back home Angus had got fed up lying on the beach and generally passing his time doing nothing. So he'd got himself a job as a clerk with a local building firm.

He liked the job and having a quick, not to say inquisitive mind, was soon picking up a great deal about the building trade. So much so that the boss, a man called Bill Pettigrew who was another ex-patriate Glaswegian, took him under his wing. The two of them became good pals outside working hours, drinking together and Angus often visiting Bill's home.

Bill was desperately homesick, although with his new-found prosperity was sensible enough to know he'd never go back to Glasgow except perhaps on holiday after the war. For hours on end he and Angus would sit talking about their beloved city. After a while Bill came to look on Angus almost as a son.

When O'Rourke got home from the hospital Mrs Boo had held a cookout for him in the middle of which O'Rourke had announced his big news. Because of his wounds, he would walk with a limp for the rest of his life and he'd been honourably discharged from the Navy.

It was at that cookout O'Rourke had introduced Angus to Eric Petersson, an Australian of Scandinavian descent, who was pursuing what O'Rourke called 'the digger's dream'.

By rights, Petersson should've been in the armed forces but due to a stomach condition and poor eyesight he'd been rejected.

'Gold!' Petersson had said. 'I know it's up there on the western slopes of the Great Divide. When I was there last I could smell it.'

'Gold!' O'Rourke whispered, his eyes taking on a far away look.

Angus sat entranced as Petersson went on to talk about his two previous prospecting expeditions, the last of which he'd only returned from the week before.

'You're sure it's there?' Angus asked.

'It's there all right. You take my word for it.'

'Eric knows what he's talking about,' O'Rourke said. 'And so he should after the years he spent studying the subject at the university.'

'You're a geologist, then?'

Petersson nodded.

That fact impressed Angus considerably, elevating Petersson to something more than a mere story teller or enthusiastic amateur.

By the time the cookout was over the three of them were well drunk. Petersson said his goodbyes and slouched off.

Alone by the remains of the fire, Angus sat staring up

at the velvet sky thinking about what Petersson had told him.

'Gold!' he said in a voice that was a loving caress. The very word had a magic about it that made the hair at the nape of his neck stand on end.

And with the stars shining down on him he began to fantasize about what it would be like to become a prospector himself.

The next day after work he and O'Rourke went down to the pub for a couple of beers where he discovered it had been a yen of O'Rourke's for many years to go prospecting. In fact if it hadn't been for the war, O'Rourke would've already tried his hand at it.

By profession, O'Rourke was a sub-editor. His last position had been with the weekly *Bulletin* which was basically an outback paper. There was a job waiting for him there now but with his eyes gleaming he confided to Angus he had no intention of going back to spend the rest of his life poring over boring copy.

Angus finished his middy and ordered up another round. 'You're going to Queensland with Petersson, aren't you?' he said.

O'Rourke nodded.

Angus sipped his ice cold beer and studied his friend. 'If Petersson's so sure he knows where there's gold how come he's taking you along? Surely that must mean divvying up the profits?'

'Money, me old sport,' O'Rourke replied with a grin. 'Eric's right out of the stuff. His choice is simple: either he stays over in Sydney for some months putting a new grubstake together or else he takes himself a partner, one who can supply the wherewithal for them both to get going more or less straight away.'

Angus thought about the savings he had stashed. He'd managed to put some money by from his job as clerk and then there was still the bulk of his winnings from the card games aboard the *Wahroonga* – all in all a fair amount.

'Would you and Petersson consider taking me with

you?' he asked suddenly.

O'Rourke looked amused. He'd known this was coming. 'You'd need to put up your ante.'

'How much?'

O'Rourke mentioned a sum well within Angus's means and Angus replied that was fine by him.

'What about your health? I thought you couldn't do any hard work which is precisely what prospecting and mining are?'

Angus replied that was the one big fly in the ointment. Obviously he couldn't do any digging or anything like that. But surely there must be other lighter duties which would need attending to? It would be up to O'Rourke and Petersson to agree to it, of course, but if they would he would do everything that didn't include heavy manual labour.

O'Rourke laughed suddenly. 'Christ almighty, talk about three bloody cripples!' he said. 'You with your bad lungs, me with my gammy leg and Petersson with his rotten eyesight and stomach condition. What a three-some!'

Angus joined in the laughter. It was funny when you thought about it.

They saw Petersson later that day. He said if he was going to take one partner, then why not two? And anyway, the extra money would come in very handy indeed.

All three of them shook hands on it and Petersson produced a bottle of Corio whisky to cement their new partnership.

It took them several weeks to get everything sorted out and during that time Angus took an intensive course in driving. He passed his test first go.

Bill Pettigrew was most upset when Angus told him he'd be leaving, speaking scathingly of the prospectors he'd seen in downtown Sydney, tramps for the most part bumming the price of a beer and only too willing to pay for it with the story of how close they'd come to striking the big one.

Prospecting was a disease, Bill said. It ate into you like a cancer till you could neither live with nor without it. Like the alcoholic who knows only too well that one day the booze will kill him but in the meantime he'll just have one more drink to see him through.

Sure there was gold in the outback. But for every prospector who struck it lucky there were a hundred who didn't.

Petersson was a trained geologist, Angus replied. And what's more O'Rourke believed in him and O'Rourke was well known to be nobody's fool.

Shaking his head, Bill said if Petersson was so damned clever then why hadn't he come up with a strike before now? And from what Angus had told him, Petersson had certainly had enough chances. Once the outback gets hold of you you're lost, Bill went on to say. The outback was the most seductive of mistresses who rarely lets go. And that was where O'Rourke and Petersson were wrong in thinking they'd be the exceptions, that they could get in and out again with the big one under their belts and lie from then on in a bed of roses. •

It was the same self deception nearly every prospector starts out with. Eventually they learn the truth that they aren't the exception at all. And that there's nothing left for them but to keep on prospecting and trekking till one day the land claims them and they vanish forever.

And wasn't Petersson already lost to that way of life? Everything Angus had told him about the man indicated that was so.

Angus had to admit he was shaken a little by the strength and vehemence of Bill's argument. The last thing he wanted was to end up the sort of bum Bill had described. He thought again of the now countless conversations he'd had with O'Rourke and Petersson and Petersson's absolute certainty that there was gold up there on the western slopes of the Great Divide.

His mind was made up, he said, the opportunity too good to miss. Nothing Bill or anyone else could say would dissuade him from going to Queensland.

But forewarned was to be forearmed. Angus swore to himself he wouldn't let the outback get into his blood the way it obviously had Petersson's

He'd give it a year. If they hadn't struck paydirt by then he'd return to Sydney.

Angus brought his thoughts back to the present as he watched Molly emerge from the shower and start to towel herself dry.

She was a barmaid in the hotel they were now in, the Southern Cross. He'd met her the first day he, O'Rourke and Petersson had arrived in Bundegai.

During the first proper conversation they'd had together she'd told him she was from Perth in Western Australia and was gradually making her way round the entire continent. She barmaided mainly but if that wasn't available then she'd do whatever presented itself.

He'd made a rude comment about that and come close to having his face slapped as a consequence. After that he'd been a lot more careful about what he said to Molly Hotblack.

'How's the prospecting going?' she called out as she started dressing.

'Nothing exciting yet. But hell, we haven't been at it all that long.'

She smiled. 'That's what they all say.'

Angus shifted uneasily at that. Her words were too reminiscent of Bill Pettigrew.

'We'll get there in the end,' he said.

'That's what I'm counting on. And you won't forget me when you strike it rich, will you?' she retorted.

'You sound like you're just after my money?'

Her eyes twinkled. 'Too right, sport. Except at the moment you don't have very much.

'Someday I'll be another Carnegie.'

'So you keep saying.'

'I will. I've sworn it.'

She laughed. 'Crazy bloody Scotchman. But I like you.'

'And I like you too. A lot.'

She paused briefly to stare at him. 'Yeh. I reckon you do.'

Angus knew he was falling in love with her – the first time he'd felt anything for another woman since Rosemary.

He couldn't think of two more contrasting women: Rosemary with her elegance and sophistication as opposed to Molly's aggressiveness and sheer volcanic charisma. Both were full-blooded women but in completely different ways.

He put Rosemary from his thoughts. Even after all this time there was still too much pain in thinking about her.

'Come on, let's be having you,' Molly said. 'Time I was downstairs pulling a few schooners.'

Angus rolled from the bed and quickly dressed. His body was lean and tanned, his hair several shades lighter than when he'd first arrived in Australia.

With every passing month he felt better and better, and even more so since coming north to Queensland. The round the clock fresh air and continual sun did him the world of good. Even if they didn't strike gold the experience would've been worth it for his health alone.

He finished dressing the same time she did and together they went downstairs to the huge tiled bar. It was more like a public convenience than a saloon, Angus always thought. He had a quick beer before saying goodbye to Molly and arranging to meet her on her night off two nights hence.

Out in the hot, pounding sun he made his way across to the post office thinking there might be some mail for Petersson who got a considerable amount of correspondence. To his surprise and delight there was a letter for him from home, the first to reach him since the *Almuria* went down.

He made his way back to the Holden station wagon that was owned jointly by him and his two partners. Seating himself comfortably in the driver's seat, he ripped the envelope open. Eagerly he read.

According to Carrie everyone, including herself, was fine. Hugh had joined the a.my and was currently abroad although exactly where she didn't know. Albeit well past retiring age, Donald was still foreman moulder at Armstrong's, and would no doubt continue in harness until either unable to carry on or the war ended.

Winnie was just the same while Harriet was doing extremely well with the Scottish Amalgamated Insurance Company, having far more responsible duties than previous thanks to the acute shortage of men.

Everyone sent their love and Harriet the message she'd once very nearly emigrated to Australia and would be eager to hear all about his stay there once he returned home.

Carrie was naturally concerned to learn of his illness and most relieved to hear he'd recovered all right with only minor after effects.

He'd mentioned, but played down, his lung damage in his letters to her.

She went on to say what a shock it had been to them all to learn of Kitty's death and that his parents had taken it badly, Mrs Kirkpatrick in particular.

The rest of the letter was chit chat but the most significant thing as far as Angus was concerned was not once did his mother either mention or refer to Archie Marjoribanks. That could only mean things were bad between them.

Relief at finally having re-established contact with home was overwhelming, even if there was the worry of his mother and Archie.

He whistled merrily all the way back to camp.

Months passed and two things happened to Angus; on the one hand he became more and more dejected that so far they hadn't even come across a trace of gold, and on the other, he fell more and more deeply in love with Molly Hotblack.

There was something about Molly that drew and held

him like filings to a magnet. He could never get enough of her company and it was always his complaint that their time together passed far too quickly.

Five times now he and the others had resited their camp as they worked themselves away from Bundegai in a sort of semi-circle.

Petersson's spirits remained high despite the fact their money was rapidly dwindling. The gold was out there, he maintained. He could smell it.

Although O'Rourke hadn't said anything to him, Angus knew he too was beginning to have doubts about Petersson. And it would be a long time before O'Rourke would say anything, not being a man who admitted to a mistake or misplaced faith lightly.

What Angus didn't realize about Molly was that she wasn't in love with him. She enjoyed his company and going to bed with him, but as far as she was concerned love had never entered into it.

The other thing Angus didn't know about her was that she was getting itchy feet again. She'd been in Bundegai far too long, she thought. It was high time she was moving onto her next port of call which she'd already decided would be the Alice.

Unaware that the cookout she'd suggested was to be the scene of her telling him she was leaving, Angus drove into Bundegai early on her day off to find her lying on her bed sipping from a cold can.

She'd made up a basket of goodies which he loaded into the back of the car alongside the cold beers he'd bought downstairs in the bar.

'You're quiet today,' he said with a smile as the Holden bounced its way out of Bundegai.

She returned his smile and laid her hand on his thigh. 'Where shall we go, then?' she asked.

'You choose.'

It was a scorching day with the sun really blistering down. There was a heavy smell of eucalyptus in the air mingled with the warm, earthy odour that the ground exuded.

'Somewhere there's a bit of shade,' she replied. 'Otherwise we'll fry.'

They'd had many cookouts and picnics together and it had been their practice to tend to head in the general direction of the camp. This time however it was decided they'd go more west. They stopped finally by an outcrop of rock beside which a small stream tinkled by.

A helluva long way from Sauchiehall Street, Angus thought as he unloaded the car.

'Koala!' said Molly, pointing to a nearby gum tree. And sure enough, there was one of the small bears sitting in the gum's branches regarding them quizzically.

Molly opened a couple of cans while Angus gathered a number of rocks for the fire surround.

While he was doing this Molly kept glancing at him surreptitiously. She knew she was going to hurt him badly and was sorry about that.

It didn't take Angus long to get the fire going and once it had died down a little he put on the steaks and sausages.

After they'd eaten they stretched out in a patch of shade thrown out by the rock. The heat and meal had made Angus langorous but sleep was the furthest thing from his mind.

Catching Molly by the halter he drew her to him. His hand sought and cupped her breast.

'Angus,' she said in a soft voice.

Smiling, he laid his lips on hers and kissed her deeply, enjoying the scent of her hair and flesh crowding his nostrils.

Somewhere a kookaburra laughed, a loud raucous noise that caused Angus's eyes to jerk open. He was about to close them again when a yellow glint from the dying fire caught his attention.

Gently Molly pushed him away. 'I want to speak to you,' she said.

Angus's brow was puckered in a frown. 'About what?' he asked vaguely, his attention elsewhere.

'There's something I have to tell you.'

There it was again, the same yellow glint as before. 'Wait a minute,' he said, and rising, made his way over to the fire.

Molly sighed. He wasn't making it easy for her.

Angus knelt and, using a twig, poked at one of the rocks he'd used for the fire's surround.

'What is it?' Molly asked, coming to stand beside him.

'I'm not sure yet.'

Using the twig, he pulled the rock he was interested in away from the others. It was still extremely hot so he kicked it down to the stream and into the water.

The jagged yellow line was less than half an inch long and appeared to disappear into the depths of the rock. Not having a pick handy Angus smashed the rock against another lying on the stream's bank.

The rock from the fire split wide open and what was revealed caused the breath to catch in Angus's throat.

'Bloody Ada!' he swore.

Lifting the two sections of rock he showed them to Molly. The split open surfaces of each were riddled with thin yellow streaks.

Molly licked her lips and then stared at Angus with eyes huge as saucers. 'Is that what I think it is?' she asked.

There was sweat on Angus's forehead that had nothing to do with the heat. He stared in fascination at the dully gleaming yellow streaks. 'You ever seen gold in this state before?' he asked.

Molly shook her head.

'Me neither. Although Eric's described it to me often enough. And from what he's told me, well. . . this could be just that.'

'What are you going to do?'

Angus grinned suddenly. 'I'm going to jump in the car and drive like hell back to camp.' And throwing back his head he let out the most enormous yell after which he swept Molly into his arms and kissed her.

Within minutes they'd loaded the car and were on their way, the two split sections of rock lying in Molly's lap.

They were halfway to camp when Angus remembered she'd been going to say something to him back there under the overhang of rock.

She shook her head when he asked her what it was. 'Nothing important,' she said. 'Nothing important at all.'

'Well?' Angus demanded.

Petersson lifted his glasses off his nose and using two fingers massaged the corners of his eyes.

'So it isn't then?' Angus said, his voice heavy with disappointment.

'On the contrary,' Petersson replied. 'It is and from the looks of it very best quality.'

'Oh my God!' said O'Rourke. Then looking directly at Angus, 'You beauty! You absolute beaut!'

Petersson's hands were shaking as he spread a map before Angus. 'Now pinpoint exactly where you found it,' he said.

Angus studied the map for a few seconds. Then his forefinger stabbed downwards. 'There's the stream and I'd say . . . just about here would be the place.'

Very carefully Petersson marked the indicated spot on the map with a pencil. 'Right. Let's go and have a look,' he said hoarsely.

Angus drove. And as he was later to remark his driving that day was probably the worst of his life.

The next morning found Angus and O'Rourke sitting round a table in the bar of the Southern Cross Hotel with a jug of beer in front of them. Every few minutes Angus glanced nervously at his watch. They were waiting for Petersson.

When they finished their jug Molly brought them a fresh one. 'He's taking his time,' she whispered.

O'Rourke topped up his glass which he proceeded to glower into.

Molly and Angus exchanged a few words and then she moved away to serve a customer who was loudly demanding her attention.

Another half an hour passed and then suddenly the doors swung open and Petersson strode into the bar. Seeing Angus and O'Rourke, he crossed swiftly to sit at their table.

'It's a bitch,' he stated flatly.

O'Rourke groaned. 'Let's have it,' he whispered.

Petersson glanced round to make sure they couldn't be overheard. Then he said softly, 'The strike is on private property. Belongs to Rawlestone who owns the haberdashery shop here in town.'

'Damn!' Angus swore.

Petersson went on, 'A quarter of a mile further east and we could've staked a claim. It's bastarding bad luck but there we are.'

'You're absolutely certain of this?' O'Rourke asked.

'Positive. It's a small property comprising a little over four thousand acres that the Rawlestones sheep farmed at one time. But apparently Rawlestone's stock got wiped out in the drought of a few years back. The story is that sickened him of sheep which he'd never been madly keen on anyway. And he went into haberdashery instead of restocking.'

'Then he should be willing to sell?' O'Rourke asked.

'I don't see why not as from what I'm told he rarely bothers to even go near the place. But two things, Sean. Number one, where would we get the money to buy a property like that? And two, we're known around here now so the moment we start making inquiries about a purchase he'd be bound to realize we were onto something.'

The three men sat in dejected gloom.

Petersson said, 'I've sent samples off to Sydney for analysis and we should get the results back within the week. I'm pretty certain they'll confirm the ore is of highest quality.' His face suddenly contorted with fury. 'Hell and damnation!' he said vehemently.

'Well, there's no use hanging around here,' O'Rourke said. 'We may as well get back to camp and talk things through there.'

'Wait a minute,' said Angus. 'Now look, I know little enough about prospecting but is it possible at all that as the vein is almost slap bang on that small stream there might well be nuggets in the stream itself?'

Petersson looked thoughtful.

'Well?'

'There's a damn good chance of nuggets *and* dust I'd say.'

'So why don't we have another look at that stream and if we're right, then what's to stop us doing some panning there? If the place if virtually abandoned as Eric here says then who's to know providing we're careful?'

'I'm still not with you?' said Petersson.

But O'Rourke was. 'Jesus, that's smart,' he said admiringly. 'You mean pan enough gold out of the stream to be able to buy the property?' he said.

'If it's possible,' replied Angus.

Petersson whistled.

'And of course once we own the place then we can get down to mining in earnest,' added Angus.

'It could just work,' said Petersson.

'Except for one thing,' interjected O'Rourke. 'Let's say we do get enough dust and nuggets to be able to buy the place, there's still the problem that Eric has already mentioned. An inquiry from us is sure to make Rawlestone suspicious.'

'There's a way round that as well,' said Angus, a smile twisting his mouth upwards. 'I've always rather fancied myself as a farmer and now that I'm about to get married and settle down – and as I've taken a great shine, or should I say, my future wife and I have taken a great shine to Bundegai – wouldn't it be the most natural thing in the world for me to approach Rawlestone to see if he'd be interested in selling?'

'I like it, I like it a lot,' said Petersson.

'But *would* you actually get married?' asked O'Rourke.

'Why not? It's been in my mind for the past few

months anyway.'

'Have you asked her yet?' O'Rourke went on.

'No. But I doubt she'll refuse. We're in love, you see.'

O'Rourke sighed. 'Love. There's only one thing better.'

'What's that?' Angus asked frowning.

'Gold!'

The three of them laughed. Then Petersson said,'I don't know that I quite agree. But I'd sure as hell hate to have to make the choice.'

'Poor Rawlestone,' said Angus shaking his head. 'We'll be paying the poor sod with what is in reality his own money.'

'Beautiful,' said O'Rourke. 'Absolutely beautiful.'

They talked further and it was agreed Petersson and O'Rourke would get back to camp leaving Angus to speak to Molly.

Molly took her lunch break and together she and Angus went up to her room where he recounted to her Petersson's news plus the two solutions he'd come up with.

'Hold on a minute,' she said. 'Let me just get this straight. Providing the three of you can pan enough gold out of that stream, assuming there *is* gold to be panned out, that is, you'll use what that realizes to buy the Rawlestone place, the excuse being you and I are going to set up home there?'

Eyes shining, Angus replied, 'I was going to propose to you anyway. This just gives me the excuse to do it sooner rather than later.'

Molly's mind was whirling. To cover her confusion she took her time about lighting a cigarette. And to think how close she'd come to giving him the elbow! She shuddered inwardly.

At long last, her luck had turned as she'd always believed it would. Her ship was about to come home.

Nor was Angus such a bad catch. He was young and fairly good looking. And there was certainly no hardship about going to bed with him.

'You're not going to turn me down, are you?' Angus asked in sudden alarm, thinking she was taking an awful long time in giving him his answer.

Instantly she was in his arms. Her lips brushed against his cheek and then nibbled at his ear. 'I thought you were never going to ask me,' she whispered.

'Does that mean you accept?'

'Of course.'

His hands swept down the length of her spine to encompass her backside. 'You'll never regret this,' he said.

She smiled over his shoulder. 'I hope not.'

'Let's go down to the bar and announce the news.'

'Later,' she whispered huskily. 'For the moment I've got a better idea.'

And pulling him over to the bed flopped onto it with him on top of her.

'Could you just show me again exactly what I'll be getting,' she whispered provocatively, adding, 'And take your time. There's no hurry.'

While Angus made love to her she dreamed behind closed eyes of fancy clothes. A smart car. A big house. All the things she'd ever wanted and never been able to afford.

It wasn't till it was too late that she remembered her contraceptive device which in the elation of the moment she'd forgotten to use.

After further consideration Petersson, O'Rourke and Angus decided only Petersson would pan the stream where dust and nuggets *were* to be found as Petersson had soon established.

The routine they fell into was that every morning just before dawn Angus would drive Petersson to the stream where he would drop him off, returning to pick him up again after dusk and taking him back again to the camp.

In the meantime Angus and O'Rourke kept up the pretence of prospecting round the site where their camp was pitched. They created the impression everything was going on precisely as it had been before.

On several occasions they altered the routine by taking Petersson into Bundegai so he could show his face as he would normally have done.

By this time Angus had started putting it about that he was rapidly becoming disillusioned with prospecting and was seriously considering looking for another line of work.

Then one night Angus came into town expecting to find Molly serving behind the bar of the Great Southern Hotel only to be informed by another of the bar staff that she was upstairs in bed having been taken ill.

He found her pale and wan with a bucket beside her bed into which she'd thrown up several times.

He immediately said he'd get a doctor but she restrained him saying she'd already been to see one. The doctor had confirmed what she'd suspected for the past few weeks.

It hadn't been too difficult for her to put two and two together, she said. Her breasts had swollen considerably and she'd put on weight round the tummy. She'd also taken to feeling nauseous at various times of the day.

'I'm pregnant,' she stated seeing the penny still hadn't dropped.

For a moment Angus was speechless and then his face lit up with joy. 'A baby!' he whooped. 'We're going to have a baby!'

First the gold and now this. Truly his cup was running over.

'That's bloody marvellous!' he cried, kissing Molly on the cheek and then hugging her.

The pregnancy was a mistake, of course. Molly hadn't intended it happening, children not figuring at all in her plans.

If she'd been able to have herself aborted locally she would have done so without telling Angus. But in a small community like Bundegai abortions just weren't to be had.

'We'll have to get married as soon as possible now,' Angus said striding up and down the room. The plan had been to wait until they nearly had enough dust and nuggets to buy the Rawlestone farm and then have the ceremony. But as far as Angus was concerned that was now out. The sooner they were wed the better.

'How about this Saturday?' he asked. When she agreed, he added she was to leave everything to him. He would do the organizing.

'I can't tell you how happy I am,' he said, sitting on the edge of her bed.

'Me too.'

'I love you Molly,' he murmured awkwardly.

A smile lit up her pallid face. 'And I love you,' she lied.

The ceremony itself was a quiet affair with only Petersson and O'Rourke in attendance, O'Rourke as best man.

But the reception held in the largest room The Great Southern could provide was a marvellously noisy do with what seemed at times like hundreds of people drinking and dancing and having themselves a grand time.

Early on, before it all got out of hand, Petersson and O'Rourke took Angus and Molly quietly aside. Acting as spokesman, Petersson said they hadn't known what to give the couple as a wedding present, but they hoped this would do.

He then handed Molly a gold nugget the size of a small prune which was by far and away the largest he'd so far panned out of the stream.

Molly was enthralled by it, staring at it in the palm of her hand as though it were the Holy Grail.

'We thought maybe later we'd get it mounted for you and make it into a pendant or bracelet, whichever you prefer,' O'Rourke said.

But in the meantime don't show it to anyone,' Petersson added cautioningly.

'I understand,' Molly whispered.

'The other thing is,' O'Rourke went on, 'when everything's set up we want to call it the Lucky Molly Digging. What do you say to that?'

Her reply was to give O'Rourke and Petersson each a kiss on the cheek.

'The Lucky Molly Digging,' she said, her eyes shining, 'I think it's terrific.'

Their conversation was interrupted by Sam Keller, the hotel owner, calling out to them that the band was about to strike up the Gay Gordons, a Scotch dance in honour of a Scotch bridegroom, was how he put it.

'Feel up to it?' Angus asked.

Molly slipped the nugget into her bra. 'Try and stop me,' she replied.

Laughing, Angus led his new wife onto the floor where despite her pregnancy she wheeched and danced with the best of them.

Well Mister McBain what can I do for you?' Con Rawlestone asked. He was a small man with a bald head and a face that had the map of Ireland written all over it.

'Angus, please.'

'All right, Angus, and you can call me Con.'

They were sitting in the Rawlestone's front parlour, Angus having called after the shop was shut.

It was over four months since Petersson had started panning the stream. It had taken him that long to get enough dust and nuggets together to cover the cost of what they'd worked out the Rawlestone place was worth.

'As you know I recently got married,' Angus started, 'and now we've got a family on the way ...'

'Congratulations!' Rawlestone interjected.

'Thank you,' Angus smiled, then going on, 'I've decided it's time I settled down and stopped prospecting which, to tell you the truth, I've been getting rather tired of anyway.'

Angus then went on to give Con Rawlestone the spiel that had been agreed on and refined over the past few months by his two partners and Molly.

When Angus had finished Rawlestone rubbed his chin and looked thoughtful. 'If I was willing to sell, and I'm not saying I'm not, would you be able to afford it, Angus? I'd be wanting the full market value you understand.'

'Oh aye, of course,' replied Angus, nursing the small whisky Rawlestone had handed him. 'Well what would be your asking price then?'

Rawlestone named a figure which was slightly less than Angus had been expecting. There was more than enough in a Sydney bank – the money had been deposited in Sydney by O'Rourke a few weeks previously. He'd gone on the pretext of seeing his mother but in reality to cash in the gold Petersson had panned and to credit the money to an account in Angus's name.

Angus nodded slowly, as though turning the price over in his mind. Finally he said, 'Aye, well I think that's fair enough, Con. You stick to that sum and we'll call it a deal.'

Rawlestone looked surprised. 'You've got that much?'

'It certainly hasn't come from prospecting, I can tell you,' Angus replied, laughing.

'No, it's money from home in Scotland, a legacy I've had put by for years for just such an occasion as this,' pretended Angus.

That explanation obviously satisfied Rawlestone who poured more whisky, after which it was agreed they'd start proceedings for the sale the very next day.

Leaving Rawlestone, Angus went straight to the Great Southern Hotel where he found an anxious O'Rourke and Petersson in the bar.

'We're on,' he said with a smile.

The three of them looked gratifyingly at one another.

'For us, the digger's dream is about to come true,' Petersson said in a soft voice.

'Amen,' added O'Rourke.

Angus went up to the bar from behind which Molly had been watching him anxiously.

'We'll soon have a home of our own,' he said.

Big as his smile was, it didn't match hers.

The day after the sale was completed Angus picked Molly up from the Great Southern and drove her out to the farmhouse. Her days as a barmaid were now over.

He'd been out to the farmhouse twice that day already, dropping off bits and pieces of furniture and other household items they'd acquired.

Shooing Angus out the door, Molly set about putting everything just the way she wanted it.

As houses went it was a bit of a dump, she thought. But it would do for a start, considering what went with it.

'The Lucky Molly Digging,' she mused aloud. It was music to her ears.

One day a few weeks later word spread like wildfire round Bundegai that gold had been discovered on the old Rawlestone property now owned by Angus McBain.

Con Rawlestone was beside himself with anger when he heard and the first thing he did was consult a solicitor.

He was even more furious when the solicitor told him there was no legal action he could take. Angus had bought the place fair and square. Con had no comeback whatever.

Con then went about telling everyone he'd been cheated as Angus and his cronies must've known there was gold on the place before Angus bought it.

But rather than gaining sympathy for himself all he accomplished was to make people admire Angus. As one of the townfolk put it, who amongst them wouldn't have done the same thing had they been in Angus's shoes.

When Con heard that he thought about it for a while. Then with bad grace he accepted the situation: in his heart he knew Angus hadn't done anything he wouldn't have had the positions been reversed. Still, it was a bitter pill to swallow.

Molly was dishing out the evening meal to Angus,

O'Rourke and Petersson when the first pain came.

Gasping, Molly staggered and clutched onto the sink for support. Instantly Angus was by her side. 'The baby?' he asked anxiously.

She nodded, grinding her teeth together as a second pain seared through her.

O'Rourke came to his feet. 'You get her to bed and I'll get the doc.' Without further ado he was out the front door and seconds later the Holden roared into life and drove off.

Angus helped Molly through to their bedroom where as gently as he could he stripped her and managed to get her into a clean nightie.

'Jesus, these pains are coming quickly,' Molly said. 'I only hope the doc gets here before the baby does.'

'Me too,' said Angus. The thought of having to deliver the child himself was too awful even to contemplate.

Despite her pain, Molly couldn't help but laugh at the expression on Angus's face. She couldn't remember ever having seen a man look so terrified in such a comical way.

While Angus waited with Molly, Petersson put some water on to boil. Having done that, and with nothing else to occupy him in the meantime, he got down to doing the digging's weekly figures and accounts.

The digging was doing excellently, especially since some heavy equipment they'd sent to Brisbane for had arrived, enabling them to work far more efficiently and at greater speed.

Another six to nine months at their present rate and yield and the money would really be rolling in. By then the work would be far too much for the three of them and they'd have to hire more men.

Through in the bedroom Molly jerked her head back and screamed.

Where's the bloody doctor! Angus thought. Knowing even as he did so that O'Rourke and the doctor would be making as good time as was possible.

'There, there, love,' he soothed, holding Molly's

shoulder as her lips stretched back into a fearful grimace, the prelude to another excruciating pain.

Angus was only too well aware that Carrie had had a most difficult birth in delivering him. Indeed she'd come close to losing her life as a result of his having been in an awkward position. He knew this from having overheard a conversation between his mother and Winnie when he was a young lad. His worry now was – and it had been preying on his mind for the past few months – that being his child Molly was carrying she might somehow experience the same difficulty.

'It'll be all over soon,' he said, the smile on his face belying his sweat drenched forehead.

A little later the pains went off and Molly was able to relax somewhat.

'How do you feel?' he asked.

'What a bloody stupid question! How do you think I feel? Like a screeching bloody sheila whose insides are being ripped apart and whose backside feels like it's getting all set to drop off, that's what!'

Angus grinned. It *had* been a bloody stupid question.

Suddenly Molly grinned back. 'This'll teach me to get so hot and bothered I forget my cap,' she said. And they both laughed, relaxing the tension that had been built up in the room.

Ten minutes later O'Rourke arrived with the doctor who banished Angus from the bedroom while he got on with it.

For the next hour and a half Angus paced up and down, watched silently by O'Rourke and Petersson. Twice the doctor called for things which Angus immediately sprang to get. Neither time was he allowed back into the bedroom but handed the articles over to the doctor at the bedroom door.

Suddenly the screams stopped. Those waiting were in no doubt that something had happened. A strange calm settled on the house, a calm that was shattered a few seconds later by the thin, piercing wail of a newborn child.

A few minutes later the doctor emerged looking hugely pleased with himself. 'Congratulations,' he said. 'You've got a son.'

'A son!' Angus echoed.

'As fine a boy as any man could wish for.'

Shaking as though he was the father himself O'Rourke reached for the whisky bottle that had been put out in preparation and poured four large ones.

'Was there any particular trouble?' Angus asked.

'Nope,' the doctor said, accepting a glass from O'Rourke. 'Everything was completely straightforward.

Relief welled through Angus when he heard that.

'To the boy!' toasted Petersson.

'John McBain,' said Angus. It had been agreed between him and Molly that if they had a son they'd call him after his father.

'To John McBain!' O'Rourke, Petersson and the doctor toasted in unison.

'I think you'd better go away in and see them now,' said the doctor.

Squaring his shoulders Angus went through to tell his wife how well she'd done and to see his newborn son.

The months after young John's birth passed quickly for all those involved at the Lucky Molly.

Molly discovered what a full time job it was looking after a baby. With Angus giving what help he could, O'Rourke and Petersson spent long hour after long hour delving ever deeper into the ore bed.

But after such a marvellous beginning things were going from bad to worse, the yield continually decreasing and falling off in quality.

Petersson became gaunt and hollow-eyed with worry, assuring Angus and O'Rourke over and over this had to be a temporary setback and that both yield and quality must pick up again.

Molly lost her exuberance and flamboyance to become more and more withdrawn. When she and Angus found themselves alone during the day he was always aware of her gaze riveted to him as though he was some sort of specimen on a microscope slide.

Then one day their worst fears were realized when the ore bed suddenly and quite dramatically came to an end.

Stunned, the three men stood in the huge excavation they'd created looking at one another.

Petersson attempted a smile which never even came close to coming off. 'Perhaps it's only a break in the bed or then again it might well be that . . .'

'Bullshit!' O'Rourke interjected. 'The fucker's played out. You know that as well as I do.'

'No,' said Peterson, his voice trembling. 'You're wrong.'

'He's right,' said Angus. Then tapping his heart, 'I can feel it here.'

'What do you know about it?' said Petersson scornfully. 'Are you the geologist or am I?'

'You are. But right now you're talking with your emotions and not your head.'

'There *is* more gold down there,' sad Petersson dogmatically. 'There has to be.'

'It looked so promising too,' said O'Rourke wistfully. 'From the way it started I was sure it would go on forever. Just shows how wrong you can be.'

'A bust,' said Angus, shaking his head. 'Who would have thought it?'

Petersson lumbered across to the mechanical digger and climbed into its cockpit. Without another word he set the neanderthal looking machine in action, a look of fierce determination on his face as the digger's metal claw tore and savaged into the hard packed earth they'd discovered beneath the ore bed.

O'Rourke gestured to Angus and together they climbed out of the excavation.

As they walked towards the house O'Rourke said, 'Petersson told me months ago that was the only ore bed on the property. With the quality and yield we were getting then that didn't bother us unduly as we were convinced the bed was a deep one. It seems we were wrong. You might say the Lucky Molly just ran out of luck.'

Angus hated the thought of breaking it to Molly. They'd made so many plans together, built up so many dreams.

Angus said, 'Well we haven't come out of it with nothing at all. There's the property which we can sell plus whatever we can get from the equipment we bought.'

Although the property had originally been in Angus's name it had shortly after purchase been stipulated in the deeds that it was jointly and equally owned by the three of them.

'I think I'm going to get drunk out of my skull,' said O'Rourke. 'And if ever a man needed an excuse for doing that then I reckon we three have a beaut.'

Angus was bemused by what had happened. Although he'd seen it coming it was still a profound shock that it had actually happened. Like the condemned man, he'd been secretly convinced there'd be a last minute reprieve.

Once in the house O'Rourke took himself off to his bedroom with a bottle of brandy. Angus found Molly in the kitchen feeding John.

He sat heavily beside her, slumping forward and cradling his head in his hands.

'The bed's run out,' he said.

The colour drained from her face. The threatened nightmare of recent weeks had become reality. 'That's it, then?' she croaked.

'That's it.'

'You're absolutely certain?'

'Petersson seems to think he can pick it up again but he's kidding himself. The Lucky Molly was a nine day wonder and today was day ten.'

Anger bubbled in Molly which she swiftly brought under control. 'What happens now?' she asked.

'I don't know. We'll have to discuss that.'

Molly plucked the now empty feeding bottle from John's mouth who immediately began to cry. Irritation creased her face as she jiggled him up and down on her lap.

Angus stared lovingly at his son. The wee fellow was the spitting image of him which naturally enough tickled him pink.

'Want me to take him?' he asked.

Molly passed John over and then went looking for a cigarette. 'What a mess,' she said through a cloud of smoke.

'It isn't the end of the world,' Angus replied. 'Nothing ever is. And let's look on the bright side. We've got one another and the baby. As far as I'm concerned, that's worth more than all the gold that was ever dug out of the ground.'

Molly looked sour, her expression making it quite clear she didn't agree.

O'Rourke appeared from his bedroom holding the brandy bottle by the neck. 'You've told the little lady I take it,' he said.

Angus nodded.

'A sad day Molly, eh?'

'You can say that again. And are you going to hold onto that bottle forever or are you going to pass it round?'

Molly coughed as the liquor burned its way down her throat. Handing the bottle back, she crossed to the window and stared out, her eyes taking on a faraway look as though she was seeing something way beyond the horizon.

'Penny for them?' Angus asked eventually.

'Nothing important,' she replied. Her voice sounded as though it came from a far distance.

'Come on, tell me,' he coaxed.

She turned and stared at him. 'I was just thinking of all the things we were going to do. Places we were going to go. The house we were going to have. The clothes. The cars.'

'I'm sorry Molly,' Angus said softly. 'I'd cut off my right arm for you if it would change things. But it wouldn't. The digging's a bust and we're just going to have to learn to live with the fact.'

'These little things are sent to try us,' said O'Rourke. 'Very character building you know.'

Molly looked as though she was about to retort angrily when suddenly John was sick all down his front.

'I'll deal with that,' she said wearily, taking John from Angus and crossing over to the sink where she began changing the wee lad.

'She's a wonderful mother,' said Angus proudly.

O'Rourke swallowed some more brandy.

For another week Petersson worked at the digging on his own before finally admitting defeat.

That evening the three men and Molly held a conference during which it was decided to advertise the property statewide in the hope they'd quickly come up with a buyer.

The equipment Petersson would sell through various private contacts he had.

The night Angus and Molly lay wide awake in bed. 'I think we should go to Sydney,' Angus said after a while. 'We'll stay with O'Rourke's mother till we can find a small flat of our own.'

Molly winced at the word small. 'And what about work?'

'I've told you about Bill Pettigrew who employed me as a clerk. Bill was very fond of me, looked on me as a son almost. He said when I left that I could have my old job back any time.'

'A clerk,' said Molly softly, a hint of contempt in her voice.

'There are big prospects in the building trade, Bill says,' Angus went on. 'Give it a couple of years and who knows? I might even start my own firm.'

To Molly it all sounded like pie in the sky. And suddenly she was feeling trapped and deathly afraid. She could see the years stretching ahead of her. No more fun. No more laughter. Instead the worry of having a child and husband to care for with little money coming into the house. What did a clerk earn? She didn't know but she was sure it was hellish little.

As for the brat now fast asleep in his cot at the far side of the room, she'd never wanted him in the first place. Oh, the idea of a child had been bearable when it had seemed she wouldn't be tied down to him indefinitely. A nanny or baby nurse had been high on her list of priorities once the money started flooding in.

But with the collapse of the Lucky Molly there would now be no nanny or baby nurse which meant she personally would have to continue looking after the brat who seemed to be never endingly performing at one end or the other.

And as for Angus, her knight in shining armour had turned out to be like so many other men she'd known in the past. Namely a dead loss. Big on promises but very short on delivery.

Angus with bundles of money was one thing. But Angus as a clerk in a small building firm was quite another.

Christ! she raged inwardly. What a Godawful mess she'd got herself into. Well she was damned if she was going to let herself be sucked into playing the suburban housewife with sprog. The very thought was anathema.

What she wanted was freedom. Laughs. Fun! God-almighty she was still young yet with her whole life stretching ahead of her. And who knew what might be waiting for her round the next bend? Or should she say *who?*

'Molly, you still awake?'

'Uh-huh.'

His hand slipped up her thigh and into the nest of her crotch.

Despite what she'd been thinking she found herself wanting him.

'I'll give you all the things we talked about Molly. I'll find a way. I promise you.'

'Of course you will,' she replied, wriggling under his

probing fingers.

She accepted him into her arms, enjoying what he did to her and how he made her feel.

And as they made love she worked out the best time for her to leave next day to catch the mid-morning bus that went through Bundegai.

Directly after breakfast next morning Molly said she wanted to go into Bundegai to get some things from the chemist's. And as Angus wasn't working would he mind looking after John?

The three men had already decided during breakfast that they'd spend the morning drafting letters to the various agents and newspapers with whom they were going to advertise the property. Petersson had the additional job of writing to his personal contacts regarding the equipment. So it was no great trouble for Angus to take care of the wee lad.

Angus did wonder briefly why Molly was taking a small case with her but at the back of his mind put it down to some other business she probably had in town.

''Bye then,' Molly said when she was finally ready.

'Don't I get a kiss?'

Smiling, she came back from the door and kissed him on the cheek. Then as an afterthought she bent and kissed John.

'Don't be too long,' Angus said.

Molly smiled again, but didn't reply.

With John cradled in his arms Angus stood and watched the Holden roar off towards Bundegai.

'Now shall we get down to it,' said O'Rourke who was seated at the table beside an extremely morose looking Petersson.

Angus turned his attention to the drafting of the advertisements.

Lunchtime came and went. She must've got tied up, Angus thought. But when afternoon gave way to evening he began to get worried.

'Maybe she's had an accident?' he said to O'Rourke.

'Car's broken down most likely,' O'Rourke replied.

'Aye, no doubt you're right,' said Angus, relieved at this most obvious of explanations. After all, hadn't the same thing happened to Petersson a few weeks previously?

A little later Angus put John down for the night, after which the three men sat playing cards.

At one Petersson went to bed shortly followed by O'Rourke.

For hours Angus kept vigil in a chair facing the door. He dropped off just as dawn was breaking.

The next thing he knew he was being shaken by O'Rourke saying John was awake and crying.

He changed the baby's nappy and fed him. Then the three men had breakfast.

'That's the trouble with not having a phone,' O'Rourke said over coffee. 'Makes situations like this a lot more dramatic than they are.'

'I was thinking just before I nodded off,' Angus said slowly, 'if Molly did have to leave the car in the garage overnight surely they would have loaned her one till she picked the Holden up again? I mean isn't that what they usually do when someone lives out of town?' And when O'Rourke didn't have a reply to that he added, 'I'll give her till ten then if you'll watch John for me I'll start walking into town.

On the stroke of ten Angus set out for Bundegai. He trudged for an hour and a half before being picked up by a passing vehicle which dropped him outside the Great Southern.

There were three garages in Bundegai and he was en route to the nearest one when he spied the Holden parked outside the post office. The car's doors were locked but there was a piece of paper jammed up against the inside of the windscreen which said: 'Angus, keys in post office.'

Having retrieved the keys he opened the car door and slid inside. The piece of paper in the windscreen turned out to be a letter.

As he read his head grew numb. It seemed as though he was standing in the middle of an ice cold wind although it was broiling out.

He read the letter through twice, then folded it and put it into his trouser pocket. Seeing and hearing nothing, he drove the Holden out of Bundegai and back to the farmhouse.

As he drew up O'Rourke came out onto the porch with John in his arms. 'Has she been taken crook then?' he called out on seeing Angus was alone.

Angus joined O'Rourke on the porch, taking John from him and holding the wee fellow close.

'She's gone,' he said, his voice trembling.

'What do you mean, gone?'

'Just that. Lit out for parts unknown.'

'You mean she's left you and the baby?'

Angus nodded.

'Why, the rotten galah!' O'Rourke exploded.

'I found the car with a letter in it,' Angus said after a few seconds. 'She says she's sorry but she couldn't yet face life as a suburban hausfrau as she put it. Before leaving she withdrew what money we had in our joint account. She apologized for that but pointed out I'd have my share from the sale of this place to keep me going.'

'I don't understand,' said O'Rourke.

'I do . . . now. I thought she loved me but I was wrong. What she was in love with was the money she saw The Lucky Molly bringing in.'

O'Rourke swore vehemently, his face flushing and his eyes sparking with anger.

Angus stared down at John who was gurgling happily in his arms. 'Well I'll never desert you, boy. You can stake your life on that,' he said.

'You mean you're going to look after the kid all by yourself?' O'Rourke asked.

'I may need some help. But I'll never have him adopted or fostered. He's my son and we're staying together.

That's the way it's going to be.'

O'Rourke remained on the porch while Angus took
John inside. He couldn't remember when he'd last been
so moved.

During the next month several people turned up to look
the property over but none of them made an offer.

In the meantime Petersson had sunk into a deep
depression and had taken to camping out at night all on
his own. Going walkabout at one point, he disappeared
for over a week.

O'Rourke tried his hand at panning the stream but his
efforts produced little dust and no nuggets. Petersson
had taken out nearly all the gold there was to be had
there.

One month became two and still they hadn't found a
buyer. Then one afternoon while Angus was changing
John and O'Rourke was busy trimming the lamps an
excited Petersson burst into the house.

'We've done it! We've done it! We've bloody well
done it!' he yelled, dancing on the spot like an Irishman
trying to keep pace with a demented fiddler.

'Done what?' queried Angus.

'All this time staring me in the face and me not having
the wit to see it!' crowed Petersson.

O'Rourke caught Petersson by the arm and forced
him to stand still. 'Will you please tell us just what it is
you're raving on about?' O'Rourke demanded.

With eyes seeming about to burst from his head
Petersson said, 'I first noticed it early last week. Although God knows I should've seen it long before then.
The trouble is I suppose when you're looking specifically
for one thing you just don't take in what else is there. Or
at least I didn't.'

'I'm lost,' said Angus.

'When it finally did dawn I took samples from all over
the property and sent them to Sydney for analysis. I've
just come from Bundegai now. The results of those
analyses were in today's mail.'

'You haven't found more gold?' O'Rourke asked quickly.'

'Not gold. Bauxite!' Having said that, Petersson looked from O'Rourke to Angus. But if he was expecting a reaction then he was disappointed. Angus and O'Rourke both stared at him blankly.

'Bauxite,' Petersson repeated.

'What's that?' Angus asked.

'The stuff they smelt aluminium from.'

Again there was no reaction.

'Alufuckingminium!' Petersson shouted in desperation. 'There's a war on and that's one of the metals the government is crying out for. And this entire farm is sitting square on top of a mountain of the stuff.'

Slowly it dawned on Angus just what Petersson was saying.

'Does that mean we're going to be rich after all?' he asked.

'Rich! The three of us are going to be each as rich as Croesus!' Petersson roared.

O'Rourke made a sort of gobbling sound and sat heavily on the nearest chair. He looked like a man who'd just been hit over the head with a sledgehammer.

Like O'Rourke, Angus was completely stunned by this bolt out of the blue. 'You're sure there's no mistake?' he asked in a whisper.

'Not this time,' Petersson replied, and whooped with joy.

Angus took a deep breath and then glanced down at John cradled in his arms. That was who the money would benefit in the long run. He'd make sure of it.

The very best of everything. That would be John's life thanks to a mountain of Bauxite and Petersson's unswerving digger's dream.

He thought of Molly then and the irony of her having left when she did. He could just imagine her face when she heard the news.

Then suddenly O'Rourke was on his feet screaming and yelling and dancing an impromptu jig with Petersson.

Angus hugged John tight against his chest. Later a great deal of serious thinking would have to be done, plans to be made, but for now he was content to give himself over to the madness Petersson had brought into their midst.

Part IV

Goodbye Yesterday

1946–1947

18

Carrie was dying and was reconciled to the fact.

She lay in bed thinking of the letter Harriet, on her instruction, had written Angus a few months previously informing him of the situation.

His reply had come by return saying he and John would be sailing on the first available ship.

Carrie gritted her teeth and stifled a groan. The plaster corset round her middle was giving her gyp. It had done ever since it had been put on. The corset was to help the sciatica the doctor said she had.

But there was a lot more to her condition than merely that. Her body was completely worn out. The ravages of years of TB and mistreatment at the hands of Archie Marjoribanks had finally taken their toll.

She was forty-five years old and looked sixty.

There was a photograph standing on her bedside table which she glanced at occasionally. It showed Angus holding up young John outside the farmhouse where they lived. It had pleased her enormously that Angus had called his son after his father. Thinking of it never failed to bring a lump to her throat.

Over at the window Harriet stood staring out. She was dressed in her inevitable black with her hair drawn severely back in a bun. Like Carrie, she was thin and wasted, but in her case it was entirely self-inflicted by her almost constant diet of cigarettes and tea. Her thoughts were with the Scottish Amalgamated Insurance

Company and its Glasgow branch, in particular. She'd been in charge of the branch for a number of years now. But with the war over and the men returning home she would soon have to step down and resume her previous position of secretary.

She was going to miss dreadfully the power and responsibility. But there was no way the company was going to promote her officially into an executive position, albeit her ability was well proven.

It was one thing for her to step into her boss's shoes in wartime. Another entirely for her to stay there or assume another position of that nature once peace had been achieved.

She saw it as one more major frustration in a life filled with them.

Carrie started coughing, dry, racking spasms that shook her entire frame. The hand she held to her mouth was skeletal, each bone distinct. The skin covering those bones was yellowishly opaque and like an old leaf to the touch.

Harriet immediately left her vantage point by the window to help Carrie reach a glass of water. As she held Carrie close she knew the only thing keeping her sister alive was Carrie's dogged determination to see Angus again and hold her grandson for the first time.

When the coughing fit was finally over Carrie lay back on the bed and closed her eyes. As she drifted off she thought how much more comfortable she'd be without the damned corset. But she also knew she wouldn't order Dr Robertson to remove it in case she somehow reduced the precious time left her.

When she fell asleep she dreamt of the happy days when she'd been married to John McBain and life, though hard, had been glorious for the pair of them.

Through in the living room Donald was sitting in his chair reading the day's paper. He was retired now having been told directly after VJ day his time at Armstrong's was finished.

He had taken over an allotment after Winnie had gone

on at him incessantly to do so. But his heart wasn't really in it. Growing vegetables on a wee plot was fine as a hobby but it was hardly a day's work for a man.

He missed unbearably the bedlam of the foundry, the roar of the blast furnaces, the dazzling liquidity of molten metal, the pride of a job – his type of job – well done.

Rising, he made his way through to the hall where he stood wondering whether or not to go through and see Carrie. He decided against it when he heard the sound of soft snoring coming from her room.

With Harriet in the house to look after Carrie should she wake he decided to take a dauner along by the Cart. That should fritter away a good hour which would bring him home just as Winnie returned from getting in the messages.

As he walked down the close stairs he thought about Alex being the first of their brood to go. And now Carrie was about to be the second.

The one blessing was she wasn't in the least scared of dying. If any thing, she was looking forward to it as she was convinced somewhere in some form John McBain would be waiting for her.

He could only hope and pray she was right.

Clad in a badly fitting demob suit Hugh stepped off the train at the Central Station. He still couldn't believe he'd emerged from the war completely unscathed. After what he'd been through it seemed a miracle to him he was actually home again in one piece.

Not only that, but there was a wife waiting to greet him and a wee baby daughter whom he hadn't yet seen.

It had been a great disappointment to him to learn Janey had given birth to a girl. But he'd consoled himself in the knowledge the wee lassie was perfect in every detail. And there was nothing to stop him and Janey having a boy next time round.

He made for the Broomielaw from where he'd be able to catch a tram for Muirend. On a sudden impulse he continued on down to the suspension bridge which took him over the gently flowing Clyde and into the Gorbals.

To another's eyes, the dirty, squalid tenements – the air hard and rasping from the sooty smoke belching out of their innumerable chimneys – might have jarred. But to Hugh they were a joy to behold as they confirmed he was home again in the city where his roots ran deep and which he so loved.

He walked as far as the Star Bar and Plaza dancehall opposite. My God, he remembered that night all right! He ran the last few yards to a stop where he caught a tram. As the tram rattled on its way he thought of Kenny White who'd introduced him to Janey. He'd been killed in North Africa.

Janey was scraping potatoes when she heard the front door open and close again.

At first she didn't recognize the man standing in the kitchen doorway staring at her in such a quizzical fashion. Then with a cry she dropped the knife and potato and rushed across the floor into his arms.

There was so much she wanted to say but for the moment no words came.

Lifting Janey's chin, Hugh kissed her, not a passionate kiss but rather one of sheer pleasure at their reunification.

Breaking away, Janey used the edge of her hand to wipe the tears from her face. Still too overcome to speak, she beckoned him to follow and hastened towards the door.

The child lay fast asleep in her cot, her face pink and angelic, the mouth puckered up as though she was blowing him a kiss on this the event of his seeing her for the first time.

'Mary Agnes,' Janey said, the words trembling from her mouth.

She was a bonnie baby with a definite look of the Chisholms about her. His heart went out to the wean and he quickly put to the back of his mind the regret she wasn't a boy. A lassie would do him just fine – for the moment.

Janey would have woken Mary Agnes but Hugh restrained her. They returned to the kitchen where Janey busied herself brewing a pot of tea.

She was putting this by to mask when he asked her where Greta Paterson was? He was looking forward to seeing his old friend again.

Janey turned a suddenly stricken face towards him and asked if he hadn't got her recent letters?

He replied that the last letter he'd received had been a little over six weeks previously.

Janey poured him a cup and as she handed it to him said Greta had been dead and buried a month now. Death, according to the autopsy, was due to kidney failure.

Janey went on to say how close she and Greta had become during the past few years, particularly after Mary Agnes had been born as Greta had doted on the child. She'd seized on Mary Agnes as a substitute for her own grandchildren so tragically killed by German bombs.

Janey said Hugh had taken the place of the dead Stewart in Greta's mind with herself replacing Stewart's wife. Greta had come to think of and refer to their small family as her own.

Hugh was well pleased his old friend had found some comfort in having Janey and Mary Agnes to stay with her. That at least went a little way to repaying the multitude of kindnesses she and Aly had lavished on him.

Hugh frowned suddenly, the thought striking him their position here at Muirend was now extremely precarious. After all it was unlikely the new owners – presumably Greta's next of kin – would be keen on their presence in the house and no doubt they'd be given notice to quit.

It was also quite feasible a new manager would be appointed in his place – new broom and all that.

A soft, loving smile curled the corners of Janey's

mouth as she stared at the dejected Hugh. It was almost worth her last letters going astray so she could tell him the good news herself.

Her smile widened as she told him that directly after the funeral she'd received a communication asking her to call on Greta's solicitors. On presenting herself she'd been ushered into the presence of the senior partner who'd told her in accordance with his late client's will the entire Muirend estate plus the farm on the East Kilbride road had been left to one Hugh Chisholm, a Paterson employee currently serving with His Majesty's Armed Forces.

So taken aback was Hugh he made Janey repeat what she'd just told him.

'My God!' he whispered when she'd finished for the second time. Crossing to the window, he stared out over the yard to the stables beyond. To think all this was now his was simply unbelievable! And the last thing in the world he'd expected.

He knew Greta had some distant relatives but Janey said that Greta hadn't wanted them to have the place as they would've only sold it. And anyway, they were more than comfortably off and didn't need any addition to their bank balances.

Hugh and Janey both loved the house and dairy and because of this she preferred everything to go to them, just as it would've gone to Stewart and his family had they still been alive.

Hugh was suddenly aware of Janey standing by his side, her face beaming as she stared up at him.

Catching her in his arms he announced his intention of taking her upstairs to bed to celebrate his safe return and their stroke of stupendous good luck.

They were halfway up the stairs when Janey remembered to tell him on top of everything else there was also £2653 in a joint bank account she'd opened in their names. This was the cash savings Greta had left and which had also come their way.

Their combined laughter was so loud it woke Mary

Agnes so they didn't get to bed right away after all. . . .

Three weeks to the day after Hugh arrived back in
Glasgow the late train from London brought Angus and
John. With them was a girl from Bundegai called Dawn
Schroeder who'd been acting as nanny to John since
shortly after Molly had flown the coop.

Having disembarked from the train Angus booked
them into the Central Station Hotel where Angus had no
trouble getting them a suite with two bedrooms, one for
him and the other for Dawn and John.

After being shown to their suite Dawn busied herself
with John who'd been fractious during the latter part of
their long journey up from Southampton.

While Dawn got John ready for bed Angus stood by a
window looking out on the city, which gave the impression of having had its life juices bled from it. The people
he'd seen so far had thin, pinched faces as grey as the
buildings surrounding them.

Tanned and fleshed out, he might have belonged to
another species altogether so stark was the contrast.

Sighing, he poured himself a glass of whisky. As he
sipped, his mind flew back to Australia and his affairs
there. The bauxite strike had been everything, and
more, Petersson had said it would.

The original digging had been abandoned and a new
site opened. This had grown rapidly into what was now
known as the Lucky Molly Bauxite Mine – LMBM for
short – employing close on a hundred people.

O'Rourke had taken over as overall administrator and
was proving superb at the job. As for Petersson, once
the mine had been opened, he'd moved on to pastures
new. He'd been last heard of up on the Northern Territory prospecting for silver he was convinced was to be
found there.

Of course Petersson didn't need to do any further
prospecting as he, like Angus and O'Rourke, was now a
very rich man with the prospect of those riches reaching
mind boggling proportions. But with the outback and

prospecting deep in his blood he needed – as Bill Pettigrew had once warned Angus nearly always happened to prospectors – to keep up his erstwhile mode of life the way a junkie needs another fix.

O'Rourke also had caught the bug although to a lesser degree than Petersson. With him it was merely the outback. As he often said, he could no more imagine himself going back to live in an urban situation than he could flying in the air.

If asked, Angus would have had to admit he too had almost fallen for the seductions of the outback. But what had saved him was an older love and craving – that for his native Glasgow which surmounted all else.

As for Molly, and he smiled grimly thinking about it, she'd been back like the proverbial shot once she'd learned of the bauxite strike. In vain she'd pleaded with him for them to take up where they'd left off but he'd have none of it.

He'd loved her once. But that love had been blown away like so much chaff in the wind the day she deserted him and John. Stripped of the emotional tie he'd even come to feel quite repulsed by her.

In agreement for a divorce he'd made a reasonable settlement on her, far more than she deserved, he reckoned. But she had given him John and for that he owed her something.

Angus's musings were interrupted by Dawn calling out to say John wanted to be kissed goodnight. This he did with all the warmth and love he bore his son.

It didn't take John long to drop off, worn out as he was by the journey and excitement.

Dawn joined Angus for a drink. The relationship between Angus and Dawn was strictly a business one. They liked one another, enjoyed one another's company, but that was as far as it went. The truth was that physically neither was particularly attracted to the other.

Angus nervously paced up and down the room, desperate to go out to Tallon Street and see Carrie.

When he told Dawn he was considering going on his

own she pooh-poohed the idea saying it was far too late and all he would succeed in doing was waking his mother when no doubt what the poor woman needed was all the sleep she could get.

Dawn was right, he decided reluctantly. It was best be bided his patience till the morning when he could take John with him.

It was a decision he'd regret for the rest of his life.

Tallon Street was smaller and meaner than he remembered it.

His heart was thudding as he rapped on the so familiar door at the top of the close. Behind him Dawn wiped John's nose and checked the wee fellow was neat, tidy and a credit to his father.

The door opened and Winnie was there staring at Angus as though he were a stranger. Then the penny dropped.

'Oh, son!' she said in a tremulous voice.

He knew then he'd come too late. 'When?' he asked.

'Last night,' Winnie replied. Had he come to Tallon Street when he'd wanted to he would have caught Carrie just before she'd died.

Realizing she was keeping them standing on the doorstep Winnie brought them in, gesturing towards the living room where she said Donald and Harriet were.

Hugh had already been but had returned to Muirend to see to the milk. He'd be back as soon as he could.

The family knew all about Dawn, Angus having carefully explained about her in the last letter he'd written.

As John came abreast of Winnie she bent and swept the wee fellow into her arms. Kissing him on both cheeks. Then holding him at arms' length she said, 'A fine lad, the living image of his dad. Carrie would have been so proud.'

Donald was waiting just inside the living room door and the first thing he did when Angus entered the room was to throw his arms round Angus's shoulders and squeeze his grandson tightly. All he said, was 'Aye, well there we are, then.'

Harriet had been crying as was obvious from her red rimmed eyes. She embraced Angus after her father had let him go.

When everyone had been introduced and a bit of a fuss made of John, Donald said to the very last Carrie had been smiling and joking, assuring everyone they weren't going to get rid of her until she'd seen Angus again and held the wee chap named after her John in her arms. But she'd been wrong.

When she died Angus's name was on her lips.

Dawn was distraught remembering it was she who'd dissuaded Angus from coming the previous night. But he dismissed her self condemnation saying the argument she'd put forward had been a valid one.

If he blamed anyone it was himself. He should've followed his instincts.

He asked to see his mother's body and Harriet volunteered to take him through to the bedroom where Carrie was laid out.

He'd brought a number of presents along and one of these he now sorted out from the rest.

It was a leather handbag he'd scoured Sydney for, knowing precisely the type and design Carrie would like.

Entering the bedroom, he came to an abrupt halt, his face plainly registering shock. If he'd met his mother alive in the street he'd have walked straight past her.

She was so *old* looking! A crone nearer Winnie's age than the actual forty-five she was.

Stiff-legged, he walked forward to sit on the edge of the bed. Slowly he unwrapped the handbag and laid it on the pillow beside her head. 'A wee minding, Ma,' he said.

Coldness gave way to heat which exploded into a blast furnace of bubbling anger. 'What happened to her?' he demanded, his voice a thrumming stretch of wire.

Harriet wilted under his terrible gaze.

'It was Archie, wasn't it?' he hissed taking hold of the front of Harriet's dress.

All this while Harriet had kept her dark secret, never

once breathing a hint of it to anyone. Time had pushed it to the back of her mind where, like a bad dream, it had gradually faded to nothingness.

But seeing Carrie dead had brought it all rushing back. Her skin crawled with the memory of what the animal had done to her. And how many awful times had Carrie endured the same?

Her nerve shredded. It came out in a rush, the words tumbling from her mouth.

When she finally finished speaking she gave a great shudder as though an enormous weight had been lifted from her.

Angus whimpered. His mind filled with dreadful pictures. It was unbelievable. Inconceivable. And yet Harriet said it was true.

He dashed from the room and before anyone realized what was happening was through the front door and running down the close stairs.

Behind him Harriet wept volubly.

Once out in the street, he hesitated, not quite knowing what to do next. Then remembering it was a Sunday and there was a good chance Archie would be at home, he ran, all the while thinking of the life Archie had given his mother. It had transformed Carrie into the raddled corpse now laid out in Tallon Street.

The time had finally arrived for the reckoning. He was no longer the wee boy Archie could contemptuously knock to one side. It would be man to man and he doubted there were many could have stood up against him the way he felt right then.

Reaching the front door he formed a fist and hammered. And hammered. And hammered.

'Christalbloodymighty, I'm coming!' the well remembered voice called out followed by a dragging sound as though Archie was pulling something heavy across the floor.

The moment the door started to open Angus leapt at it, hitting it hard with his shoulder so it was thrust suddenly and violently back in on itself.

For an instant he glimpsed Archie's startled face. Then, with a cry, Archie toppled backward to fall heavily onto the manky floor.

Angus advanced on his quarry. He was going to enjoy this.

'You!' Archie exclaimed, his face contorted with what Angus mistakenly thought was hate.

'Get up!' Angus spat.

Archie's hands scrabbled for two rubber tipped sticks lying next to him. Using these he tried valiantly to regain his feet.

Angus frowned, wondering what his step-father was playing at. Why the sticks?

For the first time he noticed how twisted and grotesque – the legs especially – Archie's limbs had become.

Raising his eyes he saw a wheelchair standing further along the small hallway.

Finally, having tried repeatedly and failed, Archie sank back onto his bottom. Glaring, he said he couldn't get up under his own steam and that Angus would have to help him.

Sitting there almost helpless as a babe Archie was a pitiful sight, and one which drained the tumultuous anger out of Angus. It just wasn't in him to ladle into a man in this condition.

Angus took Archie by the hand and after something of a struggle got him back on his feet.

Angus asked what had happened and Archie replied his old pains which had bothered him for years had been the early stages of arthritis. He turned and shuffled – making the dragging sound Angus had heard while waiting for the door to be answered – to the wheelchair which he sank into with a sigh of relief.

There was a certain classic irony about all this which wasn't lost on Angus. That Archie's arthritis caused him continual, excruciating pain was plainly evident. The man who'd caused so much misery and suffering to others was now doomed to suffer miserably himself.

Staring at his step-father Angus could find no forgiveness in himself. The picture of Carrie was too fresh in his mind. And anyway he wasn't the forgiving kind.

He hoped Archie lived to a ripe old age, and during every day of the time left him suffered all the pains and agonies of hell.

'She died last night,' Angus said abruptly.

Archie blinked and frowned. 'Who?'

'My mother.'

Archie's lips shrivelled into a thin line and he dropped his head to stare at the floor. Nor did he lift his head again until Angus turned to go.

Revenge had already been exacted on Archie and in a far more terrible manner than anything Angus had had in mind. His hand was on the doorknob when Archie suddenly spoke softly behind him.

'You may be grown up but don't think you know it all yet. In my own way I loved your mother even though I did treat her badly from time to time. For what it's worth I'm truly sorry. She'll be sorely missed for she was a good woman.'

When Archie had finished speaking Angus walked from the house out into the street where he stood feeling sick. He wondered why Harriet hadn't told him about Archie's condition.

The simple answer was she hadn't known. Archie Marjoribanks had become virtually a taboo subject in Tallon Street as Carrie couldn't bear to hear his name mentioned. Consequently Harriet had been in the dark about his illness.

Just then a face from the past arrested Angus's gaze and instantly rekindled his anger.

He watched as Tod Gemmill strolled by on the opposite side of the street. Tod was another he owed and now was as good a time as any to repay that debt.

Crossing the street he hurried after his man. When they came to Angus's old primary school, Angus maintaining a respectable distance behind Tod while he waited his chance, Tod suddenly headed off at a tangent.

Being Sunday and at a time of the morning when most

folk were either still abed or else getting ready for church the streets were more or less deserted, which suited Angus down to the ground.

Breaking into a trot he caught up with Tod in front of the Rialto picture house and tapped him on the shoulder. 'I'm claiming you,' he said.

Recognizing Angus, Tod's jaw literally fell open.

Angus jerked his thumb towards the ash and cinder track leading round the back of the picture house and Tod got the point. With a shrug Tod walked in the direction indicated.

Angus had always had extremely fast reflexes and it was these that saved him now.

In a well practised movement Tod whipped the cap from his head and flicked the brim straight at Angus's face.

Angus registered the blur and hastily jerked his head back. The cap brim missed his eyes by a few inches. Realizing what it was Tod had tried to hit him with he closed on Tod.

Tod flicked the cap again and this time its brim brushed against Angus's outstretched hand. A large gash suddenly opened up from wrist to little finger.

Grunting in surprise, Angus backpedalled.

The next time the cap sliced the air in front of him he glimpsed a flash of metal which told him the brim had been doctored in some way.

The two men circled one another, Tod swaying from side to side holding the cap bunched in his hand with its brim projecting outward.

The rim contained a row of razor blades stitched between the two layers of fabric so only their cutting edges protruded.

Suddenly Angus's opening was there as Tod overreached himself and stumbled. His hands automatically dropped to steady himself and as they did Angus leapt.

He got round behind Tod to put a crushing stranglehold on Tod's windpipe at the same time securing the hand holding the cap.

For a few seconds they struggled. Then Angus brought his heel smashing down on Tod's right instep.

Tod screamed and bucked. Dropping the cap, he reached back with both hands to tear and claw at Angus's face.

Angus exclaimed as a thumb jabbed him in the eye. Shifting his grip, he grasped Tod by a shoulder and using a combination push/pull movement, knocked him off balance. Then he threw him over his leg onto the ground.

He dropped his full weight onto Tod's chest, landing on his knees, which brought another scream from Tod.

'I give up! I give up!' Tod pleaded.

'Like fuck you do,' Angus said, drawing his fist back with the intention of bursting Tod's nose.

'I can tell you about your Da!' Tod wailed.

Angus's fist stopped in mid punch. He thought he couldn't have heard correctly. 'What did you say?' he demanded.

'Your Da,' Tod sobbed.

'What about him?'

'Promise you'll let me go?'

'If it's worth it,' Angus said slowly.

Tod sucked in a breath and groaned. He licked his lips. 'Well?'

'Your Da on the gantry, no one ever knew why he was up there.'

There was a vice in Angus's chest. 'Go on,' he whispered.

'Armstrong himself gave the order. It was to inspect something or other. I know for a fact because *my* Da overheard.' Tod gulped. 'He could never tell your Grandpa or speak up. It would've meant his job.'

So there it was. Sir Alan *had* owed Carrie compensation and the bloody man had never said a dickey bird. He'd kept stum to save himself a pittance, for that's all it would have been to him.

'Please?' Tod pleaded. 'You'll keep this to yourself? If Armstrong was to find out. . . .'

But Angus had stopped hearing. Rising, he started

back for the street, his anger completely gone leaving a great calm behind.

'He'll pay, Ma. I promise you,' he whispered.

He'd never meant anything more in his life.

19

In Scotland the best summer months are often May and September. It was the middle of May now and the sun was cracking the skies.

Diane Armstrong stood in the downstairs bay window of her sister's house in Bearsden watching several blackbirds squabbling over a worm one had dug up.

Rosemary was sitting by the fireplace mending a slight tear in one of Iain's best shirts. Diane said, 'By the way, an old friend of yours has been making inquiries about buying a house that's up for sale in Newton Mearns.'

Rosemary was engrossed in her task, nimbly sewing the tiny stitches required. 'Who's that, then?' she asked.

Diane sprung her bombshell. 'Angus McBain.'

The shock that swept through Rosemary was like having a bucket of ice cold water emptied over her head. 'Is that a fact?' she replied and somehow continued sewing.

In a quiet voice Diane went on to say Angus was apparently interested in buying a mansion that had only recently come onto the market. It was an old property with something like twenty rooms, a conservatory and outhouses.

Rosemary said it couldn't be the Angus McBain they knew as he couldn't possible afford anything like that.

But Diane was adamant. It was the same Angus McBain who'd lived in Holmlea Road and run off leaving Rosemary in the lurch.

A lump filled Rosemary's throat as she pretended to be still interested in her sewing. But she wasn't fooling Diane one little bit and she knew it.

She asked Diane if she knew where Angus had been and what he'd been doing? But these were questions her sister had no answers for.

All Diane could tell her was that Angus was back. And if he was able to consider buying a house like the one in Newton Mearns it was to be presumed he wasn't still the poor lad he'd been when they'd known him.

Rosemary smiled grimly to herself. Angus had always sworn he'd one day be a somebody with lots of money. It would seem he'd at least got the money.

Further discussion was halted by Iain's entrance.

Now he was back in civvy street Iain was being reluctantly drawn more and more into running his father's property business. Both his parents had virtually lost all interest in everything since the night he'd returned home from hospital to give them the combined shock of seeing the ruin his face had become and telling them the news of Peter's death.

Hyper-sensitive about his looks, he'd become something of a recluse, only leaving the house when absolutely necessary. The telephone was his lifeline through which he conducted the vast majority of his dealings with the outside world.

His personality had changed considerably since leaving hospital. He'd always had a tendency to be brooding and introspective: Now it wasn't unusual for him to spend days locked away in his study.

After Iain had left them the two women chatted for some time about the reappearance of Angus McBain.

Then, having seen her sister off, Rosemary went into the garden where she strolled deep in thought. Questions crowded her mind. Had Angus altered much? And if so, what did he look like now? How had he made enough money to be able to contemplate buying a mansion?

And, of course, the big question that had plagued her this long time – why had Angus run off the way he had?

As Rosemary wandered through her garden thinking about Angus, he was mounting the stairs to the solicitors who were dealing with the sale of the Newton Mearns property.

The house was an old one with an enormous amount needing done to it. But rather than being a black mark against it this appealed to Angus as it gave him the excuse to have the place modernized to his own specifications

The house was to be the first stage of the promise he'd made the day Petersson announced the bauxite strike. His son was going to have the very best of everything which naturally included a place to live.

Having stated to the solicitor that he wanted to purchase, he was entertained with sherry and digestives over which he was informed the legal documents would be drawn up in due course.

Before leaving he inquired about rented accommodation and was told the matter would be looked into right away.

Feeling well pleased with himself and the way things were going, he drove out to Cathcart and Tallon Street. Winnie was in but Donald whom he'd really come to see was at the allotment.

Over a cup of tea Winnie told him Hugh and Janey's big news. He said he'd drop by Muirend and see them after he'd had a word with Donald.

Angus found his grandfather at the plot. The two sat on an old wooden bench and for a wee while they blethered about inconsequentials, Donald using the respite to enjoy a pipeful of tobacco.

Retirement was proving a heavy burden for Donald to bear. Despite constant nagging from Winnie he was beginning to neglect himself. It was this personal neglect which was worrying Angus and had given him the idea of how he could help his grandfather and at the same time do himself a good turn.

In a mild voice Angus asked Donald if he'd be interested in holding down a job again?

Donald slowly took the battered briar from his mouth and turned to stare at his grandson. Trying desperately hard not to betray his eagerness he asked just what it was Angus had in mind?

Angus explained about buying the house in Newton Mearns and the state the place was in. Once an architect had drawn up plans for modernization a gang of workmen would have to be employed to carry them out. What he wanted was Donald to be gaffer over this lot.

Rubbing his jaw Donald said it was certainly an interesting proposition but had Angus forgotten all his experience was in the foundry?

It was fair comment and one Angus was pleased his grandfather had made. What he wanted Donald on the payroll for was Donald's expertise in handling men and getting the best out of them. Any problems over the job in hand and all Donald had to do was refer back to him. He'd soon get on site and work it out. After all, Donald was a practical man who'd worked with his hands all his life. He didn't have to be a journeyman in a particular field to know if a job was well or badly done. Common sense and a craftsman's eye would tell him that.

Donald nodded. Taking out his smoker's knife he busied himself cleaning the briar's bowl and while doing so quietly asked about money.

Angus replied he'd pay his grandfather a pound more per week than whatever Donald had been earning at Armstrong's

Donald was completely taken aback by this generous offer and for a second actually gawped. Pulling himself together, he resumed cleaning his pipe. After a suitably dignified time had elapsed he cleared his throat and said he'd be happy to accept.

Angus said Donald could consider himself on pay as from the following Monday although it would be a wee while yet before actual work started.

Together the pair of them left the allotment. Donald walked very straight and with his head held high. Back at Tallon Street an excited Donald broke the good news he was a gaffer again.

Angus made it quite clear to his grandfather the job had a limited life span after which he couldn't promise anything.

Donald said he fully understood. Then he hurried away through to the hall cupboard to root out his boiler suit for Winnie to wash and get ready for when it was needed.

Out on the landing Winnie drew the door behind her and Angus. There was more than a hint of tears in her eyes. 'Thank you, son. God bless you!' she whispered. Then wiping her face with the hem of her pinny she retreated swiftly to the hall where a voluble Donald was demanding to know where in the name of the wee man his boiler suit was!

As he dove out to Muirend Angus reflected Donald was a gaffer *par excellence* and would see to it every man jack gave a full day's work for the full day's pay they'd be collecting. Furthermore, with Donald in charge, he could rest assured no materials would go for a walk nor would there be any other petty finaglings of that ilk. The money and time saved would more than cover his grandfather's wages.

Humming to himself he arrived at the dairy to find Hugh in the stables attending to the horses. He loved coming to the dairy for the marvellous memories it held for him.

Looking round it wasn't difficult to hear and see himself and Kitty as young lads. There was a choke in his throat when he congratulated Hugh on Janey expecting again.

They found Janey in the kitchen baking and the first thing Angus did was to sweep her into his arms and give her a big hug and kiss.

Hugh was jubilant he was to be a father again. He kept

saying this time it was sure to be a wee boy.

After ten minutes non-stop talking about the forth-coming baby Hugh was told to shush by Janey who said he was beginning to sound like a big jessie the way he was going on.

Hugh mumbled something about not being able to help how pleased he was. To change the subject he said a little defiantly he was regularly attending classes down at the chapel where he was doing just fine. The priest had told him only the other day if he continued at his present rate of assimilation it wouldn't be too long before he was eligible for confirmation into the Catholic church.

Screwtops were opened and while Hugh did the honours Janey said she'd had some worrying news about Thistle Street. One of her sisters had been over to say her mother and father were near beside themselves because of the rumours flying round that the entire area had been bought up and the new owners intended giving them all notice to quit.

There were a dozen conflicting stories about what was to happen once the rows of tenements were finally empty.

One said they were to be demolished and new private middle-class accommodation built in their stead, another that a huge works was to be constructed on the site. Yet another rumour was that a Corporation scheme was to be erected in which many of the former inhabitants were to be rehoused.

As to who'd been buying up the area there were as many candidates as there were rumours to support them.

Those who favoured the housing scheme idea natur-ally enough said it was the Glasgow Corporation while others were adamant it was a titled Englishman out to exploit Scotland the way his hated race had always done.

Those believing the works story insisted it was a con-sortium of Scottish businessmen, the most well known of whom was Sir Alan Armstrong. Angus's ears pricked up the moment Sir Alan's name was mentioned.

Janey went on to say her father was terrified of losing

his job. At his age and with the surplus of young man-power suddenly swamping the market as a result of thousands of demobbed soldiers looking for work, the chances were he would never get another job again.

Hugh's bonhomie and wellbeing gradually faded as he listened to all this. Much as he liked his in-laws he didn't particularly want them descending on him for what might turn out to be an indefinite period. He chided himself for the unworthy thought. Nonetheless it was how he felt.

Angus decided he was going to have to have Arm-strong's rumoured involvement in the Gorbal's investigated. Anything Armstrong had his snout into interested him.

As it happened he already had a private investigator called Otis Bitu under hire. When he next saw Bitu he would ask him to take on this new assignment.

They spoke about the McIvers possible predicament a little while longer, then Angus excused himself, saying it was high time he went.

Motoring up the drive he decided on impulse to visit Carrie's grave which was close by.

Having parked the car, he walked down an incline past row upon row of graves until he came to the one where Carrie and his father were buried.

The gold lettering recently scored into the marble headstone shone and glinted in the sun. The grave itself still had a freshly dug look about it.

To have come all the way from Australia only to miss her by a few hours! It was heartbreaking.

There had been little of Carrie's he'd wanted to hang onto: her wedding ring, the one his father had given her and not Archie's, several hand stitched pictures she'd done herself, and the tug-of-war medal his father had won against the City of Glasgow police.

What had been his other treasured possession, his father's wallet with the faded initials J.McB. on its front, was at the bottom of the sea, having gone down with the *Almuria*.

All in all not a lot to be the only keepsakes he had of his parents, but for Angus they were enough.

Sir Alan Armstrong was being entertained by his mistress in the house he'd bought her in Partickhill.

Margaret Cunninghame was twenty-four years old, the same age as Rosemary, whom she'd been to school with. Margaret had been the other girl with Rosemary all those years ago when Angus and Kitty had saved the two Parkie lassies from the toughs in the Queen's Park reccy ground.

She was a tall woman with mouse brown hair, frightfully well spoken, and languid in all her movements.

She was a war widow. Her husband, an officer in the Scots Guards, had been blown to smithereens by a German landmine.

Her family were landed gentry, at least they had been until just before the war when everything they owned had disappeared into the open maw of the Glasgow stock market which her father had played addictively and badly.

As a result of her family's penury Margaret had married for money. But her husband had been killed before he'd come into his inheritance and, as she hadn't got on at all well with her in-laws who'd guessed her reason for marrying their son, she'd found herself more or less back to square one.

Being Sir Alan's mistress was a solution to her problem. It was an indolent life she led but then she was an indolent person. Her only worry was keeping Sir Alan happy when he visited her every Tuesday and Friday nights.

His permanent alibi was that he travelled through to Edinburgh on those nights to stay with friends with whom he conducted east coast business. And in case Cordelia ever decided to ring him there a plan had been worked out whereby his friends would say he was tied up and would ring her back. They would then contact him and he would ring her from the Partickhill house pretending he was speaking from Edinburgh.

The reason Sir Alan had taken a mistress was a quaint one: having made a great deal out of the war he had to think of new ways in which to spend and enjoy his money. The idea of a mistress had originated from one of his friends who'd let drop in conversation that a third party they both knew had installed a fancy lady in the West End.

Now Sir Alan's marriage was a happy one with which he was well pleased. Nonetheless the thought of another woman was an exciting one. So there and then he'd decided he too would have a mistress.

Propositioning Margaret had taken him ages and caused him much anxiety in case he was making a mistake as to the sort of person she was.

In the end it was Margaret, no fool at seeing what was in a man's mind and what his intentions were, who'd steered a conversation between them in such a way it had seemed the most natural thing in the world for him to suggest she became his mistress.

Later he'd wondered just who had propositioned whom?

Sir Alan sat back and gazed into his glass of whisky while through in the bedroom Margaret went about making down the bed. He reflected life had been extraordinarily good to him of late, thanks to the war.

Business in the works was falling away, of course, now the conflict had come to an end. But he'd diversified his capital into property. He positively swelled with pride and pleasure thinking of the amount of property he now owned. Nearly half a square mile belonged to him and soon it would be time for the tenements to be razed and the new constructions started.

The one fly in the ointment was there were still several streets eluding a Phoenix takeover.

With a smile of gratification he pictured the plans his architects had drawn up for the area. Once those bright, shiny houses were built they would radically alter the face of south Glasgow, at the same time earning Phoenix

Development Ltd a massive fortune.

The Gorbals would return to what it had been originally – an area where decent middle-class folk lived rather than the appalling, festering blot on the landscape it had degenerated into.

A frown creased his face at the thought of that pocket of resistance holding out on him. It was owned by a cantankerous old besom called Miss McCallum with whom he'd crossed swords in the past, and who, despite a number of most generous offers, steadfastly refused to sell.

Unfortunately the streets owned by her were situated slap bang in central Gorbals, occupying the prime site of the redevelopment area.

The one good thing was she was eighty-six years old with one foot in the grave from stomach cancer. It was thought she wouldn't last out the year.

Once she died he intended stepping in and buying her properties from her next of kin, a nephew in Inverness whom he'd ensure would be only too happy to sell.

The Gorbals! A name as hard as the people currently living there. Well, he was going to arrange it so the name was eradicated forever. It would become a mere historical reference.

Hutchesontown was the correct name for the district and the one he intended it to be known as in the future.

Leaving John and Dawn in the excellent rented accommodation, a house in Barrhead the solicitors had acquired for them, Angus drove into town to Otis Bitu's office. He rather liked Bitu, tiny, dark-haired, swarthy American of Middle European ancestry.

Otis Bitu had come to Scotland as a flyer with the United States Air Force and had married a Scots lassie by the name of Morag. Tall as he was short he worshipped her as though she was a goddess come to earth.

When Morag had announced at the end of the war she had absolutely no intention of leaving Glasgow – she wanted to stay near her Mammy – he'd seen no alternative to remaining behind while the rest of his comrades went home.

Born and bred in Lansing, Michigan, he'd done well for several years until being drafted.

Finding himself a civilian again and unable to practise his profession in Scotland, he'd elected to work as a private investigator for the simple reason it was a crazy sort of job which suited him down to the ground.

He enjoyed getting out and about and meeting people from all walks of life, finding it a sort of balm after the rigours of war.

It was through having performed some minor services for the Central Station Hotel that he'd come to be recommended to Angus. For here Angus had stayed on his return from Australia.

Angus knocked on Bitu's office door, letting himself in when Bitu called out the door was open. Bitu was on the phone and gestured he sit in the visitor's chair. Cradling the phone, Bitu launched into a verbal report outlining the results of his investigations on Angus's behalf.

To begin with he'd gone to the address Angus had given him down by the Govan Docks where he'd found the house still inhabited by prostitutes. But none of them had ever heard of Sheena Marjoribanks.

In a local shebeen where only red biddy –a lethal concoction of rough red wine and meths – was served he'd come across a played out brass called Wild Irish Maeve who for the price of a Parazone bottle filled with the nightmare mixture told him Sheena had left the Govan address to move to the Gallowgate.

Again it had been doing the rounds, asking in shops, speaking with the local police.

He'd come up with another address which had taken him out to Pollokshaws where he'd learned Sheena had moved on to Egypt, an area between Shettleston and Tollcross.

In Egypt he'd discovered Sheena had flitted yet again, this time to the centre of town because she'd landed a job as a barmaid in a boozer called the Capitol Bar.

Angus had never actually been in the Capitol Bar but knew it had a reputation as being a place where a lot of hard men drank. At least that's what it had been like before the war.

Angus was pleased with Bitu and said so. Producing his cheque book, he wrote out the balance of the American's fee, adding a tenner because he appreciated a task well done.

Handing over the cheque, he asked if Bitu would be interested in doing another job for him?

Bitu was only too happy to oblige and hurriedly got out some scrap paper and a pen to take down the details.

Leaving Bitu's office, Angus drove up Sauchiehall Street to just before Charing Cross where he turned off left.

The Capitol Bar was grimy outside but then so was nearly all of central Glasgow. He parked the car and went inside to discover there was an upstairs and downstairs bar. Sheena was in neither.

Thinking she might appear at any time he stayed in the downstairs bar and ordered a pint of heavy. He could have asked for Sheena but didn't want to, preferring to give her a surprise. When at the end of an hour she still hadn't put in an appearance he decided to leave it and return later.

After the evening meal he drove back to the Capitol Bar which was packed.

Downstairs he found an arty crafty crew far different to the hard men he'd been expecting. The clientele had been so sparse in the morning it had been difficult to judge what sort now frequented the place.

He squeezed past two young lads talking about Cubism and sidled up to the bar.

She was dressed entirely in black and standing directly facing him pulling a pint. As she lifted the pint onto the bar she looked straight into his eyes. As she did so her own eyes filled with amazement, then pleasure.

'Another pint of that when you're ready,' he smiled.

When she took his money their hands briefly touched.

She nodded as if to say it was as though he'd never been away.

Handing him his change, she whispered, 'Can you hang on until we're closed?'

He replied that he could. So she added if he'd wait for her outside the front door she'd meet him there.

At a quarter past nine the doors to the pub opened and she slipped out. Without any hesitancy she came into his arms and he held her close.

'A long time, Angus,' she said.

'It is that,' he replied. 'Did you know Carrie's dead?'

She stiffened and then pulled herself away from him. Slowly she shook her head.

There was far too much to talk about standing out in the road like this so he asked her if there was somewhere close by where they could go? She replied she had a wee place only a few streets away.

The room was a large kitchen with a box bed tucked away at the far end. It was neat and tidy and shone like a new pin.

While she hung up her hat and coat Angus sat and studied his step-sister. She was certainly older looking with a few splashes of grey in her hair. She was carrying a little more matronly weight than he remembered. And the stamp of a terrible loneliness was on her.

She produced a bottle of gin from which she poured two generous measures into tumblers. They drank it neat because she had no mix.

Missing nothing out he told her all that had befallen him since they'd last been together.

After he'd finished they sat for a few minutes in silence. Then he prompted her to tell him what had happened to her during the long years of separation.

At first she was reluctant. But he got round her with a bit of coaxing and slowly she began telling him her tale.

She'd remained on the game for quite a while after he'd gone to sea until getting an awful scare by coming down with a bad dose of VD.

The cure had been excruciatingly painful but had

brought her to her senses. When she was discharged from hospital she'd gone looking for a straight job, ending up as a conductress on the trams again.

For a time there had been a man. Then one day he just wasn't around any more and she'd had to accept he'd gone for good.

The funny thing was she hadn't been sleeping with him, having insisted they wait until after they were married. What she'd wanted more than anything was his respect.

She could only think he'd disappeared out of her life because he'd got fed up being denied sex or else had somehow found out about her past. She was inclined to think it was the latter.

'If you're interested I'd like you to be John's nanny,' Angus said. 'That's been in my mind since I knew I was coming home and Dawn who looks after him now, wants to go travelling.'

'Look after your wee boy?' Sheena said, her voice cracking with emotion.

'Would you like that?'

'Oh yes,' she whispered. 'You know damn well I would.'

'Then it's settled. When can you start?'

'I've got to give forty-eight hours notice at the pub. I wouldn't run out and leave them, you understand. They've been decent to me.'

Angus nodded. He would've expected nothing less.

There were tears in Sheena's eyes as they made the arrangements. She would overlap with Dawn for a week and then Dawn would be free to start her tour of Europe.

Later, when Angus had gone, Sheena went to bed taking the remains of the gin with her. And there she cried her eyes out. Thanking God time and time again for this new chance.

In the morning she felt a woman reborn.

Donald stood with his arms akimbo staring up at Craiglea – the name of the Newton Mearns house –

which now belonged to Angus. It was a handsome place albeit in his estimation a wee bit dark and forbidding.

He couldn't help but be filled with pride to think *his* grandson was the owner of such a fine mansion. My God, it was a far cry from the hovel he'd been born into in Invershuie or the one Winnie had first seen the light of day in in Fanagmore!

The family had come a long way in three generations. There was Angus with his grand Newton Mearns mansion and his Australian bauxite mine. And Hugh the owner of a prosperous dairy as well as an equally thriving farm out on the East Kilbride road.

Mind you, Hugh had been enormously lucky in having Greta Paterson leave him the dairy and farm but that didn't detract one whit from the achievement. After all, Hugh had grafted damn hard to get in her good books in the first place and Greta had left him what she had knowing full well he'd make a go of it.

He'd come to think an awful lot of his son these past few years although it still pained him greatly that Hugh had married a Catholic and even worse, was in the process of turning one himself.

Not that he could fault Janey on anything bar her religion. Apart from that flaw he couldn't have asked for a better daughter-in-law.

With regards to Angus, it saddened him enormously that Angus's marriage had folded, and so quickly too. The poor boy's mother had gone through so much in that department you would've thought he'd be spared similar problems.

Donald was inordinately proud of what Angus and Hugh had achieved but there was another side of him that was highly suspicious of the way in which they seemed to be joining the capitalist classes.

He still considered it wrong and grossly immoral for individuals to be so well off when countless others in the world were either starving or else barely getting by on subsistence level. In Britain, at least, with a Labour government under Clem Attlee in power, the future

looked good and getting better all the time for the
working classes. He firmly believed the corner had been
turned and what the country was now witnessing was the
dawn of a glorious socialist age.

In the meantime he had a job to get on with – and the
irony wasn't lost on him – thanks to his capitalist
grandson.

He made his way across to where the first of the
workmen he'd hired were waiting to be told what to do.

20

Angus was whistling as he parked his car and ran up the
stairs leading to Bitu's office, where he found the
American primed and ready for him.

Bitu said his inquiries about the Gorbals had thrown
up the name Phoenix. He'd gone to London where he'd
spent an entire day in Companies House in the City
Road where a record is kept of every company formed in
Britain. Eventually he'd turned up a company called
Phoenix Development Ltd which had two directors, Sir
Alan Armstrong and Sir Hamilton McLaren. Between
them these two gentlemen now owned nearly all of the
Gorbals.

Angus nodded his satisfaction. Bitu had again done
well. The question now was what did Sir Alan and Sir
Hamilton – whom he knew to be Rosemary's father-in-
law which made it even more interesting – propose doing
with the properties they'd acquired?

Bitu's new brief was to find out precisely what these

348

proposed plans were. It seemed a safe bet to assume something had to be in the wind to account for the many rumours currently flying round the area.

They shook hands at the door as Bitu promised to be in touch as soon as he'd come up with something.

Back on the street Angus walked round the corner to a little coffee shop he'd fallen into the habit of frequenting at this time of day when he'd been living at the hotel.

The coffee shop was in the rear of a barber's and was extremely masculine. It was mainly patronized by businessmen who in their pin-striped suits and starched collars blended in perfectly with the wood-panelled decor and faded genteel atmosphere.

He was surprised to see a woman sitting alone at a table. Even a woman in the company of a man would've been unusual as it was just not that sort of establishment. He was even further surprised when she smiled at him.

For a moment he thought she was a high class tart. Then with a start he realized he recognized the face.

'Hello Angus,' she said, extending her hand to be shaken.

She'd changed a lot since they'd last met but then so had he. 'Hello Diane,' he replied. And having sat, he waved to the hovering waiter to bring coffee for him and a refill for her.

They smiled and stared at one another. Finally Diane said, 'I heard on the grapevine you'd bought Craiglea so I went out there this morning hoping to see you but met your grandfather instead. He told me if I was to come here at around this time I might well run into you.'

Angus raised an eyebrow. 'Does Grandpa know who you are?'

'Oh yes. He's seen me many times in the past.'

Angus wondered about Donald knowing he frequented this particular coffee shop. He couldn't remember ever having mentioned the fact to his grandfather. But then that was Donald all over, always full of surprises.

Her voice suddenly betraying her eagerness, Diane

asked if Kitty had returned to Glasgow with Angus and, if so, how was he?

'Kitty's dead,' Angus replied and watched her face crumple in on itself. She and Kitty had been extremely fond of one another.

Angus had always presumed the Armstrong girls would have found out he and Kitty had gone off to sea, but apparently not.

Starting with the *Almuria* he spoke briefly of what had befallen them up to the point where Kitty had died from eating poisoned pickles aboard the *Wahroonga*.

'My God!' said Diane, shocked at the absurdity of Kitty's death.

Angus could hold his own question back no longer. Affecting a nonchalant attitude he asked, 'How's Rosie?' adding what he hoped appeared as an after-thought, 'Didn't I hear or read somewhere she'd got married?'

'She's fine, And yes she is.'

Angus lowered his head and sipped his coffee. He didn't want Diane to see his face.

Diane knew only too well she'd been manipulated by her sister into this meeting. Rosemary's intention was that while Diane was inquiring about Kitty she'd also find out the answer to the question tormenting Rose-mary all these years: namely, why had Angus run off and left her the way he had? Without frills or preliminaries Diane now put it to him point blank.

Angus blinked and sat back in his chair. That Diane had needed to ask the question gave him a great jolt.

He remembered the intense anger and wounded pride he'd felt that day in the Old Castle Road when he'd witnessed Rosemary kissing the man later to become her husband, and whom he'd presumed ever since she'd been two timing him with.

And yet staring into Diane's frank, open face the first suspicions of doubt began to niggle him. If what he'd believed was true all these years then why was Diane demanding an explanation from him as though *he* were the guilty one?

He knew then he was going to have to tell Diane his side of the story. He started with the episode of the cuff links.

As his tale unfolded Diane's reactions couldn't have been more genuine. Disbelief was followed by incredulity which in turn gave way to anger.

In a voice cold as winter she said her father would never have done such an underhand trick and he must be mistaken!

But Angus continued describing how feeling wretched and completely distraught he'd gone to Arnprior House only to witness Rosemary and Iain McLaren kissing in a way that could hardly be described as platonic. It hadn't been difficult to put two and two together.

Diane's face creased in a frown as she searched her memory. As for the reason behind the kissing she couldn't say. But she was certain Rosemary and Iain hadn't been involved at that point.

They sat in silence for a while, accusation and denial having given them both a great deal to think about.

Finally Diane said she would do her best to get to the root of all this and when she'd done so she'd contact Angus again and tell him of her findings.

Then by mutual consent they changed the subject.

For a while Diane talked of herself and what she'd done during the war. Then she tried to pump Angus as to how he'd come by enough money to be able to afford a house the size of Craiglea.

He skilfully parried all her questions with vague answers. For the time being he didn't want any of the Armstrongs, even friendly ones, knowing how wealthy he'd become.

They said goodbye on the street corner.

Diane was nearly a block away when, like a bolt from the blue, it came to her her father did indeed own a pair of cuff links horribly similar to the ones Angus had described.

Furthermore, unless her memory was playing her

false, they'd been a present to him from her mother the very Christmas before the January during which Angus and Kitty disappeared.

She would go straight to Rosemary's to relate everything Angus had told her.

Sir Alan knew the moment he walked into the room and saw Rosemary's face something was dreadfully wrong.

When he asked her if she'd care to join him in a drink she didn't reply, instead holding out her right hand on the palm of which lay two small objects.

Intrigued, he came closer until he could make out what they were. When he recognized them he knew immediately what this was all about.

'Well?' she snapped, her eyes flashing cold fire.

'How did you find out?'

'So it's true,' she said.

He shrugged and busied himself at the decanter. Almost casually he said, 'It was for your own good, lass. McBain was a nothing, a nobody. And you after all are *my* daughter.'

She'd realized long ago he'd manipulated her into marriage with Iain but she'd always believed he'd merely capitalized on Angus's disappearance. It had never crossed her mind he'd engineered that disappearance.

Bile churned in her stomach and it took every ounce of self control she possessed not to fly at her father and rake him with her nails.

Through the open window she could see the very spot where Iain had parked Sir Hamilton's car that fatal day she'd kissed him as Angus had looked on.

If only Angus had come to her she could've explained. Instead he'd run away to sea and out of her life.

Her hand whipped in a savage sideways motion to send the cufflinks sailing out the window to fall somewhere in the garden.

Without another word she walked stiffly from the room.

She was halfway home when the dam broke and her

pent up emotions overflowed in a flood of hot, salty tears.

Iain banked the Tiger Moth and brought her onto a course that would take him directly over Stirling Castle. The plane was a recent acquisition he'd been lucky enough to snap up at a bargain price.

The sky was duck egg blue with clumps of cumulus moving at between 4000 and 5000 feet. He was flying at 3000 so the cloud wouldn't interfere with the splended panoramic view spread below him.

He tried to get up as often as he could for only in the air did he feel whole again and at peace. In the confines of the cockpit he could forget about his face for a little while.

If it had been possible for him to remain airborne for the rest of his life he would've elected to do so. His only regret would have been losing Rosemary who was his strength and whose very strength he found so comforting.

Once over Stirling he executed a wide turn, bringing him onto a south-westerly course that would take him back to the small aerodrome in Renfrew where he kept the plane.

It was worrying him that Armstrong was insisting they start demolition work in the Gorbals as soon as possible, albeit they hadn't yet been able to acquire Miss McCallum's properties.

He wasn't at all convinced starting work at this juncture was wise. He much preferred the prudence of actually waiting till the old woman was dead and Phoenix actually owned her properties.

It also bothered him how obsessive Armstrong was becoming over this particular project.

As a means of self-preservation he'd learned to be extremely chary about this type of subjectivity while in the RAF. Fanatics might make excellent Kamikaze pilots but were hardly the best co-pilots when you yourself weren't interested in becoming part of the Divine Wind.

If only he'd been able to turn to his father for advice. But Sir Hamilton absolutely refused to discuss business, declaring that side of things to be his responsibility now.

He considered his father's attitude a great pity as there was so much he could have learned, and indeed desperately needed to learn, from Sir Hamilton, whom Iain was convinced wasn't long for this world.

During the war he'd become sickeningly familiar with the peculiar aura exuded by many people who have an approaching rendezvous with death. His father had been exuding that aura for months now.

When Otis Bitu met up with Angus some weeks after being instructed to find out what Phoenix Development Ltd had planned it was to report failure.

Try as he might, he just hadn't been able to uncover what Sir Alan Armstrong and Iain McLaren – whom he'd established was acting on behalf of Sir Hamilton McLaren – intended for the Gorbals

Demolition had already started near Ballater Street where a great many families had been evicted and a sizable area razed in the short time the bulldozers and wrecking crews had been at work.

Bitu went on to say he'd even gone as far as making inquiries of the Clerk of the Dean of Guild Court. But according to that worthy, Phoenix hadn't yet submitted plans for re-development.

While Angus digested this Bitu coughed and, looking vaguely embarrassed, shifted several times in his seat.

When asked by Angus what was on his mind he replied he'd accidentally stumbled across a piece of information which if Angus cared to exploit it might just be the key to solving the problem.

Prompted by Angus to continue he went on to say he'd discovered Sir Alan's chief accountant, a man called George Hetherington, was deeply in debt to a bookie by the name of Joe Field.

Angus grinned to hear Hetherington, whom he remembered well, had taken to playing the gee gees. A dry stick of a man, Hetherington always gave the appearance of being the very epitome of self-righteous presbyterianism. It seemed Hetherington wasn't such a dry stick after all.

It was a few minutes past eight pm when Angus knocked on the door of Hetherington's house in the smart district of Clarkston, not all that far from Muirend where Hugh and Janey lived.

Hetherington himself answered the door and asked in a not particularly friendly manner what Angus wanted.

It was plain Hetherington didn't recognize him so he introduced himself and asked if he could come in as he had a business matter to discuss.

Hetherington was startled to find out who Angus was and after a moment's hesitation started closing the door in Angus's face.

He exclaimed in surprise and annoyance when Angus first jammed his foot in the door, then leant heavily against it. Smiling softly, Angus told Hetherington he wasn't being very polite towards someone who'd come to do him a good turn.

Extremely agitated, Hetherington wasn't at all sure what to do next. Finally he decided prudence was the better part of valour and with bad grace invited Angus through to the parlour where they could discuss whatever it was Angus had in mind.

Angus had already been to see Joe Field – spinning him a yarn that had opened the bookie's mouth – to get the facts and figures right. So he came straight to the point.

'How would you like to earn £419?' he asked.

Hetherington gulped and had to hold onto a chair for support. The figure was too precise for there to be any mistake.

In a trembling voice he asked how Angus had found out about his gambling debts and what Angus intended doing about it? Both he and Angus knew if this came to

Sir Alan's attention he'd be sacked immediately.

Before Angus could reply the door opened and Mrs Hetherington entered. She was a kindly looking soul although shockingly thin with a positively haggard face. She was the sort who is always cheery with never a bad word to say about anyone. Angus warmed to her right away and wondered how she'd got tied to such a dreich colourless man as her husband was.

Seeing Hetherington wasn't going to do the honours, Angus introduced himself and shook Mrs Hetherington by the hand.

She was taking her leave to put the kettle on when she started to cough and wheeze simultaneously, causing her to stop and bend over in an effort to catch her breath.

Straightening up again she said to Angus it was just a wee dry tickle she had in her throat. Throwing him a beaming smile, she hurried away through to the kitchen.

Angus sat unbidden facing the accountant and while Hetherington stared concernedly after Mrs Hetherington he went over what he'd learned from Donald that afternoon regarding the man.

During the many years he'd been with Armstrong's Hetherington had made a name for himself as being highly conscientious and exceptional at his job. He thrived on anything to do with figures, having a natural understanding of money matters and all their various facets.

He also had a shrewd head on his shoulders and was often consulted personally by Sir Alan. And more often than not his advice was acted upon.

As chief accountant he was naturally in charge of the Armstrong books. What Angus was hoping was that he was also in charge of the Phoenix ones, or at least privy to their contents.

Hetherington slowly brought his attention back to bear on Angus. As he did so guilt and apprehension crept over his face.

Licking his lips, he asked what Angus intended doing,

adding dourly that if it was money Angus was after then Angus was out of luck as he didn't have any.

Angus shook his head. On the contrary he was hoping to give Hetherington some in exchange for a little information.

Hetherington was clearly puzzled and asked how an ex-apprentice fitter could afford to hand over the sort of money he was in debt to the tune of? Unless, of course, Angus was working for someone else, in which case who?

Angus replied he was working for no one but himself. When he saw Hetherington didn't believe him he crossed to the telephone and gave the operator the number which would connect him with the solicitor who'd handled the purchase of Craiglea for him.

When the man came on the line Angus told him what was required. Then gesturing Hetherington over, he left it to the solicitor to confirm his financial *bona fides*.

Hetherington returned to his chair to admit grudgingly it would seem Angus was now a man of considerable means.

Angus wrote out a cheque for £419.00 which he passed over to Hetherington. He wanted the accountant to hold his salvation in his hands for the psychological effect it would have on him.

The door opened and Mrs Hetherington wheeled in a trolley overflowing with goodies. She helped Angus and her husband to what they wanted and was about to help herself when Hetherington said gruffly he wanted to be alone with Angus.

Without a word of argument or dissent Mrs Hetherington left the room. Hetherington stared after his wife. There was something very poignant and touching in his expression which impressed Angus.

Hetherington's gaze dropped to the cheque still clutched in his hands.

Angus smiled and said for reasons of his own he wanted a friend – Hetherington winced at the euphemism – in Sir Alan Armstrong's camp and was willing to pay handsomely for the service.

If Hetherington agreed the £419 would only be a down payment with regular monthly sums to follow.

When Angus mentioned the sum of fifty pounds Hetherington looked startled for a second, then quickly nodded.

There was something wrong here. Angus could feel it. Although having little choice in the matter of capitulation Hetherington, for the man of honour and integrity Donald assured him he was, had done so too easily. That bothered Angus so before putting his question about the Gorbals he demanded to know why it was so?

Hetherington took so long in replying that Angus was beginning to think he wasn't going to. But suddenly he started to speak in such a low voice that Angus had to strain to hear.

Hetherington said his wife had always been asthmatic but her condition had worsened drastically during the war years as a direct result of the prevailing conditions. Her asthma was now so bad that unless they could move to a warm climate within the next year her chances of surviving much beyond that were extremely slim.

As Hetherington spoke Angus felt awful about how he'd misjudged the man. He'd presumed Hetherington to be just another punter with gambling fever whereas the truth of the matter was it had been a frantic effort on Hetherington's part to try and raise the money to take Mrs Hetherington to the sort of climate the doctor said was necessary for her survival.

Angus asked if they owned the house, thinking they could have sold and raised capital that way. But the answer was no. Like the vast majority of Glaswegians the Hetheringtons rented.

What little savings they'd had had gone on financing his gambling venture which Hetherington had hoped and prayed would bring them in the sort of return to solve their problem.

It had been clutching at straws, of course. And Hetherington had come horribly unstuck when, after a short winning streak, he'd hit a seemingly non-stop losing one.

That left the obvious question. Why hadn't Hetherington gone to Sir Alan for the sort of money that would enable him to send Mrs Hetherington abroad while he remained behind until the loan was repaid?

Hetherington replied he had indeed approached Sir Alan only to be callously turned down. He thought Sir Alan considered him far too valuable an employee to lose which would've eventually happened had the loan been forthcoming.

As an afterthought, Hetherington added he'd actually considered embezzlement and would have committed it had he thought there was any possible chance of getting away with it. But there wasn't thanks to a checking system he himself had introduced.

Angus asked why Hetherington had elected to try Joe Field's when surely the Stock Exchange would have been a far more suitable hunting ground for a man of his abilities?

Hetherington's reply was that the Exchange was still very firm after the conditions imposed on it during the war. As such it would've been virtually impossible, in the relatively short time available to him, to turn his small amount of savings into the capital sum needed.

Angus now appreciated why the poor bugger had caved in so easily.

Much as Sir Alan prized Hetherington as an employee he would be forced to sack him, especially if Joe Field made the matter public as Field was threatening to do.

Besides, from Sir Alan's point of view Hetherington would now be untrustworthy. Not only would Hetherington be sacked but undoubtedly there would be no letter of recommendation – and how that brought back memories for Angus! – which would mean the middle-aged accountant would never work again.

Angus's proposal was this. He would advance Hetherington over and above the £419, one year's money which amounted to £600, enabling Mrs Hetherington to go abroad right away.

Hetherington was dumbfounded. He stared incredulously at Angus, hope dawning joyously in his eyes. 'Why?' he croaked.

Angus explained it was merely a case of each of them having something the other wanted; Hetherington money, himself access to Sir Alan's innermost financial secrets. It seemed stupid for them not to help one another to their mutual advantage.

There had been a time when Hetherington would've refused outright in the name of loyalty to have anything to do with such a deal. But Sir Alan had forfeited that loyalty in turning down his plea for a loan, and condemning his wife to an early grave.

Angus and Hetherington shook hands on the agreement. Then Hetherington told Angus everything he wanted to know about the Gorbals project.

En route home it came to Angus there were parts of Australia – although unfortunately not Queensland – ideal for Mrs Hetherington's condition. He would put it to Hetherington the next time they spoke that she go there.

It had been a fruitful night which had brought him one step closer to Sir Alan's jugular. He wasn't quite sure yet just how he was going to effect his revenge. But he was certain that he was on the right track.

The next morning Angus was up early and, having breakfasted alone, collected the mail from the postman as he made his way out to the car.

It was a beautiful day so he thoroughly enjoyed the run down to Largs on the Firth of Clyde's coastline.

Arriving in Largs he embarked on the P.S. *Jeanie Deans* for Rothesay on the Island of Bute.

Halfway across a sudden squall came up. Leaving the outdoor passenger deck, he made his way to the aft saloon where he settled himself amongst the rose pink furnishings and light oak woodwork.

Remembering the letters he'd stuffed in his pocket earlier, he pulled them out. It was the last letter which interested him most coming as it did from Diane Armstrong and suggesting they meet again in the same coffee shop where she'd previously waylaid him. She said she'd be there on the following day at the same time unless she heard from him – her telephone number was enclosed – to the contrary.

As she'd said she would contact him again when she'd investigated the allegations he'd made about her father, Angus was curious to hear what she had to say.

When the boat docked Angus drove ashore. He had to ask directions twice before he found the house he was looking for.

He knocked, knocked again, and then again.

He was on the point of turning away thinking there was no one at home when the door opened to reveal an ancient, gnarled crone with a crabbit face.

'Miss McCallum?'

'Aye, sonny. What do you want?'

Angus hated people who called him sonny in that patronizing way. Nonetheless he fixed a smile on his face and introduced himself, asking if he could come inside as he had some business to discuss.

Miss McCallum looked suspicious and it was only when she realized he had a car – he could only wonder what association that had in her mind! – she agreed to let him in.

The place stank appallingly which was hardly surprising considering the clart and general debris littered everywhere.

There were the remains of a multitude of meals now covered in a virulent looking fungus atop a table. The sink was stacked high with unwashed dishes. There was another load piled in a cracked and mottled basin under the open-faced sink stand.

From the state of the house's interior it wasn't difficult to believe it had been many years since a cleaning hand had been raised in anger against it.

The *piece de resistance* was a rabbit hutch complete with long-eared rabbits tucked away in the far corner of the living room.

Miss McCallum asked if he'd like a cup of tea which he hastily refused. She sat down in a threadbare armchair whose bottom was threatening to fall out. A grizzled scotty dog nuzzled at her feet until she picked it up and deposited it in her lap. Gently she stroked the animal.

Angus wasn't quite sure what he'd been expecting – probably some genteel old lady amid a quaint Victorian setting. Instead he was faced with someone who might have stepped straight out of the first scene of *Macbeth*.

Opening the conversation, he said he understood she'd been ill and in the circumstances had been surprised to learn she was still at home. Surely she would have been far more comfortable in a hospital?

Miss McCallum replied waspishly that might well be so but hospitals didn't take in dogs and she had no intention of leaving dear Bella here to fret and pine which the beast would do if the two of them were parted.

In a whisper she added – perhaps she thought Bella would overhear and understand – her wee friend was also getting near the end of her days. They chatted for a while about Bella.

Then Angus brought up the object of his visit. He was interested in purchasing the properties owned by Miss McCallum in the Gorbals and was prepared to make a generous offer for them.

Miss McCallum snorted, replying he was the second person who'd wanted to buy those houses in recent years, the other being a certain Sir Alan Armstrong whom she couldn't abide at any price, being a rude and horrid man.

Angus said he knew Sir Alan and stressed he and Armstrong were far from friends.

Suddenly and without warning Bella was sick all down Miss McCallum who exclaimed in sympathy. She explained Bella had been suffering from a gyppy tummy of late which she thought had been cleared.

Leaving Bella whining in the chair, Miss McCallum hurried to a cupboard to fetch a far from clean cloth.

Hating to see the animal in distress Angus crossed to it and stroked its head. Then Miss McCallum was back wiping away the sick and fussing over the stricken beast.

Angus recalled a conversation he'd once heard between some Australian associates, both of whom were mad keen on dogs. It included a tip for canine upset tummies which he told Miss McCallum about. The mixture was warm milk with a tablespoonful of bicarb of soda stirred into it.

Miss McCallum had never heard of this particular cure and decided to give it a try. Luckily she had both ingredients to hand.

When the mixture was ready it was placed in a saucer before Bella who after a tentative sniff and taste eagerly lapped it all up. The dog appeared a little eased after that, soon curling up and falling asleep.

Miss McCallum was full of Angus's cure and insisted he take a glass of sherry with her. The sherry was sickly sweet and cloying, the glass it was served in manky. Somehow he got it down.

Again he broached the subject of the Gorbals properties to be told although he was a nice young man who'd just done her a service she had absolutely no intention of selling.

She'd originally purchased these properties on the advice of her man of business, a Mr Tait, now deceased, who'd told her never to part with them under any circumstances as they were the best possible investment a body could have.

The more she talked about this Mr Tait, who came over as having the wisdom of Solomon and the business acumen of a Rothschild, the more it became obvious she'd been a wee bit in love with him.

She said she sympathized with Angus and would like to have helped him as opposed to Sir Alan who in his efforts to get her to sell had caused her severe harassment in the past. But what it all boiled down to was her

Mr Tait had sworn her to holding onto these properties for the fine investment they represented and the regular income they provided.

She was adamant. She would hold onto these properties until her death after which they would go to her only surviving relative, a nephew living up in Inverness.

Angus asked if she was sure the nephew wouldn't sell to Sir Alan? But she pooh-poohed the idea, saying she'd written to him a number of times making it quite clear he was to abide by her wishes in this matter.

Angus could see there was no use discussing the subject further. So having left Miss McCallum his rented Barrhead address with the instructions to contact him should she ever change her mind, he climbed into his car and returned to Rothesay Pier where he awaited the next boat to Largs.

He was bitterly disappointed for he'd seen this as the perfect opportunity to initiate an attack on Sir Alan. Still it would seem Armstrong was going to have enough problems to contend with if Miss McCallum's nephew kept faith with her wishes.

According to Hetherington Sir Alan was confidently expecting to pick up the properties at bargain prices once Miss McCallum was dead and the houses transferred into the nephew's name.

With massive initial investment already sunk into the project and demolition work under way it was going to be a terrible headache to Phoenix to discover things weren't going to quite fall out as they'd planned after all.

During his return trip to Glasgow Angus tried to be philosophical about his failure. Other ways of getting at Armstrong would present themselves. All he needed to do was recognize and grab hold of them when they did.

He suddenly burst out laughing at a thought which flashed through his mind. Wouldn't it have been marvellous to have knocked down Miss McCallum's properties and built a glue factory in their stead!

He would love to have seen Phoenix try and sell their middle-class houses with that little lot belching out the most noxious fumes right in their midst.

Mid-morning the next day at precisely the time Diane had stated in her letter Angus presented himself in the coffee shop.

He was halfway to the table where the solitary woman was sitting before he was able to glimpse her face. The moment he did so it was as though he'd been hit a sledge hammer blow in the solar plexus.

He stood by the table and they stared at one another. Angus drank in every well remembered feature of her face.

'Hello Rosie,' he said and sat.

A waiter approached and, seemingly from a long distance away, he heard himself ordering coffee and biscuits.

'I was very upset to hear about Kitty's death,' Rosemary said.

Nothing had changed between them. It was the same as it had always been, the same empathy, the same ease. They fitted.

Taking a deep breath he launched into the tale which ended with Kitty's death aboard the *Wahroonga*.

The impulse to touch her, to hold her, was almost overpowering.

When he finally concluded she was sad and withdrawn. She said she hoped he didn't mind her coming in Diane's place but she'd felt it only right she did.

Jesus, the smell of her was so good! Time had dulled his memory of it. He inhaled to let it wash through him.

Continuing, Rosemary said she'd challenged her father about the cuff link incident which he'd admitted to.

Angus grunted.

The entire affair had been a complete set-up to get rid of Angus and have her married to Iain McLaren.

'And the kiss?'

She smiled bitterly and said she had, indeed, kissed Iain McLaren that day. But not for the reasons Angus had thought.

The kiss had been a purely spontaneous action because she'd just talked Iain into taking her flying again. That was all it had been. She gave him her oath on it.

'Aye, well there we are then. We were both played for a right couple of mugs,' Angus said, his intense hatred for Sir Alan Armstrong deepening even further.

That Rosemary hadn't been two timing him was a relief on the one hand and galling on the other. If only he'd kept his head how differently things might have turned out! As it was, he'd played right into Armstrong's hands.

Rosemary said Diane had told her Angus had married an Australian girl from whom he was now divorced. And that he'd brought his boy back to Scotland with him who, from all accounts, was a right smasher.

Angus dug in his wallet for a snapshot he carried of himself and John. John was positively beaming into the camera: it would have been impossible to find a bonnier or more appealing wee laddie anywhere.

Rosemary smiled as she stared at the snap. But it was a smile belying the pain lancing through her. She couldn't help but think if only circumstances had been different this wee chap might well have been hers.

'I'm sorry about the divorce,' Rosemary said.

Angus shrugged. 'Just one of those things.'

'Are you over it?'

'Oh yes.' Then to change the subject Angus said, 'He's a good looking chap, your Iain. I hope you've had and continue to have a lot of happiness together.'

For a split second she thought he was sticking the knife in. Then she realized from his expression he genuinely didn't know about the tragedy that had befallen Iain.

She considered telling him and decided not to. The last thing she either needed or wanted was his sympathy.

They talked for a little while longer, each dragging the minutes out and hoping the other wasn't noticing.

Finally after four cups of coffee and being nearly awash they ran out of excuses for prolonging the meeting any further.

Angus paid and then ushered Rosemary outside where they stood blinking in the harsh sunlight. There were creases round her eyes and mouth he hadn't noticed inside. She too had aged.

She pecked him chastely on the cheek and, without further ado, turned and went.

His heart in his mouth, he watched her till she'd rounded a corner and disappeared from sight. He'd thought she might look back. But she hadn't.

He remembered then Otis Bitu kept a bottle in his office for emergencies. If feeling the way he was didn't constitute an emergency he was damned if he knew what did.

A few weeks later Angus received a letter date stamped Rothesay. It came from Miss McCallum.

Miss McCallum had given a great deal of thought to their conversation and as a consequence had written her nephew in Inverness ordering him to travel down and see her. The nephew had come hot foot only to find himself subjected to an immediate interrogation. Riddled with guilt, he'd soon confessed to having been approached recently by Sir Alan Armstrong's partner with whom he'd made a gentlemen's agreement regarding the Gorbals properties once they became his.

Miss McCallum had been furious and lambasted the poor unfortunate who in an effort to make her see his side of things had explained he wanted to expand the wee grocery shop he owned and if possible open up another. The income from the Gorbals properties, while steady, was low whereas what he wanted was a lump sum in his hand.

After thoroughly vilifying her nephew for planning to go against her wishes Miss McCallum dispatched him back to Inverness with a gigantic flea in his ear, threatening to leave everything to a charity for dogs should he have anything further to do with Phoenix Development Ltd.

The upshot of all this was Miss McCallum was more determined than ever Sir Alan wouldn't get his hands on her properties. The cheek of the man and his partner going behind her back like that!

So to spite Sir Alan and this Iain McLaren she'd decided to sell to Angus, the proceeds of which would go to her nephew whom she still had a soft spot for. And his wish for a lump sum would then be fulfilled.

Angus was delighted by this. It meant it was now possible for him to move against Armstrong and hit the man where it would hurt most – in the pocket.

This operation he would tie in with another, something he and O'Rourke had discussed at length and come to agreement on before he left Australia. A great deal of what LMBM was producing was being exported. The bulk of what was going abroad came to Britain.

What Angus and O'Rourke intended was for Angus to set up a UK office of LMBM to handle the importing of the bauxite ore and its distribution. With the various middle men cut out they reckoned the company's British profits would leap by as much as one hundred per cent.

Angus intended setting up the company office in Glasgow for two reasons. The first was that he would be the chief executive of that office and Glasgow was where he wanted to live. For the time being, though, he would remain anonymously in the background, not wanting Sir Alan to know he was the puppeteer pulling the strings. His second reason was that LMBM ore coming into Clydeside would be work for the Docks, his small contribution to the prolonged life of his beloved city's main artery.

What he needed now was a front man, a lieutenant who'd apparently be in charge but in reality be under his command. And he was convinced he'd found just such a man in Otis Bitu whom he was sure would grab at the opportunity as Bitu's private investigation line of work – outside what Angus was putting his way – wasn't proving too lucrative.

The idea of the glue factory came back to Angus

making him laugh out loud. Glue factory it would be!

21

Sir Alan Armstrong stared lovingly at the plans for the new Hutchesontown spread before him.

These plans had actually been ready for some time but he'd always managed to find some small additional improvement to suggest which necessitated sending them back to the architects for incorporation.

When he finally came to submit the plans to the Dean of Guild Court he wanted them perfect in every detail. He wanted to submit a work of art which would reflect on him personally.

He started slightly, then smiled benevolently as Margaret Cunninghame slid her arm round his waist.

She said she enjoyed seeing him this way when he was so obviously happy, but thought sometimes he derived more pleasure from these plans of his than he did from her company.

Breaking away, he crossed to a trolley laden with drinks and poured them each a stiff one.

Handing Margaret hers he told her to sit and he would try and explain what the Gorbals project meant to him.

The engineering works was his father's creation. Sir William had conceived and brought into being the works of which he was now owner.

Armstrong's might be his responsibility but it wasn't his brainchild. The Gorbals project was. The fact he was deriving enormous self satisfaction out of it was enough.

But there was a lot more to it than that.

By building this whole new housing redevelopment scheme he was leaving his personal mark on Glasgow. For the next hundred years or so there would be a great slice of the city owing its existence to him – his memorial so to speak.

Not that he wouldn't be making a huge profit out of the redevelopment. He would. But the money wasn't primarily what this was all about.

The project was going to be the pinnacle of his life – what he would be *remembered* for.

Angus discussed the matter thoroughly with Hetherington who'd advised him to exploit without further delay the fact Sir Alan hadn't yet lodged the plans for the redevelopment of the Gorbals with the Dean of Guild Court.

Angus had therefore instructed the same architect working on Craiglea to cannibalize a past design into one for an animal by-products factory.

The reason it was necessary for him to lodge his factory plan first was by doing so he would have precedence over anything coming after, even something on such a grand scale as Sir Alan's plans. The smaller wouldn't have been allowed to intrude on the larger had the larger already been established.

Speaking further with Hetherington, Angus had been able to establish that one member of the Dean of Guild Court if approached the right way – by which Hetherington meant the man took backhanders – could be persuaded to argue their case, more or less ensuring LMBM's factory plan won aproval.

Otis Bitu – who'd accepted the job and who to all intents and purposes was now the UK representative of LMBM (Pty) Ltd – had consequently approached a civil engineer called Graeme McAskill who'd agreed to give LMBM's case due consideratioon.

This was McAskill's way of saying he was waiting to see what was offered before committing himself. Bitu had then suggested he and McAskill get together for a few drinks to solidify the situation. McAskill readily agreed.

McAskill's sweeteners usually came in the form of hard cash. But Angus intended introducing another element into the proceedings which he was convinced would really win McAskill over to LMBM's cause.

Angus explained to Sheena what he needed and asked if she could help? Sheena laughed and replied with her contacts from the old days it was the easiest thing in the world for her to arrange.

That Saturday night Bitu met McAskill in a pub. The pair of them made their way to a hotel where Sheena and a beautiful prostitute were waiting for them in the best suite the hotel had to offer.

Janice was what is known in Glasgow as *a right brammer*. She was petite with finely chiselled features and a figure any movie actress would've been proud of.

Perhaps her most winning asset – bearing in mind many middle-class Scots such as McAskill are most impressed by this sort of thing though they deny it – was her accent which was so refined as to be almost good enough to pass for a southern English one.

One look at the gorgeous Janice and McAskill was completely smitten. Glancing across at Bitu he was tipped the wink he wasn't misreading the situation.

For appearances sake and to help matters along Bitu had been paired with Sheena. But this was only a façade for McAskill's benefit. Neither Bitu nor Sheena intending anything other than a few drinks and conversation.

McAskill wasn't a widely experienced man when it came to women and Janice was something out of his wildest dreams. She had tricks to her repertoire that left him pop-eyed and gasping for more.

And more he got in abundance. When morning finally came McAskill was a man who'd already tasted paradise.

After the women had left, Bitu handed McAskill a wad of used fivers with the promise there would be more plus another party with Janice as soon as LMBM's plan for an animal by-products factory was given the go ahead.

As Bitu later reported to Angus, they could be certain McAskill would wax most eloquent on their behalf. Janice had seen to that.

The same night McAskill was being entertained, Hugh and Janey were wakened a little before midnight.

They lay in silence for a few minutes listening. Then they heard quite distinctly the chink of a foot knocking against a stone followed by the furtive whisper of voices.

Thinking burglars were paying them a call, Hugh swung out of bed and reached for his dressing gown.

In a whisper Janey asked if she should ring for the police?

Hugh replied he didn't think that necessary. He crept downstairs to the hall stand where a stout walking stick was kept. Grasping this, he stepped out into the night chill.

Again he heard voices, this time off in the direction of the dairy. Being as quiet and stealthy as he could he tip-toed towards them.

Suddenly a dozen or so figures erupted out of the darkness to go hurtling past. Although he managed several good swipes with his stick he failed to make contact with any of the ducking and weaving bodies.

Several of the figures turned in the driveway. It was evident they were teenage lads. They called out:

'Fenian bastards!'

'Left footed whoor!'

'Ya fuckin' turncoat!'

Hearing these vitriolic mouthings, Hugh knew with a sinking heart what this was all about. Taking a deep breath, he returned to the house, confident whoever those boys were they wouldn't return that night.

Janey was waiting for him at the top of the stairs to say Mary Agnes hadn't been disturbed.

They went back to bed where he told her what had been shouted at him downstairs.

Suddenly he was deathly afraid, not for himself but for

Janey, Mary Agnes and the unborn child.

Next morning they were up at their usual early hour.

When Hugh stepped outside what he saw stopped him dead in his tracks.

The sides of the house plus stables and dairy had all been daubed with various slogans in bright orange paint.

Catholics ya bass!

King Billy won at Benwater!

Remember the Boyne!

Clutching Mary Agnes to her bosom Janey came out to stand at Hugh's side. 'Holy Mary Mother of God!' she whispered.

Hugh felt sick. He'd secretly dreaded this happening.

The news of his defection to the Catholic church had finally come to the ears of those who weren't prepared to sit back and allow such a thing to happen without exacting some sort of revenge. The bully boys and wild element had become involved.

'Hugh?' Janey whispered. Leaning close and staring up into his face, she was remembering the terrible sights she'd witnessed in the Gorbals and elsewhere when the Green and Orange had clashed.

Men with faces shredded by razors. Others being carted away with hatchets embedded in various parts of their anatomies.

Quite clearly she recalled the awful picture of a man lying dead with a knife sticking out of his chest. Mindlessly drunk, the silly bugger had worn a bright blue suit and shouted 'Up the Gers!' at a dance where those present had been predominantly Catholic.

'Never mind, lass. It'll soon scrub off,' Hugh said. And giving her a squeeze he went in search of a bucket to fill with hot water. He wanted to erase as much of the daubings as possible before the milk boys came.

As he worked up a sweat scrubbing it came to him it would be a good idea to get a guard dog to let loose on the premises at night when they were all indoors.

He laughed suddenly thinking he would get a brute of an alsatian whom he would call King Billy.

Let those lads come back and he'd give them King Billy all right, a mouthful of slavering fangs where it would hurt like hell, in the arses of their trousers.

Whistling, he bent to his task, the situation not appearing nearly as black as it had done a few minutes previously.

King Billy! He couldn't wait to tell Janey.

Iain McLaren sat across from Rosemary in the drawing room of his parents' house. Upstairs with his mother and a specialist in attendance his father lay dying. According to the specialist it was doubtful if Sir Hamilton would last till morning.

He and Rosemary had been with Sir Hamilton for some hours but had broken their vigilance to come downstairs for a much needed cup of tea and smoke.

There was a knocking on the outside door which the butler answered. Sir Alan's voice filled the vestibule.

Sir Alan burst into the room with a face like fizz. He was about to launch into a tirade when, remembering the solemnity of the occasion, managed to keep himself under control long enough to ask what the up-to-date position on Sir Hamilton was?

Unable to contain himself any longer and not even making a pretence of listening to Iain's reply, he exploded with his news.

The old bitch Miss McCallum had gone and sold to some Australian firm who that very afternoon had been granted permission to build an animal by-products factory on the site where her properties now stood.

'A bloody glue factory!' he fumed.

Purple with rage, he stalked over to the whisky decanter and poured himself a large one.

Staring at the irate Sir Alan, Iain was filled with contempt for the man's insensitivity.

Sir Alan strode up and down the room furiously trying to think.

He would have to put in a bid to this LMBM (Pty) Ltd for the properties involved. Perhaps they would be understanding once he explained the situation to them. After all, there had to be a hundred places in Glasgow where such a factory could be sited without causing undue inconvenience.

What he could suggest was he give them the benefit of his local knowledge in their purchase of an alternative strip of land. Naturally he would ensure it was worth their while financially obliging him this way.

Coming up with a possible solution mollified him somewhat and whirling on the whisky decanter he poured himself another.

Turning back to Iain he began to explain what he had in mind only to be brought up short by Iain saying firmly no business would be discussed in this house that night.

Sir Alan had been somewhat dismissive of Iain in the past but hearing the steel now in Iain's voice caused him to pause and look at Iain afresh.

Part of the trouble was Iain's badly damaged face was so damned difficult to read because it so rarely betrayed the emotions behind it.

In a flash of insight Sir Alan realized there was far more to Iain McLaren than he had previously given him credit for.

Iain rose and stared at Sir Alan who was suddenly acutely aware their business relationship had just undergone a shift of emphasis.

Never again would he be able to ride roughshod over Iain who was on the brink of succeeding to the family title and, more importantly from his point of view, fortune. A large part of that fortune was pledged to the building of the Gorbals project.

Rosemary sat quietly amused by this silent interplay. It was a rare sight to see her father stopped dead in his tracks.

Sir Alan coughed, using that as an excuse to turn his eyes away from Iain.

He laid his glass beside the decanter. Then acting as though nothing had happened, declared he must be getting on his way as it was getting late and Cordelia would be worried.

At the door Sir Alan said if there was anything he could do Iain wasn't to hesitate getting in touch. But it was an offer he should've made on entering the house rather than on leaving.

Iain had just seen Sir Alan out when the specialist appeared at the top of the stairs. 'You'd better come quickly,' the specialist said.

Iain took the stairs two at a time with Rosemary coming up behind him as fast as she could. He was only a few feet away from his parents' bedroom when an agonized wail erupted from within.

They found Lize lying prostrate over her husband's body. She was weeping profusely, quite beside herself with grief.

Next morning tragedy struck the McLaren family afresh when Lize, the shock of losing her husband having proved too much for her, was discovered dead in bed.

Her face was in repose, a soft smile on her lips, as though she'd just seen someone she hadn't expected to see again so soon.

Angus wheeled his car in Craiglea's front drive. Switching the engine off, he sat back to listen to the cacophony of sound made by hammers and saws all going nineteen to the dozen.

It pleased him that within forty-eight hours of LMBM having been granted permission to build an animal by-products factory an approach had been made to Bitu by Phoenix Development Ltd.

Bitu's reply to the letter had been LMBM hadn't been aware of Phoenix's plans. But now these had been made known to them he was certain Mr O'Rourke, LMBM's head man in Australia, would view Phoenix's offer with sympathy.

This was a purely delaying tactic to allow Angus to come up with the next move.

Angus made a fist and gently bashed his thigh. Now he

knew what was niggling him.

All this was very well but where was it ultimately leading? Was he merely going to use the former McCallum properties to eventually extort a monstrous profit out of Armstrong or was there a way in which he could use this lever to hurt the man even more?

What he wanted was a gutting stroke – the infliction of maximum pain combined with maximum damage.

Suddenly what his goal should be came to him and the very rightness and irony of it caused him to exclaim. It should have been obvious to him all along!

It would be an incredibly difficult coup to pull off, and one that in the end might even prove impossible. Only Hetherington would know its feasibility so the sooner he saw the chief accountant the better.

Hetherington was full of the letter he'd received in the morning's post from his wife who'd arrived safely in Perth, Western Australia.

According to Mrs Hetherington her health had picked up almost immediately she crossed the equator. And now she had experienced the warm, dry Westralian climate she had no doubt it would improve her condition immensely.

Angus allowed Hetherington's excited chatter about Mrs Hetherington to run its course before sitting the man down and disclosing his idea.

Hetherington was dumbfounded. Then ever so slowly his face cracked into a grin and he began to laugh.

'You really do hate Sir Alan, don't you,' he said: it was a statement, not a question.

Angus thought of his father, dead without compensation; his mother married to that sadistic bastard, Archie Marjoribanks, and the life he and she had undergone as a consequence; and at last but hardly least, the incident with the cuff links which had cost him Rosemary.

'Yes, I hate him,' Angus replied grimly.

Hetherington wouldn't be rushed into giving an answer and insisted on making a pot of tea in order to give himself time to think.

Finally he said what Angus had in mind was possible if handled the right way and luck was on their side.

Armstrong's weakness lay in being short of ready capital, having only a fraction of the works' war profits left. The rest had been ploughed into buying up the Gorbals.

Some time ago Sir Alan had gone to the London Merchant Banks and various private financiers in the hope of raising building capital. Much to his consternation he'd been turned down flat by each and every one of them.

The general consensus of opinion had been the Gorbals project was not a viable one and could only be doomed to failure. None of them could believe with the terrible name the district had that middle-class people would ever be persuaded to live, far less buy private homes there.

Despite a great deal of correspondence and to-ing and fro-ing on Sir Alan's part, he'd been unable to make the money men change their minds. Rebuffed by London, Sir Alan's solution to his problem had been to approach Sir Hamilton McLaren – already involved in a minor way – and propose Sir Hamilton put up the money.

The Phoenix partnership had then been drawn up with each director having equal standing. Sir Alan's capital had bought the Gorbals. Sir Hamilton's would redevelop it.

Excited now, Hetherington leaned forward to say Sir Alan's dependency on the McLaren fortune was the key to his possible undoing. If one could somehow be separated from the other, Sir Alan would have to fall back on his own resources which would leave him with only three options.

The first was to abandon the project altogether and in time recoup his investment by selling off the Gorbals piecemeal. This Hetherington was convinced he wouldn't do as he was so committed to the project that as long as there was a way open for him to continue he would use it.

Apart from the Gorbals, Sir Alan's other major asset was the works on the River Cart and this he could raise money on by either mortgaging buildings and plant or else going public. These were his second and third.

In his privileged position as chief accountant Hetherington would be expected to give advice on the matter. He would strongly advise the latter which Sir Alan would undoubtedly plump for once it had been explained to him a greater amount of capital could be raised that way.

Angus asked why Sir Alan hadn't approached Sir Hamilton in the first place? Hetherington's reply was that Sir Alan had never wanted to share the glory of redeveloping the Gorbals: this he would be forced to do with another prominent Glaswegian in partnership with him.

Hetherington went on to say a detailed plan of action would be needed and this he'd get cracking on from the financial point of view. It was agreed they'd meet several days hence to discuss the matter further.

On an impulse Angus drove down to the Cart where he stopped, facing Armstrong's. Emerging from his car he crossed the road to stand by the iron railings over which he'd climbed to get to the river countless times as a boy.

Lines from an old street song he'd sung in his youth came suddenly to mind: 'I'm the king of the castle, and you're the dirty wee rascal!'

He glanced across to the brooding pile on the opposite bank – the king of that particular castle was about to discover just how dirty this ex-wee rascal could be.

And it wasn't hygiene he was referring to.

When Angus and Hetherington next met, the accountant had already drawn up rudimentary financial plans for Angus's eventual takeover of Armstrong's. These he would continue to work on.

In the meantime, phase one of their ultimate realization was to cause a breach between Iain McLaren and Sir Alan.

Angus had been thinking about the correspondence Sir Alan had conducted with the London Merchant Banks and private financiers. He was now able to verify from Hetherington that the contents of this correspondence had never been disclosed to Sir Hamilton either before or after Sir Hamilton had pledged McLaren money for the Gorbals project.

What Angus wondered was if Sir Iain (Iain having succeeded to the title) were to see that correspondence now would it persuade him to pull out of the Gorbals venture?

For a start, withholding vital information was hardly conducive to inspiring future trust within a partnership.

Secondly, London were certainly no fools when it came to matters of investment. So if it was their opinion the Gorbals project was a non-viable one that opinion just had to be given deep and careful consideration.

According to Hetherington this correspondence was kept in a locked filing cabinet in Sir Alan's office to which Sir Alan had the sole key.

Hetherington was in a position to remove this correspondence but for him to do so, and it subsequently turning up in Sir Iain's possession, would necessitate giving himself away. His future use to Angus within Armstrong's would be non-existent which was the last thing Angus wanted.

So Angus decided to call in an expert to acquire the correspondence for him. But before going into action he had a little ploy up his sleeve which would be the opening shot in his bid to sunder relations between Sir Iain and Sir Alan.

It was the morning of Sir Hamilton and Lize McLaren's funeral: Sir Alan was dressing to attend when he was informed there was an urgent telephone call for him.

Otis Bitu was on the line to say he'd received a telex only minutes previously informing him Mr O'Rourke was ringing through at eleven am and wanted to speak personally with Sir Alan about the former McCallum properties.

This put Sir Alan into a terrible quandary as he naturally wanted to settle the McCallum business – and from Bitu's tone he guessed it was going to be in his favour. On the other hand, it would be a dreadful insult to the McLarens if he was to turn up late for the funeral.

Bitu expressed sympathy with Sir Alan's position, then pointed out as the funeral service didn't start until twelve-thirty surely Sir Alan would have time to speak with Mr O'Rourke *and* attend the service?

Sir Alan was uncertain. Bitu said he could understand if Sir Alan didn't come into the office but O'Rourke might not.

The insinuation was crystal clear. Sir Alan assured Bitu he would be on his way shortly.

Angus was in the new LMBM office which Bitu had moved into listening to Bitu on the phone to Sir Alan. When Bitu hung up and turned to him with a smile he knew the bait had been swallowed.

As it would be a little while before Sir Alan arrived they lingered over a cup of coffee. Then Angus left the office to go across the road to where his car was parked. He settled back to wait the arrival of his adversary.

The Rolls Royce was different to the one he remembered. As Sir Alan climbed out of the Rolls he was afforded a clear view of the face he hated so much – the face he'd last seen the day he'd been framed for the supposed theft of the man's cuff links.

As Sir Alan disappeared into the building where the LMBM office was Angus got out of his car and crossed to the Rolls. It was a trick he'd learned as a lad, effective now as it had always been. He waited till the coast was clear. Then bending down to the nearside front tyre, he whipped the valve cap off and rammed a matchstick into the valve itself so it was jammed in the *on* position.

He did this with all four tyres, waiting a little way off

until the last one was flat. Hastily he removed the match-stick evidence before returning to his car.

When he was again settled in the driving seat a glance at his watch told him it was one minute to eleven.

At eleven am precisely Morag Bitu dialled her husband and, pretending to be the operator, said a call was coming through for LMBM on the radio link with Australia. It would be delayed for a few minutes due to trouble on the Australian side.

Bitu relayed this to Sir Alan and then urged him to tell him more about the alternative site for the animal by-products factory Sir Alan had discovered out in Polmadie.

Sir Alan went on at length praising the virtues of the site which in his estimation was ideal for LMBM's purposes.

Morag called again at eleven fifteen to say the call from Australia was still delayed but should be coming through any minute now. This an apologetic Bitu relayed to Sir Alan.

At eleven thirty Morag rang to say the call was on the line but due to appalling interference they were holding it for a few minutes more in the hope the interference would clear itself.

By now Sir Alan was becoming extremely agitated and kept glancing repeatedly at his gold hunter.

Bitu talked non-stop, pointing out again and again it would be ridiculous for Sir Alan to leave now and jeopardize the Phoenix position when Mr O'Rourke would no doubt be getting through at any moment.

Outside the next phase of the charade had appeared in the shape of a black cab whose driver Angus had sought out and bribed earlier. The driver would now wait a little way up the street until Angus tipped him the wink.

The minutes ticked by and as they did so Sir Alan became more and more frantic. When yet another look at his hunter told him it was noon he knew he was going to be late for the service.

And still Morag kept ringing to say the call was being

variously held or detained and should be coming through loud and clear directly. Finally at twelve fifteen she rang to say the Australian party had cancelled.

Sir Alan was apoplectic, Bitu full of apologies but argued that no fault could be attached to him for what had happened. The blame rested fairly and squarely with the telephone people.

At the door Sir Alan muttered hasty goodbyes, then went galloping downstairs intent on getting out to Carmunnock to join the other mourners who'd been invited back to the McLaren house.

The moment the Rolls started forward he knew something was wrong.

Bringing the car to a halt, he got out to examine the tyres thinking one of them had gone soft. When he saw all four were completely deflated he jibbered with anger.

Cued by Angus, the taxi moved forward to be hastily flagged down by a relieved Sir Alan. The taxi disappeared in the direction of Carmunnock – not that it was ever going to arrive there.

Once out of the city and at a rural spot previously agreed on, the driver would suddenly take ill and insist on dropping Sir Alan so he could return to Glasgow and his bed. From there, Sir Alan would have to walk a good two miles to the nearest public transport which was infrequent at the best of times and downright non-existent at others. It would be a miracle if he succeeded in reaching the McLaren house before the mourners dispersed.

Angus was well aware there were elements of farce about all this and it seemed more like a schoolboy prank than the action of one grown man against another. But there was a serious side to this apparent frivolity concerned directly with loss of face.

Even though Lady Armstrong had been present at the service and gathering after, the fact Sir Alan had elected to go off and attend a business meeting would be seen as a lack of respect for the deceased. Sir Iain couldn't fail but take offence.

Returning to the LMBM office, Angus found Bitu on the phone congratulating Morag on her successful excursion into amateur dramatics. Angus congratulated her also.

Hanging up, he announced what he needed now was a first class burglar and could Bitu please find him one?

The smile on the American's face changed fractionally to become a trifle strained. So far Bitu had done everything Angus requested with no questions asked. But now he thought it time to be told what all this was about.

Angus had been intending to confide in Bitu as more and more he was coming to think of him as a friend rather than employee. So he started at the beginning with his father's death.

In Angus's estimation Hetherington had done a brilliant job on the financial plans. If they worked as well in practice they would make him, as majority shareholder, head of Armstrong's.

This was going to take an enormous amount of capital so to ensure enough was available he'd approached the Bank of Scotland to arrange an advance set against his future earnings from LMBM which were guaranteed into the next century.

He'd also asked the Bank of Scotland to act on his behalf regarding a large number of shares he intended purchasing in the new year.

Besides the Bank of Scotland he'd also approached a number of other Scottish banks, none knowing about the other's consent to act on his behalf with regards to shares yet unbought, and all of them had agreed.

Another part of Hetherington's plan called for Angus to set up a construction company which Angus duly did, registering it under the name of Jocar Ltd whose directors were listed as D. Chisholm and W. Chisholm. Donald and Winnie had only reluctantly agreed – after Angus had pleaded with them, saying it was of vital importance to him to have people fronting the firm whom he could trust implicitly.

The name Jocar was a play on words as well as being a combination of parts of Angus's parents' Christian names, Jo/hn and Car/rie coming together to make Jocar. Angus's joke was to be at Sir Alan's expense.

As Angus intended they would never meet, he thought it highly unlikely Sir Alan would tumble to the fact D. Chisholm and W. Chisholm were his retired foreman moulder and wife.

Hetherington had explained to Angus in the first instance Sir Alan would no doubt retain fifty-one per cent of the shares issued, thereby giving him the majority holding. Jocar had been brought into existence to trick him deviously later into relinquishing this majority.

In the meantime there was still the business of engineering a split between Sir Iain and Sir Alan which the success of everything else depended on.

The man Bitu eventually found was called Shughie Reid who'd been a cat burglar all his life.

A layout of Armstrong's office and the exact location of the filing cabinet containing the correspondence was drawn by Hetherington.

To disguise the real motive behind the burglary Shughie was instructed to take other bits and pieces including the petty cash kept in Sir Alan's secretary's office.

One week after Bitu had first contacted Shughie Reid the burglary was successfully carried out and Bitu able to hand over the correspondence to Angus.

The correspondence verified everything Hetherington had said. London was unanimous in its opinion that the Gorbal's project was non-viable in its present form and could only turn out to be a white elephant.

Certainly if Angus himself had been considering investing money in the project this would have turned him completely against it. He could only hope it would have the same effect on Sir Iain McLaren.

*   *   *

The ball was being held in the home of the Duke of Renfrew, a stately mansion just outside the small village of Carmunnock.

Angus had received his invitation at Craiglea the previous week and after dithering over it had finally decided to attend. Now that he belonged to this strata of Glasgow society he might as well find out whether he liked it and vice versa.

The ball was on behalf of the area Conservative and Unionist Society. The night it fell on was Hallowe'en.

Angus parked his car amongst the Rollses, Bentleys and Armstrong-Siddeleys, then made his way to the front door and the liveried flunkey in attendance there.

Standing beside Iain with whom she'd had a terrible battle earlier on in order to get him to attend, Rosemary saw Angus the moment he entered the great hall. Although she continued making the correct responses to a couple talking to her and Iain, her eyes were riveted on Angus.

Sensitive to all his wife's moods, Iain noticed immediately the change in her focus of attention. When he was able to, he glanced swiftly across at the man she was staring at but failed to recognize him.

Diane Armstrong was talking to her mother and father when out of the corner of her eye she spied Angus. Initial surprise gave way to pleasure and, excusing herself, she crossed to where he was hovering on the periphery of a group who were talking about what a disaster it had been for Winnie to be defeated at the polls the previous year.

Angus was delighted to see someone he knew, greeting Diane warmly and affectionately. He was brought up short when she asked him if he'd spoken to Rosemary yet?

Just as he was shaking his head he caught sight of Rosemary and a man with a hideous face moving slowly in their direction.

He knew from Bitu's report – compiled since his meeting with Rosemary in the coffee shop – that Sir Iain had been disfigured in the war. But it was a shock to see just how hideous the actual disfigurement was. He couldn't help but feel sorry for the poor sod.

A few minutes later he sensed Rosemary intended to joining them and wondered if Sir Iain knew about him.

'Angus, what a pleasant surprise!'

The moment Iain heard Angus's name he knew why Rosemary had been showing such great interest in the man.

She believed he didn't know about her and Angus McBain but he did, having learned it from his brother Peter who'd wormed it out of Diane when she'd inadvertently let something drop one night during the early war years.

He'd made discreet inquiries and found out Angus McBain had vanished suddenly from Glasgow although for what reason he'd been unable to determine.

Since then he'd come to suspect Rosemary retained a great deal of feeling for McBain which hadn't bothered him unduly as McBain was safely out of the way and out of her life.

Only now McBain was back.

During the ensuing chat Angus turned to Sir Iain and said he understood Sir Iain was interested in flying?

Replying, Iain told Angus about the Tiger Moth he'd recently bought and what a joy she was to fly.

Throwing leading question after leading question, Angus encouraged Iain to talk about flying which he did with enormous keenness and passion.

Sir Iain was waxing lyrical about Mosquitoes which he'd flown during the war when he was interrupted by a new voice asking to join their circle.

Angus went ice cold inside. Glancing across at Rosemary he saw she was frowning sympathetically at him.

The muscles in his face were rigid as he turned towards Sir Alan and Lady Armstrong.

Sir Alan stared directly into Angus's face, his brow creasing in thought as he tried to place where he knew this young man from.

Unable to help herself, Rosemary smiled sweetly and said, 'Surely you remember Angus McBain father? You loaned him a pair of cuff links once.'

Inwardly Sir Alan cursed her for her impertinence. McBain! Where in God's name had *he* come from!

The atmosphere between Angus and Sir Alan was almost a static crackle. They were like two fighting dogs suddenly come face to face in an alley.

It was Sir Iain who saved the explosive situation from erupting altogether. His scarred and mangled face lit up in a gruesome smile as he asked Diane for the pleasure of the next dance. Casually he suggested Angus might like to take the floor with Rosemary.

The ferocity of the looks Angus and her father were exchanging sent shivers racing up and down Rosemary's spine. Hurriedly she took Angus by the arm and steered him in the direction of the dance floor

The arm in hers was like a steel pole.

Later that night as Rosemary sat brushing her hair in front of her dressing table Iain approached her from behind to put his hands on her shoulders.

'Tell me about the cuff links?' he asked.

She started but swiftly recovered her composure. Shrugging, she said it was something that had happened a long time ago and wasn't worth talking about now.

'I'd still like to know,' Iain said softly. Adding when he saw she intended to prevaricate, 'I know all about what went on between you and McBain if that's what's holding you back.'

This time she wasn't able to recover her composure. She was rattled and clearly looked it. 'How did you find out?' she whispered.

He told her. Then he asked again.

Rosemary nervously lit a cigarette. She had enormous affection for Iain and didn't want to hurt him in any way. But if he knew part of the story it was probably best he knew all.

Hoping she was doing the right thing she started at the beginning – the time Angus and Kitty had saved her and Margaret Cunninghame from the louts in Queen's Park Recreational Ground – and told him everything with the exception of having met up with Angus in the coffee shop. That and the fact she was still in love with Angus.

For Angus the night at the ball had proved constructive in one respect: he'd discovered just how passionate Sir Iain was about flying.

He therefore continued to hold on to the burgled correspondence while Bitu went on yet another quest for him.

Some LMBM business had come up which took Bitu to London anyway and while he was there he contacted a number of planemaking firms and flying organizations whom he enlisted to his aid.

It was finally through the Handley-Page people that he came to hear of a young man call John Muir who lived in Kilwinning, a small village in Ayrshire.

Like Sir Iain, Muir had been in the RAF during the war only instead of flying as Sir Iain had done he'd been one of the backroom boffins.

Since the war and working entirely on his own Muir had come up with a design for a revolutionary new passenger plane intended for the Middle and Far East runs. He'd tried every planemaker in Britain but his design had been turned down flat by all of them.

The simple reason for this was that money was desperately short in the planemaking world and what capital the planemakers had was already committed to schemes of their own.

According to Handley-Page who'd kept tabs on Muir he was now back in Kilwinning where he was contemplating going to America to see if they would buy his design.

What Angus had been looking for, and was sure he'd now found, was an alternative investment to the Gorbals project for Sir Iain. And where better to look for that potential investment than in the world of aeroplanes in which Sir Iain was so interested?

Janey was kneading dough when the pains started. She gasped and bent over the table till the first one had passed. Then very carefully she crossed to a chair and sat.

She gritted her teeth as the second searing pain tore at her insides. When that pain had passed away she came to her feet and stumbled to the door and out into the front yard. There was no need to worry about Mary Agnes for the moment. The wean wasn't long down for her sleep.

Hugh was in the stables mucking out.

Yet another pain exploded in her. As she lurched into his arms her fingers dug deeply into his flesh.

'It's coming!' she whimpered.

She was a hefty lump but Hugh would've managed had she been twice the weight. Staggering, he carried her back to the house and up to their bedroom where he laid her on top of the bed.

He flew down the stairs to the telephone and rang Dr Robertson's surgery to be informed by the receptionist the doctor was out doing house calls but should be ringing in soon.

His second call was to a neighbour in Tallon Street who'd go and tell Winnie that Janey's labour had started and she was needed right away.

He was filled with a curious combination of fear and elation as he raced back up the stairs to Janey. The baby was several weeks early.

Winnie and Dr Robertson arrived almost simultaneously to find Hugh with the situation well in hand. Mary Agnes was playing quite happily down in the kitchen on her own while Janey was sitting up in bed wearing a clean nightie and sipping a cup of tea between spasms.

Banished to the kitchen, Hugh strode up and down like the proverbial cat on a hot tin roof. Winnie told him to go back to work and she would give him a shout when there was news. But he would have none of her suggestion.

Suddenly he burst out he and Janey had agreed to call the baby Alexander after his dead brother providing it was a boy which of course it would be.

Winnie was most touched by this gesture and said it was a grand idea. She knew Donald would be pleased and said so.

Exactly six hours after the pains had started the baby was born without any complications.

When Dr Robertson handed it to Janey there were tears streaming down his face as a result of what he'd had to tell her after his examination of the wee one.

'I'll send Hugh to you,' Robertson said, turning in the doorway to add, 'I'm awful sorry, lass.'

The moment Hugh saw the doctor's face he knew something was wrong. 'Well?' he demanded, his voice suddenly harsh and ugly.

There were times Robertson hated being a doctor and this was one of them. 'Janey and your baby daughter are both well,' he said.

'A girl?' Hugh replied quickly and Robertson nodded affirmation.

Hugh was bitterly disappointed but consoled himself with the fact they could always try again and next time it was *bound* to be a boy.

As though reading Hugh's mind Robertson said unfortunately Janey wasn't going to be able to have any more children.

The he dropped the real bombshell. The wee girl was a mongol.

For a few seconds the whole world spun and the only thing Hugh was aware of were the doctor's pitying eyes.

'Oh, son!' said Winnie.

'I think you'd better away up and see Janey,' Robertson said. 'She needs you now.'

'Aye,' said Hugh.

He trudged up the stairs with shoulders hunched and head low. His face was grey and lined. He seemed to have aged a dozen years in the past few minutes.

He knew it was selfish but the thought running

through his mind was there would be no immortality for him after all.

'Why are you crying, Granny? Aren't you happy I've got a new babby sister?' Mary Agnes asked.

Winnie couldn't answer, the words sticking in her throat when she tried.

Dr Robertson let himself out.

John Muir wrote to Sir Iain McLaren who replied asking him to present himself at Carmunnock which Muir duly did.

They started talking mid-morning and became so involved in the conversation they missed lunch. Undoubtedly they'd have missed dinner as well had Rosemary not interrupted to demand their presence at table.

After dinner they disappeared back into Iain's study where they continued talking till well after midnight when Rosemary interrupted again to say Muir had better stay the night and that a bed had been made up for him.

Iain's conversation with Muir resumed over breakfast and continued through till late afternoon, at which time Iain suggested they go for a walk to clear their heads with a breath of fresh air.

On the return leg of this walk Iain thought to ask about the American Muir had mentioned in his letter who'd recommended Muir to contact him.

Muir explained the man had arrived at his door one day out of the blue with some knowledge of his design. To begin with he'd thought the man represented one of the American aero firms but it had transpired this wasn't the case.

The man had been extremely vague about just who and what he was. His one definite action was to recommend in the strongest terms that Muir contact Sir Iain McLaren whom the American was convinced would be interested in the design, perhaps even to the extent of financing its production.

Sir Iain was intrigued by this report and couldn't help but wonder who this mysterious American was who seemed to know so much about him.

Then he thought of the correspondence that had arrived anonymously through the post a few days previously regarding dealings Armstrong had conducted with London banks and financiers.

Suddenly he began to smell a rat. All this was too pat and far too coincidental.

Over a month had passed since the correspondence burgled from Sir Alan's safe had been mailed to Sir Iain. According to Hetherington there was as yet no sign of discord between these two worthies.

Angus was beginning to despair that his plan had failed and that he would have to find some other way of splitting the two Phoenix directors when suddenly his telephone rang one morning with Sir Iain on the line suggesting they meet.

Angus was taken aback by this invitation, but nonetheless agreed to do so the following afternoon.

Angus arrived dead on time to find Sir Iain waiting for him. They strolled for a little while in silence. Then Sir Iain's glittering, snake-like eyes swung slowly round to fix themselves on Angus's face.

They were cold as ice those eyes and made Angus wilt a little inside. In a voice as chilly as his gaze Sir Iain said he would be obliged if Angus would tell him just what in the hell Angus was up to?

The fact Sir Iain was accusing him meant the man knew something. But how much?

Angus phrased his reply in such a manner he neither pretended innocence nor committed himself in any way.

With a sigh, Sir Iain said he'd been able to prove conclusively that Otis Bitu of LMBM and the mysterious American who'd visited John Muir at Kilwinning were one and the same. And weren't Angus and Bitu often to be found in one another's company?

Furthermore, a cablegram to an Australian contact

had eventually resulted in this contact discovering that one of LMBM (Pty) Ltd's directors, who employed Bitu in Glasgow was one Angus McBain. And hadn't Angus recently returned from Australia?

Taking all this into consideration plus the fact LMBM owned the former McCallum properties which Phoenix Development Ltd were desperately after – not to mention some incriminating correspondence he'd received regarding his Phoenix partner whom Angus quite understandably hated – had led to the logical conclusion. Angus was the common denominator in all these events with the exception of the correspondence which Iain suspected Angus was also involved in but couldn't prove. Angus was up to something and would Angus please tell him precisely what that was?

Angus digested this, thinking his convoluted machinations had come to naught. Or had they?

He asked Sir Iain quickly if Sir Alan was aware of his connection with LMBM?

'Not as far as I know. I've certainly said nothing to him,' Sir Iain replied.

That was an enormous relief to Angus as it meant all wasn't yet lost. If only he could win Sir Iain to his cause he might still carry off the plan Hetherington had devised.

They walked a little further, Angus with head bowed in thought as he tried to work out how best to put what he wanted to say to Sir Iain.

Finally Sir Iain said, 'I found out about you and Rosemary a long time ago although it wasn't till recently I discovered how Armstrong separated the pair of you. Will that make it any easier?'

Angus nodded, grateful to Sir Iain for clarifying the position.

'Let me say I bear you personally no malice whatsoever. It was hardly your fault the way things happened and how they turned out. It's Armstrong I'm after. Him and him alone.'

And having said that, Angus launched into an explanation of his recent actions.

* * *

Iain was jealous of Angus and had been ever since Peter had told him of the milk boy who'd been having it off with the girl who was later to become his wife. Of one thing he was now certain – Rosemary and Angus still hankered after one another. The signs were all there and not too difficult to read.

So what should he do? Should he put a spoke in Angus's wheel by ensuring the Gorbals project went ahead as planned? Or should he follow the dictates of common sense and jettison Armstrong as Angus had been trying to manoeuvre him into doing?

There were no words to describe what he felt at the thought of losing Rosemary. On the other hand he didn't want her staying with him out of pity and doubly so when there was another man she wanted to be with.

He decided the best thing he could do was not to put the boot in as far as Angus was concerned. He wouldn't do anything against Angus that could later be held or used against him in any way.

He was only too well aware this course might prove disastrous in the long run. But it was the one he was determined to pursue.

Iain heard Angus through to the end, then said he would see Armstrong the following week and dissolve their partnership.

He'd never been happy in property anyway, and especially since Armstrong had become so fanatical about the Gorbals project.

John Muir's aeroplane was far more to his taste as an investment and it was into that he would now channel his energies and capital resources.

Nor was he doing this for Angus's sake but rather because of the correspondence Angus had sent him.

He wouldn't allow himself to remain in partnership with a man he didn't trust to be as honest with him as he was in return.

Angus asked Sir Iain to keep his own involvement in all this quiet, which Sir Iain promised to do.

They shook hands on what had passed between them and without a further word Sir Iain strode off.

Angus's breath misted the air as he rubbed his hands together in self congratulation. He would telephone Bitu with the good news immediately and later Hetherington.

His head whirling with plans, he followed Sir Iain out of the park.

22

Angus and Bitu waited till the end of the week after Angus's meeting with Sir Iain before Bitu telephoned Sir Alan to say he'd now had the go-ahead from Australia to sell the former McCallum properties to Sir Alan provided terms could be agreed.

Sir Alan was still in a state of shock when Bitu rang. He had been since Sir Iain McLaren had confronted him with the various letters stolen from his office which Sir Iain had said had come to him anonymously through the post.

It had been a terrible blow to have the McLaren money withdrawn from the project which, in a momentary panic, he'd suddenly seen as having to be abandoned.

Then he'd somehow pulled himself together again and forced his benumbed brain to consider the financial alternatives.

In grey despair he turned over all the possibilities in his mind – which individuals he could approach with a view to making them a partner, including the proposal put forward by Hetherington that he turn Armstrong's into a public company.

His initial reaction to this had been one of rejection. But the more he thought about it the more it appealed.

He'd never wanted the McLarens or any other local individuals involved in the first place. And it was only dire necessity that had made him approach Sir Hamilton.

But here was a viable alternative which would ensure all the eventual credit and glory would fall squarely to him. It would be just as he'd always seen it. His project and his alone. The new Hutchesontown. *His* creation!

He summoned his secretary and told her to fetch George Hetherington. He had a host of eager questions to ask his chief accountant about the technicalities and ramifications of going public.

The Monday following his telephone call Bitu was ushered into Sir Alan's office. Bitu repeated what he'd already told Sir Alan on the phone – O'Rourke had finally agreed to resiting the proposed animal by-products factory and selling the former McCallum properties to Sir Alan.

However, there would be several stipulations, one of which was that the actual sale didn't take place until after the old woman's death, as knowing how she felt about Sir Alan, they didn't want to cause her any further upset and pain.

Bitu then mentioned the price LMBM wanted for the properties. Sir Alan replied hoarsely that such an astronomical sum was way above their real value.

Bitu smiled thinly and said of course it was way above their real value. But what Sir Alan had to consider was their value to *him*.

Sir Alan made some rapid mental calculations. He could just afford to buy the properties out of the remainder of his capital. But it would mean his financial resources were more or less wiped out.

Still smiling, Bitu stuck the knife in even further by saying if Sir Alan wasn't agreeable to an immediate purchase his instructions were to raze the site and start building the factory within the month. Once that happened, the opportunity to buy would be lost forever.

Fearing the worst, Sir Alan asked what the remaining stipulations were?

There was only one, Bitu declared, which was that a construction firm called Jocar Ltd whom LMBM had connections with be given the overall contract for the Gorbals project.

Sir Alan naturally seized on this second stipulation as a bargaining point – as Angus had foreseen, hence the outrageously high asking price – to beat down the figure for the former McCallum properties to a little over half what had been initially demanded.

Angus didn't really care what price he got for the properties as they were now merely a device to secure Jocar the contract.

As it transpired he still made a substantial killing.

It was a Saturday afternoon when Angus drove John and Sheena into the driveway at Craiglea to find Donald waiting for them. Only hours previously the finishing touches had been completed and Craiglea was now ready to be moved into.

After the tour of inspection was over and the appropriate comments made, Angus sent Sheena and John into the kitchen to make tea while he took Donald to one side.

'You've kept on the Craiglea workforce like I told you?' he said.

'Aye, that's right.'

'Good. Now what I want you to do is expand that gang to at least ten times its present size.' Angus laughed a little when he saw the mystified expression on his grandfather's face. 'Jocar's been contracted to rebuild the Gorbals.'

'Help ma bob!' exclaimed Donald.

'But somehow I don't feel it's going to be a very long job,' said Angus mysteriously. He hadn't yet confided in Donald as to what his ultimate goal was nor what part Jocar was to play in achieving that goal.

'Are you going to tell me what this is all about?' Donald demanded.

'Not yet. I want it to be a surprise.'

'Always did have a mind like a bloody corkscrew,' Donald muttered later after the tea had come.

Angus smiled broadly. 'Flattery will get you everywhere.'

'Away to hell!' Donald retorted but secretly he was highly chuffed as it meant he was still in a job.

Later that night after John had gone to bed Sheena came to sit opposite Angus by the fire.

Although Angus had the evening paper up in front of him he was actually thinking about Hannah – Hugh and Janey's new wee girl – whom he was in the habit of dropping by to see whenever he could.

He felt so sorry for Hugh who, although trying to put a bold front on things, was a changed man since Hannah's birth.

He thought again of that little face and shuddered.

According to Dr Robertson a mongol could live a good twenty years or more. Poor soul, he thought, then poor Hugh and Janey.

'Angus?'

Dropping his newspaper, he discovered Sheena smiling at him.

'I've never really thanked you for asking me to look after John. Doing so has made me very happy, in fact happier than I've ever been before,' she said.

He returned her smile, a wealth of understanding between them.

Crossing to his chair she kissed him tenderly on the forehead, then left the room for her bed.

Angus stared after his step-sister. Next to Rosemary he loved her more than any other living female.

*   *   *

Sir Alan was in his dressing gown having just enjoyed a piping hot bath. He sat now on the toilet seat with a glass of whisky in his hand watching in admiration as Margaret climbed into a freshly drawn tub.

From time to time he enjoyed talking to her about business which was what he was now doing.

That very day the manifesto for the new public Armstrong's had been issued. It had finally been decided between himself and Hetherington there would be 1,500,000 one pound shares selling in the first instance for fifteen shillings per share of which he would retain a majority holding of fifty-one per cent.

The remaining forty-nine per cent would be made available on the Glasgow and London Stock Exchanges on a day still to be decided the following month.

There would be a board of directors of which he would be chairman. And to accommodate the monthly and annual general meetings he was having a boardroom built as an extension onto the side of his office.

There was also good news concerning Miss McCallum who'd finally reached the stage of being unable to continue on her own. She'd been admitted to a hospital in Greenock: her end was evidently imminent.

All of a sudden he grunted in agony and bent over double, his face suffused with blood.

'Alan!' Margaret exclaimed in alarm. Clambering from the bath, she quickly crossed to enfold him in her wet, soapy arms.

'It's nothing, lass,' he wheezed. Disentangling himself from her embrace, he sucked in a large lungful of air,

She wore a worried frown as she studied him. 'Can I get you anything?' she asked.

'Have you any antacid powder or milk of magnesia?'

She shook her head.

'Then a glass of water,' he smiled.

While she got the water he massaged his chest.

Within a minute his face was back to its normal colour. And within five they were laughing at the terrible fright he'd given her.

It was only a bad attack of indigestion he assured Margaret. And not the first he'd had like it either.

Usually the antacid powder or milk of magnesia cleared it up. But as she had neither he was just going to have to settle for another glass of whisky.

He started talking about the Gorbals project again and soon the incident had passed from both their minds.

Angus entrusted the drawing up of the Jocar contract to Otis Bitu.

There were two important clauses incorporated into the contract. One featured reasonably prominently while the other was buried deep in the mass of small print comprising the latter part of the document. The first clause stated all aluminium used in the constructions to be built had to come from bauxite ore originating from LMBM (Pty) Ltd.

The reason Bitu would give Sir Alan for the clause's inclusion was that LMBM wanted to encourage the importation of their ore into Britain and this was a device to set the ball rolling.

Angus, Bitu and Hetherington all agreed that Sir Alan would accept this clause as he would think it the reason why LMBM had stipulated Jocar get the Gorbals contract. He would imagine it was a case all round of 'If you scratch my back then I'll scratch yours'.

The trick was going to be to get Sir Alan to sign the contract without tumbling to the timebomb ticking away in the small print.

Directly Angus learned Miss McCallum had been taken into hospital he drove to Greenock to check she was being properly looked after and to see if there was anything she needed.

'Oh it's yourself, sonny,' she whispered out of the crabbit face he remembered so well.

He'd brought her a bunch of flowers plus a bottle of

lavender water which he'd suspected correctly she would like.

She thanked him for these gifts then launched into a tirade against the tyranny that insisted on carting her off to hospital away from the rabbits and poor Bella whom she missed so much and was so worried about it fair made her heart hurt.

Angus inquired who was looking after the animals? A distraught Miss McCallum told him that having collapsed in the street she'd been wheeched off to hospital without being allowed home to make arrangements for the poor beasties.

Angus earned her eternal gratitude by saying he would go to Rothesay straight from the hospital and, having collected Bella and the rabbits, would take them back to his house where he would see they were well provided for.

When he added he had a wee boy who'd be delighted at the prospect of having pets to play with Miss McCallum replied she couldn't have asked for anything more for them. 'And God bless and look after you, sonny.'

He stayed and chatted with her for about half an hour, then as he'd promised, he left the hospital to drive down to the quayside from where he caught a boat for Rothesay.

He found Bella in a pitiful state lying whining in the old woman's bed. It was patently obvious neither dog nor rabbits had been fed or watered since Miss McCallum had last done so.

Once Bella and the rabbits had been attended to Angus put the hutch into the back of his car. Then with a satiated Bella lying beside him he made the journey back to Craiglea where he and the animals were welcomed by an ecstatic John.

That night Angus wrote to Miss McCallum assuring her all was well with her animals and she could now set her mind at rest.

He also wrote to Sean O'Rourke telling O'Rourke what he wanted done, when it was to happen and why.

O'Rourke's brief was to arrange matters so that on a signal from Angus all LMBM ore to Great Britain would be blacked indefinitely by the Mine Workers' Union.

The actual securing of the Armstrong shares when they appeared on the exchanges was conducted by Angus with all the thoroughness of a military operation.

A number of brokers in Glasgow and London were instructed to snap up the shares the moment they became available, which the brokers did with such success that within one minute of their appearing Angus owned forty-six per cent of the forty-nine sold.

The remaining three per cent somehow eluded Angus's brokers to be bought on behalf of a Major Cattermole residing in Richmond, Surrey who, despite the offer of a most handsome profit, stubbornly and steadfastly refused to sell.

This didn't worry Angus unduly as he considered forty-six per cent a more than satisfactory haul..

The next step was to parcel the shares out to the various banks he'd previously approached and whose managers would now be acting as his nominees.

None of the nominees knew the others were also acting on his behalf or that they all had the same instructions – to rubber stamp *everything* Sir Alan proposed.

When Armstrong's board of directors was finally announced it consisted of Sir Alan as chairman, four men of his choosing of whom one was Hetherington, and the four bank managers acting as nominees on Angus's behalf.

At the beginning of December the Greenock Hospital phoned Angus to say Miss McCallum had sunk into a coma the previous day and had passed away in the night.

He thanked the Sister for ringing him and asked if she'd let him know what funeral arrangements were made as he wished to attend.

Three days later he went to Miss McCallum's funeral

in the local Greenock œmetery where he was the only mourner.

It seemed the nephew hadn't wanted the additional expense of shipping the body back to Rothesay. Nor had he even bothered to put in an appearance, having arranged everything by telephone from Inverness.

'Bastard!' was Angus's sole comment when he found this out.

A week after Miss McCallum's death the contract from LMBM for the sale of the former McCallum properties plus the Jocar contract arrived simultaneously on Sir Alan's desk, both of which he immediately handed over to Hetherington for perusal.

The same morning Bitu rang Sir Alan to give LMBM's reasons for the inclusion of the ore clause in the Jocar contract. This explanation Sir Alan readily accepted.

Hetherington sat on the contracts for several days, then returned them to Sir Alan saying as far as he could see they were both perfectly straightforward.

Hetherington had already warned Angus that Sir Alan would give the contracts to a solicitor whose job it would be to go over the documents with a fine tooth comb. To prevent this happening and the delay clause being discovered Angus had come up with a plan which now swung into operation.

Informed by Hetherington that the contracts were now back with Sir Alan, Bitu made another phone call to Armstrong, consisting in the main of a well rehearsed speech.

With panic in his voice Bitu said he'd just received an urgent cablegram from Mr O'Rourke saying for reasons unspecified there had been a change of heart about the former McCallum properties which were not now to be sold under any circumstances.

Sir Alan reacted exactly the way Angus anticipated in replying it was too late for LMBM to go back on the deal as the contracts had already been signed and witnessed.

Having inveigled Sir Alan into committing himself,

Angus further pressured the man by having Bitu announce he was leaving for Armstrong's right away and would expect to see the signed contracts on arrival.

Hanging up, a smiling Sir Alan immediately signed both contracts. Hetherington witnessed them. They were then laid aside for Bitu who arrived half an hour later seemingly frantic and consumed with worry.

Within days of the contracts being signed Donald and the Jocar workforce started building on part of a Gorbals site previously razed by a demolition firm contracted to Sir Alan.

Word went swiftly round that Jocar were looking for time served men. Within hours of work being started there were long queues of eager applicants.

Acting on Angus's instructions, Donald hired a large number of these hopefuls to further double the Jocar manpower before the week was out.

As was traditional, the Jocar men toiled over Christmas then got three days to themselves at Hogmanay, *the* festival in the Scottish calendar.

Normally Donald wouldn't have dreamt of leaving his own house on that night of nights. But when Hugh and Janey invited him and Winnie up to Muirend they decided to go for wee Hannah's sake.

Harriet was also invited, as was Angus. So too were Sheena and John but she swiftly declined saying she'd had enough of partying to last her the rest of her life. And anyway John should be in his bed, Hogmanay or not, and not up to all hours. So Angus left Craiglea on his own on Hogmanay and drove to Muirend where he was the last to arrive.

Nobody spoke much about Hannah but it was understood they were all there as a sign of family unity and strength for which Hugh was pitifully grateful.

After a while it was suggested by Hugh the men go to the pub for an hour to allow the women to have a good old blether amongst themselves.

The pub was jam-packed with alcohol being consumed as though it were going to be banned come morning.

A group of men started to sing but were told to keep quiet by the landlord as they knew damn well singing was against the law.

Donald insisted on getting the first round in so while he fought his way to the bar Hugh asked Angus how John was getting on?

Angus gave Hugh a quick rundown on the wee fellow's latest exploits and activities then subtly changed the subject, thinking that the wisest thing to do in the circumstances. He knew only too well what a bitter and compounded disappointment Hannah had been to his uncle.

While they chatted Hugh was thinking about the gang of teenage boys who'd daubed his walls earlier in the year. They'd tried again another night only to encounter King Billy, a huge fearsome black beast whose very growl was enough to chill the marrow.

He didn't think he'd be seeing them or their like back again which was a relief. But it was still depressing to be the object of so much scorn and hatred. Nor could he even emigrate now as no country would accept a family which included a mongol. For better or worse he would have to stand his ground and take whatever was dished out.

When the pub closed they drove back to Muirend where they settled down to await the bells which would start to dead on the final stroke of twelve.

At ten to twelve Janey decided she wanted Angus to be their first foot. So armed with shortie, a lump of coal and his bottle he had to go out into the yard where he would have to wait till the bells.

Earlier in the day it had been freezing cold. But during the past few hours the temperature had risen considerably making Angus think they might well be in for a fall of snow.

He took a deep swig from his bottle then listened lovingly to one of the horses snickering in the stables. He had so many fond memories of this place which had been such an oasis to him in the dark days of Archie

Marjoribanks.

He remembered again the many mornings he and Kitty had cycled here to run with the milk.

Thinking of those times inevitably brought Rosemary to mind. As it did now. Raw emotion rose in his throat which he forced down again with several more swigs from his bottle.

'Oh, Rosie love,' he whispered to the wind. Having met up with Rosemary again he'd come to realize that what he'd felt for Molly Hotblack was a mere counterfeit when put up against the real thing.

Suddenly the bells were pealing in the far distance. With the broadest of smiles plastered all over his face he chapped the door.

'Happy New Year!' he said to Janey when she answered.

And having been solemnly invited in he equally solemnly presented her with the shortie, coal and whisky after which he swept her into his arms and hugged her tight.

For the next several hours Angus drank with a savagery awesome to behold. Dram after dram vanished down his throat. And each time it seemed to those watching he must surely have reached his capacity. But he dumbfounded them by again reaching for the bottle.

Hugh was another hitting the cratur as though he intended drowning himself in the stuff. And the more he drank the more morose and sullen he became.

At a little past three Winnie and Donald decided they'd had enough and, overhearing this, Angus insisted on driving them home.

A few friends and neighbours had dropped by so there was something of a party going on. Angus announced to Janey that he wouldn't be long.

His excuse for taking a bottle along with him was he might bump into someone he knew en route in which case he'd have to exchange drinks as was the custom.

There were quite a few people out and about first footing and visiting but luckily not many cars on the road. Angus drove with a drunken concentration and somehow – much to their obvious relief – managed to deliver Donald and Winnie home all in one piece.

Waving goodbye he turned the car around and headed back the way he'd come.

His thinking was completely muddled and confused now. Every so often he spoke aloud addressing Kitty as though Kitty was sitting there in the car with him.

He confided to Kitty he was on his way to the bear cave where he was to meet Rosie just like in the old days.

He swung the car away from Muirend in the direction of the Linn Park. Things became indistinct and hazy after that. But he was aware of parking the car and then climbing a wall down which he dropped on the other side.

The River Cart was black and ominous as it moved silently on its way. A slight wind had sprung up causing the denuded trees to rustle and sway. Somewhere close by rooks were cawing.

He staggered through the long grass almost to the water's edge. Something wet hit and clung to his face again and again. In his befuddled state it took him a little while to realize it had started to snow.

Within minutes the snow had intensified to such an extent it was difficult seeing more than a few yards ahead.

His foot slipped once and he went tumbling over and over to end up sprawling only inches from the lapping water. Luckily he wasn't hurt nor was his bottle broken. To celebrate he treated himself to another drink.

The snow had started to lie immediately and even before he reached the bear cave the world had turned white and he was a stumbling snowman.

It was warm inside the cave where he sat huddled listening to tiny rivulets of melted snow running down its sides.

She would come soon he told himself. And when she did they'd make love just like they used to.

Once he thought he heard her and smiled in anticipation. But it was only a fall of snow or else some creature being less stealthy than it should.

After a while he could fight the tiredness no longer. His head slumped forward as he pitched into a deep and troubled sleep.

Sheena was in the process of giving John a late breakfast when Angus stumbled into the kitchen.

His face was grey and pinched, his eyes red rimmed with red bags under them, his clothes muddy and wet as though he'd been rolling around on the ground.

A long shuddering spasm wracked his body. 'Christ, I'm so cold,' he mumbled. Then suddenly all arms and legs, he slumped to the floor.

The briefest of examinations confirmed he had a raging temperature. Grasping him under the arms, Sheena dragged him across to the fire and there began stripping him.

John stared in horror at his prostrate father. He began to wail in a high, shrill voice.

Angus was soaked through and positively stinking of alcohol. Sheena stripped him stark naked, then getting a large towel from the press, rubbed and buffed him dry.

Somehow she got him into clean pyjamas which, within minutes, were wringing wet from the sweat suddenly oozing from him.

He was a good fourteen stones to her eight and a half but alternatively coaxing and shouting at him she managed to get him to his feet where he stood swaying and clinging to her for support.

Buckled under his weight, she manoeuvred him out of the kitchen and into the hall. Ascending the stairs to the first floor landing, in through the door of the closest bedroom and onto the bed.

His teeth began chattering as she wrapped the bedclothes round him. Every so often his body jerked as though an electric current had been shot through it. Each time that happened he gave a horrible groan.

Running downstairs she hurriedly put the kettle on for hot water bottles. Picking up the telephone she rang Dr

Robertson's surgery, to get no reply.

Cursing, she hung up and redialled, this time the doctor's home number.

She was profuse in her apologies in disturbing him at a time like this but she was sure it was an emergency.

After hearing her description of Angus's condition Dr Robertson said she was quite right to ring him and he would be at Craiglea within the hour.

With that weight off her mind Sheena hung up to find John standing by her side clutching her pinny. His face was streaked with tears and his eyes huge with concern as he asked her what was wrong with his daddy?

She replied she didn't know but the doctor was coming to find out. So John would have to be a big man and let her get on with organizing things for the doctor's arrival.

When she returned to the bedroom she found Angus writhing deliriously repeating the same word over and over again.

'Rosie . . . Rosie . . . Rosie . . .'

On arrival Robertson gave Angus a thorough examination at the conclusion of which he looked most grave.

In his opinion Angus had a pleurotic involvement compounded by an almost certain local pneumonia. Angus should really be in hospital but he was against moving him as to do so now would undoubtedly cause further complications.

He intended giving Angus an intra-muscular penicillin injection for the pneumonia. He would return in several hours with further medication.

John bit his lip and clung to Sheena as the needle slid into Angus's flesh. He whimpered when the needle was withdrawn and a spot of blood spattered the sodden whiteness of the bed's bottom sheet.

'Is there any chance of him . . . ? I mean, is it possible he could . . . ?' Sheena stumbled over the words, not quite knowing how to put the question without it seeming over-melodramatic.

Robertson looked up from where he'd stooped to

ruffle John's hair. 'Yes, it is possible,' he said evenly.

After the doctor had gone she rang Hugh and Janey to say she needed help and could Hugh go and fetch his mother for her? Hugh said he'd leave for Tallon Street right away.

Harriet was still at Muirend and offered to come over. But Sheena declined, thinking the domineering Harriet would try and take over, which she didn't want.

In his delirium Angus talked of many things. But time and time again he came back to Rosemary, calling for her and asking where she was.

Winnie and Hugh arrived and sometime after that Dr Robertson returned with a freshly charged syringe of special anti-toxin.

Robertson injected Angus after which he contrived to make him swallow several pills. He then took Angus's temperature.

Robertson perched himself on the edge of the bed and said he would hang on for a wee while as he wanted to observe the effects of the jab.

Half an hour later Robertson again took Angus's temperature, shaking his head when he saw it was unchanged.

There was a look in his eyes which told Sheena and Winnie he was becoming more and more concerned for Angus's life.

They were sitting drinking tea Winnie had made when Robertson asked who this Rosie was Angus was continually asking for? And was it possible to get this Rosie here as her presence just might help?

Sheena's gaze was riveted to Angus's sweat slicked face as she considered that. 'It's worth a try,' she said eventually. She went in search of Angus's address book.

When Rosemary came on the line Sheena explained who she was and why she was ringing.

Rosemary was taken aback to get this call so out of the blue. When she mentioned Angus by name she was aware of Iain raising his head from the book he was reading to stare at her.

Her heart was thumping when she finally hung up.

Iain sat apparently engrossed in his book but his eyes remained fixed to one spot on the page.

'Iain?'

'Yes, my dear?' he replied, looking up and smiling.

Rosemary sat and related precisely what Sheena had told her. When she was finished she waited for Iain's reply.

That the telephone had announced a crisis point in their marriage Iain had no doubt. He could feel it with a certainty that was absolute. His smile became strained as he considered what his reaction should be.

Finally and with a lightness he certainly didn't feel he said if Angus was as ill as his step-sister purported then Rosemary had better get over there to be of what assistance she could.

Rosemary's heart went out to Iain. She knew how difficult this must be for him. Kissing him quickly on the forehead, she turned and strode from the room.

For a long time after she'd gone Iain stared at the doorway through which she'd vanished. He'd known since the night of the Ball this moment was going to come when Rosemary would have to make a choice.

When he tried to concentrate on his book again what he saw was a blurred page from which Angus's face stared up at him.

On arriving at Craiglea, Rosemary was met at the door by Sheena. For an instant the two women stood eyeing one another. Then Sheena stretched out her hand and said how good it was of Rosemary to come.

As they walked up the stairs Sheena explained that Angus had needed someone to look after him and John and had very kindly asked her to be his housekeeper.

Rosemary had known Angus and his step-sister were close but hadn't been expecting whatever it was she now saw in Sheena's face.

In a moment of insight it came to her that Sheena was in love with Angus in a more than sisterly way and yet less or perhaps differently than she herself felt towards him. Surprisingly she sensed in Sheena she had an ally.

Angus lay bathed in sweat, his eyes open but unseeing, his face flushed to a ripe shade of candy pink.

Rosemary's stomach flipped as she stared down at him. Her whole instinct was to take him in her arms, gather him to her and tell him everything was going to be all right now she was here.

'He's been desperate for you to come,' Sheena said.

'I'll stay as long as I have to,' Rosemary replied simply.

Sheena nodded. They understood one another. 'I'll be downstairs if you need me. Just call,' she said, and flitted from the room.

Angus didn't know where it was he'd been but he'd wanted to stay there forever. But someone had called him back. He wasn't ready for that other place yet. There were still things to be done here.

'Rosie?' he croaked.

A hand tightened round his. 'I'm here,' she replied.

He blinked, feeling so weak it was an effort even to open his mouth.

When he tried to focus, his vision became blurred and watery. 'Is it really you? I mean, I'm not dreaming, am I?'

'You're not dreaming,' she replied.

Closing his eyes to stop his head going round and round he said he'd gone to the bear cave to wait for her but she'd never come.

She replied softly no such arrangement had been made between them.

'Must have been the bevy then,' he said. 'So many dreams and imaginings. Hard to know just what was real and what wasn't.'

She bent over to wipe his forehead and suddenly found their lips scant inches apart.

'What have we done to one another?' he asked in a whisper.

She bent her head further and their lips met in a kiss.

There were tears in her eyes when she finally drew away.

He struggled higher up the bed onto his pillows, a fever in him now that had nothing to do with the illness. 'It's still not too late,' he said urgently. 'Leave Iain and come to live with me. We'll get married just as soon as you can get divorced.'

Before she could reply the door opened and Sheena ushered Dr Robertson into the room. They both exclaimed with surprise and pleasure when they saw Angus was sitting up and talking.

Dr Robertson felt Angus's forehead, then said he'd prescribed the right medicine in asking Rosemary to come. A check with the thermometer confirmed Angus was now on the road to recovery.

Sheena announced Winnie had some leek and potato soup on downstairs and Angus was going to have some whether he wanted it or not.

'Bully!' Angus called after her and grinned.

Rosemary was in a turmoil inside. There was nothing she wanted more than to come and live with Angus. And yet she couldn't help but think of the poor man she'd left at home. She knew Iain would be sitting there, watching the clock, fearing the worst.

Before taking his leave Robertson gave Angus another injection. To observe the proprieties Rosemary stepped outside while Angus bared his bottom.

She was just about to go back into the bedroom when Sheena appeared with the bowlful of soup.

Thrusting the bowl into Rosemary's hands Sheena told her to take it, adding Angus was probably too weak to feed himself so she would have to do it.

Sheena was at the top of the stairs when she suddenly paused to say over her shoulder, 'And thank you for what you did. I think we might have lost him if you hadn't been there for him to come back to.'

As Rosemary rejoined Angus and Robertson it was to hear the doctor say he'd return the next day but from now on he expected it to be all uphill for Angus. What Angus needed was rest and plenty of it.

After the doctor had gone Rosemary sat on the edge of the bed with the intention of feeding Angus. But before he would accept any soup he demanded to know the answer to his question. Would she leave Iain for him?

They were right together and always had been, he said – like bacon and eggs they fitted. They were a natural couple.

'Well?' he demanded, and when there was no reply, 'It's now or never, lass. Let this moment go and we'll both rue it the rest of our lives.'

She was so choked with emotion she could hardly get the words out. But eventually they came in a tight crackling whisper. 'Yes, I'll live with you,' she said.

'When?'

With her thoughts whirling she replied it would be best if they waited a little while, at least until Angus was better.

Telling Iain she was leaving him wasn't going to be easy. She needed time to work out just how she was going to do it.

Angus wanted to kiss her again but she said there would be more than enough time for that once he was better. What was important now was he got this hot, nourishing soup inside him to build his strength back up.

He laid his head against the headboard and accepted the first spoonful into his mouth. With Rosemary feeding him he ate every last morsel.

Over the next fortnight Angus grew steadily better until finally Dr Robertson announced he could be taken off the sick list.

During those two weeks Rosemary came to see him every day and each visit was an inspiration to him. He was happier than he'd been in years which went a long way to aiding his recovery.

Early on he told Sheena that Rosemary would be coming to stay and eventually they planned to marry.

Sheena was genuinely pleased to hear this news. She

knew what Rosemary meant to him.

She said it would be best if she left as she wouldn't be needed now. But Angus wouldn't hear of it and nor would Rosemary.

As the days passed Angus pressed Rosemary to tell Iain. Again and again she put it off saying it was her prerogative to choose the right moment.

Iain grew desperately morose and despondent during this time, sitting in his study and staring vacantly at the wall for hours on end.

Even his enthusiasm for John Muir's aeroplane waned as he became more and more resigned to the fact Rosemary had taken up again with Angus McBain and consequently it was only a matter of time before she left him.

Finally Angus forced Rosemary into naming the date she would come to Craiglea.

On the coming Saturday she would ensure she and Iain were alone for the evening and tell him then. Angus would be outside waiting for her in his car.

On the Friday Rosemary paid her daily visit to Craiglea to discover Sheena had gone into town taking John with her to do some shopping. This meant she and Angus were alone in the house.

When she saw the gleam in his eye she knew right away what he had in mind. Nor was she averse to it providing his health was up to it which he assured her it was.

He took her by the hand and led her up to the bedroom where they both stripped and hurriedly crawled beneath the bedclothes.

He was nervous to begin with as was she. But soon those barriers fell away and it was even better than it had been all those years previously.

Life was truly wonderful after all, Angus decided.

By lunchtime on Saturday Iain knew this was the day Rosemary had chosen to tell him she was leaving. He could feel it. Sense it. Read it in her face.

He'd already decided he'd make it easy for her. There would be no row or vain pleadings – merely the statement he wanted her to be happy and if she thought being with Angus McBain would bring her happiness then so be it. He wouldn't stand in her way but rather wish her well.

Dinner that night was a sombre affair, the main course a great favourite of his, a last minute sop, he thought grimly.

After the meal they sat round the fire, he waiting for the prepared speech she was so obviously working up to.

Eyeing the clock, Rosemary knew Angus would be outside waiting for her. Upstairs she had a small case packed ready for the moment of departure.

All that was left for her to do was speak. And yet, for some reason she couldn't.

She loved Angus and always had done. There was absolutely no doubt about that. If things hadn't turned out the way they had she would've undoubtedly married him all those years ago.

As coldly as she was able, she examined her feelings towards Iain. She didn't love him in the grand manner she loved Angus. But she was inordinately fond of him – loved him in a minor way.

Over the years she'd come to accept her situation and together she and Iain had built a successful life by many people's standards. If Angus had never reappeared their marriage would have gone marching on without even a hiccup to disrupt it.

There had been the time she was going to leave Iain. But that had been before his disfigurement.

If the break had been made in those early years it would've been neat and clean. But she'd been unable to bring herself to leave him after his crash, knowing to do so would be to literally sign his death warrant.

The intervening years had altered Iain, however. He was now far tougher mentally and had come to terms with his disfigurement. This time there would be no question of him killing himself.

Staring into the fire's cheery blaze she thought of the good times she and Iain had enjoyed together. There had been many.

She remembered the innumerable kindnesses he'd done her, the way he'd always been there to give her strength and support whenever she'd needed it, the love he'd unabashedly and unstintingly lavished on her.

It came to her that their marriage was a number of daily bricks they'd built together and which formed a bond between them, a bond consisting of many little things put together to comprise a whole.

And it surprised her, thinking of it like that for the first time, just how strong and worthwhile that whole was.

Then there was the question of need. Angus loved and needed her. That was indisputable.

But Iain loved and desperately needed her too – and if she was honest about it – undoubtedly more than Angus did. For it was always possible Angus could find someone else whereas in Iain's case it was either her or no one.

Another item to be taken into consideration was that Angus was a born survivor. Naturally he could be wounded and deeply. But he was the type who would overcome that wound and flourish despite it.

Iain, on the other hand, like some plant whose roots have been badly damaged, would eventually fade and wither away.

She would be happy with Angus but her happiness would be marred by the knowledge that it had been achieved only at Iain's expense. She would be forever feeling guilty and might that not be the fatal flaw that would ultimately destroy her relationship with Angus?

For she knew herself only too well. Once her guilty conscience was activated it would gnaw and gnaw away at her with never any relief except the eventual one of death. She just wasn't the sort of person who could walk out on a marriage and conveniently forget the devastation she'd left in her wake.

What had seemed so easy only hours before, and

especially the previous day in bed with Angus, was now a skein of complications.

However, of one thing she was certain. Angus had been right when he'd said it was now or never. If she didn't make the break tonight she never would.

She glanced across to where Iain sat apparently immersed in a newspaper. He didn't fool her. They'd been together too long for that. She knew he knew and was even now waiting for her to utter the death knell to their marriage.

It was funny how she'd grown accustomed to his face over the years, she thought. To begin with it had horrified and revolted her. Now she hardly even noticed it.

She knew then she was going to stay with Iain and not go off with Angus.

For better or worse she was married to Iain. That was where her commitments lay.

With a sigh she rose and straightened her dress. For a few brief moments she considered going out to the car and telling Angus her decision face to face. But in the end she chose not to, whether because of cowardice or a reluctance to put her decision to such an immediate test she wasn't quite sure.

'I'm going to bed. Are you coming?' she said.

Iain tried to hide his surprise. Had he been wrong? Had her intended decamping been a product of his imagination?

Looking deep into her eyes he saw he'd been right and for some reason she'd changed her mind and was staying with him.

Pity? He didn't think so. He could see many things in her eyes but pity wasn't one of them.

'I'll be right behind you,' he replied, his voice not betraying one whit of the drama that had just passed unspoken between them.

He checked the gas and electricity as he did every night. And only when he was certain everything was as it should be did he climb the stairs to his wife whom up until minutes previously he'd been convinced he'd never sleep with again.

Outside in his car a chilled Angus frowned as the lights in the house went out one by one. His frown deepened to puzzled perplexity when the last one blinked off to leave the house in total darkness.

Something must have gone wrong. There had been a fight. Iain was forcing her to stay against her will.

These and a dozen other explanations for Rosemary's continued non-appearance flashed through his mind.

The minutes ticked by and, as they did so, came the horrible realization Rosemary wasn't going to come with him after all. Nor was she being held against her will. She'd *elected* to stay on with Iain. That had to be the way of it.

His head sagged forward to rest against the wheel. His breath was laboured and there was a burning sensation in his chest.

He would be daft to stay here further considering he wasn't all that long out of a sick bed, he told himself.

But still he hung on, hoping against hope he was wrong and she would suddenly appear full of apologies and saying she'd been detained for some reason or other.

Midnight came and went. Then one o'clock and finally two.

At the back of two he admitted defeat. He headed for Craiglea and the bed that was going to seem empty even when he was in it.

The drive home remained a blank in his mind for the rest of his life.

By June of 1947 Angus had Sir Alan over the proverbial barrel.

Jocar had built a considerable amount of houses in the Gorbals by this time, none of which were finished thanks to the fact all aluminium bits and pieces – and there were a great many in each unit – couldn't be installed due to LMBM's ore being blacked at source from coming to Britain.

O'Rourke had done his job well.

Sir Alan grew more and more worried as his remaining capital rapidly dwindled. His plan had been to sell off blocks of units as they were completed thereby financing the next section to be built. With nothing being sold it was all outgoings and no incomings.

In vain did Sir Alan contact D.Chisholm and Bitu – he spoke to the former a number of times on the telephone and never recognized the voice as being that of his one-time foreman moulder – to try and get them to use British aluminium in the meantime until the Australian ore could reach this country and be processed.

But Donald and Bitu – carefully stage managed by Angus – were adamant. According to the contracts only aluminium derived from LMBM ore could be used. And that was the way it was going to be.

Feeling he had no other recourse left to him, Sir Alan notified Jocar that all further construction was to be cancelled until such time as the Australian ore was in this country and processed ready for use.

Angus then played his trump card – the delay clause buried deep in the Jocar contract small print.

From now on until construction started again all costs incurred by Jocar – including the wages of the entire Jocar workforce – were the responsibility of Sir Alan who as contractor was liable.

Beside himself, Sir Alan had looked up the named clause. Apoplectic with rage, he consulted his solicitor to be informed the contract was wholly binding in law and as such he was liable for all Jocar's delay costs whether he liked it or not.

At the end of the first delayed week a massive wages bill was sent to Sir Alan which he had no option but to pay.

By the end of the second delayed month Sir Alan had been so reduced financially he was actually considering approaching the Glasgow Corporation to try and offload his Gorbals holdings for whatever price they would pay.

At this point word arrived from Australia – again

carefully orchestrated by Angus – that the end of the union's blacking was imminent. All being well, the first consignment of ore should be on the high seas within the next few days.

This news put Sir Alan into a terrible quandary. If only he could lay his hands on enough capital to tide himself over until the ore arrived in Britain, was processed and made up, all could yet be saved.

It was Hetherington who again came up with the solution. He pointed out that the members of the Armstrong's board had proven themselves to be a most accommodating lot; without exception they'd approved of everything Sir Alan had either suggested or put before them. With so much control over the board, why didn't Sir Alan put it to those directors representing outside interests that he sell them a further twenty-five per cent of his shares with the proviso that those shares would never go on the open market and could only be sold back to him?

According to Hetherington's calculations, the money so raised would be sufficient to allow Sir Alan to ride out his current financial nightmare.

Of course this would necessitate Sir Alan losing his majority holding in Armstrong's. But with such an amenable and malleable board of directors what did that matter as he would always get his own way anyway?

In desperation Sir Alan came to the conclusion that Hetherington's suggestion was his only salvation.

So he called an extraordinary general meeting of the board in which he put it to them he was willing to sell another twenty-four per cent of his shares – this a further refinement of Hetherington's – and would offer each director acting as nominee for outside interests the option on six per cent of them.

This way he could still retain – so Hetherington had smoothly argued – the most individual shares and therefore the right to the position of chairman.

The nominee directors agreed to inform their various clients of this development. All came back saying their clients were willing to take up the options.

It was a day Angus had long been looking forward to. It was the first of August and on the twelfth of the month he would be twenty-six years old. He felt twice that age.

The day dawned warm and sunny with blue sky stretching from horizon to horizon. He ate a leisurely breakfast before returning to his bedroom where he dressed himself in a brand new suit he'd had made especially for the occasion.

Outside in the drive stood something else he'd bought especially – a 1932 Rolls Royce in immaculate condition.

When it was time to leave he went downstairs where he shook John solemnly by the hand and kissed Sheena on the cheek.

Whistling merrily, he went out to the Rolls and eased himself behind the wheel.

En route, he thought of George Hetherington now on his way to Australia where his wife was eagerly awaiting his arrival.

Hetherington had taken with him a nice little additional nest egg courtesy of Jocar and Angus. Angus reckoned he'd earned a good bonus.

At the gate into Armstrong's Angus was automatically waved through by the guard. The guard was someone he'd known all his life and yet he went by unrecognized. It seemed guards didn't look too closely at the faces of those who drove a Rolls, the car being credential enough.

He drove slowly across the yard, glancing briefly at the spot where Tod Gemmill had bumped into him and planted the cuff links in his overalls. He smiled grimly at the memory.

He parked the Rolls beside Sir Alan's and climbed out into the sunshine. A glance at his watch told him the meeting was scheduled to have started one minute previously. He had timed it to perfection.

He strode up the stairs that brought him to Sir Alan's office where in a small reception area a middle-aged secretary asked him what his business was?

He replied he'd come for the board meeting and he looked so much the part he was shown straight through. When he entered the boardroom he did so as though to the manner born.

As he expected, there were four of them grouped round the table – Sir Alan plus Sir Alan's three tame directors. He stared boldly at Sir Alan.

'You!' Sir Alan exclaimed and looked thunderstruck.

Angus took his time about walking to the seat furthest away from Sir Alan. He smiled softly and waited.

'Just what in God's name do you think you're doing here, McBain?' Sir Alan demanded angrily.

Angus laid his brief case on the table and slowly opened it.

The penultimate twist of the screw had been applied to Sir Alan that morning in the form of a telegram from O'Rourke informing him the Mine Workers' Union had reconsidered their position. As a result they were once more blacking all LMBM ore to Great Britain.

This was in effect the death blow to the Gorbals project for it was impossible for Sir Alan to financially survive the consequences of this action.

Angus leant across the table to hand the man nearest him certificates and statements showing the absent four nominee directors had all been acting on his behalf. With seventy per cent of the Armstrong shares he was now the majority shareholder.

Having noted the contents of these papers Sir Alan closed his eyes. It was as though he'd been reduced to a shell with a cold wind blowing through the empty spaces where flesh and blood had once been.

Angus reached into his pocket and pulled out an old pair of cuff links which he threw down on the table where they came to rest about a foot in front of Sir Alan. 'Also for Rosemary and the compensation you owed but never paid my mother,' Angus said.

The three directors watched spellbound the drama being played out in front of them. From the expressions on their faces Angus might have been the very devil incarnate.

Angus went on, 'As the new majority shareholder I claim the position of managing director and as such will assume responsibility for the running of the firm. As you, Armstrong, still own twenty-seven per cent of the shares I hereby offer you the post of assistant managing director which your holdings entitle you to.'

Having said that, Angus swung his gaze onto the three directors sitting gawping at him. 'In the circumstances there will now be no further need for a board of directors which makes you redundant, gentlemen,' he added.

Sir Alan squared Angus's certificates and statements into a neat pile before coming to his feet.

Without uttering further he walked from the board-room into his office. His secretary's voice was heard a few moments later asking if he was all right as he looked awful.

Mumbling something incomprehensible, Sir Alan took a last fond look round his office, then left it for his car parked outside.

The three directors took their leave almost directly afterwards. En route one of them explained to the secretary there was a change of management and Mr McBain was now in charge.

After the directors had gone Angus strolled through to what had been Sir Alan's office, plonking himself down behind the man's desk.

Strangely there was no feeling of elation but rather a sense of the anti-climactic.

There was a framed photograph on the desk which he picked up and studied. It featured a grown woman and two young girls – Rosemary and Diane as youngsters with their mother.

His heart crowded into his mouth as he stared at the young Rosemary's face. With a sigh he slid the photograph into a desk drawer and called out for the secretary to come through.

The woman entered all wide-eyed and timorous. He

introduced himself and told her to take a memo, copies of which were to be distributed throughout the works.

In the memo he informed the workforce of the change of management, then went on to allay any fears they might have had regarding the sort of internal upheaval often occurring in circumstances like these.

He instructed her to tell all heads of departments and gaffers to present themselves in his office in half an hour's time. He wanted to introduce himself to these men without delay.

When Miss Morrisson had left he crossed to the window and stared out. There was an enormous amount he was going to have to learn about running a business like this. But learn it he would and quickly.

He was going to see Armstrong's prosper like it had never prospered before. Before he was finished Armstrong's was going to be a by-word not only in Glasgow but throughout Britain and beyond.

'Mister McBain?'

He turned to find himself staring at a pretty blond lassie of about twenty-two or -three.

'I'm Miss McPhail, Miss Morrisson's assistant. I was wondering if you'd like a cup of tea? We usually have one about this time.'

There was something about the girl, a certain unmistakable Glasgowness, that appealed to him. 'What's your Christian name, Miss McPhail?' he asked.

She blinked in surprise. 'Irene.'

'Well, Irene, I'd love a cup of *coffee*,' he said.

She smiled hesitatingly, then was gone.

Angus rubbed his hands briskly together. The sun was shining outside and he'd achieved what he'd set out to do. True, he'd lost Rosemary but then perhaps there was a law somewhere which stipulated a man couldn't have everything he set his heart on.

Looking on the bright side there was an awful lot he had to be thankful for including a smashing wee son whom he idolized and would have sold his soul for.

Returning to his desk he mused he was going to need a

personal assistant-cum-secretary now, someone clever and efficient to be by his side as he constantly flitted between LMBM and Armstrong business.

He wondered if the pretty Irene McPhail would be interested?

For three days after Angus's coup Sir Alan sat at home and brooded. Surly and taciturn, he refused to discuss the situation with anyone, including his wife, Cordelia.

He drank a great deal, consuming bottle after bottle of his favourite malt.

On the evening of the third day he announced abruptly that he was going out.

He drove to Partickhill, having a desire to see Margaret Cunninghame, and as this was one of his usual nights for going there he'd decided to keep the tryst.

Not feeling the same sense of shame with Margaret as he did with Cordelia he was telling her everything within minutes of his arrival.

Appalled, Margaret fetched him a stiff drink, made sure he was sitting comfortably and generally fussed over him.

They talked and drank, he downing the whisky as though it was water. The more alcohol he consumed the more flushed and agitated he became.

Like many courtesans, Margaret eventually related most things to sex and bed. To her, intercourse was the great panacea which, if not exactly the cure for all ills, couldn't fail but help.

With that in mind she began coaxing Sir Alan to come to bed.

To begin with he wasn't interested but when she began touching him in a way he especially liked he soon became aroused.

As she'd intended, all thoughts fled from his mind other than lust and bodily satisfaction. Hand in hand they hurried to the bedroom where they both quickly undressed.

Their lovemaking was fiercely urgent – far more so

than normal.

Suddenly, he gave a long, shuddering sigh and collapsed on top of her where he lay heavily pressing her into the bed.

'Oh love, that was wonderful,' Margaret crooned, stroking the side of his sweat slicked neck.

She continued stroking him, then frowned when she got no reply.

'Alan?'

For the first time it dawned on her there was something peculiar about the way he was lying so heavy and unmoving.

'Alan?'

Her hand groped for the bedside table and the lamp sitting atop it.

His face was suffused with blood, the way it had been when he'd had the previous attack in her bathroom.

His eyes were wide open and bulging as though being forced outward from internal pressure of some kind. The expression was a grotesque parody of sexual ecstasy.

There could be no mistaking he was quite dead.

A few days after Sir Alan's funeral Angus stood by the man's grave in the Linn Park Cemetery with a huge bunch of magnificent red roses in his hand.

For a long time he stared down at the grave. Then turning he made his way to another part of the cemetery where his mother and father were buried together.

On top of their grave he laid the roses.

It was a puerile thing to say but he said it nonetheless. 'You got your compensation at last, Ma. Armstrong finally paid up. And with interest.'

Tears oozed from his eyes which he hurriedly wiped away. It wouldn't do for anyone to see a grown man greeting like a wean. They'd think him a big jessie.

Taking a deep breath, he thought Armstrong's death was the passing of a personal era. Yesterday was now gone. Tomorrow lay fresh and inviting before him.

It was with a light heart that he made his way up the

path to the cemetery gates beyond which his Rolls was parked. Off on the horizon he could see the grey pall of chimney smoke that hung forever lowering over central Glasgow.

It might be a dirty horrible violent place but he loved it.

It was home.

Street Song

'Alley balley balley balley bee
sitting on your mammy's knee,
greeting for a wee bawbee
tae buy some coulther's candy . . .'

Glasgow street song (Trad.)

SUSAN

Susan's eyes were wide with fear and apprehension as she stepped through the door into Miss Buchan's school. She was flanked on either side by her parents.

'Captain and Mrs Gibb, how nice to see you again,' Miss Buchan said, stepping forward to shake their hands. 'And how are you today, Susan?'

Susan stared at Miss Buchan, not attempting to reply.

'Are you looking forward to your stay with us? We're certainly looking forward to having you here.'

Susan's gaze left Miss Buchan to travel round the wood-panelled entrance hall. She might have been a small animal plucked rudely from its nest.

'Answer Miss Buchan,' Jean, her mother, prompted.

But still Susan said nothing.

'Quite understandable in the circumstances,' Miss Buchan smiled. 'She'll soon come round though. She does know why she's here, doesn't she?'

'Oh yes,' Jean replied. 'It's all been explained to her quite thoroughly. Hasn't it, my angel?'

Susan moved closer to Jean, reaching out to clutch her mother's coat.

'Would you like to help her settle into the dormitory or do you think it best to leave right away?' Miss Buchan asked.

Jean looked at her husband Keith for an answer.

Keith was hating this, feeling guilty as hell. Ever since learning the regiment was to be posted abroad, and deciding to leave Susan behind, he'd been trying to convince himself he'd have arrived at the same decision if she'd been a boy.

'I think we should leave right away,' he said.

Trembling, Jean reached down to kiss Susan on the cheek. 'Mummy and Daddy will write to you every week and Miss Buchan or one of her staff will read the letters to you. Now be a good girl and do as you're told and we'll see you again when we come home on leave.'

Keith opened his wallet and extracted a fiver which he pressed into Susan's hand. 'Pocket money,' he said, 'which I think Miss Buchan better look after in the meantime.'

'I'll see she gets it as she needs it,' Miss Buchan said, taking the fiver from Susan.

'Well, that's it then, I think,' Keith said. Swinging Susan into his arms he pecked her on the cheek. Having deposited her back on the ground again he cleared his throat.

'Jenny!' Miss Buchan called out to a hovering girl. 'You take Susan's case up to dormitory C. Bed fourteen will be hers.'

'Yes, Miss Buchan,' Jenny said obediently. Lifting Susan's small case she walked with it towards the staircase at the rear of the entrance hall.

'Charming girl,' Miss Buchan said. 'Parents died tragically so now we look after her.'

Jean clucked sympathy.

''Bye 'bye, angel,' Jean said, her eyes brimming over with tears.

Susan stared up at her mother, a profound betrayal written clearly across her face.

Keith reached down and shook his daughter's hand. This was even more difficult than he'd anticipated. Taking Jean by the arm he turned her round and marched her to the door. Miss Buchan put her hand on Susan's shoulder in case she tried to bolt after her parents. But she didn't. Jean had one last look over her shoulder at the door. Then it closed behind her and Susan was cut off from sight.

'You and I are going to get on just fine,' Miss Buchan said. 'You have my word on that. Now, how about a nice cup of tea and a cake? And while we're having it you can tell me all about yourself. What you like and dislike, that sort of thing.'

As though in a trance, Susan followed Miss Buchan to her study, where she was told to sit on a chair in front of a cheery fire.

With the cake there were scones, pancakes and crumpets. But Susan ate nothing, mumbling she wasn't hungry.

Miss Buchan did her best to draw and distract Susan, to no avail. Susan sat staring into the fire as though seeing strange sights in its depths.

That night Miss Buchan personally saw to Susan getting ready for bed.

When all the girls in the dormitory were ready, Miss Buchan led them in prayers, shortly after which the lights were turned out. Susan lay in the darkness listening to the breathing all around her. After a while she pulled the blankets over her head and there, securely muffled in her womb-like cocoon, she broke down and quietly cried her eyes out.

It was a day she'd remember for the rest of her life.

The first holidays to come up were the Christmas ones. The girls, with the exception of seven, either went home or to friends and relatives whom they'd spend the break with.

Susan was one of the seven.

Miss Buchan did her best by those with nowhere else to go. She bought them individual presents and there was a goose and crackers. After Christmas dinner they all sat round in a circle drinking lemonade and singing carols. Then they played charades and blind man's bluff.

By far and away the youngest of the seven, Susan received extra special attention from Miss Buchan. Several of the older girls made a fuss of her and generally mothered her.

Susan said little, as was her wont, her large doe eyes drinking everything in.

Before coming to the school she'd been a happy, vivacious, extroverted child. Now she was withdrawn and painfully shy, forever trying to blend into the background as though she didn't want anyone to notice she was there. Naturally, neither

5

Miss Buchan nor any of the staff knew there'd been such a big change in her as they hadn't known what she was like beforehand.

When the small party had subsided somewhat Miss Buchan took Susan to one side.

'Would you like me to read the letter that came with your Christmas card now?' she asked.

Susan's eyes lit up. The letter readings were the highlight of her week, Jean having kept her word and written regularly. Susan sat with her hands cupping her chin as she avidly listened to her mother's words.

Mummy and Daddy were missing her. Daddy was frightfully busy while there never seemed enough hours in the day for all the things Mummy had to do. The letter ended with the promise, as it always did, that Mummy and Daddy would see her during the summer when they'd be returning home on leave.

When she fell asleep that night Susan dreamed the same dream she'd been having regularly since arriving at the school. Mummy and Daddy were arriving home – home being the house they'd all lived in before Mummy and Daddy went abroad – and Mummy was saying they were never ever going to leave their daughter again and when Mummy and Daddy went overseas at the end of Daddy's leave they'd be taking their darling Susan with them.

Miss Buchan laid the letter down and sighed. There were times she hated running a school and this was one of them.

She passed a hand wearily over her face. Well, she thought, she may as well get this over and done with. That was always the easiest way in the long run, she'd learned. She opened the door to her study and hailed a passing girl.

'Find Susan Gibb and bring her to me right away,' she said.

'Yes, Miss Buchan,' the girl replied and scuttled off.

She settled herself back behind her desk again and folded her hands in front of her. She was still in that position when there was a timid knock on the door.

'Come in!' she called out.

Susan entered, closing the door behind her as she'd been taught to do.

'You wanted to see me, Miss Buchan?'

'Sit down, child. There's another letter from your parents which is addressed to me as well as yourself.'

'Has Daddy been hurt?' Susan asked quickly.

'No. Nothing like that.'

Miss Buchan spread the letter in front of her and smoothed it with her hand.

Susan sat expectant, waiting.

Slowly Miss Buchan said, 'Due to circumstances beyond their control your parents won't be coming home to Scotland this summer, after all.'

To Susan it was the end of the world. Since entering the school her entire life had become geared to the forthcoming summer and the reappearance of her parents from abroad.

Miss Buchan lifted up two white fivers which she showed Susan. 'The Captain has sent this as pocket money. I, of course, shall be looking after it for you. Would you like some now?'

Susan shook her head.

Miss Buchan came round from behind her desk to kneel beside Susan. 'I'm awfully sorry,' she said. 'We all know how much you were looking forward to their coming back.'

Biting back tears, Susan came to her feet. 'May I go now, Miss, please?' she asked.

'Wouldn't you like me to read the letter to you?'

Susan shook her head. At the door she paused. 'Did they say when they'll be coming home?' she asked.

'No, they didn't.'

Susan closed the door quietly behind her.

Miss Buchan stood at her study window gazing out into the garden. She was watching Susan who was standing by a tree apart from the other girls.

What a sad and lonely little creature, Miss Buchan thought.

There were times when she wanted to take Susan in her arms and hug her, but of course she couldn't do that. That would have been showing favouritism, which she strictly disciplined herself against.

She watched Susan pick up the wild hedgehog that often came to that part of the garden and which Susan had made friends with. The girl stroked the hedgehog and whispered endearments to it, talking to it as though it was a person rather than an animal.

So much love to give, Miss Buchan thought. So much love.

'I saw Blackie yesterday,' Susan said to the hedgehog, whom she had christened Spike. 'He came and sat in the tree and sang to me. He told me his wife has had three little blackbirds and when they're old enough he's going to bring them over and show them to us. Isn't that marvellous?'

Spike's little brown eyes gazed up at Susan. She was the only girl in the school whom he uncurled for.

Susan gently stroked his snout. If Spike had been a cat he would have purred.

'When are you going to meet a nice lady hedgehog and have a family, Spike? I think it's high time, don't you? And when you have your family will you bring them to show to me just like Blackie has promised to do? We could sit round in a circle and have a pretend tea party, which I think would be ever so much fun. Perhaps squirrel would come if we asked him nicely. You like squirrel, don't you? Yes, of course you do, even if he is a bit crotchety at times.'

The squirrel referred to was an old red one who often came to the tree in the garden. All the other girls were scared of the squirrel because of its sharp teeth, but not Susan, who on a number of occasions had actually hand-fed the rodent.

The idea that Blackie had a family, far less that he was going to bring them to show to her, was pure fiction on her part. When it came to animals Susan had an extremely vivid imagination.

One of the teachers, called Miss Cairncross, came out of the

8

school and rang the handbell to announce the resumption of classes.

'I'll have to go now, Spike,' Susan said. 'I'd much rather stay and talk to you but I'm afraid I have to go and do my lessons. Will you be here tomorrow? Well I'll be here looking for you hoping you've been able to make it. Goodbye now and make sure you look after yourself.'

She stroked the hedgehog's snout one last time before very carefully setting him back on the ground.

''Bye Spike. Be a good boy now!' Actually she didn't know for certain that Spike was a male. She just assumed he was.

She retreated a few steps before turning and breaking into a run. She felt happy as she always did when she'd been with her friends the animals.

'Yes, Susan?' Miss Buchan asked. Susan was in her study having requested an interview.

'Please, Miss. The money my Daddy sent me.'

'Yes?'

'Could I use some of it to buy a pet with? A dog or a cat? I'd look after it all by myself so it would be no trouble to anyone else.' Susan looked expectantly at Miss Buchan, her face radiant with hope.

Miss Buchan knew her reply was going to hurt Susan but for the moment she couldn't see how she could do otherwise.

'I'm afraid a personal pet is out of the question,' she said.

Susan's face dropped.

Her heart went out to the little girl. She continued softly, 'You see if I allow one personal pet in the school then lots of the girls might want one. And then where would we be? We'd be a menagerie instead of a school. If I could make an exception I would, Susan, but you must understand there can never be exceptions. It just isn't fair on the others.'

Susan's lower lip trembled.

'I appreciate only too well what a pet would mean to you but you must see my position. I'm sorry Susan.'

Susan nodded, not trusting herself to speak. The animals in the garden were all very well but her time with them was extremely limited. Depending on when she could get into the garden and when they would put in an appearance. Sometimes a whole week could go by without her seeing Spike or Blackie or squirrel.

A pet of her own would have been totally different, however. She would have been able to be with it every evening and all weekend when there were no lessons.

After Susan had gone Miss Buchan twiddled her pencil, which she finally threw on to the desk in front of her.

'Damn!'

She was a woman who rarely swore.

Miss Buchan marched into the assembly room with a box under her arm and the assembly room fell silent.

She placed the box on the table at the end of the room and then turned to face the girls.

'A mouse was seen last week and another yesterday!' she said.

Some of the girls gasped while others giggled.

'I will not have mice in my school!' Miss Buchan said sternly. 'They are unhygienic. What are they, girls?'

'Unhygienic!' the girls chorused in unison.

'What does that mean, Agnes McDonald?'

'Unclean, Miss.'

'Quite correct. Unclean. And I will have nothing in my school which is that. So ... we have a problem: mice. What's the solution to the problem?'

Several hands shot in the air.

'Mary Geddes?'

'Traps, Miss. Baited with cheese.'

'Very good, Mary. But I think we might do even better than that.'

Her gaze swept over the room. 'Helen Moyes?'

'A cat, Miss.'

'The solution I favour myself, Helen. A good mouser.'

Turning to the table she lifted the top off the box and reached inside.

'Oh!' the girls said, when they saw the kitten Miss Buchan held.

'Now Mr Samson, the janitor, says he hasn't time to look after a cat, which leaves it up to us. I myself would undertake the task of maintaining this kitten but unfortunately I spend so much time looking after you girls I have absolutely none left over for the training of an animal. This being the case I'm hoping one of you will volunteer to look after and train our little friend here. Someone who is good with animals and knows how to handle them. Now, any volunteers?'

Several dozen hands were lifted.

'Hmm ...' said Miss Buchan, pretending to consider each eager face in turn.

Finally she gestured at Susan. 'Stand up, Susan Gibb.'

Susan stood, a tiny figure almost lost amongst some of the taller girls.

'Do you think you'd be able to train this kitten, Susan?'

'Oh yes, Miss!'

'You'd have to spend a great deal of time with him you understand?'

Susan's eyes shone. 'Yes, Miss.'

'And he's to be a working cat. Not a pet.'

'Yes, Miss.'

Miss Buchan pursed her lips and furrowed her brow as though deep in cogitation. Finally she said, 'Members of the staff have noticed how good you are with the animals out in the garden, Susan, so I think you might well be the right person to look after the school cat.'

There was a pause and then she went on, 'Well, come along girl, don't just stand there gawping. Come and collect the beast.'

Later, when she was back in the privacy of her study, Miss Buchan smiled. She hummed gaily as she set about marking some papers.

*

That night, Susan installed Tiddles, as she'd decided to call the kitten, in a cardboard box by the side of her bed.

'Goodnight, Tiddles,' she said, kissing the kitten on the head. 'Sleep tight and don't let the bugs bite.'

'He'd better not have bugs,' the girl in the next bed said. Several other girls tittered. Susan patted Tiddles, soothing him to lie still. The kitten mewed contentedly.

Susan slipped into bed feeling the happiest she'd been since her parents had gone abroad. She wasn't alone any more. She had something to care for which would care for her in return. Something to help fill the huge aching hole her parents' departure had created in her.

Keith and Jean Gibb did manage to take leave in Scotland the second summer after they'd enrolled Susan as a boarder in Miss Buchan's School for Young Ladies.

As they were home for four weeks, and rather than stay in a hotel, Keith rented a house, which came complete with servants.

Susan hated the house on sight, thinking it dark and gloomy. A cheerless, friendless place with echoing corridors and high vaulted ceilings which often as not were hidden in shadow.

However, that didn't really matter. All that did was that her Mummy and Daddy were home and the three of them were together again.

She was so excited that for the first few days she hardly stopped talking and followed Jean nearly everywhere she went. To begin with, Jean found this charming but after a little while it began to grate on her nerves. It seemed to her she could hardly turn round without falling over Susan, who was continually under her feet.

Keith too became irritated with Susan. Her constant questions seemed to go on without end.

'What was it like there, Daddy? Why did you do this, Daddy? Why did you do that? How does this work, Daddy? How does that ... ?'

12

'For God's sake, stop bothering me!' he exclaimed angrily one night as she'd innocently asked him yet another question while he was in the middle of knotting his black tie.

Tears sprang into Susan's eyes as she backed away a little from him.

'Can't you see I'm busy?' he said irritably.

'Sorry, Daddy.'

'And don't snivel. I can't stand children who snivel!'

'Sorry, Daddy.'

'And do stop saying sorry Daddy.'

'Sor ... yes, Daddy.' Head bowed, she left the room.

With a sigh of exasperation Keith left his tie. His concentration was broken, he'd never do it now. He'd get Jean to knot it for him when she came through. She always made a better job of it than he did, anyway.

A little later, when Jean appeared, he told her what had happened.

Jean pulled a face. 'I think we've just become unused to having a child around,' she said. 'One of the drawbacks of having her at boarding school.'

'And another thing,' Keith went on, 'she's forever wanting to be picked up and cuddled. It's positively unnatural.'

'It's no such thing! If anything, it's the contrary. She hasn't seen us for two years, after all!'

'Well, I still don't like it,' he grumbled. 'It doesn't feel right.'

'Stop being such an army stuffed shirt! It's a little girl of six we're talking about, not some hulking lad of sixteen or seventeen.'

'I am not a stuffed shirt!' he exclaimed.

'You are sometimes. And pompous with it.'

Keith spluttered with indignation, his deep tan turning pink in places.

Jean laughed and kissed him which mollified him somewhat. 'You don't mind *me* cuddling you,' she teased.

'That's different. You're a woman. My wife.'

'And she's your daughter.'

13

He looked thoughtful and his eyes took on a faraway look as he poured them both sherries.

'I'm sorry she wasn't the boy you really wanted,' Jean said softly. 'But if a boy wasn't to be, then he wasn't to be.'

'I know that,' Keith replied, staring into the deep brown of his drink.

'Let's just be thankful we've been blessed with a child at all.'

'If only she wouldn't ask so many questions and keep pestering me all the time.'

'I'll speak to her about it,' Jean said.

Jean knew then she was right. They had become totally unused to having a child around. Not only that, they'd become set and selfish in their ways.

'What!' exclaimed Gerald, Keith's older brother. 'You mean the child's been in Glasgow all this time without us knowing about it? What were you thinking of, man?'

Keith knew fine well what he'd been thinking of. Drat Susan for coming out with the fact she'd been spending all her holidays at school.

'I don't see why you should be inconvenienced. After all,' and Keith relished saying this bit, 'you're both getting on a bit now. Hardly up to active young children, I wouldn't have thought.'

'We might be old but we're hardly decrepit yet,' Emmaline, Gerald's wife, retorted.

Keith put the hint of a knowing smile on his face calculated to convey to his sister-in-law that he thought otherwise. He knew it would infuriate her. Like many once beautiful people he knew, Emmaline hated the thought of the ravages of time.

Susan sat very still, aware she'd somehow angered her father – although for the life of her she couldn't think how.

'Next Christmas Susan must come and stay with us,' Emmaline said firmly. 'And I won't hear otherwise.'

'That's not fair on you,' Keith said.

'Nonsense!' Gerald replied. 'We'd love to have her. Would do us both the world of good to have someone young around

14

the house again. She'd be the one doing *us* a favour, I can tell you.'

'Would you like to come and stay with us at Christmas, Susan?' Emmaline asked.

Susan hung her head and nodded.

'Imagine her spending Christmas at school! How ridiculous!' Gerald said.

Keith remembered then the stories he'd heard from the dead Michael and James about what a good father Gerald had been. Both his boys had positively doted on him. His own guilt at being irritable and snappy with Susan rose up in him. And this guilt he somehow transformed in his mind into being Gerald's fault. He glowered at his brother, all the old feelings of inadequacy and being second best coming crowding back.

Everything Gerald touched or was connected with turned to gold. Women, business, conversation. Whereas he ... 'We'll sort something out before Jean and I go back abroad,' he said, thinking, like hell he would! They hadn't found out the name of Susan's school yet and that's the way he'd try and keep it.

'What beautiful pearls those are,' he said, changing the subject. 'They caught my eye the moment I saw them.'

'They were a present from Gerald,' Emmaline replied smugly.

The topic of Susan and Christmas was gradually forgotten.

Susan was playing with Tiddles in the garden when one of the girls came rushing up to say she was wanted right away in Miss Buchan's study.

'Come in!' Miss Buchan's voice called out when she knocked on the door.

For a moment she failed to recognise the figure sitting across from Miss Buchan. Then the penny dropped.

'Mummy!' she squealed and rushed into her mother's arms. It was only the second time her mother had been home during the five years she'd been at school.

'My, how tall you've grown!' Jean said, a catch in her voice. 'Here, let me have a look at you.'

She held Susan at arm's length and shook her head wonderingly. 'I wouldn't have known you. You're a young lady now, not a child any more.'

'Is Daddy with you?' Susan asked excitedly.

'He's had to stay on in London for a few days. Army work. I've come on ahead as we felt one of us should be at Aunt Emmaline's funeral. She died unexpectedly a few days ago.'

'Oh!' said Susan, not knowing what else to say. She'd thought of her Aunt Em and Uncle Gerald several times in the intervening years, having been expecting them to contact her as they'd promised they would, but they never had.

'How long are you and Daddy home for this time?' she asked.

A worried frown settled on Jean's deeply tanned face, a face that had begun to wither from too much exposure to tropical sun.

'Times being what they are, Daddy thinks it best I stay on in Glasgow for a while, at least until we see what's what.'

'Very sensible in the circumstances,' Miss Buchan said.

Jean turned to Miss Buchan. 'That man Hitler, you understand. The Army are extremely worried about him and what he might do.'

'I think we all are,' Miss Buchan said.

'So,' Jean said turning her attention back to Susan. 'That means I'll be renting a house for six months at least. Now what do you want to do? You can either live with me and attend here during the day or else remain on as a boarder, coming home at weekends. The choice is up to you.'

Susan thought that an odd question to ask. How could there be any doubt but that she'd want to live with her mother? Anything other would have been unthinkable. Didn't her mother understand that?

'I'll stay with you, Mummy,' she said excitedly. 'Starting tonight if you like.'

Jean laughed. 'Hey, hold on a minute! Let me find a house to rent first.'

Susan suddenly thought of Tiddles and her face fell.

Officially Tiddles was the school cat which would mean she'd have to leave him behind.

'What's wrong?' Jean asked.

In a rush of words Susan explained about the cat.

'Hmm!' said Miss Buchan.

'I'm sure we can buy you another cat,' Jean said, thinking that would resolve the problem. But it didn't.

'It wouldn't be the same, Mummy. Tiddles is Tiddles.'

'I think I have the solution,' Miss Buchan said. 'Tiddles hasn't been a great success as a mouser despite your valiant efforts to teach him, Susan. So I think it best I retire him and we'll buy another school cat.'

Susan beamed. 'Oh thank you, Miss Buchan!'

'We'll gave to find a good home for him of course. Any suggestions?'

Susan whirled on Jean. 'Please Mummy?'

'You bring Tiddles with you when you come home.'

Susan's day was complete.

'I'm sorry about Em,' Keith said to Gerald. 'I did my best to make the funeral but it was just impossible.'

Gerald nodded. He looked gaunt and haggard and there were dark circles under his eyes. He'd taken the loss of his wife badly.

'At least it was quick,' he said. 'That was a blessing.'

Keith tried to look sympathetic. In reality Emmaline's death meant nothing at all to him.

Gerald poured two very large whiskies. He'd been drinking heavily since his wife's death. As he and Keith drank his eyes misted over in introspection. He was thinking about his two sons, Michael and James, who'd been killed at Ypres. He'd been thinking a lot about them lately.

'Is there going to be another war?' he asked abruptly.

'Some people in the Army think so but I personally don't believe it'll come about. It would be insanity on Herr Hitler's part.'

'There are a lot of people say he is insane.'

17

Keith snorted. 'About as insane as you or I. Cunning is the word I'd use. And devious.'

'And yet you're insisting Jean stays home for a while?'

'There's no harm being on the safe side. Just in case I'm wrong.'

'You were always the cautious one,' Gerald said smiling. 'Even as a little boy.'

They drank for a little while in silence and then Gerald said, 'You know what Em's death means, don't you?'

'No?'

'When I go everything will come to you. My half of the brewery, our house, my entire estate. All yours, Keith.'

Keith couldn't meet his brother's steady gaze. 'Let's hope it's a long time before it comes to that,' he said.

'What'll you do with the brewery? Sell?'

Keith pondered that. It wasn't something he'd given a lot of thought to. 'I don't know,' he replied eventually.

'It's not as easy to run as you once thought. I hope you realise that.'

Keith bridled. 'Are you saying I couldn't do it?'

'I'm saying no such thing. All I'm doing is warning you that if you do decide to take over my seat, do so with your eyes wide open.'

Keith made up his mind there and then. When the time came he would take over the brewery and what's more he'd make an even better job of running it than Gerald had!

Gerald smiled inwardly. He could see from the expression on Keith's face that he'd succeeded. He'd grown very fond of the brewery over the years. It was only right and proper it stay on in the family for as long as that was possible.

Three months later Hitler invaded Poland.

Susan hated the house her parents had rented. If anything, it was even gloomier than the previous one.

She clutched Tiddles to her as she stared in dismay at what was to be her bedroom. It was small and pokey and there was a funny smell in the air which she later identified as damp.

18

'Oh, Tiddles!' she said, clutching the cat to her. 'This place is horrid.'

Tiddles mewed his agreement.

The one bright spot was the garden, which was an overgrown jungle perfect for keeping pets in. She wondered if her parents would allow her to keep rabbits and a tortoise. That thought cheered her a little.

At the beginning of the war, Keith was seconded from his regiment and posted on to the General Staff in London. He was promoted to the rank of Major and given a desk. He was back in admin again. Nothing more than a bloody glorified filing clerk, was how he described himself.

He and Jean debated whether or not she should join him in London. But for various reasons, including the fact he steadily maintained it would be a short conflict, it was decided best for her to remain in Glasgow with Susan.

He came up to Scotland when he could and occasionally she journeyed down to spend the weekend with him. When Jean went south Susan was looked after by the old housekeeper Jean had employed, a Mrs Sinclair.

It was during one of her infrequent visits to London that Jean brought Keith the news of Gerald's death from cancer.

Keith's eyes gleamed when he heard this. If it hadn't been for the war he would have resigned his commission instantly and gone straight back to Glasgow to take over the brewery. But as things were, that would have to wait.

Susan lay on her bed with Tiddles curled up beside her. Her eyes were wide as she read an American film magazine Mrs Sinclair the housekeeper had managed to get hold of for her. The magazine was pre-war and concerned mainly with the films of Clark Gable, whom she adored.

Susan loved films and went as often as she was able – which was frequently – as much as three or four times a week. She went on her own and sometimes with Mrs Sinclair who was as nearly as big a film fan as she was. She would have liked to go

19

with her mother but Jean was always busy with either socialising or voluntary war work. It was a rare week when Jean spent an evening at home.

The truth was, Susan was exceptionally lonely outside school hours. She had one or two friends locally whom she visited and played with and occasionally even stayed the night with. Those nights were treasured in her memory and she often wistfully wished there were more of them. There could have been, as her friends' Mummies liked her and said she could stay as often as she liked but Jean had objected, saying she mustn't make a pest of herself.

The best times of all were when Daddy came up from London and they were all together again. But sadly these times were few and far between, becoming even fewer as the war dragged on and on.

Then there were her friends in the garden, whom she adored and lavished a great deal of time on. There was Soppy, the long-eared rabbit, who had a bad leg and an adorable expression. And the frogs she'd reared from tadpoles, who lived in the culvert at the very end of the garden. And Caw-caw the rook, who had fierce glinting eyes and a vicious way of stabbing with his beak.

Susan sighed and laid down her magazine. Lying back she closed her eyes. Someday, she told herself, her Prince Charming would come along. He'd look just like Clark Gable and be ever so romantic. He would open doors for her and always see that she walked on the inside of the pavement. He would gaze long and steadily into her eyes and his kisses would burn like fire. His name would be Clark or Tyrone, and he would be the most handsome, dashing man there had ever been. He would be madly in love with her and as a result never leave her side. And when he came along she'd never ever be lonely again.

At twelve years of age she was in the throes of puberty.

Keith smiled jubilantly to himself as his car swept through the front gates of Black Lion Brewery. With the war over and his commission resigned he was now ready to take over where Gerald had left off.

He'd arranged for a board to look after the brewery in the interim and his first job now would be to get rid of them. Their usefulness was over. He no longer needed them.

He parked his car and then sat to savour the moment. He'd been looking forward to this ever since Gerald had died. At long, long last he was now coming into his own.

He thought grimly of his Army career and especially the last war years. He'd never really got on in the Army. In his estimation, events had conspired against him. To begin with, he'd lost out by being kept in India during the first war, and then during the second he'd been anchored to a desk.

Still, if nothing else, he'd learned a great deal about admin and running things, which would stand him in good stead now.

A member of staff materialised to open his car door for him.

'Good morning, Mr Gibb,' the man said. 'And a pleasant one it is too.'

Keith got out of the car and straightened himself to his full height. Turning to the man he said in a cold, steely voice, '*Major* Gibb.' He intended starting as he meant to go on.

Keith sucked on his pipe contentedly. He'd had a hard day at work but only because everything at the brewery was going so well.

He glanced across to where Susan sat reading one of the trashy magazines she forever seemed to have her nose buried in. At seventeen she was a fully developed young woman who would soon be leaving school and going to college. She wanted to be a vet, which pleased him fine. There were a lot worse professions for a young woman to take up than that.

Not that he expected her to be a vet for long. Surely some eligible young man would come along and snap her up? And what sort of young man would that be? he wondered.

21

He remembered then he'd seen a notice displayed at the Conservative club the other night, saying there was to be a dance this coming weekend. It might be an idea for him to encourage her to attend not only that dance but other functions the Conservative club held for its young folk. For there he could be more or less assured she would meet the right sort of young man from the correct sort of background.

His heart warmed to the idea of her marrying someone rich and influential, and, what was more important, one day having a son who would inherit from both sides of the family.

A son! His grandson! A wee lad who could restore his family to the wealth and position they'd once enjoyed and which his father had gambled away and lost by bad speculation.

If he could live to see that, he'd die a happy man.

'Would you like to dance?'

Susan turned round to face a young man a little older than herself. He was good-looking but not excessively so.

'Thank you,' she replied.

They walked on to the dance floor and he put his arms round her. The dance was a waltz.

'I haven't seen you here before,' he said.

'I've been a few times.'

'It's nice to see a new face. Especially a pretty one.'

She liked that as she did all flattery.

'Isn't it exciting?' she said.

'What?'

'Princess Elizabeth getting married.'

'Oh *that*!'

The dance was being held in honour of the occasion.

'I think *he's* ever so attractive. Real yummy.'

The young man laughed. 'I'm sure he'd love to hear himself described as yummy.'

'You say that as though you know him.'

'I do. Sort of. We've met on a number of occasions.'

Susan's eyes opened wide. 'Really?'

'I play in London from time to time and as he's very keen on sport he sometimes comes to watch. When he isn't at sea, that is.'

'What do you play?'

'Squash. Have you ever seen a game?'

She shook her head.

'Very fast. Very exciting. And definitely not for girls.'

'When are you playing again?'

'Next week at a little club I go to called the Hillhead and Kelvinbridge Sports Club. Know it?'

She shook her head again.

On a sudden impulse he said, 'Would you like to come and watch the game? I could pick you up in my car and we could have a coffee or a drink afterwards?'

She laughed at the suddenness of his proposal. 'I don't even know your name!' she said.

'It's Nigel. What's yours?'

'Susan.'

'All right Susan. Is it a date?'

'Which night is it?'

'Friday.'

She was free Friday night and didn't think her parents would object. 'You'll pick me up?' she said.

They made the arrangements after which they danced together for the rest of the night.

'Have a nice time then!' Keith said, he and Jean having escorted Susan and Nigel to the door, which he now shut behind the young couple.

'Nigel McBeth!' he said delightedly to Jean. 'Son of Geoffrey McBeth, head of McBeth shipping line. Which only happens to be one of the largest shipping lines in the country. Why, the man must be a millionaire many times over.' He paused to chuckle before adding, 'I'll say this for Susan. When she picks them she *certainly* picks them.'

'Very nice boy, I thought,' Jean said, nodding her approval.

'I wonder if he's an only child?' Keith mused.

He escorted Jean back to the room where they'd been

23

entertaining Nigel while Susan got ready and poured them both drinks. He couldn't remember when he'd been so excited.

'We'll have to do everything to encourage the pair of them,' he said.

'Isn't it a bit early for that?'

'Perhaps. But a little encouragement certainly won't do any harm.'

'Give it a week or two and I could invite him for tea,' Jean said.

'Or better still, his parents as well!'

Jean looked thoughtful. 'We must be careful not to appear too pushy. That would do far more harm than good.'

'Hmm!' replied Keith.

'Anyway,' Jean said practically. 'This might be so much conjecture on our part. It's their first time out together, after all. They might well discover they don't like one another or don't particularly get on.'

Keith made up his mind to have a word with Susan the next day. She must be made to see what an advantageous match this would be. If she and Nigel did start going out regularly she must do everything in her power to develop and deepen the relationship. And if everything went well and they did decide to get married perhaps he could persuade them to add Susan's family name to that of Nigel's.

McBeth-Gibb, he thought. Yes, it had a ring to it.

A smile crept over his face. If they agreed to the joining of the names it would go a long way to help make up for the disappointment of Susan's being born a girl and, despite every effort on his and Jean's part, an only child to boot.

Combined with McBeth, the Gibb name would go on bigger and more glorious than ever. And that would be a far greater achievement than anything Gerald had managed.

He prayed to God in His Heaven everything went well tonight. A good start would be most important.

*

Susan and Nigel had been going out for six months when he decided to show her over his father's private yacht, which was at that time lying anchored in the Gare Loch.

They motored down on a sunny Saturday morning with the intention of picnicking aboard before travelling back sometime round about late afternoon or early evening.

Susan loved the run to the coast insisting the car windows be wide open so she could drink in the fresh tangy air that became progressively saltier the closer they got to the sea.

The yacht was a sixty-footer, painted sparkling white from stern to bow and flying the McBeth shipping pennant.

'She's beautiful,' Susan said as they clambered aboard.

'Shall we take her out?'

'Could we?'

Nigel smiled, 'Of course. There's a resident crew of three and that's what they're paid for.'

He left her standing by the wheel while he went below to issue orders.

Within five minutes they were under way.

'Want to steer?' Nigel asked as they rounded Kilcreggan Point heading for the Clyde.

'I wouldn't know how.'

'I'll show you.'

He stood behind her, his hands over hers as she took the wheel.

'It's awful heavy and it keeps trying to drag to the left,' she said, a frown of concentration on her face.

He eased the yacht back on course. 'You must control it. Not it you,' he said.

Flying spume lashed her face, making her feel tremendously exhilarated. Her feet tingled to the reverberations of the engine, while overhead gulls screamed and squawked having mistaken them for a fishing vessel.

'I could get to like this,' she said.

'Our whole family love boats and ships,' Nigel said. 'Always have, which is no doubt how we originally got into the business.'

25

Susan already knew he had an unmarried sister and that there had been an older brother killed at sea during the war, drowned in the south Atlantic after his ship had been torpedoed. But she didn't know anything about the rest of his family.

'Lots of aunts, uncles and cousins,' Nigel replied when she asked him. 'Some of them in the family business, others doing all sorts of things. I've even got an uncle who has a factory which makes lamps and lampshades. Does quite well out of it, too.'

'I envy you your large family circle,' she replied wistfully. 'I had two cousins an awful lot older than me but they were killed in the first war. Daddy had a married brother but I never saw them much. They asked me to go to their place for Christmas once when I was quite young but somehow that never materialised. Uncle Gerald and his wife, Aunt Em, are both dead now, as are all Mummy's family.'

'It's a shame you never had a brother or sister.'

'Daddy desperately wanted a boy. I don't think he's ever forgiven me for being a girl.'

'That's an exaggeration surely?'

Susan shook her head.

'Poor Susan,' he said, and kissed her neck.

She shivered, suddenly aware of their closeness.

'Shall we go below and have that picnic you brought?' he asked in a voice that had gone thick and husky.

'I am a bit peckish.'

'Then lunch it is.'

He called out to one of the crew to take over the wheel and after issuing the man instructions took her down to the yacht's main cabin.

Lunch was cold chicken, tomatoes, salad and apples. There was also château-bottled red wine. Nigel ate, tasting nothing. His eyes were riveted to Susan's, as hers, although a lot more coyly, were to his.

Susan enjoyed the wine. It relaxed her and put warmth in her stomach. When the meal was finished she languidly

26

started to pack away what was left and in doing so turned her back on Nigel.

She stiffened a little as his arms encircled her and his hands cupped her breasts. She closed her eyes as he caressed her. He turned her to him and brought his mouth to hers. As he kissed her he dropped a hand to rub the front of her dress where her crotch was. Susan sighed and pressed herself against him. It was such a nice feeling.

He had to stoop a little in order to get his hand under her dress. When he rubbed the front of her knickers he could feel crinkly hair underneath.

'Oh Nigel,' she said, moaning.

His hand wriggled inside her knickers to find her. It was the first time she'd allowed him to get this far.

'What about the crew?' she whispered.

'They won't bother us.'

'Draw the curtains anyway.'

Reluctantly he withdrew his hand to comply with her wishes.

When the portholes were covered he turned back to her and she came into his arms.

'I want to make love to you, Susan,' he jerked out.

'No,' she replied.

'Please?'

'What if I got pregnant?'

'I have contraceptives with me.'

She smiled. 'So this was what you had in mind all the time?'

'I won't think any less of you if that's what's bothering you. I ... I ...' He trailed off.

'Go on,' she whispered.

He laid his head on her shoulder. His breath hot and rasping in her ear.

'I love you,' he said in a tiny voice.

Susan closed her eyes. It was the first time anyone had ever said that to her – and that included her parents. Not even as a little girl had they ever said they loved her.

'Do you really?'

27

'Yes.'

'You're not just saying it because you're after *that*, are you?'

'No,' he said in an anguished tone of voice.

'Oh my darling,' she replied. She wasn't sure whether she loved him or not, but she certainly liked him an awful lot.

His hands fumbled with the buttons at the back of her dress. Susan knew if she was going to stop him going further this was the moment. Then she thought of what her father was always saying to her, which was that she should do everything in her power to consolidate her relationship with Nigel. Well, what could be more consolidating than letting him make love to her?

'Here let me,' she said, and reaching behind her deftly undid the buttons. Her dress slid to the floor and she stepped out of it. Picking it up she threw it across a table. Smiling, she then unhooked her bra.

Nigel tore off his clothes, which he left lying in an untidy heap. When he was naked he went to her and held her in his arms.

'I'm a virgin,' she whispered.

He reached down to fondle her, praying to himself that everything would go all right and that he'd be able to get it up and in.

Susan wasn't the first girl he'd been to bed with. Far from it. But unfortunately his first time he'd been so nervous he'd had trouble getting an erection, much to the girl's chagrin. And what he had managed hadn't been enough for him to get into her.

The girl hadn't said much after he'd given up but the look in her eyes had wounded him deeply, filling him with humiliation. The incident had scored itself deep into his psyche and now every time he went to bed with a girl for the first time he was more than half-convinced history would repeat itself. And so much did he worry about it, it often did.

Not that there was anything wrong with him physically. There wasn't. And after he'd managed it once he relaxed and usually had no trouble from there on in, albeit the fear was always there lurking just under the surface.

Because of this his lovemaking was invariably a hurried affair. For once he got it up he was in a hurry to get on with it in case his erection died on him and he couldn't get it up again.

They lay on the bunk side by side. 'Be gentle,' she whispered.

He stroked her flank and nuzzled her bosom, excitement mounting in him with the realisation he was getting hard.

'Hold me,' he said and guided her hand to him.

He spread her legs and worked frantically to make her wet. Come on, come on, he muttered under his breath.

Panic flared in him as he felt what erection he had begin to sag a little. Swiftly he crawled on top of her. If he could just get it in he'd be all right, he told himself.

Susan grimaced as he succeeded in entering her. She was still dry and what he was doing was sore. But because of her inexperience she thought the pain was due to her virginity.

He thrust and thrust. He wasn't going to fail after all. He was going to manage it with her first time. Uttering a groan he climaxed and then with a sigh laid himself gently on top of her.

Despite the initial discomfort Susan had enjoyed it, although she did wish it had gone on a bit longer. Gathering him to her she pressed his chest against hers. 'That was lovely,' she said.

'I'm not very good to start with but I get better as I go along,' he said.

'Then we must practise very hard.'

He laughed. 'Well I'm all for that.'

'You used the contraceptive, didn't you?'

His face was suddenly stricken. 'Christ I forgot!'

'Nigel!'

'In the heat of the moment it slipped my mind.'

'Well if I'm pregnant you'll just have to marry me.'

'I think I might marry you anyway,' he replied softly.

'Be careful what you say. I might hold you to it.'

'And I might want you to.'

They stared long and hard at one another. Then he bent down and kissed her.

29

Susan closed her eyes, happiness and sheer pleasure welling inside her.

A little later Nigel looked up as the boat started to turn to port. That meant they'd crossed the Sound of Bute and Sannox was in sight.

'We're on our way back,' he said. But he was talking to deaf ears. Susan had fallen asleep.

'Do you mind if we're excused, Father? Susan and I would like to go through and play some records.'

Geoffrey McBeth glanced across at his wife Fiona who smiled and nodded.

'Jean? Keith?'

'We don't mind at all,' Keith replied. 'Let the youngsters enjoy themselves. I can quite understand their preferring to play records than listen to the boring talk of old fuddy-duddies like ourselves.'

'Run along then,' Geoffrey McBeth said, giving a rather royal wave of his hand, 'but please keep the music down to a mild roar.'

'You won't hear a thing in here,' Nigel retorted.

Geoffrey raised an imperious eyebrow. 'I'd better not.'

Nigel held the door open for Susan and, laughing, they escaped the room.

Keith positively beamed after them. This was the second visit the Gibbs had paid to the McBeth household. The McBeths had been twice to them as well, and the foursome were rapidly becoming good friends, having discovered they had a great deal in common.

'If you don't mind my saying so, they make a lovely couple,' Keith said.

'They certainly seem to be very fond of one another,' Fiona replied.

Jean smiled and Geoffrey looked thoughtful.

'We've all taken to Susan,' Geoffrey said after a while.

Keith nodded.

'Very intelligent and sensitive young lady,' Fiona added.

Keith nodded again. The message was coming over loud and clear. The McBeths approved. Should Nigel and Susan decide they wanted to get married the McBeths wouldn't stand in their way.

'We enjoy having Nigel around,' Jean said. 'In fact we've almost come to think of him as our own son.'

'Always wanted a boy in the family. But unfortunately we weren't blessed,' Keith said.

'Well, who knows what time may bring?' Geoffrey replied.

'God can work in mysterious ways,' added Fiona, who liked to think of herself as a religious person and indeed regularly went to church, if that's anything to go by.

'He'll be working for you when he leaves university, I presume?' Keith asked.

'That's his intention, I'm happy to say,' Geoffrey replied.

Keith puffed with satisfaction on his cigar, that being very much the answer he'd wanted to hear.

'And Susan's going to be a vet?' Fiona said.

'She's always been fond of animals. Ever since a tiny thing. Can't think where she gets it from as it doesn't run in either of our families,' Jean said.

'Admirable quality that,' Geoffrey remarked.

'She'll make a marvellous mother and I *do* know where she gets that from,' Keith said, winking at Jean.

Everyone laughed.

'Have you ever been round a brewery?' Keith asked suddenly.

Geoffrey shook his head.

'Then perhaps you'd like to? Might interest you, if you can stand the pong.'

'I think I'd rather like that,' Geoffrey replied.

'Good we'll arrange it.'

There was a slight pause and then Geoffrey said, 'I'm taking a small party out on my yacht a fortnight this weekend. A run up to Oban and back with hopefully a spot of fishing on the way.'

'Sounds marvellous,' Keith said.

'Then we'll be glad to have you aboard.'

'Jean and I will look forward to it,' Keith replied.

'Let me get you another drink,' Geoffrey said, rising.

Seeing Fiona's attention was elsewhere, Keith flashed Jean a triumphant glance. Things couldn't be going better.

'Hell and damnation!' Hector swore. 'Nige is going to let us down. I just know it.'

'He is rather late,' Hector's girlfriend Mary said.

'I'm sure he'll be along,' Susan said. 'Something must've happened. Can't we extend our time on the court?'

''Fraid not,' Hector replied. 'I've already inquired and it's booked.'

'Is there anyone else around who could fill in for Nige?' Mary asked.

'No one we know,' Hector said. Then, clicking his fingers, 'Wait a minute, I did see someone in the changing room. Haven't a clue who he is but he might fancy a game.'

'No harm in asking him, whoever he is,' Mary said, reluctant to abandon the game, having been looking forward to it.

'Susan?'

'Why not?'

'All right, I won't be a minute.'

Hector loped off in the direction of the male changing room.

'I can't think what's happened to Nigel,' Susan said, worrying a fingernail.

Mary practised a few swings with her racquet.

'Well, we're in luck,' Hector said on reappearing. 'This chap's going to help us out.'

'Jolly good!' enthused Mary.

The chap gave them all a friendly smile.

'Kirk, meet Susan and Mary,' Hector said.

'Hello.'

'Shall we get on with it then?' Mary said.

Susan matched Kirk's smile. 'You'll be partnering me – if that's okay?'

'Fine by me,' he replied.
They walked on to the court.

KIRK

'For God's sake, stop nagging, woman!' Walter Murray pleaded. 'That's all you ever seem to do. Nag, nag, bloody nag!'

'It's the only way I can ever get you to do anything,' his wife Lizzie replied hotly. 'Left to your own devices, nothing would ever get done.'

Walter groaned and slumped further into his chair. He was dead beat having just come off duty at the restaurant His Lordship's Larder, where he was employed as a waiter. He'd had one difficult cover after another that day and the last thing he needed now he was home was for Lizzie to go on at him. Why couldn't she understand that all he wanted out of life was some peace and quiet!

And his lungs had been playing him up all day as well. He'd gone through two handkerchiefs with his coughing and spluttering. Once he'd had to stop and stand still for a full minute in order to get his breath back.

'Now I'm pregnant, it's our duty to the child for us to better ourselves. I want my child to be somebody. To get on and have money and position and mix with grand folk.' A fanatical gleam glinted in her eyes as she gazed inwardly at her own private vision of the life her child would lead when grown up.

If it was a girl, Lizzie saw her married to a professional man. A solicitor or banker, perhaps. Living in a big house with fine clothes to wear. And if it was a boy – well! He would go to a public school and on from there to university. And when he was qualified he'd be an accountant or a manager or something equivalent.

But that could only come about if the wee lassie or boy was given the right start in life. And it was up to her to see that's what happened.

'So what are you going to do about it?' Lizzie demanded, unconsciously rubbing the swell of her rapidly ballooning belly. She was five months gone but looked more.

'I'm a waiter to trade, Lizzie,' Walter said patiently. 'That's all I know. And at my age I'm too old to learn anything else.'

'Nonsense!' she retorted. 'That's defeatist talk.'

'It's being practical.'

'If we got the money together maybe we could run our own restaurant. You know all there is to know about running restaurants. You'd be bound to be a success.'

'Oh, I could do it all right,' he replied. 'The only problem, and an insurmountable one as far as I'm concerned, is the money. Where would I possibly get hold of the money it takes to buy and equip a restaurant? Not to mention the capital needed to keep it operational over the first few months until trade is established and it starts to make a profit.'

'You could go to the bank.'

'Which bank did you have in mind?' he asked, a tinge of sarcasm lacing his voice.

'I don't know. Any one.'

'As we live from week to week on what I bring home and have never had any previous dealings with a bank it would *have* to be any one. But let's say I did go to one. Put yourself in the manager's shoes. Would you lend anything to a waiter who wanders in off the street with no money of his own, and with no property or anything else like that either, who to boot has half his lungs burned away thanks to mustard gas inhaled in the trenches? Now be honest, Lizzie, what would you say to such a man who'd be asking to borrow hundreds off you?'

Lizzie sniffed.

'Well?'

'I'm not a bank manager. What do I know what he'd say?'

38

Walter smiled thinly. 'Well I know. It would be: there's the door, Jimmy, and please close it behind you on your way out.'

It was Lizzie's firm belief that if there was a will there had to be a way. The way was there, they just weren't seeing it, that was all.

'We'll just have to put our thinking-caps on,' she said, adding, 'The trouble with you is you've no ambition, no drive. No "get up and go"!'

She was right, he thought. He hadn't always been like this. In his youth he'd had plans and dreams like everyone else. But the war had done for those. He closed his eyes and thought back to France. How could anything ever seem important again after all that carnage and death and waste? To have come through it all alive had used up a whole life's ambition. Peace and quiet and an easy life were all he wanted now.

'I've just had an idea!' Lizzie said excitedly. 'Now listen . . .'

He forced himself to open his eyes and pay attention.

Walter sat patiently on the hard-backed wooden chair. He was dressed in his Sunday suit and best shirt and collar. His shoes had been so well cleaned they sparkled like black glass.

A glance at the clock ticking on the wall told him it was twenty-five minutes past his appointment time. He frowned fractionally but never dreamed of complaining. He was too grateful for being seen at all.

Thirty-five minutes past his appointment time a prim-looking secretary arrived to say Mr Gibb would see him now.

The owner of Black Lion Brewery was a dapper man in his early fifties. He had steel-grey hair parted in the middle and swept backwards. The steel in his eye matched that of his hair.

'Sit down, Murray,' Gerald Gibb said, picking up and rereading Walter's letter of application, 'And what makes you think you're suited to running one of my pubs?'

Thoroughly coached by Lizzie, Walter spoke his reply.

Christ, but he looks a hard and mean bastard, Walter thought to himself. He wilted a little when Gibb's penetrating gaze fastened itself on him.

'You'll be expected to live on the premises,' Gibb said.

'I understand.'

'And the hours are damn long. It means you wouldn't even see as much of your family as you do now.'

Walter smiled inwardly. Seeing less of Lizzie was an attraction as far as he was concerned. Not that he didn't love her – he did – but she was a gey, demanding woman with a tongue on her as long and sharp as a German bayonet.

'I want to get on,' Walter replied.

Gibb nodded his approval.

Gibb sat at his desk and pretended to reread Walter's application. Frankly he was in two minds. Walter just didn't seem physically tough enough for the pub he had in mind. And why did the man keep coughing like that?

'Mustard gas,' Walter replied when Gibb asked him.

Gibb grunted, softening a little toward Walter.

'I lost both my sons in France,' Gibb said, adding, 'At the second battle of Ypres.'

'I was there.'

'It was pretty horrendous from what I've been told.'

Walter nodded. 'I don't think anyone over here can really imagine just what it was like. Let's only hope and pray the world never sees its like again.'

There was a few minutes' silence during which both men sat lost in their own thoughts.

Gibb's eyes stole across his desk to where a small double-leafed leather-bound photograph holder stood. His two boys in uniform stared back at him. He remembered arguing at the time they shouldn't both join the same regiment but they'd insisted, maintaining they wanted to be together. And on the same day, in the same battle, within yards of one another, they'd both been mown down. Together they'd wanted to be and together they now were for all eternity.

Gibb named his sons' regiment but Walter had been in another, fighting with his lot further down the line.

Gibb made up his mind. If Walter wasn't suitable then he

could always replace him. But he couldn't find it in his heart not to give the man a chance. He would have done the same for anyone who'd been at Ypres.

'When can you start?' Gibb asked.

Walter blinked. 'I have to work a fortnight's notice.'

'Shall we say the first of the month, then?'

'That would be fine.'

'Consider it settled, then. You'll be contacted at home and given the relevant details. Good day to you, Mr Murray.'

'And good day to you, Mr Gibb.'

After Walter had gone Gerald Gibb again stared at the pictures of his two sons. Then, shaking his head in sorrow, he got back to the work in hand.

Lizzie was appalled. The inside of the pub was filthy dirty, and as for the living accommodation! She would've considered it a health hazard for pigs. Walter himself was disappointed. He'd been hoping for a lot better than this.

Lizzie stared out of a cracked window. The district was even worse than the one she'd left. Instead of going up in the world it seemed they'd actually come down.

She watched ragged urchins run up and down the street, only one of whom wore footwear and that carved wooden clogs. Her heart hardened within her. She'd move heaven and earth to ensure her child to come and any others that followed didn't end up like those ragamuffins out there.

With a shudder she remembered her own childhood. There had been times when there was no food at all and she, like the rest of her family and their friends, had got so thin their bones had stuck out like bare branches on a winter tree. She'd been nineteen years old before she'd owned a single article of clothing bought specifically for her and not handed down.

The fact she was plain to the point of verging on being downright ugly hadn't helped matters much, either. And for a long while it had been feared by herself and the rest of her family she was going to end up an old maid.

Then at the eleventh hour, so to speak, along had happened Walter Murray who, far from being the best catch in Glasgow, was certainly far better than none at all.

Lizzie dragged her attention back to the room she and Walter were now standing in. Hot water and soap would attend to the filth and dirt. Give her a month and she'd have this place sparkling like new from top to bottom.

'If we make a success maybe they'll give us a better pub in a better area next time,' she said.

'The cellar's a bloody mess,' Walter replied.

'Then fix it. You can, can't you?'

'Oh aye. It just needs some sorting out, that's all.'

She took off her coat and threw it over a chair. 'Then we'd better get started. You down there and me up here. As you say, there's a lot to be done.'

'Do you think we've made a mistake?' he asked slowly.

'No. Your job as a waiter was a dead-end one. This pub may be the bottom of the barrel but at least there's the opportunity to work your way up. And who knows? With a bit of luck there's no reason why we couldn't own our own one day. No reason why we couldn't own two or three, even.'

'Jings crikey, don't get carried away now girl,' he replied.

'Nothing's impossible, Walter,' she said. 'It all depends how much you want it in the first place.'

Which wasn't a great deal, he thought mournfully.

'Right then, let's get to it!' she said.

He made his way down to the cellar.

Walter wiped his hands on a towel and glanced at the clock on the wall. Lizzie had been upstairs in labour for twenty hours now. At the moment there was a doctor and midwife with her.

He'd leave it a wee while longer and then pop up again to see how she was. Despite assurances from both the doctor and midwife, he was beginning to worry everything wasn't as it should be.

He was in the middle of pulling a pint when the midwife appeared in the bar. The woman was smiling and nodding to him which immediately set his mind at rest. He called to George the other barman to take over.

'Well?' he demanded.

'A smashing big boy. A real whopper at ten pounds,' the midwife said.

'And Lizzie?'

'Fair played out but nothing a few days in bed won't cure.'

He shouted to George to give the midwife a gill and then, snatching up a bottle and two glasses, he rushed upstairs.

Lizzie's face was sunken round the cheeks and she looked totally exhausted. When she saw him she managed a wan smile.

'A boy,' she said.

'Aye, I was told. Would you like a dram?'

Slowly she shook her head.

'Well how about you, Doctor?'

'I won't say no. It's been a long hard pull. Or should I say push,' the doctor replied with a laugh. He hadn't been with Lizzie the entire time but had been popping in every hour or so to see how she was doing.

Walter poured two very large whiskies. 'Ach well, it's not every day you get a son,' he said and handed the doctor a glass. Walter stuck his chest out, pride oozing from every pore. 'To the baby!' he toasted.

'To Kirk,' Lizzie interjected weakly. 'That's what I want to call him.'

She pulled the wean even closer to her and gazed down at him adoringly.

She had plans for this big son of hers.

The years passed and Walter worked hard at running his pub but despite his efforts the pub never did really well. The sad truth was he just didn't have the sort of personality a good publican needs. And although he worked hard his heart was never really in it.

As Gerald Gibb had said, the hours were extremely long and taxing. Never in the best of health anyway since being gassed, Walter soon looked pale and drawn, while his coughing grew more and more frequent.

Lizzie despaired. She hated the area and was mortified at the thought of her Kirk having to grow up here. She scrimped and saved every penny she could, with her mind always on the pub they would buy for themselves one day.

How different their life was to what she'd imagined. There was money in pubs, she'd always said that. The trouble was all the profit went to the brewery with them being paid a mere pittance by comparison.

Again and again she nagged Walter to ask Mr Gibb for a new pub and once Walter actually did write the man a letter. The reply had been curt in the extreme. There were no better pubs available from the brewery and that was that.

There were other breweries, she'd pointed out to Walter. Why don't they approach one of them? But Walter didn't want to know. He was in a rut and didn't want to move out of it.

Sexual relations between them deteriorated, to become non-existent. To begin with she'd hoped that by denying him she'd force him into taking a bolder stand, but as it had transpired, it hadn't bothered him to go without.

In the end she was the one who'd suffered most by the abstention. Not that she would have admitted it, mind you. And being as full of pride as a Highlander, Armageddon would come sooner than she'd make the first move to repair matters. She'd made her stand and that was where she'd stay until he capitulated. Lizzie Murray was a woman who never admitted defeat.

Kirk was eleven years old when Walter received a letter from Gerald Gibb saying he was going to be in the area on such and such a day and intended calling into the pub.

'You can't let this opportunity go,' Lizzie said at once. 'You must ask him again for a transfer. Perhaps a wee pub on the outskirts or a country pub. Just so long as it's not in a slum like this.'

Walter groaned. Did she never stop?

'Have you heard the way our Kirk's beginning to speak? I've done my best but it's those hooligans he's forced to associate with at school. He's starting to sound as common as they do.'

'He's working-class like me and you, Lizzie. How else would you expect him to speak?' Walter said patiently.

'Like the gentleman he's going to be someday.'

Walter shook his head. 'You live in a dream world, so you do. He's got about as much chance of becoming a gentleman as I do of going to the moon.'

'He'll be a gentleman all right and do well in life,' Lizzie snapped in return. 'I've promised him.'

'You shouldn't make promises you might not be able to keep.'

'I'd be able to keep them if you weren't the failure you are.'

'I do my utmost to make a success of this place,' he retaliated, making a vague gesture which took in the pub. 'I want Kirk to go to public school and university after that. We have to give him that chance. It's our duty. Why, you've heard his teachers yourself. They all say what a fine brain he's got. He's streets ahead of anyone else in his class.'

Walter had grudgingly to admit she was right. Kirk had ability, there was no doubt about that. But this public school and university she'd been harping on about for years. That cost money, a lot of it – he'd inquired – and was way and beyond their slender means.

'Go down on your bended knees if necessary,' Lizzie went on, 'but make Mr Gibb give us a better pub and preferably a bigger one. I'm not asking for my sake but for the boy's. He's your son too, after all.'

'You make it sound as if I didn't love the lad.'

'Then prove it! Talk Gibb into giving us a better place and with it the wherewithal to take Kirk out of that dreadful school he's forced to go to now.'

Walter sighed, 'I'll speak to Gibb when he comes.'

'And you'll do your best?'

'As best I'm able. You have my word.'

'Right then,' she replied. She was at the door when she turned. 'Would you like me to be there?' she asked.

'Would you shame me, woman, by speaking for me? I'm a man and can speak like one when I have to.'

'Aye, all right,' she said and left him to it.

The day Gerald Gibb arrived at the Murray's pub had been possibly the most traumatic of his life.

He hadn't been feeling well of late, losing weight and off his food. Consequently, the previous week he'd been to the doctor's, who'd sent him to the hospital for some tests.

He'd been summoned back to the hospital that morning where a consultant had broken the news to him. He had cancer.

After learning this, a great anger had started burning inside him. There was so much left to do in life, minor things as well as major. He'd always wanted to go abroad and never had. He'd always wanted to go on a long sea cruise but due to business pressures and commitments had postponed it year after year. And now he would do none of these things. Putting off till tomorrow what he should have done today he had simply run out of time.

At least he was leaving a thriving business behind him, which was something. But what consolation was that, when he had no direct heirs to leave it to? Anger turned to bitter resentment and that in turn to a cold malevolent fury.

That was his mood when he entered the Murray pub.

Kirk was down in the cellar where he often played. Here among the beer barrels it was easy to imagine himself a knight in Camelot or a soldier in enemy terrain or a host of other characters in whatever situation those characters required.

The only trouble was he always played alone. His mother did not allow him to play with the boys from school, either out in the street or down here. Consequently, although used to his own company, he was often lonely, wishing there was some boy roundabout his mother would allow him to be pals with.

He was down on the cellar floor sneaking up on a couple of

46

imaginary Red Indians when he heard his father come down the stairs. He was about to jump up and make his presence known when he became aware there was someone with his father. When he heard the man addressed as Mr Gibb he froze and remained hidden out of sight.

'You'll remember I wrote to you asking for us to be considered for a new pub, Mr Gibb,' Walter said. 'And you replied saying there was nothing going at the time. Well, the wife and I were wondering if there was anything in the offing now? We really would be most grateful for promotion.'

Gibb turned a baleful eye on Walter. He had to vent his fury, at the card life had dealt him, on someone. And Walter, by unwittingly making his request at the worst possible moment, made himself the perfect target.

'I beg your pardon?' Gibb asked.

'The wife and I were wondering ...'

'What makes you think I would entrust you with a better pub when you've made such a hash of this one?'

Taken aback, Walter blinked. 'We haven't done that badly.'

'No?'

The look in Gibb's eye made Walter suddenly deathly afraid. He felt like someone who'd run on to what appeared to be a lovely sandy beach only to find himself, before he knew where he was, up to his neck in quicksand.

Gibb went on. 'I own four other pubs in this area. All of them in worse condition than this one and all of them taking more money. Why do you think that is, Murray?'

'I couldn't say,' Walter mumbled in reply.

'Well I'll tell you. Because as a publican you're a disaster.'

Walter cringed.

'And I rue the day I ever gave you the chance here. I've been through your figures and do you know something? At the moment you aren't even doing half the business my other four round about are.'

'I work hard, Mr Gibb, sir. Honest I do.'

'Sometimes hard work isn't enough, Murray. And for God's sake stop coughing and spluttering like that!'

47

'I can't help it, sir.'

'Well stand away from me then. I don't relish having your spittle all over my suit.'

Walter backed hastily away. 'I'm sorry, sir.'

Gibb's lips thinned. 'You're a horrible little man, Murray. Disgusting, I'd call you. No wonder the customers keep away from here. Who'd want to come and be served by that sour face and no doubt be coughed over half the time?'

Walter screwed his hands together. This was rapidly becoming a nightmare.

'What are you, Murray?'

'A horrible little man, sir.'

'That's right. And don't you ever forget it.'

'No, Mr Gibb, sir.'

Gibb took his time about lighting a cigar, enjoying watching Walter inwardly writhing in agony. He knew Walter now thought he was going to lose his job.

'The best thing I could do would be to have you replaced,' Gibb said.

Walter was appalled. Jobs were so scarce that at his age and in his condition he would probably never find work again.

'Please don't do that to me, sir. I have a wife and family to keep.'

A wife and family? It was more than he had, Gibb thought bitterly, Emmaline having died several years previously.

Tears squeezed out of Walter's eyes. Lizzie had told him to go down on his bended knees. Well so he would, only not for what she'd had in mind.

He sank to the floor. 'Please?' he pleaded.

The sight of Walter in such a state pleased Gibb. It made him feel better, for by making Walter suffer so, it was as though he was unloading some of his own pain.

'Please?' Walter repeated, and grovelled.

From his vantage point behind the barrels Kirk felt sick watching his father's humiliation. At that moment he didn't know whom he hated more, his father for allowing himself to be so humiliated or Gibb for doing it to him. For years he'd listened to his mother's derisory remarks and comments about Walter but up until now he hadn't fully realised what a weak and pathetic creature his father was.

One thing was certain: no one would ever speak to him like that. No matter what the consequences.

He sank further back into the shadows and turned his face away. He didn't want to see any more. It was bad enough he had to hear.

Walter was sobbing now, a flood of tears rolling down his face from where they went spilling to the floor.

Gibb stared down at Walter. He wasn't being quite fair in saying his other four pubs in the area were on equal terms with this one. Each of them had factories and other small firms close by while this one didn't. It just proved Murray's stupidity for not realising that. The truth was this particular pub had always been a problem one and several times he'd considered selling it. But as long as it continued making a marginal profit he supposed it was best to hang on to it rather than give one of his competitors another outlet.

'All right man, get back on your feet,' he said.

Slowly Walter climbed upright. His lungs were hurting like hell, burning as though filled to overflowing with molten lava.

'I don't want to hear any more nonsense from you about promotion. Is that clear?'

'Does that mean I can keep the pub?' Walter asked eagerly.

'Lord knows why I'm being so lenient but I suppose you can.'

Seizing Gibb's hand Walter pumped it up and down.

'Thank you. Oh thank you, Mr Gibb,' he said.

Gibb shook him off and stalked to the stairs. Walter ran after him like a whipped cur after its master.

Kirk emerged from the shadows. The skin on his face was drawn tight and both his hands were clenched into fists. He stared down at a crate bearing the legend Black Lion Brewery stamped across one side. In place of the black lion insignia he saw Gibb's face.

His foot lashed out again and again.

Upstairs Gibb had just gone and Lizzie was eagerly confronting Walter. She fretted impatiently while he poured himself a large whisky which he gulped down. He poured himself another.

'Well?' she demanded.

In a harsh strained voice he related to her what had occurred in the cellar. When he had finished she sat, her ample backside spilling over the seat. She was numb through.

'Oh shite!' Walter jerked out. His coughing had started up again.

Lizzie looked at her man. But there was no sympathy in her expression. What had she ever done to be landed with the likes of him? she wondered. Well, whatever it was it must have been really dreadful for she was certainly paying for it now. Why, she was twice the man he was! Oh, if only she'd been born male she would have shown them! There would have been no holding her.

'There will be no public school now for Kirk,' she said, the words almost choking her.

'I'm sorry, girl.'

'Sorry! What good's that? It was a better pub and more money I wanted, not bloody sorry!'

Walter hung his head in shame. Why did everyone make life so complicated when it could be so easy? If they could just let him alone to get by without too much fuss or worry. All he wanted out of life was some peace and quiet. Surely that wasn't too much to ask?

'I've always said Gibb was a hard-hearted bastard but I've never seen him like that before,' Walter said.

'At least he's a man. Not some cowering wee mouse,' Lizzie retorted, her voice dripping venom.

'Let it be.'

'All my dreams, everything we've worked for out the window and you say let it be! Christ sake, have you no red blood in your veins at all, Walter Murray, or are you filled with nothing but piss and vinegar?'

He closed his eyes and thought of all his friends dead in the

50

war. Men hanging on the wire, men drowned in mud, men with limbs and bellies and faces blown away, men shrieking in unbelievable agony, and the sanctimonious padres who tried to tell you in the middle of all that there was still a God! How could anything possibly be important after France? If only Lizzie could see how mean and petty everything she worried about was. So what if Kirk didn't get to public school? He was a bright and healthy lad, what more could anyone ask for?

He came out of his dwam to the realisation she was asking him something.

'If we can't afford public school at least let me send him to elocution lessons.'

He nodded. 'If that's what you want.'

'It's not much. But at least it's something.'

She rose to return upstairs. Half-way to the door she paused and turned. 'Did you really cry in front of him?'

'Yes,' he replied in a whisper. 'I thought for sure we were going to lose the pub and be out on the street. And where would I get another job, I ask you?'

Cynicism settled heavily on her mouth. 'And you're the man who can speak like one when he has to?' she said.

Laughing hollowly she left him alone.

When the time came for Kirk to leave school the war was over and Lizzie's fear that he'd have to participate in it laid to rest.

Of the twenty-seven applications for jobs Kirk lodged he got three interviews. Out of the three interviews, he was offered one position, that of a junior clerk in an import/export firm.

Lizzie was furious. This was a far cry from what she'd had in mind for her Kirk. But after discussing the matter at length between them it was decided he would accept the position. The plain fact of the matter was unemployment was high and jobs hard to come by.

During the time between leaving school and starting work Lizzie took Kirk into town and got him kitted out with clothes. To start with there was a suit, absolutely *de rigueur* for office work. A stout pair of shoes to match the suit. A topcoat for the winter weather. And a trilby hat.

Some of the neighbours watched in amazement the morning Kirk left the pub to start his new job. He had this peculiar way of walking, what might be best described as a most pronounced swagger of the hips, which the neighbours found ludicrously pompous now that it had been combined with, or it might be said topped off by, a trilby hat.

'My God, will you take a look at that!' Mrs McMahon said, leaning out of her window.

'Help my Bob, what does he look like!' Mr McMahon said on joining her.

Mrs McMahon sniggered. 'Talk about having a big tip for yourself!'

'First day on the job and already he's dressing like a gaffer.'

'Ach well, he was always like that. Too good for the likes of you and me and the others around here. Say hello to him in the street and he nods down at you as though he was Lord God Almighty and you were something that had just been dug up.'

'Office work,' Mr McMahon, a riveter currently unemployed, sneered. 'Just right for our Kirk. He'll no' be dirtying his hands on that.'

'Kirk dirty his hands – don't talk daft, man!' Mrs McMahon replied.

And with a laugh they both came back into the house, closing the window behind them.

Out in the street Kirk swaggered on his way to the tramstop.

Kirk hadn't been working long when disaster struck at home. He returned to the pub one evening to find Lizzie in tears and his father sitting ashen-faced staring into space.

'What's wrong?' he demanded.

Walter shook his head, unable to speak.

Through her sobs Lizzie managed to get out, 'The new owner of the brewery's been here. A Major Gibb, Gerald Gibb's brother. He's given your dad the sack.'

'Holy Christ!' exclaimed Kirk.

Lizzie went on. 'It seems he's got rid of the board who's been managing the brewery since his brother's death. And now he's taken over personally he says he intends cutting away all the old dead wood.'

'When do we have to get out by?' Kirk asked.

'The end of the month. There will be a new manager installed by then.'

'What can I do?' Walter asked.

'Nothing,' Kirk replied. And he was right. As sole owner of the brewery Major Gibb could do as he damn well pleased.

Walter wrung his hands. 'Where will we go?'

'You'll never get another pub at your age so we'll have to find a house,' Kirk replied, adding, 'It's best you do that, Mum. And if you run into trouble then I'll just have to take a couple of days off my work to see what I can come up with.'

Lizzie nodded.

'There were no hints or prior warning,' Walter said. 'He just marched into the pub, announced who he was, took me round the back and came out with it just like that.'

'A military man,' Lizzie added. 'They don't beat about the bush.'

Bastard! Kirk thought. This Major sounded about as choice as his brother. A real nasty piece of work.

'Maybe I'll get a job as a barman. I don't see what else I can do,' Walter muttered.

'Either that or go back to being a waiter,' Lizzie said.

Walter buried his head in his hands.

Kirk stared angrily at his father. Weak as dishwater, he thought. Not one ounce of backbone. God, how he pitied his mother having to put up with him all these years. She'd deserved far better than the likes of that.

Walter started to cough. Wracking coughs that seemed to be coming from the very depths of his being. He covered his mouth with the large white handkerchief he was never without.

Kirk recoiled inwardly. You would have thought he would be used to his father's coughing by now but he wasn't. He still

53

found it as disgusting and filthy as he always had.

'We might have to rely on your wages for a while till your father gets fixed up somewhere,' Lizzie said.

'Have you any savings?'

'A few pounds, that's all.'

'*Can* we get by on my wages alone?' he asked.

'We'll have to, son. Let's just hope and pray it won't be for too long,' Lizzie replied.

There was silence for a while after that and then Kirk said, 'What a bloody mess!'

Walter continued spluttering into his hanky.

It took Walter months to find another job, which he eventually did in a pub not that far away from where his own had been. When the regulars discovered why he coughed so much he was immediately nicknamed Mustard Murray. Walter took this in good part – not that he could have afforded to do otherwise – and soon became quite a favourite with the customers, something he'd never succeeded in doing in his own pub.

It was working simply as a barman and not having the responsibility of being manager which made Walter more cheerful in his dealings with the public. Although now making even less money than he had been before – and that had been little enough – he was far happier within himself.

The house Lizzie had managed to wheedle out of the Corporation factor was in the same area. The close they lived up was badly in need of repair and all the walls were damp. The communal toilets on the half-landings stank and were forever clogging up.

The first night in their new home Lizzie broke down and wept. Sitting by the fireside she cried buckets while Kirk did his best to comfort her.

Walter went through to the bedroom where he stood staring out the window. Some wee boys were playing 'kick the can' in the rubbish-strewn street. Some other wee boys were hurling round in a broken-down pram they'd found in a midgie somewhere. Above the tenements the chimneys belched

54

smoke into an already polluted atmosphere. Everywhere Walter looked he saw the colour grey. The buildings, the streets, the sky, even the faces of the wee boys.

'Ach, well, it could be worse,' he said, adding, 'At least we're alive, and that's the main thing.'

Having been brought up so much on his own, and continually dissuaded from making pals with any of the lads at school by Lizzie, Kirk continued being a loner now he was working. He would have considered making friends at the office but unfortunately there was no one there his own age, the closest to him being a man of thirty-two who was married with a family.

Therefore it was his habit to go on his tod to the Saturday night dancing up the town where he soon became an accomplished dancer.

Following the custom he would stop off at a boozer first where he'd sink a couple of pints before continuing on to the dance hall.

He lumbered, which is to say took home, quite a few lassies whom he later took out to the pictures and other dances. But none of these relationships lasted long, as his interest in the individuals concerned was always short-lived.

Till the night he met Minnie McKie, that is.

He knew the moment he saw her across the dance floor that he was going to ask her up. She was tall with close-cropped dark hair and finely chiselled features. A gem shining out from amongst the dross.

He strode forward, pushing his way through the standers till he was by her side.

'Would you like to dance?' he asked.

A half-smile lit up her face while she took a moment or two to study him. 'That would be nice,' she replied.

He was disappointed to hear her accent was quite broad. From the looks of her he'd been expecting something more refined.

Some young men find it difficult to chat up a girl, especially a particularly pretty one. But not Kirk. Lacking confidence was a problem he'd never been bothered with.

She fitted easily into his arms and they moved well together. When the first dance finished he asked her if she'd stay up for the second. Soon he had her laughing.

'You've got good patter,' Minnie said.

'I'll take that as a compliment,' he replied.

She eyed him quizzically. 'There's something different about you. Maybe it's the way you talk, all posh like.'

Kirk talked 'posh' as a result of the long stint of elocution lessons he'd had as a child. Having failed to send him to public school Lizzie had made sure she'd had her way about that. She adored the fact he spoke with what she considered to be an upper-class accent. Others, unkindly, had described it as a plum in the gob.

'Then again, perhaps it's just me? What you might call a natural charisma,' Kirk replied.

'What's charisma?'

He smiled in what some people would have thought was a patronising fashion. 'A sort of magnetism,' he said.

'Well nobody could ever accuse you of being shy.'

'No,' he replied, 'that they couldn't.'

Sweat was running down both their faces as the hall was becoming more and more packed. Up on the platform the band was giving it big licks while from time to time a female vocalist went up to the mike and sang. Every so often lights were brought to bear on a many-faceted silver ball hanging twirling from the ceiling. The effect was to send blobs of light dancing over every available surface.

'What do you do?' Kirk asked.

'I work in a shipping office as a shorthand typist.'

'I'm with an import/export firm. It might be we deal with you?'

'Donaldson shipping?'

'Know them well,' Kirk replied.

Somehow that was a bond between them. Something to start off from and build on.

He asked her then where she stayed and was relieved to hear

it wasn't all that far from where he himself lived. With trams stopping relatively early it was always important to establish where a lassie lived in case you landed yourself with a long walk home.

They danced on to the last waltz during which he asked if he could see her back to her place.

'I'd like that,' she said, and laid her head on his shoulder.

During the tram journey home he discovered she lived with her mother and an older sister. Her father had been killed in the war. He didn't tell her much about his own family, preferring not to go into that.

When they got to her close he took her firmly by the hand and marched her round to the back where it was dark.

There they kissed and cuddled for a good twenty minutes before she said she just had to go in.

'Can I see you again?' he asked.

'If you like.'

'What about one night through the week?'

'Wednesday would be the best,' she said.

'That suits me fine. I'll meet you at your front close at seven.'

She took his face in her hands. 'I like you,' she said, well aware she was being awfully forward.

'And I like you too.'

'Till Wednesday then.'

She kissed him one last time before running up the stairs.

As he walked home through the gas-lit streets Kirk whistled a jaunty tune. It was good to be winching – which means taking out -- someone he had a real fancy for.

It was just a pity she was working-class, though. Otherwise she might have suited him in the long term just dandy.

After a couple of months of winching Kirk and Minnie started meeting one another at lunchtime. There was a cheap little restaurant they would go to while other times they would find a quiet spot to eat the sandwiches they'd agreed to bring with them.

It was during one such sandwich-eating session that Minnie said, 'My mum's boyfriend has come back from America and she's having a wee party for him at the house. Would you like to come?'

Kirk nodded. 'An American?'

'Aye, he's stationed over here with their Air Force. Hank the Yank we call him but his real name's Harry. I think you'll like him.'

'I'll look forward to it.'

'It'll also give you a chance to meet my mum and sister,' she said coyly.

Kirk grinned. 'Is this me getting my feet under the table?'

'See it as you like.'

'As long as you don't start talking about engagements,' he said.

Innocently she studied her sandwich. 'Oh it's far too early yet for that.'

Kirk told himself he was going to have to watch it with this one. Well he'd string her along for as long as he could. And if he played it correctly that could be quite some time.

He wondered if there would be some way he could get her alone at the party. He was getting awful fed up, and frustrated, by the restrictions of her back close.

Harry, whom all the Scots called Hank, Hydelman was a shortish, very hairy, American who looked like he had a lot of Italian or middle European blood in him. He laughed a great deal and was forever slapping people on the back – a habit which Kirk personally found very irritating.

Minnie's mother, Judy, looked to be in her mid-forties. Reasonably well groomed, she was still in good nick despite having had two children and lost a husband.

The sister Irene was an older version of Minnie but hadn't nearly such a nice personality.

'Have another Scotch,' Harry said and topped Kirk's glass up to the rim.

'Hey, go easy!' Kirk said, thinking it was something new to

58

see so much whisky being thrown around. Whisky was still as hard to come by as it had been during the war.

'How about you, Min?' Harry went on. 'There's plenty more where this came from.'

'Just a little one then,' Minnie replied, gasping when her glass got the same treatment Kirk's had done.

'Call that wee?' she said.

'It is in Texas, where I come from,' Harry replied with a laugh before moving on.

'Idiot!' Minnie smiled. 'He doesn't come from Texas at all. He's from Ohio.'

Kirk sipped his drink. Like most Glaswegians he wasn't a whisky connoisseur. As long as it was the real McCoy and came in a glass, that was fine by him. But he did know enough about whisky to appreciate that what he'd been drinking since arriving at the McKies' was deluxe quality of a standard he'd only ever tasted once before.

Music from a gramophone started up and he and Minnie danced. To show his manners he also danced with Judy and Irene – the former was already well on her way to being sloshed.

There were half a dozen Americans present, all of whom seemed amiable men eager to be liked.

Every time Kirk's glass was even half empty Harry appeared to fill it to the brim again.

'Enjoy! Enjoy! I like people to enjoy!' Harry called out.

'Quite a character,' Kirk said.

'Mum likes him.'

'Is marriage in the air?'

Minnie shook her head. 'He's already got a wife and kids in the States. That was why he was back there. He goes home to see them every so often.'

'What does he do in the Yank Air Force? Fly a plane?'

'No. He's in charge of the B.X. on their base.'

'What's a B.X?' Kirk asked.

'It's a big shop called a Base Exchange where the men and the families living on the base can buy things at a reduced

59

price. According to Hank they've even got washing machines and fridges there, although I find that hard to believe.'

'Is that a fact?' Kirk said thoughtfully. 'And Hank's in charge of the whole kit and caboodle?'

'So he says.'

'Let's dance again,' Minnie added a few seconds later. George Formby singing 'Chinese Laundry Blues' had just been put on the gramophone and it was one of her favourites.

About an hour later Judy came up to Minnie. 'I'm getting a bit woozy so Hank's taking me out for a spin in his car. I'm just letting you know in case you can't find me and start worrying.'

Harry joined them. 'If we're late getting back don't feel you have to wait up,' he said.

'Fine,' Minnie said.

Judy kissed Minnie on the cheek and then she and Harry were making for the door.

Kirk smiled. He'd just been presented with a Heaven-sent opportunity. He gave Harry and Judy a good fifteen minutes to get under way before whispering in Minnie's ear he wanted to speak to her out in the hall.

Once there he said, 'Which is your bedroom?'

'Why?'

'Why do you think?'

She looked uncertain so he took her in his arms and kissed her.

'Just for a little while,' he whispered.

'All right then,' she said, and taking his hand led him to one of the several doors lining the hallway.

'Don't put the light on,' she said once inside.

There wasn't a lock on the door but there was a small chest of drawers close by. This Kirk lifted and placed in front of the door. If anyone tried to come in they'd get the message.

He kissed her and was still kissing her as he manipulated her on to the bed. Deftly he undid the top buttons of her dress so he could get at her breasts. Hot and sticky, she squirmed under him.

'Oh!' she said when his hands went under her knickers to find her.

Her knickers were half-way down her thighs when suddenly she stopped him. 'Tell me you love me,' she said.

'I love you, Minnie. I swear it,' he answered.

'I've never done it before, Kirk.'

'Neither have I.'

'I'm pleased about that.'

Her knickers slid off and then he pushed his trousers and underpants down to his knees.

She sucked in her breath and throwing her arms around his neck drew him close to her. 'Oh, my darling love,' she whispered.

He got on with it.

Lying in his own bed the next morning Kirk began to think about Harry Hydelman.

Harry was in charge of the B.X. and judging from last night this B.X. seemed to have an abundance of whisky, a commodity most sought after in Glasgow, being the Glaswegians' favourite tipple. There was some to be found in most pubs and occasionally to be bought over the counter but, since the war when the bulk of that produce had started to be shipped to America in return for warships, weapons etc., and latterly to repay some of the vast debt Britain had run up with the States, never ever enough to satisfy the demand.

It seemed to him this was a situation ripe for exploitation. The big question was, would Harry play ball? And if so what sort of quantities might be involved? It was an exciting thought and one he dwelled on over breakfast.

After the meal was finished he walked round to Minnie's where he was in luck. Harry had come back and stayed the night and had not yet returned to base.

Minnie welcomed him with a kiss and a knowing wink. In a whisper she said Judy was still in bed having the most God Almighty hangover. Harry was still with Judy.

61

Kirk said he would wait as he wanted a word with the American. Minnie and Irene got on with the clearing up while he sat by the fire and thought.

'It's all right for some,' Irene said, not entirely jokingly.

Kirk beamed her a smile and sat on.

Eventually there were sounds from the bathroom and a little later Harry appeared, having washed and shaved.

'Some party,' Harry said and whistled. Then noticing Kirk, 'You still here?'

'I've been home and come back again,' Kirk replied.

Minnie handed Harry a cup of coffee, which he accepted gratefully. She asked him if he'd like breakfast but he said no, the coffee was enough.

'It's you I've really come to speak with,' Kirk said to Harry. 'Perhaps we could take a walk while I explain what I have in mind.'

'Couldn't we talk here?'

Kirk smiled. 'I think it best we take a walk.'

Harry looked curious. He glanced at his watch and then nodded. 'Okay, I got a while before I'm due back on base. A walk it is.'

Kirk waited briefly in the hallway while Harry disappeared to have a word with Judy. Then Harry was back and side by side they descended the tenement stairs.

'You sure sounded mysterious up there,' Harry said when they were out on the street.

They passed Harry's flashy American car standing conspicuously at the kerb. Kirk wondered what the neighbours would make of that if it wasn't moved soon. But perhaps Judy McKie was the sort of woman who didn't give a damn what the neighbours thought. On reflection he decided that was probably the case.

'Minnie told me last night you're in charge of the B.X. out at your base,' Kirk said.

'That's right.'

'And amongst the other things you sell there is whisky.

Hence the liberal supply there was at the party.'

Harry came up short and his eyes narrowed. 'What are you getting at?' he demanded.

Kirk licked his lips which had suddenly gone dry. He wasn't at all sure he wouldn't get a punch in the face for what he was about to suggest.

'I was wondering if you'd be interested in us coming to some sort of arrangement? Literally any amount you can supply I can sell.'

They walked for a little while in silence, Harry's brow furrowed in thought. Every so often he glanced at Kirk.

'Supposing, just supposing mind you, I had a mind to sell the stuff off base, why go through you when I could do it myself?'

'For the simple reason you're an American and they stand out like sore thumbs here. You'd have everyone talking about you and what you were doing. I, on the other hand, am a local and I know the trade. I was brought up in a pub and it would be to pubs I'd be selling. Try it on your own and you'd be committing suicide. But with me on the inside, so to speak, there's no reason why we couldn't have a nice profitable little fiddle going without any of the authorities being any the wiser.'

'What sort of cut did you have in mind?' Harry asked.

'Fifty-fifty, straight down the line, as I believe you people say.'

Harry was tempted. But he needed time to think it through.

'I'll need a few days before I can give you an answer,' he said finally.

'Take as long as you need.'

Harry nodded. 'Okay then.'

They turned around and walked back to Harry's car, the door of which Harry opened.

'Aren't you going back upstairs?'

'Naw, I got to get back to the base. I have some paperwork I can't put off any longer.'

Harry climbed into the car, rolled down his window and stared straight into Kirk's eyes. 'Are you sure you could make your side of it work?' he asked.

'Absolutely positive,' Kirk replied.

'As much as I could supply you could sell?'

Kirk nodded.

'I'll be in touch through Min,' Harry said, putting the car into gear and driving off.

Kirk took a deep breath. His hands were trembling fractionally as he put them into his pockets.

He'd said he knew what he was doing. He just hoped he did.

Harry took his time about driving back to base. Kirk's proposition had been so unexpected that it had caught him off guard.

There was no doubt about the fact he could use some extra money. His elder boy was in college and the second one wanted to go too after he graduated from high school later in the year. He could manage both but it would be an awfully tight squeeze. And he had to remember it wasn't that long till he'd be leaving the Air Force. He still hadn't decided what he was going to do then but any additional dough he could get together in the meantime couldn't help but come in useful.

Could he trust this Kirk, though? What if the kid turned out to be all mouth or, worse still, tried some sort of double-cross?

But then why *should* the kid try a double-cross? He was the goose who'd be laying the golden eggs and it would be only stupid to try and screw him in any way. And Kirk hadn't struck him as stupid, in fact quite the reverse.

He smiled suddenly. It was a crazy notion, all right. Scotland making the goddamn stuff, selling it to the States, the States in turn sending it back to Scotland, then he, in tow with a Scotsman, selling it back to the Scots.

The idea appealed to him.

'I think the split should be sixty-forty,' Harry said. 'After all,

64

as supplier I'm the one who could really be putting his ass in a sling.'

Kirk shook his head. 'We're both dependent upon one another. You need me just as much as I need you. Equal partnership or nothing.'

Harry pretended to consider that but his mind was already made up. 'Okay, it's a deal,' he said finally.

Kirk stuck out his hand and they shook on it.

'When can I have the first delivery and what sort of quantity will it be?' Kirk asked.

Harry got out a notepad and pencil. He wrote down a figure which he showed to Kirk. 'That's the cost per case to the B.X. Right?'

Kirk nodded.

'So you tell me what you'll be selling it for and we'll go from there.'

They got down to the business of hammering out the details.

The arrangement was Harry would deliver personally every Saturday afternoon, as this time suited them both.

Kirk found and rented a brick-built garage which was so situated it wasn't overlooked. This made it perfect for loading and unloading.

The first delivery consisted of ten cases. It was Harry's idea for them to start relatively small and see how they went from there.

That night Kirk started on the first of the independent pubs he'd decided to approach. Going up to the bar, he asked to see the publican, who turned out to be a Mr Fowler.

'I'm a rep, Mr Fowler,' Kirk said, shaking Fowler's hand. 'Is there somewhere private we can go? I'd like a confidential word.'

'This way,' Fowler replied, and led Kirk through to a back room.

'Now, what can I do for you, lad?' Fowler said.

Kirk opened his briefcase and pulled out a bottle of whisky

which he handed Fowler. 'I'm selling, if you're interested in buying.'

'What? The one bottle?'

Kirk smiled. 'By the case.'

Fowler sat down and regarded Kirk. 'It's knocked off, I take it?' he asked.

Kirk disregarded that. 'This isn't a one-off affair,' he said. 'Give me your order and I'll deliver it weekly.'

'What price?'

Kirk stated the price agreed upon between him and Harry.

'That's more than I normally pay,' Fowler said slowly.

Kirk shrugged. 'But not much more. And think how your business will pick up when it gets around you've got a regular supply of the cratur to sell. Why, I wouldn't be surprised if you doubled your beer profits, and what's a few extra quid against that?'

Fowler considered Kirk's argument. The truth was, he was desperate for more whisky. His customers were always moaning that there wasn't enough for their needs. Like every other publican he did his damndest to get more but inevitably he ended up with his quota and that was that.

'Can you do me five cases a week?' Fowler asked, blinking when Kirk said that was all right.

'Cash on delivery,' Kirk said.

'Fine by me.'

'I'll be round Monday night, then,' Kirk said. 'Delivery straight into the cellar just like any other.'

'I'll be expecting you,' Fowler replied.

Once he'd left the pub Kirk allowed a broad smile to light up his face. One up, one down. If the rest were as easy as that one had been, it would be like knocking ducks off the proverbial pond.

The second pub on his list was several streets away from the first. This one was a great cathedral of a place doing far more trade than the other.

When he emerged yet again into the night it was having taken an order for the second five cases and knowing the publican would take an additional five when he could supply them.

As he strode for the bus to take him home, his swaggering walk was even more pronounced than usual.

He was most pleased with himself.

There was a wee man Kirk knew from the Black Lion Brewery pub his father had run as manager. John, the man's name was, and he owned a van.

The van was old but not so old as to be unreliable, dilapidated but not so dilapidated as to be particularly eye-catching. In other words just perfect; the sort of van seen every day making deliveries and which passers-by would never look at twice.

John was only too delighted to help Kirk out and a bargain was struck between them.

'You can rely on me, Mr Kirk,' John said with a leer and a wink. 'I'll not let you down.'

'We'll drink to that,' Kirk replied and, producing a ten-bob note, told John to away up to the bar and fetch another two pints.

Kirk sat back and watched John getting the order up. It was a good feeling to have other people obsequious to you and so keen to do your bidding. He liked the feeling a lot.

At the end of the first month Kirk was taking delivery of twenty-five cases a week and was supplying five pubs. Outlay was minimal. Just the rent of the garage and paying John for his muscle and the hire of his van.

After the divvy Kirk was already making more than twice what he earned from the import/export firm where he worked, and as far as he was concerned he and Harry had hardly even scratched the surface.

'A wee something extra for the housekeeping, Mum,' Kirk said that Friday night when he handed over what he paid for his keep.

Lizzie's eyes widened. 'Are you sure you can afford it, son?'

67

'Oh aye.'

Lizzie sat down and counted the money again. 'What are you up to then?' she asked.

He smiled and tapped his nose.

'You wouldn't be doing anything daft, would you?'

'Who, me?'

'Well whatever it is just make sure you take care.'

'Careful's my middle name,' he said, and crossing to her kissed her cheek.

She laughed suddenly. 'Have they made you managing director of that firm you work for?' she asked.

'You mean I forgot to tell you?'

'Get away with you!' she said, playfully punching his shoulder.

'It's just a wee deal I've got going,' he said. 'And as long as it's on, there'll be something in it for you every week.'

Moisture misted her eyes. 'I always knew you'd come up trumps, son. I always said someday you'd make it to the top. Right up there with all the big cheeses.'

'I've a long way to go before I'm that,' he replied, grinning. 'But let's just say I feel I've got my toe on the first rung. Now, do you mind if I get changed? I'm going out with my lassie tonight.'

'I'll lay out a clean shirt for you right away.'

A few minutes later as she was handing the shirt to him she said, 'And when are we going to meet this lassie of yours then?'

'Not this one, Mum. Maybe someday there will be one I'll bring home. But not this one.'

'I understand,' Lizzie said. And she did, perfectly.

While he knotted the new tie he'd treated himself to that day he thought of the night before him.

Judy and Irene were away out which meant he and Minnie would be left alone for a few hours, allowing them to have one of their 'sessions', as Minnie called them.

He was thoroughly enjoying sleeping with Minnie. The only trouble was he was beginning to find her a little hard-going when they had nothing else to do but talk to one another.

If things had been otherwise he would already have been on the lookout for someone else to replace her. But as her mother was being knocked off by Harry, and Harry and he had such a nice little thing going together, he didn't want to tempt fate by upsetting the applecart in any way.

The idea he had then caused him to stop what he was doing and stare at himself in the mirror.

Of course! Why not? With money starting to roll in it was a natural progression. If he could find himself a small flat, or a single-end even, that would give him a great deal more freedom than he now enjoyed. And how was Minnie to know what he was up to when she wasn't there?

The smile that curled his mouth upwards gave him the appearance of a friendly shark.

'Oh, you beast!' he said to his reflection.

Chuckling, he reached for the cologne bottle. He loved smelling nice.

Five months after they'd started, Kirk and Harry were selling a hundred and fifty cases a week to twenty-eight pubs.

Although Kirk had bought himself a small motor and learned to drive he retained the services of John, upping John's wages in accordance with the expansion of the amount of work involved for the man.

He'd also moved into a tiny but luxurious West End flat; an excellent address that pleased him no end.

Early one evening he was in bed with Minnie when there was a knock on the door.

'Who's there?' he called out.

'Harry.'

'Wait a moment.'

He slipped into his dressing gown before admitting Harry. It was the first time Harry had been in the flat.

'I hope you don't mind me barging in but I'd like to have a talk about the Scotch,' Harry said.

Kirk placed a finger over his mouth and gestured with a

sideways motion of his head towards the bedroom. Harry got the message.

'Minnie!' Kirk shouted. 'Get yourself dressed and come on out here.'

Kirk poured them both drinks and they talked about this and that till Minnie appeared. Neither she nor her mother, Kirk and Harry having decided it was prudent, knew the two men were doing business together.

'How about some fish suppers?' Kirk suggested, knowing full well that was Minnie's favourite food. Personally he found the meal somewhat vulgar.

'Great!' said Minnie and clapped her hands.

'Look, I've just poured Harry and me drinks so what about you toddling off down and getting them?' Kirk suggested.

'All right.'

He handed her a pound note and then he and Harry had to wait a further few minutes while she shrugged herself into her coat and made sure her hair was in place.

'Anything wrong?' Kirk asked anxiously once Minnie was on her way.

'Far from it. Quite the reverse in fact,' Harry replied.

'Thank God for that,' said Kirk sagging back in his chair. 'So what's this all about?'

'I've been having some correspondence with a couple of friends of mine stationed in England. Men who also run B.X.s. They're both open to an arrangement.'

Excitement surged in Kirk. Excitement that was tinged with a little fear.

'What sort of arrangement?' he asked.

'Well, I've reached a ceiling on what I can ask to be supplied to my B.X. If I was to up the ante any more it would only arouse suspicion.'

'The last thing we want,' Kirk said.

'Right,' Harry agreed. 'But if instead of being supplied by one B.X. you were supplied by three, then it's possible the amount you're currently offloading could be tripled. What do you think about that?'

70

'Four hundred cases a week!' Kirk said and gulped, his mind reeling at the thought.

'Can you handle it?'

'Yes,' Kirk said promptly.

'Are you sure? I don't want you to make a mistake about this. Rather we make do with what we've got than we blow it and end up in the hoosegow.'

'I can handle it,' Kirk said.

'Okay then. Of course our profit won't be so high on what we get from England. On those consignments it'll be a third each. You, me and the other party.'

'Agreed,' Kirk nodded. 'How do we get their stuff brought up here?'

'You leave that to them and me. Your problem is distribution this end.'

Kirk sipped his drink and thought furiously. John and the van would still be adequate but he was going to need more storage room. Furthermore, with the amount of time that was going to be involved now he would have to give up his job with the export/import firm so that he could distribute and collect cash during the day.

He would tender his notice at the first opportunity. And by God, how he was going to enjoy that! It was going to be marvellous to be rid of that dreary boring job.

Mentally he totted up what his share was going to be out of all this. The figure he arrived at caused his breath to catch in his throat.

He poured more drinks and raised his glass in a toast.

'To the United States Air Force and its most marvellous B.X.s!'

They drank to that and then Harry said, 'And here's to rye and bourbon and the fact that the vast majority of Air Force personnel in this country at the moment are drinking those rather than Scotch.'

'I'm not quite with you,' Kirk said. 'How does that affect us?'

'Because I have a natural in-built ceiling, as I've just told

71

you, beyond which I daren't go without running the risk of questions being asked. Now my ceiling is two hundred cases a week for the base, fifty of which is drunk by the personnel, and a hundred and fifty which comes to you. But if they wanted to consume a hundred cases then I'd have to give it to them, which would only leave us fifty. And so on. Savvy now?'

'I see,' Kirk replied. 'The less they demand the more for us?'

'On the button.'

'To rye and bourbon!' Kirk toasted.

'Amen,' added Harry.

Kirk grunted as he struggled out of bed. He went through to the bathroom and stared at himself in the mirror there.

There was flab on his shoulders and upper arms. The spare tyre round his belly filled both hands when he grasped it. His backside looked like two lopsided haggises filled to bursting. Too much booze and good food was taking its toll. He decided he was going to have to do something about it.

During that week and the next he made inquiries, the Hillhead and Kelvinbridge Sports Club being the one to emerge most highly recommended.

One afternoon he drove round there. He had difficulty at first finding it as it was most discreetly tucked away. He chatted to the club secretary who helped him fill out the necessary application form. When he said he didn't know a member of the club to sponsor him the secretary was only too happy to oblige.

Armed with a temporary membership card, until his proper one came through, he went on a tour of the facilities. The voices he heard were all very well spoken, the men and women they belonged to clean cut and obviously out of the top drawer.

Instantly he felt right at home. This was the sort of place where he belonged and the type of company he should keep.

There was a cool marbled pool which he swam in for half an hour before dressing again and returning to his flat.

He couldn't wait to get back.

EDDY

It was pay night and Frank King was having his usual celebratory bucket. He drained off his pint and then made his way through the press to the bar where he waited patiently till he could catch Sammy McCafferty, the barman's, eye.

'Remember the Boyne!' a drunken voice shouted, causing Frank to frown.

'Death to all Fenians!' another voice added. And a small roar of approval rose to batter the high ceiling.

Frank glanced round to see the knot of Orangemen who'd invaded the pub. All of them wore sashes and looked as though they'd been on the batter since early that day.

It was 12th July, the day the Orangemen took their annual walk. Wearing their sashes and playing their flutes they traversed Glasgow in a defiant show of strength against what they considered to be the Catholic menace.

Out on his coal-round that afternoon, Frank had seen a woman's accordion band, the noise from which had given his usually placid cuddy Damson a fright. And no wonder: the so-called music had been a dreadful din.

Frank slid his empty glass across to Sammy who gave him a fly wink. Sammy was also a left-footer.

'King Billy slew the Fenian crew at the battle o' Benwater ...' the Orangemen sang, banging their feet on the floor while several of them raised their clenched fists aloft. Frank decided it was time he was making tracks for home, which he would do as soon as he'd finished this last pint. He paid Sammy the correct money and then raised the beautifully headed pint to his lips. He was on his first swallow when the elbow dug savagely into his side, causing him to choke and splutter beer.

'What in the fuck do you think you're doing, Jimmy?' the angry voice demanded.

Frank caught his breath before turning to face the man addressing him.

The man was short with extremely broad shoulders and a face that was booze-flushed. His eyes were small and vicious-looking.

'You bumped into me,' Frank said quietly.

'Like fuck I did,' the man retorted, adding, 'You spat at me.'

Suddenly the atmosphere in the pub had changed. There was potential trouble afoot and everyone was aware of it.

'You jabbed me with your elbow, causing me to splutter. That's what happened,' Frank replied.

'Are you calling me a liar, pal?'

'I'm not calling you anything. I'm just telling you what happened.'

The man grunted and peered into Frank's face. He took in Frank's liquid brown eyes topped by a thatch of thick black curly hair. 'A fucking Mick,' he breathed.

The hubbub that had been all around quietened; it was as though the air had suddenly been shot through with electricity.

Frank was in deep trouble and knew it. Out of the corner of his eye he could see the Orangemen inching closer. He stood his ground for the simple reason there was nothing else he could do. The man and the rest of the man's Orange cronies were between him and the door.

'See the likes of you,' the man said and prodded Frank's chest with a stubby finger. 'You're a dirty lot who come over from fucking Ireland to work for cheap wages. You undercut good Protestants and put them out of work, so you do.'

A growl rose from the hovering Orangemen.

Frank kept his mouth shut. To say anything could only exacerbate matters. He reckoned in a man-to-man fight he might well be able to take his opponent, but tough and strong

76

as he was, there was no way he could take on all the Orangemen and possibly win.

'No speaking, eh?' the man snorted, and prodded Frank again.

'There's a streak of yellow through all Micks,' the man added, underlining his point by hawking between Frank's feet.

Frank had been slightly drunk before but he was stone-cold sober now. His eyes flicked round the pub but he saw no help there. Most of the drinkers were studiously looking away, in fact anywhere but in his direction. They didn't want to get involved.

'Okay, break it up, break it up!' a new voice said.

The newcomer wore a black cotton jacket denoting he was someone in authority.

The man turned on the newcomer and snarled, 'This Mick cunt here spat at me.'

'Well that's worth a pint and a half-gill on the house any day,' the manager said, signalling to a barman to put it up.

'I'm still not satisfied,' the man said, still bristling.

'Look do me a favour, Jim, and let it go,' the manager said. 'Any trouble in here and I could lose my licence. You wouldn't do that to me, would you?'

The man instantly backed down a little. It would be a terrible thing to deprive another good Protestant of his living.

'Aye, well then,' the man said and reached for his free pint and whisky.

The manager took Frank by the arm. 'Right, come on you,' he said and hustled Frank toward the door.

Outside in the street the manager whispered, 'I know it wasn't your fault. Sammy told me. But I had to do what I did to get you out in one piece.'

'And I appreciate it,' Frank replied.

'See you another night,' the manager said before turning and bustling back into the pub.

Frank took a deep breath. Then he cursed himself for going into a boozer on Orange night. He should have had more sense. Hurrying down the street he headed for where he could catch a tram home.

To get to the tram stop he had to cut through an alleyway. Half-way up it and surrounded by darkness he became aware of the hurrying feet behind him.

There were five of them headed by the man from the pub.

'So you thought you'd get away with it, did you?' the man said as he swung the first punch.

An arm took Frank round the throat and seconds later his legs were kicked out from under him.

He landed heavily and as he did so the metalled working boots started to rain down on him.

There was a lot of pain until one lashing boot took him behind the ear.

Oblivion was instant.

Josie King was sitting knitting in front of the empty grate when there was a knock at the front door. Her sixteen-year-old son Eddy sat facing her, reading a cheap western novel he'd borrowed from one of his pals at the small repair shipyard where he worked as an apprentice boilermaker.

'I'll get it,' said Josie rising. She thought it was probably one of the neighbours round for a blether.

The two police constables both looked grim. One of them asked if they could come in.

A coldness swept through Eddy as he watched the two policemen enter the room. He dropped his book to the floor and stood up. Josie reckoned she knew what the trouble was. Frank had got drunk and been picked up. It had happened before but not for a couple of years now. He could be a wild man at times, her Frank.

'Mrs King?' the elder policeman asked.

Josie nodded.

'Wife of Francis Connelly King?'

Josie nodded again.

'I'm sorry to have to tell you your husband was in a fight of some sorts. A patrol found him and called an ambulance which

78

took him to hospital. He died before he could get there.'

Numbness enveloped Josie. She couldn't believe what she'd just heard. 'What, do you mean he's dead?' she asked, her voice trembling.

The elder policeman looked at Eddy. 'I think you'd better make your ma a cup of tea, son,' he said. 'Or maybe something stronger if you have it in the house.'

'Oh my God!' said Josie. Tears welled from her eyes to run streaming down her face – a face that had suddenly gone milk white.

When Eddy didn't move the younger policeman went to the sink and ran water into the kettle, which he then put on the cooker.

Josie came apart. A strangled wail of anguish erupted from her mouth. She started to shake all over.

'Who did it?' Eddy asked.

The elder policeman shook his head. 'We've no idea yet. When your father was found he was alone in an alleyway. Whoever his assailant or assailants were, there was no sign of them.'

'You will find them though?' Eddy demanded.

'Oh aye.'

With that promise Eddy moved to comfort his distraught mother. Later she would want to see the body.

Summer dwindled into autumn, which in turn gave way to winter, and still the police failed to come up with anything. It was as though whoever had murdered Frank King had vanished into thin air, leaving the police completely mystified.

At first Eddy believed the promise the policeman had given him. But as time passed he came to realise the cynical view held by many of his Catholic friends was well founded. The reason the police weren't finding his father's killer or killers was for the simple reason they weren't pursuing their inquiries with much vigour.

A bastion of Protestantism, the Glasgow police didn't deem it worth their while, or in their best interests, to hunt down the killer or killers of a Catholic murdered on Orange night.

What was one Fenian more or less, after all? Good riddance to bad rubbish, they probably secretly thought.

With Frank dead and buried, Eddy's money wasn't enough to keep the house running so Josie had to hire herself out as a skivvy. She found two families of well-to-do Jews in the West End whom she did for six days a week.

Eddy hated the thought of his mother working but there was nothing else for it if he were to make ends meet. He considered it just as well he was an only child as he didn't know what they would have done had there been children younger than him.

It was unusual for a Catholic couple to have only a single offspring but as Josie had often said, God had only seen fit to smile on her and Frank the once.

Christmas was looming on the horizon when one Saturday, walking down the street, Eddy bumped into Sammy McCafferty.

'How are you then?' Sammy inquired, thinking Eddy looked a lot more grown up since his father's death. Before there had still been some of the boy in Eddy but there was no sign of that now. The boy had become a young man.

Sammy had been to the funeral but hadn't spoken to Eddy at the time. Nor had he seen Eddy since.

'How are the police getting on?' Sammy asked.

Eddy shook his head.

'I told them about that bastard who claimed your da the night it happened. I even called round at the station to tell them when he reappeared but whether they followed it up or not I couldn't say.'

'What bastard?' Eddy asked. This was news to him.

Sammy related to Eddy what had happened on the night of 12th July when Frank King had fallen foul of the Orangeman and his friends. He went on to say the Orangeman had been back into the pub three times now, twice on a Friday night and once on a Saturday.

Eddy considered going to the police and kicking up a stink.

But second thoughts told him he probably wouldn't get very far. Which left the ball in his court.

Of course there was always the possibility the police had spoken with this Orangeman, but somehow he doubted that.

He and Sammy walked a little way in silence. Finally he said. 'If I was to come into your pub the night would you give me the nod should this bloke appear?'

'Aye, sure, Eddy. Only be warned, he's a real mean sod if you're thinking of chiselling him yourself.'

Eddy wasn't at all sure of what he was going to do. He would play it by ear and see what happened.

'Just you give me the nod, Sammy. That's all I ask.'

When they parted on the corner Eddy called out, 'See you opening time, Sammy!'

And Sammy McCafferty waved back.

That night when the manager of Sammy's pub opened the front doors Eddy was one of those waiting to be let in.

He ordered up a pint and then found himself a corner in which to stand. And there he stood without even going to the toilet till closing time when last orders were called. Amongst the first in, he was last out. The Orangeman hadn't showed.

The next Friday and Saturday nights he was back but again had no luck. The following Friday he presented himself yet again. By half past eight his attention had wandered – he was half listening to a football conversation going on behind him – when suddenly Sammy was by his side.

'Him at this end of the bar trying to get a drink,' Sammy whispered out the side of his mouth, at the same time gesturing fractionally with his head.

Eddy sidled closer and took a long hard look at the man he'd come to find. And he didn't like what he saw.

Gloag, for that was the Orangeman's name, was still in his working clothes, having just knocked off. As he drank his pint he thought about the big Coventry Eagle motorbike he'd recently bought. He'd got it cheap as there was a lot of work needed doing on it. But he didn't mind that. He enjoyed

81

working on bikes. He'd have the bike ready for when the good weather came again, Gloag thought. Then he'd take a run down to the coast, Saltcoats or Dunoon maybe. That would be grand.

For half an hour Gloag stood at the bar drinking pints and whiskies, then, turning abruptly, he carved his way through the crowd for the door and the street beyond.

It was bitter cold outside and snowing. Eddy huddled into his overcoat as he hurried after Gloag. He still hadn't made up his mind what he was going to do next.

The tramcar clattered out of the night and Gloag leapt aboard. His heavy boots rang on the metal steps as he ran upstairs. Eddy settled downstairs and bought a ticket for a maximum ride. His eyes were glued to the steps leading to the top deck as the tram rattled on its way.

Gloag got off the tramcar in a part of Glasgow Eddy had never been in before. There was a lot of bomb damage about including a church they passed which had only one wall left standing and, curiously enough, the font.

Gloag walked along a wasteland between two rows of houses. He paused by a snowed-over midden where he had a pee. Still doing up his flies he made his way behind the midden to vanish round the side of a wash-house.

For a moment or two Eddy panicked, thinking he'd lost Gloag. And he would have, too, if it hadn't been for the man's wet, clearly distinguishable footprints leading through a back close. Eddy followed the footprints up two flights of stairs to the door through which they'd disappeared. The name on the side of the door said 'Gloag'.

He now knew the Orangeman's name, which was a start. Standing outside the door he heard the thin cry of a wean from within, which told him Gloag was married with a family, which was something else.

But what should he do next? He went down to the front close where he stood watching the snow fall and thought about it.

82

Next morning Gloag woke with gummy eyes and tacky mouth. He thought of his Coventry Eagle which he would soon be working on, and smiled. Beside him his wife Margie snored with her mouth wide open. The teeth on view were without exception rotten.

Without any preliminaries Gloag hiked her nightie up and then rolled on top of her. Grasping her fat waist he savagely thrust into her.

Margie gasped and came awake. She was like sandpaper down there but knew better than to complain. To do so would have earned her a cuff round the chops. She closed her eyes again and tried not to grimace as he squeezed down on her breasts. She thought about the day's housework while he got on with it.

When it was over Gloag sat up in bed and scratched himself.

'Breakfast, woman,' he growled and headed for the sink to wash and shave.

After he'd eaten his bacon, eggs and fried bread he said he was off out. He didn't say where he was going nor did Margie expect to be told. A man's business was his own affair.

Outside in the street Eddy was stiff and cold through. He rubbed his hands and listened to his stomach rumble. He was dead-beat, almost dropping with tiredness having kept watch on Gloag's close all night.

He lit his last fag, more for something to do than anything else. It tasted like old socks in his mouth.

It was still dark, and would be for a good hour yet, when Gloag appeared in his close mouth. He was smiling at the prospect of what lay before him, as he headed up the street.

Eddy followed at a safe distance.

The garage where Gloag kept his motorbike was a ramshackle affair at the back of a stables. There were about a dozen horses kept in the stables which belonged to a local dairy. When Gloag arrived all the horses were out delivering the milk.

Gloag unlocked the garage door and let himself in. As there was no electricity he lit a paraffin lamp which cast a warm

83

friendly glow round its immediate vicinity.

Gloag was taking down his overalls when he became aware there was someone in the doorway watching him. 'Who the hell are you and what do you want?' he demanded harshly.

Eddy stepped forward a pace. Now he was face-to-face with Gloag, the numbing coldness that had seeped into his bones during his long night's virgil began to thaw. 'I've come about Frank King,' he replied.

'Who's he when he's at home?'

'The man you tried to pick a fight with in Chapman's pub last Orange night.'

Gloag's eyes narrowed as did his nostrils. He lifted the paraffin lamp so he could get a better look at Eddy. 'And who's this Frank King to you?' he asked.

'He was my da.'

Gloag smiled; a gruesome leer that lit up his face which, combined with the glow from the lamp, made it like an ogling Halloween lantern.

'The Fenain's brat, is it?' Gloag hissed.

Eddy knew then beyond all doubt Gloag had been in on his father's murder. Despite himself moisture misted his eyes. Anger like a ball of fire burst in his belly but for the moment he was able to keep it contained.

'Did the police ever bother to question you about the murder?' Eddy asked, his voice croaking a little.

'Why should they?'

'Don't play funny fuckers with me, Gloag. I'm telling you.'

'Oh you are, are you?' Gloag replied, laughing, adding contemptuously, 'I'd wait till I was fully grown before I start talking like that, sonny.'

Eddy swallowed hard. 'Were you alone or were there others with you?'

Gloag lit a cigarette which he drew on while studying Eddy. 'Why don't you piss off? You're beginning to annoy me,' he said.

'Why Gloag? Why? He never did you any harm.'

Gloag listened but there were no noises to be heard apart from his own breathing and Eddy's. He knew the pair of them were quite alone.

'Because he was a Catholic cunt and I hate Catholics,' Gloag said and spat. 'If I had my way I'd rid this country of every last one of the dirty swine. The answer to your question, sonny, is that your da got what he did because he was what he was. A dirty stinking Fenian who the world's well rid of.'

Gloag laid the paraffin lamp on the workbench and striding forward very quickly grasped Eddy by the lapels of his coat. He jerked Eddy up till Eddy was dancing on his tiptoes.

'And for two ha'pennies I'd do the same to you except it would spoil the pleasure I've been looking forward to of working on my bike. So why don't you do as you're told and fuck off while you're still in one piece.'

Having said that, Gloag threw Eddy from him. Eddy twisted to fall sprawling across the workbench.

With a contemptuous laugh Gloag turned to gaze lovingly at the Coventry Eagle thereby presenting his back to Eddy. It was the worst, and last, mistake he ever made in his life.

A berserk rage swamped Eddy. The ball of anger became a tidal wave which flooded through him in an instant. His hand closed over a heavy adjustable spanner.

The first blow split the back of Gloag's skull wide open. The second caused a section of bone to penetrate the brain killing Gloag were he stood.

The all-enveloping rage only lasted for a few seconds. When it passed Eddy found himself towering over Gloag's corpse, which lay huddled at his feet. Trembling, Eddy tottered over to the motorbike and sat on its pillion. He didn't have to examine Gloag to know the man was dead. That was blatantly obvious.

He sucked in a few breaths to steady himself while staring in fascination at Gloag's body. After a few seconds he rose and went outside to where he'd noticed a tap before entering the garage. The water was icy cold which was just what he needed.

He splashed handful after handful over his face till he was feeling better. Then he carefully washed the spanner and returned it to the workbench.

It was still very early but being a Saturday morning it wouldn't be long before people were out and about.

He crossed to the other buildings which a quick investigation revealed to be stables. Behind one of the buildings he discovered an evil-smelling pit three-quarters full of horse dung and dirty straw.

Returning to the garage, he grasped Gloag under the arms and dragged him to the side of the pit. Sitting back on his hands he put both feet against Gloag's and pushed.

There was a glopping sound as the corpse made contact with the pit's contents. The feet and legs were the first to disappear from sight, the horrible staring eyes and blood-matted head the last.

Eddy ran some more water from the tap and, using rags he found under the workbench, did his best to clean up the blood that was splashed over the garage floor. What stains remained he covered with oil and grease so that they were indistinguishable from the rest of the general muck and clart. The rags he wrapped round a half brick which then followed Gloag to the bottom of the pit.

Satisfied he'd done everything he could, he rehung Gloag's overalls on the peg where they lived and locked the garage door. This latter he achieved by simply snapping a padlock shut.

He then hurried out into the street and set off back the way he'd come.

Josie was worried stiff when Eddy didn't come home all night. Thinking something had happened to him, she was several times within an ace of going to the police but in the end decided to wait till morning before reporting the matter. It was lucky for Eddy she did.

'Where have you been?' Josie demanded angrily the

moment he let himself into the house. 'I've been out of my mind!'

He was pale and shaken and every few seconds his hands would tremble uncontrollably. 'I killed him,' he said.

Josie was taken aback. 'Killed who, son?' she asked.

'One of those who murdered my da.'

Josie could see from Eddy's face that what he said was true. 'Holy Mary, Mother of God!' she ejaculated, and having crossed herself sat down.

Eddy told his mother the whole story, starting from when he'd bumped into Sammy McCafferty right up to the bit where he'd dumped Gloag in the muck pit.

On completion Josie told him to get out of his clothes. With blood stains on them it was best they were burnt in the grate so they could never be used in evidence.

Eddy stripped down to the skin while Josie looked out a fresh set of togs. While he was putting them on she heaped those he'd just taken off on to the fire where they were soon consumed.

She then insisted he eat breakfast and much to Eddy's astonishment he found himself ravenous.

Over the meal they discussed what he should do. At no point did it cross either of their minds that Eddy should go to the police and meekly confess to what he'd done. That would have been tantamount to suicide. The options open to him were limited and clear. Either he stayed on and tried to bluff it out or he took to the road. He decided on the latter.

Josie packed a small case for him and from a secret place produced two five-pound notes which she made him take. This ten pounds was what she'd managed to save from her skivvying.

At the door she held him close but didn't cry. There would be time enough for that after he'd gone.

He promised to write but she said it was best he didn't for some time in case the police intercepted his letters and learned his whereabouts from them. He admitted she was no doubt right. If still free, he would drop her a note after six months and sign it as a fictitious relative. She could play it by ear from there.

Josie thought her heart would burst as she gave him a last kiss and told him to take care of himself.

On the half-landing he turned to smile and wave. Then he disappeared from view to go clattering down the rest of the stairs. Closing the door Josie went through to kneel before a statue of Our Lady. She prayed long and hard, at the conclusion of which hot scalding tears came.

'This is it,' the driver said with a yawn.

Eddy awoke and stretched as much as the confines of the lorry's cab would allow. He looked out the lorry window and liked what he saw. The surrounding houses were very alien in appearance to him but somehow they gave the impression of being friendly.

'Fulham,' the driver said. 'End of the line for me.'

'Thanks,' said Eddy and got out.

'There's a caf round the corner there if you feel like a wad. I can recommend it.'

Eddy nodded his appreciation and decided a bite was precisely what he needed.

He found the caf where the driver said he would and after a cup of tea and a couple of slices of bread and thinly scraped marg decided he would have a wander round the area.

As he walked he decided this would be an ideal place to settle in digs for a little while. After all, when the police did start looking for him, where better to lose himself than amongst this teeming humanity called London?

At the first newsagent's he stopped and bought a paper, which he anxiously scanned for news of a murder hunt. But there was nothing, which didn't surprise him unduly as it might well be months, if he was lucky, before that pit was dug out and Gloag's body discovered.

On the other hand, the police might well come looking for him sooner than later. When Gloag was reported missing, as was bound to happen in the next few days, some bright spark might well remember what Sammy McCafferty had reported and put two and two together.

A number of postcards were pinned in the newsagent's window advertising various items, one of which was board and lodging. Upon inquiring of a passer-by, Eddy discovered the address to be close at hand.

The woman who opened the door was tall and willowy. Eddy judged her to be in her late twenties or early thirties.

'Yes?' she asked, looking him up and down.

'I'm after digs,' he stated.

'Hmm!' she said. 'You'd better come through, then.'

The kitchen he was ushered into was neat and clean. He sat when she invited him to do so.

'You sound Scotch,' she said, eyeing him up and down yet again.

Eddy squirmed, embarrassed by the close scrutiny. 'Cumbernauld,' he lied, naming a small village outside Glasgow.

He accepted the cigarette she offered him.

'How long would you intend staying?' she asked.

He shrugged. 'That depends.'

'On what?'

'What sort of work I find. Whether I like it. A number of things.'

'So you haven't come down to a job?'

'No,' he said.

He was doing a bit of eyeing himself now. She was a good-looking woman of a finer, more delicate type than had been his experience up to now. The vast majority of Glasgow females might well have hearts of gold but they also had figures, to put it kindly, sufficiently padded to keep out the biting Scottish winter weather.

There was a leanness and breeding about Mrs Grimes which reminded Eddy of a picture of a racehorse he'd once come across in a book.

'Have you run away from home?' she asked suddenly.

Eddy had a winning smile when he cared to use it, which he did now. 'Not at all,' he replied. 'I just fancied coming to the big city. Who knows? After a while I might even go abroad.'

Mrs Grimes digested that. She'd taken an instant liking to this Scottish lad with the marvellous accent. There was something indefinable about him which excited her. Something wild and barbaric that was so utterly refreshing and new.

'There's not all that much work about at the present,' she said. 'Before the war ended there were jobs galore but when the soldiers came home these were all snapped up. Still, I'm sure there's something you can find. Do you have a trade or profession?'

He shook his head.

'So you're unskilled?'

'I'm afraid so.'

'Well you're young enough which'll probably be in your favour.' She paused, waiting for him to volunteer his age but he didn't oblige.

'Do I have digs then?' he asked.

She told him the rent and demanded two weeks in advance. He paid there and then.

En route to his room at the back of the house she said, 'I'll let you have your own key but on no account are you to try and sneak women in. Is that quite clear?'

She smiled inwardly when she saw he was blushing.

During the next four days Eddy tramped the streets of Fulham and nearby Walham Green to no avail. There was no work to be had, or if there was he couldn't find it.

Returning home discouraged, he threw himself on his bed and stared at the ceiling. He was still lying there when there was a tap on the door.

'Come in!'

Mrs Grimes entered, clad in her housecoat. 'How did you get on?' she asked.

He shook his head. 'Not a sausage.'

She looked at him thoughtfully. 'I had an idea this afternoon. Do you like cars?'

'Yes.'

'Can you drive?'

'No,' he replied. 'Although I'd love to learn!'

She smiled at his enthusiasm. 'I have a brother who sells used cars over in Warren Street. He mentioned about a week back he was going to have to look for someone to help him. Think that might appeal?'

'Sounds marvellous,' Eddy said.

'Then we'll go over there first thing tomorrow and see what's what. Mind you, I'm not promising anything. He might well have found somebody in the meantime.'

'I understand perfectly,' Eddy replied, adding, 'It's awful good of you.'

She sat on his bedside chair and crossed her legs, exposing a length of thigh in the process. She seemed blissfully unaware of this, although Eddy certainly wasn't, as she went on, 'The other thing is I need your ration book. I've been feeding you so far from the household rations which are short enough, goodness knows.'

This was an eventuality Eddy had been expecting and was prepared for. Rising from the bed he opened a drawer from which he extracted his book.

'Sorry the front's a bit of a mess,' he said apologetically. 'I spilled a cup of tea over it some time back.'

The name on the front of the book had originally read E.F. King. Eddy had doctored it since his arrival in London to read E.F. Kingsley which was the name he'd given Mrs Grimes.

As he handed the book over he couldn't help but see down the front of her housecoat. She wasn't wearing a bra which meant her small breasts were fully in view.

The breath caught in his throat. He had never seen a woman's breasts in the flesh before. The truth was he was still a virgin.

From the expression on his face Mrs Grimes guessed that to

be the case, thinking further that if he had any experience at all it was extremely limited.

'I'd better be getting on then,' she said. Standing she was only a fraction smaller than him.

This close and in such a confined space her personal scent was extraordinarily strong and sent Eddy's head whirling. He would have given anything in the world to be able to reach out and take her in his arms but of course he never dreamed of actually doing so.

'You can call me Annie,' she said, and with one last smile was gone, closing the door behind her.

Heart hammering, Eddy lay back on the bed. He tried to think about the job in Warren Street but instead his mind was filled with thoughts about Mrs Annie Grimes.

That night he slept fitfully, waking a little after midnight having dreamed he was back in the garage killing Gloag. He wiped sweat from his brow and then groped for his cigarettes.

He was half-way through his smoke when he heard the unmistakable patter of feet in the hallway. He knew from their lightness they belonged to Annie. A door softly opened and then just as softly closed again, causing him to frown. All the rooms on this floor belonged to lodgers, with the toilet downstairs where Annie's quarters were.

The room she'd entered was the one next to his and belonged to a Yorkshireman called Crosthwaithe. Besides himself and Crosthwaithe there were three other lodgers, bringing the grand total to five.

For a few minutes there was silence and then a bed began to creak. Soon the creaking changed to a rocking sound. There was no doubt in Eddy's mind what was going on through the wall and it surprised him how affected he was by the knowledge. Why should he be jealous? She was nothing to him, he told himself. But jealous he was.

He thought of Crosthwaithe and Annie making love together and the image conjured up in his mind brought the sweat back to his brow. He stubbed out his cigarette and buried his head beneath his pillow. But that didn't help much. He could still hear the rocking sound.

And then with a final bump it was over and silence reigned once more.

Later she left. The same pitter-patter of her feet on the linoleumed floor.

For what seemed like hours after her departure he tossed and turned before finally sinking into an exhausted and fervered sleep. He dreamed again, only this time Gloag killed him and it was his body the muck pit claimed.

Next morning at breakfast Annie was chirpy and full of beans whereas Eddy was morose and sullen.

Several times he threw baleful glances across the table at Crosthwaithe, whom up till the previous night he'd rather liked. He decided now the Yorkshireman wasn't at all his cup of tea, noticing for the first time several mannerisms of Crosthwaithe's which he found irritating.

After breakfast the other lodgers left immediately for work. He had to wait till Annie washed up.

While she was busy at the sink he sat smoking a cigarette and studying her back-view. He had to stop the latter when the same sweat he'd had the night before reappeared on his brow.

On the bus they had a fight over who would pay the fares. He insisted that as the man he should do so while she argued that was all very well but he was unemployed whereas she was earning an income.

In the end she let him have his way, smiling secretly to herself as he stared huffily out of the window. The more she saw of Eddy the more she liked him. Part of her mind thought of him as a son figure. But only part of it.

Gilbert Crabtree – 'Everybody calls me Gil!' – looked every inch the salesman he was. Exuding charm and confidence and *bonhomie*, he showed Eddy round the showroom after Annie had explained Eddy was looking for a job.

Eddy instantly felt right at home in the showroom. Running

a hand over a highly polished car he said if Gil would have him, he'd love to work there.

Behind the façade Gil Crabtree was an extremely shrewd and capable man. He was also an excellent judge of character. He could tell Eddy was honest and trustworthy, which counted for a great deal in his book. He could also see Eddy had a natural charisma, which was a potential customer winner.

'You start at the bottom. You understand that?' Gil asked.

Eddy nodded, eyes shining in anticipation.

'Thirty bob a week to begin with and we'll see how you go. Deal?' he asked, proffering his hand.

It was considerably more than Eddy had expected. 'Deal,' he replied. And they shook.

'When can you start?'

'Right away if you like.'

Gil laughed and put his arm round Eddy's shoulder. 'You and I are going to get on just fine, kiddo,' he said.

'I'll leave you two to it,' Annie said.

Gil saw her to the door where they stood talking for a few minutes. When she finally swung off down the street Eddy raised his hand in farewell but she never looked in his direction. He found that upsetting but didn't show it.

Eddy enjoyed the next few weeks more than any previous part of his life.

He missed Glasgow dreadfully and doubted if he'd ever get over the loss. In a way he felt the loss of Glasgow even more than that of his da.

But London was different: cheery and exhilarating. His time at work was spent either polishing and cleaning the cars or else answering the telephone when Gil was out.

He wanted to try and deal with some of the customers but Gil said it was too early for that. Selling wasn't as easy as it looked and Eddy would have to learn the art – for art it was, as Eddy soon discovered.

If he was happy during the day he was wretched at night,

however. He'd lie awake listening for the pitter-patter of Annie's feet on the linoleumed floor and all too often he heard it.

He began to hate Crosthwaithe, finding it increasingly difficult even to be civil to the man. He would dearly have loved to give vent to his feelings and punch Crosthwaithe on the nose.

In fact he often imagined that happening; Crosthwaithe lying vanquished on the floor with bloody nose with Annie looking on at him adoringly.

One night when Annie was in his bed and they were sharing a cigarette, having just made love, Crosthwaithe said, 'I don't know what I've done to offend young Eddy but he sure as hell hates my guts for some reason or other.'

This was news to Annie, who hadn't noticed anything untoward between the two.

'When I said hello to him this morning the look he gave me would have sunk a battleship.' Crosthwaithe had been in the Navy during the war and often used naval references and allusions.

'Do you want me to have a word with him?' Annie asked.

'If you don't mind. The bad feeling's getting on my wick.'

'And what a wick it is,' Annie said coarsely. And they both laughed.

She was padding back down the corridor when it suddenly dawned on her what the problem might be. She turned to stare thoughtfully at Eddy's door.

She knew of course that Eddy was daft on her. It was blatantly obvious, the way he looked at her. And she fancied him. The trouble was when Eddy showed up she'd already embarked on a most satisfactory affair with Crosthwaithe.

Perhaps if she shifted the rooms round that might help. On reflection she didn't think so.

She waited till the following Sunday afternoon when Crosthwaithe had gone to a cricket match and the other three lodgers were out, before confronting Eddy in his room.

She found him lying sprawled on the bed reading a western

novel. A type of literature she'd come to know he was fond of.

'Sit down, Annie,' he said, a smile lighting up his face.

She came directly to the point. 'What's between you and Crosthwaithe?' she asked. And when he didn't reply, she added, 'I won't have any bad feeling in this house. I can't stand atmospheres.'

He gazed sulkily down at the book in his lap, refusing to meet her gaze.

She smiled to herself, seeing he was wearing his petted-lip expression. When he looked like that he became so boyish she wanted to gather him in her arms and mother him.

'Well?' she demanded.

'I can't,' he mumbled.

'I think maybe it's my fault,' she said. 'It never dawned on me till the other night you might be able to hear.'

He shot her a glance and then looked hurriedly away again.

'Is that it?'

He nodded.

'I thought so.'

Eddy was the picture of abject misery. 'Maybe I should find other digs?' he suggested, although it was obvious from his voice that was the last thing he wanted.

'I don't think it's necessary to go that far,' Annie replied.

'It's awful hearing you two at ... through there.'

'I can imagine.'

At that moment he was despising himself for a weakling. Men didn't behave like this in front of women where he came from. He was acting like a big softie. If his pals at home could have seen him they would have had a right good laugh.

But there was something different about Annie Grimes. Something he'd never seen in any of the women he'd been friendly with in Glasgow. Perhaps it was her age or her Englishness. But he didn't think it was either. It was something, a quality, in the woman herself. A sort of added dimension that kept giving him the feeling she knew something he didn't.

Annie realised she was going to have to make a decision.

And the time to make it was here and now.

'Eddy?'

There was a throatiness in her voice which made him look up instantly.

'Do you want me?'

He couldn't believe his ears. 'Do you mean ... ?'

'That's precisely what I mean.'

'Oh Annie,' he said, but still didn't move.

She stood up and crossing to the door turned the key in the lock. Then she closed the curtains as the window was overlooked.

Standing by the bed she smiled staring down at him. 'Well?' she asked.

He took her into his arms awkwardly and clumsily, still not able to believe this was actually happening. Their mouths met and when their tongues touched he literally staggered as his legs seemed to turn to jelly.

'Take your clothes off,' she whispered in his ear.

He tore at his pants and shirt while she regarded him with amusement.

'Don't look at me like that,' he said.

'I'm sorry. I didn't mean to.'

'Do you find me funny because I'm so much younger than you?'

'You mustn't take offence,' she replied. 'There's none meant.'

'All right then,' he said. 'But don't laugh at me again. I don't like it.'

'I was smiling not laughing.'

'You know what I mean!' he said.

'I know,' she replied and took off her blouse to reveal she wasn't wearing a bra.

Her skirt slid to the floor to be kicked to one side. She sat to remove her stockings, garter and belt and pants.

Eddy was suddenly embarrassed and shy. The last woman to see him with his clothes off had been his mother and that had been years ago when he was a wee boy.

97

Annie could tell she'd been right about his lack of experience. 'Have you had many women?' she asked teasingly.

'Oh aye, lots,' he lied.

'I see.'

His eyes devoured her as she moved to the bed. Her personal scent was stinging his nostrils and he suddenly knew what it reminded him of. She smelled just like gin. A peculiar odour but an attractive one.

She could see how nervous he was. His chest was rising and falling while the skin on his upper arms rippled from time to time. His expression was studiedly casual as though this sort of thing happened to him every other day.

She circled his neck with her arm and drew him to her. His hand came up to cup her breasts.

She gasped in astonishment as he leapt on top of her. His hips ground against hers as he desperately, and with no success at all, tried to enter her. She knew then she was his first woman.

'Hold on a minute,' she whispered.

He was panting while sweat slicked down the side of his face and along his nose. He jerked when she took him in her hand to help him.

And then he was off as though it was something that had to be done as quickly as possible and he was out to break the world record.

The way he leapt up and down causing the bed to bang convinced Annie they were going to break it. Talk about being heard in the next room! The way he was carrying on they'd be heard in the next bloody street!

When it was all over Annie said, 'I can honestly say no one has ever made love to me like that before.'

'I thought it was good, too.'

She lifted herself on to one elbow to stare into his face. He looked like a cat who'd fallen into a bowl of cream. 'There's no need to go at it like an express train,' she said.

Instantly his face fell. 'Did I do something wrong?'

'Not exactly wrong.' Then teasingly, 'Have none of your other girls ever said anything?'

'No,' he said hesitatingly. Very unsure of himself now.

'Well they should've done. They should have told you to relax and enjoy it more. Draw it out. Make it last.'

He thought about that. 'That's decadent,' he said finally.

She couldn't help the guffaw which erupted out of her. 'You're in a class of your own, Eddy. You're absolutely priceless!' she said.

'Are you laughing at me again?'

'Yes. What are you going to do about it?'

'I could, eh ...'

She laid her hand on his thigh. 'Biff me one, is that it?'

'I never said that.'

'You Scotchies are all so tough. Tartan terrors, all of you,' she said, tongue in cheek.

He liked the image of that. Like most working-class Glasgow men he fancied himself as a hard man.

'I could tell you things that would wipe the smile off your face,' he retorted, thinking of Gloag.

'Then go ahead.'

He shook his head and wouldn't be drawn. That was a secret iron bars wouldn't have prised out of him.

She caressed him, thinking what a magnificent raw animal he was. Nor did she mean that in a derogatory way. He wasn't stupid, far from it. But his mind was still very unformed, amorphous in its lack of experience and sophistication. He thought he knew a lot but in reality he was still a child.

There was also an arrogance about him which was deeply rooted in the Glasgow thing. Annie saw, and was attracted by, the manifestation of this arrogance but was wrong in thinking it a personal trait. The root-cause went far deeper than her understanding of it.

She fingered the small crucifix dangling from his neck. 'Are you a Catholic?' she asked.

He nodded, suddenly wary. 'Why?'

'Nothing. I just wondered.'

'Does it make a difference that I am?'

She frowned. 'Why should it?'

'Where I come from it might.'

'You get all sorts round here,' she said. 'All religions and colours of the rainbow. We don't bother too much about it. The rule is if they don't bother you, you don't bother them. Live and let live.'

Eddy sighed. 'Where I come from you can end up dead for kicking with the wrong foot.'

'Kicking with the wrong foot?'

'Catholics with the left and Protestants with the right. It's a saying.'

'You're exaggerating, surely?'

He thought of his da done to death in an alleyway. And for what reason? No other than he'd been a Mick on Orange night.

'No exaggeration,' he said softly.

There was a wistfulness in his voice which reached deep inside to touch her. 'Why don't we try again?' she asked.

The surprised look on his face told her he hadn't thought of a second time.

'Just relax,' she said soothingly. 'Leave it all to me.'

This time the bed was only in half the danger of being broken.

For years now Annie had been sleeping with a succession of her lodgers, having been lucky in as much as there had always been one who'd taken her fancy and vice versa. But this was the first time she'd actually taken up with a new one while the old was still in residence.

That night she told Crosthwaithe to stay behind in the communal sitting room after the others had gone to bed. She wanted to speak to him.

When they were alone she took him through to the kitchen and made a pot of tea. Handing him a cup she said bluntly, 'I'm afraid you're going to have to find another place to stay, Eric.'

Crosthwaithe was flabbergasted. 'What do you mean?'

'What I said. I want you to find another place to live. It's all over between us.'

Crosthwaithe's face twisted into an ugly scowl. He wasn't a man who took kindly to being chucked over.

'Is there someone else?' he demanded.

Annie shrugged. 'That's none of your business.'

'And what if I make it so?'

'There would be no point. It's finished, Eric. Now let it go. I know of a few places round about that are nice and comfortable. I'll put in a good word for you.'

But Crosthwaithe had no intention of letting the matter drop. Reaching out, he grabbed Annie's arm, twisting it so that she cried out.

'That hurt!' she said.

'Where do you get off thinking you can treat me like this?' he demanded. 'Why, you're nothing but a bloody slut!'

Using the open palm of his free hand he cracked her hard several times across the face. On one of her cheeks he left a red-wealed imprint.

'Let me go, you bastard!' she hissed, badly shaken. She'd known he had a temper but had never figured this to happen.

'You heard her,' a new voice called from the doorway. 'Let her go.'

Crosthwaithe turned to find himself staring at Eddy, who was clad only in pyjamas. He barked out a laugh. 'Get lost, kid,' he said.

Eddy closed the door and moved closer to where Annie was struggling in Crosthwaithe's grip. 'I meant what I said. Let her go.'

'Or else what?'

Eddy picked up the bread knife. It was a vicious-looking weapon that had been sharpened so many times it was hooked slightly in the middle of the blade giving it a scimitar-like appearance.

'I'll stick this in you,' Eddy said simply and quietly.

Crosthwaithe laughed again, but this time the laugh died

somewhat. There was an expression in Eddy's eyes which told him Eddy meant precisely what he said.

'So *you're* the new one, are you?' Crosthwaithe said in a taunting voice. 'Well, you're only the latest in a long line. And I mean a *long* line. She's anybody's who'll give her the time of day.'

Annie sobbed at that and averted her head.

Eddy desperately fought to keep his rage under control. He'd already murdered one man. The last thing he wanted was to up his tally.

'No wonder you've been giving me such filthy looks of late,' Crosthwaithe went on at Eddy. 'Christ, was I slow! I should have guessed marmalade thighs had been at you.'

Eddy frowned, not understanding the allusion.

A cruel smile stretched Crosthwaithe's mouth. 'Why marmalade?' he asked. 'Because it's a well-known early-morning spread.'

Annie cringed and seemed to shrivel where she stood.

'Pack your bag and go. Tonight. Now,' Eddy said, his grey Glasgow-accented voice thickening when he added, 'or so help me God, you're a dead man. I swear it.'

Crosthwaithe released Annie, who staggered away from him. She stood with her face to the wall and her back to both men.

Eddy gestured with the knife towards the door. 'You've got five minutes,' he said.

Wearing a contemptuous leer Crosthwaithe walked stiff-legged from the kitchen.

'Annie?'

'Not yet. Wait till he's gone.'

'I understand,' Eddy replied.

Tears ran down Annie's now red cheeks to fall splashing to the floor. She looked years older than she normally did.

Eddy stood by the outside door with the knife held ready in his hand. His breath was laboured as though he'd been running. The fire in his belly was like a red-hot cone trying to burrow its way through his flesh.

When Crosthwaithe appeared with a battered suitcase in his hand nearly a quarter of an hour had passed since he'd left the kitchen.

Eddy didn't say anything about that. The important thing was Crosthwaithe was going. He stepped aside to allow Crosthwaithe access to the door. 'One other thing,' he said. 'You bother Annie again after this and I'll come looking for you. And it won't be a knife I'll have. It'll be a brace of razors.'

Crosthwaithe blanched and some of the defiant cockiness oozed out of him.

Eddy went on. 'I'll carve you so badly there's not another woman will ever look at you.'

Crosthwaithe opened the door and walked out into the night.

Back in the kitchen Eddy tried to take Annie in his arms but she'd have none of it. She dabbed her tear-streaked face with a tea-towel. She felt old and horrible and, above all, dirty. If the water had been hot she would have had a bath. As it was she would have to make do with dousing herself with perfume when she went through to her room.

'I'm sorry you had to hear that,' she said.

'The man's a pig.'

She nodded her agreement.

He laid the knife on the table and helped himself to two of her cigarettes. She mumbled her thanks when he pressed one between her cold and colourless lips.

Again he tried to take her in his arms and again she broke away from him.

'Maybe it would be best now if you left as well,' she said.

'I don't want to, Annie.'

'Even after what you heard?'

'Was it true?' he asked.

Her eyes were full of pain. 'Yes,' she whispered in reply.

He drew heavily on his cigarette and then bit his lip. 'It's different now I'm here,' he said after a while.

The ghost of a smile lit up her face. 'You're lovely, Eddy. Truly lovely. Perhaps things might have been different if I'd

103

met you years ago instead of now. But I didn't.'

He said awkwardly. 'I know you're a lot older than me but we can still make a go of it, can't we?'

'There's a lot you don't understand, Eddy. A lot I haven't told you.'

'Then tell me now.'

'No. Tonight isn't the right time. Certainly not the way I'm feeling.'

'Can I come to your room?' he asked.

She came to him and laid her hand on his cheek. 'You really would have killed Eric, wouldn't you?'

'Yes.'

She shivered, then kissed him on the side of the mouth. 'Thank you for being my protector. My knight in shining armour.'

'I'd do anything for you, Annie,' he said – and meant it.

'Not tonight, Eddy. Tomorrow night if you still want me. But not tonight.'

'I'll want you all right.'

'Then I'll come to you.'

'Promise?'

'I promise,' she said.

He felt a tremendous warmth and affection for this woman called Annie Grimes. He'd only known her a short time and yet already he couldn't imagine life without her. It was as though he'd known her always.

He went to sleep alone but smiling.

The following week Gil announced it was high time he learned to drive. After all what damn good was a car salesman who couldn't demonstrate the vehicles!

Eddy was therefore given time off from the showroom to go and apply for a provisional licence, and the night of the day it arrived Gil personally gave him his first lesson.

Eddy found he loved driving. There was a thrill about it he found exciting in the extreme. Furthermore it turned out he was a good driver, having a natural rapport and feel for cars.

104

Gil also started teaching Eddy the administrative side of the business, showing him how to keep the accounts and fill out the various forms that bureaucracy demanded.

At the end of the month Gil was so pleased with the speed of Eddy's progress he increased Eddy's wages to two pounds ten shillings a week. Eddy was naturally delighted, saying he felt like Carnegie with all that loot.

Annie was insistent he save some of it which he did by opening a Post Office book. He considered sending some of it home to Josie but after a great deal of thought decided against that. It had been agreed between him and his ma he wouldn't contact her for six months, so that's the way he'd leave it.

He still hadn't got over the daily fear of having his collar felt at any moment. But as time went by and nothing happened his fear began to die down a little.

He was amazed to discover Annie could drive – he'd never heard of any woman in Glasgow capable of that! – and several weekends Gil lent them a car which they drove out into the country.

On one such occasion Annie took along a picnic which they had to eat in the car as the weather was still cold.

He asked her to tell him about the things she'd promised to tell him the night of Crosthwaithe's departure but she demurred, saying not yet. He was left wondering what deep and dark secrets she had that she was so loath to confide to him.

Every night she came to his room and into bed with him. Most nights they made love but not every night. Sometimes it was sufficient for them to have a cuddle and just be with one another. Several times he asked to come to her room but she always refused. That was her private place, she said. Her sanctuary. Her Holy of Holies.

Once when he was home alone he was tempted to go into her room and have a look around. In the end he decided against it. It would have been betraying her confidence as well as his love for her which daily grew more and more strong.

He firmly believed she loved him in return.

The shock was therefore profound when one night she took him into the kitchen to announce her husband was coming home that Sunday.

He'd known right from the start she was a 'Mrs' of course, but somehow he'd assumed she was divorced or her husband had been killed in the war. There was enough of the latter, by God, war-widows being thick on the ground.

'His name's Toby,' she said. 'And he's an actor.'

'An actor!' Eddy exclaimed. That was the last thing he'd expected. The only actors he knew anything about were those he saw at the pictures, like James Cagney or Errol Flynn. And what chance did he have up against a man like Errol Flynn!

Annie laughed when he mentioned Flynn. 'Toby's not at all like that,' she said. 'He's a theatre actor, which is a different breed entirely. He's about your height, not at all good-looking and certainly not dashing. He plays character parts, which means he's forever having to be an old man or a hunchback or something.'

'And you mean you two are still together?'

'Yes. Although he spends most of his life away in rep while I keep the house running.'

Eddy was mystified. To him, a husband stayed with his wife, or if he absolutely had to go away, like a soldier or a sailor, he wrote or kept in touch or came home at every opportunity, which certainly wasn't the case between Annie and this Toby.

'Tony's hobby is betting on the horses,' Annie explained. 'That's why he only ever does seasons at reps like Cheltenham or Windsor or Wolverhampton where there's a racecourse nearby. Even between seasons he often stays on just to be at the track. If it wasn't for acting, which he's also mad on, I do believe he'd spend twenty-four hours a day there.'

Eddy was angry. She should have told him about all this when they started. Not left it to what was almost the last minute before the husband arrived back.

Anger and resentment churned together. He felt he'd been played for a mug although in his heart of hearts he knew that wasn't so.

'How did you meet an actor?' he asked.

'He was in rep in Worcester, where I come from, and where there's a track of course. I had a girlfriend who worked at the theatre, and who invited me to a first-night party. At the party I met Toby, he asked me out, and it all snowballed from there.'

'Did you love him?'

'I wouldn't have married him otherwise.'

Hopefully, 'But you don't any more?'

'I'm afraid I do, Eddy. And I always will.'

He felt dreadful when he heard that. Each word was a spike driven into his brain. 'I see,' he mumbled.

Annie stared into space, a peculiar lopsided smile disfiguring her face. She was seeing the past, reliving old memories.

'At our first anniversary I discovered I was pregnant. We were both overjoyed and decided to establish ourselves in a permanent base. This house was it. We settled in and got it all sorted out and then six months into the pregnancy I lost the baby. Right here in the kitchen.'

'I'm sorry, Annie.'

The lopsided smile grew deeper and even more pronounced. Lines Eddy had never noticed before appeared round her eyes and mouth.

She went on. 'It happened and we got over it. He went into the Army but not before I was pregnant again. I had to write to him telling him I'd lost that one at five months. Eighteen months later, after he'd been home on leave, I got pregnant yet again. I kept that one for twelve weeks before I miscarried. The doctor at the hospital told me I'd never be able to get pregnant again. Which was just as well, I suppose, as it seemed I just couldn't hold on to them.

'When he came back from the war we were both changed. He more than me to begin with, though. The loss of the children coupled with what he'd been through had affected part of his mind. Oh he wasn't crazy or anything like that! He just didn't want to know about sex any more.

'At first I held out hope he would get over it. But he never

107

has. Believe me, I tried everything I could think of, and I'm quite inventive that way when I want to be, but nothing worked. He's utterly and totally impotent.'

There was a long pause during which Eddy stared at Annie and she continued to gaze into space. Finally she went on.

'I wanted to go with him when he went back to acting but he wouldn't have that. He said it wasn't fair on either of us. And I suppose he was right. So now he keeps away for most of the time and I stay on here.'

Eddy didn't know what to say. He couldn't think of any words which seemed adequate.

'I won't sleep with you while he's at home,' she said.

'I understand.'

'Which won't be for long. It never is.'

'I'm glad you told me,' Eddy said. 'All of it, that is. I might have hated him otherwise.'

Annie sent Eddy to bed early after that. She sat for a while alone in the kitchen thinking of the early days with Toby when they'd been happy together.

Then she went to her own bed in the room no man other than her husband was ever allowed to enter.

On the Sunday, Toby appeared, having taken a taxi from the station. He was just in time to join Annie and the lodgers at the communal supper table.

He didn't look much like an actor, Eddy thought. And certainly nothing at all like Errol Flynn! Annie had been right about that.

He had an anonymous sort of face which looked vaguely pale and drawn. He was slim and rather athletic in his movements, with eyes which had a rather brooding quality about them. He alternately smoked and chewed a pipe, or its stem rather. And except at meal-times this pipe was more or less a permanent fixture in his mouth.

After supper, which was a rather subdued affair, Annie and Toby disappeared into her bedroom, leaving Eddy feeling wretchedly alone.

He lay on his bed trying to read a western but just couldn't settle to it. He desperately craved Annie's company but that would be denied him at night from now on until Toby went back into rep again. And judging from what Toby had said at supper he had no immediate prospects.

Rather than lie there fretting Eddy decided to go down to the local pub for a drink. So he consequently put on a collar and tie and took himself off.

He enjoyed English boozers, finding them as different as chalk and cheese to their Scottish counterparts. The atmosphere was generally more friendly and relaxed and you could take your ease over a drink without having to worry about very early closing time.

He ordered a pint from a new bird behind the bar. At least she was new since the last time he'd been in which was a few weeks back.

'One for yourself?' he asked.

She smiled and thought about it. 'A half of shandy would be nice,' she said.

He laid the money on the counter.

The pub wasn't too busy so they had a chance to talk. At first she was reluctant to be drawn but using all his charm on her – the same charm Gil was so impressed with when it came to dealing with customers – he soon had her chatting.

Her name was Michelle and she lived nearby. During the day she was a shorthand typist but was doing this evening job in order to save up enough money to buy a car. She softened towards him considerably when he told her he was a used-car salesman and might be able to put something worthwhile at a reasonable price her way.

She offered to buy him a drink in return but he refused. A man should always pay for the drink, he said, muttering into his beer the English had some bloody queer notions about what was proper, right enough.

After a while business picked up and he decided to head for home. He paused by the door to give her a wave and got one in return.

That went a long way to making him feel a lot better.

The next night he returned to the pub and the night after that. During a lull when they were able to talk he asked her if she'd like to come to the pictures with him.

'There's a new Humphrey Bogart movie on,' he said.

'Marvellous,' she replied.

'In here or outside the picture house?' he asked.

'Outside the picture house.'

'When?'

'It'll have to be next Monday night. That's my only night off.'

'Next Monday at seven-fifteen outside the Odeon.'

'It's a date,' she replied. And they both laughed.

She showed up promptly to find him already waiting in the queue. He said it would only be another couple of minutes and they'd be allowed in.

She wore a lot more powder and paint than Annie did. And he couldn't help but think how much younger than Annie she was. He later found out she was eighteen, a few months older than himself.

Although the picture was later hailed as a classic, Eddy remembered little of it. They sat in the back row where the lovers went. And, after holding hands for a few minutes, started to kiss. The kissing went on almost non-stop till the end of the programme.

She lived in a house the exact same type as Annie's. He took her round the back and behind a garden shed.

They kissed some more and then he put his hand on her breast. When he tried to undo her bra she objected, asking him what he thought she was? It was their first time out, after all.

He apologised immediately while cursing inwardly at not being able to go any further. First dates and having to sneak behind garden sheds had never been a problem where Annie was concerned, he thought ruefully. He kissed her one last time and said he'd see her in the pub the next night. When she was indoors he trudged off home.

He found Annie in the kitchen making some cocoa.

'Toby's already in bed,' she said.

He was still excited from his encounter behind the garden shed. Hungrily he eyed Annie, desperately wanting her.

'Would you like a cup?' she asked.

Her gaze flickered from his face to his neck and she frowned. 'You're bleeding,' she said.

'Eh?'

She hurried to his side and touched what she'd thought was a wound. But it wasn't blood that stained her probing finger.

'Lipstick,' she said.

He was thrown into confusion, cursing inwardly for not having had the sense to go to the bathroom first to check for tell-tale marks.

Annie was upset and looked it. Biting her lip she turned away.

'Annie, I ...'

'You don't have to say anything,' she cut in frostily. 'I have no claim on you, after all.'

'You've got it all wrong.'

'Have I?'

He tried to but couldn't meet her gaze when she swung it on to him.

'What's her name? Or don't you know?' she asked. Her voice dripping acid.

'Michelle.'

'Pretty?'

'Not as much as you,' he replied gallantly.

Annie's features settled into an inscrutable mask. 'You weren't able to wait very long, were you?'

He felt like a little boy caught in the biscuit tin. He was flushing and that made him furious with himself.

'I got the impression Toby's going to be home for quite some time,' he mumbled.

'That still shouldn't have made any difference,' she replied softly. 'Even if your assumption was true – which it isn't. I've already told you, he never stays for any length of time and there's no reason to believe this visit will be any different from the others. He always makes out that it'll be ages before he gets work again. Actors are all like that. No matter how good or successful they are they all have this terrible fear they're going to be sitting on their backsides for goodness knows how long if indeed they'll ever be re-employed again. From the work point of view, the acting profession is the most insecure race there is.'

'I didn't know that,' Eddy muttered; then suddenly erupting, 'What difference does it make who I go out with anyway? It's *him* you love, not me!'

'Maybe I was expecting too much,' Annie replied. 'But you're wrong too. You should stop seeing everything as either black or white. It's not. There's a whole spectrum in between.'

Eddy thought he understood what she was saying but he didn't really.

Annie poured two cups of cocoa which she put on a small tray. 'Goodnight then,' she said.

'Goodnight.'

She gave him the briefest of smiles and then left, carrying the cocoa.

He made his own which he couldn't drink because he felt so sick.

'Eddy, have you got a moment?' Toby inquired, smiling behind his belching pipe.

Eddy was just getting ready to leave for the pub. He'd arranged to take Michelle home after she'd finished behind the bar.

'Sure, what can I do for you?' he replied.

'I'm taking Annie to a party in Kensington Sunday night. Actors, directors, angels, that sort of thing.'

'Angels?'

The smile widened. 'People who back plays. They're called angels.'

'Oh!'

'Anyway I was wondering if you'd like to come with us. You might find it amusing.'

Eddy hesitated. 'Did Annie suggest I come?' he asked.

The minutest hint of steel crept into Toby's smile. 'No, it was my idea,' he replied.

Thinking about it, Eddy decided he liked the idea of mixing with theatricals. The prospect was an exciting one. 'I'd love to come,' he said. 'I'll look forward to it.'

'No need to get overdressed. Actors and the like aren't noted for their formality.'

Eddy didn't detect the tinge of mockery in Toby's voice.

He left for the pub in high spirits determined that tonight was the night he was going to make Michelle behind the garden shed. But he was wrong.

'Not here,' she hissed, pulling his hand down from where it had been up her skirt.

'Then where?' he demanded.

'I don't know,' she replied. 'But certainly not outside like this, like some common street woman. You might have a bit of respect.'

'But I do respect you!'

'Well you don't show it when you act like this.'

Eddy boiled over with frustration. 'There must be somewhere we can go. Don't your parents ever go out at night?'

She shook her head in the darkness.

'Fuck it!' he swore.

'That's what you've been trying to do,' she giggled.

Her giggle caused him to laugh, allowing some of the tension to ease out of the situation. He drew her to him. She was incredibly well-built, busty with lots of delightful curves that rarely failed to draw an appreciative ogle from the male customers in the pub. Her flesh had a spongy quality about it so that it gave easily to the touch. Cuddling her was rather like embracing a large soft cushion.

'I like you,' he said.

'I should hope so too when you've just been feeling me tits and had your hand up me knickers,' she retorted.

He laughed again.

113

'I wish you had more nights off,' he said.

'You and me both.'

'Pictures again on Monday?'

'Unless you can think of something you'd rather do?'

He chuckled. 'Oh I can think of something I'd rather do, all right. It's finding the place to do it.'

'You're sex mad,' she teased.

'If I'm mad it's from the lack of it.'

'Go on, I bet you say that to all the girls.'

'Only the pretty ones,' he replied.

'Flattery will get you everywhere. But not here.'

'I'll think of something,' he said. But for the moment anyway it certainly seemed an insoluble problem.

He explained then he wouldn't be in the pub Friday night as he was going to a party with his landlord and landlady.

When he told her the 'do' was in Kensington she made a remark about his going up in the world now he was mixing with the toffs.

He kissed her one last time on her doorstep, leaving her squealing with indignation as he had a final quick feel of her bum.

The block of flats where the party was being held was very grand. There was a doorman and a reception desk, both of which impressed Eddy no end.

He was dressed in the suit he'd bought for the showroom, which Annie had assured him was the right thing to wear. He was a bit mystified by that, not seeing how a suit could be classed as informal. But then he'd never heard – as Toby had so rightly guessed – of black tie.

'Darlings!' spouted a stunningly good-looking lady who was introduced to Eddy as Milly Tilson their hostess. He was later told she was a well-known West-End actress.

Eddy tried not to gape at the furnishings and decorations. He'd never been so close to anything so splendid. He kept thinking it must be something like this inside Buckingham Palace.

114

Annie's apprehension as she watched Eddy's reactions was coupled with concern. Although nothing had been said she knew Toby had cottoned on to the fact Eddy was, or had been, her latest lover. She also knew Toby was setting Eddy up in the hope Eddy would make a fool of himself. It was Toby's revenge for Eddy's being able to do what he couldn't.

In different circumstances she would have warned Eddy and possibly persuaded him not to come. But she was still hurt and smarting over the fact Eddy had so quickly gone and found himself another woman.

One part of her wanted Eddy to fall into Toby's trap. Another part of her didn't.

For what she realised about Eddy, which few other people did, was how sensitive he was. Behind the hard Scottish exterior there was a quite different person to the outward portrayal.

'Darling, wasn't it absolutely divine! I thought I would corpse rigid when the old roué whispered that in passing.'

Eddy wondered what a roué was and why did they call one another darling all the time? And by God if there wasn't two pansies over in the corner actually holding hands! He tried, but couldn't take his eyes off them till they moved away and were lost to his view.

He stood by an oaken sideboard and stared at it in open admiration. It was beautiful and must have cost the absolute earth. His mother loved good wood and in a flight of fancy he imagined turning up on her doorstep with this very sideboard as a present.

'Are you in antiques?' a voice beside him asked.

He turned to find himself staring at an extremely distinguished-looking elderly gentleman.

'Not me.' Eddy replied. 'I deal in used cars.'

'But you obviously have an eye for beauty.'

Across the room Eddy could see Annie staring at him. 'I know what I like,' he replied.

The man regarded Eddy quizzically. 'It's a Glasgow accent, isn't it?' he asked.

Eddy was suddenly wary. 'A little place just outside,' he replied.

'One of the most difficult accents for an English actor to do, you know, especially southern English. The voice placing is so different.'

'Is that so?' Eddy said, wondering what in hell a voice placing was. 'I take it you're an actor, then?'

'That's correct.'

'I'm afraid I don't know much about the theatre. Films are about my limit.'

'Nothing wrong with films,' the man said; then, glancing round, 'although I'm sure there are many of my colleagues who wouldn't agree.'

'Snobs, eh?'

The man chuckled. 'Precisely.'

'It's all entertainment surely, whether it's Shakespeare or the Keystone Kops?'

The man regarded Eddy with new interest. 'Wisely put, if I may say so. Have you ever seen any Shakespeare?'

Eddy laughed. 'Christ, no. But I have been to the theatre once.'

'Ah! And what did you see?'

'Harry Lauder. He was very good.'

For a moment or two the man wasn't sure whether or not Eddy was pulling his leg. But the straight face Eddy kept finally convinced him he wasn't.

'Harry Lauder's what we call variety. Have you ever seen a straight play?'

Eddy shook his head. 'Where I come from people want a good laugh not culture.'

'But you can get a good laugh as you call it from a straight play. A comedy play, that is.'

'I'm sure you're right,' Eddy said politely.

The man looked thoughtful. 'Why don't you come to the theatre next week as my guest?' he asked finally. 'You can bring a partner if you like.'

116

Eddy was taken aback. 'That's very kind of you,' he replied. 'I think I'd like that. Is it Shakespeare?'

'No, a comedy.'

'Better still.'

'What's your name?'

Eddy became wary again. 'Why?'

'So I can leave tickets for you at the box office.'

'Oh! Eddy Kingsley.'

'Fine,' said the man, noting the name in a small black pocketbook he'd produced.

'Can you make it tomorrow? Monday's the only night my girlfriend get's off.'

'Tomorrow it shall be,' the man said.

They both looked round as Toby joined them.

'Everything all right?' Toby asked.

'Would you believe this fella's never seen a play in the theatre? Extraordinary!' the man said. 'Coming as my guest tomorrow night.'

'Well, well, well,' Toby said, lost for words.

'And come round after for a drink, dear boy,' the man said. 'I'll tell the stage doorkeeper to let you through.'

And with that the man was off to talk to someone else at the other end of the room.

'Nice old duffer that,' said Eddy.

Toby rolled his eyes heavenwards. 'That "old duffer", as you call him, happens to be one of the most important respected actors in British theatre.' And he went on to name a name even Eddy had heard of.

'Bloody hell!' exclaimed Eddy; then, remembering the man had been to Hollywood before the war to make several pictures, 'I wonder if he knows Errol Flynn.'

Toby stood, looking totally baffled.

The play was by Noel Coward and Eddy didn't think much of it, probably due to the fact it was set against a social background he knew nothing about.

Michelle thought the play marvellous, however, and sat enraptured for the duration, eyes wide, drinking everything in.

As promised, the stage doorkeeper was expecting them and gave them explicit instructions how to get to number one dressing room.

'Dear boy, I'm so glad you could make it!' the knighted actor said. He had already changed out of his stage costume and was now wearing a magnificent gold robe over his own clothes.

'Do help yourself to champagne while I take my slap off.'

Slap, it transpired, was his make-up.

Eddy felt it only right he said he enjoyed himself. But if there was any reticence in his praise it was more than made up for by Michelle, who fairly gushed compliments.

There was a second glass of champagne to follow the first and then the knight was ready to leave.

At that moment there was a knock on the door and the stage doorkeeper handed in a note.

'Dash!' said the knight, having read it. 'I've been let down.'

'Anything I can do to help?' Eddy asked.

The knight considered that. 'Yes, there is,' he said, having come to a decision. 'I was supposed to be taking several friends out to supper and now they can't make it. And as I was looking forward to it and the table's already booked, how about you two joining me in my other friends' stead?'

Michelle gasped.

'Oh we couldn't!' Eddy said.

'Why not?'

'Well, eh ...'

'Have you anything else planned?'

'No, we haven't,' said Michelle quickly.

'Then supper it is,' the knight said. 'And I'll brook no further argument.'

All the way to the restaurant Michelle beamed fit to burst.

The Ivy wasn't far away and was, the knight confided to them, a great haunt for actors.

Having been shown to a table, the knight ordered a bottle of French wine which he said he hoped they would enjoy.

Eddy gazed around, the same open admiration stamped all over his face as had been there when the knight had caught him staring at the sideboard. This sort of lifestyle was about as far removed from what he'd been brought up to in Glasgow as the Gorbals is from the moon. The tablecloths were crisp white linen, the cutlery heavy silver. Everything screamed taste and quality and money.

He was suddenly aware how cheap his suit looked compared to the one worn by the knight. A discreet glance confirmed the rest of the male diners were as well and expensively attired as the knight.

And as for Michelle! Alongside the ladies present she appeared coarse and vulgar. She was wearing far too much make-up and her dress looked positively gaudy. But the worst thing was when she laughed. He'd never noticed her laugh being particularly different before but now he could hear it was more of a strident cackle than a laugh. He hoped and prayed it was just his imagination that several of those diners closest to them had glanced disapprovingly their way.

He wouldn't have felt like this if it had been Annie he'd come with, he thought. She had class and would have been right at home here.

The wine when it arrived was delicious, an absolute delight on the palate, as were the fish he had for starters and the beef he had to follow. The pudding was a caramel and gâteau concoction and absolutely out of this world.

At the end of the meal Eddy felt like someone who'd just spent an hour and a half in fairyland.

If he thought he and Michelle were out of place it certainly didn't seem to bother the knight, who maintained a steady flow of sharp and witty conversation.

For a while the knight quizzed Eddy about Glasgow and its people, saying that the two times he'd played Glasgow he'd died the death.

'And such antagonism everywhere you go,' the knight said.

119

'You can almost feel it crackle in the air like an electrical force. Antagonism and violence.'

'The antagonism was probably because you're English,' Eddy said; then quite simply, 'they hate the English.'

'Even yet?' the knight asked wonderingly.

'Even yet.'

The knight shook his head in amazement.

'And they'd hate you even more because you're upper-class English,' Eddy added.

The knight chuckled. 'If only they knew.'

'What do you mean?'

'I was born and bred in Stepney,' the actor said.

'Never!' Michelle exclaimed. 'You don't arf talk posh now.'

The knight smiled enigmatically. 'Marvellous institution, the theatre. You can be anything you want in it. A king, a prince, a knight of the realm.'

'But you *are* a knight of the realm,' Eddy said.

The smile deepened. 'That's what is so particularly nice about the theatre. Sometimes the fantasy becomes reality.' His eyes twinkled. 'But it all started in Stepney and I never allow myself to forget that.'

For the first time in his life it consciously came home to Eddy that just because you had been born in the slums didn't mean that had to be your lot for life. There were ways and means of self-advancement. What the knight had just told them proved that.

He weighed the silver knife and fork in his hand and stared appreciatively at the crisp linen table cover. The food he was eating and the wine he was drinking were far superior to any he'd ever eaten or drunk before.

Yes, he decided. He could get to like this way of life. He could get to like it a lot.

After the meal the knight drove them home in his Rolls which had been parked close by the restaurant.

Eddy and Michelle were profuse in their thanks. The knight replied saying the pleasure had been all his.

After the Ivy the last thing Eddy wanted was a quick grope

and cuddle behind the garden shed so he said goodbye to Michelle on her doorstep. She reminded him about the promise he'd made her the night they met about his getting her a car. He said he hadn't forgotten and was merely waiting for the right sort of vehicle to show up.

As he walked slowly back to the Grimes' house he thought again how out of place Michelle had looked in the Ivy. Like a lump of coarse clay set against best Dresden.

His trouble was, he concluded, Annie had spoiled him. And he cursed himself for being so stupid and hasty in taking up with Michelle when he could have had Annie back in his bed again if he'd only had the patience to bide his time.

The trouble was, and what had motivated him to take out Michelle in the first place, he loved Annie but she loved her husband.

How could he ever have made love to her again knowing she loved somebody else? That he was merely a sex substitute for Toby who couldn't do it any more?

Feeling miserable as sin he went to bed, where it was a long time before he fell asleep. Going to bed miserable and having difficulty getting to sleep was becoming a habit with him.

A few days later Toby announced he and Annie were going to spend the weekend with his parents.

Eddy was half way to work before it dawned on him that meant he would be able to bring Michelle back to his bedroom, which he naturally hadn't been able to do with Annie in residence.

That very afternoon they got a car in which he knew was exactly what Michelle was looking for. He spoke to Gil about the price and Gil said he would be happy to let Michelle have it for what he'd paid for it with only a few nicker on top to cover overheads.

He kept the car at work till Friday when after knocking-off time he got Gil to drive it round to Michelle's pub, where Gil parked it outside the front door.

He had to make his own supper that evening, as had the

121

other lodgers, Toby and Annie having caught a late-afternoon train.

After supper he went out and bought a bottle of whisky which he placed by his bedside along with two glasses and a jug of water.

Humming, he set off for the pub. With access for the pair of them to his bedroom and a car to hand over to Michelle, tonight couldn't help but be the long-awaited night!

He kept the news of the car secret till closing time when he announced to Michelle that he had a surprise for her. When she was cleared from her duties he took her outside where he handed her the keys and logbook.

'Yours,' he said indicating the car with a flourish.

Michelle squealed with delight, squealing again when he told her the price, which was well within the limit she'd allowed him.

'Oh Eddy!' she said throwing her arms round his neck. Her kiss was one of excitement rather than passion.

'Let's go for a little drive,' she said, having settled herself in the driver's seat.

But he had other plans. 'You can drive us round to my place. I have another surprise for you there.'

'Another surprise?'

'A big one,' he said and smiled.

En route he told her about Annie and Toby's being away for the weekend.

Once they were in the bedroom he closed and locked the door.

'Are you sure no one will disturb us?' she asked.

'I'm positive.'

She came into his arms, shivering a little as his hands cupped her backside.

'Let's get stripped,' she whispered.

He was only too happy to agree.

Naked, she was a magnificent female animal. A cat who stretched out lazily on his bed before beckoning to him.

The weeks of pent-up sexual frustration welled up within him.

'I see what you mean about it being a big surprise,' she joked.

He lay down beside her and soon joking was the furthest thing from both their minds.

He came back to sit on his bed having seen her out to the car. He poured a large whisky which he knocked back in one. Then he poured himself another.

It hadn't been a success. Not that anything exactly had gone wrong. It hadn't.

For him it had just been nowhere near as good as it was with Annie. More of a base metal experience than the gold making love with Annie was.

In bed as well as out, Annie had that indefinable something which put her in a far different and higher league to the one Michelle was in.

He drank more whisky and lit a cigarette. He thought how strange the house seemed without Annie in it. Lacking her presence it was as though the house was a dead thing, a mere shell, empty and lifeless, waiting forlornly for her return.

He lay back on the bed, which now smelled of Michelle. How often that self-same bed had smelled of Annie and how he had taken for granted that which had been something extraordinarily worthwhile in his life.

He didn't realise it but he was going through the painful process of mentally growing up.

Annie Grimes was his catalyst.

A few weeks after the visit to his parents, Toby secured himself another job in rep. He left almost immediately, having said he would he gone for at least six months.

With Toby's departure Eddy hoped things between him and Annie might go back to what they had been before. But she would have none of it.

His great fear, in fact it made him sick just thinking about it, was she'd take another lover from the ranks of the other lodgers. But much to his relief she didn't.

He'd dropped Michelle as soon as she'd paid for the car and now stayed home most nights reading. His tastes in that department had begun to widen and he found himself ploughing through writers of the calibre of Thomas Mann and James Joyce. True, he didn't understand an awful lot of what they said but he persevered and as time passed more and more began to sink in.

During this period Annie was friendly enough towards him but that was as far as it went. There were no nightly visitations although once he lost control of himself to actually plead with her.

'I don't think it would be for the best,' she'd replied firmly. And that was that.

He'd been left feeling extremely embarrassed and hating himself for having pleaded with her.

Then one evening he'd come rushing home with the news he'd passed his driving test at the second attempt. He was quite beside himself with excitement, and on finding her in the kitchen swept her off her feet and whirled her round.

'I've passed my driving test!' he exclaimed and then whooped like a Red Indian.

'Oh Eddy, I'm so pleased for you!'

'Isn't it bloody marvellous?'

Setting her down again he did a funny little jig to the accompaniment of a strangulated vocalisation which was supposed to sound like bagpipes.

Annie laughed. 'You're daft as a brush,' she said.

'We must celebrate. Will you come out with me for a drink?'

'Depends which pub you have in mind.'

He recognised that for what it was: a dig at his relationship with Michelle.

'That was all over ages ago, Annie. I swear.'

'So you say.'

'I give you my word.'

'All right. Accepted.'

He took hold of her hand. 'Michelle was merely a reaction against you having told me you still loved Toby. That went deep, very deep.' He paused before continuing. 'Anyway, aren't you being just a little bit selfish about all this?'

'How do you mean?'

'You love Toby but you wanted me as well. When Toby came back I was supposed to sit meekly on the sidelines while you took up with him where you left off.'

'Hardly "taking up" when there's no sex involved!' she exclaimed.

'Well I for one certainly wouldn't agree with that. You both love one another so whether there's sex or not it's taking up again as far as I'm concerned.'

She bit her lip and frowned.

Eddy continued, 'And when I react by going out with someone else you pull the rug from under my feet as if I was the one who'd promised to love and cherish you till death us do part.'

'Did you sleep with Michelle?' Annie asked.

'Yes.'

'So there you are! You betrayed me, us.'

'Did you sleep with Toby?'

The frown returned to her face. 'We were in the same bed together, that's all.'

'Then answer me this. If he was still capable of getting it up, would you have had it off with him?'

'That's hypothetical ...'

'Would you have had it off with him, Annie?'

She looked at the floor. Then nodded.

'So the only reason you didn't betray me was because it wasn't possible to do so. How then can you justify your attitude towards me?'

When she looked up at him there was new respect in her eyes. This was a far more mature Eddy than the one she'd known to date. She began to appreciate just how traumatic an experience her disclosure that she was still in love with Toby, and their consequent break-up, had been to him.

Eddy had only reacted in the way any red-blooded man would have done. And in the light of what had just been said, if there was a villain in the piece, wasn't it her?

'I think we should go and have that drink,' she said.

He knew then he'd won her back. Furthermore he'd come out of all this a far stronger and more knowledgeable person than he'd been before, which pleased him greatly.

Later they returned to the house and went straight to his bed where she remained all night.

Their lovemaking wasn't quite the same as it had been before, the subtle difference making it even better.

For the first time Eddy felt he was the more dominant one. He liked that. He liked it a lot. A man should be on top.

And when next morning going to work he thought of the *double entendre* contained in that last bit, he laughed long and loud.

Six months to the day he'd fled Glasgow, he wrote home to his mother. In his letter he pretended to be a relative who'd just heard his father had died and was writing to tend his condolences.

Josie's reply came by return of post.

First of all she was desperately relieved to hear from him and know he was all right. With regard to the Gloag matter, whatever inquiry there had been, if there had been one at all, certainly hadn't involved the police questioning her. Nor had there been anything in the papers. To the neighbours and the yard where he'd worked she'd said he'd had a sudden opportunity in Canada which he'd had to take up on the spot otherwise he would have missed it.

This explanation of Eddy's overnight departure had been accepted without undue comment, Glaswegians having a long tradition for grabbing opportunities whenever and wherever they arose.

Eddy read his mother's letter through several times and then sat back to think about it. It seemed to him more or less certain that Gloag's body hadn't yet been discovered. For it if had there would surely have been something about it in the papers.

This was excellent news as far as he was concerned. The longer that body remained in the muck pit the less likelihood the police would tie it in with him.

Of course he wasn't in the clear yet. Far from it. But he could now afford to entertain a lot more hope than he would have dared up to now.

From then on in he kept in constant correspondence with Josie, both of them having agreed it was best he remain in London for the present just to be on the safe side.

During the next eighteen months Eddy learned all Gil could teach him about selling cars. His earnings rose considerably, allowing him to send money home to Josie every week, which was just as well as she had to give up work due to failing health.

His relationship with Annie settled into a regular pattern. She slept with him most nights, the exception being when Toby returned from rep as he did four times during the eighteen months.

He and Toby even came to like and respect one another. And he got the definite feeling, although he never asked Annie if he was right, that Toby approved of him as Annie's lover.

He desperately loved Annie but was reconciled to the fact she would never fully be his woman. The reconciliation had been a hard one but he'd managed it in the end.

Then one day when he returned home from work there was a letter waiting for him from Josie telling him if he ever received it it meant she was dead.

Practical as ever, Josie had arranged for a neighbour to hold on to the letter with instructions to send it at the appropriate time.

The letter was addressed to Mr Kingsley so the neighbour didn't know it was going to Eddy.

Eddy was deeply upset to hear of his mother's death. Although he'd known her health was bad enough to stop her working, he hadn't realised her condition might be terminal. Thinking about it in the past he'd imagined her to have ten or fifteen years left to her at least.

This meant he would have to make a trip back to Glasgow. Josie would need burying and, as her only surviving relative, the task naturally fell to him.

He ate a hurried supper while Annie packed his case. Then together they went to Euston where he bought a ticket on a sleeper.

It was a brief parting and an unemotional one as he only intended being gone a few days.

They kissed and she told him to take care. He didn't even bother to watch her while she walked back along the length of the platform.

He was already asleep when the train pulled out. When he awoke he was back in Scotland.

It was like slipping into a much-loved old garment which had been misplaced and then refound. Or meeting an old friend whom you hadn't seen for a long time.

Slowly he drew in a deep breath. Dirt, soot, salt air and a dozen other things which combined to give Glasgow its distinctive smell filled his nostrils.

An enormous love and warmth for this place, this horrible dirty city straddling the Clyde, swept through him.

A lump rose in his throat. Time and Annie Grimes had combined to make him forget how much he missed Glasgow. But now he was back it was all too apparent to him. This was his true home and no matter where he was forced to roam or had to go, this was where he really belonged.

He caught a taxi which took him back to the grey lowering tenement he'd been born in.

The next-door neighbour – the same one who'd sent the letter to him without realising it was him she was sending it to – had the keys of the house and was also able to tell him Josie's body had been taken off to the city mortuary.

At the mortuary he told them he'd be having Josie buried

privately and they were good enough to recommend an undertaker. He therefore duly went on to the undertaker's where it was arranged the burial would take place two days thence, from the funeral parlour.

She was to be laid to rest beside his father as she would've wanted to be.

He returned back to the house after that, from where he put it about to the neighbours that he'd returned home from Canada because of his mother's failing health and it had been a shock on arrival to learn he was too late and she was already dead.

That afternoon he returned to the city centre to attend to a few matters relating to the forthcoming funeral. After which he felt he'd well and truly earned a drink.

The boozer he chose was a little one just off Argyle Street.

'Pint of bitter,' he said to the man behind the bar, making the mistake because his mind was on other things.

'We call it heavy here, Jim,' the barman retorted.

Eddy smiled. 'Oh aye, of course. Sorry, I've been away.'

'Just come back, then?

Eddy nodded.

'You'll be pleased to be home?'

He sipped his pint appreciatively. 'I never realised how much I'd missed the place till I got off the train this morning. That was when it hit me.'

'I was away from Glasgow for four years at one point during the war. Fighting the Jerries was nothing. It was the homesickness that got me. The day I arrived back I swore I'd never leave again and I never have and I never will.'

Eddy raised his glass. 'To Glasgow!' he toasted.

The barman smiled and a loving expression appeared on his face. 'You'll not find a better place anywhere, pal. I tell you.'

Eddy drank to that.

The morning after the funeral Eddy received a letter from Annie. In it she said she thought it best their relationship be ended and this seemed an ideal opportunity for a clean break to be made. She went on to say how fond she'd become of him and that their two years together would be something she'd remember for the rest of her life.

But it was because she'd been so selfish to him in the past that she was trying not to be now. As she'd made clear all along, she was Toby's woman and always would be. She couldn't expect him to continue playing second fiddle with no hope of becoming number one in her life.

With the break he'd be free to find his own woman who would love him the way she loved Toby. And she fervently hoped and prayed he'd find that woman soon.

As for her, the last two years had been most therapeutic and it was directly thanks to him this was so. She only hoped she'd given him as much as he'd given her.

She'd come to accept the fact of Toby's impotence and that she wouldn't have any children. From now on she would travel with Toby round the reps, the pair of them living together on a full-time basis as man and wife.

Eddy was her last affair. Perhaps with them back together again Toby might regain his sexual potency; if not, she'd do without. But that there would be no more men outside the marriage bed she was certain. Her mind was fully made up on that.

In the last paragraph, she wished him all the luck in the world for the future.

He read the letter through twice, then folded it carefully and put it in his wallet.

In his heart he knew what Annie said was right. Things couldn't have gone on for ever as they had. This way was best.

Best, but not easy.

For a while he sat in darkness crying his eyes out. When he'd brought the crying under control he washed his face. Then he went into town to the pub with the friendly barman where he got drunker than he'd ever been in his life before.

He'd been home a week before he managed to screw up the

courage to do what he had to. Namely return to the scene of the crime.

He caught the same tramcar out to the stop where Gloag and he had alighted and there got off. He then retraced his steps to Gloag's house, having trouble doing so as much of the area had been earlier rebuilt or was in the process of being so.

He recalled then the extensive bomb damage he'd noticed the night he'd followed the Orangeman home. It seemed since his last visit the majority of the damage had been cleared and a large rebuilding programme got under way.

He came up short when he came to where the dairy and ramshackle garage had been.

For a moment or two he thought he'd come to the wrong place but a quick recheck convinced him he hadn't. The dairy and garage had fallen victim to the planners. They were now gone and in their place stood a long line of brand new shops.

As best as he could work out, and his calculations were very rough indeed, where the muck pit had been was now underneath the back of a fruiterer and greengrocer's.

Eddy just didn't know what to make of it. Surely some sort of foundations had been laid down in which case the muck pit must have been dug up? Or had it been filled in?

Well whatever had happened, Gloag's body hadn't been discovered. Or if it had and had further been identified then no suspicion had fallen on him.

He ran a hand over his face and then lit a cigarette. The weight that had just been taken from his shoulders was an enormous one.

He'd got away with it. Of that he was absolutely certain.

There was now no reason why he couldn't remain in Glasgow. He wasn't only home. He was home to stay.

He'd managed to save quite a bit from his job with Gil and this he now put to use. He scoured various parts of the city until he found what he wanted. A centrally situated lot that would be ideal to sell used cars from.

He then went to the motor market and bought six cars all at excellent prices.

He was now in business for himself.

It was in his third week of trading that a rather posh-looking bloke with a plummy voice asked if he thought he could get hold of a particular Alfa Romeo which the bloke wanted.

Now Eddy didn't think there would be many Alfa Romeos knocking around Glasgow, which was obviously why the bloke was having difficulty getting hold of one, but London was a different kettle of fish entirely. He was pretty certain he knew where in London he could lay his hands on the particular Alfa the bloke was after. What he would do would be to get Gil to buy it and send it up by train, for which trouble Gil would receive part of the profit.

'I think I can get the car you want but it'll take me at least forty-eight hours to verify it,' Eddy said.

'Fine,' the bloke replied. 'When you know you can contact me here.'

He handed Eddy a card upon which various details were printed.

The name above the address was Kirk Murray.

KEITH AND JEAN

THE YEAR 1911

Keith Gibb was just dozing off when the first shot banged out. Sitting up in bed he rubbed his eyes, wondering if he'd fallen asleep without realising it and had dreamed the shot. Then the second one boomed and he knew it had been no dream or figment of his imagination.

Long and lean he slipped from beneath the covers and hurriedly shrugged himself into his dressing gown. The thought uppermost in his mind was that burglars must have broken in and father was taking pot shots at them with one of the several shotguns the family owned.

Snatching up a spike-ended shooting stick and carrying it like a sword, he ran from the bedroom. At the head of the stairs he met Ferguson the butler, who was incongruously clad in his black jacket hastily thrown over thick flannel pyjamas. Ferguson was out of breath, having just come galloping up the stairs.

'I think the shots came from Master Gerald's old room,' Ferguson gasped, his chest heaving like some ancient bellows.

'Right then,' Keith replied, grasping the shooting stick even tighter. 'Let's take a look then.'

Slowly Keith stalked forward, with Ferguson following a few paces behind. The lights were already on.

At what had been Gerald's room he stopped and placed his ear against the door. There was no sound from within. Gripping the door handle he counted to three, then threw the door wide open. Flicking on the light switch he strode forward with the shooting stick held waist high before him.

A quick check of the various cupboards and under the bed revealed the room to be quite empty.

'Well it sounded like it came from here,' Ferguson said.

Keith grunted. His parents' bedroom was across the hallway. That was where he'd go next.

The door was locked. 'Father? Mother?' Keith called out, rattling the doorknob. But there was no reply.

He placed his ear against the door and listened. As in the previous room, all he heard was silence.

'Father, are you in there?' he called out, rattling the doorknob again.

He suddenly had a terrible thought. What if the burglars were in there holding his parents captive? His father might have been overcome and had the shotgun taken from him, in which case that very gun might well now be pointed at the door. His mouth was suddenly desert dry.

'What are you going to do?' Ferguson whispered. He'd had the same thought as Keith.

'I'm going to break the door down,' Keith whispered in reply. 'You stand back and give me room.'

Ferguson scuttled out of the way.

Keith threw himself against the door, only to bounce off it. He prepared himself for another charge, trying not to think of the third shot, which might ring out at any moment.

On the fourth attempt the lock gave and the door crashed open. Carried on by his momentum Keith stumbled into the room, got tangled up with his shooting stick and went tumbling to the floor. He cursed volubly as he rolled on the carpet.

In the doorway Ferguson stood rooted, eyes bulging as he stared at the bed.

Keith came to his feet and seeing Ferguson's expression whirled round to face his parents' bed. 'Oh my God!' he whispered at the sight which greeted him.

Numb with shock he walked to the side of the bed and gazed down at its contents.

The sheets, blankets and headboard were covered in blood

and a pinky-greyish matter which he took to be brains. His mother was lying on her side with the back of her head shot away. His father was sprawled across her, the entire top of his head completely blown off.

Obscenely the shotgun still dangled from his father's big toe, the latter obviously having been used to fire the piece's second barrel.

Keith sat on the edge of the bed, picking a tiny triangle that miraculously wasn't spattered with blood and gore.

'Why?' he asked the two bodies. 'Why?'

Only several hours previously they'd all been downstairs together enjoying a marvellous dinner. His father had been in a particularly good mood that evening, laughing and joking like some music-hall comedian.

Mother had been a little restrained, that's true. But then a quietish woman by nature, that was nothing exceptional or out of the ordinary for her. Neither had given even the slightest hint that they were contemplating suicide. For suicide was what it clearly was.

With tears streaming down his face Ferguson came to the bedside to lift the turned-down covers and gently drape them over the corpses. He'd been in Roderick Gibb's employ for over twenty-five years.

Keith forced himself out of his reverie. His brain started to function again as he watched Ferguson remove the shotgun and lay it on the floor beside the bed. The first thing he had to do was ring his brother Gerald. And after that, the police.

'You stay here with them, Ferguson. I won't be long,' he said.

Then, rising, he padded downstairs to the telephone his father had installed only the year before.

'Where are they?' Gerald said, bursting into the bedroom. Keith turned to face his elder brother who'd already come up short on having seen the bloodstained and gore-covered bedclothes.

'Sweet Jesus,' Gerald breathed.

He walked to the bed and drew back the coverings, gagging at the sight of what lay underneath.

'They couldn't have killed themselves. You must be wrong,' he said.

Keith shook his head. 'Father shot Mother first then himself. There's no doubt about it.'

'But why?'

'That's precisely what I've been asking myself since I broke in here.'

Gerald took a deep breath and then replaced the covers. 'Where's Ferguson?' he asked.

'Below stairs trying to calm the servants. He's already broken the news to them.'

'Sweet Jesus,' Gerald repeated.

Keith shivered. The shock of the night's events was beginning to seep into his very bones. He felt cold all the way through.

'You say you've informed the police and they're on their way?' Gerald asked thoughtfully.

'Yes.'

'Well when they arrive you'd better let me do all the talking.'

Anger flared in Keith. It was just like Gerald to try and take over. There might be a huge gap between them but that was no excuse for Gerald's always treating him as though he were still a child.

'As I found them and I still live here, and you don't, I think it's best I handle this,' Keith replied.

Gerald blinked. 'Now look, young Keith ...'

'Don't you young Keith me. I'm twenty-one now and have attained my majority, don't forget! I won't be patronised by you or anyone!'

Gerald lit a cigar, taking his time about doing so. He sometimes forgot how touchy Keith was about his age and the difference there was between them. After all, his own two boys were contemporaries of Keith's, being two and three years respectively younger than his brother.

138

The voice of Agnes, one of the maids, came from out in the hallway. 'Please Master Gerald, Mr Ferguson has sent me up with a decanter he says you might be wanting to use. He also said I wasn't to come in.'

'I'll get it,' Keith said, and strode to the door.

The decanter contained Glayva, which had been a great favourite with his father – and indeed he and his father had drunk a glass each after dinner.

He poured large ones, a lump sticking in his throat at the memory of having seen his father do precisely the same thing with the same decanter and glasses so many times before.

'There was no hint at all, you say?' Gerald asked.

Keith shook his head. 'None. What about you?'

'Nothing.'

There was a pause and then Keith said, 'Do you think maybe they were ill or something?'

'That's possible.'

'I can't think of any other reason. At least none that makes sense.'

'There was no note?'

Keith frowned. 'I haven't seen one. But then neither Ferguson or I thought to look.'

Together Keith and Gerald searched the obvious places in the room and then the not so obvious. On turning up nothing, Gerald went downstairs to search various rooms there. But of a note there was no sign.

Gerald was on his way back up the stairs again when the police arrived.

'What!' Gerald exclaimed. 'Surely you must be wrong?'

Dan Ritchie, the family lawyer, shook his head. 'I'm afraid not,' he replied.

Keith sat dumbfounded, for the moment unable to speak. What remained of his world following the death of his parents had just collapsed around his ears.

'I think you'd better tell us how it happened,' Gerald said.

Ritchie leaned forward on his desk and made a pyramid with

his hands. He spoke slowly and evenly as he always did. He was a dour, dreich sort of a man.

'Your father had been speculating heavily in the past year as well as investing a considerable amount of capital in various overseas projects. All of which, I'm unhappy to say, proved to be disasters. He could've ridden these out, mind you, if they hadn't coincided with a long, bad run he was having at the tables. In the end it was gambling, your father's little weakness, that did for him, gentlemen.'

'Not so little,' Gerald said bitterly.

'Aye,' said Ritchie, nodding. 'You have a point.'

'How much is left?' Keith asked, his voice a croak.

'Virtually nothing. There are debts as well, you see ...'

'Debts!' Gerald exclaimed.

'Gambling ones. Not legal, mind you, if you feel you don't want to pay them.'

'We'll pay,' Gerald said. 'I won't disgrace his name. Right Keith?'

Keith nodded.

'Well then,' Ritchie went on. 'Once those are met, all that will be left which is yours is the Black Lion Brewery.'

'What about the house?' Keith asked.

'That'll have to be sold as well, I'm afraid.'

'Can't we sell the brewery and keep the house?'

'No!' Gerald said emphatically. 'Neither you nor I, having no income of our own, can afford the upkeep of the house. The brewery on the other hand gives us the means to earn something.'

'What do you know about running a brewery?' Keith asked scornfully.

'Nothing. But I can learn. After all, Father knew nothing about breweries either and yet it made money for him.'

'Not a lot,' Ritchie said, 'and I always blamed the fact your father never took a personal interest in it as the reason. A business like that needs personal handling if it's really going to amount to anything.'

'So we'll both be working at this brewery then?' Keith asked.

'Certainly. If you don't mind me being boss,' Gerald replied.

'Why should you be boss?'

'For the obvious reason. I'm nearly twenty years older than you. Also, as elder brother, it's my right.'

Keith hated the idea of having to take orders from Gerald. That would be too much. All his life he'd lived under Gerald's shadow, at home, at school, everywhere. The wonderful Gerald, who was so clever, so witty, who at school had been such a marvellous sportsman, not to mention head boy.

He, on the other hand, wasn't clever, nor was he witty or good at games. And when it came to sheer personality he wasn't a patch on Gerald, who could tell such fabulous stories – risqué and otherwise – in company, while the best he could do was blush and stammer and invariably fall over his words. Especially if there were young women present.

'Then you can count me out,' Keith replied. 'For I'm not working under you and that's that.'

'I understand,' Gerald said. And he did.

'You'll have to make some remuneration to your brother in that case,' Ritchie said, 'the brewery being left jointly between you.'

'Half whatever profits I make suit you?' Gerald asked.

'That would be fine,' Keith replied, pleased with himself for having taken such a positive stand.

Gerald sat back in his chair. 'Having to work for a living for the first time at my age!' he said. 'What a turn-up for the book that is!'

For up until that moment both Gerald and Keith had led lives of leisure as befitted gentlemen of their social standing.

Keith frowned, thinking about that. Even with some money coming in from the brewery – and Ritchie warned him that certainly for the next few years it wouldn't be all that much – it was going to be impossible for him to maintain himself in even

141

a semblance of his present lifestyle.

But what to do? Working for a wage seemed demeaning. And especially in the south of Scotland, where he was well known.

There was the law and medicine, of course, both honourable professions he could go into. But neither appealed. Nor was he certain he had the particular talents required for either.

Then the idea came to him, bringing a smile to his face. It would be the Army for him!

The Army was the ideal solution, he thought. The perfect answer to his problem.

And there and then he resolved to take up a commission.

Gerald was also thinking, but about his wife Emmaline. She was beautiful and came from a proud old Scottish family. Sadly, however, the family were also poor as church mice which hadn't bothered him one bit when he married her but which he now slightly rued.

After all, there had been so many beautiful women he'd been attracted to, and they to him, it was a pity, seen now in hindsight, that he'd chosen one without money of her own.

He shrugged mentally. There was no use crying over spilt milk. What was done was done and that was that. And hadn't Em given him two fine boys of whom he was inordinately fond? He wouldn't have traded either for a fortune. They were going to find things tough going also from now on in but like him, no matter how painful, they were going to have to learn to adapt.

Thank God his own house was bought and paid for. A present from his father years ago. That at least was something to be thankful for.

And Em had a few bits and pieces of jewellery that could go to tide them over the first few years until he got this brewery really onto its feet and providing a substantial living for them.

What an amazing occurrence this was to happen at his age, he thought. And beer of all things for him to get involved with. Not only hadn't he a clue how it was made, he positively loathed the stuff as a drink!

Second Lieutenant Gibb was in the ward-room of a troop-ship bound for India drinking pink gin with other officers of his regiment, when the news came through.

The ship's captain was handed a radio message which he read from beginning to end twice before looking up. Crossing to the Colonel of the regiment, he handed him the message.

'Gentlemen,' the Colonel said, having, like the ship's captain, stared long and hard at the message. 'I have an announcement to make.'

The hum in the ward room stilled as every eye was turned to the Colonel.

'Yesterday the Germans invaded Belgium and as from that date we are at war with Germany.'

Pandemonium broke out in the ward-room as neighbour excitedly turned to neighbour.

'The King!' someone shouted.

'The King!' the gathering toasted.

Spontaneously they began to sing.

'God save our gracious King ...'

The date was 4 August, 1914.

Keith took to India the way a duck does to water. He loved its heat, smells, alienness, its colour and inherent treachery – the latter both of the land itself and the indigenous peoples inhabiting it.

Fort Victoria was north of Peshawar and south of the Khyber Pass. The billets and other various buildings were made of local brick, the compound surrounding them of stone.

In the distance the hills loured, brooding and menacing. Hills filled with hostile natives who'd never made their peace with the Raj.

The regiment's brief, as had been the regiment's before them and the regiment's before *them*, was to be the continued British military presence in the area, stopping the wild hill brigands from sweeping down to rape and pillage the broad lands of the Punjab.

143

*

'The Gay Gordons, if you please!' Captain Rintoul called out, smiling broadly at the company.

The various dancers formed into two lines and the band struck up. Several wheeches rent the air as the dance got under way.

Keith Gibb stood not far from the punch bowl, talking to another second-lieutenant with whom he shared a quarter.

'Surely they won't keep us festering out here much longer,' Second-Lieutenant Dick said. 'It's been four months, now, after all.'

'Who knows how they think?' replied Keith.

'Och man, we're a Jock regiment. We should be in the thick of it giving those Jerries what for.'

It was a conversation every soldier in the fort had already been through a thousand times or more.

'They say the casualties are dreadful,' Keith said.

'Aye. I hear the lads are taking awful punishment.'

'Well for every one of ours that gets it, we're getting two of theirs,' Keith said, repeating what an officer had told him.

Dick smacked his palm with a clenched fist. 'It's damnable being out here nursemaiding brownies when we should be in France where the action is. They say promotion is so quick out there you can go up several ranks in a week.'

Keith shook his head in wonderment.

They both sipped some punch and then Dick said, venomously, 'I hate India. It's a filthy place. Nothing but flies and the pox.'

'I like it. Could live the rest of my life out here and be quite happy.'

'Really?'

'Yes.'

'No accounting for taste, is there,' Dick replied. 'And talking of taste, what do you think of Miss Jean Ogilvie? That's her over there.'

Keith gazed at the female in question. He'd never seen her before.

144

'Major Ogilvie's daughter. Came out with us but went on to Poona where the family have friends. Only joined us at the fort last week.'

Jean Ogilvie was a somewhat dumpy girl who could never have been accused of being beautiful. Homely and saucy was the best description for her.

Keith didn't particularly like beautiful girls, finding their beauty off-putting. Besides, all the handsome young men monopolised the beauties, which meant he, shy and awkward, never got a look in.

The more homely variety was far more up his street. With them he didn't feel nearly so bumbling or thick-tongued.

'Not bad,' he said.

'If you like her, away and ask her up, man! She's free now but won't be for long I shouldn't think.'

Keith considered the matter, rarely making decisions on impulse.

'Aye, why not?' he said, after thinking it over.

He laid down his punch glass, minutely adjusted his uniform and then moved towards where Jean Ogilvie was standing watching the dancers.

'Would you care to go on the floor?' he asked, bowing slightly from the waist.

Her eyes took him in. And then a soft smile curled her mouth upwards. 'I'd love to, Lieutenant,' she replied.

He didn't dislike dancing, but then he didn't particularly like it either. He moved swiftly and without grace.

Jean thought Keith gauche but pleasant. When it soon became apparent he wasn't very good at small-talk, she chattered on. And the onus of having to make the conversation flow lifted from him, he relaxed considerably.

At the end of their third dance together it was obvious to both of them that they'd clicked. At his suggestion they took some refreshment, after which they strolled out on to the verandah.

There, under her gentle probing, he started telling her about himself. Her face expressed concern and sympathy

145

when he related how his mother and father had killed themselves in a joint suicide pact.

She was the first person he'd confided that to since joining the Army.

'How awful,' she said.

'It was rather. Even more so when my brother and I discovered the family fortune was no more. Still, one has to make the best out of things, eh?'

'I think you're very brave,' she said.

He pushed his chest out a little. No one had ever called him that before. It brought a warm glow to his insides.

'I say,' he said. 'Do you think I could see more of you after tonight?'

'I don't see why not.'

'Can you ride?'

'I was brought up on a horse.'

'Good,' he said, smiling. 'Then riding it is.'

They talked some more and then went back to join the others.

Jean laughed as her horse broke into a full gallop. She felt gloriously alive as her hair streamed out behind her like a banner in the wind.

Keith urged his mount forward but try as he might he just couldn't catch Jean. Being lighter than him and with the better horse was proving an advantage he just couldn't overcome.

By a grassy knoll Jean drew rein and there she had to wait for a few seconds till Keith caught up.

'Slow coach,' she teased.

Keith dismounted and then helped her to the ground. They held hands as they walked their horses a little distance.

'I've got a new job,' Keith said, pulling a face. 'They've given me a desk and put me on to the administrative side of things. It's excruciatingly boring.'

'I wouldn't have thought of you as being good at that sort of thing,' she replied. 'You seem to me to be far more the man of action.'

'Some man of action who can't even catch up a lassie on a horse!' he joked, causing her to grin.

He stared at the hills and then slowly took in the surrounding terrain. Out here away from the fort it always paid to be careful. There were standing rules about that.

'Do you wish you were in France?' she asked suddenly.

'Of course.'

Jean looked sad. 'So many good men gone already. The papers seem filled with endless lists.'

'The Navy's doing well anyway.'

'Are they? I wouldn't say so, with the *Good Hope* and *Monmouth* being sunk.'

'Ah well ... perhaps you're right. At least the Turks have been defeated in the Caucasus which is something.'

'I know it's a terrible thing to say, but I hope the regiment never gets sent to France,' Jean said.

'You're thinking of your father?'

'Yes. But not only him.'

'I see,' Keith replied, squeezing her hand.

When the horses had had their breather he helped her to mount. But not before shyly taking her in his arms and kissing her.

When they raced back to the fort she allowed him to win.

A year passed, during which Keith and Jean continued seeing one another. Their relationship went from strength to strength as they grew closer and closer together.

In the May of that year Keith had learned of the deaths of Gerald's two sons at the second battle of Ypres. He'd written Gerald and Emmaline a long letter expressing his condolences. He'd been fond of Michael and James, who in a way had been more like brothers to him than Gerald ever had.

Gerald's reply said he and Emmaline were distraught but were somehow coping, he mainly by throwing himself into his work at the Black Lion Brewery, whose business and profits were expanding all the time. Keith was naturally pleased about the latter, as the more profit the brewery made the more money was credited to his bank account.

Financially his fortunes were beginning to revive somewhat, although still far from what they had been before his parents' death.

And then one morning the word spread round the fort like wildfire. The regiment was being posted to France.

Once off duty he went straight round to see Jean, finding her sitting crocheting with her mother. He could tell at once from the expression on her face that she'd already heard the news.

'Tea?' Mrs Ogilvie asked. And diplomatically left the room.

'Daddy came home an hour ago to tell us,' Jean said.

'They say we're shipping out within the fortnight.'

Jean nodded. 'That was what Daddy said.'

'We're going straight to the front, apparently.'

Jean's eyes filled with pain. 'Yes. So it seems,' she said.

'There will be plenty of scope for promotion.'

'I've no doubt,' she replied softly, turning her face away so he didn't see the look of anguish which twisted her features.

He was suddenly embarrassed, clumsy and awkward again. Nervously he twisted his fingers. 'Jean ... I ... eh ...'

'You want me to marry you, don't you?'

'How did you know that?' he asked surprised.

'You've been working yourself up to ask me for some time now. And don't look at me as though I could read minds or something. It was quite obvious really.'

'Well? What do you say? I think we're made for one another.'

She rose and crossed to a window to stare out. Her mind was a turmoil. Finally she said, 'If it was peacetime, Keith, I'd marry you gladly. But it's not. And now the regiment's off to fight in France.'

Sick with disappointment, Keith lowered his eyes.

'I'm sorry, Keith. But that's the way I feel. If you're still alive and want to ask me again when the war's over, then I'll say yes.'

148

'I understand,' he said miserably. 'It was selfish of me to ask.'

'No. It's selfish of me to refuse.'

He went to her and circled her waist with his arms. 'I love you, Jean,' he whispered.

Tears filled her eyes. 'And I love you too.' Breaking from his grasp she fled the room.

Keith couldn't believe it. 'Are you sure?' he demanded.

Second-Lieutenant Dick nodded. ''Fraid so, old chap. The entire regiment with the exception of second battalion is off to jolly old France. We're staying behind to maintain the British presence in the area.'

'Well I'll be a son of a gun,' Keith said.

'Feel the same way myself. Let's just hope it won't be long before we join the others over there. I'm itching for action, I can tell you.'

'But we can't patrol this entire area with only one battalion,' Keith said. 'That's impossible.'

'We're being reinforced with a battalion of brownies. Gunga Din, what?'

'That makes it more reasonable then.'

'Brownies,' Dick said in disgust. 'I want to scratch every time I'm near one.'

'Oh come on, they're not that bad!'

'Tell me that again after you've had a faceful of curried breath.'

Keith laughed. 'Well, that *can* be a bit much at times.'

'My aunt Sally and it can!'

Keith picked up his hat and swagger stick. He must get over to break the news to Jean right away.

'So you'll be staying on then,' Keith said.

Jean nodded. 'Daddy says that would be the safest thing for Mother and I, what with the U-boat menace and all. He says it's best we remain in India until the war's over.'

'I quite agree. It's by far the most sensible thing to do,' Keith replied.

'From what Daddy's been told we'll be allowed to remain in the fort – all the families who wish to stay on, that is – as with the number of personnel greatly reduced there'll be no trouble about quarters.'

'There's tremendous excitement in the regiment,' Keith said. 'They're positively champing at the bit, dying to get to grips with Jerry.'

'You're sick at not going, aren't you?'

'Yes.'

She took his hand. 'Well, I'm glad you're not. It's bad enough Daddy's got to go without you as well.'

'Well if I have to remain on here with the battalion the fact you're staying on too is the best consolation prize I could have. Are you sure you won't change your mind?'

'About what?'

'Marrying me.'

Her face clouded over. 'Not till the war's over, Keith. I'll never change my mind about that.'

'Then I'll just have to wait.'

She kissed his cheek. 'Let's just hope it's over soon.'

'But not too soon. Otherwise I might not get a chance to get into it.'

'Men,' she said reproachfully. 'What children they all are!'

News of the big battle came over the telegraph on the direct line with Peshawar and being on duty and in administration Keith was one of the first to know.

He and Second-Lieutenant Dick stood looking at one another, aghast at what they'd just heard.

Captain 'Robbie' Roberts repeated what he'd just read out.

'The regiment was decimated,' he said. 'Overall British losses were approximately four hundred thousand men.'

'Four hundred thousand,' Dick said, and shook his head. It was a mind-boggling figure.

'How many of our regiment came through?' Keith asked.

Roberts scanned the message. 'Two hundred and fourteen,' he replied.

All those in the room looked from one to the other, each thinking of the many friends and comrades-in-arms they'd never see again.

'Do we know who these two hundred and fourteen are?' Keith asked.

'That's coming through in a later message,' Roberts replied.

'All those bonny lads,' said McPherson, an old sergeant who'd been in the Boer War. There were tears trickling down his stone face as he rose and stalked from the room. Keith thought of Jean and her mother. It was best he told them himself what had happened.

It was late that night before the second message came humming over the telegraph.

For hours the families who'd remained behind mixed with many of the soldiers standing outside the telegraph hut waiting to find out who'd survived.

For a long time they sang hymns, 'Abide With Me' and 'Rock Of Ages' being repeated several times.

But eventually the singing ceased and those gathered waited on in a stolen silence only broken by night sounds.

Finally the message came through and a notice was pinned to the door of the telegraph hut. The notice contained a list of the names of the two hundred and fourteen survivors.

Major John Fergus Ogilvie was not among them.

'The regiment's being reformed in Scotland but still we're to remain here!' Second-Lieutenant Dick said in disgust.

'Surely not!' Keith exclaimed.

'So the orders say.'

'And what about promotion?'

'If you mean for us, then forget it. It'll be the usual slow grind for you and me, just as though there wasn't a war on.'

'But that's not fair!' Keith said angrily. 'In France there are chaps our age who are majors by now.'

'So when was the Army ever fair? Anyway, France is France and India is India.'

'But we should be forming the nucleus of the new regiment.'

'That's not how the War Office sees it, apparently,' Dick replied.

Keith sat and sulked.

After a while he rose and strode out in the warm sunshine. A good ride was what he needed to blow his anger and frustration away.

'If the regiment's gone back to France then there must be a new offensive brewing,' 'Robbie' Roberts said.

Keith chalked his cue. He and Roberts were playing billiards. He lined up his shot and potted well.

'Good shot!' said Roberts. And swallowed some port.

'I'm dying to see what these new tanks are like,' Keith said. 'They sound quite something.'

'First gas and now huge metal monsters that crush a chap to death,' Roberts sniffed. 'War's becoming dashed uncivilised, what?'

'All that matters in the end is winning,' Keith replied thoughtfully. 'Nothing else.'

His cue stroked forward and another ball disappeared.

There was a new look in Robert's eye as he stared at Keith. It was as though he was seeing Keith for the very first time.

Face flushed, Keith burst into the room. 'We're going at long last!' he said, and taking Jean in his arms whirled her round.

'I don't have to ask where,' Jean replied when she'd finally caught her breath. 'It can only be France.'

Keith nodded excitedly.

'Well, I suppose it was inevitable,' she said in a resigned tone of voice.

'Aren't you thrilled?'

'Don't be stupid,' she retorted bitingly. 'How could I possibly be thrilled about you being sent to that slaughter-house?'

152

'I'm sorry,' he said, calming down. 'I suppose that was thoughtless of me. I mean, your father and ...' He trailed off.

Her eyes filled with tears. 'I know I shouldn't say this but if you go I know I'll never see you again. It'll be just like Daddy. A final wave at the railway station and then with a toot-toot of the engine you'll be taken out of my life forever.' She dabbed her eyes with a handkerchief. 'I've just read the names of four boys I knew back home in the last papers which arrived this morning.'

'All dead?'

She nodded.

'I'm sorry.'

'Oh, Keith!' she said rushing into his arms and hugging him tight. 'What did we do to deserve what's happening in the world today?'

'God alone knows,' he replied softly.

And in silence they stood hugging one another for a long time until finally Mrs Ogilvie appeared, when they broke apart.

'It's unbelievable!' Second-Lieutenant Dick said, taking off his cap and throwing it on to his bed from where it slid to the floor.

'Word came through less than an hour ago,' Keith said. 'Our orders are cancelled. We're not going to France after all.'

'The blooming Ruskies have had a revolution you say?'

'So it seems – which makes this area even more strategically important than before. The War Office must think there's the possibility that whatever government comes into power might try and sweep down to have a go at taking India from us. Which would be easy enough for them when you consider that due to the war in Europe our army in India is probably at its lowest strength since the beginning of the Raj.'

Dick lit up a cigarette, having first carefully placed it in the ivory holder he affected. 'If they do come we certainly don't have enough troops here even to attempt a holding action. It would be like a gnat trying to stave off a vulture.'

'We're to be reinforced,' Keith said.

'More brownies?'

'No, troops from Blighty. An English regiment but we don't know which one yet.'

'Well that's something at least,' Dick replied.

'We'll never get to France now,' Keith said. 'That was our last chance.'

'Bloody bolsheviks!' Dick swore.

At long last it was all over. The Kaiser had abdicated and escaped to Holland. The Armistice had been signed by the Germans.

Keith took Jean out into the velvet night and together they strolled, hand in hand.

'You said I was to ask you again when the war was finished,' he said. 'So I am. Will you marry me?'

'As soon as you like, my darling.'

He caught her in his arms and kissed her.

'Keith! Someone might see!'

'Let them. Who cares?'

'I do, for one!'

'Isn't a man allowed to kiss his fiancée?'

'Yes. But not out here where everybody can see! One has to be discreet about these things. And as a second-lieutenant you have to set an example to the men.'

'That's the other good news,' he said. 'It's now Lieutenant.'

'Oh Keith! I'm so happy for you.'

'For *us*, Jean. From now on it's us.'

She smiled and slipped her hand back into his. She thought she'd never been more happy or contented.

For the umpteenth time Keith cleared his throat and then examined his appearance in the mirror. He was more nervous than he'd ever been in his life before.

There were places in Peshawar where one could go to learn these things but he never had. Nor had he done it before joining the Army and coming out to India.

Tonight, his wedding night, would be his first time ever.

He sipped some gin and then glanced yet again at his watch. She'd had half an hour on her own through in the bedroom to get ready. Was that enough time or should he wait a while longer?

He sipped more gin and then started to pace.

In his mind he went over all he knew about lovemaking. It didn't take long.

Through in the bedroom, Jean lay propped up in bed waiting for Keith to come to her. If anything she was even more nervous than he was. Her hand crept behind one of the pillows supporting her to touch the large white hanky she'd placed there. Although what on earth she was going to need it for she didn't know.

But that had been her mother's sole advice to her when she'd blushingly asked about sex.

'Just keep a large white handkerchief under your pillow, my dear,' Mrs Ogilvie had said, as embarrassed about the subject as her daughter was.

And that was the end of that conversation.

The door to the bedroom opened and Keith entered, looking splendid in his silk pyjamas and silk dessing gown.

'Everything all right?' he asked.

'Fine, fine,' she replied, trying to sound casual.

'You don't mind if I join you, then?'

'No, of course not.'

He cleared his throat. 'I thought everything went jolly well today, don't you think?'

'Yes.'

'Dick was a laugh.'

'Always is at a party.'

Keith inched slowly towards the bed, very conscious this was the first time he'd ever seen Jean in her night attire.

'Thought the chaplain made a good speech after,' he said. 'Quite witty which surprised me.'

'Me too.'

'The chaps were trying to get me sloshed, you know, but I

was having none of it. Wouldn't do to be stinko on one's wedding night, what?'

Jean smiled.

He knew he was prattling on but felt he had to. Silence would have been even more disconcerting and embarrassing.

Taking off his dressing gown he threw it across a chair, at the same time saying, 'Dashed decent of the C.O. to lay on the champagne, I thought.'

'Yes, I thought so too.'

He slid into bed beside her. 'Well then ...' he said, and cleared his throat.

It wasn't till morning that it dawned on Jean what the hanky was for.

'Keith! How marvellous to see you!' Gerald said. 'And this must be Jean.'

Jean and Gerald shook hands. Then he ushered her and Keith through to where Emmaline was waiting.

'First time home in ... how long is it?' Gerald asked.

'Eight years,' Keith replied.

'Is it really?' Emmaline said, shaking her head.

Gerald had aged considerably, Keith thought. And so had Emmaline but she was still an incredibly beautiful woman all the same.

Gerald passed round sherry.

'How long are you home for?' Emmaline asked Jean.

'Four months, and then it's back to India.'

'You like it there, I believe.'

'Yes, we both do.'

'It has a way of getting into the blood,' Keith said. 'We'll both be upset when we have to leave.'

'Is that likely?'

'Oh yes. As you know my regiment was posted back there after the war but we're due to be moved on again any time now. Singapore and the Far East I should think.'

'Sounds terribly exciting,' Emmaline said.

Keith smiled. 'There's a lot to be said for the Army. It's certainly been good to me.'

'Kept you out of the war, eh?' Emmaline went on, the merest hint of wickedness in her eyes. When she saw the expression on Keith's face she added hastily, 'I don't mean you to take that the wrong way. I only wish our Michael and James could have sat it out in India. They'd be alive today if they had.'

'If I didn't get to France I can assure you it wasn't for the lack of trying,' Keith said.

'Of course. I didn't doubt otherwise.'

'More sherry?' Gerald asked.

'Yes please,' Jean replied emphatically.

'Losing the boys was a terrible blow,' Gerald said. 'And one we haven't recovered from yet.'

'If we ever will,' Emmaline added.

'It's a pity you're too old to have had another family,' Jean said.

Emmaline turned an icy stare on to Jean. 'Yes, it is rather. But what about you two? Surely it's high time for a son and heir?'

Bitch, Jean thought.

This was a sore point with Keith. He'd hoped Jean would fall pregnant soon after their marriage but so far nothing had happened in that direction.

He glanced across at Gerald. That was another thing Gerald had scored over him, he thought bitterly. Michael and James had come quickly after Gerald had married Emmaline.

Gerald smiled back, as though aware of what Keith was thinking.

'It won't bother us not to have a family for a year or two yet,' Keith lied. 'That sort of thing is always difficult when you're in the Army and abroad a lot.'

'Quite,' Gerald agreed.

The death of her two sons had turned Emmaline into a shrew, Keith thought. Underneath that still beautiful face she was as sour as acid.

Mind, you, to be fair, he had some sympathy for her. He hated to think what he'd have been like had he lost two sons in the conflict.

Plain as a suet pudding, Emmaline was thinking, while smiling at Jean. Typical of Keith to marry a woman like that. A proper little *hausfrau*.

Turning to Keith she said, 'And what rank are you now?'

'Still Lieutenant.'

'Really? I would've thought you'd be a Field Marshal at least!' And having said that she gave vent to a derisory cackle.

A blush crept over Keith's features while Jean's lips thinned in anger.

'She's only teasing,' Gerald said. 'A great one for that, my Em. There's no harm meant by it.'

Like hell there isn't, Keith thought.

'Promotion's very difficult in the Army at the moment,' Jean said.

'You mean so many young officers holding comparatively high rank with still the great lump of their military career stretching before them?' Emmaline asked sweetly.

'Precisely,' Keith replied.

'Those young officers were promoted on the battlefield,' Jean said, determined to get it in before Emmaline did.

'That must be very frustrating for you,' Gerald said to Keith.

'It is.'

'Enough to make you pack in the Army?'

Keith shook his head. 'No.'

'How do you feel about that, Jean?' Emmaline asked.

'I'm only too happy to agree with whatever Keith wants or thinks is best. I believe very firmly in family loyalty, you see.'

Emmaline disregarded the barb. 'But doesn't it upset you, never having a permanent place of your own? I know it would me.'

'One has to make sacrifices in life,' Jean replied. 'I thought we all learned that in the war.'

'Oh well, there's always a job for you at the brewery any time you want it,' Gerald said to Keith.

'No, thank you.'

'Well it's always there, should you ever change your mind.'

'I don't think I will,' Keith said softly and emphatically. In fact I'd rather sweep the streets first, he added under his breath.

A maid arrived to announce dinner was ready to be served. They all smiled at one another as they went through.

'What do you think then?' Gerald demanded.

Keith shrugged. 'I never saw it before so I can't really say.'

'Production's up three hundred and fifty per cent since I took over,' Gerald said proudly. '*And* I've doubled the number of pubs I own.'

'*We* own,' Keith corrected.

'Of course. That's what I meant.'

His brother was obviously extremely good at the business of running the brewery and that rankled with Keith. Why did Gerald have to be so damn good at everything he did!

'You do check how much goes into your personal account every month?' Gerald asked just a trifle sarcastically. He had been expecting Keith to be just a little bit more enthusiastic.

Keith nodded.

'Then you'll appreciate how much the profits have increased.'

Keith was damned if he was going to say 'well done' or anything like that.

'What are your plans for the future?' he asked instead.

'Keep on expanding, I suppose.'

'Why not?' replied Keith somewhat vaguely, and was delighted when a flash of irritation crossed Gerald's face.

They walked along a gantry overlooking some fermenting vats. Keith walking ramrod stiff, every inch the officer and gentleman. It amused him to note Gerald had become round-shouldered and developed something of a slouch.

'Mind you, I suppose running a brewery isn't all that difficult. I would imagine the stuff almost sells itself,' he said.

'It's not quite as easy as that,' Gerald replied disdainfully.

'No?'

'*No*,' Gerald said with emphasis.

'That surprises me,' said Keith.

They stopped by a set of metal steps descending to the floor below.

'I don't suppose you'd be interested in selling your half of the place?' Gerald asked hopefully.

''Fraid not, old bean,' Keith replied, a soft smile curling his mouth upward. 'I'm very happy with things the way they are.'

Using his swagger stick he touched Gerald on the lapel.

'Very happy.'

He used his swagger stick again to gesture that Gerald could lead the way down the metal steps.

Should an accident occur, and he fell, he wanted Gerald below him.

The regiment spent six years in the Far East and two in southern Africa before finally being shipped home to Glasgow's Maryhill barracks.

During this time Jean visited a number of doctors, all of whom told her the same thing. There was no physical reason whatsoever for her not to have a child.

Secretly Keith feared he was to blame, thinking there must be something wrong with him.

Until one evening he returned home to their quarters to find a bottle of champagne cooling in a bucket and a special dinner laid on.

'What's all this for?' he asked, having hastily confirmed to himself that he hadn't forgotten either her birthday or their anniversary.

Jean produced two glasses and told him to open the champagne. When their glasses were charged she clinked hers against his and then said, 'Here's to the three of us!'

Keith frowned. 'What three?'

160

'You, me and the baby.'

'What baby?'

'You're not being very quick on the uptake, Keith.'

A few seconds passed and then his frown cleared. 'You mean ...?'

'Yes. I'm pregnant.'

'You're sure? Absolutely?'

Smiling she nodded.

'Oh Jean!' he exclaimed, and, taking her in his arms, kissed her.

'After all these years it just happened,' she said excitedly.

He drank off his champagne and then poured himself some more. His eyes were shining fiercely with pride.

'I'd almost given up hope,' he said; then, 'Dammit, I *had* given up hope!'

'I'm three months gone and the doctor says everything's just as it should be. It should be a straightforward birth with no complications.'

'I'm going to have a son!' he said and whooped.

'Now hold on, Keith. I can't promise that.'

'Don't be daft, woman! Of course it'll be a boy. They run in the family. Didn't my father have two and didn't Gerald?'

'Still ...'

'There's no "still" about it. A boy it'll be. Anything else would be unthinkable.'

He paused and his eyes gleamed. 'A boy, who'll turn out to be a better man than any of us. Better than me, Gerald, Michael and James. A man who'll restore the family fortunes to what they once were!'

Chest heaving, he sat down. He was quite overcome with the vision he saw.

'A son,' he whispered. 'A son!'

Jean bit her lip.

Keith paced up and down the hospital corridor, a tall slim man of what had become in the past few years a hawkish appearance.

161

He glanced at his watch. God, how much longer? he thought. And continued pacing.

Several nurses hurried by. He searched their faces for some sort of sign as to how things were going. But they knew nothing.

'Keith?'

He turned to find Gerald standing beside him.

'Any news?'

'Not yet.'

'She's certainly taking her time about it. I expected it to be all over by now.'

Keith grunted, sure from Gerald's tone that was an intended jibe.

Gerald went on, 'We were lucky with Em's births. Both were short labours.'

They would be! Keith thought. Out loud he said, 'And how is Em?'

'Fine. You know you and Jean really should try and manage to come over more often.'

'We keep meaning to,' Keith lied. 'But you know how things are. What with Jean being pregnant and one thing and another.'

'Well, maybe after the baby's born?'

'We'll try and arrange something,' Keith said, having absolutely no intention of doing so. Then to change the subject, 'How's the brewery doing?'

'Excellently. Profits up again. Can't complain about that, eh?'

Keith knew fine well profits were up as he kept a close watch on what was deposited every month in his bank account. 'No, we can't,' he agreed.

A door opened and the Ward Sister appeared. 'Captain Gibb?'

Keith hurried to her side.

'I'm happy to tell you you've got a smashing wee daughter. Both she and your wife are doing fine.'

Keith blinked. 'There must be some mistake,' he said quickly. 'We were expecting a boy.'

The Ward Sister smiled.

Keith realised what he'd said and how ludicrous it must have sounded. 'What I mean is . . .' he stumbled on.

'Congratulations Keith!' said Gerald, clapping his brother on the back.

'We were just convinced it was a boy,' Keith said lamely to the Sister.

'As long as the baby's healthy that's the main thing,' Gerald said.

'Quite so,' the Sister added.

Keith was completely shattered. It just hadn't crossed his mind that it wouldn't be a boy. They'd chosen the name months ago. Roderick Keith Gibb. They hadn't even thought of one for a lassie.

'Cheer up!' Gerald said. 'I'm told anyone can produce a boy but it takes a man to produce a girl.'

For two peas Keith would have belted Gerald then. Instead he forced a smile on to his face – it came out as something of a grimace – and nodded.

'When can we see mother and daughter?' Gerald asked.

'In about half an hour,' the Sister replied.

'Right! That gives us time for a wee celebratory dram first. Eh, Keith?'

'Half an hour?' Keith said, looking at his watch. 'All right then.'

They went to a pub round the corner which, being owned by Black Lion Brewery, meant Gerald was received like Lord God Almighty.

To Keith that was like rubbing salt into an open wound.

The regiment was going abroad again and Keith, still bogged down in the administrative job he loathed, was naturally going with it.

As usual Jean would accompany him.

163

'If we have to leave Susan behind she could stay with Gerald and Em,' Jean suggested.

'Do they know we're going yet?'

'No, I haven't told them.'

'Fine,' said Keith, nodding. 'We can't take the lassie with us, it just wouldn't be fair to her where we're going. And I'm not having Gerald doing a takeover bid on her. Susan's ours and she's going to stay that way.'

'So what do we do then?'

'There's a school I've heard of in Kelvinside. Miss Buchan's School For Young Ladies. It has an excellent reputation and I thought she might go there as a boarder.'

'But she's only four!' Jean said, feeling absolutely wretched.

'I appreciate that, woman, but what else can we do? She'll be well looked after, a home away from home, they say. And so it should be at the price they charge.'

'I can't help feeling it's wrong somehow,' Jean said, wringing her hands. 'She's such a wee mite, after all.'

'Do you have any other suggestions?'

Jean shook her head.

'Well then?'

'I suppose it'll have to be ... What did you call it?'

'Miss Buchan's School For Young Ladies.'

'Miss Buchan's it is, then. But I can't say I feel happy about it.'

'Neither am I. But everything in life doesn't just go as we would want it, as you well know.'

'I'll have to see the place and meet this Miss Buchan and her staff before I agree, Keith.'

'Naturally,' he replied. 'I wouldn't have expected otherwise.'

Outside, it was typical Glasgow weather. Grey and dreich with soft rain smirring down.

'I can't wait to get back to the sun,' Keith said.

Jean sighed. She missed the sun dreadfully as well.

SUSAN AND KIRK (1)

'What's your game then, Jim?' the publican demanded.

'I'm only trying to sell you some whisky, that's all,' Kirk replied.

'And where would you get whisky when most of us can't get the bloody stuff for love or money?'

'That's my business,' Kirk replied.

The publican was a small man with an inturned eye. There were two very old razor scars down his left cheek.

'Fell off the back of a lorry, I suppose?' the publican said sarcastically. Then suddenly reaching forward he grabbed Kirk by the lapels of his coat. 'Are you trying to get me back in the Bar-L?' he demanded, referring to Barlinne Prison.

'Why should I do that?'

'Because you might be the polis. What with your fancy clothes and la-de-da accent and flashing bottles of whisky under me snoz with the promise as much as I need to come if only I'll give you an order. Do you think I came up the Clyde on a bicycle or something?'

'I'm not the police,' said Kirk, beginning to sweat a little. This was turning ugly.

'Sez you!'

Kirk picked up his sample bottle of whisky and slipped it into his briefcase.

'I think I should go now,' he said.

'Damn right,' the publican replied angrily. 'And don't come back again. Neither you or any of your pals. And you can tell them from me there's no way they're going to get me back

167

inside again. I'm going straight. That's the word. Got it?'

'Got it,' Kirk replied.

'Now fuck off!'

The publican followed him through the saloon to the door and closed it firmly behind him.

Kirk walked down the street a little way before stopping and drawing in several deep breaths. He might well be making a lot of money but by God there were times when he didn't half earn it. For a few moments back there he'd thought the skelly-eyed nutter was going to carve him. The bugger might have been wee but often the smaller they were the more dangerous they were.

He was suddenly aware he was soaking wet under his arms and all around the crotch. He'd had quite a fright back there. Quite a fright indeed.

He decided to call it a night. He'd more or less made the calls he'd set out to make anyway.

Half-way back to the flat he suddenly thought it would be a marvellous idea to go to the sports club and have a swim. The way he felt now that was just what he needed.

He stopped off at the flat to pick up his trunks and other sports equipment, then continued on out to the club.

The place was less busy than usual and the pool was empty. He swam contentedly for a while and then, coming out, went through to the male changing room to put his clothes back on again.

'I say, you wouldn't care for a game of badminton, would you? We were supposed to have a mixed foursome and the other chap hasn't turned up.'

Kirk looked up at the young man poking his head round the changing-room door. 'Badminton?' he queried.

'It would be awful for us to come out and then not get a game. Won't you help?'

Although Kirk had never actually played badminton he knew the rules, having watched a number of matches since joining the club.

'All right,' he replied. 'I'll be out in a minute or two.'

'Jolly good,' said the chap and disappeared from view.

It was the first time Kirk had been asked to join in any of the activities since taking up his membership, so he thought it a good idea to show willing. The sooner he got to know some of these people the better.

The chap was called Hector and Hector introduced him to the two girls, one of whom was Mary and the other Susan.

His partner was Susan.

She was a girl he judged to be roughly the same age as himself, with shoulder-length blonde hair and warm blue eyes. She wasn't beautiful as such, or a stunner even, but she was certainly attractive and he found himself drawn to her right away.

'I hope I don't let you down,' he said. 'I'm afraid my experience is strictly limited.' He thought it best not to mention he'd never played before.

'That's all right.' She smiled. 'As long as we can get a game in, that's the main thing.'

The other three played expertly while he sort of lumbered along doing the best he could. Fiercely competitive by nature, he hated it when he lost points and made errors. And the more graceful Susan and her companions seemed, the more cumbersome he felt by comparison.

'Well, we didn't do too badly,' Susan said politely when it was all over. Actually she and Kirk had been thrashed by the other two.

Kirk felt like a limp rag. He hadn't had so much exercise in a long time and felt the better for it.

'I could use a drink after that,' he said.

'Well we usually have one in the bar afterwards. Won't you join us?'

'I'd love to,' he said, smiling.

'We'll see you and Hector there in about fifteen minutes then,' Susan said.

She and Mary marched off to the ladies' changing room while he and Hector went to the men's.

After they'd showered Kirk established from Hector that it

was Susan's boyfriend, somebody called Nigel, who'd failed to show earlier on.

When he and Hector arrived in the bar, feeling it was the proper thing to do he placed the first order, extending the order when the girls showed up.

He'd just started to chat to Susan when suddenly there was a shout and a halloo! from the entrance to the bar.

'Nige, old son!' Hector called and waved.

'I'm frightfully sorry, Susan,' Nigel said when he joined them, 'but my flaming bus went and conked out miles from anywhere and it's taken me till now to get here.'

'Nigel, Kirk. He very kindly stepped in to make up the foursome.'

Kirk shook hands and forced a smile on to his face. He could have seen Nigel far enough, for by now he'd decided he fancied Susan.

'New to the club, are you?' Nigel said in a friendly manner.

'Yes.'

'It's a good old place, eh?'

'I like it. The club itself, that is, anyway. I'm afraid I don't know anyone here yet.'

'Well, now you know us,' said Susan.

'That's true,' he replied, looking her straight in the eye and smiling.

Nigel frowned fractionally when he saw that.

'I'm not really keen on badminton myself,' Nigel said after a few moments. 'Always considered it more of a ladies' game than anything else.'

'He's a squash man,' Hector said. 'One of the best players in the south of Scotland.'

'That a fact?' said Kirk.

'Squash is a man's game,' Nigel said. 'Do you play?'

Kirk shook his head.

'Pity. I would have liked to have got you on the court.'

Kirk knew then Nigel was aware he fancied Susan. 'Maybe someday,' he said softly.

'I'd like that,' Nigel replied.

Susan's gaze drifted from Nigel to Kirk and back again. The hint of a smile lifted the corners of her mouth.

While Hector was ordering another round Mary asked Kirk where he lived.

'With your parents?' she asked.

'No, I have a small flat of my own.'

'How lovely!' said Mary. 'I wish I had one.'

'Do you live with your parents?' Kirk asked Nigel.

'Yes.'

Kirk nodded in such a way as to give the impression to Nigel he found that secretly amusing.

Nigel looked furious.

'Who does your cooking?' Susan asked.

'Me.'

'Really?' she said surprised.

'I'm actually quite good at it. But then one usually is quite good at what one enjoys doing.'

Nor was it cooking he was talking about now, as she well knew. She blushed a little and turned her attention back to Nigel who was looking as though he would love to have a go at Kirk.

Susan thought she liked Kirk, although she found him somewhat brash. But there was no doubt there was something very exciting about him. Something extremely vibrant and alive. And he had wicked eyes. There were moments when he was looking at her when she knew precisely what was in his mind.

'I think we should be getting along. Look at the time,' said Nigel.

'Where's the car parked?' asked Susan.

'It isn't,' replied Nigel. 'At least not round here. I had to leave it where it broke down and thumb a lift in part of the way. The rest I came by public transport.'

'I can't take you both home,' said Hector. 'I haven't got enough petrol in my tank and I'll never find a garage open this late.'

'Then you'd best take Nigel as you three live relatively near

171

one another and I'll either catch a tram or a bus,' Susan said.

'I won't hear of it!' said Nigel.

'If you take me home then how will you get back?' Susan asked.

Nigel chewed his lip. He had no answer to that.

Kirk thought the gods must be smiling on him that night. It was a heaven-sent opportunity.

'I could drive Susan home if she'd like,' he said casually.

Nigel opened his mouth to object but before he could speak Hector said, 'That would solve everything!'

Kirk turned to Susan and raised an eyebrow.

'All right then,' she said. 'It seems the easiest way out of the problem.'

When he heard that, Nigel put a brave smile on his face. But he seemed to be having difficulty swallowing.

At the front entrance to the club they split into two groups. Hector, Mary and Nigel going off in one direction, Kirk and Susan in another.

'It's not much of a car,' he said apologetically when they arrived at his motor, 'but at least it goes.'

Susan laughed when he said that.

Once inside the car she gave him her address and they moved off. It was a small car so they were squashed together. When he shifted gear he couldn't help but occasionally brush her leg.

Once, she looked at him to see if he was doing it deliberately. Deciding he wasn't, she turned her attention back to the road and the directions she was giving.

He parked the car and turned to her. 'Can I see you again?' he asked.

'I don't know you.'

'Go out with me and you'll get to know me.'

'You're quite a pushy person, aren't you?'

'I've had to be,' he said in the darkness.

He put his arm round her and drew her to him. She didn't resist but then again she didn't exactly melt in his arms either. He kissed her long and hard, enjoying the experience. When he put his hand up to touch her breast she pushed his hand away.

'How long have you been going out with Nigel?' he asked.

'A little over a year now,' she replied.

He caressed the side of her face. Drawing a finger slowly along her cheekbone.

'You're a ladies' man, aren't you?'

He laughed. 'What does that mean?'

'Amongst other things, you're not scared of them in any way.'

'No,' he said, 'I'm not.'

'Nigel is. He tries not to show it but deep down he's scared of women.'

'A lot of men are. I could never see why myself.'

'What do you do?' she asked.

'I'm in business.'

'What sort of business?'

'My own.'

'You're not exactly forthcoming, are you?' she said.

'There's not a lot to be forthcoming about. I have a small business from which I earn my living. I'm what you might call a middle-man.'

'You make it sound mysterious.'

He laughed. 'I don't mean to. And what do you do?'

'I'm at college studying to be a vet.'

'I'd never have guessed that,' he said, surprised. 'You don't look the type.'

'And what *is* the type?'

'Big and butch or horsy. That's hardly you.'

'And what's me?'

'Extremely feminine and attractive,' he said, and kissed her again. This time she responded more, putting her arms round him and returning his kiss.

When they broke apart they were both breathing more heavily than they had been.

She studied what she could see of his face in the darkness.

'I think you're dangerous,' she said after a while.

'In what way?'

'I'm not sure yet.'

'You mean you think I might be a homicidal maniac?' he said jokingly.

She laughed. 'No, I mean towards women. What is usually referred to as a right proper bastard.'

'Why don't you go out with me and find out?'

'Maybe.'

'That's neither yes nor no.'

She fumbled in her pocket to produce a lighter which she flicked into flame. She wrote in a small diary, tearing the page out and handing it to him.

'I'll be home tomorrow night. If you still want to take me out ring me and we'll talk about it.'

She got out of the car and closed the door.

He rolled down the window.

'I'll ring. You have my promise on that,' he said.

'Thanks for the lift home.'

'My pleasure.'

He watched her walk across the pavement and into the drive which led to her house. He couldn't see much of the house because it was screened by some trees. But what was visible was imposing and very, very large.

'She's worth a few bob,' he thought to himself as he drove away.

He would telephone all right.

He racked his brains to think of somewhere different to take her, wanting them to get off to the best possible start. Idea after idea was discarded until a possible solution suddenly dawned on him.

He drove to the BBC where he was in luck. His inquiry procured him two tickets for a well-known wireless comedy programme several days thence. They would be part of the audience.

He rang as he said he would and told her about the tickets.

She said she'd love to see the show as she listened to it often. It was a date.

Their evening out together was a huge success, and in more ways than one.

The episode with the skelly-eyed publican had put the wind up Kirk and had been worrying him ever since. And thinking about it he realised he was bound to run into the odd nutcase from time to time. But how to protect himself?

The solution was suggested to him in a hilarious sketch about the infamous old-time gang called The Billy Boys who terrorised Glasgow in the twenties and early thirties. He would hire himself a bodyguard, and what's more he knew just the right man for the job.

After the show Susan declared she'd thoroughly enjoyed herself. He suggested they go for coffee. They found a small café that was open and having bought their coffee settled themselves at a wooden table.

'I don't even know your last name yet,' he said.

She smiled. 'Gibb.'

'Susan Gibb?' he said. 'I like it. It has a nice ring about it.'

'Susan *Euphemia* Gibb. But I'm not too keen on the Euphemia part.'

'I'm not surprised,' he said.

And they both laughed.

They sat staring at one another in silence for a few seconds while in the background the Italian proprietor's voice could be heard issuing melodic instructions to his staff.

'Will you go out with me again?' Kirk asked.

'If you like.'

'I like.'

'There's a dinner-dance I've been invited to next week. A small thing my father's throwing for some members of his firm. Nigel was supposed to be taking me but he's had to cry off. Some squash fixture or other that was originally postponed and has now been rescheduled for that night, which he says is just impossible for him to break.'

'Sounds like Nigel's loss is my gain.'

'You'll take me then?'

'I'm already looking forward to it,' he said.

They made the arrangements there and then, after which he said, 'Now, tell me about studying to be a vet. I'm absolutely fascinated.'

'Are you taking the mickey?'

'Who me?'

He tried to keep a straight face but couldn't.

She joined in his laughter.

Kirk felt decidedly nervous as he chapped the tenement door. The man he'd come to see had a reputation a mile long. Amongst all the city hard men, he was one of the – if not *the* – hardest.

'Who is it?' a gruff voice demanded from behind the door.

'My name's Kirk Murray and I've come to see Mr McGhie.'

'What about?'

'I have a proposition which might interest him.'

'Who did you say you were?'

'Kirk Murray.'

'Never heard of you.'

'You're quite right, we've never met.'

There was a fractional pause. Then, 'Are you alone?'

'Yes.'

'Just wait a minute. I've got to get my clothes on.'

Kirk took a step backward from the door. Further along the front close a marmalade cat had its tail up and was having a pee against the wall. He watched that with interest.

'Turn round very slowly, Murray, and keep your arms by your sides,' the voice that had come from behind the door said now from behind him.

He did as he was told and inched round.

The man confronting him was in his early thirties with a face like a bashed-in turnip. His hair was cut extremely short and there was a small puckered scar on his chin. He was wearing a blue shirt and waistcoat, two ivory-handled razors clearly

176

protruding from the top pockets of the latter.

The eyes that took Kirk in were palest blue and had a dead, glacial quality about them. Kirk looked into those eyes and found them absolutely terrifying.

With a shrug McGhie dismissed Kirk. Here was no threat.

'Can't be too careful you understand,' McGhie said. 'There are some right bampots around.'

As McGhie's house was on the ground floor, Kirk presumed McGhie must have climbed out a back window and come round on him that way.

'Can we talk inside?' he asked.

'Aye, sure. Proposition, is it?'

Kirk nodded.

McGhie opened the door and led the way.

Kirk was well acquainted with the stink of tenement houses but even so this one was worse than usual. It was like walking into a long-unwashed underarm.

Mrs McGhie was a lot younger than her husband and pretty in a common way. There were two half-naked children crawling round the floor.

'What can I do for you, Murray?' McGhie asked, sinking into a fireside chair that had seen better days. He gestured for Kirk to sit.

Mrs McGhie collected the two children and dragged them squawling from the room. She wouldn't return until her husband shouted for her.

'What I have in mind, Mr McGhie, is this –'

'Call me Turk. Everyone else does.'

Kirk started again. 'Are you working, Turk?'

'Hell no! Who'd employ the likes of me?'

'I might. If you were interested.'

McGhie leaned forward. 'Doing what?'

'Hopefully nothing more than just keeping me company. I'm looking for a bodyguard.'

Turk McGhie smiled. 'I like the sound of that. A bodyguard? Against whom?'

'Nothing professional. Just the odd headcase who might

want to have a go at me. And who I'm hoping won't because you'll be there.'

'Sounds like money for old rope. What sort of wages did you have in mind?'

Kirk mentioned a figure he'd already decided on, adding, 'Cash in your hand every Friday night and no one the wiser. What do you say?'

'When do I start?'

'Tonight if you can.'

'Just tell me where and when and I'll be there.'

They shook hands on the arrangement and Kirk left the house feeling hugely pleased with himself. As far as he was concerned, employing Turk McGhie had been inspirational on his part. For now his personal safety wasn't only assured, it also meant he was in a position to bring a certain pressure to bear on those publicans he was dealing with.

He was thinking of expanding his empire, and his plans, although dependent upon the whisky Harry Hydelman and Harry's friends down in England were supplying, did not include them.

The whisky was his cake. Give it a few more months for the English side of things to reach full capacity and he would start going for the icing, which would be his and his alone.

After all, Lizzie had always drummed it into him that if he was going to think at all then he should always think big.

Which was precisely what he intended doing.

The dinner dance was held at the Covenanters' Inn in Aberfoyle. The décor was Jacobean; tartan and weaponry were everywhere.

Kirk was looking forward to the evening ahead of him as he escorted Susan through to the roped-off area reserved for her father's party. This sort of 'do' was right up his street.

'Kirk, I'd like you to meet my father, Major Gibb,' Susan said.

Major Gibb was a tall slim man with a definite military

bearing about him. He spoke in clipped tones and everything he said somehow sounded like an order.

Mrs Gibb was a pleasant, faded sort of lady who might have at one time in her life spent too long in the sun and consequently dried out as a result.

'Let me introduce you around, my boy,' Major Gibb said. 'Then we'll all have another drink before we sit down.'

And still it didn't click with Kirk. Nor did it until he was about to sit down at the table when his eye was caught by a piece of white cardboard leaning against a pepper pot.

The cardboard bore the legend, 'Reserved for Black Lion Brewery'.

He felt as though he'd been doused with ice-cold water.

'They've got venison on tonight. I just love it, don't you?' Susan said at his side.

Kirk stared at the man who'd so cold-bloodedly sacked his father and whose dead brother, Gerald, had once dreadfully humiliated Walter that afternoon long, long ago in the cellar of what had then been Walter's pub.

'Kirk?'

He turned to her. 'Sorry. Did you say something?'

'Your eyes have gone all poppy as though you'd just seen a ghost.'

He smiled. Unwittingly she'd just come up with the perfect allusion. 'In a way I have,' he replied.

'How so?'

He continued smiling and didn't reply.

For the rest of the meal he was strangely silent, often staring quizzically at Major Gibb and occasionally sideways at Susan.

Once, she asked him what he was thinking.

'That it's a small world,' he replied. And although she pressed him he wouldn't elaborate.

After the meal came the dance part. More drinks were brought while the table was cleared. In another part of the room a small band struck up.

By now Kirk had established that the majority of men in the

party were senior personnel with Black Lion Brewery while the others had outside connections.

One of these was a man called Andy White who worked for a small distillery which supplied a variety of spirits to the pubs owned by Black Lion Brewery. Although whisky was in short supply there was no shortage of other spirits such as gin and brandy, and it was mainly these Andy White, the area rep, supplied to Black Lion.

Kirk made a point of chatting at length to White, saying confidentially he would like to talk to White at a later date on a business matter. On hearing that, White was only too pleased to give Kirk his card. Kirk said he would phone White the following week.

Kirk had been planning to contact a distillery soon but up until that evening hadn't decided on any particular one. Now that he'd met White it would have been foolish of him not to have taken advantage of the fact.

He and Susan had a few dances together after which they were summoned over to where Major and Mrs Gibb were sitting.

'It's most kind of you to escort my daughter when Nigel couldn't make it,' the Major said. Then, turning to Susan, 'You did say he'd met Nigel, didn't you?'

'Yes,' Susan replied.

'Marvellous fellow, Nigel,' Major Gibb went on. 'Very fond of him.'

Kirk could see only too clearly which way the wind was blowing. Nigel was favoured and the Major was letting him know it.

Mrs Gibb said, 'He comes from a very well-connected family. They're in shipping, don't you know.'

'No, I didn't,' Kirk replied.

'And what is your family in?' the Major asked.

It was on the tip of Kirk's tongue to say his father had been killed in the war or come out with some other fanciful, and acceptable, story. But at the very last moment he changed his mind.

Very slowly and with a smile on his face he said, 'Actually my father works as a barman in a pub. He used to run a pub of his own once but the owner sacked him.'

'And which brewery owner was that?' Major Gibb asked.

Kirk's smile thinned. 'You,' he replied softly.

Susan looked quickly at Kirk but he kept his gaze riveted on the Major, who now suddenly looked quite put out. A blush crept into Mrs Gibb's cheeks and her hands fidgeted in her lap. Kirk sipped his drink, said nothing and waited.

'I hope there are no bad feelings?' the Major said after a while.

'From my dad or myself?'

'Both of you. Business is business, after all.'

'Well, there's certainly none from me,' Kirk lied, adding a trifle acidly, 'as you say, business is business.'

Susan placed a hand on his arm. 'Shall we have another dance?' she asked gently.

'Why not?' he replied and led her back on to the floor.

'You're certainly a cool one,' Susan said when they were dancing.

'Do you want me to go?'

'Not unless you feel you want to.'

'I didn't know who your father was until tonight,' he said.

'I know that,' she replied. 'Do you hate him?'

'He put my mother, father and myself out on the streets so I'm not exactly enamoured of him. But if I hated anyone in your family it was your Uncle Gerald, who owned the brewery before your father. He was a real choice specimen.'

Susan registered surprise. 'You knew him!'

'No. But I had first-hand experience of him at work. He once humiliated by father like you wouldn't believe. Made my father beg like a dog. There was no need for that, none at all. Neither of them was aware that I overheard.'

'I'm sorry,' Susan said. 'It must have been awful for you.'

'I've never forgotten the incident. Things like that leave a mark on you.'

'Did your father deserve to be sacked?'

181

'To be honest, he wasn't exactly the best publican in the world. But he didn't deserve that sort of treatment, not after the years he'd put into that pub. Your father could have at least placed him elsewhere as a head barman or something.'

'And now he works as an ordinary barman?' she asked.

Kirk nodded. 'He was far too old to get another pub. Especially having been sacked, which meant he didn't have any references. He was idle for quite some time during which we lived off my wages till he landed the job he's got now.'

They danced for a while in silence. Then Kirk said, 'I got the message loud and clear from the Major that he more than approves of Nigel.'

'He wants us to get married.'

'And will you?'

'I haven't made up my mind yet.'

Kirk smiled. 'Shipping and beer. It could be the foundation of something really colossal.'

'I rather think my father sees it that way too.'

'I thought he might.'

'But when I marry it'll be because I want to and not because he's forced me into it.'

'And how does Nigel feel about all this?' Kirk asked.

'He loves me.'

'But you don't love him?'

'I never said that.'

Kirk smiled. 'You didn't have to. It's obvious from the way you speak about him.'

Susan furrowed her brow and looked thoughtful. 'I like him, there's no doubt about that.'

'But liking isn't loving. There's an awful big difference between the two.'

'Have you ever been in love?' she asked, looking up at him.

'No.'

'Not even a little bit?'

He gently squeezed her waist. 'Is that supposed to be a leading question?'

'Of course not. How could you even possibly begin to feel

182

that way towards me? You've only known me five minutes.'

'Precisely,' he replied.

'I suppose I was just trying to pry into your past,' she said.

'There's no one else, if that's what you're trying to find out,' he lied smoothly. God, Minnie would've had a fit had she heard him say that!

Susan smiled and seemed to put more vigour into her dancing.

They stayed for a further hour and then Kirk suggested they go, to which Susan agreed.

'Thank you very much for the evening,' he said to Major Gibb. 'I thoroughly enjoyed myself.'

'It was a pleasure to have met you,' the Major replied, looking as though it was anything but.

Kirk shook hands with Mrs Gibb and then moved away to wait until Susan had said her goodbyes.

Once in the car Susan snuggled up to him. The drone of the engine and the darkness all around soon took their effect by sending her off to sleep.

As they headed for Glasgow, Kirk had time to reflect on the evening. To begin with he thought he'd been a bloody fool to come clean with Major Gibb the way he had. But thinking on it further he came to the conclusion his reaction had been the right one. If he was going to continue to see Susan, and he certainly had every intention of trying to, then to have lied would only have got himself horribly enmeshed in a skein of untruths which could have unravelled at any time very much to his detriment.

'We're here,' he said later, shaking her by the shoulder.

Susan blinked and sat up. 'Where are we?' she yawned, looking out the car window.

'Outside my flat. I thought you might like a cup of coffee.'

'Coffee?' she mocked gently.

'Genuine Blue Mountain. You can't get better than that,' he replied, pretending not to have picked up her inference.

He held the door open for her while she got out, then, taking her hand, led her upstairs.

Once in the flat she gazed around. It was the first time she'd ever been in a bachelor flat.

'What do you think?' he asked, taking her coat from her.

'It could do with a bit of redecoration.'

'Couldn't agree more. Unfortunately I just don't seem to have had the time.'

'It's a bit plebian as it stands now.'

He treated her to a mocking smile. 'But you've forgotten. My secret's out. I *am* plebian.'

'Nonsense. You might have come from the masses but you're not one of them.'

Busy getting out the coffee, he said over his shoulder. 'If my mother could hear you say that she'd go down on her knees and kiss your feet.'

'You sound like you're fond of her.'

'I am. She's the original pillar of strength. If she'd been born a man she could've become Prime Minister.'

'And what about you, what do you want to become?'

'Rich,' he said and laughed. 'Filthy stinking rich. I have an aim in life: to be top dog.'

'Top dog at what?'

'Whatever I'm doing,' he replied.

'That's quite an aim,' Susan mused. 'And you know something?'

'What?'

'I think you'll probably succeed.'

He laid out two cups. 'If I don't, it won't be for the lack of trying, I promise you.'

Susan sat and regarded him steadily until the coffee was made. They drank in silence, each watching the other, both knowing what was coming next.

When their cups were empty he took hers and placed it along with his on the side of the sink. He liked to be tidy, that being something else Lizzie had instilled in him.

He crossed back to Susan and hoisted her into his arms. He kissed her while at the same time caressing her body. She

184

moulded herself against him and moaned deep in the back of her throat.

He pulled his lips from hers and gazed into her eyes. He saw assent there.

In the bedroom he took his time stripping her. As he worked, she stood staring at him, the bird hypnotised by the stalking cat.

When she was naked he laid her across the bed and caressed her some more. She twisted and writhed under his knowing fingers.

'Get your clothes off,' she gasped, perspiration dotting her brow.

The waiting was almost unbearable for her as he slowly undressed and then carefully folded his various articles of clothing over a nearby chair.

When he finally came to her she'd worked herself up into a fever pitch. Eagerly her hands grasped him, urging him on.

But Kirk had learned a great deal with Minnie, part of which was that he had a natural talent for sex. Instinctively he knew what to do and how to go about it. Nor did he ever allow himself to become totally subjective during the preliminaries and the act. There was always that part of him he kept apart.

He soothed her now. Tamping down the fires he had lit and her imagination had fanned into a roaring furnace.

When she was calm and once more in control he started again, secretly amused and pleased with himself at having such power over the female body.

When her flesh was burning to the touch and her neck was stained with passion he went into her. Slowly, deliberately, the maestro putting bow to his violin.

And all the time he made love he smiled like some benign god looking down from on high.

Later that night, Susan sat before her dressing-table mirror thinking of Kirk and his lovemaking.

What he'd done to her, and how he'd made her feel, had

been absolutely fantastic! Right out of this world! Compared with him Nigel was a ham-fisted clod.

Goose-bumps played up and down her spine at the memory of the orgasms she'd had. What she'd experienced previously were mere minor sensations, not even in the same league as those which had racked her body causing her to cry out in exultation and ecstasy.

Earlier, she'd talked to him about love. Well surely what she and he had experienced on his bed was love. What else could it be?

And it was glorious.

'Pleased to meet you again, Kirk,' Andy White said, rising from behind his desk, where he'd been busy with paperwork. 'Now, how about a dram?'

'Bit early for me, thanks all the same,' Kirk replied. It was ten in the morning.

'Tea or coffee, then?'

'Tea please.'

'Right. I'll just send the girl to make it.'

Andy left the room and Kirk gazed around. The Carswell Distillery was situated on the outskirts of Glasgow and dealt mainly with Glasgow and the surrounding area. Still small, it nonetheless was ambitious and was trying to muscle in among the larger distilleries with the intention of one day being counted as such itself.

To Kirk's way of thinking, this made them ideal for his purpose as it meant he stood a far better chance of getting a better deal with Carswell's than he would with its larger competitors.

'Now, what can I do for you?' Andy White asked on his return.

'I want to know the discount terms you'd give me if I bought from you in bulk?'

White smiled just a little patronisingly. 'Whisky's very tight, if that's what you're after.'

'I want everything but. Whisky doesn't interest me.'

'And what sort of size order did you have in mind?'

Kirk handed White a sheet of paper on which he'd written his weekly requirements.

The smile vanished from White's face as he read the paper.

'That's only for starters,' Kirk said. 'I hope to double and then triple it within the month.'

'That's a lot of drink,' White said.

'I'm dealing with a lot of thirsty people.'

White fiddled with a pencil. 'What sort of discount did you have in mind?' he asked.

'Twenty-five per cent.'

White looked up, shocked. 'That's ludicrous!'

'Oh, I don't think so. It still leaves you enough to make a fair whack out of it. And don't forget it's your product that'll be going into the pubs and once people get used to a certain product they tend to keep on using it. Off-sales, that sort of thing.'

'So this would be going into pubs, then?'

'Yes.'

'That makes a difference.'

Kirk smiled gently. 'I thought it might.'

'Do you ... eh ... own these pubs?'

Pub ownership had never occurred to Kirk before. He decided he liked the idea.

'No,' he replied. 'Let's just say I have influence with them.'

'It's a helluva big single order if you manage to triple it,' Andy White. 'It would make you our second largest customer.'

'Who's the largest?'

'Major Gibb's Black Lion Brewery.'

'Second to them, eh?' Kirk said. That was another idea he liked.

'Of course you realise I can't give you an answer on this myself. I have to put it higher up.'

'How long before you can tell me?'

'A couple of days. Shouldn't be more.'

'Fine. I'll wait to hear,' Kirk replied.

The tea arrived and for a while they talked about football. White, it turned out, was a Clyde supporter.

'Masochist,' said Kirk.

With Turk McGhie bringing up the rear, Kirk entered the pub. This was the last on the long list of those he supplied whisky to. The owner was a man called McAlpine.

McAlpine was behind the bar, and when he saw Kirk come in through the door he gave him a friendly nod and gestured towards the back room. When he saw Turk was with Kirk, a nervous expression flitted across his face. Turk tended to have that effect on people.

'This isn't your regular day,' McAlpine said, breaking open a bottle. He poured three half-gills which he handed round.

Turk downed his in a single gulp. As far as he was concerned, whisky was for swallowing and not for playing with.

'How's business?' Kirk asked.

McAlpine was no fool. He knew something was coming. 'Can't complain,' he replied.

'I've been in a few of the boozers round about. You're doing better than them.'

'Aye, I'd say that was probably so.'

'Can you say why?'

He's going to put up the price of his bloody whisky, McAlpine thought bitterly.

'Because I've always got whisky and they haven't,' he replied looking grim.

Kirk nodded. 'Quite.'

'How much a case?'

Kirk looked puzzled. 'Pardon?'

'How much are you putting it up a case?'

Kirk grinned. 'No, no, you've got the wrong end of the stick entirely, Mr McAlpine. My price stays the same. But whether the whisky stays with you is another thing entirely. Tell me, what do you pay for a case of gin?'

McAlpine mentioned a price.

'Aye, that's about right. You see, what I want you to do is buy all your spirits from me. Same price as you're paying now, so you're not out of pocket any. The only difference, as far as you're concerned, would be that I'd be your sole supplier, instead of me and the other people you're dealing with now.'

'Same price on everything?' McAlpine asked, wanting to hear Kirk say it again.

'You show me your invoices and I'll match the prices. Of course, if you don't scratch my back here then I won't feel obliged to continue scratching yours. In other words, there'll be no more whisky.'

McAlpine was over a barrel and knew it. He was one of four pubs supplied whisky by Kirk in the district and all of them were doing far better than their competitors. He'd be cutting his own throat not to agree. And as Kirk had pointed out, it wasn't going to cost him anything.

'You're on,' McAlpine said.

Kirk sighed. That was the last pub wrapped up and not a bit of difficulty in convincing any of them.

'Another half?' McAlpine asked.

Kirk nodded. 'And while I'm drinking it I'll read through your invoices so I can make a note of what you're now paying.'

While McAlpine fetched the invoices, Kirk thought about how much more money all this was going to mean for him.

On top of his whisky profit he was going to collect a cool twenty-five per cent on every other bottle of spirits supplied by him. At the very minimum his income was going to increase by at least seven hundred and fifty per cent. It was a staggering thought.

There was no use leaving that amount of money lying in a bank collecting a derisory interest. He had to make it work for him, and Andy White had given him the idea of just how to do it.

It was time he bought his own pub, which would be even more grist to his spirits mill.

It was true what was said about money, he thought. Once you had it you couldn't help but make more.

But first he was going to give himself a well-deserved treat. He'd taken Susan to the pictures the other night and one of the films had featured an Alfa Romeo which she'd enthused about.

He'd find and buy one of those. And he'd start looking in the morning.

Kirk lay in bed with Minnie snoring gently by his side. God, he was bored to tears with her, he thought. He knew it to be his imagination but daily her empty chatter seemed to get more and more inane.

He was finding it damned difficult running two birds at the one time though he was managing it. The trick was to make sure neither came up to the flat unless specifically invited. Both had strict instructions to telephone rather than call round if they wanted to speak to him.

The other problem was that for a large city Glasgow had an amazingly small centre which was where most of the amenities were. It always worried him that when out with one he'd bump into the other.

Still, that was a risk that had to be run, for he had no intention of giving up either – for the time being, that was.

He put his hands behind his head and pictured Susan. She was still seeing Nigel but, so she assured him and he believed her, only at her father's insistence. The Major still wanted to marry beer to shipping.

'Black Lion Brewery,' he said out loud. Christ, what a coup it would be to marry Susan and fall heir to the whole shebang!

For Susan was the Major's only heir and when he popped his clogs the brewery would come to her, and through her to whoever she was married to.

What a magnificent opportunity there was for him here if only he played his cards right. The Major was dead against him of course, wanting the merger with Nigel. And he daren't alienate the Major, who might spike his guns – should he succeed in marrying Susan – by putting all sorts of complications in his way.

That meant that anything sudden and without the Major's blessing, like an elopement say, was definitely out.

He hadn't proposed yet but he would soon. And when Susan accepted, as he had no doubt she would, they would then both have to work at getting her old man to agree.

That might take quite some time and would depend entirely on Susan's sticking to her guns and not giving in to pressure to marry Nigel instead.

This time-lapse suited his purposes admirably. For the goose that for the moment was laying such marvellous golden eggs for him wouldn't be around forever. And when the goose flew back to America his entire spirit empire would collapse virtually overnight.

He'd already spoken to Harry about continuing with the blokes who man the P.X.s down in England but they'd turned down the idea. They'd only work the fiddle through Harry because they knew and trusted him.

When that happened he could get shot of ratbag snoring beside him, her usefulness being ended, and get on with marrying Susan.

'Black Lion Brewery,' he said again out loud. What a perfect revenge on that sod Gerald Gibb who'd humiliated his father so badly and cruelly. And what a deliciously ironic twist against the Major, that the son of the man he'd fired so callously would end up in the Major's seat.

It was a lovely dream but there was still an awful lot could go wrong. In the meantime he must get on with investing the substantial amount of money he was earning. And in fact he was going to see a pub in the morning that had been recommended to him as a good buy.

The other thing was to get hold of the Alfa he'd promised himself. He'd tried a dozen dealers so far and not one of them had come up with the particular model he wanted.

He remembered then passing a new used-car lot that had

only opened recently. As it was on the way to the pub he had to go and see, he would stop in there.

Whoever ran it couldn't do any worse than the other dealers he'd tried.

'What?' Walter Murray exclaimed, and sat down.

'I've bought a pub and I want you and Mum to run it for me,' Kirk said.

'You mean you actually own it?'

'Lock, stock and water engines.'

'Since when?'

'This afternoon.'

Pride blazed from Lizzie's eyes. 'You're on your way, son. You're on your way,' she said, and going to him hugged him tight.

Walter scratched his head. This was the last thing he wanted. He was happy being an ordinary barman. No worries, no problems, just pulling pints and letting life roll over him.

'I thought I'd run you over to see the place. What do you say?' Kirk asked.

Walter shifted uncomfortably. 'I've got to be on duty soon. It's not really all that convenient at the moment.'

'To Hell with your shift!' Lizzie exclaimed. 'This is far more important. Walter, you're going to be running your own pub again! Just think of it!'

'Aye,' he replied miserably. 'I am.'

'When do we take over, son?' Lizzie asked.

'I've given the chap I bought it from a few days to move out and you can get in directly he's away.'

'Is it a big house?' Walter asked.

Kirk grinned. 'Huge.'

Walter groaned inwardly.

Kirk wasn't surprised by his father's reluctance. He had been expecting it. En route to the pub in his car, he stated it was his idea for it to appear that it was Walter who was running the pub while in actuality it would be Lizzie who'd be pulling the strings from behind the scenes. Walter would be out front managing the bar itself, while Lizzie would be doing all the paperwork and actual management.

Walter brightened considerably when he heard that. Lizzie nodded her approval. This arrangement would suit her down to the ground.

As Kirk had said, the pub was huge – barn-like; there was a predominance of tiles everywhere, which gave it the appearance of a public toilet.

As far as Lizzie was concerned, the biggest mark in its favour was that it was situated in a part of the city that, although still working-class, was definitely far superior to the area they were in now. Definitely several steps up, she said, nodding her approval.

While Lizzie and Walter were being shown round by the man who up until that afternoon had been the owner, Kirk took himself down to the cellar, wanting to see again the extremely large storeroom situated at its rear. It was this storeroom which had clinched the buy for him. There was plenty of room to store his spirits, whisky and otherwise, prior to their distribution. And with his mother and father above the storeroom, like two dogs guarding a buried bone, his spirits were as safe and secure as drink can ever be said to be in a city renowned for an extremely high incidence of alcohol thefts.

Whistling, he made his way back upstairs. If the result of today's work didn't call for a celebratory drink, then nothing did.

'Oh my God, my God . . . my God!' Susan gasped, her body convulsing.

Breath hissed from beneath Kirk's teeth as he collapsed on to her.

Her face was awash with sweat, various strands and locks of her hair wet and plastered to her skin.

'Ooooohh!' she groaned. The sound seemed to come up from her very toes.

Kirk lay where he was for a few seconds and then gently pulled himself away.

'That was the best yet,' Susan said.

'Happy?'

'Hmm. You?'

'If you are, I am.'

There was a pause and then she said, 'I never knew it could be like this. So ... so satisfying.'

'I love you, Susan.'

She rolled over to face him. 'And I love you, too.'

He smiled in a way he knew she found disarming. 'Fancy getting married?'

She blinked, caught off guard. 'Pardon?'

'Would you like to get married?'

'Is that a formal proposal?'

'As formal as you'll ever get from me. What's wrong? Was I supposed to go down on one knee or something?'

She shook her head. 'I'm just ... I don't know what to say!'

'The customary reply is yes or no.'

'Of course it's yes! What I meant was, it was a bit of a shock coming out the blue like that.'

He drew her to him and kissed her on the mouth. Putty in his hands, he thought. Sheer bloody putty.

'I think I knew the moment I first saw you it was going to end up like this,' he lied smoothly. 'There seemed a sort of inevitability about us. As though it had been decreed from on high.'

'Mrs Kirk Murray,' she said aloud, but as though talking to herself. 'I like the sound of it.'

'When shall we tell the Major?'

Susan frowned. 'That isn't going to be easy. He won't be exactly mad on the idea.'

He stroked her flank causing her to shudder. 'If he does make strong objections, the thing is for you to stick to your guns. It may take a while, and there's no great rush for us to get married, after all, but we must bring him round to seeing it our way in the end.'

'He's going to be awfully disappointed. He has his heart set on my marrying Nigel.'

'His heart or his sporran?'

Susan laughed. 'That's wicked!'

'But true. And you know it.'

She looked wistful. 'He so desperately wants to be a big success in business like his older brother Gerald was. He was always under Gerald's shadow, as far as I can make out, the way some younger brothers are. He sees my marrying Nigel as laying the foundations for something far larger and grander than anything Gerald achieved.'

'Well we must persuade him your happiness is more important than empire building,' Kirk said.

'We can try.'

'And we'll succeed. You leave it to me.'

'I don't care about anything else, Kirk. Just so long as I have you,' she whispered.

'That's how I feel about you. But we must be practical. I mean, there's no use being silly about these things. Besides, it would hurt me to think I'd caused any sort of rift in your family. That would be getting off to a bad start and I don't want that for us.'

'When shall we tell him, then?'

'If he's in, why not tonight? There's no use putting off till tomorrow what we can do today.'

Her leg curled round his and she reached down to stroke him. 'I couldn't agree more,' she said.

He laughed before saying, 'And before we go to see him I've a surprise for you I've got to pick up.'

'What sort of surprise?'

'Wait and see.'

'Oh! That's unfair!'

He rolled over on top of her, pinning her to the bed. Slowly he sank on to and then into her.

Within a minute she'd forgotten all about the surprise.

'It's absolutely beautiful, Kirk!' Susan exclaimed, clapping her hands in delight.

'She's a beauty right enough,' Kirk said. 'Just what I had in mind.'

Eddy King smiled. There was nothing like a happy, satisfied customer.

'The engine's in excellent nick,' Eddy said. 'I've checked it out myself so you can take my word on that.'

'How clever of you,' Susan said to Kirk. 'It's just like the one we saw at the pictures.'

'I'm glad you like it. It was a bit of a problem getting hold of one but seeing your face now makes it all worthwhile.'

'Are you taking it with you?' Eddy asked.

'Of course,' Kirk replied, extracting a packet of money from a side pocket. He already knew the price, having been told by Eddy on the telephone earlier.

'What about my old car?' Kirk asked. 'Will you take that off my hands?'

Eddy crossed to the car and looked at it. He named a sum he thought fair in the circumstances, which Kirk accepted on the spot.

After money and log-books had been exchanged, Eddy waved to Kirk and Susan as they drove off in the Alfa Romeo.

Not a bad-looking bit of skirt that, Eddy thought to himself after the Alfa had disappeared from view.

What looked like a potential customer appeared on the lot to stare at an old Lanchester. Eddy hurried over, Kirk and Susan already fading from his mind.

Major Gibb stared long and hard at Susan before turning his gaze to Kirk.

'Naturally we want your blessing, sir,' Kirk said.

'Do you, now,' the Major replied, his voice steely with overtones of anger.

Susan bit her lip.

'We love one another very much,' Kirk added.

Major Gibb poured himself a small whisky, which he sipped, rather like a bird of prey delicately tasting blood. He didn't offer a drink either to Kirk or his daughter.

Inside he was fuming. How dare this ... this upstart, this guttersnipe, propose marriage to Susan! And how dare she accept him when she knew damn well it was his dearest wish she marry Nigel.

'What do you say, sir?' Kirk asked.

Major Gibb stared straight ahead and didn't reply. The tension in the room mounted and mounted.

Kirk looked at Susan, who pulled a face. He shook his head and gestured everything was going to be all right, doing that to calm her more than anything as she was obviously becoming very agitated.

'Susan?' the Major said at length. 'Do you trust me?'

'Yes, Daddy.'

'And have I not always tried to do my best for you?'

She nodded.

'Then listen carefully to me now. I'm a lot older than you with far more experience in life. What you feel for this man here is mere infatuation that will soon pass as all these things do. A marriage with him would be a disaster. He has no stock, no breeding. In other words, albeit he might speak like a gentleman, he's as common as muck.'

Kirk went white. He'd been expecting a set-to but this was below the belt.

'What's he got to offer you apart from this infatuation, eh? Well the answer's nothing.'

'I own a pub of my own!' Kirk said hotly. 'And I have other interests.'

'A pub,' the Major said scornfully. 'One pub. And what are these other interests?'

'Spirits,' Kirk replied. 'I buy and sell in bulk.'

'That's interesting. So you deal in spirits and own a pub. And of course I own a brewery plus a great many pubs, all of which Susan will inherit one day. I don't suppose that ever crossed your mind, did it?'

'We love one another and that's why we want to get married,' Kirk insisted.

The Major smiled. 'I met lots like you in the Army, young man; you're a breed I know well. Adventurers, we used to call them. They'd do anything to get on.'

Kirk was furious now. He hadn't expected the old fart to see through him like this – at least not quite so clearly.

'Father I . . .'

Susan was forced to shut up when the Major interrupted her. 'Has it crossed your mind, my girl, that it could well be your inheritance he's after?'

'Not Kirk, Daddy. Honestly, he's not like that.'

He smiled patronisingly. 'What a naïve child you really are!'

'I am not a child, nor am I naïve!'

'If you're not a child then stop acting like one. Can't you see he's trying to take you in?'

'It's just not true!' Kirk said.

'So you say,' the Major replied. 'But I don't believe you.'

'You can't make me marry Nigel,' Susan said.

'No, that I can't.'

'And I won't, Daddy. Not now I've met Kirk. He's the one who's right for me.'

'How can you be so sure about such a thing at your age?'

'I just can,' she replied defiantly.

The Major went on, 'Nigel's people have position, power, status. They're one of Scotland's leading families. You'll never do better than that.'

Kirk barked out a laugh. 'And you accuse *me* of being an adventurer! What do you think you are? Why, you're trying to do exactly the same thing you're accusing me of!'

'It's not the same,' the Major replied coldly.

'Why not? Because I'm common as muck, as you put it, while you're a few rungs higher up the social ladder? Christ, but that's the most two-faced, hypocritical attitude I've ever heard.'

'What I'm proposing is a marriage between social equals,' the Major said, 'with advantages to both sides. The way these things have always been done. I will not, repeat, *not*, have Susan marry beneath her and to someone who is so obvious and blatant an opportunist and adventurer.'

Kirk clenched his hands into fists. The last thing he'd

wanted was for this to happen. His bitter retort died in his mouth as Susan suddenly burst into tears. Going to her, he took her in his arms.

As Susan sobbed on Kirk's shoulder and the Major glared at them, the door opened and Mrs Gibb entered. She'd been out and had just that minute returned.

'What's going on here?' she demanded.

'He's proposed to Susan,' the Major said.

'Susan hasn't accepted, has she?'

'She has.'

'Quite impossible. Completely out of the question.'

On hearing that Susan burst out wailing.

'Precisely what I've been telling them,' the Major said jubilantly.

At that moment Kirk saw himself back in his father's pub cellar and heard his father being cruelly humiliated by Gerald Gibb. And now the same thing was happening again, only this time he was the one on the receiving end. Well, the Gibbs wouldn't find him such an easy mark as Walter. By God and they wouldn't!

The intense hatred he'd felt towards Gerald Gibb when he was a boy was born in him again, only this time it was directed at Gerald's brother, the Major.

'There there, lass,' he crooned, stroking Susan's hair. 'They won't break us apart. You have my word on that.'

'Your *word*!' the Major sneered. 'The word of a guttersnipe.'

'If you weren't an old man and Susan's father I'd punch your head in for some of the things you've just been saying.'

The Major stuck out his chest. 'Don't let my age deter you. I'm more than capable of looking after myself.'

'Right then!'

He tried to let Susan go but she clung on to him. 'Please Kirk, not that. Please!'

Her pleas made him pause.

'Hiding behind a lassie's skirts now, eh?' the Major taunted.

With a roar Kirk tore himself from Susan and leapt forward. All deviousness and previous good intentions were swamped by anger.

As Kirk charged at him the Major leant down and picked up an object that had been standing against the back of a chair.

'No!' Susan screamed.

The Major's hand flicked and there was a brown blur through the air.

Kirk's cheek was opened from ear to mouth as neatly as though a scalpel had been run along it. Blood spurted to blind one eye.

The Major darted to one side and the brown object blurred through the air again.

This time Kirk managed to get a hand in front of his face. He grunted in agony as a section of skin was flayed from the side of his hand.

The Major raised his swagger stick to strike again but that blow never landed. He staggered backward as Kirk's head took him full in the chest.

Kirk and the Major tumbled to the floor with Kirk managing to get himself on top of the Major. His undamaged hand grabbed the swagger stick and tore it from the Major's grasp.

Kirk was dimly aware of Mrs Gibb pounding on his back as he raised the swagger stick to strike. Beneath him the Major struggled, but to no avail.

'Kirk?'

Susan's hand closed around his. 'Please don't. For me.'

He swallowed and then took a deep breath.

'Please?'

He took another deep breath and then another. Blood from his cheek fell splashing on the Major and the carpet.

'All right,' he said, his voice trembling. 'I won't touch him.'

Very slowly he brought the swagger stick down till it was resting across the Major's throat.

'You've just made the biggest mistake of your life,' he said.

The Major's look was one of contempt.

Kirk rose to his feet, leaving the swagger stick across the Major's throat, where it rested for a few seconds more before the Major snatched it away.

Susan peered at the wound on his cheek. 'You'll have to go to the hospital with that. It needs stitches,' she said.

'Get out of my house,' the Major said, coming to his feet.

'You riff-raff are all alike. Cause trouble wherever you go,' Mrs Gibb spat.

Susan found a hanky which she pressed to Kirk's cheek, and for the present anyway this stopped the flow of blood. There was also blood dripping from Kirk's hand, the damaged part feeling as though it had been immersed in boiling water.

'Will you come with me to the hospital?' Kirk asked.

Susan nodded.

'You'll stay here! I forbid you to go!' the Major said.

'Susan dear, Daddy knows best,' Mrs Gibb added.

Susan looked undecided.

'Well?' Kirk demanded softly.

Susan made up her mind. She knew if she deserted Kirk now their cause would be lost forever.

'I'll get the coats,' she said. And without looking at either of her parents she left the room.

Kirk stared hard at the Major, as though trying to imprint the man's face in his memory for all time, the hatred between them so strong it almost seemed a physical entity.

'You sacked my dad but you'll never sack me,' Kirk said.

'Peasant,' Mrs Gibb commented after he'd gone.

'Now just try and relax,' the doctor said, priming the hypodermic.

Kirk stared at the needle in fascination, his insides turning as the doctor brought it close to his flesh. He closed his eyes and waited for it to bite.

Within seconds the anaesthetic took effect and his lacerated cheek grew numb. While this was happening, nimble fingers were cleaning and bandaging his hand. 'This'll be as right as rain again in a few weeks,' the pleasant-faced nurse said as she worked on the hand.

Kirk mumbled his thanks.

'Right then, let's get you sewn up,' the doctor said.

After a while Kirk asked, the words coming out most peculiarly due to one side of his face being frozen, 'Will there be a scar?'

The doctor stopped what he was doing and took a step back. His eyes locked on to Kirk's.

'I'm doing my absolute best but I'm afraid there will be. I'll try and make it as fine a one as possible though.'

'Thank you,' Kirk replied. He closed his eyes again and let the doctor get on with it.

In his mind he conjured up the image of Major Gibb. One way or another he'd get that bastard, if it was the last thing he ever did. On his mother's life he swore it.

He'd marry Susan, not because it was a way at getting the brewery but because it would hurt the Major and his dreadful wife. They desperately wanted Susan to marry Nigel. Well, he would deny them that.

And that would only be the start.

Susan dropped him off at the flat in a taxi.

'You'd better not come up,' he said. 'All I want to do is go to bed and sleep.'

'I understand. Oh, my poor Kirk,' she said laying her hand on his injured cheek.

'It only hurts me when I laugh,' he joked. And they both smiled in the darkness.

'I'll ring you in the morning,' she said.

She kissed him on the lips and then sat back in the seat as he climbed stiffly from the cab.

The first thing he did when he was inside the flat was to pour himself a large drink. He drank that off as though it was lemonade and poured himself another. The alcohol went straight to his head, making him feel woozy. He swayed and had to catch on to the mantelpiece to steady himself.

There was a mirror above the mantelpiece which he now gazed into. Although no Adonis, he'd always been proud of his looks, knowing himself to be a little bit more handsome than the average. Well, that was all changed now that he was to bear a scar for the rest of his life. What hurt most was the fact people would be bound to think it was a razor scar, the mark of the criminal and lower classes.

His reverie was broken by a knock at the door. 'Who in hell's that?' he said to himself, seeing off yet another drink.

When he opened the door a smiling Minnie stood revealed.

'Hello, love,' she said, her smile turning to a frown when she saw his bandaged cheek and hand.

'What happened to you?'

He gestured her inside. 'I got done over and robbed by a gang,' he said, that being the story he'd earlier decided to tell everyone.

'Did they put the boot in?'

'Aye,' he said pouring himself yet another drink and one for Minnie. He suddenly rounded on her as a thought struck him.

'What do you mean coming here without ringing first? You know I told you never to do that.'

'I was just so excited,' she replied eagerly. 'I just had to come right up and tell you the good news.'

'What good news?'

'I'm expecting a wean.'

The words hit him like a thunderbolt. 'Hell's teeth!' he exclaimed. He swallowed his drink and poured himself another large one. His head swam and Minnie went out of focus. He remembered then the nurse had told him not to drink on top of the pills she'd made him take.

'Are you sure?' he demanded.

'Aye. There's no doubt,' she nodded.

Minnie came to him and took him in her arms. 'Now you're doing so well there's no reason we can't get married is there?' she asked.

The laughter rumbled out from deep within him. 'Marry

203

you?' he said contemptuously, breaking away. 'Don't be so bloody daft!'

Minnie caught her breath, the beginnings of tears in her eyes. 'Why not?'

The alcohol rose up and swamped him. All his pent-up fury and rage exploded. He wanted to hurt someone, to humiliate them the way the Major had humiliated him.

He lashed out verbally, hardly conscious of what he was saying.

'Because you're hairy Mary, that's why. A bloody hairy who lives with her slag of a mother in the gutter. Do you actually think I'd marry the likes of you? Why you must be out of your effing skull, woman! I never said I intended marrying you. And as for this brat you say you're carrying, how do I know it's mine, eh? Answer me that!'

'Oh, Kirk,' she whispered, standing transfixed.

He raved on. 'I've no guarantee that I'm the father, after all. God knows who could've been through you, the whole male population of the district for all I know. And anyway how *can* you be up the clout? You always told me you took precautions.'

'Something must've gone wrong,' Minnie mumbled.

'I'll bet it did. Gone wrong intentionally. Well, if you think you're going to nail me with this brat you say you're carrying, you've another think coming.'

He stumbled to the bottle and poured himself another, slopping quite a bit on the floor in the process.

'Now get out!' he said, reeling where he stood.

For the space of a few seconds Minnie stood staring at Kirk. Finally she said, 'May God forgive you for tonight because I never will.'

Then with great dignity she walked from the flat, pulling the outside door quietly closed behind her.

Kirk stumbled through to his bed and fell across it. 'I'll never marry hairy Mary,' he muttered thickly. 'It's the Gibb lassie for me.'

His snoring filled the room.

When Susan returned from the hospital she found her parents waiting up for her. She knew right away from her father's flushed face he'd been drinking more than usual.

'The doctor told Kirk he'll carry a scar for the rest of his life,' she said accusingly.

'Marriage with him is, as your mother said earlier, *completely* out of the question,' Keith thundered. 'Can't you see that?'

'You'd live to regret it, dear,' Jean said, a pleading tone in her voice.

Keith went on. 'Nigel is such a nice boy ...'

'I'm not disputing that,' Susan cut in. 'But it's Kirk I happen to love.'

'Love!' Keith spat scornfully. 'What do you know about love at your age!'

Susan coloured a little. 'I'm not a child any more ...'

'Then stop behaving like one.'

'I would say you were the one doing that, Father.'

His hand flashed to crack against her cheek. Crying out, Susan staggered backwards.

'I won't be spoken to like that by anyone, far less you,' Keith said.

'Perhaps you'd like to take your swagger stick to me as well?'

'Susan!' Jean warned.

'I never realised before tonight what a bully you really are. That and selfish through and through.'

Keith advanced a step, his face suffused with anger.

'When I think of everything we've done for you ...'

'Like what?'

'You've had nothing but the best in life.'

'Oh sure! Except my parents when I needed them.'

'Don't talk nonsense,' Jean said guiltily.

'You abandoned me when I was four years old. Twice I saw you, twice only between then and the beginning of the war.'

'It was unavoidable,' Jean said. 'Your Daddy was in the army ...'

'My "Daddy" wanted a boy. What he didn't want to know was me.'

'That's just not true,' Keith said.

'When have you ever shown any affection for me? When have you ever shown you loved me? Well, I'll tell you. Never! Not once!'

At long last the dam had well and truly burst and all the bitter years of loneliness and frustration came pouring out. Tears ran down Susan's face washing her make-up away. Her eyes took on a peculiar staring quality.

'Neither your mother nor I are particularly demonstrative,' Keith said. 'You must have realised that.'

'You managed to be demonstrative with one another, all right. It was only when it came to me that you were suddenly unable to be.'

'We did, and still do, love you very much,' Jean said.

'Then why did you never tell me?'

Jean hung her head in shame.

Susan rounded on Keith. 'And the only real interest you've ever taken in me is since I've met Nigel. And why is that, I ask? As if I didn't know.'

'He's the perfect match for you,' Keith said.

'You mean his money and assets are the perfect match for ours.'

'Think of the children you'll have. Think of the marvellous position they'll be in,' Keith urged.

'And what about *me*? Don't I count?'

Keith threw up his hands in exasperation. 'Everything was all right until this Kirk Murray appeared!'

'You'll break your father's heart if you don't marry Nigel,' Jean said softly.

'Both you and he broke mine often enough when I was a child.'

Jean had no answer to that.

Susan continued. 'I like Nigel well enough and if Kirk hadn't happened along I no doubt would have married him. But I did meet Kirk and love him, and no one, not you,

Mother, nor you Father, is going to make me give him up. As far as I'm concerned he's the only decent thing that's happened to me in this life and I have no intention of sacrificing what we've got together merely to further Father's family ambition.'

All Keith had dreamed of since Susan met Nigel was collapsing round him. He just couldn't believe it was actually happening.

'We gave you everything,' he said in a piqued tone of voice.

'You gave me pocket money and Miss Buchan's School For Young Ladies,' Susan replied.

Jean was crying as Susan left the room.

Kirk groaned as he came awake. His mouth felt like a sand-pit and his head was filled with cotton wool inside which someone was playing a big bass drum.

'Christ!' he said, sitting up. He had a thirst on him he felt the entire Clyde wouldn't slake.

It was his own fault, of course. He shouldn't have forgotten the nurse's warning about taking alcohol on top of the pills.

Then he remembered Minnie's visit and slowly, in bits and pieces, what had been said came back to him.

Groaning again, he buried his head in his hands. First the Major fiasco and how he'd gone and bombed out Minnie. Not that he gave a monkey's about her but if he was to lose Harry Hydelman because of it then his entire business would vanish down the plughole virtually overnight.

He mustn't let that happen without at least trying to save the situation. He'd explain to Minnie about the pills and how, combined with the alcohol, they'd put him out of his mind. He'd tell her he hadn't known what he was saying. Anything, as long as it gave him a chance to continue stringing her along until Harry was due to return to the States. The kid was going to be a problem but that was something he'd worry about once he was reconciled with Min.

He washed some aspirin down with tea which made him feel fractionally better. Then he set about getting dressed, not an easy task, feeling the way he did and with a bandaged hand to boot.

Minnie's elder sister Irene answered his knock. 'Is Min home?' he asked, forcing a smile on to his face.

Irene looked daggers. 'Aye, she is. Away ben.'

Minnie was in bed, with her mother, Judy, sitting on a chair beside her.

'Oh, it's you,' Judy said scornfully.

'Is she having a long lie or something?' Kirk asked.

At the sound of Kirk's voice Minnie's eyes flickered open. Slowly she turned her head to stare at the wall.

'I'm sorry about last night,' Kirk said. 'I'd taken these pills at the hospital you see and . . .'

'You meant every word you said. I could see it in your face,' Minnie said.

'That's not true. Honest!'

'Don't lie, Kirk. Not ever again.'

'Hairy Mary?' Judy said. 'Oh, you sod!'

'Listen, about the baby . . .'

'There is no baby now,' Minnie said, tears welling from her eyes.

'But you said . . .'

'There was one last night. But not this morning.'

'She went to an abortionist,' Irene said from the doorway.

'Oh, God Almighty!' Kirk said, holding his head which was still throbbing violently.

'The first we knew of it was when she came home bleeding like a stuck pig. I know well the butcher she went to and it's a wonder she survived,' Judy said.

'He uses a knitting needle,' Irene added.

Kirk felt sick then. Bile rose in his throat but he managed to swallow it down again.

'Is there anything I can do?' he asked.

'It cost a fiver,' Judy said.

'I don't want his rotten money. Let him stuff it,' Minnie said vehemently.

'It's the least I can do,' he said fumbling for his wallet.

'I tell you, I don't want it!' Minnie yelled, half rising from the bed. With a sob she fell back again.

'There, there, lass,' said Judy.

'It's all a horrible mistake,' said Kirk.

Minnie wiped tears from her eyes. 'I never ever want to see you again. Do you understand?'

'You'll change your mind. You're naturally fraught,' Kirk replied hopefully.

'No. You and I are finished. Just the thought of you ever laying your hands on me again makes me want to vomit.'

'All right then. I'll go.'

'And don't ever come back! As far as I'm concerned, from now on in you're as dead as the wean that man howked out of me.'

Having said that, Minnie pulled the blankets over her head and gave herself over to her grief.

At the door Kirk handed Irene two fivers. 'To pay for the abortionist,' he said.

Irene handed one of the fivers back and without saying anything further shut the door in his face.

He walked downstairs to stop at the close mouth. What a bloody shambles! Yesterday he had everything, today ...

I must ring Harry, he thought. Maybe I can still salvage something out of all this.

But knowing how thick Harry and Judy were, he didn't hold out much hope.

They met in a café not far from the base where they'd met several times previously. Kirk arrived first and had already got through two cups of coffee by the time Harry showed, dead on three o'clock as agreed.

'Now what's the panic?' Harry demanded once he'd got himself a coffee and sat down facing Kirk.

'It's about Min and I,' Kirk replied, and went on to tell Harry a version of what had happened.

Harry listened attentively while puffing on a stogie he'd lit up. During the entire story his eyes never once left Kirk's face.

As Kirk talked he sweated, under the arms and between his legs. His stomach felt as though there was a pound of lead sitting on it.

'So there we are then,' he said, coming to the end of his tale.

'A bad business,' Harry said.

Kirk nodded.

Carefully Harry knocked ash into the ashtray. 'So why come all the way out here to tell me? What's your reason, Kirk?'

'I want to know how this affects us. Judy and you being so close and all.'

'Hell, shit! She's just a handy piece of ass as far as I'm concerned. There's certainly nothing she would say to me would affect what you and I have got going.'

A tidal wave of relief surged through Kirk. Grinning, he said, 'And there I thought it was love between you two.'

'That's what she thinks as well,' Harry smiled. His smile broadened when he added, 'Truth is, I wanted to dump her a few months back but decided against it, thinking it might upset you in some way. You see I thought *you* were in love with Minnie. The real thing, wedding bells and all that horse manure.'

'You thought ... ?'

'I guess we were both wrong,' Harry said.

Kirk sat back in his chair and shook his head. 'Bloody hell!' he said.

Harry continued, 'So now you've split with Min that leaves me free to give Judy the heave. You see, I got the sweetest little soldier lady back at the base. A real hot momma who just can't get enough of ole Harry here!'

'So things can go on between us just as they have been?'

'Darned tooting, kid. Darned tooting!'

This was unbelievable luck, Kirk thought. Just when he'd thought everything was lost the tables had turned and he'd come out ahead – for that's how he saw getting rid of Minnie.

Of course, he was still losing, as far as the Major and Black Lion Brewery were concerned, but he'd just have to live with that for the moment. The important thing was the whisky fiddle was still secure and in the short-term that mattered above all else.

He felt a tinge of regret that the child was gone; he rather fancied himself as a father, but what the hell! There was plenty of time ahead of him for babies. Ones that Susan would give him.

And now that Min was off the scene there was no reason from his point of view why he and Susan couldn't get married more or less right away.

Of course this went totally against all the plans he'd had in that direction but it was just impossible for him to carry those out after his scene with the Major and Mrs Gibb.

He'd put it to Susan first chance he got, he decided, which turned out to be sooner than he'd imagined. When he got back to the flat, she and several suitcases were on the doorstep waiting for him.

She'd left home, and come to move in.

'It's working out a treat,' Kirk said, closing the books his mother kept on the running of the pub.

Lizzie folded her arms under her substantial bosom. 'I enjoy it. As does your dad not having any worries other than managing the bar.'

'Good,' he nodded.

'Mind you, I am a wee bit disappointed.'

'In what way?'

'We're doing well but not as well as I thought we would've.'

'And why's that?' he asked.

'It's that pub, the Belle Vale, round the corner. Because they're so close to the subway station they get all the people coming home from their work. Friday nights between six and eight that place is a wee gold mine.'

'Is that a fact?' Kirk said thoughtfully.

'If we could just get that trade our figures would be up fifty to seventy-five per cent at the end of the week. But there's no hope of that, I suppose. After all, the Corporation's hardly likely to move the subway just to oblige us!'

Kirk laughed with his mother. 'Hardly!' he agreed. 'But then if the mountain can't come to Muhammad, then it might just be possible for Muhammad to go to it.'

'I don't follow you, son.'

'Is the pub brewery owned or independent?'

'Independent,' she replied.

Kirk smiled. 'Well you know the old saying, if you can't beat them join them. Or better still take them over.'

'They'd never sell,' Lizzie replied, pursing her lips.

'You never know until you ask them, do you?' Kirk said. And left it at that.

He waited till early Friday evening before paying a visit to the Belle Vale and it was just as Lizzie had said. The place was packed to the gunnels, with the four barmen on duty working flat out.

He left, to return early Saturday morning, ordering a soft drink and asking to see the owner, who turned out to be a Mr Muir.

'What can I do for you?' Muir asked. Although well on his way to seed he still had a hard look about him.

Kirk introduced himself and shook Muir's hand. Then, coming directly to the point, he made a gesture which took in the Belle Vale.

'I was wondering if you'd be interested in selling?' he asked.

Muir shook his head. 'Not a hope. I like the place fine.'

'I'd give you a good price.'

'The answer's still no.'

Muir stood up to walk away but Kirk restrained him by placing his bandaged hand on his arm.

'Why don't you think it over? There's no harm in that.'

'The answer's still going to be no, Jim, even if I think it over till kingdom come. Now do you mind? I've got work to be getting on with.'

Pity, Kirk thought as Muir strode away. For now he would have to send in Turk McGhie.

On the previous night he'd decided he was going to have this place.

212

*

It was just after closing time and Muir was out the back of the pub stacking crates of empties for the early morning pick-up. He looked up as a figure loomed out of the darkness.

'Mr Muir?'

'Aye, what is it?'

Muir screamed as the bicycle chain wrapped itself round his head. He screamed again when the chain was savagely jerked, causing its many sharp edges to rip his face to shreds.

He fell to his knees, desperately tearing at the chain. Breath whooshed out of him as the boot went into his kidneys. Knocked off balance, he fell forward to land sprawling in a puddle.

Many men would have been finished then but Muir wasn't. Blinded by blood and chain he none the less rolled over and tried to climb back to his feet.

He grunted as his legs were kicked from under him and again he fell sprawling into the puddle. A hand grabbed the hair on the back of his head and pushed. His nose and mouth went under water.

Just when he thought he was going to lapse into unconsciousness his head was pulled clear of the water and life-giving air rushed into his lungs. The effect was to make him cough and splutter.

A voice in his ear said, 'This is only the start. Things can get a lot worse, I promise you. We'll wreck your pub, drive your customers away, and with my razor here I could carve your bonnie wife just like a Christmas chicken. And if you went to the polis, well ... nothing would happen for a while like and then she'd just disappear one day. For ever. Get my meaning?'

Muir nodded.

'Good. So why don't you just save yourself all that trouble by talking sensibly to my friend Mr Murray when he calls to see you again? He's the one who wants to buy the Belle Vale, remember?'

Muir nodded again.

'He'll give you a fair price so you can buy another boozer

elsewhere. It's just that he's decided he wants the Belle Vale for himself. Understand?'

'Yes,' Muir croaked.

'Right then,' Turk said.

And to make sure the point was fully driven home Turk drew back his foot and kicked Muir full in the testicles.

Muir was howling and scrabbling on the filthy ground as Turk faded back into the night.

'You've got to carry me over the doorstep,' Susan said. 'It's traditional.'

'Bloody hell!' exclaimed Kirk. 'Carry a big fat lump like you!'

'Beast!' replied Susan, laughing.

'You haven't even begun to see the beast in me, Mrs Murray. That comes once we're inside and I can have my wicked way with you.'

'Oooh!' she said, pretending to be frightened. 'I think I might like that.'

He swung her into his arms and kissed her first before carrying her into the house. Once inside he unceremoniously dumped her into a chair.

'Now, how about some of that champagne I paid an absolute fortune for?' he asked.

'Yes, please.'

He popped the cork off the ceiling and then proceeded to pour more champagne over the floor than he actually got into the glasses.

'Some publican you are,' Susan sniffed.

'Champagne isn't my normal line. I'm more used to pouring pints of heavy,' he retorted.

'Then we'll have to ensure there's more champagne from here on in.'

'Damn right!' he said.

He handed her a glass. 'To us!' he toasted.

'To us!'

He sipped appreciatively, absolutely adoring champagne.

'Are you upset your folks didn't come?' he asked.

'I didn't expect them to. Did you?'

He shook his head.

'They'll get over it. In time.'

Kirk's eyes glittered. 'I don't think so somehow. To put it mildly, they hate my guts.'

'I thought it was nice of Nigel to send a telegram to the registry office.'

'Maybe we should have had a church wedding, but with your folks acting the way they've been, a ceremony in the registry office seemed the best thing in the circumstances.'

'The main thing is we're married,' Susan said. 'That's all I wanted.'

'Me too.'

He poured more champagne and then, kneeling beside her, said, 'Bed?'

'But it isn't even noon yet!'

'Spoken like a good Protestant,' he said.

She uncurled herself from the chair and stood up, drawing him with her. 'I love you,' she said simply.

'And I love you too.'

He led her to the bedroom, his mind already on the appointment he had later that afternoon when he was to sign the final papers transferring ownership of the Belle Vale to him.

He'd done down the Major and acquired his second pub at a rock-bottom price all in one day!

Starting to undress Susan, he thought that what he was about to do to her wasn't the only screwing he excelled at.

'That's it then,' said Harry Hydelman. 'I fly back Stateside middle of next week.'

Kirk sighed. It had been a damn good run and now it was over. The shipment of whisky Harry had just delivered was the last one.

He opened a bottle and poured them both a stiff one. 'We couldn't have gone on much longer, anyway,' he said. 'More and more whisky's being made available. A few more months and who knows? The publicans and the punters might well be able to get as much as they want just for the asking.'

'It's good to take it philosophically,' Harry said.

Kirk stared into his drink. He had an Alfa, a house and four pubs. What did he have to complain about? And the pubs were coining it in for him. Jesus, but they were money-spinners!

He and Harry talked for a little while longer and then Harry took his leave.

'Goodbye, kid,' Harry said at the door.

'Goodbye, Hank the Yank.'

He closed the door and Harry Hydelman went out of his life.

Another week, he thought, and that would be the end of his spirit business. He grinned, thinking Harry had never found out about the deal he had going with Carswell's Distillery.

Harry might have made on their fiddle, but he'd made an awful lot more.

He picked up the latest letter he'd received from the Army and read it through again. For over a year now he'd been successfully using one excuse after another to postpone his call-up. He would have considered it an unmitigated disaster to have had to go while Harry was still in Britain.

But with Harry now going home there was no reason for him to keep up his delaying tactics. He'd notify the Army in a fortnight's time and let events take their course from there. It was a real bitch that he had to go but since the Army medic had logged him A1 fit he'd known it was inevitable.

He'd put his mother in overall charge of his pubs while he was away. She'd see no fast ones were pulled on him by any of his managers or staff. And if anyone tried, well . . . there would be Turk McGhie to back her up.

He made a mental note to increase Turk's wages. He needed the hard man's loyalty while he was away and as far as he was concerned nothing secured loyalty better than money.

'You'll write to me as soon as you can?' Susan said, dabbing at her tears with a handkerchief.

'The first moment I get. I promise.'

'Oh Kirk, I'll miss you.'

'I should get leave after basic training and anyway two years isn't for ever.'

'At this moment it seems like it.'

He held her close and whispered in her ear, 'I know what it is you'll be missing most. Old Henry one eye.'

'Don't be crude,' she said. But his joke had brought a smile to her face.

'Now away with you. And I'll write the first moment I get.'

He kissed her and then propelled her from him. He gave her a wave before turning abruptly into the door of the assembly point. He reported to a sergeant who told him gruffly to sit down. He chose a bench on which a solitary figure sat hunched.

The figure straightened and lit a cigarette.

'I know you,' Kirk said. 'But I can't put my finger on it for the moment.'

Eddy King smiled. 'I sold you an Alfa Romeo. How's it going?'

Recognition flooded Kirk's face. 'The Alfa, of course. It's still going well.'

'Glad to hear it.'

They shook hands and reintroduced themselves.

'It's good to see a friendly face in a situation like this,' Kirk said.

'Aye, it is that,' Eddy agreed.

Susan walked away from the assembly point looking neither left nor right. She might have been a zombie or a robot.

She didn't know how long she walked for but suddenly she was aware she was standing outside a teashop. She went inside and sat at a table.

'A pot of tea and a cake please,' she said to the waitress.

She looked at the faces around her and saw nothing. All she could think of was that Kirk had gone away and for most of the next two years she was going to be on her own again.

She was still attending college, which would help fill the days and her mind. But the nights. Oh, the terrible nights that lay ahead of her.

The loneliness she remembered only too well from her childhood settled back on her, causing her shoulders to sag a little.

Without Kirk's presence and lovemaking it would be as though she was dead. For these two things were very life-blood to her.

Rising, she made her way through to the toilet where, once in the cubicle, and having locked the door behind her, she bent down into a squatting position.

She threw up into the bowl.

KIRK AND EDDY

'Mean by name and mean by nature,' the corporal spat, drawing himself up to his full five feet two inches. His eyes, like something out of the reptile house, swept round the room taking in everyone and everything.

'We've got a right one here,' Kirk muttered to Eddy who was standing beside him.

'Silence!' Corporal Meany bellowed. 'Anyone utter again and I'll have all your guts for garters.' He paused before adding spitefully, 'And maybe I'll have them anyway. Just to keep in practice, like.'

Stiff-legged, he stalked forward. The men of his previous section had given him a nickname. They'd called him the meanest poison dwarf of all. It summed him up precisely.

There were eight in the section and they'd all just arrived in from Scotland, having completed their basic training. Billeted at Schloss – which is to say 'castle' – Schwartzberg, they now formed part of the BAOR, or British Army of the Rhine.

Meany stopped in front of a soldier. 'Name?'

'McKenzie, sir.'

'You're a horrible shite of a man, McKenzie. Know that?'

'Yes sir.'

'Now what are you?'

'A horrible shite of a man, sir.'

'Good.' Then very softly, 'And don't you ever forget it.'

Meany passed the next man and then stopped at the next. 'Your name?'

'Napier, sir.'

'You sound Edinburgh.'

'I am, sir.'

Meany grinned. 'Well you must be a poof then. Only poofs ever come out of Edinburgh.'

A man laughed.

'Shut up!' Meany screamed.

The man stopped laughing instantly and swallowed hard.

Meany turned his attention back to Napier. 'What did you do in civvy street? I take it you are a conscript?'

'Yes, sir. I was a musician, sir. Played clarinet.'

'Clarinet, eh? So I was right. You are a poof.'

'No sir.'

'Are you contradicting me?'

'No sir. I'm only ...'

'Only what?'

Napier started to look scared. 'I'm not a poof, sir,' he said in a voice that was little above a whisper.

Meany brought his face to within inches of Napier's. 'If I say you're the fucking abominable snowman then the abominable snowman you are,' he hissed.

Napier nodded.

Meany moved on.

'Now what have we here?' Meany said, stopping in front of Eddy. 'Name?'

'King, sir.'

'King, is it? Not Dunphy or O'Toole or O'Houlihan?'

Eddy stared straight ahead, not rising to the bait.

Meany went on. 'The map of Ireland written all over your face. A Mick, is it? A Fenian? A fucking left-footer?' He waited a few seconds and then screamed, 'Well?'

'I am a Catholic, sir.'

'Aaahhh!' breathed Meany. 'One of those. Well, well, well.'

Pursing his mouth, Meany walked round to the side of Eddy's bed where his kit was stacked.

'Show it to me. I don't want to touch it,' Meany said.

Eddy did as he was bid. Holding each piece of kit up for inspection.

'Dirty,' Meany said. 'Dirty ... dirty ... dirty ... dirty ...'

Meany drew in a deep breath. 'Your entire kit's dirty, King. Almost crawling, you could say.'

With a sudden motion his arm swept sideways to send Eddy's kit clattering over the bare wooden boards that comprised the floor.

Meany grinned viciously. 'You have an hour, soldiers. When I come back I want to see your kit shining, and I mean shining. And of course the floor will be filthy now, thanks to King's kit contaminating it, so that will have to be cleaned. You, King, that will be your responsibility. Floor and kit for you. Kit for the rest of you.'

He paused and his grin grew even wider. 'One hour. Precisely.'

Humming jauntily, he strode from the room, slamming the door behind him.

The men slumped where they stood.

'Welcome to Germany,' Napier said.

'That man's unbelievable,' McKenzie said.

Norrie Smart nodded his agreement.

'I suppose we'd better get on with it,' Kirk said.

Eddy looked in dismay at his kit strewn across the floor. He was thinking of his father and Gloag and praying history wasn't about to repeat itself.

'I'll never get all this done in time,' he said.

'Yes you will,' Kirk said. 'We'll divide your kit amongst the rest of us which will only leave you with the floor.'

'Hold on a minute,' Pete Rennie said. 'I don't see why in the hell I should help him out.'

Eddy blushed. 'I'll do it all myself then.'

'No, no!' Kirk said, waiting till the full attention of the section was focused on him. He then went on.

'The way I see it is this. We've been unlucky to draw a first-class bastard for corporal. Well, that's tough on us. But if we don't all pull together as a unit it'll be even tougher. One for all and all for one like the musketeers, that should be our motto. Because you see, Rennie, it might be Eddy here just now but

223

who's to say who it'll be next week? It might be you, pal. Or you McKenzie or you Kirkwood.'

'I think what you say makes sense,' said Napier. 'I'm certainly willing to help Eddy if he helps me. If Meany doesn't like Catholics, he certainly doesn't like Edinburgh folk either.'

'One for all and all for one,' Smart said approvingly.

'Well?' Kirk demanded.

Napier nodded. 'I think maybe you're right.'

'I *know* I'm right.'

'Let's get on with it then,' Ogle said, picking up a piece of Eddy's gear. 'Time's a-wasting.'

The men galvanised into action, Eddy hurriedly starting to change before making for where the buckets and hot water were kept.

In the midst of all this, Ogle said suddenly. 'Tell me, Napier, are you really a poof or do you just walk that way natural, like?'

'Get me a bird and I'll show you whether I'm bent or not!' Napier retorted.

Everyone burst into laughter.

On time to the minute the door to the room opened and Meany strode in. He came up short and his eyes slitted when he saw the men were standing to attention by their beds.

The inspection was thorough, done by an obvious expert.

'Hmm!' said Meany, grudging approval in his tone, when it was all over.

The men stood rigid, staring straight ahead. Not a muscle moved or eyeball flickered.

'When did you last sleep?' he asked Smart.

'Over twenty-four hours ago, sir.'

'Well then, big hard men like you won't be tired yet, will you?'

Smart wasn't sure whether to reply or not.

'Will you?' Meany barked.

'No sir.'

'I'm glad to hear it. Because in an hour and a half we leave on all-night patrol. I suggest you get yourselves something to eat in the meantime. You're going to need it.'

Chuckling he quit the room.

'Bastard!' said Smart.

'But an NCO,' Kirk said.

Muttering and grumbling, the section left for the cookhouse where Sergeant McQuarrie – affectionately known as the Glasgow poisoner – held sway.

The pine forest was dark as the inside of a coal bin. In single file, with Meany in the lead, the section moved forward.

'I can't see a bloody thing,' Eddy whispered.

'You're not alone,' Kirk's voice came whispering back out of the blackness.

'Damn!' said Ogle, who'd just fallen over a tree stump.

'Quiet!' Meany's voice scythed through the night air from ahead.

Eddy's eyes were drooping and his eyelids felt as though there were grains of sand under them. It was bitterly cold, which was affecting him even more than it normally would have done, due to lack of sleep.

The thought uppermost in his mind was that if they didn't get a break soon he'd drop in his tracks. And he shuddered to think what Meany would do to him should that happen.

Soon the trees started to thin and then they disappeared altogether. The section found themselves moving along hillside with thick bracken underfoot.

The moon was a pale sliver high in the sky. The clouds were low, many and scudding in the biting wind that had sprung up.

Meany stopped and waited till the section had come alongside him. Using his sten he pointed to a clump of trees several hundred yards away.

'The boundary between us and the Russian sector,' he said. 'Cross over and you'll have Ivan breathing down your neck *tout de suite*.'

All in, the men leaned on their rifles. Breaths rasped as they tried to catch their wind.

'Not tired, are we?' Meany taunted in a low voice. He was

still fresh, thanks to the full eight hours he'd had the previous night coupled with the fact he was used to this patrol having been doing it for the past eighteen months.

The men kept silent, deeming that the best policy.

Meany chuckled. 'Only another couple of miles and then I'll let you have a smoke. All right?'

Kirk, who was closest, nodded.

'Then let's go.'

To try and keep himself awake Eddy thought of Annie Grimes as he walked. A smile came to his face as he remembered the good times they'd had together. He didn't think he was ever going to find another woman like her.

Kirk was idly thinking about Susan, wondering how she was getting on.

He'd been home on leave the previous week, a forty-eight hour pass and his first since coming into the Army, which had been marred by Susan being down with a bad attack of the flu.

That had been a big disappointment to him as he'd been looking forward eagerly to those two days. She'd told him to go out and enjoy himself, but apart from checking round his pubs, which were all doing very nicely thank you, and having a few drinks here and there, he hadn't bothered.

When he left her her face was still all puffed up, her nose red and streaming. A repulsive sight, he'd thought, but had naturally refrained from saying so.

The worst thing of all was he hadn't been able to have sex with her. She had offered but quite frankly she was in such a state it would have been a form of sadism, and masochism on his part, to have gone ahead with it.

He couldn't remember when he'd been so randy and couldn't wait to get amongst the Kraut fräuleins, or 'frats', as he'd heard they were called.

One thing was certain. Irregardless of what he'd said to Susan, he wasn't going to be going without while he was over here. The very idea was ludicrous. If he had to be in Germany then he was damn well going to make the best of it ...

There was a secluded dip in a hollow and this was where

Meany led them. From beyond the dip could be heard the sound of running water.

'We'll have a brew up,' Meany said, slumping to the ground. 'Ogle, you go up to the top there and watch. I'll have your char brought to you. Napier, you go down to the burnie over by and fill the kettle.'

There was a rattle and then a clank as a small kettle came tumbling over the ground to land at Napier's feet.

'All the comforts of home,' Meany added.

With a sigh, Eddy sank on to his backside. He couldn't remember when he'd been so whacked.

'King? What do you think you're doing?'

Eddy was instantly wary. 'Taking a break, Corporal.'

'Wrong, Mick. You've got a job to do.'

Eddy struggled to his feet. He was coming to hate Meany albeit their acquaintance had been a short one to date.

'What do you want me to do, Corporal?'

Meany took his time lighting a cigarette. He sighed with satisfaction as he blew smoke into the air.

'I want you to cross that burnie and report back to me what's on the other side.'

'What sort of thing am I looking for, Corporal?'

Meany smiled in the darkness. 'I've been wondering for some time whether or not the Ruskies have mined the far bank. Now seems as good a time as any to find out.'

Eddy's mouth went dry. 'Mines?'

'Aye. You know the things? When you step on them they go bang.'

Eddy wasn't at all sure whether Meany was having him on or not, playing games with him.

'That's a direct order,' Meany said softly.

'Right then, Corporal,' Eddy replied, now very wide awake.

'Then get on with it.'

Meany closed his eyes and lay back. 'Murray and Rennie can make the fire,' he added as an afterthought.

Eddy glanced at Kirk, who looked back sympathetically. Hefting his rifle he headed for the burn.

He found Napier just straightening up having filled the kettle. 'I've to go for a walk on the other side to see if it's mined,' he said.

'The man's a bloody headcase,' Napier replied.

Eddy couldn't have agreed more.

He stared at the burn, realising with a shock it was more than that. It wasn't exactly a river but neither was it a burn. Fast-flowing, it had the breadth of a British canal.

He went in tentatively, feeling with his feet to see what sort of bottom it had. Holding his rifle above his head he waded out towards the middle.

The water came up to mid-thigh and then stopped. The surface beneath his feet was still fairly solid as he continued across.

Then it happened. His right foot came down, only instead of being arrested it continued going down and down. With a muffled cry he pitched forward.

Water closed over his head as he sank feet first. Despite his alarm he had wits enough to hang on to his rifle.

He kicked for the surface, using his free hand to make a doggy-paddle sort of movement. He gasped in a huge lungful of air as his head broke water.

The flow of water carried him a few yards by which time he was able to reach out and grab hold of the grassy bank. Digging his fingers in, he managed to drag himself up on to the bank where he collapsed, coughing and spluttering.

When he'd caught his breath he'd have given anything for a cigarette but his packet was sodden. He cursed through clenched teeth.

He allowed a few minutes to go by before coming to his feet. Carefully keeping close to the bank he walked upstream. As far as he was concerned, this bank was as far as he was going. He found the broken branch of a tree which he used to test the depth of the water for nearly a hundred yards upstream, from where he'd landed. But nowhere was the water as shallow as it had been on the other side. Finally he decided there was nothing else for it but to swim back across to where the water became shallow again.

He slung his rifle round his shoulders before sitting on the bank. He submerged his feet in the water and then sort of slipped and slid in. He struck out strongly, doing the breaststroke. In less than a minute he was clambering to his feet, having come again into shallow water.

'Dear, dear me,' said Meany when he saw the dripping and bedraggled Eddy looming out of the darkness. 'And what happened to you, soldier?'

'Nobody told me your burnie was deep at the far end,' Eddy replied.

'Is that a fact?' Meany said, pretending to be surprised. 'I'll have to make a mental note of that for future reference.'

'Were there any mines over there?' Smart demanded eagerly. Intellectually he was the complete opposite to his name.

'Oh aye, hundreds and thousands of them,' Eddy replied sarcastically. 'Didn't you hear them going off?'

'Oh!' said Smart. The penny dropping.

'How far over the other side did you go?' Meany asked casually.

Eddy squatted by the small fire and tried to warm himself. His teeth were chattering.

'I went up and down a hundred yards and in about a hundred feet,' he lied smoothly.

'So we can safely say it isn't mined,' Meany said.

'Or else he was lucky,' Kirkwood added.

'Are we all going over?' McKenzie asked anxiously. The last thing he wanted being to end up soaked through like Eddy.

'Here,' said Kirk putting a steaming mug of tea into Eddy's hands.

'No we're not,' said Meany, replying to McKenzie's question as he rose to his feet. 'And there's no time for that now, King,' he added. 'You can use it to put out the fire.'

Eddy trembled, and it wasn't from the cold either.

Kirk reached out to place a restraining hand on Eddy's arm. 'Do as the man says,' he said gently.

Eddy upended his mug, causing the small fire to expire in a billow of steam and angry hisses.

'Right then, single file as before,' Meany said. 'And I think we'd better double it up so King here doesn't catch cold. You look the delicate type to me – are you, King?'

'Not particularly, Corporal.'

'We'll double it up anyway. Nothing like getting the old blood coursing, especially on a cold morning like this.'

Clutching his sten in front of him, Meany led the way at a trot.

'Can you make it?' Kirk asked quietly.

'Do I have an alternative?'

Kirk grinned. 'That's the lad.'

'Besides, if I stood still I'd probably freeze to death.'

The rest of the section had now started after Meany.

'I'll bring up the rear,' Kirk said.

Unslinging his .303 Eddy followed the dim shape of Ogle while behind him the still overweight Kirk was soon puffing and panting.

Before long, the run began to take on a nightmare quality for Eddy. A cold, clammy perspiration appeared on his brow and his breath became harsh, like sandpaper, in his throat.

Weakness settled on him, sapping his strength and will. To combat it he thought again of Annie Grimes. Talking to her, laughing with her, the pair of them making love together. And when that was exhausted he thought back to his young days in Glasgow. Going guising at Halloween. Playing street-games of which there had been a multitude. The first time he'd kissed a lassie down a back close dunny.

He thought of his father, whom he'd idolised and whom that bastard Gloag had murdered for no other reason than his father was a Catholic. In his mind he tried to conjure up a picture of Gloag but the face he saw was Meany's. A man he hadn't even known existed until the previous day.

His feet pounded beneath him while his senses swam. He

knew he had a temperature and guessed he was either already delirious or else well on the way. The heat of his fevered body was causing his clothes to steam, the steam puffing off him in wisps and clouds.

From somewhere ahead a voice began to sing and amazingly was allowed to continue to do so. The voice was Norrie Smart's.

> *'Three German officers crossed the Rhine,*
> *Parlez-vous?*
> *Three German officers crossed the Rhine,*
> *Parlez-vous?*
> *Three German officers crossed the Rhine,*
> *Fucked the woman and drank the wine.*
> *Inki pinki parlez-vous?'*

Napier, in a most untuneful voice for a professional musician, sang the next verse.

> *'Oh landlord have you a daughter fair?*
> *Parlez-vous?*
> *Oh landlord have you a daughter fair?*
> *Parlez-vous?*
> *Oh landlord have you a daughter fair,*
> *With milk white tits and curly hair?*
> *Inki pinki parlez-vous?'*

Up ahead Meany started to laugh as it began to rain.

'Jesus Christ Allbloodymighty!' Kirkwood said, collapsing on his bed. 'I never ever want to go through the likes of that again.'

Eddy sat on the edge of his bed. He was wide-eyed and staring.

'The best thing is for us all to get stripped off and towelled down,' Kirk said, to which there were murmurs of agreement.

'See that Meany!' Ogle said. And a few of the section

laughed when he mimed strangling the corporal.

Kirk threw off his top clothes and then turned his attention to Eddy. 'Come on, let's be having you,' he said.

Eddy grinned weakly but didn't move.

'You feel as though you're burning up,' Kirk said, having felt Eddy's brow.

'Perhaps we should report him sick?' Ogle suggested.

Eddy shook his head. 'I won't give him the satisfaction. Just help me get into my kip, Kirk, and I'll be all right.'

'I have a couple of aspirins,' Pete Rennie said, crossing to his locker.

Kirk helped Eddy strip down to the buff. Then, using a thick coarse towel, he rubbed Eddy vigorously from head to toe. Eddy stood as though in a dream, shivering and occasionally shaking. Even after the rub-down his flesh was still bluish and mottled.

Kirk assisted Eddy into pyjamas after which Eddy gulped down the aspirins Rennie handed him.

'Bed and sleep,' Kirk said.

Eddy's head touched the pillow and his eyes closed. Before Kirk had finished drawing the bedclothes up over him he was snoring.

'Rise and shine, you horrible lot. Come on, out your stinking pits!' And walking down one line of beds, Meany pulled the covers from each. He repeated this when he walked up the opposite line of beds.

'Come on, come on, come one!' he yelled with relish. 'What do you lot think this is, a holiday camp or something?'

Eddy's eyes flickered open. His fever had gone, leaving him still weak, but apart from that he was all right. Constitution of a bloody horse, he told himself as he swung his legs out of bed.

Meany strode down the room to stand in front of Eddy. 'And how's our intrepid swimmer this morning?' he asked.

Eddy stared up at Meany, thinking of Gloag. 'Intrepid, Corporal? I'm afraid that's too big a word for me,' he replied.

Meany's eyes glinted. He knew he was being got at.

'A smart bastard, eh?' he hissed.

Eddy smiled. 'That's the point, Corporal. I'm not. I never had the advantages of education you've so obviously had.'

A hint of a red flush crept up Meany's neck. 'I went to the ragged school, sonny, where we knew how to deal with the likes of you.'

'I'll bet you did,' Eddy replied softly.

'Where I come from in Glasgow we had Catholics for breakfast,' Meany said.

'Where I come from in Glasgow we were lucky to *get* breakfast,' Eddy retorted.

'Oh, so you think yourself a bit of a hard man, do you?'

'Not me, Corporal. I leave that for the bampots and headcases. Life's hard enough without added aggravation.'

'You haven't even begun to understand what aggravation is, sonny.'

'Are you trying to tell me I'm about to find out, Corporal?' Eddy asked, a trace of insolence in his tone.

'I think you could take my word on that.'

Eddy nodded. The position was crystal clear.

Meany strode into the centre of the room. 'We go out on patrol every other night,' he said. 'Always covering the same ground we did last night and this morning. Understand?'

Smart grunted something in the affirmative.

'Now, it became obvious to me during last night's patrol that despite your basic you're all still soft. And it's going to be my task, indeed pleasure, to toughen up you load of namby-pamby jessies and poofs.'

He paused to puff out his chest and stride up and down a few steps before continuing.

'First off, I think we'll start with PT, as I'm sure you're all stiff after your wee stroll out there in the German countryside. So you've got forty minutes for ablutions and something to eat before reporting to me on the exercise yard. Right then, get to it!'

Heels drumming a tattoo on the wooden floorboards, he marched from the room.

'I wouldn't push him if I were you,' Kirk said to Eddy. 'Don't forget he's got the stripes up, which gives him the power of God as far as we're concerned.'

'Aye, I shouldn't let him rile me,' Eddy agreed.

'How are you feeling?'

'Well, not exactly fit to take on the world but an awful lot better than I was last night.'

'I really thought you were going to come down with pneumonia or something. You looked dreadful.'

'And I felt it too, I can assure you.'

Kirk fingered the scar on his cheek. It was something he often did when he was thinking. 'You were lucky,' he said.

'Lucky? To have been landed with a corporal like Meany? That's hardly what I'd call it.'

'You have a point there,' Kirk admitted, as side by side they headed for the ablutions.

'I hope there's hot water,' Eddy said.

There wasn't.

Punctual to the second, Meany strode on to the exercise yard. Like his section standing waiting for him, he was dressed for PT.

'Flat on your faces, you load of nancies,' he shouted. 'And we'll begin with push-ups. Thirty to start with and then in batches of twenty. And if any man stops before I give the order, he has to start all over again.'

Meany threw himself flat on the ground. 'Arms – raise!' he said. Then, counting out the push-ups, 'Hup ... hup ... hup ... hup ...

'All right, come to your feet and run on the spot.'

Kirk came slowly erect. Never an athletic person at the best of times, the push-ups had just about done for him.

Weak to start with, Eddy considered it a miracle he'd got through that first exercise. Gritting his teeth, he ran where he stood. He would drop before he gave in.

The exercises went on and on till finally, with a groan, Napier keeled over.

234

'Get up!' Meany screamed.

Napier shook his head. 'I can't Corporal. Honest!' he somehow managed to get out.

'The poofs always give in first,' Meany smirked to the rest of the section. 'No guts, you see. No stamina. No backbone.'

He paraded up and down in front of them. 'Now, look at me and you'll see a man and a soldier. And that's what this army's all about. Men and soldiers. Which, God help me, I'm supposed to turn you lot into.'

Smart reached down to help Napier back to his feet.

'What do you think you're doing?' Meany demanded.

'I just thought I'd ...'

'You're not here to think! You're here to do as you're told. What I tell you. That and nothing else! Understand?'

'Yes, Corporal.'

'And come to attention when you talk to me!'

Smart snapped to attention.

Napier dragged himself to his knees. His face had gone a pasty colour and veins stood out on his arms and legs.

'Smart!'

'Yes sir?'

'As you've got so much energy you may as well wear some of it off. Ten times round the exercise yard, starting *now*! Double time! Double time!'

Smart doubled off to sympathetic looks from the rest of the section.

'And what are we going to do with you, clarinet player?' Meany mused.

Napier climbed to his feet, his thin chest heaving.

'What a specimen,' Meany said scornfully. 'Typical Edinburgh, all pish and water.' Rounding suddenly on Kirkwood, he said, 'And just what do you think you're staring at?'

'Sorry sir. I didn't realise I was staring.'

'Well, you were, you nasty little shit. What are you?'

'A nasty little shit.'

'A nasty little shit, *sir*.'

'A nasty little shit, *sir*!' Kirkwood echoed.

'And don't you ever forget it!'

'No sir!'

Meany walked up and down in front of them several times and then glanced at his watch.

All eyes were on Smart as he doubled past.

'Faster! faster! faster!' Meany shrieked.

Smart positively sprinted on his way.

Meany turned to the rest of the section. 'You've got half an hour and then I want you on the training compound, kitted out for armed combat. Got that?'

'Yes sir!' the section chorused in unison.

'Attention!'

They came smartly to attention.

'Right turn. Dismiss!'

'Phew!' said Kirk when he and Eddy were out of range of Meany's hearing.

'Between last night's patrol and now this, I feel as though I've tangled with a road roller and lost,' Eddy said.

Kirk gave a small grin. 'I know exactly what you mean.'

A few minutes later, as they were changing, Kirk added, 'You know, that man's not only off his chump, he's downright bloody dangerous as well.'

'My da once met someone who I'm sure was just like Meany,' Eddy said, pausing and staring off into space.

'What happened?'

'He murdered my da.'

'God above!' exclaimed Kirk softly. 'Was he caught?'

'He paid the penalty all right,' Eddy replied in a peculiar tone of voice.

Kirk was fascinated by the strange expression on Eddy's face. It sent shivers up and down his spine, as though someone was walking across his grave.

Meany was already waiting for them when they arrived at the training ground, which was situated at the rear of the castle behind the kitchens and stores.

The castle itself was a towering Gothic edifice built on a sort of black rock, the latter giving it its name, Schwartzberg, meaning literally 'black mountain'. There was a magnificent view from the ramparts. On one side there was a sheer drop to a tree-studded valley, while on the other side a rolling plain stretched for several miles until it ran into tree-covered foothills. In the far distance there was the silver glint of water.

The road from the castle gates ran downward until it became the main thoroughfare of the small town of Welsdorp.

'Now, as you all know, this is a rifle,' Meany said, brandishing a .303. 'And this is a bayonet, the bayonet being affixed to the rifle so.'

There was a click as the bayonet slotted into place. Levelling the rifle, Meany brought the tip of his bayonet on to a level with Kirk's belly.

'I think I'll have you to start with, Murray,' Meany said.

Without taking his eyes off Meany, Kirk fixed his bayonet.

'That's a clever laddie. Now come at me.'

Kirk advanced tentatively.

'Not like that, you stupid great nana. Come at me like you meant it. Like you intended doing me some damage.'

Kirk's mouth twisted into a leer. That was going to be easy.

The two men circled one another, eyeball locked to eyeball. Suddenly, and shouting the way he'd been taught, Kirk lunged.

The bayonet stabbed forward, but where only moments before Meany had been standing there was now only empty air. Kirk stumbled by, grunting as the butt of Meany's rifle rapped him in the side.

'You're dead,' Meany said.

Kirk lumbered round, ready to have another go. But Meany waved him back to join the others.

'Now, how about you, Rennie? Let's see if you can do any better.'

Rennie couldn't, being, if anything, slower and more awkward than Kirk.

'Ivan would have you lot on toast,' Meany said scornfully. 'A bunch of bloody Girl Guides could do better.'

For a full five minutes Meany demonstrated, using Smart as an opponent and foil, the intricacies and techniques of the bayonet in close combat.

'Think you've got any of that?' he asked when he'd finished his demonstration. And when there was no reply, 'I said have you got that, you load of imbeciles!'

'Yes, sir, Corporal!' the section chorused.

'Well, let's see if you have then. King, step forward.'

Eddy fixed his bayonet and then stepped towards Meany.

Meany grinned. 'Now if there's one man in this section who looks as though he'd really like to use his sticker, it's you, Mick. Present!'

Eddy levelled his weapon, the tip of his bayonet about six feet from the tip of Meany's.

'Come on then, sonny Jim,' Meany said, crouching fractionally.

Eddy went in slowly. They circled one another, first one way and then the other.

Kirk and rest of the section looked on anxiously. During the last few minutes the atmosphere had changed to become taut and charged.

'Papishers, if I had my way I'd shoot the lot of them,' Meany whispered just loud enough for Eddy to hear. 'I've never yet met one who was worth a monkey's wank.'

Eddy blanked out what Meany was saying, keeping his concentration fixed on waiting for an opening. The tip of his bayonet wove a small figure of eight in the air in front of him.

'And they're usually cowards. Back stabbers,' Meany whispered.

Eddy lunged fractionally but didn't follow it through. Meany danced out of the way.

Meany was certainly quick on his feet, Eddy thought. The man would have been a big hit in the Locarno in Sauchiehall Street any Saturday night.

'What's the matter? Want me to tie a hand behind my back?' Meany whispered. And having said that, he laughed.

Eddy gritted his teeth. He was damned if he'd be drawn. Let the bastard come to him.

'*One, two, three, O'Leary, I saw Wallace Beery,*
Sitting on his bumbeleree, kissing Shirley Temple-O!' Meany sang, and waggled his rifle.

Eddy started to circle again, his concentration homed on Meany's eyes.

'What's the matter? Don't you want to play?' Meany whispered.

Eddy didn't reply, biding his time. As far as he was concerned he could go on like this just as long as it took.

Irritation flashed across Meany's face. He was beginning to get annoyed.

'Come on, you stupid Mick,' Meany said.

Eddy went back to making a figure eight pattern with the tip of his bayonet. He could see his continued silence and refusal to make the first move was getting through to Meany.

'Oh all right then!' Meany said, straightening up and bringing his rifle into a vertical position.

Heaving a sigh of relief, Eddy brought his .303 into the same position, which was a mistake. Too late, he realised Meany had conned him.

'Ha!' cried Meany jubilantly, viciously swinging the butt of his rifle round and lunging forward at the same time.

Breath whooshed out of Eddy as the rifle butt took him full in the kidneys. He pitched to the ground when the rifle barrel smashed across the back of his neck.

He hit the ground with a jarring thump, his own rifle flying from his hands to clatter away. He was trying to struggle on to his knees when the cold metal of Meany's bayonet came to rest against his right cheek. He immediately froze.

'You're dead, King. What are you?' Meany said.

'Dead, Corporal.'

'In combat never ever trust the enemy. No matter what he does or says. Anything could be a feint or ruse to give him the advantage. And once he gets that you end up just so much meat. Got all that into your thick skull?'

'Yes.'

'Yes, *sir*!' Meany screamed and lashed out with his foot.

Eddy groaned as Meany's foot smashed into his side. For a brief instant he saw red and an awesome fury started to envelop him. But luckily, before the fury could overcome him, he remembered Kirk's words about the corporal's stripes making the man God as far as they were concerned. Biting his lip, he brought himself back under control.

'Well?' Meany demanded.

'Yes, *sir*,' Eddy croaked.

'Now stand up.'

Slowly Eddy came to his feet.

'Pick up that rifle.'

Eddy did as he was bid.

'Let me see it.'

Eddy handed the rifle over.

'This is filthy, King. In fact I've never seen a rifle so filthy. What have you been doing with it? Kicking it round the parade ground?'

Eddy came to attention and stared straight ahead.

'Answer me, you horrible shite of a man!'

'I dropped it, sir.'

'Tch! Tch! Very careless of you, King. The Army doesn't like its property being treated in such a manner. In fact it gets downright upset. These ...' and he waggled the rifle under Eddy's nose, 'cost money, a great deal of money, which the Army is very short of. So Army property has to be treated with the utmost respect. Is that clear?'

'Yes sir!'

'I think you'll have to make up for your carelessness, King. Report to Sergeant McQuarrie after I've dismissed the section.'

'Yes sir!'

Meany thrust the rifle at Eddy so that it banged hard against his chest.

'And after McQuarrie's through with you you'll clean and

polish that rifle like you've never cleaned and polished it before.'

'Yes sir!'

'Right then, rejoin the section.'

Meany strode up and down, his eyes glittering as he surveyed the men standing before him.

'You're a slovenly lot. A horrible, nasty, slovenly bunch who need their arses kicked from here to kingdom come and back. And I'm just the corporal to do it. God knows what I've done to deserve eight misfits like you but having drawn you I'm going to make something out of you. And do you know why? Because I've a reputation to think about. A reputation, I may add, that took me a long time and a great deal of sweat to acquire. And no bunch of clarinet-playing Edinburgh poofs and left-footed morons are going to bugger it up for me.'

He paused to take a deep breath. 'You're a bunch of fucking toerags! What are you?'

'A bunch of fucking toerags, sir, Corporal!' they responded in unison.

The man's demented, Kirk thought.

'What are you smirking at?' Meany demanded.

'I wasn't aware I was, sir,' Kirk replied.

'I don't like the way you talk,' Meany said. 'You speak with a plum in your mouth like an officer. So why aren't you one?'

'I don't want to do any more than two years, sir!'

'I suppose you're one of those born with a silver spoon in your mouth? Daddy with a Rolls and cucumber sandwiches for tea?' Meany laughed, finding himself amusing.

'My father manages a pub,' Kirk replied. 'And before that he was a barman. And there was no silver spoon, sir.'

'So why do you talk that way?'

'I had elocution lessons when I was young, sir.'

'Elocution lessons!' Meany exclaimed, and guffawed. 'Help my bob, another poof!'

'It was my mother's idea, sir. Not mine.'

'A right little mother's boy, I'll bet you were. Did you wear a sailor suit when you went to your elocution lessons?'

241

'No, sir.'

'My, my, this mother of yours must have cried when someone razored your pretty face.'

'I wasn't razored, sir. I had an accident. And yes, she wasn't very happy about it. In fact she was quite upset.'

'I'll bet she was. What sort of accident was it then?'

'I prefer not to say, sir.'

Meany glowered. 'When I ask you a question you'll answer it.' Adding onimously, 'Or else.'

Kirk racked his brains for something to say, having absolutely no intention of telling what had really happened.

Finally he said, 'I was in a car crash. The windscreen shattered and it was that which ripped my face.'

'Hmm!' said Meany, thinking that was plausible enough.

Eddy glanced at Kirk. He'd been wondering, since meeting Kirk again how he had come by that scar. He'd never asked and Kirk had never volunteered the information. He didn't believe the explanation Kirk had just given Meany.

'You're pals with King here, aren't you?'

Kirk was wary. 'Our beds are next to one another, if that's what you mean, sir.'

'Don't play at words with me, sonny,' Meany replied threateningly.

'I wasn't trying to, sir. I mean I wouldn't presume as much. I was only trying to answer your question. You see, we're all pals together in the section. We all get on.'

Meany came forward to tap Kirk on the chest. 'I get the feeling from you sometimes that you're trying to take the piss. Well don't. It would be a big mistake on your part.'

'Yes sir!'

'And just so you've got time to think about that, you'd better join King when he presents himself to Sergeant McQuarrie at the cookhouse.'

'Yes sir! Thank you, sir!' Kirk snapped.

Meany's eyes narrowed. He suspected Kirk was taking the piss again. And he was right.

'Section, attention!'

Sixteen feet came smartly together and eight backs went ramrod straight.

'Right turn! . . . Dis – miss!'

When they were out of Meany's hearing, Kirk came alongside Eddy. 'How are you?' he asked.

'Sore. That was a belter I got in the kidneys. And the kick I got in the side wasn't too helpful, either.'

'There was a moment back there when I thought you were going to haul off and hit the sod.'

Eddy nodded. 'There was a moment I thought so too.'

'Well don't ever do it. No matter what the provocation. Believe me, you'd be playing right into his hands.'

'That's what I keep trying to tell myself.'

'I have a suspicion we're both going to be prime targets from now on in,' Kirk mused. 'As you heard, he doesn't like the way I speak.'

Tongue in cheek, Eddy said, 'He's a horrible little shite of a man. What is he?'

'A horrible little shite of a man!' Kirk replied.

And they both laughed.

'You can wash, Murray, and you, King, can dry,' Sergeant McQuarrie said. He was large and fat with only a few wisps of hair to cover an otherwise bald head. He smiled a great deal and was extremely popular with the men.

Kirk groaned when he saw the mountain of dishes confronting him.

'And when you get through with that lot there's more to come,' McQuarrie added.

'We haven't eaten,' Eddy said hopefully.

McQuarrie nodded. 'I'll see you don't starve.'

'Thanks, Sarge.'

'Here we go then,' Kirk said, plunging his hands into a huge sinkful of steaming water.

Eddy picked up a drying-cloth.

For the next two and a half hours they worked flat out, no sooner clearing away one pile of dirty dishes, pots and pans, than another took its place.

McQuarrie appeared every so often to check up on how they were getting on, once instructing Kirk to fill a very badly crusted pot with water and leave it to steep – for which Kirk was most grateful, having been scrubbing away at the pot for a good ten minutes.

Finally it was all over; the last dish and item of cutlery had been dried and put away.

'You did well,' McQuarrie said. 'Now come away through and mess with the rest of us.'

There were eight of them round the table over which McQuarrie presided, sitting at its head.

Kirk goggled when he saw what was served up. He hadn't seen food like this since joining the Army.

'Perks of the job,' McQuarrie said, attacking a huge piece of steak.

'Wine?' a cook asked Eddy, proffering a bottle.

'Yes, please,' Eddy replied eagerly.

'Breakages from the Officers' Mess,' McQuarrie said, giving them a sly wink. 'It's just amazing how butter-fingered some of our boys can be.'

A general laugh ran round the table.

As a man who loved his food, Kirk was most appreciative of the spread he was now tucking into. 'I could almost forgive Meany anything for this,' he said.

'Aye, of course it was Meany who sent you to me,' McQuarrie said. 'What did the pair of you do?'

'He doesn't like me because I'm a Catholic,' Eddy replied.

'Nor the way I speak,' Kirk added.

'Well, he certainly doesn't like Catholics,' McQuarrie said. 'Which means we'll be seeing a lot of you here.'

'Is he an Orangeman?' Eddy asked.

'No, I don't think so.'

'So why does he hate Catholics?'

McQuarrie poured himself a huge glass of hock. The

244

redness of his nose gave it away that he was a man fond of his drink.

'There was an incident some years back. The good corporal came home one night to find a note from his wife telling him she'd run off with some bloke called O'Malley. Don't ask me what O'Malley did or how she came to meet him, but ever since then Meany's had a down on Catholics. What's your name?'

'King.'

'Just thank your lucky stars it isn't O'Malley. If he's bad on you now he'd be ten times worse then.'

'He certainly takes liberties with his men,' Kirk said.

McQuarrie leaned forward to emphasise his point. 'You'd better understand this. Meany is well liked and respected by the officers. He turns out good soldiers, whatever his methods, which is what the officers like. If he is a bit overenthusiastic at times, the officers turn a blind eye towards it. You see, there's a lot of them, regulars who fought in the war, think the Army's becoming too soft and would like to see it toughened up again back to wartime standards.'

'He's a sadistic sod all the same,' Kirk said.

'But *careful* with it,' McQuarrie added. 'He'll never be caught out because he's far too fly for that. Anyway, the officers *don't want* to catch him out which gives him an awful big advantage.'

'So what you're saying is no matter what happens we can never complain about him?'

McQuarrie pulled a face. 'Murray, the last thing you ever do in the Army is complain. It just isn't done.'

One of the cooks sang dolefully, causing them all to smile,

'They say that in the Army the prunes are mighty fine,
A prune fell off a table and killed a pal of mine.
Oh, I don't want to lead an Army life,
Gee ma, I want to go, but they won't let me go,
Gee ma, I want to go home!'

'Bugger it!' Eddy said when he and Kirk got back to the room where the section slept. He'd just remembered he still had his rifle to clean.

'No rest for the wicked,' Kirk said, starting to pull off his clothes.

'I wouldn't do that if I were you,' a voice said from the doorway.

They turned to find Meany staring at them. The rest of the section were already fast asleep.

'We're just this minute back,' Eddy said.

'I know that, sonny. I've been waiting for you.'

Eddy picked up his rifle and sat on his bed. With Meany watching him he started disassembling it.

'You want me for something, Corporal?' Kirk asked.

'I thought your friend King here might get lonely so I've decided you can keep him company. Go through to my room, pick up my gear which is stacked on my bed, bring it back here and clean and polish it.'

'Now?' Kirk asked.

'*Now*,' Meany replied, a faint leer twisting his mouth upwards.

Meany's room was down the corridor. As Meany had said, Kirk found the gear ready and waiting for him.

When they were alone Kirk said to Eddy, 'I don't know how, yet, but we're going to have to deal with that man because there's just no way I'm going to take two years of his riding me.'

'That's also been in my mind,' Eddy replied. 'But like you, I haven't yet thought of a way without landing myself in it.'

Kirk spat and buffed. 'My mother used to always say "where there's a will there's a way". It's a problem we'll just have to think about long and hard. And if we do we'll find the answer in the end. I promise you.'

An hour later Meany returned to find Eddy finished but Kirk still hard at work. He picked up Eddy's rifle and minutely examined it.

'Call this clean?' he said scornfully. 'Why, I've seen

middens cleaner than this. It's an absolute fucking disgrace! What is it?'

'An absolute fucking disgrace, sir!' Eddy chorused.

Meany threw the rifle at Eddy who caught it deftly. 'Now try again and let's hope you get it right this time otherwise you'll be up on a charge.'

Grinning malevolently he turned and strode from the room.

'The answer will come,' Kirk said softly, staring at the door through which Meany had vanished. 'It just needs lots and lots of thinking on.'

'Can't a bloke get some sleep around here!' Ogle grumbled from his bed.

'Piss off!' replied Kirk.

Spitting, he buffed some more.

'Right wheel! Left right ... left right ... left right ... left right!' Meany shouted.

Although it was bitter out, the sweat was pouring from Eddy as he marched and counter-marched to Meany's orders. The section had been on the parade ground for two and a half hours now and the strain was beginning to tell.

'Right turn! ... right face! ... Halt! ...' And before they had time to even catch their breath, 'By the left ... quick march! Left right ... left right ... Pick up your feet, Rennie, it's the British Army you're in, not the bloody American one! Left right ... left right ... Shoulders back, Kirkwood! You look like the hunchback of Notre Dame! ... left right ... left right ... Right wheel! ... left right ... Squad halt! ... Squad present arms! ... Squ ... aadd slope arms! ... Squaaddd ...'

Eddy glanced at Kirk, who shot him a weak grin. Then he was doubling up, the pack on his back feeling as though it weighed a ton. He sought solace in thinking about his bed, frowning when he remembered they were on patrol tonight. It would be tomorrow morning before he'd get some kip.

'Double up! Double up! Double up!' Meany screamed.

Eddy groaned.

*

There was no moon in the sky, which rendered the night black as pitch. The section was in a pine forest, Eddy hurrying along behind Kirk knowing if he once let Kirk out of his extremely limited vision he'd be lost and have to call for help – Which was the last thing he wanted as it would give Meany an excuse to punish him some more. If Meany needed an excuse, that is.

Twigs snapped underfoot as he pushed forward. It was eerie in the forest. Trees and branches making weird and grotesque shapes. He kept telling himself not to be so bloody silly but despite that he couldn't help but keep imagining the shapes were, or concealed something, waiting to pounce on him.

He wouldn't have been at all surprised if a whole battalion of Ruskies had suddenly materialised, tanks and all.

'Corporal? Corporal, where are you?' Napier's voice said from somewhere ahead. Napier had been behind Meany who'd been in the lead.

Eddy came up short, as ahead of him Kirk stopped.

'Corporal, can you hear me?' Napier called out, this time more urgently.

Eddy was just about to move up and join Kirk when suddenly a kick in the backside sent him sprawling. He yelled as he nose-dived into a soggy mixture of wet leaves and earth.

'Ivan!' he thought, rolling to one side. He desperately tried to scramble to his feet only to be knocked sprawling again by a boot kicking him in the belly.

Lying on his side, doubled up with pain, he stared in fascination at the sten's muzzle inches away from his forehead and pointed straight between his eyes.

'Asleep on our feet, were we?' Meany asked jovially. 'Or just lost in thought?'

Kirk and Rennie appeared, to stand staring at Meany.

'I didn't hear you,' Eddy replied.

'Oh I know that!' Meany said sarcastically. 'Otherwise you wouldn't be lying there like the stupid tit you are. What are you, King?'

'A stupid tit, sir.'

'Well, if it's any consolation to you, you're only one tit

248

among eight. What were you dreaming of, eh? Answer me!'

'I wasn't, Corporal.'

'Don't lie to me. Of course you were dreaming, for you sure as hell didn't have your mind on what you were about.'

By this time the rest of the section had gathered around. Meany swung on them. 'None of you did. You were all content to play follow the leader with what you laughingly call your minds elsewhere.' He sighed. 'Make soldiers out of you lot? I'm beginning to think it's impossible.'

Somewhere an owl hooted, causing Napier to jump.

Meany laughed when he saw that. 'Frightened of being out in the dark, poofter?' he asked.

'No sir.'

'What about you, plum in the mouth?'

'How could I be scared when you're with us Corporal?' Kirk replied.

Meany's eyes slitted fractionally. 'I told you before, don't try and get funny with me or by God you'll live to regret it.'

'It was a statement of fact, sir. Nothing else,' Kirk lied.

Meany came up close to Kirk. 'I don't trust you, Murray,' he said. 'You're a devious bastard who thinks he's more clever than he is. I know the type.'

Kirk stared into Meany's eyes and didn't reply.

'Just watch it, that's all. Especially your mouth. I suggest from now on you keep a tight rein on it.'

They stared at one another for a few seconds and then Meany swung round.

'Right, you dozy bunch of diddies, that was your smoke break. Now let's get cracking again. And this time try and keep awake!'

'I could get to hate that man,' Ogle muttered to Eddy.

'You wouldn't be alone, mate,' Eddy whispered back.

When the patrol was finally over they made their way back to their room in the castle where they all collapsed on to their respective beds. It seemed no time at all before Meany was striding into the room crying, 'Rise and shine! Rise and shine!' and, as he always did, pulling the covers from their beds.

'Atten . . . tion,' Meany shouted, and waited till they'd done so at the end of their beds before continuing.

'What day is it, Kirkwood?'

'Saturday, sir.'

'Correct. But it's also something else. Rennie?'

Rennie screwed his face up in a frown. 'I don't know, sir,' he replied eventually.

Meany beamed. 'Of course you don't because I haven't told you yet. Funny eh?'

They all dutifully laughed, knowing it was expected of them.

'Well I'll tell you. It's not only Saturday, it's your day off. What is it.'

'Our day off, sir, Corporal!' they chorused.

'Did I hear "For He's A Jolly Good Fellow"?'

Smart led the singing 'For he's a jolly good fellow, for he's . . .'

When the song was over Meany went on, 'Now I suppose most, if not all, of you will be going down to Uelsberg. Right?'

'Yes sir, Corporal.'

'So what I want to say to you is this. If anyone is naughty or misbehaves himself in any way, which would reflect on me as your NCO, I will personally make his life not worth living. And that, I can assure you, is no idle threat. Now gather round for your passes.'

Meany manipulated it so that Eddy and Kirk were last in line. When finally it was Eddy's turn he said. 'Ah, King! I'm afraid you won't be going along.'

Eddy's heart sank.

'Nor you, Murray. I was asked for two volunteers for a most demanding job and you two are them.'

He cupped his hand to his ear. 'Did I hear you say something? Like, "I volunteer, Corporal"?'

'I volunteer, Corporal,' Eddy said dully, the others looking at him and Kirk in sympathy.

'Murray?'

'I volunteer, Corporal.'

'Lovely!' said Meany rubbing his hands together. 'I'll be back in ten minutes and I'll expect you to be dressed for a dirty job.'

'Don't we get time for something to eat, Corporal?' Eddy asked, adding, 'I'm starving.'

'Plenty of time for that afterwards,' Meany replied, pausing by the door to say over his shoulder. 'Nine minutes, now.'

'Hard luck,' said Ogle when Meany was gone.

'We'll tell you all about it,' Rennie said.

'Thanks a lot,' Eddy replied sarcastically. 'That's just what I need, a lurid account of your day off to keep me going.'

He and Kirk began dressing for a dirty job.

Prompt as usual, Meany strode into the room to find Eddy and Kirk waiting for him. He checked that they'd washed and shaved before telling them to follow him.

He led them to another part of the castle which was the officers' quarters. Stopping by a door he opened it and a toilet was revealed. He ushered them inside.

The stench was appalling, causing Eddy to gag. He didn't have to be told to know what was coming. Meany told him anyway.

'Your job's to unbung this lot and when you've done that I want the bowls, the floor, everything, cleaned out like new.' He gestured across to where various buckets, brooms and tools were either lying or propped against a wall. 'I think you'll find everything there you need,' he added.

Eddy glanced at Kirk, who looked as though he was going to throw up. He felt that way himself.

'I'll be back in a while to see how you're doing. Any questions?'

Eddy shook his head and Kirk did likewise.

Meany made to go and then paused. 'Oh!' he said, pretending he's just remembered something. 'Happy day off!'

Chuckling, he left them to it.

Eddy cautiously approached the first bowl. Water and urine

were dripping down its sides on to the floor. Its inside was filled with what looked like diarrhoea. Close up the stench was, if anything, even worse.

'Any ideas about how to go about this?' he asked.

'Not a clue,' Kirk replied.

Eddy crossed to the tools and picked out a plunger. 'I suppose this is as good as anything to start with,' he said.

'Christ!' exclaimed Kirk a little later when some of the mess slopped over his boots.

Trying not to be too aware of the smell they both got on with it.

Two hours later a grinning Meany arrived back in the toilet. Hands on hips he surveyed what they'd done.

Eddy and Kirk were down on their hands and knees scrubbing the floor. The toilets were unbunged and functioning properly.

'Not bad,' Meany said grudgingly.

'Phew!' said Eddy when they were finally all finished. 'I stink like a pig.'

'You stink *worse* than a pig. We both do,' Kirk added.

Meany laughed.

Kirk stared at the corporal, careful not to let what he felt about the man show in his eyes. Just keep on thinking, he told himself. Just keep on thinking.

When they'd stacked the buckets, brooms and assorted tools, Meany told them to fall in behind him and with him leading the way they marched back to their room. Once inside, Meany picked up Eddy's rifle and threw it to him. 'I believe that's still dirty from last night. What are you going to do about it?'

'Clean it, Corporal.'

Meany nodded. 'You're an awful one for getting your rifle dirty, King. I've never known the like.'

'Perhaps I'm accident-prone?' Eddy suggested.

'Perhaps. In which case you should pray to one of those plaster saints of yours.'

'I might just do that, Corporal, seeing as how you've suggested it.'

'You do that, sonny. For all the good it'll do you.'

Meany took two passes from his pocket and threw them on to Eddy's bed. 'The rifle gets cleaned first,' he said. 'And be sure you're back by twenty-three hundred.'

Eddy picked up the passes, gaping at them in astonishment. This was the last thing he'd expected and, judging from the incredulous look on Kirk's face, the last thing Kirk had expected as well.

'One last thing,' Meany said, 'whatever you do, don't go to the Blue Pig bierkeller. It's not off bounds or anything like that. I just don't recommend it.'

When Meany was gone Eddy said, 'Well I'll be a son of a gun! He gave us passes after all. Do you think we've misjudged him?'

'Not a chance,' Kirk replied. 'He's a bastard through and through. If he gave us those passes then he had a reason, and one that suited him, not us.'

'Well, I'm not looking this gift horse in the mouth.'

'Me neither.'

Eddy's face fell. 'Bloody rifle. That'll take a good half-hour.'

'Quarter of an hour. I'll help you.'

'Thanks, mate.'

'One for all and all for one, eh?'

'Pass the cleaning gear, D'Artagnan,' Eddy said, grinning.

Once out of the castle they hurried down the road that led straight into Uelsberg. Both were excited and champing at the bit to enjoy themselves.

'First thing I want is a beer,' Eddy said.

'What I want is me hole. Us married men miss that sort of thing you know.'

'I wouldn't say no myself.'

'I'll bet you wouldn't, you randy bugger. Did you have someone at home?'

Eddy shook his head.

'Footloose and fancy free?'

'That's one way of putting it.'

A gleam came into Kirk's eye. 'Before getting married I had a bit called Minnie. A real looker, and Christ could she screw! I get horny just thinking about it.'

'I had a woman down in London when I was staying there. My landlady. She and I ... well ... we were having it off together.'

'You sound like you were fond of her?'

'I was. There was only one problem. She was married and still loved her husband.'

'Too bad,' Kirk said sympathetically.

'Her name was Annie and she was quite a bit older than me. Tall, slim, dark-haired.'

'Do you write to her?'

'No point,' Eddy said softly.

They walked for a little while in silence, Eddy's initial excitement having turned to introspection.

Kirk gazed about, taking everything in. He was loving this.

'My first time abroad,' he said. 'You?'

Eddy nodded.

'I miss Glasgow, mind you. I even dream about it at nights.'

'You'll miss the wife more than anything I'd imagine?'

'Oh aye, her as well,' Kirk replied, eyes riveted on a girl passing on the opposite side of the road. 'Look at the bum on that!' he exclaimed.

'I'm still starving,' Eddy said. 'Don't forget we haven't had anything to eat yet.'

'Food and beer first. Then, when the inner man's satisfied, we'll see what we can do about the rest of us.'

They found a small bierkeller which served them frothing steins of lager, after which they had lavish helpings of sausage and sauerkraut.

Kirk ogled the waitress who was blonde, buxom and dressed in a traditional peasant-type outfit cut low at the top.

When she returned to clear away their dishes he tried to chat

254

her up but she would have none of it.

'Can't win them all,' he said as she swayed away from them.

They paid at the bar and then made their way out into the street. 'What now?' Eddy asked.

Kirk smiled. 'I can't help wondering why Meany didn't want us to go to this Blue Pig. Probably because it's the best place in town.'

'You could be right.'

Kirk stopped a passer-by and asked for directions.

The Blue Pig turned out to be a subterranean dive at the end of an alleyway. They ordered beers and then settled themselves at a table.

'More like it,' said Kirk. 'Look at the spare bint flying around.'

There were a number of unescorted girls sitting at tables, standing at the bar and even dancing together on the small dance floor.

There were roughly a dozen other soldiers about, all of them with girls whom they'd obviously picked up there.

'This place is a whore house,' Kirk said. 'No mistaking it.'

Eddy gazed about him with renewed interest. He'd never been in a brothel before.

'Either of you two gentlemen spare a lady a cigarette?'

Kirk and Eddy stared up at the female standing beside their table. She was no Rita Hayworth but then she wasn't exactly ugly either.

Eddy held out his cigarette case. 'Be my guest,' he said. He suddenly felt nervous and a bit embarrassed.

The female helped herself to a cigarette, put it between scarlet painted lips and waited for a light. Eddy obliged.

'You're new, aren't you?' she said.

Kirk nodded. 'How do you know that?'

She smiled secretly. 'It's not difficult to tell. My name's Gottfried.'

Kirk rose to his feet. 'Perhaps you'd care to join us for a drink?'

She looked from one to the other. 'I have a friend,' she suggested.

'Which one?' Kirk asked.

Gottfried pointed out a girl sitting a few tables away. 'Magda,' she said. 'Very nice.'

Kirk glanced at Eddy, who nodded.

'Fine,' he said. 'Perhaps you'd like to ask her over.'

Gottfried smiled and moved away.

'We've cracked it!' Kirk said enthusiastically.

Eddy was still nervous. 'I'm not so sure,' he said.

'What do you mean you're not sure?'

Eddy cleared his throat. 'I've never ... I mean a whore before.'

'Me neither. But there's always a first time for everything. And the way my hormones are jumping I don't care what she is as long as I get it up her.'

'Well if you think it'll be all right ...'

'Of course it'll be all right. If it wasn't, those other blokes wouldn't be here.'

'That's true,' Eddy murmured.

They both rose as Gottfried and Magda joined them.

Introductions were made all round and they sat. Kirk waved to a passing waiter, who came instantly to their table. The order was four beers.

'Can Magda have a cigarette as well?' Gottfried asked.

'Of course,' replied Eddy and again proffered his case.

Magda took the cigarette hungrily, smiling gratitude to Eddy when he lit it for her.

'So ...' said Gottfried. 'You are new up at the *Schloss*, yes?'

'Yes,' said Kirk.

'And this is your first time into Uelsberg?'

'Right again.'

Gottfried's eyes gleamed. 'The price is two packets of cigarettes or half a pound of coffee. *Each*,' she said.

Kirk blinked. 'What happened to good old-fashioned money and army vouchers?'

'Money and vouchers no use unless you have sterling. In which case it is two pounds.'

'Each,' said Kirk.

'*Each*,' she replied emphatically.

'What's all this cigarettes and coffee business?' Eddy asked.

'Everything is cigarettes and coffee nowadays,' Magda said.

'Christ, look who just came in!' Eddy exclaimed.

Kirk glanced up to see Meany staring at them.

'We're for it now,' Eddy added. But he was wrong.

Meany continued staring at them for a few seconds before making his way to the bar where he stood with his back to them.

'What's he up to?' Kirk said quietly. 'Because I'm certain the bugger's up to something.'

'Well, he only said he didn't recommend we come here,' Eddy said.

Magda laid her hand across Eddy's. 'I like you. You're nice,' she said.

'You've got an American accent!' Eddy said in surprise, having just noticed it.

She caressed his hand, stroking it as though it was a thing of great beauty.

'I lived in the American sector for some years. I have only recently moved to Uelsberg.'

Kirk brought his attention back to Gottfried. 'As I don't smoke I haven't any cigarettes on me, so it'll have to be sterling,' he said.

'Fine.' She nodded.

'And you?' Magda asked.

Eddy had picked up his Naafi ration the previous day and consequently had a number of packets on him. 'I'll pay in fags,' he replied.

'What about a bottle to take upstairs?' Kirk asked.

'We can get slivovitz but that would mean more cigarettes.'

'How many?' Eddy asked.

'Twenty.'

He shook his head. 'No can do. Another ten's my limit.'

'For that you get half a bottle.'

Eddy passed ten cigarettes across to Gottfried and while she went to the bar he, Kirk and Magda made their way to a door beyond which Magda had told them were the stairs to their rooms on the upper floors.

En route, Kirk caught a glimpse of Meany watching them in a large ornate mirror. Meany was smiling.

'What's slivovitz?' Eddy asked as they climbed the stairs.

'A sort of plum brandy,' Kirk replied. 'I've heard of it but never tasted it.'

'I would have preferred whisky myself,' Eddy grumbled.

Magda laughed. 'It is very rare to see a bottle of whisky. And to buy it would be very, very expensive.'

'How many fags?' Kirk asked, curious.

Magda shrugged. 'Two hundred maybe. Maybe more.'

Kirk thought of all the whisky he'd had from Harry Hydelman. Christ, if he could have pulled that stunt again he could really have cleaned up here.

The room Magda told him to wait for Gottfried in was small and cramped. There was a large quilt on top of the bed, which looked as though it had already been put to use, and not long since either. The thought didn't put him off at all.

Gottfried arrived to say she'd given half of the half-bottle to Eddy and Magda.

What was left she poured into two tumblers and handed Kirk one.

'*Prosit!*' she toasted.

'*Prosit!*' he replied.

She sipped hers appreciatively.

He swallowed some and then coughed. He thought it must be like drinking bloody paraffin.

Gottfried laid her glass down and immediately started to strip. She did this in a clinical way and without any overtones of sex whatsoever. When she was totally nude she turned to Kirk.

'Now we have the fuckings!' she said gaily.

'Now we have the fuckings,' he agreed.

Later that night Kirk and Eddy lay in their own beds in the darkness.

'I certainly enjoyed that,' Eddy said. 'Just what I needed after a week of Meany. Mind you, I'm not looking forward to the morning. That bastard will take it out on us for going to the Blue Pig after he advised us not to.'

'Cigarettes, coffee and whisky. There's a fortune to be made out of those, it would seem.' Kirk's mind ticked over with the possibilities.

'Unless you've got an outside source, you can't get enough of either to really make it worth your while,' Eddy replied.

Kirk smiled. 'So you were thinking along those lines as well, eh?'

'Once a dealer always a dealer,' Eddy replied, going on to say, 'Magda told me the redcaps are sheer murder on anyone trying to deal in the *schwartz*, as she called it. That's the black market to you and I. She says several of the lads have tried in the past but the redcaps quickly got hold of them. Uelsberg's a small place and is already carved up by one or two local operators. It seems if competition tries to start up the redcaps quickly get to hear of it, or are given heavy hints, that sort of thing.'

'And if the competition's civilian?'

'The operators deal with it themselves. And from what Magda said, they tend to be heavy-handed in a fatal sort of way.'

'It's still a thought,' Kirk mused.

'But where would you get the commodities?'

'Where there's a will ...'

'... there's a way,' Eddy finished for him.

They both chuckled.

'I hate to see an opportunity go by,' Kirk said. 'It upsets me.'

'I know what you mean. And you were rooked tonight. Two packets of fags against two quid!'

'I won't be caught short again,' Kirk said. 'From now on I'll be taking up my Naafi ration. Too right and I will.'

The next thing he knew Meany's voice was shouting that it was time to get up. He shivered as his coverings were whipped from his bed.

'Rise and shine! Rise and shine, you horrible lot of shits. What are you?'

'A horrible lot of shits sir, Corporal!' the section responded.

'Aaatten ... tion!' Meany yelled.

The section scrambled to the end of their beds, where they lined up.

Grinning, Meany walked up one line and then down the other.

'Did we enjoy our day off?'

'Yes sir, Corporal!' they chorused.

'Good! I'm glad to hear it.' He paused before saying, 'Murray, King, one step forward, march!'

Here it comes, Eddy thought.

'Who were naughty boys, then? Who went to the Blue Pig when nice Corporal Meany told them not to?'

'We didn't realise that was it until we left,' Kirk lied.

'A little mistake, was it?'

'Yes sir,' Kirk said.

'A bigger mistake than you realise,' Meany said with relish.

Kirk frowned. There was something here he was missing. And from the look on Meany's face he was about to be enlightened.

Meany was enjoying this so he teased it out.

'Do you know why I recommended you didn't go to the Blue Pig?' he asked.

'No sir,' Eddy replied.

'Murray?'

'No sir.'

'You did appreciate I must have had a reason though, didn't you?'

'Yes, sir,' Eddy said.

'And yet you elected to disregard my advice. Very foolish, King. Not very clever, Murray.'

He chuckled, his eyes twinkling with amusement.

'Get your nookie?' he asked.

Ogle tittered.

'Well?'

'Yes, sir,' Eddy replied slowly. He knew there was no use pretending otherwise. Meany had seen Kirk and him go upstairs with the two whores.

'And you, Murray?'

'Yes, sir.'

'Oh dear, oh dear me!' Meany said, grinning from ear to ear. He stepped back a pace as though wanting to put distance between himself and them.

'Been to the bog yet this morning?' he asked.

Eddy glanced at Kirk. He couldn't think what all this was leading up to. But a glimmer of light was beginning to dawn with Kirk.

'No, sir,' they both answered.

'Then you'd better go now. Come on, hurry up. I'll be waiting for you when you get back.'

Eddy and Kirk left the room and made for the toilet where they both relieved themselves.

'What's this all about?' Eddy asked.

'I just hope to God I'm wrong. But I think I might know.'

'Well come on, tell me!'

'How's your pee?'

Eddy stared in astonishment. 'What do you mean how's my pee! Same as it always is.'

'Then let's just hope it stays that way.'

'I'm still not with you.'

'Don't be dense, Eddy. We went out with two whores last night and now Meany's getting us to slash. Put two and two together.' And when Eddy still looked blank. 'VD man!'

'Oh Christ!' exclaimed Eddy.

'It must be that. What else?'

Eddy hastily examined himself but it looked the same as it always did. 'How about you?' he asked.

'Normal. No sensation of pissing over broken glass, which I'm told is how it feels.'

'Oh that bastard! He watched us climb those stairs.'

'And he was smiling all the time,' Kirk added.

They took themselves back to their billet, both angry and a little scared.

'Everything all right?' Meany asked when they entered the room.

'Yes Corporal,' Kirk replied.

'Ah!' Meany said, nodding at some private thought. After a few suspenseful seconds he asked, 'Penny dropped yet?'

'You think we've caught a dose, sir,' Kirk replied.

'I don't know for certain, mind you. But I'd say the chances are fairly high. You see I'm rather friendly with the particular medic who deals with these things. And he told me yesterday morning that it had been confirmed to him only hours previously that the recent run of VD cases he's had have all been traced back to the one source: the Blue Pig.'

Eddy sucked in a breath.

'Bloody hell!' exclaimed Rennie.

Meany went on, 'The civilian authorities will have been informed by now and by tomorrow the place will have been closed down. The thing is, were only some of the girls infected or were they all?'

'Is there some way of finding out?' Eddy asked. 'I mean surely they'll be examining every female who worked there?'

Meany smiled sadistically. 'That's got nothing to do with the Army, King. I presume you're asking me to inquire about the two you and Murray were with?'

Eddy nodded.

'No can do, sonny boy. Right out of my jurisdiction.'

Oh you're really lovely, Kirk thought. A real gem.

'So I suppose you'd better make your way to the medic for the cure. Which I am assured is most painful. Socking great jabs of penicillin up the arse two or three times a day. I've heard it said strong men have broken down and cried during the treatment. Needle like a bicycle spoke, I'm told.'

Eddy blanched. He had a thing about injections.

Meany went on, 'Just one other item. Once it's been established you have a dose, you're put on a charge. Ten days in the guard house at the tender mercy of Sergeant Marnoch. Who also is a great friend of mine, by the way. I know a word from me to him will ensure things are made interesting for you.' Meany rocked back on his heels and sighed. 'So there we are then. You see, you should have listened to what I told you.'

Kirk was thinking furiously. If the medic was a friend of Meany's, what guarantee was there, knowing how devious and underhand Meany was, that Meany wouldn't have fixed it with the medic to say they had contracted VD, whether they had or not? It was a risk he was damned if he was going to take unless he absolutely had to.

'Are you ordering us to go to the medic?' Kirk asked.

'Noo ... oo,' Meany replied slowly. 'Merely advising it.'

'Then I prefer to wait until there are some definite signs.'

Meany pursed his lips and frowned. 'And you, King?'

Eddy glanced at Kirk who imperceptibly shook his head. 'I'll hang off as well,' he replied.

Meany regarded the pair of them thoughtfully. Suddenly his brow cleared and he was smiling again. 'It'll take six months for you to be absolutely certain,' he said. 'And in the meantime if you do have it it'll be getting deeper and deeper into your system. And the deeper it gets the harder, and more painful, it is to cure.'

Kirk knew Meany was right and that he was taking an awful risk. But he still preferred that to the almost certainty of a cure followed by ten days hell, if ten days was all it was, at the hands of Sergeant Marnoch. He'd heard tales of men who'd gone into the guard house for a week and hadn't reappeared till months later, it having been alleged they'd been 'difficult' while inside. Men who'd come out relatively fine in body but completely broken in spirit.

'I'll chance it,' Kirk said.

'King?'

Eddy knew Kirk had to have a good reason for making this decision. 'Me too, sir,' he replied.

'Right then. I'll leave you two lepers and the rest of you to get on with it then,' Meany said, throwing over his shoulder at the door, 'You've got an hour and then it's outside for drill.'

When Meany was gone the section relaxed. Eddy sat on the edge of his bed and Kirk on his.

'Why?' Eddy asked. And Kirk explained his reasons, which Eddy was forced to agree with.

'Why don't you go and see a civilian doctor?' Smart asked.

Kirk replied. 'You don't think he's going to let us out the castle, except on patrol, until this is all over, do you? He must know we'd think of that.'

'I'm sure six months is wrong,' Kirkwood said.

Ogle said, 'There's a chap down the corridor, Randy Ronnie Ralston they call him, who I was told has had a dose several times. Why don't we check with him to see what he knows?'

'Good idea,' Eddy nodded.

'I'll see if I can catch him before he goes to breakfast,' Ogle said and left the room.

'That Sergeant Marnoch is terrible,' Rennie said. 'Some of the lads were talking about him in the Naafi the other night. He's real bad news.'

Eddy sat fretting until Ogle returned with Randy Ronnie, who turned out to be a small ferret-faced man.

'Meany's talking a load of garbage,' Randy Ronnie said straight off. 'Three weeks is absolute maximum for it to show itself. After that your worries are over.'

Kirk heaved a sigh of relief. That was something, anyway. There was one helluva big difference between six months and three weeks.

'Good luck, mates,' Randy Ronnie said and left.

Napier said, 'Look I don't want this to be misconstrued or anything. But while you two don't know, is it safe for us? Sharing a room with you and all, I mean?'

'That's a point,' Kirk said.

'How about if Kirk and I keep to ourselves. And you lot just make sure you don't touch anything of ours,' Eddy suggested.

'What about the bog? Aren't you supposed to be able to catch it from toilet seats?' Smart asked.

'When we have to go we'll make sure we never actually touch the seats. All right?' Kirk said.

Smart nodded, but reluctantly.

'What a hell of a fix,' Eddy said miserably.

'We'll get our own back. Somehow, some way. It just needs ...'

'... thinking on. So you keep saying,' Eddy said.

Kirk suddenly smiled. 'Well come on, cheer up. It isn't exactly the end of the world!'

'You won't say that when your dick falls off,' Eddy replied miserably.

The next three weeks were sheer murder for Eddy and Kirk. Every time they went for a pee they held their breath, waiting for the tell-tale burning sensation. And every morning when they woke, the first thing they did was examine themselves to see if they'd had a discharge during the night.

The rest of the section were pleasant enough about it but naturally and sensibly kept their distance.

The result of this was that Eddy and Kirk spent the whole of their free time together, becoming, in their plight, even closer than they'd previously been.

Finally the great day dawned when their three weeks was up and neither of them had shown any signs of infection whatsoever.

To celebrate, the entire section went along to the Naafi, where they had a few beers. And that was where Meany found them.

'What's all this in aid of then?' he asked.

'The three weeks are up, Corporal,' Eddy replied.

'What three weeks?'

'You were mistaken, sir. The waiting period is three weeks, not six months.'

Meany frowned, his gaze travelling from Eddy to Kirk and back again. 'Who told you that nonsense then?' he asked.

'It's general knowledge, sir,' Eddy replied. 'Quite a few of the men told us.'

That wasn't true. Randy Ronnie was the only one they'd consulted.

Meany's frown deepened. He knew then he should have ordered them to go up before the medic. It had been a mistake on his part for him not to have done, but then he'd been convinced they'd both caught a dose.

'You were lucky then,' he grumbled, admitting defeat.

Smiling, Eddy lifted his glass and swallowed off the remains of his beer. The glass had been almost full.

'I'd be careful if I was you. That stuff's alcoholic,' Meany said scathingly.

Like most male Glaswegians Eddy couldn't bear any slur on his drinking ability. 'It would take a lot more than that to get me even slightly pissed,' he retorted.

'*Sir!*' Meany warned.

'Pissed, sir,' Eddy said hastily.

'Fancy yourself as a drinker then, do you?'

'I can hold my own.'

'Amongst boys maybe. But what about up against a man?'

Eddy realised he was being goaded but couldn't help himself. 'What man did you have in mind, sir?' he asked.

Meany glanced around to make sure their conversation wasn't being overheard. 'How about me?' he suggested.

'You, sir?'

'Aye, me. I say I can drink any stinking Fenian under the table and what's more I'm willing to put my money where my mouth is.'

Hush fell round the table as every pair of eyes came to rest on Eddy's face.

'How much were you thinking of?' Eddy asked.

'What can you afford, sonny boy?'

'How about twenty?'

266

'Pennies or shillings?'

'Pounds,' Eddy said.

'Wow!' said Smart. It was an awful lot of money.

'You're on,' Meany replied. 'Tomorrow night at nine in the cookhouse. I'll tell Sergeant McQuarrie to expect us.'

'What about the drink?' Kirk asked.

'Don't worry about that. Whisky. And I tell you what, I'll even supply it myself. How about that?'

Eddy nodded.

'Twenty quid, eh?' Meany said and laughed. 'I'm going to enjoy this.'

Chuckling to himself he left the Naafi.

Eddy sat and stared into his empty glass.

'That might have been foolish,' Kirk said.

'Would you have backed down?'

Kirk pulled a face. 'You're right, I wouldn't.'

With the exception of Napier, they were all Glaswegians round the table and they all understood. Their attitude to drink had been instilled into them since they were wee. A man was expected to drink hard and often. To have turned down a direct challenge of the sort Meany had issued to Eddy would have been a jessie thing to do.

'You must drink at least a pint of milk beforehand,' Napier said. 'It lines the stomach.'

'And have a good meal before as well. That absorbs it,' Smart added.

Suddenly suggestions were being offered from all directions as everyone in the section put forward tips they thought might help.

The next morning they were drilling on the parade ground when an officer called Lieutenant Gilzean came striding up.

Meany immediately called the section to attention and saluted.

'I need four men for a job,' Lieutenant Gilzean said.

'I'll take him, him, him and him,' he said, his pointed finger stabbing the air. Eddy and Kirk were two of those singled out.

Meany gave the appropriate orders and soon the four of them – Smart and Ogle were the other two – were marching along behind the lieutenant.

When they reached a parked lorry Gilzean told them to climb aboard. He got in front with the driver and the lorry moved off.

They rattled out through the castle gates, heading towards Uelsberg. When they entered the town it was the first time Eddy and Kirk had been back since their night out at the Blue Pig.

The lorry drew up at the railway station and Gilzean ordered them out. He said they could have a smoke while he went to see what was what.

'Seems a decent sort of bloke,' Ogle remarked once the officer had gone.

'Unlike a certain NCO I could name,' Smart said. Then, turning to Eddy, 'How do you feel for tonight?'

Eddy shrugged. 'All right, I suppose.'

'There'll be no holding Meany back if you lose,' Ogle said.

'But what'll he be like if Eddy wins?' Kirk asked.

Ogle grimaced. 'I hadn't thought of that.'

'We can't win either way,' Smart added.

Gilzean reappeared and they came to attention.

'Stand easy,' Gilzean said. 'We're here to pick up a load of supplies but it seems the train is late. Just how late they're not sure yet. They're telephoning down the line now and somebody will be out to tell me as soon as they have a definite answer. So we'll just have to hang around for the moment. Sorry about that, chaps.'

Five minutes later the station master hurried out of the station. When he saw him Gilzean got out of the lorry cab where he'd spent the interim reading some official-looking documents.

The station master and Gilzean spoke briefly. Then with gestures of apology the station master made his way back into the station.

Gilzean called the men together. 'The damn train is going to be at least an hour and a half late which is a real piece of nonsense,' he said. 'Rather than return to the castle and then have to come all the way back again I think it best if we disperse and then meet up here again in exactly an hour and a half. That meet with everyone's approval?'

The four of them were quick to say that was fine and dandy with them.

'Thought it might be,' Gilzean said drily. 'All right then, hop it. And don't be late back!'

'There's a stroke of luck!' Smart said.

'How about a beer?' Ogle suggested.

But a thoughtful-looking Kirk had other ideas. 'You two go on,' he said. 'Eddy and I have a little something to attend to.'

Eddy turned in surprise to Kirk. This was news to him. But he went along with it.

'What do you have in mind?' Eddy asked after Smart and Ogle had hurried away.

'What sort of chance do you really give yourself up against Meany tonight?'

Eddy shrugged. 'I honestly don't know. I'm a pretty fair drinker when it's called for but who knows what Meany's like? He may well be the original hollow legs.'

Kirk stroked his scar. 'There's just the possibility, and it's a long shot at the moment, that we can turn tonight to our advantage. But to do so you've got to drink the sod under the table.'

'I'll certainly be trying my best.'

'I've no doubt about it. But why don't we see if we can get you some help, make the odds a little more in your favour, so to speak?'

'How?'

'Well, maybe I'm barking up the wrong tree but perhaps there's something medical that would help. A pill or something, I don't know. It's just an idea but one I think is worth looking into now that we've got this hour and a half to ourselves. What I suggest we do is find a doctor who can speak English and put it to him.'

269

'It's a helluva long shot but why not?' Eddie replied. 'I've nothing to lose after all.'

'And if it works out possibly everything to gain.'

'What haven't you told me, Kirk? I know that funny look you get in your eye. It means you're up to something.'

Kirk laughed. 'First things first. Let's find the quack and we'll go from there.'·

They made inquiries round about for a doctor who spoke English and the name they came up with was that of a Doctor Kruppermann whose address was close by. They hurried there at once.

The receptionist was a middle-aged lesbian type who primly told them to wait and the doctor would see them as soon as it was convenient.

'Leave the talking to me,' Kirk said.

Ten minutes later, they were ushered into the presence of an extremely good-looking blonde in her mid-thirties sitting behind a desk.

'We're looking for Dr Kruppermann,' Kirk said.

The woman smiled. 'I am she.' Then seeing their looks of bewilderment. 'Don't you have women doctors in England?'

'Scotland,' Eddy replied quickly. 'We come from Scotland.'

'I suppose we do. It's just I've never experienced one before,' Kirk added, thinking she wasn't a bad-looking bit of gimp at all.

'Now which one of you is sick?' Dr Kruppermann asked, waving them to seats.

'Neither of us,' Kirk replied.

The doctor frowned.

Kirk hurried on, 'The reason we've come to see you is because my friend here ...' He paused and then said. 'Oh hell! I was going to give you a cock and bull story but I think the truth's far better.'

She nodded and he smiled inwardly. He knew women always found that line disarming.

And then he went on to explain why they'd come to see her. When Kirk was finished Dr Kruppermann sat back in her

270

chair and gave a soft laugh. Her washed-out blue eyes twinkled with amusement.

'Can you help us?' Eddy asked eagerly.

'I don't know. Let me think,' she replied.

Silence reigned in the room while the two men sat looking expectant.

'Hmm!' she said eventually, and, rising, crossed to a bookcase from which she extracted a book.

'Naturally we want something that's safe. If it exists at all that is,' Eddy said.

'Naturally,' she replied.

Sitting again at her desk, she opened the book and for the next few minutes pored over it.

Kirk glanced at his watch. He and Eddy still had a considerable amount of time left before having to report back to Lieutenant Gilzean.

'Ah!' said the doctor, and then again, 'Ah!'

'You've found something?' Kirk asked.

She looked up at them. 'I thought I remembered something from my early medical studies. And here it is. Fructose is what you want.'

'Fructose?' Eddy queried.

'Fruit sugar.'

'How does that help?' Kirk asked.

'It changes the metabolic rate by up to twenty per cent, which means alcohol consumed during that period is burned off more quickly. In other words someone having taken fructose will be able to drink more than normal.'

'And it's safe?' Eddy asked.

'Oh yes. Quite.'

'Well I'll be ... !' Kirk said, looking extremely pleased with himself. 'Fruit sugar, eh?'

'I won't even have to give you a prescription. You don't need one to buy it.'

'Doctor, you're lovely,' Kirk said.

Kruppermann laughed, 'I'm glad to be of assistance.'

When Kirk and Eddy arrived back at the railway station

they had a bottle of fructose with them and full instructions on how and when to take it.

The entire section reported to the cookhouse at nine o'clock to be ushered into a back room where they found a trestle table and chairs had been set up.

Eddy felt marvellous, psychologically as well as physically. He was well primed with fructose.

A few minutes later Meany arrived. 'Is the lamb ready for the slaughter?' he demanded and laughed.

One of the cooks shook his head, confiding to Napier, 'He pulls this stunt every time he gets a new section and he's never lost yet. The man's capacity is phenomenal.'

Meanwhile Meany had started needling Eddy. 'How about upping your bet, Fenian? Or have you got cold feet already?'

Eddy stared hard at Meany, hating this man who in many ways reminded him of Gloag, whom he'd killed all those years ago. He would have given anything to be able to have a go at Meany in a fair fight. But of course that was impossible.

'You look right scared, sonny boy. Green round the gills and you haven't even had a drink yet.'

Having said that Meany laughed cruelly, at the same time fishing in his pocket for money. He slapped notes on the table in front of him.

'Twenty pounds, I believe you said. Well there's mine. Where's yours, King?'

In reply Eddy laid four fivers beside Meany's notes and then held up two more. 'Did you say you wanted to up the bet?' he asked quietly.

Meany chortled. This was getting better and better. 'Done!' he replied. And laid another ten singles out to match Eddy's two extra fivers.

Napier and the rest of the section looked on wretchedly. By now, it had passed among them what the cook had told Napier and they believed Eddy didn't have a snowball in hell's chance.

'Any more bets? I'm willing to cover them all,' Meany said.

Neither Napier nor the rest of the section were having any. With the exception of Kirk, that is. He was willing to have a flyer, knowing what he did.

'I'll match Eddy's thirty. If that isn't too much for you, Corporal?' he said blandly.

'Let's see your cash, plum in the mouth.'

Kirk laid his money on top of Eddy's.

'Consider it a bet!'

Meany covered Kirk's amount. 'Any more for any more?' he asked.

There were no takers.

The same cook who'd spoken to Napier shook his head. 'Suckers,' he mumbled.

'I think Sergeant McQuarrie should hold the money,' Kirk said. 'Just so there's no problem after.'

'There won't be any problem, I assure you,' Meany said, laughing yet again.

McQuarrie picked up the money, counted it to confirm it was all there, and then slipped it into a trouser pocket. He then went to a cupboard from which he produced two bottles, neither of which bore a label.

'What's this then?' Kirk asked.

'I said I'd supply the whisky and that's it,' Meany replied. 'Heather Dew, McQuarrie's own.'

Kirk uncorked the bottle and took a sniff. He then tipped some into his mouth. It was very strong and smoky-flavoured, rather like some of the highland malts, he thought.

'You make this, Sergeant?' Kirk asked.

'I used to work for a distillery before I joined the army,' McQuarrie replied. To Eddy he added, 'Don't worry, it's good stuff. But it's about a hundred proof.'

'If you back out now you forfeit your bets,' Meany said quickly.

'Poteen,' Eddy said.

'Which will soon separate the men from the boys,' Meany added, pleased at the flanker he'd pulled.

Kirk looked at Eddy, who nodded. He was willing to go on.

'I doubt if you'll need more than a bottle each,' McQuarrie said. 'No one's ever drunk more than that.'

'Right. Let's get on with it,' Kirk said.

McQuarrie took charge. 'I do the measuring and pouring out, gentlemen. It's half-gill at a time and both have to finish before the next tot is poured. Is that clear?'

Eddy and Meany nodded.

'The contest ends when one of you either flakes or else says he's had enough. Is that clear?'

Eddy and Meany nodded again.

'And when I declare a winner that's final. There'll be no argy-barging after or tomorrow or whenever.'

'Get on with it, man. I'm bloody thirsty,' Meany said.

McQuarrie used a proper pub measure, pouring each from the same bottle.

Meany took his first and threw it back. He smacked his lips with relish. 'Mother's milk,' he declared.

Eddy tasted his tentatively; appreciating the strength of it from the bite in his palate.

'Swallow it, don't play with it,' Meany gibed.

'There are no time rules so why don't you just shut up ... *Sir*,' Eddy replied.

Meany looked murderous, his lips thinning into a vicious downward hook.

Eddy slowly drained his glass and then nodded to McQuarrie that he was ready for another.

McQuarrie poured out two fresh measures.

Meany took more time over this one having got the message he wasn't going to pressure Eddy into drinking quickly.

The minutes ticked by and two glasses each became three and then six.

Eddy smoked, his eyes fastened to Meany's. Meany glared back, having now lost his initial jocularity.

Eddy pushed his glass forward for a seventh tot. 'Mother's milk,' he said, repeating what Meany had said earlier. As he'd guessed it would, he saw that infuriated Meany.

The alcohol was taking effect on Eddy now. His brain was

beginning to numb and he was getting a little lightheaded. But he felt he could go on for a long while yet.

At ten o'clock they were on their fifteenth drink and both men were swaying slightly where they sat. The inside of Eddy's head felt as though it was a block of ice. He had to concentrate to keep his vision sharp.

'And again, sergeant,' he said. As usual he'd finished after Meany.

Meany's face was flushed and there was sweat on his brow. Every so often he made a sort of sighing sound at the back of his throat.

McQuarrie held up the second bottle, which was now empty.

'Well there's a first time for everything,' he said wonderingly.

The rest of the section and the cooks looked on in awe.

In the functioning part of his brain Eddy was thinking that without the fructose he'd have been gone long before now.

His skin was cold on the outside but was raging hot underneath. He guessed that to be his metabolism working overtime in burning up the alcohol.

He brought the glass to his lips and drank. The smoky-peat flavour was heavy in his nostrils and a fog of it seemed to have gathered at the back of his throat. It was a taste and smell he felt would be with him for the rest of his life.

'Catholic whoor!' Meany said venomously; adding, 'the only good papisher's a dead one.'

'It's nice to be liked,' Eddy replied, and without realising what he was doing drained his glass. It was the first time he'd finished before Meany and when it dawned on him what he'd done he grinned.

'I'm waiting, Corporal,' he said.

Meany blinked and stared at Eddy's glass.

'It's empty,' Eddy said.

Meany seemed to shrink even further in upon himself and Eddy knew then he'd scored heavily psychologically.

'Fill 'em up!' Meany said with bravado, having finished his

drink. But there was something empty in his voice as though the spirit had gone from it.

The end came two drinks later. With a moan Meany's head slid sideways and he started to slip from his seat.

'Have you had enough, Corporal?' McQuarrie asked.

'Away to hell! All of you bastards!' Meany jerked out. His hands desperately clawed at the table to try and stop himself, but he couldn't. He went crashing to the floor.

Slowly and emphatically Eddy emptied what remained in his glass down his throat.

'I declare King the winner!' McQuarrie said.

The section cheered while Kirk hurried to Eddy's side. 'How do you feel?' he asked.

'Bloody.'

'I'm not surprised.'

Eddy's face broke into an expression of sheer delight. 'I beat the sod. I beat him!'

'You did that,' Kirk said.

'That was just amazing,' McQuarrie said, handing their winnings over. 'Just amazing.'

Eddy started to retch.

Kirk gestured Smart and Ogle over. 'Take him to the bog, will you. Napier and I will see to the Corporal.'

'Aye, of course. Sure,' Ogle replied.

If anyone thought those arrangements unusual or that Kirk was suddenly showing concern for Meany, they never said so. Smart and Ogle each took one of Eddy's arms and draped it round their shoulders. He managed a few steps and then staggered, his feet buckling under him.

'Hurry for Christ's sake!' Eddy mumbled. His cheeks ballooned as vomit burst from his throat into his mouth.

A cook held the door open as Smart and Ogle broke into a run with the hapless Eddy being dragged along between them.

Meany's eyes opened and closed, his lips drew back in a snarl. His body twitched involuntarily as though he had St Vitus' dance.

'What a state,' Kirk said, grabbing hold of Meany's front.

With Napier helping him he got the Corporal upright.

They held Meany the way Smart and Ogle had held Eddy. 'We'll get him into his beddy bydoe where he can sleep it off,' Kirk said.

Meany sagged suddenly between them as he flaked out.

'The sooner he's in kip the better,' McQuarrie said. 'And I'd put a bowl by the side of the bed if I was you.'

'Bugger that. Let him wallow in his own spew,' Napier retorted.

McQuarrie sighed. None of the men ever liked Meany. Which wasn't all that surprising considering how Meany treated them, he reflected.

'We're away then,' Kirk said. 'And thanks for the facilities.'

'I wouldn't have missed it for the world,' McQuarrie replied. Then, shaking his head, 'More than a bottle each. Bloody hell!'

Once outside in the cold night air Meany showed signs of reviving, which suited Kirk just fine. He didn't want the corporal totally zonked out.

'Where are you going? His billet's this way,' Napier queried. Kirk was pulling them in another direction.

'I'm going to have a go at fixing this sod,' Kirk replied. 'Will you help me?'

Napier pulled up short. 'What do you have in mind?' he asked suspiciously.

Kirk laughed softly at the expression on Napier's face. 'Well, I'm not going to stick a bayonet between his ribs, if that's what you're thinking.'

Napier nodded. 'Anything short of murder and I'm your man.'

'Right then. Let's make tracks for the Officers' Mess. And we'll keep in the shadows in the hope nobody sees us.'

'Wherewegoing?' Meany muttered, his eyes flicking open and then closing again.

'Don't worry about a thing, Corp,' Kirk replied soothingly. 'We're going to see you right.'

'That'shelluvagoodofyou,' Meany said. And a second or

two later his head dropped forward again.

When they came to the Officers' Mess they came round the side of it. Napier held on to Meany while Kirk confirmed the coast was clear. En route he'd given Napier his instructions.

The Officers' Mess was ablaze with light and the muted hum of voices could be heard.

As Kirk and Napier dragged Meany up the steps leading to the Mess, Kirk whispered in Meany's ear, 'Eddy King's coming for you, Corp. The Fenian bastard says you're nothing more than a yellow-livered snake and he's going to sort your hash once and for all.'

Kirk held Meany upright while Napier pounded on the Mess door.

'You're all a bunch of cunts!' Napier yelled. 'A bunch of fucking horrible toerags and if just one of you will step out here I'll give him what for!'

'He's coming,' Kirk whispered. 'He says he's going to give you what for!'

'Like fuck he will!' Meany snarled.

Kirk draped the Corporal over a wooden rail.

'Someone's coming!' Napier whispered urgently.

'Get on your feet man! Get on your feet!' Kirk urged.

Meany grabbed hold of the rail and stood there swaying. 'Where are you, King? Where are you, you Catholic whoor!' he slurred.

'Come on!' cried Napier vaulting over the railing.

Kirk stayed long enough to pound on the door one last time, then followed Napier over the railing.

Napier scurried round the side of the building to be joined almost instantly by Kirk.

'What's all the racket?' a voice queried.

'Let me at you, you whoor!' Meany's slurred voice replied.

There was the sound of a scuffle.

Kirk crossed his fingers.

'Having trouble, steward?' a new voice asked.

Kirk recognised the voice immediately. 'Lieutenant Gilzean,' he whispered.

'I'm afraid the Corporal's had a bit too much, sir,' the steward replied.

Meany stood swaying, blinking his eyes as he tried to focus. His hands were balled into fists.

'Now there's a good chap. Get yourself back to your billet before you're put on a charge,' Gilzean said kindly. Coming to Meany he tried to put his arm round Meany's shoulders with the intention of assisting the corporal down the short flight of steps leading to the ground.

With a roar Meany swatted Gilzean's arm away. 'Don't touch me, you Catholic whoor!' he cried. And roaring again punched Gilzean full in the face.

Blood spurted from Gilzean's nose as he staggered back. Blood that fell to spatter the front of his tunic. The steward leapt forward to Gilzean's aid but Gilzean shrugged him aside.

The door banged open to reveal the portly figure of Lieutenant-Colonel Boswell. 'What the deuce is all this, Lieutenant?' he demanded.

Gilzean, blood still streaming down his face, came to attention and saluted. In a few terse sentences he explained the situation.

Boswell's eyes blazed. 'Striking an officer, eh?' he said in an ominous tone of voice. 'All right, Lieutenant, carry on. You know what to do.'

'Yes, sir!' Gilzean replied, saluting again.

Meany shook his head. Something was desperately wrong but he couldn't think what. And where was King? The bastard had been here only seconds ago.

He blinked his eyes but still couldn't focus. All he could make out were blurred images in khaki.

Then suddenly there were more khaki figures and hands were grabbing hold of him. He was dimly aware of his feet scraping the ground.

Kirk and Napier shrank further into the shadows as the guard hauled Meany away. Kirk was jubilant; that a Lieutenant-Colonel had been involved was far far better than

279

anything he'd dared hope. Meany would have the book thrown at him.

'Come on,' he whispered, 'let's get out of here.'

When they were a safe distance away Kirk turned to Napier and said, 'We must keep stum from the rest of the section about what we've just done. I know they wouldn't do it intentionally but should one of them ever blab and it got back to the other NCO's, you and I would in for the high jump.'

'My mouth is sealed,' Napier replied. Then said excitedly, 'Jesus, what do you think they'll do to him?'

'I'm not quite sure but whatever it is it won't be pleasant. Of one thing we can be certain. He's finished as a corporal.'

'Poor sod. I almost feel sorry for him in a way.'

'Don't,' Kirk replied. 'He sure as hell wouldn't if the positions were reversed.'

Napier sniffed. Kirk was right.

The next morning the section had the unbelievable luxury of a long lie in.

It was gone half past nine when the door banged open and Corporal Forbes marched in. 'Wakey wakey!' he shouted. 'The holiday's over.'

Eddy groaned and covered his head with his hands.

'Which one of you is Murray?' Forbes demanded.

My God, Meany's remembered it was me set him up, Kirk thought. He glanced across at Napier who was looking grim and not a little scared.

'I am, sir!' he said, crawling out of bed and coming to attention.

'Troop Commander wants to see you right away so get washed, shaved and dressed as quick as you can.'

'Yes, sir!'

'The rest of you clean this room out. Further orders will be forthcoming.'

'Yes, sir!' came the ragged reply.

Turning on his heel Forbes marched from the room.

'I'm dying!' Eddy moaned. 'I really think I'm dying.'

'You look terrible,' McKenzie said cheerfully.

'Like a corpse all set for interment,' Kirkwood added.

'I'll never drink again,' Eddy groaned.

'That's what they all say,' Smart said, pleased that it raised a laugh.

'What's happened to Meany?' Ogle asked.

'Must be laid up with a hangover,' Smart replied.

'I hope the bastard suffers,' Rennie said.

'I'll drink to that,' Kirkwood said, and again everyone laughed.

Napier sat on Eddy's bed. 'Can you get up?' he asked.

Eddy's face was white as cream and his eyes were bloodshot. 'I did win, didn't I?' he husked.

'You did.'

'Where's Kirk?'

'Off getting washed. The Troop Commander wants to see him.'

'What about?'

'I've no idea.'

Eddy groaned. 'I've never ever had a hangover like this one. My head feels as though a grenade's gone off inside it.'

'A couple of pills and a shower's what you need,' Napier said.

'I don't think I could manage that on my own.'

'Don't worry. I'll help you.'

Looking like death itself, Eddy was helped out of bed and to his feet.

Ogle started to sing and the others joined in.

'For he's a jolly good pish artist,
For he's a jolly good pish artist,
For he's . . .'

'Very funny,' said Eddy.

Twenty minutes later the section were sitting on or by their beds waiting for the further orders they'd been promised.

Eddy was still in a dreadful state but feeling a lot better than he had been. His skin was clammy and oily still despite the shower, and every time he swallowed it was as though his windpipe had been scalded by boiling water.

Napier sat nervously watching the door. He couldn't think why Kirk might have been sent for other than in connection with the previous night's incident. He started sweating profusely under the arms.

Napier was first on his feet when the door opened and Kirk entered. Kirk wore a bemused expression.

'Well?' Napier asked.

Kirk smiled as he surveyed the section. 'It seems Corporal Meany disgraced himself last night,' he said. 'In fact he disgraced himself so badly the Corporal will shortly be a corporal no more.'

Relief surged through Napier. He knew from the quick look Kirk had shot him that they were in the clear.

'What happened?' Rennie demanded.

Kirk went on, 'Well, as you all know, Napier here and myself took Meany back to his billet after the drinking contest. We didn't undress him or anything, just dumped him on his bed and left him to it. Only it seems Meany didn't stay there but somehow got up again and went for a walk.' He paused before adding, 'To the Officers' Mess.'

Ogle whistled.

'I like it so far!' Kirkwood said.

'And ...? And? ...' Smart demanded.

'Nobody knows why but apparently he started banging the Mess door and shouting obscenities. And when a steward and Lieutenant Gilzean tried to talk him into quietly going back to his room, he thumped Gilzean.'

'Ah!' said Kirkwood, bliss written across his face.

'Bloodied Gilzean's nose,' Kirk added.

'Ah!' Kirkwood repeated.

'At which point Lieutenant-Colonel Boswell appeared on the scene and Meany was marched off to the guard house.'

'What are they going to do to him?' Napier asked.

'He's to stay in the guard house till tomorrow when he's

282

being flown back home. He'll be doing his detention in the Military Correction Training Centre at Colchester. Fifty-six days' worth.'

The section looked from one to the other. They'd all heard about Colchester and what allegedly went on in the MCTC there.

'What happens to him after that?' Ogle asked.

'He'll certainly be reduced to ranks, although whether that happens before or after, I'm not sure, and then he'll be returned to the regiment.'

'So we could meet up with him again, only this time on equal terms?' Smart said, a speculative gleam in his eye. 'I doubt that. From what the Troop Commander said, I definitely got the impression he'll be posted to another battalion.'

'Pity,' replied Smart, his voice heavy with disappointment.

'So with Meany gone, who's our new corporal?' Rennie asked.

'Stand to attention and salute when you talk to me, you horrible little shite of a man!' Kirk barked out, adding with a twinkle in his eye, 'What are you?'

'You don't mean ...?'

'I'm afraid so,' Kirk replied. 'I did my best to talk them out of it but you know how it is when one is so obviously head and shoulders above the common herd.'

'I'll give you common herd!' Smart said indignantly.

'He's pulling your pudding, Norrie. Don't rise to the bait,' Napier said.

'Oh!' replied Smart, then, 'I knew that!'

McKenzie and Ogle both groaned and Rennie said scathingly, 'Of course you did!'

'Life suddenly looks an awful lot rosier than it did a few minutes ago. Congratulations ... Corp!' Napier said, crossing to Kirk and pumping his hand.

The rest of the section crowded round, eager to slap Kirk on the back and get in on the hand pumping. The only one not to do so was Eddy, who was lying curled up on his bed with his back to Kirk.

Finally Kirk broke away from his well-wishers and, crossing to Eddy's bed, sat. 'Well what have you got to say to your new corporal?' he asked.

His reply was a combined grunt and snore. Eddy was fast asleep.

'I think we'll let this David kip,' Kirk said quietly and tenderly. 'It took a lot out of him beating Goliath.'

'What the hell's he talking about?' Smart whispered.

Ogle withered Smart with a look.

'Well I can't have seen every picture that's ever been made,' Smart replied waspishly.

It was the section's twenty-third patrol with Kirk as leader. It was three o'clock in the morning and they were taking their second break.

McKenzie was acting as lookout while Rennie brewed up. Smart had built the small fire which crackled fiercely. When it came to building fires there was no one in the section to touch him.

Kirk and Eddy sat side by side, both with steaming mugs in their hands. Eddy was smoking.

'Just stay where you are, gentlemen, and don't move!' a voice said, coming from the darkness beyond the fire.

Everyone froze with the complete unexpectedness of it.

'MacKenzie?' Kirk called out.

The reply was muffled and indistinct.

'Who are you?' Kirk asked, gesturing to Smart to stay where he was.

'Throw your weapons behind you, please,' the voice instructed.

'No,' said Kirk emphatically. 'I'm afraid we can't do that.'

'Then I might have to shoot you.'

'For what reason?'

'An armed incursion into Russian territory.'

Kirk frowned. The voice had an English accent. 'You don't sound Russian to me,' he said.

284

A sentence in Russian rapped out and there were vague rustlings all around.

'Okay, I believe you,' Kirk said. 'But tell me, when did the Russian sector become Russian territory?'

The voice chuckled. 'The moment we Russians took it over. We're very possessive, don't you know?'

'If we are in the Russian sector, and according to my map we aren't, then it's a genuine mistake. So rather than shoot holes in one another why not join us for a cup of coffee instead? I don't know how many men you've got but I'm sure we can cope.'

There was a brief pause and then the voice said, '*Real* coffee?'

'As real as you'll get anywhere.'

Again there was a brief pause and then the voice rapped out what could only be an order.

McKenzie stumbled out of the darkness looking sheepish and embarrassed. 'I never heard a thing,' he said.

'Did they hurt you?'

'No. Just a hand over the mouth, that's all.'

'Ivan!' Ogle whispered excitedly.

The man who came towards them was short and stocky. He was dressed in the uniform of a Red Army officer.

'Good morning,' he said.

Kirk rose and extended his hand. 'Corporal Murray,' he said, then gesturing around, 'my men.'

The Russian nodded pleasantly to the section before turning his attention back to Kirk. 'I am Captain Turushev and you said something about coffee?'

Eddy poured some into his own mug which he passed to Turushev, who accepted it gratefully.

'Sugar and milk?' Eddy asked.

Turushev laughed softly. 'All the pleasures of home,'

'What about your men?' Kirk asked.

'They can stay out there.'

'How many of you are there?'

285

'A lot more than you, Corporal.'

The section relaxed. Most eyes fastened on Turushev, others were drawn to the surrounding darkness and the Russian soldiers whom they couldn't see but who could see them.

'Ah!' sighed Turushev after he'd taken a swallow. 'It's been such a long time since the real thing.'

'Your English is very good,' Kirk said.

'I was posted in London for two years after the war. That was where I learned it.'

'You sound just like an Englishman,' Eddy said.

'I'll take that as a compliment. Although being Scottish perhaps you didn't mean it as one. The Battle of Bannockburn, Scotland v England at Hampden Park and Wembley.' And having said that, Turushev laughed.

'Did you like England?' Kirk asked.

'Loved it. I was connected with the Embassy there, which meant I attended a great many parties and then functions. I had some marvellous times I can tell you. Especially with the English women.' He leaned forward confidentially. 'Whoever said English women are cold doesn't know what he's talking about. You can take my word for that!'

Kirk smiled. 'Eddy here's our expert on English women. Had one in London for some time himself.'

That annoyed Eddy a little. He didn't like Annie talked about that way. Somehow it cheapened her. To change the subject, or to try and get away from it anyway, he pulled out his packet of cigarettes and offered the Russian one.

Turushev delicately picked out a cigarette and held it up so he could admire it. 'Senior Service,' he said. 'I haven't had one of these since I left England.'

'I thought Russian fags were supposed to be good,' Eddy said.

'Camel dung. Or if it isn't, that's what it certainly tastes like. But you can find out for yourself.' And having said that he passed one of his own cigarettes over to Eddy.

Eddy flicked a match and they both lit up.

286

'Christ Almighty!' said Eddy coughing. 'You're right.'

'And this is sheer bliss,' Turushev replied, drawing smoke deep into his lungs.

Kirk caught Eddy's eye and gave a slight gesture of his head to indicate Eddy's packet which was still out. Eddy got the message.

'Here, you'd better have these,' Eddy said. 'I've got more back at the billet.'

Turushev didn't need to be offered twice. 'You're most kind,' he said, accepting the packet as though it was some priceless item.

'Now, about this little mix-up,' Kirk said. 'According to my map we're still in the British sector.'

'Show me,' Turushev said.

Kirk unfolded his map and spread it on the ground. Using his finger he pinpointed what he thought to be their position.

Turushev shook his head. 'This is where you really are, right here!' he said.

'Are you sure?'

'Absolutely.'

Kirk chewed his lip. 'Map-reading never was my strong point,' he admitted.

'It's easily done on a night like this in country which is very similar for miles around,' Turushev said generously, adding with a wink, 'actually I've been over on your side several times myself when I shouldn't have been.'

Kirk knew then it was going to be all right. 'More coffee?' he asked, seeing Turushev's mug was empty.

'If you could spare it.'

'Our pleasure,' Kirk replied.

As Eddy was filling Turushev's mug, Kirk said, 'How about a wee dram to go with it?'

Turushev's rather slanted eyes opened wide. 'You don't mean whisky, do you?'

Kirk produced a small flask, which he always took along on patrol with him. It contained Sergeant McQuarrie's Heather Dew, which he rather liked and which was only a fraction of

287

the cost of a bottle of Scotch – when Scotch was available that is, which was rarely.

'Tell me what you think of that,' he said, handing over the flask.

Turushev took a deep swig.

'And again,' Kirk said.

The second swig was even deeper than the first.

'Well?' Kirk demanded.

'Excellent. Highland malt, if I'm not mistaken?'

It was on the tip of Kirk's tongue to say he also thought it tasted like Highland malt when in actual fact it was poteen, but something stopped him from doing so.

'Real coffee, good cigarettes and malt whisky,' Turushev said. 'My lucky night.'

Kirk glanced at his watch. Time was passing, the section really should be on its way.

Turushev noted the glance and realised what it meant. 'I too must continue my patrol,' he said.

'Is this your regular beat?' Kirk asked.

'Yes. Every night.'

'We do turn about with another section.'

'One on, one off. You're very lucky,' Turushev said wistfully.

Turushev finished his coffee and the remainder of the whisky, after which hands were shaken all round. Turushev was about to stride back into the darkness where his men were patiently waiting, when suddenly he paused as a thought struck him.

'Can we talk privately for a second?' he asked Kirk.

'Sure,' Kirk replied. And the two of them moved away from the others.

Turushev said, 'I was wondering if you could get me a few bottles of that excellent whisky. I'd be willing to pay handsomely of course.'

Kirk rubbed his scar. Why not do the Russian a favour? he thought. It was no skin off his nose.

'Roubles are no use,' he said.

'Naturally. But I think I can lay my hands on some sterling or Deutschmarks.'

Kirk nodded. 'It is a bit pricey, you appreciate?'

'How much in sterling?'

Kirk knew how much it cost to buy a real bottle of Scotch on the German black market, which was the price he now stated.

'Fine.'

'Half a dozen bottles too many?'

Turushev sucked in a breath. 'You can get me as many as that?'

'No problem.'

'Then half a dozen bottles it is. Now, when and where?'

'Night after next? Same time, same place?'

'I'll be looking for you,' Turushev said. 'Till then, Murray.'

'Till then, Captain,' Kirk replied.

After the Russians had gone, the section proceeded on its way. The men of the section had strict instructions from Kirk that they weren't to mention to anyone about their encounter with the Russians.

The men were only too happy to comply.

A smiling Turushev strode out of the darkness. 'Good morning,' he said.

'Good morning,' Kirk replied, handing Turushev a mug of coffee.

The Russian accepted a cigarette from Eddy, which he allowed Eddy to light for him before turning to Kirk and raising an eyebrow.

Kirk opened his knapsack and passed over half a dozen bottles of Heather Dew.

'No labels?' Turushev asked, examining one of the bottles.

Kirk shrugged. 'It's what's inside you're drinking, not the label.'

'Quite true,' Turushev replied, and taking the top off the bottle had a swig.

'There's no mistaking true Highland malt,' Turushev said.

Kirk nodded, thinking, like hell there wasn't!

Turushev pulled out his wallet and he extracted a wad of notes. These he handed to Kirk. 'I think you'll find that right,' he said.

'You don't mind if I count it, do you?'

'Of course not.'

The money was in Deutschmarks and correct.

'It's a pleasure doing business with you,' Kirk said.

Turushev packed the bottles away in a haversack he'd brought with him and then returned to his coffee, which Eddy had topped up. He squatted, facing Kirk.

'Is there any chance you can get me more?' he asked.

Kirk regarded the Russian thoughtfully. This was beginning to get interesting.

'How many bottles would you want?' he asked.

'As many as you can get me.'

Excitement fluttered in Kirk's insides. It was the same sort of excitement he'd experienced when he'd heard about Harry Hydelman and the B.X.

'Are we talking in terms of a dozen now, or in cases?' he asked.

'Cases if you can do it.'

Kirk rocked back on his heels. It had been galling him that he hadn't been able to deal in the Uelsberg black market. The people who did so had registered their disapproval of soldiers trying to butt in only a few weeks previously, when a soldier who'd tried to set up in silk stockings had been beaten within an inch of his life. And Kirk was damned if he was going to get mixed up in proceedings like those without a Turk McGhie to back him up.

But dealing with a Russian for a Russian market was a different kettle of fish entirely. And one that smelled hugely of profit.

'What about money?' he asked. 'Can you lay your hands on large sums of sterling and Deutschmarks?'

'I can do better than that,' Turushev replied mysteriously. 'Come, let us take a walk, you and I.'

The two men rose and strolled a little way off.

'What do you make of that?' Turushev asked, handing Kirk a small hard object.

Turushev flicked a lighter into flame and held it close to Kirk's palm so Kirk could see what it was that lay nestling there.

Yellow metal glinted in the light from the flame. Metal that had been cast into a small bar.

'Gold!' whispered Kirk through suddenly clenched teeth.

'Eighteen carat,' Turushev added.

Kirk weighed the gold in his hand. For such a small amount it was surprisingly heavy. Reluctantly he handed it back to Turushev, who was grinning in the darkness.

'How much is that worth?' Kirk asked.

'That, and the box of bars it came from, is valueless to me because I can't cash it in,' Turushev replied with a shrug.

'Why not?'

'Because all spoils of war go direct to the State. Yes, my friend, this was Nazi gold. A small cache which I was lucky to stumble upon.'

The picture was beginning to clear for Kirk. 'Gold you can't sell but whisky you can?' he asked.

'When I was in London I committed a small indiscretion, as a result of which I will never be allowed to set foot in the West again. So the gold, as I've already said, is valueless to me now and in the future. But if I could exchange it for whisky, I would then be in a position not only to further my career – "bribery and corruption", I think is the appropriate English phrase – but also to feather my nest at the same time. The latter, of course, providing we can deal in quantity.'

He paused to light a long Russian cigarette before going on. 'I take it you are acquiring your whisky from the German black market?' he asked, eyes slitted and intent upon Kirk.

'Yes,' Kirk lied.

'So you will act as middleman between them and me for which, naturally, you will make a substantial profit.'

Kirk's mind was whirling. The trouble was he didn't know what McQuarrie's still was capable of or even if McQuarrie would agree to sell to him in bulk. He needed time to think and make inquiries and work everything out.

'Look,' he said slowly. 'The contact I have is only a small one and frankly I don't know what sort of amounts he can handle. Let's agree to meet four days hence, which is my patrol after next, and I should be able to know more then. Whatever happens I'll bring you another half-dozen bottles.'

'That arrangement is satisfactory with me,' Turushev replied, handing Kirk the gold bar.

'In the meantime have that on account, as I presume you will want to have it assayed and establish its value.'

Kirk fingered the small bar lovingly before slipping it into a pocket where it would be safe.

'Now, what about coffee and cigarettes? Can you do anything for me there?' Turushev asked.

Kirk knew there would be nothing like the profit in those that there would be in the whisky. But a profit was still a profit, after all.

'I'll give you an answer on those next time as well,' he replied.

Turushev nodded his approval.

Kirk stroked his scar, his mind tumbling over at a rate of knots.

Sergeant McQuarrie sat on the edge of a table and looked long and hard at Kirk. 'Just what have you got yourself mixed up in?' he asked.

'Something that can make some extra change for both of us,' Kirk replied.

'If you're selling round about, those German black marketeers will cut your balls off, you know that, don't you?'

'I won't be selling round about.'

'Then where?'

'That's my business, Sergeant.'

McQuarrie looked sceptical. 'Now let's go over this again. You want me to up my production and you will buy the lot?'

'As much as you can sell me.'

'At the same price as usual?'

Kirk laughed softly. 'I'm not asking for bulk reduction if that's what you're thinking!'

'I was thinking more of an increase actually,' McQuarrie replied.

'How much per bottle?'

'An added one and six.'

Kirk pretended to consider that, finally saying reluctantly, 'You drive a hard bargain, Sergeant. But it's agreed.'

Rising from the table McQuarrie beckoned Kirk to follow him. He led Kirk through various rooms to the very back of the cookhouse area, all of which was his exclusive domain.

When they reached the room where the still was, McQuarrie locked the door behind him. Kirk stared in fascination at the still; it was the first he'd ever seen.

'Where on earth did you get it from?' he asked.

'I didn't. It was already here when I arrived. The Wehrmacht were billeted here during the war so I can only presume they had it installed.'

Kirk regarded the steady drip of alcohol, which was rapidly filling up a two-gallon jar. The air was pungent with the smoky odour he'd come to associate with Heather Dew.

McQuarrie went on, 'When I came across it, it had been shoved back here out the way and quite obviously hadn't been used for a number of years. Well I got to thinking. It seemed there was never any whisky available in the Mess and of course the black market stuff was way beyond what I could afford. The next step seemed inevitable, me having worked in a distillery and all and knowing how to go about making it.'

'What amazes me is how much like Highland malt it is,' Kirk said. 'I've been around pubs and whisky all my life and honestly I couldn't tell the difference.'

'It's a very high-quality poteen, and that's because I know exactly what I'm doing. But there's more to it than that. So much of the flavour and body of a whisky depends on the water used to make it with. And the water round here seems to be similar to that found in many parts of the Highlands.'

Kirk shook his head. 'Amazing!' he said.

'But there's a lot about whisky-making we don't know. Why is it, for example, that two distilleries across the road from one another and using the same stream can turn out two quite different-tasting malts? No one's discovered the answer to that one yet. It's simply one of the mysteries.'

'As far as I'm concerned, the big question is how much can you turn out per week?' Kirk asked.

'I'm not sure. At the moment I'm only producing enough for myself and a few of the lads I sell it to, which amounts roughly to about two dozen bottles a week.'

'Could you do a dozen cases?'

'Oh aye, easy. If I can get the grain that is.'

'Where do you get it from now?'

'From the supplies brought in, man. I just syphon off what's required and that's that.'

'What about enough for full production?'

McQuarrie frowned. 'That could be tricky. I don't see how I could explain how I suddenly needed that amount when I've been getting by on what I have for a number of years now.'

'All right, that's a problem I'll have to solve,' said Kirk thoughtfully. 'You just write down what you need and I'll see to it.'

'Then there's bottling,' McQuarrie went on. 'What about that?'

Kirk picked up a distinctive green bottle waiting to be filled with Heather Dew. McQuarrie always used the same type bottle for his poteen.

'Where do you get these from?' Kirk asked.

'From the laundry. They're old bleach bottles.'

Kirk raised an eyebrow. 'And you're telling me you can't get enough from the laundry if, or should I say when, we go into full production?'

'That's it.'

'Leave that to me as well, then.'

And labels, Kirk thought. He'd have to do something about

those. If he was going to do this thing he may as well do it properly.

'Right then!' said Kirk, smacking his hands together. 'I'll need half a dozen bottles for three days from now and in the meantime I'll get on with my side of things.'

'I just hope you know what you're doing,' McQuarrie said.

Kirk remembered that was a question he'd been asked once before. Well that had worked out all right, so why not this?

'Trust me Sergeant. Just trust me and I'll put an added bit of jingle in both our pockets. Making money's a talent I have.'

Humming, he went in search of Eddy.

'There you are, sir,' the jeweller said, counting the notes out into Kirk's hand.

Kirk stared at the pile of Deutschmarks in amazement. It was far, far more than he'd expected.

'Pleasure to do business with you, sir. Call again any time,' the jeweller said.

Kirk nodded and, turning, left the shop.

Outside Eddy was waiting for him. Together they walked down the street.

There was an enormous profit to be made here, Kirk thought. He would be buying whisky from McQuarrie for a pittance, selling it at black market prices plus some. And now there was the value of the gold which he could further juggle to increase his profit.

'Want in?' he asked Eddy, aware that Eddy knew full well what he was up to.

'Why not?' Eddy replied.

'I'll need a partner. It's a two-man operation, the way I see it.'

'If I'm a partner then that's fifty-fifty, I take it?'

Kirk smiled. 'It's my idea so I get extra for that. But I'll tell you what, seeing how I like you and we've been such good mates, how about sixty-forty?'

'You're on,' Eddy replied. And they sealed the partnership by shaking hands.

A few steps further down the street Eddy said, 'What about the rest of the section? One for all and all for one, as you put it?'

'This is money we're talking about. There's no one for all when it comes to that,' Kirk replied.

Eddy laughed. 'Jesus, you're a hard bastard,' he said.

'Not as hard as some I could name. But I'm getting there.' Kirk replied softly.

He was thinking of Major and Gerald Gibb.

Eddy was well pleased with himself as he stepped out of the printer's office. He'd got a good price on the labels for Heather Dew which he'd placed with the printer and which the man had promised him would be ready in two days' time.

He glanced at his watch. He had some time to kill before making his way back to the castle. He was supposed to meet up with Kirk who was somewhere at the other end of Uelsberg talking to a grain merchant.

He knew the coffee in the coffee shop was ridiculously overpriced and not very good either but for the moment he couldn't think of any other way to pass the next half-hour.

After buying his coffee he looked for a seat, spying one beside a solitary woman. He'd sat beside her and started to spoon into his cup before he recognised her.

'Dr Kruppermann, isn't it?' he queried.

She looked up to stare at him blankly.

'I came to see you some time ago about an alcohol problem I had.' Then, blushing when he realised what that must sound like, he blurted out, 'Fructose?'

'Oh yes! Now I remember!' She laughed. 'The drinking contest.'

He nodded. 'I won.'

'I'm pleased to hear it.'

'The fructose made all the difference. I couldn't have done it without it.'

She smiled and sipped her coffee, crow's-feet crinkling the corners of her eyes and mouth.

Eddy was enjoying the experience of being alone with a good-looking woman, the last having been the whore Magda. Suddenly he was self-conscious and ever so slightly embarrassed.

'Cigarette?' he asked, offering his packet.

'Thank you.'

He lit it for her and for the next few seconds they smoked in silence.

'Are you married, Doctor?' he asked, then wondered what had prompted him to do so. It was terribly forward.

What could only be interpreted as pain edged into her eyes. 'I was once,' she said, 'but no more.'

'The war?'

She smiled again, only this time there was a bitter quality about it.

'The Russian Front,' she replied.

'I'm sorry.'

'Why should you be? You never knew him and he was your enemy.'

'The worst thing about war is the ones who're left behind. Wouldn't you agree?' he said after a while.

'Yes, I would,' she whispered.

'I was lucky to miss it.'

Annie Grimes, he thought. That was who Dr Kruppermann reminded him of. They weren't physically alike at all, Annie being tallish, brunette and slim while Dr Kruppermann was quite short with blonde hair and, from what he could see, a well-padded, curvaceous figure. But they both had the same quality of femininity which he recognised but couldn't have described in words. He judged the doctor to be a few years older than Annie.

Seeing her cup was empty, he said, 'Would you like another?'

She looked undecided.

'I'd really appreciate the company,' he said.

There must have been something in his tone for she looked at him strangely and quizzically.

'I'll get the coffee,' he said and taking her cup rose and made for the counter.

On his return she said, 'Are you a regular soldier?'

'No. National Service.'

'It must be difficult for a young man like you to be away from home. You must be homesick for your parents and sweetheart, perhaps?'

He shook his head. 'There's no one.'

'No one at all?'

'Nobody,' he said, and stared into his cup.

'Me neither,' she replied. 'I was the only one of my family to survive the war.'

'We've got something in common then. Being alone in the world, that is.'

After a little while she said wistfully, 'Such strange and sad times we live in.'

His heart went out to her, and although he'd only known her a few minutes, and despite the fact she was considerably older than he was, he wanted to reach out and touch her, to take her in his arms and comfort her.

'Was your husband a doctor?' he asked.

'No, not Willi!' she laughed. 'He had his own business.' She laughed again. 'Anyone less like a doctor I can't imagine.'

They stared at one another, she cool and very self-contained.

'And what did *you* do before they made you a soldier?' she asked.

'I also had my own business.'

'Oh!' she said, surprised. 'You look too young for that.'

'Mind you,' he added, 'it wasn't all that much of one. I sold used cars. But they were my cars on my lot and that was the main thing.'

'You sounded very proud when you said that.'

He shrugged. 'I suppose I am. Where I come from that would be considered something of an achievement.'

'Oh, *ja!* The Scottish man, I'd forgotten that,' she said smiling.

'Not just Scottish. I'm from Glasgow, a Glaswegian.'

She laughed softly. 'Your eyes shoot fire when you say that. Say it again.'

'Glaswegian?'

'There we are. Shafts of fire!'

He cocked his head and looked at her. 'Are you taking the mickey?' he asked.

'No, I wouldn't do that to you. But tell me about this Glasgow of yours which brings such fire to your eyes.'

'Ach – it's a dump. A real hole in the ground. Dirty big tenements, most of them with outside cludgies ...'

'Cludgies?'

'Toilets.'

'That's awful,' she said.

He went on. 'Chronic unemployment. Terrible housing. Why, I've known whole families of six and seven crowded into a room and kitchen with the room hardly big enough to swing a cat in.'

She shook her head.

'And a terrible place for drink. Friday night, pay night, you'll see them crawling home along the gutter. A couple of screwtops in their jacket pockets, a half-bottle in their back one, and pissed as ... well, "farts", the expression is. If you'll excuse me.'

'And you like this place?'

'Oh aye. It's wonderful.'

She shook her head in amazement.

He groped for words, trying to explain. But he wasn't really articulate enough. 'It's the people, you see. They're different ... they're ... well, there's just nobody like Glasgow folk, except perhaps those in Liverpool, but I've never been there so I can't say.'

He offered her another cigarette, which she eagerly accepted. She didn't seem to have any of her own. They both lit up.

299

'And it's a violent place,' he said, continuing. 'Stabbings, razorings, broken bottles, hatchets. You never know what you might be up against if you get into a barney with someone.'

'And these are your marvellous folk?'

'I know, it does sound a bit funny when it's put that way,' he replied ruefully.

'Funny?'

'Peculiar. Odd.'

'I agree,' she said.

'But it's a wonderful city all the same. You'll not find a better anywhere, not in the whole wide world.'

Leoni Kruppermann decided she liked Eddy. She liked his youth and vitality, but above all she liked the raw enthusiasm he exuded. So different, and uplifting, to the cynicism and deep-rooted weariness of herself.

Sighing, she drained her cup. 'I really must be getting on,' she said. 'I have several calls to make, important ones. Thank you for the conversation and cigarettes. And the coffee of course.'

He didn't want her to leave. Being with her had brought back that warm glow he'd once felt with Annie Grimes and hadn't experienced since.

'I, eh ... eh ...'

'Yes?'

'There's an English picture on at the weekend. I ... eh ... don't suppose you'd like to go and see it, would you?'

He looked like an overgrown schoolboy, she thought. And his lack of sophistication was absolutely charming. So different to what she'd been used to in the past.

He was very young of course. She was probably old enough to be his mother. Well ... perhaps not quite, she pretended. And she could do with a night out. Some laughter and gaiety.

'If you're already busy I'll understand perfectly,' he said.

'I'd love to go,' she replied.

Relief, tinged with excitement, welled through Eddy. 'That's great,' he said.

She produced a pocketbook and pen, scribbling a few lines

in the former. 'That's my home address,' she said, tearing out a page and handing it to him. 'Telephone the surgery and leave a message as to what time you'll pick me up.'

He stood and gazed down into her face. 'I'll be looking forward to it,' he said.

'I also.'

They shook hands in the continental fashion and then she was hurrying away. He watched her through the large coffee shop window until she'd disappeared from sight. He looked at his watch and with a start realised he'd been so engrossed he'd forgotten the time. He too would have to hurry if he was going to meet Kirk.

'What kept you?' Kirk said when Eddy arrived at the appointed place.

'Oh, I just met someone, that's all.'

'Sounds mysterious.'

'Not really. How did you get on with the grain merchant?'

They started walking in the direction of the castle. 'Expensive sod, but he'll supply what we need,' Kirk replied. 'And you?'

'We can have the order in two days' time.'

Kirk nodded. 'That only leaves the bottles to sort out, which is being more difficult than I'd anticipated. The bleach is made and bottled in Düsseldorf, apparently, which rules out a direct approach. I'll just have to think of something else, that's all.'

'Life's tough at the top,' Eddy said and laughed.

'You'd better believe it. And what's got into you suddenly? You're all bright-eyed and bushy-tailed, as the Yanks say.'

'Can I have a pass for Saturday night, Kirk?'

'Sure. I thought we all might go into town anyway and have a few beers.'

'I actually want to meet somebody.'

Kirk stopped dead. 'A bird, is that it? I should have known.'

'She's helluva nice. I like her.'

'Not one of the brasses I hope?'

'No. Doctor Kruppermann. Remember her?'

'You fly bugger! She was quite a classy piece of skirt, as I recall.'

'Yes, she is good-looking.'

'Not too old for you? Sure you can handle her?' Kirk teased.

'I can handle her,' Eddy replied emphatically.

Kirk laughed as they continued on their way to the castle.

'Well?' Eddy demanded a little further on.

'Well what?'

'The bloody pass, Kirk!'

'Of course you can have it. Would I stop a pal, and business partner, getting his hole?'

'It's not like that,' Eddie said quietly.

Kirk smiled mockingly and snorted, bursting out laughing again when Eddy turned and good-humouredly hit him on the shoulder.

Kirk and Turushev strolled a little way off from the section. Both held steaming cups of coffee. As usual, the Russian's men remained hidden.

'Your gold is genuine all right and my contact has given me the go-ahead for two dozen cases a week. All that remains now is for you and I to haggle out a price,' Kirk said.

'Two dozen cases!' Turushev mused. 'Excellent!'

'Which I suggest I don't deliver every week but rather do a monthly delivery of eight dozen. It would be a lot easier for me that way, if it's all right by you.'

'Fine. That suits me down to the ground.'

'And with the monthly shipment there'll be five thousand cigarettes and a hundred pounds of coffee. That all adds up to quite a load so I suggest you have some sort of transport available.'

Turushev shook his head. 'Not necessary. My men are yellow-faces from Kazakhstan and Uzbekistan, peasants well used to carrying heavy loads. They could hump double that amount if needs be.'

302

'Suit yourself,' Kirk said shrugging. 'Now, I had the gold bar you gave me assayed and valued. Going on that value, and not forgetting I have to make a profit out of all this, what I propose is . . .' And he went on to state just how much whisky, cigarettes and coffee he was prepared to give against each gold bar.

When he was finished Turushev said cynically, 'You do like to make your profit, don't you?'

'I'm taking an awful risk, Turushev. And risks cost money.'

'All right then. It's agreed. And as we're going to be doing business from now on, you can call me Kolya.'

'And I'm Kirk.'

They shook hands.

'Now let's arrange a time and place for the first meet,' said Kirk, all business once again.

It was evening and Kirk and Eddy were in the still-room bottling Heather Dew. Kirk held a two-gallon jar of poteen and Eddy a metal funnel as they carefully filled bottle after bottle. Several other brimming two-gallon jars lay stacked nearby.

'So how are you getting on with your doctor then?' Kirk asked.

'All right.'

'What does that mean?'

'Precisely what it says. All right.'

'Got your end away yet?'

'To hear you, you'd think sex was the most important thing in the world,' Eddy retorted.

Kirk looked thoughtful. 'Well, – it's a toss-up between that and money. I'd hate to have to choose.'

'There are other things in life, you know.'

'Which I suppose means you haven't got there yet?'

Eddy mumbled something.

'What's that? Speak up! I can't hear you.'

Eddy mumbled again.

'I still can't bloody well hear you!'

'*No I haven't!*' Eddy yelled.

'All right, all right! No need to blast my eardrums to bits. What's wrong with you then? Lost the notion?'

'I haven't got round to it yet, I suppose.'

'So what do you do, these nights you take her out?'

'The pictures. Music. We take walks. Discuss art ...'

'What the hell do *you* know about art?' Kirk exclaimed, obviously amused.

'Not a lot. But I'm learning. Matisse, Gauguin, Rembrandt, Picasso. Leoni has books with pictures in them, pictures of paintings and drawings. I prefer Picasso myself, especially his nudes.'

'My God!' said Kirk, shaking his head. 'What next?'

'Leoni is very cultured ...'

'All Krauts love culture,' Kirk cut in. 'They have a positive thing about it. Only with the vast majority of them they see it from the outside in and not inside out.'

Eddy frowned. He wasn't quite sure he understood what Kirk meant by that.

'She'll have you going to the theatre next,' Kirk said.

'Oh we are, next week. A play by Bernard Shaw, which I won't understand a word of as it's all in German.'

'Then why bother going?'

'Because she wants to see it, that's why.'

'No hanky-panky, sitting through plays you can't understand, Picasso and Matisse! This is beginning to sound serious.'

'You're just jealous, that's your trouble,' Eddy replied, not realising just how true that actually was.

'Me? Jealous? Don't be ridiculous!' Kirk scoffed. But in truth he was greatly feeling the strain of not having sex. After his scare with Gottfried he'd decided that whores just weren't worth the risk and to date he hadn't found a decent and respectable German female to have an affair with.

There had been several who'd given him the come-on but he hadn't been sure that he could trust them not to be pox-ridden, the number of VD cases amongst the castle soldiers having risen steeply yet again.

'Anyway I like plays,' Eddy said, and went on to tell Kirk about the night he and Michelle had gone to see the famous actor knight as the knight's guest and of the meal the three of them had had afterwards at the Ivy Restaurant.

'That night gave me a taste for getting on in life,' Eddy said. 'If I can possibly get them I want the good things, the luxuries.'

'Now you're talking, Eddy. Getting on, getting ahead. That's where you and I are similar. And I'll tell you this, when you get back in civvy street, if you find you're not making as much selling used cars as you would like then think about a pub. They're little goldmines, all of them.'

Kirk patted the two-gallon jar he was holding. 'Anything to do with booze and you can't go wrong. There are an awful lot of people in Glasgow who'd give up eating before they'd give up drinking.'

'A pub, eh?' Eddy mused. Although he knew Kirk owned several of them it was a new idea that he go into that line of business.

'And by the time we've finished with Heather Dew and our friend Kolya Turushev, let's hope you'll have more than enough loot in your sky to be well able to afford one. I'll certainly be looking to add another, if not two to my string.'

That conversation stayed with Eddy and gave him much food for thought.

'"Circus Family, 1905",' Leoni Kruppermann said, then, turning the page, '"Friendship, 1908".'

The latter was a pen-and-ink sketch belonging to the early so-called Negro phase of Cubism. A note below the sketch said it had been inspired by Negro masks.

'It's amazing what that man Picasso sees in people,' Eddy said wonderingly. 'I'd hate to think how he might portray me.'

'Very romantic, I should think,' Leoni replied.

'How do you mean?'

'I don't mean in the sexual sense but rather in your overall attitude to life.'

They were sitting on Leoni's sofa with the art book spread on her lap. On the floor stood an empty bottle of wine that Eddy had brought along and which they'd drunk while talking and leafing through various art books.

'What's wrong with sex then?' he asked.

'Nothing. I never said there was.'

He found he couldn't stare her straight in the eyes that close together. Her gaze was too frank and penetrating for him. Not that he had anything to hide.

He wondered then about his reticence at making a pass at her. They'd been going out for some time now and he hadn't even as much as kissed her. He couldn't think why, except he'd got the impression that was the way she'd wanted it.

'I have a little tea. Would you like some?' she asked.

'No,' he replied quickly, taking hold of her by the arm. 'I'd much rather we just sat here for the moment.

She smiled, a faltering one that hovered round her lips.

'Leoni?'

'Yes?'

He drew her to him and stroked her hair. Her flesh against his was firm but springy, her breasts large and pressing. His right hand curled round her neck, gently pulling her head back and her face up to him. He laid his lips on hers and closed his eyes.

For the space of a few seconds she was rigid. Then with a sigh she surrendered herself. Her arms enfolded him, drawing him tightly to her. His fumbling fingers found the zip at the back of her dress. The dress split open as he pulled it down.

Still kissing her, he pulled the top of her dress over her arms so that her slip was revealed. He pulled the slip's straps and it, in turn, fell away. Shaking a little, he felt for the catch of her bra.

When her breasts were exposed he laid his face on them. It was like sinking into a deep pillow.

'*Mein liebe,*' she crooned, stroking his hair the way he had done hers.

He found a nipple and sucked.

'Have you a gummy?' she asked.

'A what?'

'A gummy?' She frowned trying to think of the English word. And when she couldn't remember it she touched him on the penis. 'A covering for that,' she said.

'Oh! Yes,' he replied.

She rose with his hand in hers so he was forced to rise also. 'Come,' she said.

The bedroom was as small and dingy as the rest of the flat but Eddy didn't notice that now. He was too busy taking his clothes off and watching while she did the same.

She had a magnificent body, he thought. And he trembled thinking he was going to make love to her.

'Are you cold?' she asked.

'No. It's just ...' He trailed off.

'I understand.'

She came to him and took the contraceptive he was holding. She knelt before him and rolled the sheath down his erection.

'Have you been to bed with a German woman yet?' she asked.

'No,' he lied.

'Then I will have to make your first an occasion to remember.'

She led him to the bed and sank down upon it with him on top of her.

Her breath was hot in his face. Her skin like warm silk. He hadn't felt like this since he'd last been with Annie Grimes.

'That's it then,' said Kirk, loading the last box of Heather Dew.

Eddy brought the lorry's back flaps into place and tied them off. He then joined Kirk in the lorry's cabin. Kirk was in the passenger seat.

'Ready?' Kirk asked. Eddy nodded. 'Then let's go.'

At the entrance to the castle they were stopped by the duty sentry. 'Rotten night you've got for it,' Kirk said with a smile, handing over the pass McQuarrie had written out for them. He was referring to the rain which was bucketing down.

'It always seems to piss down when I draw sentry duty,' the man grumbled, holding the pass under his cape and flicking his lighted torch over it. 'Taking some stuff to the station, eh?'

'That's right, mate. Sending some faulty stores back down the line and picking up a fresh consignment for the kitchens.'

'Everything seems in order, then.'

Kirk accepted back the pass. As far as he was concerned, getting past the sentry was the tricky part. The bloke might decide to have a good look in the back of the lorry, in which case they would have a hard time explaining away their load.

Eddy slipped the lorry into gear and the lorry trundled forward. He would have to drive all the way into town before turning off down a side road which would eventually lead them into open countryside.

The place chosen by Kirk and Turushev for the meet was a secluded spot rarely visited by British patrols. Kirk had reckoned this to be the safest spot, and also the most accessible for the lorry, for the exchange to take place.

They left Uelsberg behind and took a narrow dirt road in the direction of the Russian sector.

'Nervous?' Kirk asked.

'A little. You?'

Kirk thought back to the days when he'd been flogging Harry Hydelman's whisky round the Glasgow boozers. 'I've done this sort of thing before,' he replied. 'You don't get so twitched second time round.'

Eddy glanced sideways at Kirk. This was the first time Kirk had ever referred to previous nefarious activities and Eddy could only wonder what it was he had been up to. He hoped Kirk would go on to explain, but he didn't.

To take his mind off his nervousness, Eddy thought about Leoni as he drove. He'd been to bed with her on innumerable occasions now and each time was better than the last. He had the same sense of belonging with her that he'd had with Annie Grimes. As though together they formed a whole, a completely rounded human being.

He knew he was falling in love with her – if he hadn't already. At night he dreamed of her. The pair of them laughing together, making love, enjoying life and each other.

'Careful!' Kirk said as the lorry bounced and shook. One of its wheels had gone into a hole in the road. He added, 'We don't want to break that stuff back there.'

'I'm doing my best, but it isn't exactly Sauchiehall Street we're driving along,' Eddy retorted.

'Cow!' Kirk exclaimed.

Eddy swore as he braked to a halt. The cow turned to look at them before ambling on into a field.

'You don't get those in Sauchiehall Street either,' Eddy said, slipping the engine into gear and edging the lorry forward.

'Oh, I don't know. Have you seen some of the things that come out the Locarno Dance Hall on a Saturday night?'

Eddy couldn't help but laugh. 'Aye, you have a point,' he said.

'Moo-ve along there, ladies please!' Kirk giggled.

'How about, "Would you care for anudder dance, miss?"'

'To which she replied, "Aren't you the horny one!"'

It was silly and corny but it appealed to them. They both chuckled at the daftness of it.

A little later Eddy turned off the road to drive across a field. When he came to a dark, lowering wood he skirted it, heading north.

When they reached the agreed spot, Eddy flicked his lights twice. Men appeared as though out of the ground and moved towards the lorry. Eddy and Kirk climbed down from the lorry's cab, Eddy having left the engine running and the lights on.

'Good evening,' Turushev said. 'Everything go all right?'

'Hunky-dory,' Kirk replied. 'You know Eddy. He and I are going to be partners on this deal.'

Turushev nodded and shook hands with Eddy. 'Now, let's have a look at your load,' he said.

Eddy untied the flaps at the rear of the lorry and flipped them out of the way. Kirk produced a torch, as did Turushev, and all three of them clambered inside.

'You don't mind if I check, do you?' Turushev asked.

'I'd be surprised if you didn't,' Kirk replied.

Turushev selected a cardboard box at random and tore it open. Pulling out a bottle of Heather Dew, he unscrewed the top and took a swig.

'Mother's milk,' said Eddy, thinking of Meany, who had now served his time at Colchester and, reduced to the ranks, had been reposted to another battalion within the regiment.

'And labels too,' Turushev commented.

'A fresh consignment just over from Bonnie Scotland,' Kirk said.

Turushev then opened a carton of cigarettes and lit up. He smoked as he checked one of the large tins of coffee.

'Satisfied?' Kirk asked.

'Everything seems to be in order.'

'All right, get your blokes to unload while we settle up.'

The three of them climbed out of the lorry. Turushev barked an order in Russian and a number of his men moved forward. Without exception the men were all short and stocky. Their faces were flat and oriental looking. Eddy thought it must have been men like these who rode with Genghis Khan.

'Wait here a moment,' Turushev said and, striding away, vanished into the darkness.

Eddy was suddenly nervous again. He licked dry lips and glanced at Kirk who seemed quite unperturbed. All around them the yellow-faces worked silently.

A minute went by and then Turushev rematerialised holding a small, square tin. On joining them he handed the tin over to Kirk.

'You won't take offence if I check, will you?' Kirk said.

'I'd be surprised if you didn't,' Turushev replied, echoing Kirk's earlier words. They all grinned.

Kirk laid the tin on the ground and took its top off. The little yellow bars of gold inside gleamed in the light from his torch. He touched each bar to count it.

'I wonder why the Jerries cast it in such small bars,' Eddy said.

Turushev shrugged. 'There could be a number of reasons. My own theory is it was to be used as small payments for a great many people. But that's only a guess on my part.'

'Nazi gold,' said Eddy. 'It's like something out the *Wizard* or *Hotspur*.' When he saw Turushev was looking puzzled he went on to explain. 'Children's comics, *Boys' Own* sort of stuff.'

Kirk put the top back on the tin, which he then lifted to hold in the crook of his arm. 'Same time, same place next month?' he suggested.

Turushev opened a diary which he glanced at using his torch for light. 'That's the Tuesday?' he asked.

'Yes. I looked it up before we set off.'

'Then the Tuesday it is.'

Eddy glanced round and was surprised to find the three of them alone. The yellow-faces had all vanished.

'*Do sveedaneeya*!' Turushev said, having shaken Kirk and Eddy by the hand. Then he melted into the darkness after his men.

'Let's hit the road,' Kirk said.

The drive back to Uelsberg seemed to pass a lot more quickly. In the early hours of the morning they drove into Uelsberg and headed for the station, where they parked. Here they would wait for the first morning train through, from which they genuinely had to pick up supplies for Sergeant McQuarrie.

'Can I have a look?' Eddy asked.

Kirk took the top off the tin before placing it on Eddy's lap. Eddy reached down and ran a caressing hand over the gold.

'The first run of many, let's hope,' Kirk said.

'Amen,' Eddy replied.

★

Eddy was buffing his boots when Kirk stuck his head round the door.

'Eddy, can I see you for a minute?' he asked, then to the rest of the section, 'Everything all right?'

There were various comments, all of them rude, and then Napier said, 'How was Hamburg, Corp?' Kirk had been on a twenty-four-hour leave which he'd taken in Hamburg, that being the nearest big city only a few hours away by train.

'It's true,' said Kirk. 'They really do have them sitting in windows.'

'This whoor for rent,' Smart said, giggling.

'Did you, Corporal? Did you?' Rennie asked.

'You know I'm not like that.'

Everyone laughed.

'What are you like then?' Ogle demanded.

'Give me a kiss and I'll tell you.'

The section were still guffawing when he shut the door behind himself and Eddy.

'My room,' he said.

Kirk twisted the key in the lock, then went to sit on his bed. From an inside pocket he produced a large manila envelope absolutely bulging with Deutschmarks.

'I see it but I don't really believe it,' Eddy breathed.

'It's real, all right. And most of it's pure profit.'

Kirk dumped the money on the bed. 'First of all, we take out what we've had to invest so far. Bottles, labels, buying the hooch from McQuarrie and what we had to pay out to the black marketeers.'

This outlay they'd split fifty-fifty between them, both having had money transferred over from Glasgow, where their capital was.

Kirk counted out the correct amount and put it to one side. This would have to be reinvested to make up the second load due to be delivered to Turushev in a month's time. Kirk then started to divvy the profit. Sixty per cent to him and forty to Eddy as agreed.

'Did the bullion dealer ask any questions?' Eddy inquired,

for that had been the real reason behind Kirk's visit to Hamburg.

They could have sold the gold to one of the local Uelsberg jewellers but Kirk had been against that. If cashing in fairly large quantities of gold was to become a habit with them, he didn't want raised eyebrows, questions asked, and perhaps even word of the gold getting back to the castle, which would very soon result in an inquiry. Far better the anonymity of a large city and the professional retiscence of a bullion dealer used to such transactions.

'Not one,' Kirk replied. 'He took the gold, weighed it, told me to come back in a couple of hours and when I did told me the price he was willing to pay. He didn't even look curious as to where I'd got it from.'

Eddy lit a cigarette as Kirk continued counting. The money on the bed fascinated him.

'There we are then,' said Kirk finally. He picked up the smaller of the two piles and handed it to Eddy. 'Not bad, eh?'

Slowly Eddy counted his pile. He was absolutely stunned when he'd finished. 'It's unbelievable,' he whispered.

'Don't forget we're making two thousand per cent profit on Heather Dew alone,' Kirk replied. 'That's quite some mark-up.'

'And we're going to make this every month?'

'As long as Turushev wants and we can supply, then yes.'

Eddy whistled. 'Bloody hell!' he said.

'How does it feel being a capitalist?'

'Just lovely!'

Kirk laughed. 'Think big. That's what my mother always said. Think big!'

Eddy clutched the money to him. His mind was full of dreams. Dreams that all included Leoni Kruppermann.

Eddy and Leoni were lying in bed having finished making love only seconds before.

'Just what the doctor ordered,' he said languorously.

'But *I* am the doctor!' she replied, laughing.

'Then you've just had a taste of your own medicine.'

'And I liked it.'

'How about another dose?'

'Can I have a cigarette in between?'

'What a good idea!' he replied, and nipped her nipple with his teeth before jumping out of bed.

Leoni squealed and then smiled. She was a woman who occasionally liked a bit of rough handling.

Eddy padded to the table where his cigarettes and lighter were. As he was picking them up his eye was caught by an envelope lying beside them. The envelope was addressed to 'Gräfin von Kruppermann'.

'What does "von" mean?' he asked.

Leoni sat up and regarded him. She was a splendid fulsome sight with her golden-blonde hair cascading over her shoulders to partially hide her large coral-pink-tipped breasts.

'It means the person belongs to the upper classes. There isn't an English equivalent.'

'You're upper class?'

'Very much so. Although I tend not to use the "von" when practising as a doctor. It has an unsettling effect on patients.'

'And what about "Gräfin"?'

'That means "countess".'

His face dropped. 'You're joking?'

'No.'

'You? ... A countess?'

'I'm afraid so.'

'You mean I've just been ... with a countess?'

She laughed. 'You should see the expression on your face!' she exclaimed.

'You never said!'

'You never asked. Why is it important?'

'I don't know. I'm just ... stunned, that's all.'

'You are funny,' she said.

He lit two cigarettes and passed her one. To think that he, Eddy King, from the Glasgow slums, had been having it off with a countess. It was mind boggling.

'Your husband, who died on the Russian Front, was a count, then?' he asked.

'That's right. Graf von Kruppermann. He was also a general.'

Eddy whistled. 'And now here you are with a common-or-garden British private. Bit of a come-down for you, eh?'

'It's the man that interests me. Not his rank or position.'

'But a count and a general to boot!'

Her smile became wistful. 'Times change, Eddy. We in Germany have had to adapt or else go under. Before the war I was a countess and very grand with my diamonds and limousine, my great town house and our castle in the country.'

'You owned a castle?'

'Oh yes. And a drafty old place it was, too. It was picturesque though, and the view was breathtaking.'

'What happened to it?'

'It's still there but now American soldiers live in it. Just like you and the other Scottish soldiers live in Schloss Schwartz-berg.'

He shook his head in wonder.

'But as I said, all that was before the war. Now . . . ? Now I am just a doctor trying to make my way, just like everyone else.'

'I take it, then, he left you stony?'

'Pardon?'

'The count didn't leave you any money?'

'He did, but everything we had was confiscated. The town house, the schloss, the business, land, jewels, everything.'

He stroked her cheek, thinking how sad she looked. He drew her to him when tears welled in her eyes.

'Love me, Eddy. Please?'

He took her cigarette and placed it along with his in the ashtray.

'Be tender,' she whispered.

And he was.

★

315

'A countess!' Kirk exclaimed. 'She was pulling your pudding. Having you on!'

'No she wasn't. It's straight up. I saw an envelope with her full name and title on it. Gräfin von Kruppermann. "Gräfin" means countess and "von" means she belongs to the upper classes.'

'Well, well, well,' said Kirk. 'Imagine you landing a countess!'

They were in the still-room putting labels on bottles that had previously been filled. Heather Dew dripped steadily from the still into a rapidly filling two-gallon jar.

'God, she's marvellous!' Eddy said, eyes gleaming.

Kirk slapped on another label and looked thoughtful. He was remembering how he'd felt when he'd first screwed Susan, how chuffed he'd been at doing it with someone of her class. But a countess! Now that really would be something.

'Put your backs into it, you vile chaps!' Kirk bellowed. It was an expression he'd heard one of the officers use and he knew it amused the section to hear him parrot the man.

'What are you?'

'Vile chaps sir, Corporal!' they chorused back.

'And don't you ever forget it!'

'No sir, Corporal!'

The section was removing large sandbags that had been used to shore up a crumbling wall. When all the bags were removed a team of civilian masons would move in to start repair work.

Eddy was working a two-man team with Ogle.

He grunted as he pulled another bag free and twisted it on to its end. The sack and sand inside it were wet through, which made the sandbag doubly heavy.

Gripping the bag firmly, Eddy began to drag it along the ground, while Ogle began pulling another bag free.

He'd only taken a few steps when he felt something in his groin go rip. It felt exactly as though a zip there had been opened quickly.

'Oh!' he grunted and let go of the bag. Bending over, he clutched himself.

'What's wrong, Eddy?' Kirk asked, coming striding up.

Eddy couldn't stand any more so he sank to the ground. Through his pants he could feel a large bulge of flesh. God, what have I done to myself? he thought.

He'd gone pasty white and there was sweat running down his face. The pain in his groin was like that of a large aching tooth.

'Let's have a look, my old son,' Kirk said. With Ogle helping him he unfastened Eddy's trouser's and pulled them down, after which they pulled down Eddy's underpants. What he saw caused him to wince.

'I think he must have ruptured himself,' said Ogle.

Eddy stared in fascination at the bulging flesh. It was as though a small balloon had somehow got under his skin.

'It's the medics for you,' Kirk said, and gently pulled Eddy's underpants and trousers back up again.

By this time the entire section were crowded round.

'Smart, you're the strongest. Help Ogle and myself to carry him,' Kirk said.

Eddy groaned as he was gently lifted from the ground.

'Easy there, lad,' Kirk said.

Those of the section remaining behind called out good luck and well wishes as Eddy was carted off.

At the castle hospital Eddy was laid on a stretcher and taken away. Kirk told Ogle to go back to the section and carry on. He would wait till there was news of Eddy.

Kirk was kept hanging around for well over an hour before being told he could go through and see Eddy.

Eddy was lying flat out on the bed wearing pyjamas and a grim expression.

'Well, what did they say?' Kirk demanded.

'It's a hernia, right enough. I've been examined by a surgeon called Major McDougall who told me I'll have to have an operation. He's setting it up for Monday next.'

Kirk pulled a face. 'Bad luck.'

317

'After that I'll be in for ten days. Then they'll give me a fortnight's leave.'

'Will you go home?'

Eddy thought of Leoni. 'No, I think I'll take it here,' he replied. 'That way I shall be on hand to help you with Turushev's next consignment.'

Kirk nodded. 'Good.'

'There's just one thing. I need a favour.'

'Name it.'

'I'm supposed to be meeting Leoni tonight, picking her up at her place at seven. Will you go and tell her what's happened? She doesn't have a phone so I can't contact her that way.'

'Consider it done,' Kirk replied.

'You're a pal, Kirk.'

They chatted for another ten minutes and then Kirk said it was time he got back to the section. They'd all be eager to know the doctor's verdict.

The last thing Eddy did before Kirk went was to write down Leoni's address and hand it to him.

She answered his knock almost at once, a frown crossing her face when she saw it wasn't Eddy.

'Dr von Kruppermann, I'm Kirk Murray, Eddy's friend. Do you remember I came with him to your surgery?'

'Oh, *ja*!' she replied, recognition flooding into her eyes.

'Eddy's asked me to call on you. May I come in?'

She ushered him into a dark and dingy hallway. He followed her into an equally dark and dingy room.

'Has something happened to Eddy?' she asked.

'I'm afraid it has.'

Cap in hand, Kirk explained in detail about the heavy sandbags and Eddy's rupturing himself. As he spoke he thought she was certainly good-looking if a little long in the tooth.

'Poor Eddy,' Leoni said, after Kirk had stopped speaking. 'Will I be able to go and visit him?'

318

'I doubt it, Doctor. It wouldn't be appreciated in certain quarters.'

'I understand.'

There was a small pause and then Kirk said, 'Well I suppose I'd better be on my way.'

'Oh! Excuse me for being so impolite. I was thinking. Would you care for a cup of tea? I'm afraid that's all I can offer you. I have no coffee or alcohol in the flat.'

'I'd love a cup of tea,' Kirk replied.

When she left the room he looked around. What a dump! he thought. High up one wall there was a damp patch, while further along some wallpaper was peeling away. The furniture was long overdue to be scrapped and the carpet underfoot was threadbare. One of the windows was cracked, through which, because there was a wind outside, came a low moaning noise. On a sort of stand there was a very old bell-mouthed phonograph beside which was a stack of records. On an impulse he crossed and picked up the first half-dozen records, which were all in faded cardboard covers. Wagner, Liszt, Beethoven. A quick flick through the remainder of the pile showed they were all classical pieces.

'I'm afraid I have no sugar,' Leoni said, entering the room carrying two cups. 'But I have milk, if you'd like?'

'No thanks. I prefer it without.'

He devoured her with his eyes as she moved away having handed him one of the cups. He'd had sex in Hamburg with a very high-class prostitute whom he'd been certain was clean. At the prices she'd charged she'd bloody well better be! But apart from her and the brass at the Blue Pig he'd been going without since his arrival in Germany. Highly sexed by nature, he was therefore continually randy as a rabbit in heat.

He sipped some tea and then said, 'I was wondering, as you're now at a loose end as I am, if you'd care to come out for a drink? I'm sure Eddy wouldn't mind. In fact he'd probably insist, not wanting you to be left here disappointed on your own.'

319

Leoni looked uncertain. 'I don't know . . .' She trailed off.

'Or if you don't fancy a drink there's a Mozart concert on that I think I might be able to get tickets for.'

Her eyes opened wide. 'Could you really? I knew it was on, of course, and desperately wanted to attend. But when I tried I just couldn't get a ticket.'

'Maybe I can do better. I have certain connections, shall we say.' He glanced at his watch. 'But if we're going to try we'd better hurry.'

Tea was forgotten as he helped her into her coat. 'I just adore Mozart,' she said excitedly.

'Me too,' he replied. Truth was Mozart, like Wagner, Liszt and Beethoven, was just a name to him. He had no experience or knowledge whatever of classical music. He was a Glenn Miller man himself.

He took her to a small café where he left her sitting at a table while he sought out the proprietor, who lived upstairs.

Herr Goetz looked like a schoolteacher or clergyman with his freshly scrubbed, cherubic face topped by silvery white hair. He was the black marketeer Kirk dealt chiefly with.

Kirk told Goetz what he wanted. Goetz said he'd left it rather late, but Kirk said he expected to pay more for that. Goetz told him to go back downstairs and wait. He would see what he could do.

Fifteen minutes later Goetz appeared downstairs to beckon Kirk into the back of the café.

'Did you get them?' Kirk asked.

Goetz held up two tickets and then named his price. 'I don't charge too much because I expect to do a lot of business with you in the future,' Goetz said.

'You can count on it,' Kirk replied.

Money changed hands and then with the two tickets safely in his pocket Kirk hurried back to Leoni.

'Let's go,' he said.

'Did you . . . ?'

He nodded.

320

'How marvellous!' she exclaimed.

'Nothing's impossible when you know how,' he said as they made their way down the street in the direction of the hall where the concert was being performed by a touring company of German musicians.

'And if you've got the wherewithal,' she added.

He was correct when he thought he detected bitterness in her tone when she said that.

After the concert – which he found excruciatingly boring but which she thoroughly enjoyed – he walked her slowly home. At the door to her flat she thanked him but made no move to ask him inside.

'We'll be going on patrol tomorrow night,' he said. 'And the day after that I'll be going to see Eddy. If you like I could call by here in the evening to tell you how he's doing.'

'That would be kind of you. I'll look forward to that,' she replied.

He stepped back a pace and nodded. 'Till then.'

Turning, he strode rapidly off. Nor did he look round.

A countess, he thought. Yes he could see it now. She had breeding that shone like a beacon through her poverty. And if there was one thing attracted him, and always had, it was breeding.

Two nights later he was back. She led him through to the same dark and dingy room as before and asked him if he'd care for some tea.

'I hope you won't think me forward,' he said, smiling. 'But I took the liberty of bringing along a few things.' And having said that he handed her a bag he'd brought with him.

She laid the items out on the table. 'Butter!' she exclaimed excitedly. 'Coffee! Sugar! Cigarettes! A dozen eggs! Oh, how absolutely marvellous! I can't thank you enough.'

'It must be extremely difficult for you,' he said sympathetically. 'Eddy mentioned to me what it had been like for you before the war.'

'Yes,' she replied wistfully. 'There is so much I miss, in – what would you call it in English? – my reduced circumstances.'

'I hope you won't take this the wrong way but I was offered some and I was about to turn them down when suddenly I thought of you. I'm sure the good doctor could use a few pairs of these, I thought, and so I took them.'

He extricated an envelope from an inside pocket and handed it to Leoni, who regarded it quizzically. When she peered inside the envelope, an expression of sheer delight mixed with incredulity blossomed on her face.

'Nylon stockings!' she whispered.

'I had to guess your size so I hope they fit all right.'

'I must try them on right away.'

'Do you have a couple of glasses? I'll pour us both a drink while you're doing that.'

From another pocket he produced a bottle of Heather Dew.

'Scotch whisky?' she said, awed.

'And my favourite brand,' he replied, chuckling.

She handed him two glasses before hurrying off to the bedroom. He hummed as he poured.

When she returned her eyes were shining. 'They fit perfectly,' she said. 'I haven't had nylon stockings in ... well, more years than I care to remember. I can't even begin to thank you enough.'

He handed her a glass and they both drank.

'Whew!' she gasped. 'That's strong.'

'Malt whisky usually is. It's one of it's attractions. Do you like the flavour?'

'It's rather ... smoky?'

'That comes from the peat which the water runs through before it's taken up by the distillery.'

He wasn't sure whether that was right or not, with regard to real malt whisky that is, but it certainly sounded convincing.

He sat and watched her while she put a record on. She flashed him a smile as she wound up the ancient phonograph.

'Do you like Liszt?' she asked.

'There'll never be another like him,' he replied.

As the strains of the music curled round the room she sat across from him, her eyes taking on an introspective, sad look about them.

'Those records are all I have from before the war,' she said. 'There were times when they were all I had to hang on to. I think I might have died without them.'

'Can't you find better accommodation than this?' he asked.

She pulled a face. 'Dreadful rooms, aren't they? I am ashamed to ask anyone in. But better flats are ... very, very hard to come by. And expensive. Money must be given, you understand?'

'"Key money" we call it in Britain.'

'So, key money. And I am, eh ... not well off from what I earn as a doctor. I can only charge what people can pay. And believe me, they can't pay much.'

He nodded sympathetically.

'Still, things are getting better all the time. Already there is a great difference between now and just after the war. We are starting to build on the ashes.'

While she talked he imagined her in bed. He saw her naked with that splendid hair spread out on the pillow around her head. Eddy had mentioned she had fabulous breasts. His hands itched to get hold of them, straining as they were now beneath her dress.

'But here am I chattering on and I have forgotten to ask how poor Eddy is,' she said.

'He's painful round the rupture but apart from that in fine spirits. I think he's a little nervous of the operation,' adding with a laugh, 'I know I would be! I'd be having nightmares that the surgeon's knife might slip. I mean it's not exactly something you can sew back on again, is it?'

Leoni smiled. 'You laymen, what funny ideas you have of us doctors,' she said.

He poured more Heather Dew into their glasses. He could see she was already a little flushed from the first.

'It really is most kind of you to bring me the coffee,

323

cigarettes and other things. Especially the nylon stockings. I shall keep those for very special occasions.'

'I'll see what else I can do ...'

'No no, you mustn't. That would be too much,' she cut in.

'Nonsense! What else are friends for?'

'But they are so expensive!'

'I make a few bob.'

She frowned. 'I don't understand that.'

'I'm not exactly short of money,' he explained, thinking Eddy must have been a right fool not to get these things for Leoni himself. It was blatantly obvious she was desperate for them. But then, from the long talks he'd had in the past with Eddy on the subject, he'd already gleaned that Eddy was somewhat naïve about women.

Outside the wind blew causing the cracked window pane to rattle and moan.

And in that instant he had an idea.

Eddy came to, feeling as though someone had had a right go at his head with a hammer. His mouth was parched and there was a faint ringing in his ears.

His hand fumbled under the bedclothes to his groin, where it encountered a swathe of bandages. He pressed lightly and felt nothing. He pressed harder but still couldn't feel anything.

There was the patter of feet and a rustling sound. Then a Queen Alexandra nurse was bending over him.

'How do you feel?' she asked.

'Water,' he croaked.

She picked up a porcelain jug with a long spout from his bedside table and slipped the end of the spout into his mouth. Water ran over his swollen tongue and down his throat.

'I could drink ten of those,' he rasped.

'Well one's enough for the moment,' she replied crisply. She laid the jug back on his table and then proceeded to smooth down his bedclothes.

'Nurse?'

'Yes?'

'The operation. Did it go all right?'

'Of course,' she replied, looking surprised.

'It's just – I can't feel anything down there. Where the rupture was.'

'Ah!' she said. 'That's perfectly normal. The flesh has been cut, you see, which means the area surrounding it will feel dead for quite some time. But feeling will grow back there eventually.'

Eddy was suddenly panicky. No one had said anything about this to him beforehand.

'Will that affect my ... I mean, will I be able to ...?'

The nurse smiled. She considered teasing him and then decided not to. 'I don't think you'll have any trouble with the ladies, if that's what you're asking.'

Relief surged through him. 'I had myself worried there for a moment,' he said.

'It's best you try and get some sleep now. When you wake up I'll bring you something to eat and then the doctor will want to see you.'

Eddy closed his eyes and soon drifted off. He dreamed it was Leoni who would be taking care of him.

He slept for a number of hours, wakening when a voice said, 'How's the patient then?' Kirk held up a bunch of grapes and added, 'I'm told this is the thing to bring!'

Eddy managed a weak smile. 'How did you get in here?'

'It wasn't easy. But you know me. I'm irresistible. They've given me five minutes. Now, how do you feel?'

'Not too bad, I suppose. Tell you the truth, I'm not quite sure.'

Kirk leered. 'Still got it then? You have had a feel to make sure?'

'Oh aye, it's there all right. But my entire right groin feels dead as mutton. The nurse who was here earlier says it will take a while but the feeling will eventually come back there.'

Kirk laid the grapes on the bedside table, helping himself to some in the process.

'How's Leoni?' Eddy asked eagerly.

'Fine. She's asked me to drop by this evening to let her know how your op went.'

'You're a good pal, Kirk. I won't forget this.'

'Oh,' said Kirk, 'I nearly forgot.' He produced several packets of cigarettes which he slipped into the bedside locker. 'I know you're not supposed to smoke in here but I also know you'd go daft without your fags. Maybe you can get the chance of a puff when no one's looking. Now ...' he said, standing, 'I'd better get back to the section. We've got quite a bit on today.'

'Thanks again,' Eddy said.

'I'll be back when I can. And in the meantime keep your hands off those nurses.'

'That's the last thing I have in mind,' Eddy replied.

Kirk nodded, thinking Eddy meant he wasn't up to it.

But Leoni was the reason for what Eddy had said.

'What you ask is difficult,' Goetz said.

Kirk stared into the German's eyes and smiled.

'That's why I've come to you,' he replied.

'And when something is difficult it is also expensive.'

'Naturally.'

'Would this be for yourself? I ask because I have to know whether it will be a short or long let.'

'For a lady,' Kirk replied.

'Ah!' said Goetz. 'I understand.'

'How much do you charge for a bottle of Scotch whisky?' Kirk asked.

Goetz frowned, not seeing the connection. He stated a round figure in Deutschmarks.

'And malt?'

Goetz stated a higher figure.

Kirk said slowly. 'I have access to a limited supply of malt whisky. What I thought was we might agree your fee in cases. Not all payable at once, I'm afraid, but over a period of say ... six months?'

'Of course, I couldn't allow you the same figure as what I

326

would sell them for. I have to make a profit,' Goetz replied smoothly.

'Of course.'

Goetz folded his hands, put them under his chin and gazed into the distance. 'A dozen cases,' he said after a while.

'I'd want *Berchtesgarten* for that,' Kirk replied with a razor smile.

'That's my price. Take it or leave it.'

'You drive a hard bargain, Goetz.'

Goetz spread his hands. 'I have a living to make.'

'Tell you what. Because I'm going to put so much business your way, make it eight and it's a deal.'

'Twelve, Corporal Murray.'

Kirk groaned. 'I honestly doubt if I can do that many.'

Goetz went back to staring into space. A full minute went by before he spoke again. 'To maintain good feeling between us I'll settle for ten.'

Kirk extended his hand and they shook.

'A nice flat now,' Kirk said, as he was about to leave.

'Trust me,' Goetz replied.

Out in the street Kirk began to hum. He'd enjoyed that. He wasn't quite sure yet how he was going to squeeze out ten extra cases in the next six months but he'd do it somehow.

He hoped Goetz wouldn't take too long.

'You're joking!' Leoni exclaimed.

'No,' Kirk replied. 'It's all yours as from the first of next month.' And he named a rent which wasn't all that much higher than she was now paying.

'I just can't believe it,' she said.

'Come and let me show you around.'

'But you must have paid a fortune in key money for this place.'

'I happen to think you're worth it,' he replied.

The tone of his voice told her precisely what he had in mind. But then she'd known that since the first night he'd come calling with presents.

327

Eddy was sitting by the side of his bed reading a book. He looked up at the sound of approaching feet.

'And how are you today, King?' Major McDougall, the surgeon who'd done Eddy's operation, demanded.

'Dying to get out, sir,' Eddy replied.

'Hmm!' said McDougall thoughtfully, looking sideways at Sister Hardy who was accompanying him on his rounds.

'Stand up please, King,' Sister said. Eddy stood. 'Now walk over there and back.' Eddy did as he was told.

'Any pain or discomfort?' McDougall asked.

'A little stiff, sir, that's all.'

'All right then, lie on the bed and let me have a look at you.'

Sister Hardy pulled screens round the bed while Eddy clambered into a horizonal position. He unloosened his pyjama bottoms and slipped them down.

McDougall's fingers probed the long, angry-looking wound and the flesh surrounding it. 'Good . . . good,' he said, nodding to himself. 'How long have the stitches been out, Sister?'

Sister consulted the chart at the end of Eddy's bed. 'Two days, sir,' she replied.

McDougall snorted. 'Pull your pyjamas up again, King,' he instructed. He held out his hand for the chart which Sister Hardy handed to him.

Eddy retied his pyjamas and then swung his feet over the side of the bed while McDougall studied his chart.

'The thing is, King,' McDougall said, looking up, 'you're not really supposed to be discharged till tomorrow but I have a problem inasmuch as I need a bed. How do you feel about going out today?'

'That would be marvellous, sir!' Eddy grinned.

'I think he'll do, Sister,' McDougall said. Then turning back to Eddy. 'You'll be due a fortnight's recuperative leave. Will you be going home?'

'No sir. I have a friend in Uelsberg I thought I'd spend it with.'

Sister cleared her throat and looked away.

'Well, nothing too strenuous for a while, King. Do I make myself clear?'

'I understand, sir.'

'Right, well I think that's you, then. Good luck. And I hope I don't see you in here again.'

'Thank you for everything, sir.'

McDougall smiled and moved on.

Sister Hardy said, 'I'll have a nurse bring you your clothes after the doctor's rounds.' Then she hurried after Major McDougall.

An hour later Eddy walked out of the hospital area. Slowly he made his way to the billet, hoping to find the section there.

'Christ sake, look what the wind blew in!' Napier exclaimed.

'You look like death warmed up!' said Smart.

'No he doesn't. He looks great,' said Ogle, punching the large Norrie Smart on the shoulder.

'Well I'm hardly a hundred per cent but at least I'm back on my feet again,' Eddy said.

'We're all off to the Naafi for a beer. Want to come?' Kirkwood asked.

'No thanks. I've got other plans,' he replied, holding up the form Sister Hardy had signed and which entitled him to two weeks' leave.

'Jammy bugger!' said McKenzie.

'Where's the corp?' Eddy asked.

'Don't know. Around somewhere, I suppose. To tell you the truth we haven't seen all that much of him off-duty hours of late.'

Eddy nodded. Well it didn't matter. He'd catch up with Kirk later. The important thing for him now was to get into town to see Leoni.

He picked up one or two things from his locker which he added to what he'd brought from the hospital. Then he went in search of Lieutenant Gilzean whose signature was needed on the form Sister Hardy had given him. When added, the lieutenant's signature then made the form a two-week pass.

It was a long haul into town so he waited by the castle gates until he could hitch a lift, which he eventually did from a captain.

From where the captain dropped him off it wasn't very far to Leoni's. He prayed she was in. She wasn't expecting him till the following night.

Outside Leoni's flat he groped in his pocket for the key she'd given him. Quietly he slipped it into the lock and opened the door.

All the lights were out except in the bedroom whose door stood ajar.

She was singing, 'Lili of Marlene', the number Dietrich made famous during the war.

> 'An der Kaserne vor dem grossen Tor,
> Stand eine Laterne und steht sie noch davor;
> Da woll'n wir uns mal wiederseh'n,
> Bei der Laterne woll'n wir steh'n,
> Wie einst, Lili Marlene,
> Wie einst, Lili Marlene . . .'

He made his way towards the bedroom door, imagining her to be sitting at her dressing table as she was fond of doing, combing her hair or otherwise attending to her toilet.

On reaching the open door he stopped to stare in. She wasn't at her dressing table but sitting naked on her bed. He couldn't think what she was doing as hands on hips she moved up and down.

And still it didn't dawn until suddenly there was another movement and for the first time he noticed two hairy legs projecting out from underneath her.

'Oh my God, but it's good!' Kirk voice sighed.

Eddy felt sick and for a moment or two he thought he was actually going to throw up. It seemed to him as though the blood in his veins had turned to iced water.

Leoni threw back her head and stroked her hair in a downward movement. The song had become a croon now which she husked from the back of her throat.

But I love her, Eddy thought. I *love* her!

'Yes!' she cried suddenly. 'Oh yes!'

Her body spasmed as did Kirk's and then with a groan she collapsed on top of him, her large breasts squashing against his chest.

Rage rose up in Eddy. Shaking with anger he stepped through the doorway and into the room. He stood beside a wooden standard lamp.

Still panting from her exertion Leoni looked up. When she saw him she exclaimed.

'What is it?' Kirk demanded, and pulled her head out of the way so he could see.

'You bastard!' hissed Eddy.

'You're not supposed to be out till tomorrow,' Kirk said reproachfully.

'I can see I surprised you.'

'We were going to tell you.'

'That's big of you.'

With a plopping sound Leoni pulled herself free and sliding from the bed made her way to a chair, over which her dressing gown was draped. Picking up the gown she hurriedly shrugged it on.

'I'm truly sorry you had to find out this way, Eddy,' she said.

'Why?' he asked simply.

She tried to look him straight in the face but couldn't. Her eyes dropped away to stare at the carpet.

'Whore,' Eddy said quietly.

'Now wait a minute pal ...' Kirk said, coming off the bed.

'Pal?' Eddy interjected, his voice dripping sarcasm.

'Leoni and I didn't mean this to happen. It just did somehow.'

Eddy nodded, but said nothing. His rage was getting more explosive with every passing second.

'You asked me to come round and then I kept returning to give her progress reports. And somewhere along the line we just fell for one another. I'm sorry too. I'd do anything rather than hurt you.'

Kirk might just have got away with it then if he hadn't allowed a patronising glint to show in his eyes. Eddy saw that glint and knew right away Kirk was lying. Kirk had intentionally set out to steal his woman.

A berserk rage burst within him as he reached for the nearest thing to hand, which turned out to be the standard lamp. The plug came ripping from the wall as, using the lamp like a huge club, he swung its heavy base at Kirk.

Kirk tried to dive to one side but didn't quite make it. The base of the lamp took him full in the ribcage, knocking the wind from him and sending him spinning to the floor.

Eddy twisted the lamp round and with a roar brought it scything down at the sprawling Kirk. Leoni screamed. She saw murder written all over Eddy's face. The dazed Kirk rolled to one side as the lamp smashed against the floor. The base and part of the stem broke off leaving Eddy clutching what now virtually amounted to a spear, the end of the stem being sharp and jagged.

Kirk was scared and being naked felt incredibly vulnerable. Desperately he tried to scramble away from that advancing point. Eddy lunged and the sharp end of the lamp stem lanced towards Kirk's face. A split second before it struck home, Kirk managed to twist his head out of the way.

Leoni, hysterical now, ran to Eddy and wrapped her arms round him. 'Stop it! Stop it! Stop it!' she screamed.

Eddy tried to shrug her free but somehow she managed to hang on. Her feet drummed against the back of his legs.

Eddy lunged with the lamp stem again but by this time Kirk had managed to grab hold of a wooden chair which he used to ward off the blow.

'*Eddy!*' Leoni screamed in his ear.

He heard her voice from a long way off, which caused him to pause. The mists of his awful rage thinned and began to disperse as he became his own man again.

Trembling, he dropped what remained of the standard lamp. He felt so weak he thought he must surely collapse to the floor.

Her scent was thick in his nostrils and he was only too painfully aware of her body wrapped round him.

'Get off!' he said quietly.

Her face was streaked and puffed. She looked ten years older than she had a few minutes before.

Kirk still held the chair in front of him. He too was trembling and weak, the latter in his case from shock and fear.

Leoni moved away from Eddy, tugging her dressing gown tightly round her as she went.

'You were going to kill me,' Kirk said.

Eddy remembered Gloag and the adjustable spanner he'd used to smash the man's skull in. 'Yes,' he said.

'I think you'd better go, Eddy,' Leoni said, her voice more thickly accented than usual.

Eddy staggered and nearly fell. His body was covered in a cold clammy sweat and his wound was paining him. But the pain was nothing like that in his heart.

Kirk stood the chair back on its legs. Then edging round the bed he picked up his trousers and hurriedly put them on. As he buttoned up his flies Eddy watched him balefully.

Eddy dragged a breath deep into his lungs. The reason he hadn't already gone was he wasn't sure his legs would carry him to the outside door and beyond.

'I could put you on a charge for this,' Kirk said.

'You could but you won't,' Eddy wheezed in reply.

Kirk's lips thinned. Eddy was right.

Eddy took a long last look at Leoni, his countess. He never wanted to see her again. 'Whoor,' he repeated, this time using the emphatic Scottish pronunciation.

Leoni flinched and turned her head away.

'The lady told you to go,' Kirk said.

'What lady's that? I don't see any lady.'

Leoni's head dropped in shame. Eddy ran his fingers through his hair and then did his best to pull himself together. If nothing else, he would make a dignified exit. Slowly, and with great effort, he walked from the bedroom into the darkness of the room beyond. He closed the main door silently behind him, leaving the key she'd given him in the lock.

Out in the street he hobbled to where he knew he would get a taxi.

In the back of the taxi heading for the castle he sang quietly, *'Underneath the lamplight, by the barrack gate . . .'*

He managed to make it to the still room and the whisky there before the tears came.

'King, I want a word with you,' Kirk said.

The rest of the section looked up. They knew that for the past few days there had been bad blood between Eddy and Kirk. No one knew what it was about.

'I'm on leave, Corporal,' Eddy replied. He stretched out on his bed reading a book.

'I know that. I still want a word with you all the same.'

Eddy dropped his book a fraction so he could see over the top of it. His eyes met and locked with Kirk's.

'What about?'

'In private, if you don't mind.'

Eddy carefully marked his place and then put the book on top of his pillow. He winced a little as he came to his feet.

At the door Kirk said, 'My room.'

Eddy followed Kirk out into the hallway. Silently they walked in the direction of Kirk's billet.

Once there Kirk said, 'It's about Heather Dew and Turushev. Do you want to stay in or get out?'

Eddy stared at Kirk whom he now hated. The last thing he wanted was to continue in association with this man. But on the other hand it would be downright stupid to cut his nose off to spite his face. There was far too much money involved.

'I'm still in,' he replied.

Kirk nodded. 'All right. We continue as before.'

'Not quite,' said Eddy.

And left Kirk standing there.

Eight months passed, during which the Turushev run, as Eddy and Kirk had come to call it, went smoothly.

After every run, Kirk would arrange to go to Hamburg to convert the gold into cash at the bullion dealer's. And on his return he and Eddy would get together and divvy up.

It never failed to amaze Eddy how much money he made out of the run. After nine runs he considered himself a modestly wealthy man.

The relationship between Eddy and Kirk remained a stilted one, the pair of them only talking to one another when it was to do with either army business or the run. Kirk continued seeing Leoni, spending usually two or three evenings a week with her. Countess Leoni von Kruppermann was a name never mentioned between Eddy and Kirk.

Then one morning the section were roused from their beds by a new corporal called McPherson.

'Let's be having you then!' McPherson shouted, rubbing his hands briskly together. 'Lots to do today. Lots to do!'

Rennie asked the question everyone was wondering. 'Where's Corporal Murray?' he queried.

'Gone sick, lad. Don't ask me what's wrong with him because I don't know. All I was told was he was admitted to the hospital last night and is likely to be there for some time.'

'Will you be in charge till he gets back?' McKenzie asked.

'Don't know that either, lad. I've just been ordered to look after you lot until further instructed. So who knows what that could mean? It could be a day, a week, a month or until you've done your time and are sent home. Now come on jildy jai! Lots to do! Lots to do!'

The section were out on patrol that night so it wasn't till late the following morning after he'd caught up on his sleep that Eddy was able to get to the hospital.

He told a Q.A. nurse he was there on section business so she looked up Kirk's name and told Eddy where to find him.

There were six in the ward which comprised three beds on either side. Kirk was behind some screens awaiting further treatment which a nurse would shortly be giving him.

He looked up from the book he was reading as Eddy slipped between the screens.

'I've only got a minute,' Eddy said. 'What the hell's wrong with you? And is it true you're going to be laid up here for some time?'

'Nice of you to be worried about me,' Kirk replied.

'I'm thinking about the run, that's all.'

'I knew you'd come, so I've written it all out here,' said Kirk. And from his bedside locker he produced a sheet of paper on which he'd written various addresses and instructions.

'See Goetz and tell him you'll be handling the next shipment of coffee and fags. I've marked down the prices you've to pay. Watch him, he's a shark. He's bound to try for an additional mark-up. Now there's the run itself. Can you manage that on your own?'

'I think so. They're used to us making that monthly journey down to the railway station. I don't think they'll give me any trouble just because you're not there for once.'

'It may be more than once.'

'I can still manage it.'

Kirk pointed to another address on the sheet of paper. 'The bullion dealer. You'll have to do that as well. Slip McQuarrie a few quid and he'll see you get the necessary pass.' Kirk handed the sheet of paper to Eddy who folded it and put it away.

'Any problems, try and get to see me. Although that won't be easy. They don't exactly encourage visitors in this ward.'

'What's wrong with you then?'

A pink flush crept over Kirk's face. 'You may as well know now as you'll find out anyway. I've caught a dose.'

'VD?' Eddy said incredulously.

'What other sort of dose is there?'

'But I mean ... how? Who?'

'*Who* do you think?'

Eddy gaped. 'Leoni?'

'Right first time,' Kirk replied bitterly.

'But ... but that's impossible!'

'I can assure you, Eddy, there's been no one else.'

'Then why didn't I catch it?'

336

The two men stared at one another. Then Eddy's face broke into a grin. 'She's been two-timing you,' he whispered.

Kirk turned his face away. 'Looks like it. It's the only explanation as far as I can see.'

'Oh, that's rich. That's really rich!' Eddy said.

'I thought it would amuse you.'

'Does she know she's infected?'

'Presumably not. From what I gather it's far more difficult to detect in women than in us men. She'll have to be told, of course. I suppose I'll write.'

Eddy sat on the edge of the bed and chuckled to himself.

'Meany was right,' Kirk said. 'The treatment *is* bloody painful. The penicillin jabs they give you in the backside are like being stuck by a harpoon.'

'And how long does the treatment go on for?'

'Six weeks at least. And then I'm up on a charge for catching it. That'll probably be ten days in the guard house.'

'What about your stripes?'

'I've seen the end of them. It'll be plain Private Murray when I rejoin the section.'

'Well I never!' said Eddy, thinking there was a God after all.

'I mean, I thought I was safe with her. A doctor and a countess to boot!'

Eddy laughed at the expression on Kirk's face. 'A dose!' he exclaimed, the laugh becoming a guffaw.

'And it *is* just like peeing over broken glass,' Kirk said.

Eddy guffawed all the way back to the billet.

'Well well, if it isn't Romeo Murray himself,' said Smart, looking up from cleaning his gear.

'How's the old cock, then?' Ogle inquired politely.

'Hasn't fallen off, has it?' Rennie asked.

'Eff off, you horrible lot,' said Kirk.

'Now now, you can't speak like that to us any more, ex-Corporal Murray. You've lost your stripes don't forget,' said Kirkwood just a little maliciously.

Kirk dumped his gear on the one empty bed. 'And speaking

337

of corporals, what's the new one like?' he asked.

'We had a corporal McPherson for a couple of weeks,' replied Napier. 'But he moved on.'

Smart eagerly added, 'You're going to love the one who took his place.'

'Easy is he?'

'I wouldn't say so.'

'Do I know him?'

'Oh yes. You do that,' said Ogle.

'Don't tell me Meany's back with stripes up?' Kirk asked thinking how absolutely horrendous that would be.

Kirkwood smirked. 'Not Meany.'

Just then the door flew open and Eddy marched in.

'Speak of the devil,' said Napier.

Kirk stared at the two stripes on Eddy's arm. Then his gaze travelled up to Eddy's face.

'Back with us again, Murray?' said Eddy.

Kirk stood and saluted. 'Yes, Corporal,' he replied.

'There have been one or two changes while you've been away.'

'I can see that ... sir.'

'My billet, Murray. I want to have words with you in private.'

'Yes, sir.'

Eddy led the way.

Once in his room, the same one Kirk had inhabited as a corporal, he locked the door behind him. While Kirk watched, he removed a tin box from a secret hiding place. The box was crammed with Deutschmarks, most of them higher denominations.'

'What we've made from two runs,' Eddy said. 'Will you trust me or will I go through it all bit by bit.'

'I trust you. That's why I took you on as a partner in the first place,' Kirk replied.

'Pity I couldn't trust you the way you trusted me,' Eddy said.

'Money and women, Eddy. Two different things entirely,' Kirk replied.

Eddy grunted. Then he emptied the contents of the box on to his bed.

'The way I see it is this,' Eddy said. 'I've done two runs on my own on top of which the positions are now reversed. I'm the corporal and you're the private. Taking all that into account, I think we should switch the percentages. Namely forty per cent for you now and sixty for me.'

Kirk stared hard at Eddy. 'What if I say no?'

'Then I'll fix it so you end up with bugger all.'

'In which case I'll spill the beans and it'll be a long stay in Colchester for the pair of us.'

Eddy lit a cigarette and studied Kirk. 'I'm not going back to the way it was,' he stated flatly.

Kirk pursed his lips, looked at the money and then back again at Eddy. He stroked his scar.

'What if we both give a bit?' he suggested. 'Fifty-fifty, equal partners straight down the line.'

Eddy blew a perfect smoke ring. 'You count,' he said.

Having gone in on the same day they also came out on the same one.

At the Central Station they disembarked and side by side walked out into Gordon Street.

'Glasgow,' said Eddy. 'God bless her!'

Kirk glanced at his watch. Susan was supposed to be meeting him but hadn't arrived yet. The train had been early.

Kirk extended his hand. 'I know we had our differences but well ...' He shrugged. 'I suppose that's life. Will you shake?'

Eddy took the proffered hand. 'Goodbye then.'

'We'll keep in touch.'

'Oh aye, sure.'

'I'll contact you when we've both had time to settle in. I have your address.'

'You do that,' Eddy replied. And lifting his case he headed for the nearby taxi rank.

He didn't look back nor did he wave.

Kirk had no intentions of seeing Eddy again. Their original friendship had been all right when they were in the Army, but it was different now they were home.

Eddy was a workie, a peasant, and spoke like one. A different class entirely to what he'd become.

Anyway what friendship they'd had had well and truly expired that night Eddy had walked in on him and Leoni.

A car squealed to a halt and Susan stuck her head out of the window. 'Kirk!' she called excitedly.

As he went to her he put Eddy King out of his mind. As far as he was concerned, Eddy now belonged to the past.

Having moved back into his house, which the neighbours had very kindly been looking after while he'd been away, Eddy decided a celebration pint would be in order. At opening time he therefore took himself down to the nearest pub which he'd been in the habit of frequenting during his last visit home.

'That the national service done, then?' John the publican asked, setting a frothing pint in front of Eddy. 'No no,' he added when Eddy went to lay some money on the counter. 'First one's on the house.'

Eddy sipped the pint of heavy appreciatively. 'It's rare to be back,' he said. 'You can keep abroad as far as I'm concerned.'

'I'm afraid the wife and I are off ourselves,' John said miserably. 'Not that we really want to go, mind you. It's a case of having to.'

'How so?' Eddy asked.

'It's the wife's chest. It's been playing her up something awful these last few years.' He shook his head. 'Bronchitis on top of asthma. Bad.'

Eddy nodded sympathetically.

'The doctor recommended we go and live in a dry climate, which he promises will help her condition a lot. So it's Arizona for us. I've got a brother out there, you see, and I'll be working with him.'

They talked for a few minutes more and then John moved away to serve an influx of customers.

Staring into his beer, Eddy suddenly remembered the advice Kirk had given him about getting into the pub business. All pubs were goldmines, Kirk had said. And whatever else he was, Kirk certainly had his nut screwed on the right way when it came to making money.

When John was again free, Eddy called him over. 'Does that mean you'll be selling this place?' he asked.

'Aye, just as soon as we can find a buyer,' John replied; then, seeing the gleam in Eddy's eye, 'Why, are you interested?'

'I might be. What sort of price do you have in mind?'

John stated a figure which Eddy thought quite reasonable.

'Is there somewhere we can have a natter?' Eddy asked.

'Come away through the back and we'll talk there.'

John lifted the flap and Eddy went behind the bar. He had to wait there for a moment or two while John checked the staff were able to cope. Then John was leading him into the rear of the pub.

'And maybe I could have a wee look at your books? Just to give me some sort of idea what kind of trade you do,' Eddy said.

'Books? Who the hell keeps those?' John replied.

And they both laughed.

'What you'll want to know is all up here,' said John, tapping his head. 'And I'll be only too happy to tell you.'

A fortnight later the pub was Eddy's.

SUSAN AND KIRK (2)

SUSAN AND KIRK (2)

Lizzie Murray squealed with delight as Kirk popped the bottle of Dom Perignon and the cork bounced off the ceiling to fall slithering away out of sight under some chairs. Champagne frothed and foamed into two glasses, one of which Kirk handed to his mother before hoisting the other in a toast.

'To my twenty-first pub!' he said, and drank.

Lizzie's eyes shone. 'Twenty-one,' she breathed, shaking her head in amazement. 'Who would ever have imagined it?'

Kirk laughed. He was feeling marvellous, on top of the world. That afternoon he'd taken possession of his seventeenth pub since coming out of the Army only a few short years before.

'Who said you needed a university degree to be successful?' he said to Lizzie. 'It just goes to show if you've got it you've got it.'

'Aye, there's no keeping a good man down,' Lizzie added, the pride she felt for her son clearly written all over her face.

Kirk topped up their glasses and then sat down. He'd put on a considerable amount of weight since coming out of the Army. He was now very chubby, bordering on the rotund – this thanks to drink and lashings of good food, the latter always having been his weakness.

'So where do you go from here, son?' Lizzie asked.

'On and on, I suppose. Just keep buying more and more pubs.'

Lizzie sat facing Kirk, a shrewd, cunning look on her face. 'Maybe you should give things a wee bit more thought than that,' she said.

345

'How do you mean?'

'Well, there's been an awful lot in the papers of late about what's happening amongst the breweries down in England. And we all know that what happens down there tends to happen up here not all that long after.'

'Go on,' Kirk prompted softly, knowing that when his mother spoke like this it was wise to listen. He had long since come to respect her judgement and insight when it came to business matters.

Lizzie played with her double chin, she too having put on a great deal of weight during the past few years. 'There's an awful lot of buying going on,' she said. 'Where before there were five or six local breweries, one has bought the rest out and now services that entire area. Nor is it stopping locally. These big breweries are getting bigger all the time, either merging with or swallowing up their larger competitors. The way I see it the only logical end to all this will be a small number of huge breweries tending to the needs of the entire country, by which I mean Britain as a whole.'

Kirk pondered on that before replying. 'You could be right. But how do you see that affecting me?'

Lizzie reached out to take his hand. 'I always told you, son, think big. It might well be that in, say, ten years' time there will be only two breweries left in Scotland, and whoever owns these will have an awful lot of power. It doesn't matter how many pubs you own then; you'll be their lackey to jump when they say jump because if you don't they can stop supplying you and thereby put you out of business. If they don't, do so anyway, and why not? If they put you out of business they'd be able to buy up your pubs at rock-bottom prices.'

Kirk's champagne suddenly didn't taste so good any more. He swished the remains round his glass and looked at it sourly.

'You say think big? Just what do you mean by that?' he asked.

'Now's the time to be thinking ten years ahead. When the dust finally clears why shouldn't *you* be one of the two, possibly three, that are left?'

'You mean I should be making as well as selling?'

Lizzie's face cracked into a smile. 'Precisely.'

'Run my own brewery,' he said softly. It was a thought that had crossed his mind more than once but not for the reasons Lizzie had just put forward.

'The way I see it,' she went on, 'we'll end up with one brewery in Glasgow, one in Edinburgh and possibly, just possibly, one in the north, say Dundee or Aberdeen. But that third one will only be a small giant so to speak compared to the other two. And when it comes to Glasgow you know who the front runner must be at the moment, don't you?'

'Black Lion.'

'Aye, your friend and father-in-law, the high and mighty Major.'

Unconsciously Kirk reached up to touch the scar on his cheek. Over the years the scar had faded considerably but was still clearly discernible. From certain angles it gave his face a somewhat lopsided look. Slowly he traced the scar, anger burning in him as he remembered how he'd come by it. He and the Major were still bitter enemies although, for Susan's sake, they suffered one another's presence from time to time.

'What you're saying is I get him before he's in a position to get me?' Kirk said.

Lizzie nodded. 'That about sums it up.'

A wolfish grin lit up Kirk's face. He found the idea most appealing.

'You've got a mind on you that's sharp as a Blue Gillette,' he said admiringly.

'Maybe so. But you're the one can get things done. That's your talent.'

'Quite a team, eh Ma?'

'Quite a team, son,' she replied, squeezing his hand.

There was a loud yelling sound from the pub below. Lizzie cocked her head to listen, wondering if it was the portent of trouble. But the sound swiftly died away again. Walter had everything under control.

347

When she turned her attention back to Kirk he was already deep in thought.

Kirk sat in the back seat of his car gazing out at the passing scenery. Glasgow never changed, it seemed. Dirty houses, dirty streets with dirty children playing on them.

A wee boy wearing ragged clothes and wooden clogs came clattering along the pavement. He had an old rubber tyre which he was 'making go' with a stick. For a moment or two Kirk felt jealous. That was the sort of thing he'd always wanted desperately to do as a child but had never been allowed to.

As the wee boy clattered by out of sight he put the incident from his mind and concentrated on the meeting which he had requested and which he was now on his way to attend.

Turk McGhie brought the car into the brewery's forecourt and killed the engine. He turned to Kirk. 'Want me to come with you, Mr Murray?' he asked.

Kirk shook his head. Turk wasn't needed here. He climbed out of the car and made for the main entrance. Once inside, he announced who he was and whom he'd come to see. He was requested politely to sit. Mr McRae was on the phone and would see him directly.

The building Kirk was in was over a hundred and fifty years old and looked it, he thought. It had a geriatric air about it, as though at any moment it might just suddenly give up the ghost and come crashing down.

It was a month since Kirk had taken over his twenty-first pub and in that time he'd made extensive inquiries about the nine breweries currently functional in Glasgow. Thistle Brewery was the one he'd chosen, for the simple reason it was on the verge of bankruptcy and therefore it should be possible to buy it at the cheapest price.

'If you'll follow me, Mr McRae will see you now,' a pinch-faced man said, having appeared at Kirk's side. All the way along the passageway the man continually 'washed' his hands.

McRae was a bluff man in his early fifties, who rose as Kirk entered his office.

'Pleasure to meet you, Mr Murray,' he said, extending his hand. After they'd shaken and they'd both sat he added, 'I must say, you're a lot younger than I'd expected.'

Kirk nodded. That was a remark often made.

'Will you take a dram? Or perhaps you'd like a beer. I can recommend our 80/- ale. Smooth as silk.'

Kirk had already decided shock tactics were in order. He was already well known as someone who invariably came straight to the point – when it suited him, that was – and never pulled his punches.

'I never touch any of your beers,' he replied. 'I've tried all three of them. Your 70/- ale, your 80/- ale and your Scotch Ale. All three of them are dreadful, which is why I don't sell them in any of my pubs.'

McRae blinked and sat back in his chair. He'd never ever been spoken to like this before. Kirk stared at McRae, his eyes hard and unyielding. He wanted to dominate McRae, make the man buckle to his will.

McRae was completely thrown. 'I, eh ... I rather thought when you asked to see me today that you were considering putting Thistle beer into your pubs. I see now that isn't the case.' He waited expectantly but Kirk didn't reply. Finally he was forced to go on. 'What did you want to see me about, then?' he asked.

Kirk opened his briefcase, extracting a sheaf of papers which he laid on his lap. 'I've been doing a considerable amount of checking up on Thistle Brewery, Mr McRae. To put it in a nutshell, you're in one god-awful mess.'

McRae looked angry. 'You'd no right ...'

'I had every right,' Kirk cut in. 'I didn't do anything illegal.' McRae fumed. Kirk continued. 'For years now you've been lurching from one crisis to the next. During the past six years you've lost forty-four per cent of your business to Black Lion and several other brewers. On your current performance – and frankly if you haven't improved it by now, Mr McRae, you aren't going to – Thistle will go under next year or the following year at the latest.'

'That's pure conjecture!' McRae blustered.

'Like hell it is. You're mortgaged up to the hilt, you personally as well as the firm, with no other collateral or options up your sleeve to produce at the last minute. You've been running for years, McRae, and now you're on the point of running out of road.'

'How did you find out all this?'

'There are ways and means. Some of it was public knowledge; the other bits weren't too difficult to discover.'

McRae slumped at his desk and it was obvious most of the stuffing had been knocked out of him a long time since.

'What do you want?' he asked.

'To buy you out. I'll give you a fair price. Which won't be all that much, I warn you, considering the state the firm is in. But remember, it's a lot more than you'll get if you go into receivership.'

'Are you acting on your own or for someone else?'

'On my own.'

'Will ... will you continue brewing or have you something else in mind?'

'I plan to continue brewing.'

'I'm pleased about that,' McRae said, gazing off into space. 'There's been a brewery on this site for over three hundred years. Did you know that?' Kirk shook his head. 'This is the second building.' He sighed. 'It's a relief in a way. I've been at my wits' end a long time now worrying about keeping going. It's not just the firm, you see. It's the men. Some of them have been with us man and boy. If Thistle was to close down they'd be thrown out of work. And you know what unemployment's like in Glasgow. Some of them might get taken on by other breweries, the younger ones in particular. But for the majority, closure would be the finish of their working lives.'

'If they're good workmen who know their jobs they'll have nothing to fear from me,' Kirk said.

McRae crossed to a cupboard which he opened to reveal a row of bottles. 'How about a dram, then, if you don't like our beer?' he asked.

The man was a born loser, Kirk thought. It was stamped all over him.

'Fine. Then I suggest we arrange for our solicitors to get together. I'd like to get this thing sorted out as soon as possible.'

'If you'll come this way, Mr Murray,' said James Ogmore. 'Our entire creative department, including the team we hope will be eventually handling your account, are dying to meet you.'

Kirk strode along the deep-pile carpeted hallway. It was his first visit to Ogmore, McCall and Bird Ltd, Scotland's leading advertising agents, of whom James Ogmore was the chief partner.

The room he was ushered into was luxurious in an 'arty-crafty' way. The people in it, eighteen in all, rose smiling to their feet as he came through the doorway. While Kirk was being introduced around, wine was opened. When the gathering sat again everyone held a glass.

'This of course is just a preliminary meeting, a sort of "getting to know one another" occasion,' James Ogmore said. 'Now, have you anything particular in mind? Something that will at least give us a starting-off point?'

Kirk said slowly, 'What I want is the sort of advertising that will make people stop in their tracks and then go on to buy my beer. Something new and stunning. Something far better than the usual sort of beer adverts seen in Scotland today. What I want is something like the new S H Benson Guinness ad, "Down With Guinness . . ." in giant letters, while in tiny totey ones underneath, "Then You'll Feel Better."'

'That is a particularly good ad,' Ogmore said wryly, raising a laugh when he added, 'I wish we'd thought of it first.'

'Will you continue calling the brewery Thistle Brewery?' an intense-looking bearded man asked.

'No. As far as I'm concerned Thistle is associated with a rotten pint. I want a brand new name, something completely fresh.'

'Speaking right off the top of my head, how about KM Brewery?' a female suggested.

Kirk stared at the woman while he considered that. She was a striking redhead in her early twenties with large green eyes.

'Your initials,' she added softly.

'Speaking as an out-and-out egotist, I rather like it,' Kirk replied.

The others laughed and the woman grinned.

Kirk wracked his memory trying to remember her name. It was a funny one, gaelic he thought. And then it came back to him. *Ciona. Ciona ... Campbell? No ... Cran ... Cram ... Crammond. Yes, that was it. Ciona Crammond.

'KM Brewery it will be then, Miss Crammond.' Kirk smiled.

James Ogmore signalled that Kirk's glass should be refilled. 'You mentioned something about brewing new beers?' he said. 'Perhaps you'd like to elaborate on that.'

Kirk sipped his wine before replying. 'I intend selling three draught beers,' he said. 'A good pint of heavy, stronger and more flavoursome than the one Thistle do now. That'll be for the ordinary working man who enjoys his pint of wallop. The second one I want to aim more at the middle classes. Not quite so strong and lighter on the palate. The sort of beer a woman might well appreciate.'

Several in the room nodded. All were intent, hanging on his every word. He found he rather liked that. He also found he was addressing most of what he was saying directly to Ciona Crammond.

He went on. 'The third beer will be for the younger side of the market. The sub-twenties, just-over-twenties. Students. That sort of clientele which, speaking now as a pub owner, I'm finding is increasing as a corner of the market all the time. Young people nowadays, it seems, have a great deal more money to spend than did their parents, and a lot of what they

*Pronounced Shona.

352

spend goes on drink. For them, I want a beer they can identify with, something they feel belongs to their age group. For that I want an ultra-modern name; completely different to any other beer name that's gone before.'

'A very exciting and original concept, if I may say so,' Ogmore commented.

'The last two beers will be keg. The first one traditional barrel,' Kirk added.

'What's keg?' Ciona asked.

'A fairly new idea that's come out. Basically it's pasteurised beer put into a metal container which, when it reaches the pub, is delivered to the pump by CO_2.'

'Doesn't that damage the beer?' a man asked.

Kirk smiled. 'It's a slightly new taste, you might say. And incidentally, it's also a lot cheaper from the brewery point of view.'

The man looked as though he was about to add something but a sharp glance from James Ogmore caused him to change his mind.

'Keg's easier to handle and lasts longer in the pub, has a longer pub life we say,' Kirk said.

'But your first pint of heavy will remain in traditional barrels?' Ogmore asked.

'Correct,' Kirk said.

Kirk spoke for a few more minutes about his plans and ideas after which he answered a number of questions from the floor.

When the meeting was concluded, Ogmore suggested lunch and Kirk accepted.

Ogmore was in his office putting on his coat and Kirk was idly staring at some plaques on the walls when Ciona Crammond knocked and entered.

'Ciona will be in charge of the team who'll be drawing up our proposed campaign for you,' Ogmore said.

'Then I think she should come to lunch as well,' Kirk said smoothly.

Ogmore's eyes flickered ever so fractionally between Kirk

and Ciona. 'Good idea,' he replied. 'The more you two speak with one another the more insight she'll have on how to give you satisfaction.'

Kirk thought of a reply to that which brought a smile to his lips.

After lunch Kirk returned to the brewery, where he found Bill Baxter, his head brewer, by the mash tuns. Bill was an old groutchedy sort of a man well known for his sour disposition.

'How are you doing, Bill?' Kirk asked.

Baxter curled his lower lip in contempt. 'This beer 3 is more pish water than beer,' he said scornfully. Beer 3 referred to the beer Kirk would be aiming at the younger market. Beer 2 was for the middle-class market. And beer 1 was the traditional heavy.

'Let's have a taste,' Kirk said.

They moved on past the coppers and hop backs to where several small kegs had been racked and fined. Kirk waited patiently while Baxter drew off a glass of bright amber liquid, which Baxter then grudgingly handed him.

'CO_2,' Baxter muttered under his breath. 'The whole damn thing's sacrilege.'

Kirk took a swallow and then another. 'What's the gravity?' he asked.

'1034,' Baxter grunted in reply.

Kirk finished off the glass. The beer was light on the tongue, middle bodied and went down very easily.

'Drop it another four points,' he said.

Baxter shook his head in bewilderment. 'It'll be hardly alcoholic at all, then. Who's going to drink the likes of that, man?'

'*Mr Murray* to you, Baxter,' Kirk snapped in reply. 'And it's not your job to worry about who buys it. All you have to think about is making the damn stuff.'

Baxter looked at the floor, grumbling under his breath.

'And what's more, if the job doesn't suit you you can pick up your cards right now.'

Baxter looked up, fear edging into his eyes. 'It's just so different to what I'm used to brewing, Mr Murray,' he replied.

'I'm well aware of that, Baxter.'

'And as for this keg business, sir. It's ... it's immoral!'

Despite himself Kirk had to smile at the man's outrage. 'You know Thistle was on the verge of closure when I took over?' he said.

Baxter nodded. 'Aye, it had been rumoured long enough.'

'Well, a lot of the reason Thistle wasn't doing well was because of the muck you were putting out.'

Baxter spluttered, his face flaming. 'Thistle 70/- and 80/- ales won prizes forty years ago!'

'Forty years is a long time, Baxter.'

'The quality never changed. Not in my time anyway!'

'I'm sure. But tastes do change and Thistle never moved with the times. There's going to be a revolution in this industry, mark my words, and I want to be at the head of it.'

'But you'd have to drink God knows how many pints of beer 3 to get drunk!' Baxter said.

Kirk smiled. 'Precisely. And the more beer drunk the bigger the profit.'

Light dawned in Baxter's eyes. 'I see,' he said slowly. 'I hadn't looked at it from that point of view before.' Then changing back, 'I don't approve, mind you. But at least I see what you're driving at now.'

'Now, how's beer 2 coming along?' Kirk asked.

'I'm just not getting a good wort so far,' Baxter replied, and then launched into a lengthy and detailed explanation, three-quarters of which was way over Kirk's head.

Kirk got home that night feeling tired but elated.

'How was your day?' Susan asked, bringing him a whisky and water while he kicked off his shoes and sank into a comfortable chair.

'I have a feeling these advertising agents are going to work out,' he replied.

'Good.'

'I'm going to call the brewery KM Brewery. Like it?'

'KM for Kirk Murray, I presume?'

He laughed. 'Right first time. Think it's too much?'

'Do you?' Kirk shook his head. 'Then there's your answer.'

He sipped his whisky as he thought back over the day's events.

'I've been having trouble with Baxter, the head brewer. But I think I've finally got him straightened out.'

'By that I take it you've got him round to your way of thinking.'

'When you work for me that is the *only* way to think,' Kirk replied.

'Poor Baxter,' Susan said sympathetically. 'I'll bet you really gave him a flea in his ear.'

'Nothing to what he'll get if he doesn't come up with the new beers I want soon.'

'How are they going?'

'Beer 3's almost there. But 2 still has a long way to go.'

'Speaking of beer,' Susan said slowly. 'I spoke to Father today. He rang up this afternoon.'

Kirk sat bolt upright. 'He didn't know anything about the new beers or any of my plans, did he?'

'He didn't mention anything.'

'And you were careful not to ...'

'Yes I was,' Susan cut in angrily. 'You told me not to say anything to anyone and I haven't.'

Kirk grunted and sank back into his chair. 'So what did the Major want then?' he asked when he was once more in a comfortable position.

'The same old question. When are we going to give him a grandson?'

'Ah!' Kirk replied, and then his brow furrowed. 'It is peculiar how you've never got pregnant after all this time, isn't it?'

'I thought ... Well I thought perhaps I should see a doctor and get myself checked over.'

'You think something might be wrong in that department?'

'Who knows!' she shrugged. 'It's certainly possible. And if there is, it might well be something simple which can be easily put right.'

'Then you'd better see a doc.'

All this was a ruse on Susan's part. She had been to the doctor about the problem of her continuing non-pregnancy the previous year. The doctor had confirmed there was absolutely no reason why she shouldn't have a baby.

She now came to what all this was really about.

'As long as I'm going to see the doctor, why don't you as well? It can't do any harm.'

Kirk wasn't too sure he liked that idea, feeling that in some way it questioned his masculinity.

'I don't know ...' he prevaricated.

But Susan was ready for this. She went on, 'Why I think it's a good idea you go is connected with something I read on the subject. It seems a high proportion of non-pregnancies, where both partners are fertile, is due to the woman being too acidy – the acid killing off the sperms – for her mate, in which case she's given pills to reduce her level of acidity. Now the doctor wouldn't be able to tell if I was too acid for you unless he was able to test you as well.'

That seemed a fair enough argument to Kirk, and one which let his manhood off the hook, so he capitulated.

'All right, you set up the appointment and I'll be there,' he said.

Susan came across and kissed him on the cheek. 'Thank you,' she whispered.

'Of course, maybe we haven't been trying hard enough to have one,' he replied.

'You must be joking! You're forever at it.'

'Nonetheless. Perhaps I need to try just that little bit harder.'

'Dinner's in the oven. It'll burn,' she said as he nibbled her neck.

357

'Let it,' he replied, slipping out of his chair and dragging them both to the floor.

And it did.

Kirk sat beside James Ogmore, both men with large whiskies in their hands. They were in Ciona Crammond's office and she was just about to explain her proposed campaign for the KM Brewery. Several of her team sat in the background ready to add their two cents' worth if asked.

Ciona held up a large sheet of cardboard on which a pint of beer had been painted. Below the pint was the new KM logo and a line of copy which said simply: KM HEAVY - A TRADITIONAL PINT FOR THE MAN WHO KNOWS AND APPRECIATES HIS BEER.

'Beer 1,' said Ciona. 'Straightforward, basic, aimed directly at the working man who doesn't like frills or fripperies. What I would call a no-nonsense ad.'

Kirk nodded. That sort of ad would go down well with working-class Glasgow.

'Beer 1 is obviously the easiest of the lot,' said Ciona.

'All this will be going out on hoardings, newspaper ads, cinema ads, what we call give-aways, that sort of thing,' Ogmore chipped in.

Ciona continued. 'Beer 2 I thought we might call Golden Brew ...'

'Golden Brew?' muttered Kirk. He liked it.

'I think Golden has such marvellous, and indeed middle-class, connotations. Happy, healthy, sun-drenched, goodness, that sort of thing.' She held up a second sheet of cardboard on which was depicted an obviously middle-class family enjoying themselves on a seaside outing. Overhead the sun was bursting through a powder-blue sky, the two children were rosy-cheeked and bonnie, while before Dad sat a brimming golden pint and before Mum a sparkling half-pint.

'This is just one setting of which there could be many appropriate ones,' Ciona said.

'Not bad,' said Kirk. In fact he thought it excellent. It

portrayed exactly the sort of image he was after.

Golden Brew, he thought to himself. It definitely had a ring about it and was very different to anything else currently on the Scottish market.

'Now beer 3,' said Ciona, 'and the one I'm sure we'd all agree was the hardest of the lot. Well I've personally thought to call it KM '60, the drink of tomorrow here today. The '60 stands for 1960.'

'Yes, I got that,' Kirk said.

Ciona held up another cardboard picture. This one portrayed a group of older teenagers dancing to what was very obviously a rock-and-roll band.

'Or,' said Ciona, 'KM '60, the drink of tomorrow in keg, the barrel of the future.'

There was a pause and then Kirk said, 'I like both slogans.'

'If you give us the go-ahead we can develop all these ideas,' Ciona said.

Excitement gripped Kirk as he stared at the cardboard picture Ciona was holding up. His gut reaction told him she was on the right track with all three beers. He could smell money here. And that particular sense of smell had never yet let him down.

'The idea behind KM '60 would be to identify it with the new wave of international singers, musicians, bands, screen idols –'

'And sport,' Kirk interrupted. 'Incorporate sport as well.'

Ciona nodded that she'd taken his point on board, then continued. 'We wouldn't use the actual names themselves but rather associate through look-alikes, inference, that sort of thing.'

Ciona spoke non-stop for another five minutes before finally coming to a halt. When she'd done so, several of the others present added a few comments. When they were finished silence reigned.

'What do you think, Mr Murray?' James Ogmore asked eventually.

Kirk allowed a smile to light up his face. 'I like very much what you've done so far. You've got my account for a year on trial. After that we'll see.'

James Ogmore extended his hand which Kirk shook. Then Kirk shook hands with Ciona Crammond.

'I think this calls for a drink,' said Ogmore.

'I think it calls for several,' said Kirk.

Everyone laughed. While some minions fetched the booze Kirk drew Ciona down beside him.

They had a great deal to talk about.

Kirk was stunned. 'But that's impossible!' he exclaimed. 'I've already impregnated a woman.'

Doctor Goldberg adjusted his spectacles before glancing back at the report spread before him. 'The results of your tests are quite definite,' he said. 'You have an extremely low sperm-count – nine thousand to be precise. Anything below ten is considered infertile.'

'Then how do you explain what happened before?'

Goldberg took off his glasses and stared at Kirk. 'It's not completely out of the question, of course, although highly improbable.'

'But it *did* happen.'

'Not to Mrs Murray, I take it?'

'No,' Kirk replied. 'The woman I was associated with previously.'

'And how long ago was this?'

'A handful of years.'

'Hmm!' said Goldberg, looking thoughtful. He picked up a pencil and tapped its butt end on his desk. Eventually he added, 'There is the possibility that in these intervening years something may have happened to you physically to render you infertile.'

'Like what?'

'Excessive stress and strain, far too much alcohol over a prolonged period, disease ...'

'What sort of disease?' Kirk cut in quickly.

'Venereal, Mr Murray.'

Goldberg knew from the stricken look on Kirk's face that he'd struck home. He sighed; these things were invariably very sad. The callow youth sowing wild oats only to reap a great deal more than ever dreamed of. It was a story he knew only too well having heard it so many times before.

'I was over in Germany doing my national service ...' Goldberg sighed again. 'And I caught a dose. The army medics treated me.'

'That would seem to be it then,' Goldberg said. 'The disease must have fouled things up in the tubes from your testes, hence the sperm drop.'

'Is there anything you can do?'

Goldberg shook his head.

'Then I'll never be a father?'

'As I said before, it's not totally impossible. But what we're talking about is the proverbial chance in a million.'

Kirk thought of Leoni von Kruppermann. 'That bitch!' he whispered, his hands knotting into fists.

'You're sure there's no treatment?' he demanded.

'Positive,' Goldberg replied. 'I'm sorry.'

'Not half as much as I am, doctor.'

Kirk rose and shook Dr Goldberg's hand. 'Just one thing. I'd like this kept confidential between the pair of us. I don't want my wife to find out, not yet anyway. And certainly *never* what I've just confided in you.'

'I understand perfectly,' said Goldberg.

Half-way home, Kirk started to laugh. In an ironical way what had happened was very, very funny.

Susan was waiting up for him. 'How did it go?' she asked anxiously, the moment he walked into the room.

He poured them both a drink before replying. As he handed her a glass, he said brightly, 'There's nothing wrong with me. A1, top of the bill. Everything functioning just as it should be.'

'Well, that's a relief!'

'So if there's nothing wrong with either of us, it's just one of

361

these things. God's will, as they say. We'll just have to keep on trying and hope that one day something happens.'

She came to his side and put her arm round his waist. 'It's getting late. How about bed?' she suggested.

'If you don't mind I think I'll stay down here a while and have a few drinks. I've a lot on my mind at the moment, things to do with the brewery I want to work out.'

'Are you all right?'

'I'm fine! Fine! Just got a lot running around inside the old bonce, that's all.'

She kissed him on the cheek. 'Don't be too late up. And if I've fallen asleep you can wake me if you like.'

He pecked her back but didn't commit himself one way or the other.

At the door she turned to add something but didn't when she saw he was already lost in thought.

For a long time after Susan had gone to bed, Kirk sat drinking steadily, thinking about his German countess and the legacy she'd given him.

Then eventually he started thinking about Ciona Crammond, wondering, not for the first time, what she'd be like to have.

When he finally turned in, he was more than a little drunk and randy as hell.

It might have been his wife Kirk made love to, but it was another woman he had pictured in his mind.

Writing this letter was something Kirk had been looking forward to since the day he'd bought what was now KM Brewery. Of the twenty-six pubs he now owned – five more had come with the brewery – twenty-one sold Black Lion beer.

In his own handwriting he informed Major Keith Gibb that as from the first of the coming month he would no longer be selling the Black Lion product, replacing it with his own KM brews.

When the letter was finished he signed it with a flourish and then sat back in his chair to stare at it. His fingers came up to stroke the scar on his cheek. He'd sworn revenge the day the Major had given him that. Susan had been part of his revenge. The rest was about to follow.

The letter in front of him was the point of the knife going in. From now on, he'd be pressing on that knife, driving it deeper and deeper until one day ... Kirk smiled thinly to himself. Until one day the bastard was destroyed.

'Come in,' said Ciona Crammond. 'It was good of you to come over.'

Kirk shrugged himself out of his coat and, while she was disposing of it, had a quick look round the room.

At one time, the house had been one of Glasgow's grander ones, inhabited by a large well-to-do family and all the various servants needed to cater to their needs. Now it was sub-divided into a number of flats of which Ciona's was on the ground floor.

The room was extremely high, with a great deal of fancy plaster-work on the ceiling. An absolutely enormous mirror was fastened to one wall, which cleverly made the room seem larger than it actually was. There were a great many books scattered around, together with a number of other mis-cellaneous items including articles of clothing. Whatever else Ciona Crammond was, she wasn't a tidy person.

'Drink?' she said on re-entering the room.

'Please.'

'Whisky, wine ...?'

'Whisky would be fine,' he said, smiling.

He watched her as she poured the drinks. He hadn't been all that surprised to receive her phone call at the brewery. It had been only a matter of time before one of them made the first move.

'Everything going to your satisfaction so far?' she asked, handing him a whisky and water, half and half, the way she knew he liked it.

'Anybody in Glasgow who hasn't heard about KM beers by now must be deaf, dumb and blind,' he grinned.

'Slainthe!' she toasted.

'Slainthe!'

Their eyes were on one another as they drank.

'I've been working from home today – I do from time to time – which is why I asked you here rather than the office,' she said.

He nodded.

'I've been thinking: launch day. What we need over and above what we've already planned is something physical to actually take place.'

He grinned inwardly at the choice of her words.

'Something to give the newspapers good photos and copy. But more than that, something the people can actually see. Now, launch day is a Saturday, right?'

'Right.'

'Which is the day most of Glasgow comes into the town to do their big shopping.'

'Right again,' he said.

'What about a pipe band then? You know we Scots are suckers for tartan and the sound of the pipes. To use a common expression nowadays, we just lap it up.'

It was true, he thought. Nothing went down better amongst the populace than a pipe band.

'How does advertising KM beers come into it?' he asked.

'Placards, sashes, that sort of thing.'

'If it went up Argyle Street from the Trongate, up Buchanan Street and along Sauchiehall Street to Charing Cross, and then came all the way back again, say round about mid-day, it would be seen by an awful lot of people.'

Ciona nodded eagerly. 'Precisely.'

'Can you get a band?'

'I've already made inquiries. I've got one which will happily do it providing you make a contribution to their instrument fund.'

'What sort of figure?'

Ciona mentioned one Kirk thought extremely reasonable.

'We'll have them then,' he said.

'I like a man who can make up his mind,' she replied, smiling. 'Now how about another drink?'

After their refills had been poured they sat facing one another across the room. 'You've done a very good job on my campaign,' he said.

Her eyes crinkled at the corners. 'Thank you.'

'Have you been with Ogmore, McCall and Bird long?'

'Eighteen months. Before that I was down in London working for one of the agencies there. J Walter Thompson.'

'I've heard of them,' Kirk said.

'Very big, very good. I learned a great deal.'

'So why come back here?'

'The parents are getting on a bit. I thought it best to be close by.'

'Do they live in Glasgow?'

'Helensburgh now. But they only moved there a few years ago.'

'So you were born and brought up in Glasgow?'

'For my sins,' she grinned.

'Tell me about your father. What does he do?'

'Did. He's retired. He was a judge.'

Kirk raised an eyebrow. 'I'm impressed.' Then suddenly, 'Not Justice Crammond, the one they called "Hanging Crammond"?'

'He's ever such a pet really,' Ciona said. 'He just seemed to get an awful lot of murderers at one point, that's all.'

'Most of whom went to the gallows at Barlinne, hence the name.'

Kirk was more than impressed now. Mr Justice Crammond had been one of Scotland's best-known figures for many years, not only famous but also part of the establishment and one of the leading lights in the highest strata of Scottish society.

'Laurel Bank or Park?' he asked, these being the names of two of Glasgow's very best private girls' schools.

'Craigholme, just to be different,' she replied.

Well she certainly belonged to the country's cream, he thought. There could be no denying that.

'What school did *you* go to?' she asked, a mischievous twinkle in her eye.

He knew from that twinkle she was well aware he wasn't from the upper crust, as he sounded to a lot of people. The genuine article always recognises the masquerader.

'The school of hard knocks. About five million miles away from Craigholme,' he replied.

She nodded her approval. She would have been disappointed if he'd lied.

'And what about your wife?' she asked, the mischievous twinkle stronger than before.

'Ah! Of better stock than me. The rose to my thorn.'

'I've heard she's very nice.'

'She is.'

'A vet, isn't she?'

'Qualified but never practised.'

'You think a woman's place is in the home?'

His lips thinned wolfishly. 'I think a woman's place is in the bed. Whether she works or not doesn't bother me.'

'You're an extremely arrogant man, aren't you?'

'Yes.'

'And conceited.'

'Dreadfully.'

'I think I like you.'

'I *know* I like *you*.'

She laughed. 'Are you always so positive?'

'Only about women, money, business and life in general.'

'In that order?'

'Not necessarily.'

He rose and crossed to her, taking her hand and drawing her to her feet.

'Don't you think we've talked enough now?' he asked.

'What else did you have in mind?'

'The same thing you did when you asked me here.'

He kissed her hard, pulling her to him and squashing her against his chest.

366

'Have you a double-bed?' he asked, when their mouths finally broke apart.

'Yes.'

'Good. I hate being cramped.'

'Come on,' she said, her hand hot and sticky with expectation in his.

As she led him to the bedroom, he said, 'You aren't an Honourable, are you?'

'No. Why?'

'Pity. I would have liked that.'

'Are you a snob, Mr Murray?' she asked sweetly.

'Kirk, please. And yes I am. Through and through.'

The bedroom looked as though a bomb had struck it, the dressing table littered with make-up, powder – more of which seemed spilled than was actually in the box – cotton wool, toilet roll and a number of cups containing the remains of coffee. There was a table by the bed. The table-top was absolutely covered with rank upon rank of standing smoked-down cork-tipped cigarette butts.

Kirk stared at that little army in fascination. It was the first time he'd ever seen anything like it.

Ciona's hands went up behind her, and several seconds later her dress fell away. She kicked it to one side, then pulled her slip over her head. Crossing to the bed she sprawled across it. 'Well?' she demanded.

Ten minutes later the bed was rocking violently as Kirk and Ciona went at it hammer and tongs.

Suddenly she shrieked and threw her arms around his head. And as she did so the bed tilted and sort of slid away from beneath them.

'Jesus Christ!' said Kirk, as with Ciona clinging tightly to him the pair of them went rolling to one side, to end up dumped on the floor.

'I've heard of orgasms that made the earth move but that was bloody ridiculous!' he exclaimed.

Ciona giggled and buried her head in his shoulder. Her red

hair lay spread below them like a carpet of red gold.

'I forget to mention that one of the legs isn't there any more,' she said. 'That bit's held jacked up by a pile of books.'

Kirk looked and sure enough the bed only had three legs.

'We've knocked all your cigarette ends down,' he said.

'There's nothing down that I can't put up again,' she whispered in his ear.

And she was right.

The pipe band turned into Buchanan Street playing 'Scotland The Brave'. Behind the band came a dozen pretty lassies dressed up in the same tartan as the band, and all carrying placards and wearing sashes proclaiming the virtues of KM beer. Hordes of people in the middle of their shopping stopped and cheered. Wee boys ran up and down the gutter shouting various things, including, 'Kiltie kiltie cauld bum!'

'What do you think?' Kirk asked.

'Impressive. Certainly dear dull Glasgow hasn't seen anything like it since the end of the war,' Susan replied.

'I've got a great feeling about all this, you know. There'll be no stopping me now.'

'I believe you,' Susan said, and meant it.

They followed the pipe band up the street. A street which only minutes before had been grey and dreich but which was now magically transformed. The air was alive, thrumming with gaiety and excitement.

'Just listen to them,' Kirk said. KM Brewery, KM heavy, KM Golden Brew and KM '60 seemed on everyone's lips.

'Your advertising agency has certainly done you proud. No doubt about it,' Susan said.

And all thanks to Ciona Crammond, Kirk thought. She was the driving force as well as the really creative one behind this campaign.

'Come on, let's get round and ahead of them on to Sauchiehall Street,' he said, and, taking Susan's hand, pulled her off to one side and out of the throng.

On the other side of Buchanan Street, Eddy King stood in a

doorway, his gaze fixed on Kirk and Susan as they hurried away.

It was the first time he'd seen Kirk since the day they'd both come home from their national service. As he'd known at the time, Kirk had never contacted him nor he Kirk. He thought of Heather Dew and Kolya Turushev – 'the Russian run', they'd called it – and smiled. You've come a long way, Kirk my old china, he thought. A long way. But then so had he.

He waited till the press had subsided a little, before venturing out of the doorway. Making for his car, he presented a smart figure in his brand new camel coat, below which he wore a well-cut twenty-pound suit. He eased himself into a gleaming Jaguar and drove off, the very epitome of the self-made man: hard, ruthless and determined to keep getting ahead.

But at the back of his eyes, there was a sadness, the pain of memory. Annie Grimes, Leoni and Kirk had done that to him. They'd undermined the ruthlessness, given him a soft spot.

Some people would have said they'd made him more human.

George Penn and his Pennmen were in one corner blowing up a jazz storm. The room was packed with heaving bodies, all eating, drinking, smoking, enjoying themselves.

'Marvellous party,' said James Ogmore. Surrounded by a few acolytes and sycophants, he was talking to Susan.

Although she'd met him a number of times now, this was the first occasion she'd seen him really let his hair down. She hadn't realised before that he was queer.

'Kirk and I both thought it went extraordinarily well today. He was very pleased.'

'So were we at the agency, if I may say so. Mind you, most of the credit must go to Ciona. This campaign was mainly her baby.'

Susan smiled. Her throat was sore from having to shout so much in order to be heard above the din.

'And speaking of Ciona where is she?' Ogmore said, looking around.

A man from the brewery came up to Susan and said that the barrel of Golden Brew that had been laid on was now empty and should he open another.

'If they've gone through an entire barrel this quickly then I'd think you'd better,' Susan replied.

'I'll need the keys to the garage then,' the man said. That was where the various barrels and crates had been stored.

Susan pulled a face. 'We'll have to find Kirk for that. He's got them.'

'I saw him only a few minutes ago,' one of the acolytes said. 'He seemed to be heading for the rear of the house.'

'Will I go look for him?' the man from the brewery asked.

'No, you keep dishing out the KM '60 in the meantime, and I'll find and send him to you,' Susan replied.

The man nodded and moved off.

The reason Susan wanted to hunt for Kirk herself was that by going to the back of the house she could nip outside for a few moments and get a breath of fresh air. The noise and smoky atmosphere were beginning to give her a bit of a headache.

Excusing herself, she started to squirm through the mass of pressing flesh in the direction of the door, being stopped every few seconds to be congratulated on the success of the party and the launch of KM beers.

'Not here, dope!' Ciona whispered. 'What if someone walked in?'

'Bugger them!' said Kirk.

'Now, you don't mean that.'

'You're right,' he replied, removing his hand from her breast. 'Would be a bit embarrassing to be found groping my lady advertising agent in the back kitchen, wouldn't it?'

Ciona giggled. Both of them had had a fair amount to drink.

'There must be somewhere we can be alone,' he said, looking about.

'What about the rest of the house?'

He shook his head. 'People everywhere. Upstairs, downstairs, in my lady's chamber.'

'I like your lady, you know.'

'Susan? She's all right. Bit boring, mind you. Hadn't noticed that till recently.'

'Are you saying since you met me?'

'Yes ... Yes, I think I am.'

She smiled and buried her face in his chest. 'That's a lovely compliment. Thank you,' she whispered.

'Hold on a mo',' he said. 'Follow me.'

At the rear of the back kitchen was an old pantry now used as a storage room. He opened the door to this and bundled her inside.

The pantry was very narrow, and because of various sacks and boxes there was only about two feet of standing room.

'Rather cramped, don't you think?' she giggled in the darkness. 'And didn't you once tell me you hated being that?'

'I hate being randy and not being able to do anything about it even more,' he retorted.

Susan stumbled into the front kitchen, a veritable cavern of a place, to find several servants hired for the party busy making more sandwiches.

'Has anyone seen Mr Murray?' she asked.

'Sorry ma'am,' one said.

Another, a young girl, said, 'I think I might have seen him going into the back, Mrs Murray, but I couldn't be sure like. I mean it might well have been somebody else.'

Susan muttered thanks and moved on. She had intended going through to the back kitchen anyway as there was a door to the garden there.

All the lights in the back kitchen were on and there was an opened bottle of whisky on the table.

Well if he had been here he must've moved on, Susan thought. Crossing to the garden door she tugged it open and stepped outside. The air which washed around and over her

371

was cool and invigorating, like sparkling wine, she thought. She drank in a deep lungful and immediately felt better.

Wind rustled the trees and flowers in the garden. And what was that? An animal? After a few seconds it dawned on her it was somebody giggling, but where?

Her eyes and ears followed the sound until she traced it to the small projection at the back of the house which was the old pantry now used as a storeroom.

There was the murmur of a man's voice and then she understood. Some couple had wanted a little privacy and had found their way there. Probably a couple of young things after a bit of snogging, she thought. And why not? She'd enjoyed doing that sort of thing herself when she was their age.

She was about to turn and re-enter the back kitchen when suddenly, and quite clearly, the man's voice said, 'Oh that's lovely!'

The voice was unmistakable. It was Kirk's.

She closed her mouth, which she'd suddenly realised was hanging open, and swallowed hard. She felt numb all over. She considered briefly tearing the pantry door open and confronting him and whoever he was with. But second thoughts told her that would be a stupid thing to do. It was probably just some passing fancy, a young bird who'd thrown herself at him and whom he was having a couple of minutes' stolen passion with. A few kisses, a little petting. Nothing more.

She'd do herself more harm than good by making a mountain out of a molehill, she told herself. Let it go. Let it pass. And closing the garden door quietly behind her, she tiptoed back to the front kitchen, where she picked up two plates of sandwiches to take through to the party. She sought out James Ogmore and spoke to him, as he had an easy manner about him which was just what she needed then.

Twenty minutes later – she knew precisely how long it was because her eyes had kept straying to a wall clock – Kirk re-entered the room, and a few seconds after him, although apparently not with him, came Ciona Crammond.

'I don't know about anyone else but I'm thoroughly enjoying myself,' declared Kirk, his face flushed and his hair messed. He was carrying a glass containing a very large whisky.

Susan forced a smile on to her face and made herself act as though nothing had happened.

'Ciona! Come and join us!' Kirk called out.

'The lady wonder,' said James Ogmore, making a mock bow. One of his sycophants tittered.

Kirk took Ciona's hand in his and squeezed it. Susan saw the look which passed between them, and knew then that it had been no young thing that Kirk had been in the pantry with. It had been Ciona Crammond.

She raised her glass to her lips and it took all the willpower she possessed to stop it from trembling.

'A big, big day for you and Kirk,' said James Ogmore.

'Yes,' Susan replied. 'It is that.'

The last guest didn't leave till five in the morning, by which time Susan was absolutely worn out.

The house, a new one on the outskirts of Glasgow they'd moved into two years previously, was a shambles. But thank god she didn't have to worry about that. Several cleaners would be arriving later to put it all back in order again.

She poured herself a glass of cold milk which she took with her up to the bedroom. There she found Kirk had stripped off and gone through to the adjoining bathroom where she could hear he was having a shower.

She was about to strip off herself, when she suddenly noticed something peculiar about his underpants lying by the side of the bed. There was a streak of what looked like blood on the front of them. Frowning, she bent and picked up the underpants, wondering how he'd come to get blood there. She ran her finger along the mark, from which the colour transferred rather greasily on to her skin. A quick sniff confirmed her mistake.

Not blood but lipstick. And she knew then what it was Kirk

373

and Ciona had been doing in the pantry. Or to be more precise what Ciona had been doing.

Curling the underpants in her hand she angrily threw them from her. Sitting on the bed she hung her head. She desperately wanted to weep but wouldn't. At least not yet.

When Kirk came out of the bathroom shortly afterwards he found her in bed, apparently fast asleep. Humming, he got in beside her and within minutes had nodded off.

When he started to snore Susan opened her eyes and stared at the ceiling. Silently, so it wouldn't waken him, she allowed the tears to flow.

With a satisfied grunt, Kirk added the last name to the list it had taken him the best part of a week to compile. He pressed a button and a few seconds later Turk McGhie entered the office. Turk nodded and sat down facing Kirk across the desk.

'A list of every pub in Glasgow,' Kirk said, tapping the sheets of paper in front of him with his hand. 'With details of whether they're tied houses, free houses, and if the latter, which beer they sell. We'll start with north Glasgow where most of my pubs are and which is the area I wish to consolidate first. I've sectioned the north into half-mile squares so you can do a steady progression from square to square until every free house north of Sauchiehall Street is selling KM beers. Over and above your regular wages, there'll be a bonus for every pub you persuade to give its business to my brewery. Any questions?'

Turk McGhie shook his head.

'Well there's the list and a map with the sections clearly marked. Good luck.'.

McGhie accepted the map and sheets of paper, folding them and putting them into his pocket.

After Turk had gone Kirk shivered. Turk in one of his silent moods always had scared the living daylights out of him.

'Time gentlemen, please!' the publican of The Doch And Doris called. It was twenty past nine at night.

Several of those in the pub grumbled but nonetheless got on with the business of drinking up. The publican, whose name was McKevitt, came round the front of the bar to start collecting glasses. Behind the bar, his son Joe ran water into the basin in preparation for the washing up.

Fifteen minutes later McKevitt and Joe were the only ones left in the pub. Or so they thought. They both looked up in surprise when the door to the toilet opened and McGhie emerged.

'Time's been called, Jimmy,' McKevitt said. 'You're the last one.'

McGhie walked slowly to the bar where he gave McKevitt a cold, baleful, fish eye.

'I'm a representative from KM Brewery,' he said.

'Oh aye?'

'As you're a free house, we'd like you to give up the Black Lion muck you sell now and take our beers.'

McKevitt grinned as he hefted a bucketful of ullage on to the bar. 'And why should I do that?' he asked.

'Because ours is a better beer.'

'Keg?' McKevitt laughed. 'It'll never catch on. Anyway, I've been dealing with Black Lion for over twenty years now. Why should I change? I've always got on with them and they've always dealt fairly with me.'

Turk's eyes bored into McKevitt's. 'You'd find we're very competitive. In fact, it may well be we can give you a better deal than you're now getting from Black Lion,' he said.

McKevitt shook his head. 'You're wasting your time, Jim. Not interested.'

'You heard my dad. Now let's be having you,' said Joe.

'I haven't finished speaking yet,' said Turk quietly.

Irritation flashed across Joe's face. 'I think you have. My dad said we're not interested and that's that.' He then made the mistake of taking McGhie by the arm and trying to propel him towards the door.

McGhie shrugged himself free. And a second later the heel of his flattened palm scythed in a downward arc which ended on the bridge of Joe's nose. There was a cracking sound followed by a spurt of bright red blood as Joe's nose broke where bone meets gristle. Joe's hands came up to his damaged face as he hastily back-pedalled. He never even saw the vicious rabbit punch which took him on the back of the neck to send him sprawling unconscious on the cigarette-end-strewn floor.

'What sort of bloody maniac are you?' screamed McKevitt, backing off as Turk advanced on him.

'Now, about changing your beer. I think you'll find it's going to be all the rage around here soon, so I advise you to get in at the very beginning when the terms are still good.'

'Get away from me!'

'I think traditional heavy and Golden Brew would be your best bests. I doubt if you'll have much call for KM '60, the beer of tomorrow in keg, the barrel of the future,' McGhie said. Grabbing hold of McKevitt's shirt front he drew the publican to him. 'Well? What do you say?'

'I'll ... I'll call the police. They know how to deal with the likes of you.'

McKevitt screamed, his feet trailing on the floor, as Turk dragged him across to where the bucket of ullage stood on the bar. Grabbing the back of McKevitt's head, Turk then swung himself round behind the man.

'If you like Black Lion beer so much then drink it,' Turk said and forced McKevitt's head down till his face was deep in slops from ear to ear. McKevitt struggled violently but found it impossible to break Turk McGhie's iron grip.

Turk counted thirty seconds before pulling McKevitt's face free.

'What's it taste like? Good, eh?' he asked.

McKevitt's eyes were popping and his face was puce. 'I ... I ...' he spluttered.

'Still thirsty, eh? Then be my guest!'

McKevitt shrieked as his face was forced back down, this time slowly, into the beer slops. When his mouth disappeared under, a stream of bubbles broke the surface.

Turk made the second immersion a short one, fifteen

seconds only, before yanking McKevitt's head back up again.

McKevitt made choking sounds and staggered away from Turk when the grip on his hair was released.

Turk took his time about lighting up a cigarette.

'There will be another representative from KM round to see you in the morning to take your order. Welcome to KM Brewery. It's a switch you'll never regret.'

Joe McKevitt had come to his feet where he stood panting.

'And don't either of you go to the polis,' said McGhie, moving to the door. 'It would be a very, very stupid thing to do.'

There was a blur of light as he produced an ivory-handled cut-throat razor, which he held in the cocked position. Slowly, and emphatically, he drew it down the door curtain, whch parted like sliced butter. 'If you get my meaning,' he added.

The razor vanished as quickly as it had appeared.

'Good night,' said Turk. 'It's been a pleasure doing business with you.'

'Your favourite, *coq au vin*,' said Susan, placing a plate piled high in front of Kirk.

Her own plateful was tiny by comparison, as she was on a diet. She wanted to have as trim a figure as possible in case it was that which had caused Kirk to stray.

Kirk attacked the meal with relish, washing every mouthful down with a gulp of red wine. 'Sure beats the mince and tatties my mother used to make,' he said at one point.

Sweet was jam roly-poly which he absolutely adored. He scoffed down the first helping in seconds, grinning when, without asking, he was immediately given another.

'Smashing!' he said when he was finished.

He was putting on weight again, Susan thought. But she didn't want to tell him that in case it made him angry with her. It had been a long long time since he'd last been to the sports club where they'd met.

'You sit comfy by the fire and finish that bottle of wine,' she said. 'I've just got something to do first, then I'll be with you.'

Rising from her chair she slipped out of the room to the bedroom where the special negligee she'd bought earlier on that day was laid out waiting for her. She stripped naked, looking at herself in a full-length mirror. Not too bad, she thought. But there was room for improvement which was why she was on the diet. Her flesh was firm, her bust still standing up with no hint yet of sag. Her bottom was a little droopy but then it had always been like that. Her tummy and thighs were where she needed to take off a few pounds and she was working on that.

She powdered herself down and then dabbed a brand new perfume on her neck and breasts. She then shrugged into the negligee after which she patted her hair back into place.

Kirk was in an extremely contented mood as he sat by the fire sipping wine. The brewery was going great guns and, thanks to Turk McGhie and his persuasive ways, production was having to be increased every week to keep up with demands. Since the grand launch, nearly all the Glasgow distilleries had been clamouring to see him, wanting him to sell their spirits in his pubs. In the end he'd decided to do a deal with his old pal Andy White at Carswell's. Not because of any sentimentality but for the simple reason Andy had come up with the best terms.

Kirk sighed and refilled his glass. Life was certainly good. He thought of Ciona whom he'd been with before coming home. He'd called at her flat and for an hour they'd tested the new bed he'd insisted on buying her. After several spills off the old three-legged one he'd decided a joke was a joke but to hell with nonsense.

By God, she was a demanding woman, that, who fair took it out of him! he thought. An early night he decided. As usual he had a busy day ahead of him tomorrow. He had a meeting with a man up from England who wanted to try and convince him to can more take-away beer rather than bottling it.

His heart sank the moment Susan re-entered the room. The seductive nightdress, the perfume he could smell even at this distance, all added up to one thing.

Damn! he swore inwardly. He just didn't fancy her after Ciona. And what was more Ciona had drained him so much he wasn't even sure he was capable.

Susan sat by the side of the fire and curled her legs up under her.

'I was out in the park today watching some children play,' she said quietly. 'They really are tremendous fun.'

He grunted.

'It would be such a marvellous thing for us if we could have one.'

'Yes,' he said reluctantly.

She looked into the fire, a coy expression on her face. 'Perhaps if we tried it at different times of the day. Mornings, afternoons, that sort of thing. And if we varied the positions, that might also help.'

'Six days of the week I'm at work mornings and afternoons . . .'

'We could wake up early.'

'I just don't feel like it nowadays at the crack of dawn.'

'There was a time when you did.'

'I didn't have the responsibilities and worry then that I do now,' he said.

'Well what about afternoons? You're the boss. If you want to come home for a little while there's no reason why you can't.'

He barked out a laugh. 'What do you think I do in my office all day? Sit playing with paper clips? There's work to be done, Susan. A great deal of it. There never seem to be enough hours in the working day now as it is, far less taking time off in the middle of it to come home for some hanky-panky.'

'I'm sorry. I was only trying to help,' Susan said miserably.

Kirk stared at his wife, thinking how pathetic she looked. Mind you, there had always been something of that in her but it had never been so pronounced before. Suddenly he found himself repulsed by it, and couldn't help comparing her to the bubbling, vivacious Ciona. It was a comparison Susan didn't come out of well.

379

'Perhaps we should think of adopting,' she said. 'I know it's not the same but it would be an awful lot better than having no children at all.'

There she was, harping on about bloody children yet again! He knew her father was ringing her during the day from time to time. All that old fart could think about was children too!

Christ! why couldn't they just let things be? There weren't going to be any bloody kids, thanks to that German sow of a countess and the pox she'd given him. But of course Susan didn't know about that, nor could he bring himself to tell her. He felt he would lose face somehow, that his masculinity would lose credit.

What a bloody mess! he thought. For the truth was that secretly he wanted a child as well. He thought bitterly of the baby Minnie had had aborted. It might well have been a boy. His son. That thought had been preying a great deal on his mind of late. If only he'd known what lay in store he could've encouraged Minnie to have the child. He wouldn't have married her, of course, that had never been on the cards. And later, when the child was older, especially if it had been a boy, perhaps some arrangement could've been made.

'I love you, Kirk,' Susan said.

He brought himself out of his reverie. 'Eh?'

'I said I love you.'

'And I love you too.'

Wistfully, 'Do you?'

'You know I do.'

'I sometimes wonder, Kirk.'

He sipped his wine to give him time to think. Did she know something? She couldn't. He and Ciona had been most discreet. And yet there was a knowing look in her eye. Or was that merely his conscience making him see something that wasn't really there?

Susan picked up the poker and stabbed the fire. Ever since discovering about Kirk's affair she'd been unhappy in the way she'd been unhappy as a child. She felt lost, terrifyingly alone again. Abandoned.

Kirk knew he was going to have to make the effort. She'd done herself up especially. Knowing him to be the randy sod he was, she'd twig there was something wrong if he didn't make love to her. Anything else would have been totally uncharacteristic of him.

He laid his empty glass by the empty bottle and came to his feet.

'Let's go on up,' he said.

Later, as he made love to her, she closed her eyes. It was a mechanical thing he was doing to her. His mind was elsewhere.

Inwardly she wept.

Major Keith Gibb frowned as he studied the report he held. Another six free houses, making fourteen this month in all, had served the brewery notice they no longer wished to be supplied with Black Lion beer.

This was getting serious. In fact, if the trend continued this way it would be downright disastrous. For a panicky moment, he felt everything he'd built up over the years since the war slipping away from him. Then his old army discipline reasserted itself and he brought himself back under control. This was only a trend, he told himself reassuringly. A new brewery making something of a hit because of all the razzmatazz surrounding its launch, not to mention the enormous amount of advertising that had gone before and after that launch.

KM '60, the drink of tomorrow here today, he thought scornfully. The beer itself was dreadful. He'd sampled it personally.

No, all this was a flash in the pan. A novelty that would soon lose impact. What he had to do was sit tight and weather the onslaught. The tide would turn back in his favour soon enough.

There were four burly barmen and the manager had been a

well-known boxer in his day. It was the biggest challenge Turk McGhie had faced so far.

'I'm happy enough with Donaldson's beers,' McKenna, the manager, said.

'Perhaps you should take time to think it over,' Turk suggested politely.

'I know your type,' McKenna said. 'You're a troublemaker. A hard man. Well I don't like people like that in this club. In fact I actively discourage them. Do I make myself clear?'

McGhie knew he hadn't a hope, even if he was to use his razors, against these five. They were too big and too many.

'Every other free house and licence in the area has switched over to KM beers,' he said.

'Well good for them. I'll just have to be the odd man out, won't I?'

'You're making a mistake,' Turk said softly.

McKenna's eyes blazed with anger. 'If you try threatening me, you'll be the one making a mistake,' he replied.

Turk shrugged. 'If that's the way you want it.'

'We'll see you out,' one of the barmen said.

When Turk walked to the door he had three escorts. Once outside, he sat on a low wall and lit a cigarette. He blew smoke at the gun-metal grey sky and thought.

The Labour Club was a wooden barn of a place containing a large bar and a hall where fund-raising dances and whist-drives were held. Every Friday and Saturday night, with the exception of the Glasgow Fair when everyone was on holiday, it was jam-packed to the gunwales, at which time it got through an awful lot of beer.

Donaldon's, who supplied their beer, was a small brewery which had already lost most of its few outlets to KM. If it were to lose the Labour Club, it was almost certain to go under.

Turk sat for a good hour on the wall smoking cigarette after cigarette but no solution to his problem came to him. He took a tramcar to his local boozer, finding himself an out-of-the-way seat, where he drank half after half.

The next day he returned to the Labour Club but didn't go

in. Instead he walked round it, viewed it from a distance, watching those who came in and went out, all the time cudgelling his brains for the idea he knew would eventually come.

On the afternoon of the second day, he was walking past a nearby row of tenements when something he saw chalked there caused him to come up short.

The Shamrock Are The Boys! the legend proclaimed. The Shamrock was the name of the local gang. A ferocious, violent lot of youngsters who had a terrible reputation ranking that of the legendary Tongs and Cumbie. The gang held sway over a small area which was a Catholic ghetto surrounded by Protestant neighbours. Relationships between the two groups, as was always the case in Glasgow, were uneasy. The Shamrock, in common with most of the gangs, was divided into two sections. The Wee Shamrock, consisting of boys aged between roughly eight and twelve, and The Big Shamrock, lads between twelve and eighteen.

The Labour Club, situated on some waste ground, bordered on to Shamrock territory but was used mainly by the Protestants, the Catholics having a Hibernian Club they frequented.

Turk moved on to a café where he sat mulling over a cup of tea. The Shamrock was the solution he'd been looking for, he was convinced of that.

Slowly the bits and pieces of a plan fell into place.

On the Friday night, the publican of the pub The Big Shamrock used looked up fearfully as Turk entered. He'd already experienced Turk a few weeks earlier when Turk had persuaded him to take KM beers in place of what he'd sold up until then.

A group of The Big Shamrock stood grouped round the bar. Only a handful of them were of drinking age but the publican would never have dreamed of chiselling them about it. It would have been worth his life to do that. Nor did he have to worry about being prosecuted for selling to minors. Police never came into the pub. They had more sense.

Turk ordered a pint and a half-gill. He was wearing a brand-new baby-blue suit with a white shirt and a thin red tie. He wore more sober clothes when with Kirk, Kirk demanding it, but when out and about on his own he wore the sort of paraffin he liked best.

Several of The Shamrock glanced suspiciously in his direction. They were obviously wondering if he was looking for trouble. For there was no mistaking he was a fighting man. An aura of danger and violence clung to him like a cloud.

He finished off his whisky and then picked up his pint. Hooking the thumb of his free hand in his waistcoat pocket he sauntered over to where The Shamrock stood.

Instantly muscles tensed and hands edged towards hidden weapons.

'You The Shamrock?' Turk demanded.

'What's it to *you*?' one of the bigger lads replied. He had thick, greasy, black hair and beetling eyebrows.

'Heard a lot about you. That's all,' Turk replied, sipping his pint.

'We're well known. And not only hereabouts, either,' the lad said.

Turk nodded. 'That's true enough.'

'So what do you want?'

'Nothing in particular. I don't know anyone in here and then I saw you and I thought I'd just have a wee dauner over. Just to be friendly, like.'

'I've never seen you around here before,' the lad said accusingly.

This was their leader, the kingpin, Turk thought. This was who he'd work on most.

'Naw, I don't come from this part of Glasgow myself. I'm around for a while on business.'

'What sort of business?' another lad demanded.

Turk fixed the lad with a glacial eye. 'That's my affair, sonny,' he replied.

The lad stiffened and took half a pace forward.

Turk gave a frozen smile. 'I'm not looking for trouble. But I was brought up to always mind the questions I asked a body. Never to pry into anything personal. Still, I'm sure it was a slip of the tongue and not meant, eh?' He laughed. 'Tell you what, as we seem to have got off on the wrong foot with one another a wee bit, what do you say I buy you a drink? In fact, I'll buy you all a drink. I had a big win on the dogs today. What do you say?'

'Aye, all right then,' the one he'd called sonny said. Then turning to the leader, 'That okay, Frankie?'

'Sure.'

Turk called the publican over, telling the man to set up pints and whiskies for his good friends here.

'Right away, Turk,' the man replied, busily getting on with it.

'An unusual name that,' said Frankie the leader. 'Should we know you?'

'I'm Turk McGhie.'

Several of the group glanced at one another, respect registering on their faces.

'I've heard of you all right,' said Frankie.

'Aye, well don't believe everything you hear. An awful lot of it's lies,' said Turk pretending mock humility.

'I'm sure,' replied Frankie.

Turk glanced at the bar clock, working out how much time he had.

'Do you fancy the Celts against Queen of the South tomorrow?' he asked.

'Och, the Celts will walk it,' a lad said.

'Do you support them yourself?' Frankie asked.

Turk patted hs left leg and winked. 'I do that.'

The fact he was a Catholic like themselves was an instant bond between The Shamrock lads and Turk.

Whisky and pint followed whisky and pint, all of them paid for by Turk out of his mythical win at the dogs. And the more drink disappeared down their throats, the more The Shamrock accepted him as one of their own.

'How many in your gang then?' Turk asked eventually.

'Sixty in The Big Shamrock, seventy-five in The Wee,' Frankie replied.

Turk whistled. 'That many, eh? I'm impressed.'

'We control this whole area,' Frankie boasted. 'Nothing goes on here but it has our say-so.'

'That a fact? I'm surprised then you let them paint slogans about you the way they do.'

'What slogans?' Frankie demanded.

'The ones on the ... Och no, forget it. Let's have another round,' said Turk.

'No come on, what slogans?'

'The ones the prods have written over the walls of that Labour Club over by.'

Frankie glanced at his men who were already looking angry. 'What do these slogans say?' he asked Turk.

'Now I'm only repeating what I saw as you're asking me to do,' said Turk. 'There was one said, "The Shamrock are Fenian poofters", and another said, "The Shamrock are not fit to lick King Billy's boots".'

Frankie's face contorted with fury. Already flushed from drink, it became a beetroot colour.

'There must've been a dozen like that,' Turk added. 'All written in orange paint.'

'Prod bastards,' one of the gang said vehemently.

'More whiskies all round,' Turk called out to the barman. 'And make them big ones.'

'I say we go and kick their heads in,' the one Turk had called sonny said.

'Aye, give them what for!'

'Call all the boys together, Frankie. There's still time the night.'

'We'll murder the whores.'

'Any of them call me a poof to my face and I'll take my bayonet and ram it up his Khyber, so I will!' another of The Shamrock spat out. His mouth split open in a chilling leer, revealing a set of badly rotting teeth.

The last order started to arrive and Turk began passing the glasses round.

'*Could* you get all your lads together tonight?' Turk asked, pressing a glass into Frankie's hand.

'Oh aye.'

'Friday night, that Labour Club will be jumping round about now,' Turk said. 'Probably quite a few of them having a good laugh at your expense. It was the orange paint that got me. Orange! I ask you. They couldn't have got more insulting if they'd tried.'

'Right,' said Frankie, having arrived at a decision. 'We'll call the lads together and then we'll away over there and see what's to do.'

He started issuing orders and a number of those present peeled away to summon the rest of the gang.

'You'll be going in armed, of course?' said Turk.

'Too right and we will,' Frankie retorted.

'Well it looks like it's going to be a hot time in the Labour Club tonight,' said Turk. And ordered more whiskies.

McKenna, the manager of the Labour Club, sat staring into the fire roaring in the grate. His face was badly bruised and one cheek was bandaged and taped where it had been sliced open. It was six o'clock at night and he was home for his tea. He'd been at the club all day long and would be going back again after he'd eaten. The place was an absolute wreck, everything having been either smashed, ripped or broken.

Ding dong! the doorbell went.

'Can you get that, love? I'm busy with the chips,' Chrissie McKenna shouted out from the kitchen.

McKenna grimaced as he rose. He was stiff from the fight.

When he opened the front door, Turk McGhie was revealed standing there. Turk was clutching the hand of Agnes, McKenna's wee lassie of six.

'I had to ask some children playing in the street which was your house and one of them turned out to be your daughter,'

Turk said affably. 'Smashing wee girl she is too.'

McKenna's heart did a flip seeing Agnes with McGhie. 'Away through,' he said to her. 'Tea's almost on the table.'

Agnes ran past her father, calling out to her mother about the nice man who'd given her sixpence for showing him where Daddy lived.

'What do you want?' McKenna asked.

'I heard today about what happened last night. I'm awful sorry.'

McKenna nodded.

'The inside of the club's a complete write-off, I'm told?'

'That's right.'

Turk tut-tutted. 'Could I come in? I have an idea or two that might interest you.'

'We're about to have our tea.'

'It would be to your – and the club's – advantage, Mr McKenna.'

McKenna was shaken by Turk's appearing with his daughter. He didn't like that idea at all. Grimly he thought it might be best to hear Turk out.

McKenna ushered Turk inside to the living room and offered him a seat.

'At least we can be thankful no one was killed,' Turk said.

'I'm surprised no one was,' McKenna replied. 'They came in with swords, bayonets, chains, razors, you name it and they had it. It was sheer bloody pandemonium I can tell you.'

Turk shook his head in sympathy.

'Most of the men were too busy looking after their wives and trying to get them out the hall to get themselves organised properly. In a way that was the worst part of it, having all those women there.'

Turk shook his head again.

'In five minutes they just demolished everything inside that place. It's taken the club members years to get the club the way it was and now they're going to have to start all over again from scratch. It'll cost a fortune.'

'That's one of the reasons I'm here, Mr McKenna. I spoke

to my boss Mr Murray this morning, and he was appalled to hear what had happened. He has to make his offer a business one, of course, you'll appreciate that I'm sure, but he says he's willing to scratch the club's back if they'll scratch his. He'll rebuild the entire bar and kit it out if the club will take his beer as opposed to Donaldson's. That's a handsome offer that'll save the club an awful lot of money. I doubt if you'll find a wee brewery like Donaldson's are willing to do the same. What do you say?'

It *was* a handsome offer. There was no denying that. 'I'll have to put it to the club secretary. That's a decision that isn't up to me alone.'

'I'll tell you what else I'll do, Mr McKenna. I happen to know some of The Shamrock. I'll have a wee drink with Frankie their leader and tell him those daubings were all a mistake and that it wasn't any of your club members who put them there. I'll tell him it was some outsiders, mischief-makers who did it.'

McKenna was no fool. He knew then that McGhie had been instrumental in daubing the club walls. The man was almost admitting as much.

'I mean it would be terrible if the club was to be all done up again only for The Shamrock to pay it another visit. Wouldn't you agree?'

'I would,' McKenna said softly.

'That's settled then. I'll have a word with The Shamrock and you'll speak to your club secretary about KM beer. When the club's made up its mind if you just let us know the decision we'll go ahead with getting the bar rebuilt.' Turk stood. 'I think that's that, then. And I must say that's a grand wee lassie you've got there. A wee charmer if ever there was. Going to grow up to be really pretty too. You must be proud of her?'

'We are.'

'Heard a story recently about a wee lassie over in Partick who was out playing one night, just like your Agnes was now, when some animal got hold of her and took a razor to her. They say it's just awful to see her now.'

389

A cold sweat had formed on McKenna's brow. He wasn't scared in the least of McGhie, not for himself that is. But he was for his wife and daughter. They were his Achilles' heel.

'Now what sort of mind does a thing like that?' Turk demanded.

'God alone knows.'

At the door McGhie said affably. 'We'll look forward to hearing from you. And I hope it isn't too long before the club's back on its feet again. We at KM Brewery will certainly give it every support we can. Goodbye now.' And with a cheery wave he set off down the street.

McKenna closed the door and stood stock-still for a moment. He didn't have any doubts at all that McGhie would carry out the threat against Agnes should KM not get the club business. A man like McGhie didn't make idle threats.

'Tea's on the kitchen table,' Chrissie McKenna said, appearing in the hallway. 'What was all that about?'

'Just a little bit of business, that's all,' McKenna replied.

All through tea he couldn't keep his eyes off Agnes's face, thinking about what McGhie had said about the wee lassie – imaginary or otherwise, it didn't matter – over in Partick.

As McGhie passed the Labour Club he glanced up at the various daubings that had caused so much trouble. It was amazing what you could accomplish with some whisky and a can of orange paint, he thought.

And, grinning, he continued on his way.

Kirk entered Ciona's flat holding an already chilled jeroboam of champagne. 'It's celebration time!' he announced.

'What's the occasion, then?' Ciona asked, producing glasses.

'Today Donaldson's Brewery packed it in. That's one less competitor for yours truly and the first of the many who're going to go to the wall in the next couple of years.'

Champagne frothed and gurgled as he poured. 'The day's not all that far away when there will only be one beer made and sold in Glasgow. Mine!'

'You sound pretty certain of that.'

'I am.'

'So you're aiming for a monopoly in Glasgow?'

'Ah!' said Kirk, drinking. 'There's nothing quite like champagne.' Then turning his attention back to Ciona. 'That's right. That's the trend in the beer industry. Bigger, larger, all encompassing.'

He sat and beckoned her to his side. He kissed her, lingering on her lips which he'd often told her were the softest he'd ever known.

'I could eat you,' he whispered.

'You say the nicest things.'

'Especially when I'm randy.'

'When aren't you randy?'

'With you? Never,' he replied.

Ciona laughed softly and sipped her champagne. 'So when did you get this monopoly idea?' she asked.

'Had it for some time now. The way I see it, chances are high there will only be two or three breweries functioning in Scotland at the end of this decade or the middle of the next. It's already happening in England, and what happens there happens up here soon after.'

'But two or three? Surely there will be more than that?'

'It's possible, of course. It may slim down to half a dozen big breweries and stop there, if left to its own devices, that is. But I'll tell you this: having seen the possibility of there being one and one only brewery in Glasgow, I intend making absolutely sure that situation comes about, and furthermore that the brewery to whom the prize falls is mine.'

His eyes suddenly took on a faraway look. 'Why not?' he said to himself.

'Why not what?'

'Well, I saw it as two or three breweries left. But what if they were all owned by the same person?'

'Like you?'

'It's a mind-boggling thought, isn't it?'

'Don't they have laws against that sort of thing?'

391

Kirk snorted. 'There are always ways and means round laws. Especially where that sort of money would be involved.'

He lay back in the couch and gazed off into space. 'It would be a lifetime's work, but what an achievement to pull it off.'

'Well no one could certainly ever accuse you of lack of ambition,' Ciona said.

Kirk brought himself back to reality. 'But first there's Glasgow to contend with. And Black Lion Brewery in particular. They're my main competitors. I've got them on the slide but I'm still a long way from delivering the coup de grâce. But it'll come, oh yes, it'll come.'

He fingered his scar. 'And I can't tell you how much I'm looking forward to that day.'

Ciona tried to smile but the smile died on her face. There was something in Kirk's tone which made the hairs on her arms stir and rise.

Susan lay in the darkness listening to Kirk stumbling up the stairs. When he entered the bedroom the lights snapped on, causing her to blink.

He stood swaying, staring down at her. He wore a foolish grin on his face.

'You're drunk,' Susan said.

'Get away! How clever of you to figure that one out,' he slurred.

'Who were you with?'

'That's my business. But if you must know, one of my pub managers.'

Susan swung herself out of bed. 'Let me give you a hand to get undressed. You'll never manage on your own.'

The moment she came close to him she knew he'd lied to her. He'd been, as she'd suspected, with Ciona Crammond. The perfume clinging to him was one she'd come to know.

Suddenly something snapped in her. She wasn't going to take any more of this. She'd had enough. The guilt she felt at failing to conceive was swamped by anger and humiliation.

'How dare you come home reeking of another woman and

expect to get into bed with me? How *dare* you!'

Kirk blinked, the same foolish grin still plastered all over his face.

'Don't think I don't know what's been going on. You've been sleeping with that slut Ciona Crammond ever since your beers were launched, maybe before, for all I know. Do you think I'm stupid or something? That I haven't got two eyes in my head or a nose to smell with? You stink of her!'

'Now hold on a minute, Susan –' Kirk said.

'And don't try and soft soap me. I want it to stop, here and now, understand?'

'You've got it all wrong ...'

'Like heck I have,' she interrupted.

'Ciona and I are just good friends.'

Susan barked out a laugh. 'You *are* drunk if that's the best you can come up with.'

'No honestly, I've never touched her.'

'Don't lie to me, Kirk.'

Kirk's good humour began to evaporate; the beginnings of violence bubbled in his stomach.

Susan went on, her voice thinning and becoming shrill. 'It's finished after tonight. I want your word on that.'

'Aw, go to hell.'

'Kirk!'

'Stop moaning, woman. You're becoming a pain in the backside.'

'If I am moaning it's because I've got plenty to moan about. I'm sorry I can't give you a baby ...'

'Don't bring *that* up again, for God's sake!' He stopped as a thought came to him. 'Has the old fart been on the phone again to you? Has that been what's triggered all this off?'

'Daddy didn't ring ...'

'Babies! The old bugger's absolutely demented by them. Or should I say *boy* babies. There's a difference as far as he's concerned, isn't there?'

Kirk took his jacket off and threw it across a chair. He then tore his tie from round his neck and hurled it into a corner.

'That bloody man! Well I'll get him yet. You just see if I don't.

'Babies, babies,' Kirk muttered a few seconds later, holding his head in his hands. 'Why do you and he always have to be going on about them?'

'I won't let our marriage be wrecked by this affair,' said Susan.

'Shut up!' growled Kirk.

'If you haven't the guts to end it with her then I'll do it for you.'

Crossing to the bedside table Susan picked up the telephone there. She flicked open a small directory, knowing Ciona's number to be in it. There had been a number of times during the ad campaign when Kirk had had to ring her legitimately on business.

'Get away from there!' Kirk slurred.

Susan, a look of determination on her face, started to dial.

'I said get away from there, Susan!'

Susan completed dialling and waited for the rings to start. She should have done this before now, she told herself. But she'd hoped Kirk's affair with Ciona a thing that would soon blow over. Only it hadn't.

Kirk stumbled across the room. The inside of his head was numb and everything was beginning to go hazy at the edges.

'Give that phone to me!' he snarled.

Susan gasped as his hand clamped on her wrist. 'Let me go!' she exclaimed.

'Give it to me!'

'Hello?' Ciona's voice said.

Kirk desperately tugged on the phone, trying to jerk it from Susan's grasp, but she hung on doggedly, determined not to let it go.

'Hello who is this, please?' Ciona's voice asked.

With a roar Kirk backhanded Susan across the face, she screamed as her head snapped back.

'What's going on there?' Ciona's voice demanded.

Kirk hit Susan again and again till at last she fell backwards off the chair to collapse on the floor in a heap.

Chest heaving Kirk replaced the phone on its cradle, while at his feet Susan cried into the carpet.

'Teach you to do as you're told,' he said, adding after a few seconds, 'Stupid cow.' He lurched over to the bed and sat down. Everything was turning round and round, and he felt decidedly sick. Groaning, he fell sideways, where he curled into a foetal ball. The picture and sensation in his head was of himself falling from a towering skyscraper. He whimpered as the ground rushed up to meet him.

Just before he hit the ground he lapsed into unconsciousness.

'Oh my God!' Kirk said, coming awake. He'd never felt so dreadful.

He rolled onto his back and then ran a hand over his stubbled face. Dehydration had made his tongue feel twice its normal size.

Something had happened the night before, but what? Minnie kept popping into his mind. He'd had a go at her, or hit her or ... But Minnie was years ago. So what? ... who? ...

'Christalmighty!' he husked as it came back to him. He'd hit Susan. Yes that was it. The memory was jumbled but he had most of it now. A glance told him her side of the bed hadn't been slept in. So where was she?

He gasped with pain as he came to his feet. Clutching his head he staggered to the bathroom where he swallowed a couple of tablets and a number of glasses of water.

He found her in the kitchen where she was already dressed and eating her breakfast. He came up short when he saw her face.

One eye had a hideous purply-black swelling underneath it. And what had been the white part of the eye was now blood red. Her nose was swollen and there was a scratch on one cheek.

He sat facing her, noting his hands were trembling from the after-effects of the alcohol when he laid them on the table.

'Where did you sleep?' he asked.

'The lounge settee.'

'I, eh . . .' He licked his lips. 'I'm sorry, Susan. Truly I am. I don't know what came over me.'

Susan crunched toast and regarded him steadily.

'What can I do to make it up?'

'Get rid of Ciona Crammond.'

He lowered his gaze, staring at the tablecloth and running his fingers over it.

Susan said very quietly, 'The only reason I haven't gone back to Mummy and Daddy this morning is I can't bear the thought of proving them right about you. That you're the peasant they always claimed you to be.'

He cringed when she said that, as she'd known he would.

He reached out to take her hand but she snatched hers away. 'Don't touch me!' she hissed, fury and indignation in her voice.

He was genuinely appalled at what he'd done. Another look at her face caused him to grimace. Poor bitch, he thought.

'Well?' Susan demanded.

'All right. I'll end it today,' he said reluctantly.

'You swear?'

He nodded.

'And there will be no more . . . tarts?'

'No more,' he whispered.

Susan pursed her lips. She didn't know whether to believe him or not. But time would tell.

'You'd better hurry up. You're already late for work,' she said.

As was usually the case with him after a heavy drinking bout he was starving. 'I could eat a horse,' he said.

Susan rose to her feet. 'Then you'd better cook one,' she replied. And swept from the room.

Two months later, Susan knew Kirk was back seeing Ciona Crammond again. There were so many things gave it away. The odd trace of perfume. The occasional guilty look in his eye when he thought she wasn't watching him. The over-elaborate explanations of where he'd been and what he'd been doing there. And then the most significant of all. The many nights that passed without him trying to approach her sexually. With his sex drive, that was a dead give-away.

She thought of leaving him, taking a flat on her own. But somehow that idea didn't really appeal. Probably because her parents would then know her marriage had broken down, and she didn't want that.

The idea came to her when she was standing at a window watching a horse and cart trundle by. The horse was old and bowed from a lifetime's hard work. Her heart went out to the beast, making her think of the animals she'd had as a child.

That was it, she thought. She needed something to take her mind off things. And she was a qualified vet, after all, so why didn't she set up practice? It would occupy her days and she would be accomplishing something worthwhile in the process.

The idea excited her and she couldn't wait to get cracking.

The first thing was to find premises and then ... She wondered briefly if she should ask Kirk if he minded. Why should I? she thought. Why the hell should I!

When she had occasion to mention it she'd *tell* him what she was going to do.

Eddy King was doing the rounds of his pubs one night when he saw an old familiar face sitting dejectedly in a corner hunched over a pint.

He bought two large whiskies and strolled over. 'Hello Norrie, how are tricks?' he said, placing one of the whiskies beside the pint.

Norrie Smart looked up at Eddy, and on recognising him his face broke into a grin. 'Help my bob! Where did you spring from?'

Eddy laughed and sat. 'It's good to see you again. What about the others? Do you ever see them?'

'Naw. Although I did hear from somebody that Ogle

emigrated to Canada. You know about Kirk Murray, of course? I keep reading about him in the paper. He's big-time now. Owns this new KM Brewery.'

'Yes, I know about him,' Eddy replied.

'You two used to be pals when we were first in Germany. But something happened between you. The others in the section never found out what.'

'We stopped being pals and that's the way it remained.'

Smart suddenly laughed. 'Remember Meany and that drinking contest you two had? And him so pished at the end of it he started bashing up officers.'

'Mean by name and mean by nature!' said Eddy, doing his best to imitate Meany.

Smart laughed. 'Then Kirk became corporal, and when he lost his stripes because of catching a dose they made you one.'

Eddy swallowed his whisky. 'Seeing you fairly takes me back.'

Looking embarrassed, Smart pushed his glass around the table. 'Listen, I'm helluva sorry but I can't buy you one back,' he said, adding, 'I'm out of work.'

'Don't worry about it,' Eddy replied quickly. 'I've got more than enough for the two of us.'

Eddy went back to the bar and bought two more large whiskies and a brace of pints.

'You're a toff, so you are,' said Smart when the fresh drinks were placed in front of him.

'So how come you're not grafting?' Eddy asked.

'I keep getting the sack because of my headaches.'

'What headaches are these?'

'I wasn't home long from Germany when one Saturday morning I was out playing football with the boys. A real good kick-around, that sort of thing. Anyway I go charging into the goalmouth and the next thing I know I'm flat on my back having whacked my head against the post. A few weeks after that the headaches started, migraine, the doctor calls it. They're really hellish Eddy. When I have one, all I can do is lie in bed with the blankets pulled up over my head waiting for it

398

to stop. Two days, three sometimes before it goes away. As you can imagine, employers aren't very keen when you start having that sort of time off at least once a month. I'm sure most of them think I'm skiving but it's just not true.'

'I'm awful sorry to hear that, Norrie.'

'Makes life difficult, I can tell you. Especially now I'm married with a wean.'

'Congratulations!'

Smart looked pleased with himself. 'Aye, she's a real nice woman. You'd like her.'

'I'm sure.'

'And the wee fella's a right humdinger. A chip off the old block.'

Eddy thought for a few seconds before asking, 'What is it you do, Norrie?'

'Plastering.'

'I see.'

'Why? Do you know someplace I might get a start?'

'I do. But not as a plasterer. How do you fancy being a bar cellarman?'

'You mean in a pub?'

'That's right. One down the road called The Bowlers' Tavern.'

'That would be grand,' replied Smart. 'Why, do you know the owner or something?'

Eddy grinned. 'I *am* the owner. Just as I'm the owner of this place we're drinking in now.'

'You're not pulling my leg now, are you?'

'Not only The Bowlers' Tavern and this pub but thirteen others as well. All of them round about here.'

Smart whistled. 'Christ, you have got on, haven't you! You're almost as big a success story as Murray.'

'Not quite,' said Eddy. 'But I'm working at it. So – what about the job then, eh? I'll make allowances for your migraines and keep you covered at all times.'

'If you'll lend me a pound in advance I'd like to buy you a drink on that,' Norrie Smart said.

Eddy handed over a fiver. 'Get them in and then we'll away down to The Bowlers' and I'll introduce you around. You can start Monday.'

'This is my lucky day. You won't regret taking me on, honest, Eddy.'

Eddy laughed. 'I believe you.'

Smart made his way across to the bar to get another round in.

It was late that night after the pubs had closed that Eddy got a phone call from Willie Crerar who managed The Exchange Bar for him.

'Aye, what is it, Willie?' Eddy asked.

'There was a geezer in here from KM Brewery wanting me to change over to their beer. I told him it was nothing to do with me and that he should speak to you. He said he would do that and asked for your address, which I gave him. Maybe I shouldn't have done that, Mr King, but quite frankly he scared the bejeesus out of me.'

'Did you get his name, Willie?'

'No. Sorry.'

'All right Willie. Thanks for letting me know.'

'You just be careful, Mr King. Yon's the queerest brewery representative I've ever come across. He's got bad news written all over him.'

'I'll be careful Willie. 'Bye now.'

Eddy cradled the phone and stared thoughtfully at the wall. All his pubs sold Black Lion beer and he had no intention of changing breweries. And if he had he certainly wouldn't have gone to KM. It was the principle of the thing, Black Lion belonging to Kirk.

Not that he would have had all that much choice of breweries to change to anyway, he thought grimly. The number of breweries in the city was decreasing every year, with one after the other going to the wall, all of them forced out of business by KM, which was expanding at a phenomenal rate.

'Eddy, are you coming through?' a female voice called from the bedroom. Eddy grinned. Maisie was a new barmaid who'd come to work for him recently.

Pulling pints wasn't the only thing she was good at.

The following mid-morning, Eddy was sitting at the table doing some paper work when there was a knock at the front door. Some sixth sense told him the man from KM Brewery had come calling. And he was right.

'Mr King?' Turk McGhie inquired.

Eddy nodded.

'I wonder if I could come in and talk to you?'

Eddy ushered McGhie through to the front room. Willie Crerar had been right. This one positively exuded violence and mayhem.

'My name's McGhie and I represent KM Brewery,' Turk said, having declined the offer of a seat.

The man's eyes were mesmeric, Eddy thought. They reminded him of those belonging to an eagle he'd once seen at Calderpark Zoo.

'I called at one of your pubs last night and your manager was good enough to give me your address,' McGhie said. 'Neither myself nor the brewery realised that many of the pubs round about there were owned by the one man. You, Mr King.'

'Fifteen, to be precise,' said Eddy.

'Yes, that checks with the list I made up,' Turk replied.

'Did you now?'

Turk's pale blue eyes bored into Eddy. 'As you probably know we've been operational in the north, west and east of Glasgow up until now –'

'And now you want to move into central Glasgow. The town itself,' Eddy cut in.

'That's correct.'

Eddy stuck a cigarette in his mouth and lit up. He regarded Turk McGhie through a streamer of cloud. He'd wondered a number of times in the past why so many independents had

401

changed seemingly *en masse* to KM Brewery. The reason was now becoming obvious.

Eddy said slowly, 'The town pubs being the juiciest plums of all, catering as they do not only to the town itself's needs but also the entire south side, which, of course, is dry.'

'And with more and more people being moved out to south-side housing schemes, the town pubs are going to be doing even better still in future,' Turk added.

'Which is why you want them to sell your beer and not Black Lion, as most of them do now.'

'The people aren't very happy with Black Lion beer of late,' Turk said. 'It's said they put out a bad batch as a result of which two men are supposed to have died and another gone insane.'

'I've heard that rumour myself. But nobody seems to know who these men were or are. No names, just anonymous hearsay.'

'It's said that there's no smoke without fire.'

Eddy stared at Turk for a few seconds in silence. Finally he said, 'And what happens if I decline your offer to switch my business from Black Lion to KM?'

McGhie raised an eyebrow. That simple gesture spoke volumes.

'I think I'm beginning to see.'

'We can be very persuasive when we put our minds to it,' Turk said. 'I haven't yet met anyone I've failed to convert to KM.'

'There's always a first time.'

McGhie's thin smile was truly frightening. A tremor of fear ran up Eddy's back to play for a few seconds across his shoulder-blades.

'What's the brewery's number?' Eddy asked.

McGhie frowned. He hadn't been expecting that question. He spoke the number after which Eddy crossed to the phone and dialled. When through to the brewery, Eddy asked to speak to Mr Murray. And when the girl said Mr Murray might well be tied up Eddy told her to tell him it was Eddy King on the line.

Turk watched Eddy through slitted eyes that seemed never to blink.

'Eddy! How are you?' Kirk's voice said.

'Fine. Never better. And you?'

'In the pink.'

'Well, certainly in the money since you took over the old Thistle Brewery.'

Kirk chuckled. 'And how are the used cars getting on?'

'I wouldn't know. I never went back to selling them.'

'Oh?'

'I decided to take an old pal's advice and go into booze. Can't fail with booze in Glasgow he used to tell me. And what's more, he was right.'

'Well, well, well,' said Kirk, a new tone in his voice.

'I own some pubs in the town ...'

'Pubs! You mean two or three? You have done well for yourself.'

'Fifteen, Kirk. All bought, paid for and doing nicely, thank you.'

'Whose beer do you sell then? Mine, I hope. I won't forgive you if you don't.'

'Well, that's why I'm ringing you actually. I've got a representative of yours here who's trying to persuade me to ditch Black Lion and come over to you. His name's McGhie.'

There was a pause and then Kirk said. 'I'll tell you what, why don't you and I get together for lunch and talk over old times? I'd enjoy that, what about you?'

'Fine. As long as you pay.'

'It'll be my pleasure to. And listen, I am sorry I never contacted you after we got back from Germany but you know how things are? I just never seemed to have the time.'

'Same with me,' Eddy lied.

They talked for a few more minutes, making a time and date for when the lunch would take place.

Eddy hung up and turned to find those ice-cold eagle eyes boring into him. 'All right?' he asked.

McGhie nodded his head fractionally, the expression on his face telling Eddy he'd made himself an enemy.

'You know the way out,' Eddy said.

Turk McGhie left the house without saying another word. And when he was gone Eddy had the intense urge to get a duster and polish out and clean everywhere McGhie had either touched or stood.

Instead he made himself a cup of very strong tea but even the four sugars he heaped into it didn't take away the sourness McGhie's visit had left in his mouth.

He thought of Leoni and the hand gripping the cup tightened. 'Not twice, my old son,' he said aloud. 'Not bloody twice!'

'You've got fat,' said Eddy, shaking Kirk's hand.

'I wouldn't exactly say that.'

'I would. Look at your belly, it's like a rubber tyre.'

Kirk smiled daggers. It always irked him to have his ever-increasing weight referred to.

They sat and the wine-waiter appeared. Kirk ordered, without consulting Eddy, choosing a particularly heavy Bordeaux.

Eddy hated Bordeaux, always finding it sat like lead on his stomach. He decided to let it go. He'd have a few token sips and leave it at that.

'Fifteen pubs, eh?' Kirk said. 'You *have* come up in the world.'

'Not as much as some I could name not a million miles from here,' Eddy replied.

Kirk laughed. 'I've been lucky.'

'Where you're concerned, Kirk, luck rarely has anything to do with it. You were always the man to make your own opportunties.'

'Like Heather Dew and the Russian run?'

404

'Certainly gave me enough money to get started,' Eddy acknowledged.

Kirk nodded, his eyes twinkling. He seemed to find that amusing.

'Did you get married?' Kirk asked.

'Nope. Haven't found the right girl yet.'

'And you still haven't forgiven me for Leoni. I can read it in your face.'

'I was never an easy forgiver. Especially about the important things.'

'We are what we are, Eddy. There's no changing that.'

'Sounds like an excuse to me.'

Kirk smiled suddenly, but there was the hint of something far deeper than the present conversation behind the smile. 'Anyway I paid for my indiscretion. Remember?'

'How could I forget?'

'There but for the grace of God, eh?'

'I don't know. She might not have felt the need to cheat on me.'

Anger flashed in Kirk's eyes and then was gone.

'So, now you're moving into the town pubs,' Eddy said.

'That's right.'

'All my pubs are supplied by Black Lion, with whom I have no complaint whatsoever.'

'They're getting an awful bad name of late.'

'Your man McGhie mentioned that. But, as I told him, it's only wild rumour. Anonymous hearsay, Kirk. Nothing more.'

'You can say what you like. I wouldn't be too happy swallowing a pint of theirs. I care about what I put down my throat.'

Eddy shook his head. 'You're right. The leopard doesn't change its spots. Especially when it's called Kirk Murray.'

The wine arrived and while it was being poured they placed their order.

'So you don't want to switch over to KM then?' Kirk said, when they were once more alone.

'Correct.'

There was a pause before Kirk went on. 'I like you, Eddy. Always have done. And what's more I still feel a little guilty over the Leoni thing. That's why I asked you to lunch today. So I can personally make you see sense. To make amends for what I did to you in the past.'

Eddy smiled thinly. 'You persuade me rather than let your hard man try to do it. Is that what you mean?'

'Let me tell you why I bought the old Thistle Brewery,' Kirk said. And went on to tell Eddy what his mother had originally pointed out to him and how this had formed itself as a plan in his mind for KM Brewery to end up with a Glasgow monopoly.

When Kirk had finished talking, Eddy sat back in his chair and stared at Kirk in astonishment. 'Can you do it?' he asked.

'I believe so. It'll perhaps take a few more years yet, but it'll come. Once I control the majority of town pubs, on top of those already selling my beer, I will have cut the feet from under my main rival – Black Lion. By that time, they'll be in such reduced circumstances it will be relatively easy for me to buy them out, take them over, or whatever. And with Black Lion gone, there will be nothing to stop me. KM Brewery will be number one in Glasgow and the surrounding districts. There will be no number two.'

Kirk paused before continuing. 'By that time, of course, anyone who doesn't want to sell my beer will have no beer at all to sell. With no alternative, they either change their mind or close. I'd hate to see that happen to you, Eddy.'

'There's always Edinburgh beer. Or Belhaven down in Dunbar. What's to stop an enterprising publican selling them?'

'It's a possibility I've already considered. The short-term answer is Turk McGhie. It's amazing the amount of accidents there are on the Edinburgh road, for example. That stretch is a veritable death trap. Particularly with heavy waggons.'

'And the long-term?'

'With Glasgow under my belt, who's to say I won't be

casting my eye over the country as a whole? If a certain brewery was trying to ship into Glasgow then I might turn my attention in its direction. I think you would find that would deter most of them.'

'You really have this all figured out, haven't you?'

'If you're going to do something, then do it well. My mother used to always say that.'

'Along with: if you're going to bother to think at all, then think big.'

Kirk grinned. 'I see you remember.'

All this had given Eddy an enormous amount of food for thought. The flat refusal he'd come ready to give couldn't possibly be his answer now. This needed a great deal more thinking on.

Kirk went on. 'As KM gets bigger and bigger I'll need to delegate authority. Manager in control of this, manager in control of that. High heid bummers, as they say.'

'Are you offering me a job?' Eddy asked.

'Sell me your pubs and I'll make you one of the top men in the organisation.'

'And if I don't?'

'Then at least stock KM. The alternative is to end up with fifteen pubs and no beer to sell in them. Or spirits come to that. For by then, not one local distillery would dare cross me. I'll be their largest, and only, local bulk buyer then, you see.'

'I'll have to think about this,' Eddy replied slowly. 'I mean you've hit me with an awful lot today.'

'Take as long as you need. A month say, you should be able to make up your mind in that, surely?'

The meal arrived and Kirk tucked in with relish.

Eddy merely toyed with his. He'd been hungry on arrival, but he wasn't any more.

'Wh... wh...!' Major Keith Gibb mumbled, as the telephone by his bedside clamoured into life.

Switching on the bedside lamp he glanced at the alarm clock, frowning when he saw it was only a few minutes past five A.M. Who in God's teeth could be ringing him at this unholy hour?

'Yes?' he snapped into the phone.

'Major Gibb?'

'Speaking.'

'Detective Inspector Hamilton, sir. I thought you'd want to be contacted personally. Your pub The Black Lion is on fire.'

Keith was instantly wide awake. 'How bad is it?'

'Pretty bad, sir. The firemen are doing everything they can but the flames had already taken a firm grip before any of us got here.'

'Thank you for ringing and I'll be there as soon as possible,' Keith said and hung up.

'What is it?' Jean asked, raising herself on to one elbow.

In a few terse sentences he told her.

Jean's face hardened. This on top of all the other worries Was there no end to it?

Keith swung himself out of bed and started to dress. His face was drawn and haggard. What had once been a well-fleshed robust body was now thin and spindly, the belly projecting as though gas had been pumped into it. Keith had to stop when he started to cough. Groping for his handkerchief, he brought it to his mouth and spluttered into it

'Perhaps you shouldn't go?' Jean suggested tentatively.

He shook his head and then coughed again before replying 'I have to,' he said. 'It's not just any pub. It's The Black Lion itself.'

Jean nodded. She understood.

When he was gone she too rose from her bed and go dressed. Any further sleep would have been impossible.

Twenty minutes later Keith arrived at the scene of the fire Leaving his car he crossed to where a small knot of policemen stood, one of whom quickly identified himself as Detective Inspector Hamilton.

Keith stared at the roaring flames shooting high into the early-morning sky. Other flames shot from windows while yet others licked round the building.

'Everybody out?' he asked.

'Yes,' Hamilton replied.

The intense heat hammered at Keith's face. In a well-organised fashion, fireman ran hither and yon, playing out even more hoses, redirecting those already operational, shouting instructions to one another.

The pub was a write-off. There was no doubt about that. All that was left for the firemen to do was try and contain the blaze and stop it spreading to the neighbouring buildings.

'Any idea yet how it started?' Keith asked.

'Not so far,' Hamilton replied. 'There will be a full inquiry of course.'

Keith turned his attention back to the flames and the building they were intent on consuming.

The Black Lion was the biggest and best, the showpiece, of the pubs the brewery owned. For years, it had been a shining gem in the brewery's crown, an early Victorian masterpiece that had been lovingly preserved and cared for.

It was insured, of course, but money couldn't replace that Victorian interior or façade. Aesthetically, they were irreplaceable. The pub could be rebuilt. Not in its old form but a new one. But that would take time, the entire building being gutted even as he watched. And while it remained closed, yet another outlet, and the one most previous to it, had been lost to the brewery.

The heart and fight went out of Keith then. He was beaten and knew it.

The trouble was, he thought, he was an admin man. And a damn good one too! But this sort of business, and what had been happening ever since KM came into existence, was beyond him.

Gerald might have known how to cope, he thought bitterly. But then, he wasn't his brother. And that admission to himself caused his bony shoulders to slump even further.

He looked quickly up as with a great roar one of the walls caved in. Some onlookers screamed, as sparks and flaming debris burst around the holocaust like a roman candle going

409

off. Those windows remaining started to pop, sending shards
of glass flying everywhere.

'I think we'd better move back, sir,' Hamilton said.

Keith was lost in his thoughts.

'I said I think we'd better move back, sir!'

'Yes ... yes I think you're probably right,' Keith replied.

For the next four hours he and the policeman stood side by
side, occasionally talking but mainly saying nothing, until, at
long last, the fire was extinguished.

The Black Lion pub was no more, the three-storey building
having been reduced to a one-storey blackened shell, from
which the occasional wisp of smoke still rose.

Keith thanked Hamilton for calling him and then thanked
the chief fireman for the job his men had done. Wearily, he
walked to his car and drove to the brewery. He'd never taken a
day off from his work yet and, no matter that he felt wretched
as could be, he certainly wasn't going to start now.

Once in his office he sent out for a razor. And after he'd
washed and shaved he felt somewhat better.

'You've a Mr King to see you, sir. He made the
appointment yesterday but in light of what's happened I'm
sure he'd understand if you said you preferred to see him
another day.'

Keith opened his diary and glanced at the small notation
he'd made regarding the appointment. This refreshed his
memory as to who King was.

'No. I'll see him now,' Keith said. 'Send him through.'

Eddy had never met the Major before, always having dealt
with subordinates. But this time he wanted the top man
himself.

'Now, what can I do for you, Mr King?' Keith asked, as
Eddy entered the room.

'First of all, let me say how sorry I was to hear this
morning's news. The Black Lion was a grand old pub, one of
Glasgow's finest.'

'Yes,' replied Keith looking sad. 'It'll be a great loss. Not
only to the brewery but the community as a whole, I'd say

410

They just don't build public houses like that any more, nor do I think they ever will again.'

'Have they any idea what started the blaze?'

'Not yet, but I'm assured there will be an inquiry. I suspect however the verdict is going to be cause or causes unknown.'

Eddy detected the bitterness in the Major's voice, and he guessed the Major was thinking of Turk McGhie, as indeed had he after hearing about the fire.

Keith's lips thinned as a sudden pain spasmed through him. His fingers sought out his stomach which he held until the spasm had passed.

'Sorry about that,' he said, seeing the look of concern on Eddy's face. Pulling open a drawer, he groped for the pills he kept there, two of which he washed down with a glass of water.

Eddy waited till the Major had regained his composure before saying, 'I had lunch with Kirk Murray of KM Brewery a few days back. He wants me to leave Black Lion and transfer my business to him.'

'Lunch, eh?' mused the Major. 'Not like him to give the personal touch for that sort of thing.'

'We used to be friends once upon a time.'

Keith raised an eyebrow. 'Used to be?'

'We did our national service together. We ... eh ... sort of fell out. I don't wish to elaborate.'

'I understand. So if you're not friends, are you enemies?'

'Not quite to the point of hostility ... yet,' Eddy said.

'Well, he's *my* enemy,' Keith replied. This was a conversation he would previously have been unlikely to indulge in. But with the burning of The Black Lion, he just didn't care any more. He tapped his cheek. 'You know the scar he has there?'

Eddy nodded.

'Well I gave it to him.'

Eddy gawped, so unexpected had that been. '*You* did?'

'For impertinence. You do know he's married to my daughter, don't you?'

Eddy shook his head. This again was news.

411

'Married her for the brewery, I always maintained. Only he didn't get it. I made sure of that.' Then as an afterthought, 'At least I have so far.'

'That's what I've come to talk to you about, sir. Kirk is convinced he'll either buy you out or else close you down. He intends KM beer to be the only one bought and sold in Glasgow.'

'Yes. I already guessed that to be what he had in mind.'

'He wants me to sell my pubs to him. Or, failing that, at least to sell his beer. If I don't comply with either, and he gets total control of Glasgow, as he says he will, he'll eventually cut off my supply. No beer and no spirits.'

'And what do you think of that?'

'I was hoping for your assurance that Black Lion won't go under.'

Keith closed his eyes and sighed. 'Believe me there's nothing would please me more than to give you that assurance. Unfortunately I can't. You see, he's got me every way.'

'How so, Major?'

'Well to start with he's been taking away my outlets right; left and centre. I'm now down to a third of what I had when KM opened. And every week there are new outlets to add to the casualty list.'

Keith stood and crossed to a window through which he stared out over Glasgow. 'Eventually I suppose the situation will get to me having only the brewery pubs as outlets, and unless he burns *those* down, I could hang on, a rump situation of what the brewery had formerly been. Unfortunately I'm an extremely sick man, Mr King. The same sort of cancer that killed my brother Gerald. And when I go, the brewery will go to my wife and after her, our only child and daughter, Mrs Kirk Murray. I'd imagine the Black Lion label will disappear about a week after that happens, and the brewery itself will become a subsidiary of KM, the old Thistle that was.'

'I see,' replied Eddy, adding in a softer tone, 'and I'm sorry to hear about your illness.'

'I would sell,' went on Keith. 'But who would buy, given the

412

present situation? A few years ago, if I'd put Black Lion on the market, there would have been a dozen takers. Today I'd be surprised if I even got an inquiry.'

Keith sighed and knotted his fists. 'If only I was twenty years younger. If only I had more of my brother Gerald in me. I would fight that man to hell and back. I disliked Murray vehemently the moment I clapped eyes on him. He's a scoundrel through and through, and it breaks my heart to know that one day he'll get what he was after, all those years ago when he married our Susan: to own this place.'

Eddy thought of Leoni. 'He's ruthless, all right. He'll stop at nothing to get what he wants. I found that out to my cost. He knows damn well I won't work for him and be his toady so I suppose I'll have to opt for the alternative and sell his beer,' said Eddy, adding with great feeling, 'but by Christ, it's going to hurt! The very thought brings bile to my throat!'

'If only I could find a buyer for this place. Someone really strong, with the guts to defy him! I tell you, Mr King, I'd die a happy man.'

Keith was half-way back to his desk when he stopped as though he had run into a brick wall. A curious glint came into his eyes as he fastened his gaze on Eddy.

'Perhaps there is such a man after all,' he said softly. 'A man who hates Murray almost as much as me.'

'Who?' said Eddy, frowning. When the Major didn't reply but merely continued to stare at him, the penny suddenly dropped.

'*I* couldn't afford the Black Lion Brewery!' he exclaimed. 'It's way outside my pocket.'

'Maybe not. I could sell it to you at a token price.'

'But you'd be losing a fortune!'

Keith shrugged. 'You can't take it with you. And once I'm gone, my wife's got more than enough to see her through the rest of her life comfortably. And don't forget, as Susan is our heir, what we leave goes to her which is just the same as handing it on a plate to Murray. This way I not only give the brewery another fighting chance, I also deprive Murray of the money it would've raised had I been able to sell it at its proper value.'

Eddy sat back in his chair, quite overcome by the prospect of what the Major was offering. He'd come to see the man to make a simple inquiry and here he was being handed Black Lion Brewery, gift-wrapped.

'Surely there's someone else in your family could take up the fight?' Eddy asked.

Keith shook his head. 'No one. Only Susan and she's married to Murray.'

Eddy couldn't contain himself. Rising, he paced up and down while he tried to put his racing thoughts in order. It was an incredible opportunity. And one he'd be a fool not to grab. This way, rather than being at Kirk's mercy, he'd be in direct competition to the bastard, which was a sweet, sweet thought.

Keith leaned forward on his desk, his eyes gleaming. He'd lost some of his sickly pallor, there being the hint of a flush in his cheeks. 'Well?' he demanded.

'What sort of token price did you have in mind?'

Keith considered that. 'Five thousand?' he suggested.

'That's ridiculous!'

'All right then, two and a half.'

'I didn't mean it that way ... I meant ...'

'I know what you meant, Mr King,' Keith said with a grin.

Eddy extended his hand. 'Done, Major. You've just sold yourself a brewery.'

They shook hands.

'I'll get on to my lawyers and have the necessary papers drawn up right away. I suggest you work alongside me until such times as they're completed, and that way I can teach you what I can about running a brewery. Now, I know it's early yet but how about a dram? I think we both need one.'

'I'd love to see Kirk's face when he finds out,' said Eddy as the Major poured out stiff ones.

Laughing together, they drank.

Kirk's secretary looked up in alarm as he went striding by her.

Missing was the customary "good morning" or "how are you?" She thought she'd never seen him so angry looking.

'Get me McGhie,' Kirk snapped at her, before slamming his office door shut.

He threw the morning *Herald* on to his desk, then sat glaring at it. He'd read the article on page two a dozen times or more. He almost knew it by heart.

'Eddy King!' he said through clenched teeth. Eddy, of all people, to buy Black Lion Brewery!

He sat fuming, staring into space, until he was roused from his reverie by a knock on the door.

'Come in!' he snapped.

Turk McGhie entered the room.

'Have you read this?' said Kirk pushing the *Herald* to the front of his desk. 'The article about Black Lion.'

Turk picked the paper up and read, mouthing words as he did so. Reading wasn't exactly his forte. Finally, he replaced the paper on the desk and stared at Kirk.

'No more arsing around cutting the brewery down piecemeal. I want the bloody place finished in one fell stroke. Understand?'

Turk nodded.

Kirk's fist banged the desk. 'Down and out for the count. Kaput!'

'Leave it to me, Mr Murray,' said Turk, and turned to the door.

'Turk?'

'Yes, Mr Murray?'

Kirk ran a hand over his face. He musn't let his anger warp his judgement. To make a move so soon would be too obvious. It was best to allow some time to pass first.

'Not yet though, Turk. Think about it. Plan it. Give it three or more months. Then do it.'

'Will there be extra in this for me, Mr Murray?'

'There certainly will.'

Turk grinned, then strode silently from the room. Not even the door made a sound as he closed it behind him.

It was ten o'clock at night and Susan sat with a large drink in her hand. She was more than just a little drunk.

As usual Kirk was out on what he called business, but which actually meant he was with Ciona Crammond. It had got to the stage where he spent five nights out of seven with her.

Susan gazed morosely into her glass. She knew she was hitting the bottle far too much of late but when night fell, and that terrible loneliness settled on her, she needed solace from somewhere. And far too often it was the bottle which provided it.

She had no problem with the daytime. Then, she had her practice and beloved animals to occupy her and keep her busy. But the nights were something else entirely.

If only they'd had a child, things might have been different. But their marriage continued to be barren. In fact there was now no chance of her getting pregnant as for some time she'd cut Kirk off from having sex with her.

The first time she'd done it, he'd asked her why and she'd replied he knew damn well why. He'd never broached the subject again. Nor her in bed.

She listened to the clock ticking forlornly, thinking how unhappy she was and how she'd been unhappy for most of her life. Reaching for the bottle she poured herself another drink.

And when she went up to the bedroom a little later, she took the bottle with her.

Eddy was working at his desk when the secretary buzzed through to say there was a Mr Smart to see him. No appointment had been made. When Eddy didn't reply at once, the secretary added, 'A Mr Norrie Smart, sir. He said you'd know who he was.'

'Send him in,' said Eddy.

He rose when Norrie came into the room and they shook hands.

'Sorry to bother you when you're at work but I wanted to see you before the other applications came in,' Smart said.

Eddy waved him to a seat. 'What applications are these?' he asked.

'For the job of night security officer that the brewery advertised in last night's *Citizen*. I know it's a cheek on my part, considering you gave me the job I've got now, but you see we've had another wean ...'

'Congratulations!' Eddy cut in.

Smart smiled and looked generally pleased with himself. 'A wee lassie this time. We're calling her Isobil after the wife's mother.'

Eddy desperately envied Smart at that moment. He would have loved to have had a wife and child of his own. But since Leoni he hadn't met anyone he cared enough for to marry.

Smart went on, 'And, you see, the night security job offers quite a bit more than I'm making now. That extra would be an awful big help.'

'How are the headaches?'

'A lot better of late. The doctor's put me on a special diet which seems to be helping.'

'Hmm!' said Eddy thoughtfully.

'I also think working nights would help as well. It's quiet then, less noise and hassle to set the headaches off.'

Eddy could see how badly Smart wanted the job. Well – why not? The least he could do was give him a chance. And he was a big strapping fellow after all. Just the sort to deal with any intruders.

'I'll give you a month's trial and we'll see how you get on,' Eddy said. 'And if it doesn't work out you can always go back to the Bowlers' Tavern.'

'You're a right toff, Eddy. I won't let you down. And listen, congratulations to you on taking over Black Lion. Who would have thought back in the days of the section you and Kirk would end up owning rival breweries?'

'Yes, who would have thought,' mused Eddy.

'Intimidation? That's quite a charge, Mr King,' Superintendent McIlwham said.

417

'It's been going on ever since KM opened,' Eddy went on. 'A thug called Turk McGhie does the actual nasty work, and from all accounts he's brilliant at it.'

'In a case like this we're powerless unless someone will come forward and testify. Can you provide such a person?'

'I can.'

McIlwham took out a pencil and scratch pad. 'What's the person's name?'

'Danny Porteous. He owns a pub in Hillhead, The Byres Arms in Byres Road. He used to sell our beer till he had a visit from Turk McGhie. To begin with, he told McGhie to take a running jump, but he changed his mind after having a pint-pot smashed in his face. He came damn close to losing an eye.'

'Why didn't he come forward before?'

'Because he was scared to. Why else?'

'And now he isn't?'

'Oh, he still is, but now he's willing to take the chance. He's been brooding about the incident ever since it happened, finding it difficult to live with himself because of backing down. It didn't take too much persuasion on my part to make him agree. To use his own words, he wants to be able to live with himself again. He's that sort of person.'

'I see,' said McIlwham.

'Can you give him protection till this is all over?'

McIlwham laughed, causing Eddy to frown. 'Isn't that a bit melodramatic, Mr King? I think you've been watching too many American movies.'

'I'd call getting a glass in the face fairly melodramatic, wouldn't you?' replied Eddy quietly.

'I doubt if protection will really be needed. But I'll have a word with this Porteous myself and decide whether it is or not.'

'Murray and McGhie musn't find out his identity until there's a trial. McGhie would be bound to go after him then.'

'I don't need you to tell me my job, Mr King,' McIlwham stated coldly.

'I wasn't trying to –'

'You just leave the police side of things to me. I'll do what has to be done, I can assure you.'

'All right then.'

'Fine,' said McIlwham, nodding.

'You'll be in touch,' said Eddy rising.

'I will.'

Eddy left the Superintendent's office confident that Black Lion's fortunes would soon be on the turn. The Major had once gone to the police about McGhie's intimidation but nothing had come of it, due to lack of witnesses. Well, now he had Porteous willing to testify. The whole rotten can of beans that was KM Brewery was going to be split wide open.

'Very interesting indeed,' said Kirk thoughtfully. And after a few minutes' more conversation, hung up the phone.

So, Eddy was on the move, he thought. Well, he'd soon put a stop to that little ploy.

A glance at his watch told him it was three-thirty p.m. Turk would be reporting in the back of five. He'd give Turk his instructions then.

'Mr King?'

'Speaking.'

'Superintendent McIlwham here.'

'Oh good morning, Superintendent.'

'I'm afraid I've got some bad news for you, sir. Mr Porteous, who was gong to testify? Well, I'm afraid he had a fatal accident last night.'

Eddy went cold all over. 'What sort of fatal accident?'

'He fell down the pub cellar steps and broke his neck. Death apparently was instantaneous.'

'You're sure it was an accident?'

'No doubt about it, sir. Mr Porteous was serving in the bar and left some customers to whom he'd been chatting to go down and change a keg. When he didn't reappear a barman went looking for him and found him at the bottom of the cellar steps. Very bad steps those, I've since seen them myself. He must've tripped.'

'Convenient for some people, wouldn't you say?'

There was no reply.

'Thank you for ringing, Superintendent.'

'Have you anyone else will testify, Mr King?'

Eddy gave a grim smile. 'No. And if anyone was considering it, I'm sure Danny Porteous's death will convince them it's best to keep their mouths shut.'

'But that was an accident, sir.'

'Thank you again for calling, Superintendent. Goodbye.'

Eddy hung up. 'Accident, my backside!' he said. Somehow Kirk and McGhie had found out about Danny. But who could've tipped them the wink? Danny sure as hell wouldn't have mentioned to anyone that he was going to testify. And he certainly hadn't. The only person he'd spoken to about it being . . .

Acting on a hunch he picked up the phone and dialled the Major at home.

'Major Gibb?'

'Yes?'

'Eddy King here. Point of information, if you don't mind. When you approached the police previously about bringing intimidation charges against KM, who did you speak to?'

'Let me see now,' replied the Major. A few seconds elapsed before he said, 'A Superintendent McIlwham, I think his name was.'

'I thought it might be,' said Eddy, and went on to tell the Major about Porteous and Porteous' 'accidental' demise.

After his call to the Major he made another to a different police station.

There he said he had a complaint to make about the KM Brewery. The sergeant he spoke to said he would take his number and have someone ring him back.

'Who will that be?' Eddy asked.

'A Superintendent McIlwham,' replied the sergeant.

'He personally handles all complaints about KM Brewery, then?'

'That's correct, sir.'

Eddy hung up.

Very neat, he thought. Very neat indeed, and typically Kirk. It gave credence to the old joke that used to be bandied about that the Glasgow police were the finest money could buy.

The moment he'd given McIlwham Danny Porteous' name, he'd signed Danny's death warrant.

When Turk McGhie strolled into the Tam O' Shanter Inn he was noted instantly by the two men sitting with an eye on the door.

As Turk vanished into the toilet one of the men glanced up at the bar clock. Ten minutes to closing time. Turk was working to his usual pattern of staying behind in the toilet till the rest of the customers had gone.

Mike Jardine and Sandy Pettigrew were two ex-commandos, both unemployed until Eddy had sought them out and put them on the payroll. Their job was to negate Turk.

Pettigrew came across to the bar, and in a whisper told the publican Turk had arrived. The publican was to carry on in his usual fashion and leave to them what had to be done.

Jardine and Pettigrew had been sitting in the pub for two days now, waiting for McGhie to appear. It was Eddy who'd worked out that Turk was acting according to a preconceived plan, advancing from pub to pub within a given area. Once that had been established it had been easy to spot that the Tam O'Shanter was one of the next in line of independent pubs to be 'converted' to KM beers.

Last orders were called and slowly the customers started to drift off. Jardine and Pettigrew positioned themselves in a darkish corner, from where they could watch the length of the bar as well as the door to the toilet.

Grumbling, the last of the customers went off into the night, leaving the publican, a barman and the two ex-commandos. The doors were shut and locked, the glasses piled by the sink.

Turk appeared right on cue. He was gliding quietly towards the bar when he suddenly became aware of the two figures sitting watching him. He frowned in their direction, thinking they might be police.

The publican was so nervous he dropped a glass, which went crashing to the floor. He tried to smile it off but the smile somehow got twisted on his face, turning it into what can only be described as a demented leer.

'Polis?' Turk asked softly.

Jardine and Pettigrew rose and crossed to within half a dozen feet of Turk. They positioned themselves so that they formed a triangle with Turk at its apex.

There was nothing particularly startling looking about either of the two ex-commandos. Neither was over average height or more muscled or broad in the shoulder than was normal for Glasgow. In fact they looked just what they were. Two lower-middle-class family men.

But Turk had been too long a fighting man to be fooled by appearances. He knew he was being confronted by men as deadly as himself.

'Landlord!' called out Jardine. 'I think this gentleman has something to say to you.'

The publican was now in such a state a tic had started to jump at the corner of his left eye. The result was to make him appear to be constantly winking. In other circumstances it could have been very funny.

'Are you the police?' Turk asked again, thinking that if they were, Kirk would soon sort all this out through his police contact.

'No,' replied Pettigrew.

'Then who?'

'We work for Black Lion Brewery just like you work for KM.'

Turk nodded. Everything was now crystal clear.

The publican hovered behind the bar.

'Say your piece,' instructed Jardine to Turk.

For a brief few seconds Turk considered trying to take these

422

two. But in the end he decided against it. He felt the possibility was quite high that the two together outmatched him, razors and all. No, his best policy was to back off and discuss this new turn of events with Kirk.

'I'm a representative from KM Brewery,' he said to the publican. 'And I'm here to see if you'd be interested in changing from Black Lion to us.'

'No, I wouldn't,' the publican stammered.

'You're sure?' Jardine asked.

The publican nodded.

'So there you are, McGhie,' Jardine said.

'Do you get the point?' Pettigrew asked.

'You've made it quite clear.'

'I hope we have. Because we're going to be around from now on in, protecting our brewery's interests. There's going to be no more of the nonsense that's been going on up till now.'

'Because if you try it we'll jump on you from a great height,' Jardine added.

Turk bit back the anger that flared in him. He wasn't used to being talked to this way. His hands twitched involuntarily as though they had a life of their own.

When Jardine saw that, a lazy smile settled on his face. There was a number of dead Germans in the war for whom the last thing seen in this life had been that smile.

'Well?' Pettigrew asked.

'If the man doesn't want our beer, then he doesn't want it,' Turk said. And it almost choked him to do so.

Again he considered making a play here and now and again told himself not to. If these two did manage to take him he'd lose all credibility. And the job he had with Kirk was far too soft – and lucrative – a number for that to happen. There would be other ways and means.

'Goodbye, Mr McGhie,' said Jardine, making the 'Mr' part sound like an obscenity.

'I'll let you out,' said the publican, hurrying round the bar to the door.

Turk, Jardine and Pettigrew stared at one another as bolts

rattled and the key was turned in the lock.

Silent as usual, Turk strode from the pub.

'What you did was right,' said Kirk the next day.

'I thought I might find out where they live and take them individually, one after the other,' Turk suggested. He was still smarting under the previous night's humiliation and wanted this new situation resolved as soon as possible.

Kirk's mouth thinned in thought. He also wanted this resolved at the earliest opportunity.

'How long now since King took over Black Lion?' he asked.

'Eight or nine weeks.'

'All right then,' said Kirk, making up his mind. It was earlier than he'd planned but he was going to give the go-ahead just the same.

'I told you to think about finishing off Black Lion Brewery in one fell swoop. Have you done so?'

Turk nodded.

'Then do it as soon as you can. And we'll see what side of his face Eddy King smiles on then!'

It was the opening night of a new season at the Citizens' Theatre. Five minutes before curtain-up, an eager throng had gathered in the foyer. The atmosphere was one of heady excitement and expectation.

It was the first time Eddy had gone out with Jane Miller, a long leggy blonde who worked as a beauty consultant in Pettigrew & Stephens of Sauchiehall Street. He'd met her the previous week through a radio scriptwriter friend of his who held lunchtime court every Monday to Friday in a cheapish Sauchiehall Street restaurant. Eddy found the scriptwriter amusing, and not for the man's supposed witty conversation either. The scriptwriter's idea of chic and sophistication was to drink beaujolais with his cod and chips.

Jane was done up to the nines and drew many admiring glances. Beautiful she might be, but she was decidedly short of chat as Eddy was rapidly finding out.

Eddy bought them a programme and then led her to their seats in the stalls. The play they were about to see was *Dandy Dick* by Sir Arthur Wing Pinero.

'Ever been to the Citizens' before?' he asked with a smile.

She shook her head.

'How about the variety theatres then?'

'No,' she said.

'I hope you'll like the play. It's a comedy.'

She smiled back at him.

This would be their first and last date, he decided. As far as he was concerned, the lovely Jane Miller was proving to be a complete washout. She had about as much personality as a stale loaf.

After Jane had quickly glanced through the programme he took it, always liking to familiarise himself with the names of the actors he was about to watch.

He'd actually read the name and gone on before it struck him just whose name it was he'd read. His eyes crawled back up the list and there it was, Toby Grimes.

Annie had said she'd travel round the reps with Toby. If she was still doing so that meant she was in Glasgow. Perhaps even in the theatre!

It was if he'd been shot through by a bolt of pure energy. He tingled from head to foot.

Then the house lights dimmed and the curtains opened. The play had begun.

When the curtain came down at the end of the first act, Eddy couldn't have said what he'd just seen and heard. All he'd been able to think about was Annie.

'Like a drink?' he asked.

'Mmm!'

Side by side, he and Jane moved up the aisle to the bar.

Like most theatre bars in the interval, it was pandemonium trying to get served. But eventually Eddy succeeded, and clutching two glasses made his way back to where Jane was standing by a large mirror.

'Cheers!' he said and raised his glass to his mouth. But it

never got there for what he saw reflected in the mirror caused him to pause in mid-action.

The same willowy figure. The same brown hair he remembered so well. She looked as though she hadn't aged, but the distance between them might have been deceiving.

Slowly he turned to stare at her, devouring her with his eyes. She was with a young man who, judging from his clothes and manner, would seem to be an actor. They were deep in conversation, the man gesturing floridly to make some point or other.

She must have become aware of Eddy's gaze on her for she frowned and glanced around her.

When their eyes met Eddy smiled.

For a second or two he was just another stranger, and then suddenly recognition flooded her face, manifesting itself in high colour which stained her cheeks.

He wanted to go to her. Talk to her. Just look at her. And indeed, he was about to excuse himself from Jane, when with great deliberation Annie turned her back on him.

It was like being punched or kicked. Or something equally physical.

It was quite obvious she didn't want to speak to him. Nor would he force the issue. She must have her reasons, which he would respect.

The bell rang, announcing that the second act would shortly begin. Seeing little and hearing less, Eddy escorted Jane back to their seats.

Norrie Smart hummed as he made his way along the gangway. With this hourly walkaround over, it was time to get the kettle on and the sandwiches out.

He never even saw the blow to the back of his head which sent him sprawling unconscious.

The play was over and Eddy was fitting the key in the car door when suddenly the night erupted with the clamour of a fire engine with all sirens going.

'Somebody's chimney's probably gone up,' said Jane when the din had receded a little.

Eddy had just moved the car out into the street when he had to draw back into the kerb to let a second fire engine past.

'If there's two of them it's more than a chimney,' he remarked.

A little further along the street he had to stop yet again to let a third by.

As they drove in the direction of Jane's house he knew from her manner he'd proved as big a disaster to her as she had to him. Pity, he thought. She'd seemed such a bright prospect when he'd met her at the scriptwriter's table.

'Thanks for the evening,' she said when he parked outside her house, already fumbling with the door handle. Opening the door she slid out. 'You stay where you are. I'm fine from here by myself,' she said quickly.

'I'll ring,' he lied.

''Bye!' she called out. Then her feet were scrunching up the gravel path as she beat a retreat.

Eddy sighed as he engaged the gears. All the way home his mind was on Annie, remembering, as he'd done so often in the past, the time they'd spent together in Fulham.

As he let himself in the telephone started to ring.

'Mr King, is that you?'

'Yes.'

'It's Tam McFadyen here. I manage the ...'

'I know who you are, Tam.'

'You'd better get to the brewery right away, Mr King. The whole bloody shebang is going up in smoke!'

'What are you talking about, Tam?'

'Fire, Mr King. The place is on fire.'

Eddy caught his breath. In his mind all he could see was the blackened shell The Black Lion pub had been reduced to.

'Thanks, Tam, I'll be right there,' he said and slammed down the phone.

He was turning away when the phone rang again.

'Yes?' he snapped.

427

'Is that Mr King?'

'Speaking.'

'This is the police, sir ...'

'If it's about the brewery, I already know and I'm on my way.'

At the outside door the phone started to ring yet again but this time he left it. He hurtled down the stairs and into his car, which he drove like a maniac, jumping four red lights and not giving a damn. Crouched over the wheel it came to him that the fire engines he'd heard in the Gorbals must have been going to the brewery. He muttered a string of obscenities to himself as he dodged in and out of the traffic.

The sky was lit up where it hadn't been before. When he got closer he saw yellow flames and sparks. It was just like bonfire night. Only in this case the bonfire was his brewery.

He slammed the car to a halt and climbed out. A cordon of police were holding back onlookers, while firemen did their best to contain the blaze. A figure waved to him, which he recognised as Tam McFadyen. He waved back.

'You can't go any closer now, sir,' said a big Highland policeman.

'Like hell I can't! That's my brewery that's on fire!'

'You own the premises?'

'I just said that, didn't I!'

'Through you go, sir.'

He went as near to the fire as he dared, hand to face to ward off the intense heat that battered him. The building was a write-off, that was blatantly obvious.

'Who are you, sir?'

'Eddy King. You police?'

'Detective Inspector Ireland of the CID.'

'My God!' Eddy exclaimed, as there was an explosion inside the building, which sent huge shafts of flame shooting skywards.

'We've been trying to ring you at home ever since the 999 came through, sir.'

'I was at the theatre and ...' A sudden thought struck Eddy, causing him to glance around. 'Did you get the security guard out?' he demanded.

Ireland glanced from Eddy back to the building and the raging inferno consuming it. His grim expression was reply enough.

'Oh!' Eddy sighed.

'Just the one guard was there, sir?'

Eddy nodded.

'Must have been overcome by the smoke. Some of the first firemen here did get in on the ground level but there was no one there. He must've been higher up.'

Beyond the cordon a group of youths capered and cavorted, thinking the fire great sport. For two pins Eddy would have gone across and smashed their teeth down their throats.

A woman in the crowd screamed and pointed up at the building.

'Yon's a man!' somebody else shouted.

Norrie Smart stood framed in a blown-out window, his head, arms, torso, everything, burning fiercely. He was a flaming human torch.

'Oh Christ!' said Eddy, a lump suddenly clogging his throat.

Smart seemed to dance and wave to the crowd. Then he pitched forward, turning end over end, to fall to the ground below. Eddy found himself running toward the still burning figure. All he could think of was Norrie's new wee wean.

As he ran he tore his coat off and, arriving at Norrie's side, threw the coat over his body. He ripped off his jacket, which he used as a flail to try and beat the flames out.

Underneath the flames Norrie's face was a nightmare. The hair was gone as were the eyes, the latter melted. The lips had been burned away to reveal the teeth. Norrie moaned, the most pitiful sound Eddy had ever heard.

Then suddenly Eddy wasn't alone with Smart. A dozen uniforms surrounded them both as the firemen took over.

Foam spurted and other articles were brought into play. Within seconds the fire enveloping Norrie was extinguished.

Eddy and the firemen reeled under the heat from the building. Later Eddy would discover that a lot of his skin had been scalded. A stetcher appeared and Norrie was gently lifted on to it. He was covered by a blanket before being taken to an ambulance which was standing by.

'I'll follow on behind,' said Eddy to the ambulance driver. But as he was turning to spring to his car the other ambulance-man said, 'He's gone, mate. Too late for hospitals now.'

Feeling sick to the very depths of his being, Eddy stared down at the body of Norrie Smart. Big dumb Norrie who'd always seemed two mental paces behind everyone else but who'd always stand by you and do you a good turn if he could. And now, ridiculously young, he was dead, leaving a wife and two wee ones behind.

'It was best he died now rather than lingered on,' the driver said. 'With those burns they'd never have saved him. This is by far the best way for him, believe me.'

Tears rolled down Eddy's cheeks as the ambulance, with siren howling, took the burnt remains of Norrie Smart to the morgue.

Poor Norrie who'd never done anyone any harm. Who'd only wanted a wife and family and the opportunity to support them.

In the flames Eddy saw Turk McGhie's face laughing at him and behind Turk was Kirk, also laughing. His hands knotted at his side as a terrible anger was birthed in him, an anger that within seconds had blossomed into an awesome rage. He was dimly aware that Ireland was talking to him but he heard nothing. There was a roaring in his ears and a fire, as intense as that he was watching, in his belly.

Suddenly he knew what he must do. Turning abruptly he strode for the police cordon, beyond which he had to fight to get through the milling onlookers.

Once in his car he opened his wallet and extracted the card Kirk had given him the day they'd had lunch together. He memorised Kirk's address before starting the car and moving off.

*

Glass in hand, Susan sat staring into the fire. She heard the front door open and then close again, followed by the sound of Kirk hanging up his coat.

He would have been with Ciona Crammond again, she thought bitterly. How she'd come to hate that name!

'I'm home, Susan!' he called out.

'I'm in here,' she slurred. 'Having a nightcap.' Nightcap, my foot! She'd been having nightcaps since arriving in from work hours previously.

On entering the room, Kirk saw immediately that she'd been hitting the bottle again. That disturbed him but he didn't comment on the fact. After all, those who lived in glass houses . . .

'Pour me another, will you?' said Susan, holding out her empty glass.

'Think I'll join you,' he replied, hoisting a smile on to his face.

'Another busy day?' she said sarcastically, adding a second later, 'And evening?'

Kirk ignored the taunt. He handed her the refill and said he was going down to the basement for a bottle of wine. That was what he fancied and the claret jug was empty.

She watched him swagger away, a swagger that was becoming more and more pronounced as the years went by. His bottom really was getting far too big, she thought dimly. Then she shrugged. Why should she bother? Let Ciona Crammond try and get him to stick to a diet. After all, if Ciona was getting the pleasures of the front then it was only fair she get the worries of the rear. Susan laughed aloud at the vulgarity and absurdity of that thought.

She frowned as the doorbell rang. Who on earth could that be at this time of night? She'd have to answer it herself. The servants were off duty now. Sighing, she came to her feet and lurched for the door.

'Is Kirk home?' Eddy asked, his face contorted into a thundercloud of anger.

'Who are you?'

'Eddy King.'

Susan's eyes narrowed. 'Oh yes! Kirk's spoken of you. The pair of you were in the Army together.'

'Is he home, Mrs Murray?'

'Come in. He's downstairs getting some wine.'

The inside of the house was opulent and in very good taste, but Eddy noticed none of that as he followed Susan through to a drawing room.

'Kirk will be back in a moment,' Susan slurred. 'Can I get you a drink?'

Eddy shook his head.

'Then please sit down.'

'I prefer to stand.'

'Suit yourself, Mr King,' she replied, and sat herself.

Kirk entered with an opened bottle of wine. 'Susan, I . .' He came up short when he saw Eddy.

The anger Eddy had somehow managed to bring under control threatened to break its banks. He started to shake as though he had the ague.

'To what do we owe this pleasure?' Kirk asked, a hint of mockery in his voice.

'Black Lion brewery was burned down tonight.'

Kirk expressed mock concern. 'I am sorry to hear that. What a blow for you. But surely you mean it burned down?'

'*Was* burned.'

'Can you prove that?'

Eddy gritted his teeth. 'I doubt it. Same as we couldn't prove The Black Lion pub was deliberately burned down. As an arsonist your man McGhie is excellent.'

'Careful, Eddy. There's a witness present.'

Eddy took a step forward and his shaking got worse. 'Intimidation, arson, and now murder, Kirk.'

'What are you talking about? Who's been murdered?'

'Remember Norrie Smart?'

'From the section? Yes, of course I do. What's he got to do with this?'

432

'Norrie was my night security guard at the brewery. Tonight he was burned to death. He came out of a top window, a human torch, and was still alive as he fell to the ground. When I got to him it looked like every inch of his flesh was on fire, his hair was gone and his eyes – oh his eyes, Kirk.. they'd melted.'

Susan gagged and turned away.

Kirk had gone pale.

'Well?'

'Well what?'

'Nothing to say?'

'I, eh.. I'm sorry about Norrie, naturally. But it had nothing to do with me.'

'Liar!'

'I swear!'

'Lying bastard!'

Fear appeared in Kirk's eyes as Eddy advanced on him. Slowly he began backing away.

'You told McGhie to burn me out, so as far as I'm concerned you're as guilty for what happened as he is.'

'You've got it all wrong, Eddy!'

'Like hell I have!' Eddy roared and threw himself at Kirk, his anger breaking its banks and enveloping him.

Kirk smashed the bottle against the side of Eddy's head causing him to stagger. Suddenly the two of them, and the carpet beneath their feet, were covered in claret, the colour of blood.

Eddy wrapped his arms around Kirk and started to punch, his fist pile-driving time and time again into Kirk's flabby middle.

Kirk brought his head down, trying to break Eddy's nose, but he missed and hit Eddy's shoulder instead. Thrown off balance, he stumbled and then fell, dragging Eddy to the ground with him as he went. They rolled over and over on the carpet a few times, then Eddy was sitting astride Kirk with Kirk's throat between his hands.

Kirk's eyes bulged as Eddy began to squeeze.

'Stop it! Stop it!' Susan screamed, tugging frantically at Eddy's shoulder. 'You'll kill him!'

Kirk's face turned plum coloured. His legs kicked as he struggled valiantly to heave Eddy off. But Eddy hung on grimly, intent on finishing what he'd come to do.

Hysterically Susan hit Eddy again and again round the head and ears but he felt nothing. His entire world was focused on his two hands and Kirk's throat.

Kirk was convinced the next few seconds were to be his last, when suddenly the vice round his neck was relaxed. Coughing and spluttering, he sucked in life-giving breath.

With a peculiar expression on his face, Eddy rose to his feet. 'I can't do it,' he mumbled. 'I just can't do it.'

Kirk rolled over on to his side, bringing his legs up into an embryonic position, which made his breathing easier.

Eddy shook his head. When it came to the bit he was a lot different from the boy who'd killed Gloag all those years ago. Life, Annie Grimes and Leoni von Kruppermann had done that to him.

'Get out of here!' Kirk husked.

Eddy's fury was gone now, leaving him strangely tranquil inside. He stared down at Kirk, a mixture of hate and contempt on his face.

Kirk glared back.

Susan sobbed. She seemed to be trying to eat the hand stuffed in her mouth.

'I'm going to see Norrie's widow now,' Eddy said. 'Want to come along?'

Kirk dropped his gaze.

Eddy strode from the room.

The next morning Eddy woke early. He washed and shaved but couldn't face food. Getting into his car he drove out to the brewery – or what was left of it.

The building was cordoned off by ropes and two policemen were on duty to see no unauthorised person tried to go inside.

A solitary figure stood apart, staring at the still smoking ruin. Eddy recognised the Major.

Eddy joined Keith, who shook his head sadly.

'So, there we are then,' Eddy said.

'A man dead, I believe?'

'Aye. The night security guard. A bloke who was in the Army with me.'

'Married?'

'Wife and two kids. I saw her last night. You can imagine the state she was in. I only hope no idiot lets her see the body.'

'So,' Keith said squaring his shoulders. 'What now?'

Eddy laughed hollowly.

'You're not thinking of quitting, are you?'

'I don't see what else I can do. Salvage what I can out of this mess, which probably means putting KM beer into my pubs.'

'I expected more of you than that, King.'

'What else can I do? Look at the brewery, for God's sake! You know how long insurance takes to come through and then I'd have to knock down what's left and rebuild from scratch. And in the meantime every pub I have would have to be closed due to lack of beer. The whole thing would take years, by which time Murray would have the rest of the Glasgow market sewn up anyway.'

'I know of a way in which you could have Black Lion beer back in your pubs within a month,' Keith said softly.

'How?'

'Thanks to Murray, there's half a dozen breweries have closed down within the last few years, one of which was Donaldson's. And Fergus Donaldson is a friend of mine. I'm sure he'd be only too happy to sell.'

Eddy frowned. He hadn't thought of that. But then since the fire he hadn't really had a chance to think things through.

'You still have the workforce and the outlets,' Keith said. 'Your only problems are premises and equipment. Solve those and you're back in business again.'

'But I couldn't raise that sort of capital,' Eddy replied. 'At

435

least not until the insurance money came through.'

'Why don't we talk to Fergus and see what he thinks?' Keith suggested.'

'I've nothing to lose.'

'And everything to gain,' Keith added, smiling.

They used Eddy's car to drive to the outskirts of Glasgow, where they found Fergus Donaldson just about to sit down to breakfast. Eddy and Keith took coffee while Fergus ate. And while he did so, they took it in turns to speak.

At the end of the meal Fergus poured them more coffee and then sipped his, looking thoughtful.

'Well, the way I see it is this,' he said. 'There's nobody else going to want to buy it as a brewery and frankly I've had difficulty selling it at all. It's been on the market as light industrial premises since we closed down, but I've had no nibbles, far less takers.'

'Everything's still there as it was, isn't it?' Eddy asked, suddenly thinking Donaldson might have had the guts ripped out the place.

'Oh aye. Exactly as the day we stopped production,' Donaldson replied.

'Then there's no reason why Eddy couldn't have Black Lion beer back in the pumps within a matter of weeks?'

'None at all.'

'There is the money problem,' Eddy said, and went on to explain about his lack of capital.

'That's no real problem at all,' said Donaldson. 'Let's agree a price that's fair to both of us and I'll wait till your insurance money comes through to collect. You're doing me a favour taking the brewery off my hands so the least I can do is a favour in return. Tit for tat, so to speak.'

'What sort of price did you have in mind?' Eddy asked.

Donaldson named a sum that Eddy thought was more than reasonable.

'Agreed,' Eddy said, and they shook hands on it.

'I'll get my solicitors on to the matter right away,' said Donaldson. 'But as their office won't be open for a good hour yet would you like to go and have a look at the place? I'd be only too happy to show you around.'

'I'd love that,' replied Eddy, full of enthusiasm. 'And before we go, do you think I could have a piece of that toast? I've suddenly got very hungry.'

The Donaldson Brewery was a lot smaller than Black Lion had been. But then with the loss of trade Black Lion had suffered since KM came into existence, the new premises were more than adequate for the amount of beer needed to supply their outlets.

On the second day after the fire the workforce reported to the new premises, where they set about getting the brewery producing again.

That first week was the most hectic Eddy had ever known but gradually things began to sort themselves out. He estimated another fortnight and then the first of the beer would be in the pumps. In the meantime all Black Lion pubs were closed down.

A few nights later Eddy came home dog-tired and after washing and having a dram, tumbled into bed. Within seconds he was fast asleep.

In his dream he was back at the scene of the fire and Norrie Smart was standing framed in the window. He seemed to close in on Norrie's face where he saw the eyes slowly turn into a horrible gooey gel which ran down Norrie's burning face.

He woke screaming and covered in sweat, gulping in breath after breath when he realised it had only been a nightmare.

But the fact remained; Norrie was dead. Murdered by that bastard Turk McGhie. Of course there would be no police action. No doubt when the results of the inquiry into the fire came through, the cause, or causes, of the blaze would, as in the case of The Black Lion pub, be found to be unknown. Superintendent McIlwham would undoubtedly see to that.

Rising from his bed, Eddy poured himself another dram. Turk McGhie was the key to all this, he thought. Remove Turk and the reign of terror would be over. Kirk would then have to fight fair and square for his business same as everyone else.

There was no use going to the police about Turk. Both he and the Major had tried that to no avail. So if the law wouldn't help then it would have to be the other way.

McGhie was a rabid animal and the kindest thing for them was to be put down. And Turk's case, if for no other reason than Norrie Smart's horrible death, demanded it.

But how? And who?

He couldn't ask Jardine and Pettigrew. Although well capable, he had no doubt they would baulk at civilian murder. Protecting his business interests was one thing, cold-blooded assassination quite another. Anyway it would be stupid of him to ask them. That would have been putting his own neck out on a limb in a way he had no intention of doing.

The drink was sour in his stomach so he made himself a cup of tea. And while he was doing so his mind drifted back to the theatre visit and Annie Grimes.

Thinking of Annie brought a half-remembered conversation percolating up into his mind.

'Can you do me a dozen rollers by tomorrow lunchtime?' Eddy asked in a loud voice. He was standing just inside the showroom door.

Gil Crabtree blinked and turned to face the man who'd just uttered the sort of request every used-car dealer dreams about.

'A dozen Rolls Royces, sir?' Gil repeated, just to make sure he'd heard correctly.

'Assorted colours will be fine,' said Eddy.

Gil's forehead suddenly puckered into a frown which cleared again just as suddenly in an explosion of recognition.

'Eddy! Eddy King!'

'The one and only,' said Eddy.

Gil threw his arms round Eddy and hugged him tight. 'It's great to see you again!' he laughed. 'But what brings you down here from darkest Scotland?'

'To see you and buy you a pint.'

438

'Gin and tonic, if you don't mind. Nothing so vulgar as a common pint. But come on now, why have you returned to civilisation?'

'I told you. To see you.'

'You're after a special car?'

'I'm after something. But not that.'

'If it's to do with Annie, she's . .'

'She's in Glasgow,' Eddy cut in. 'I bumped into her recently but we didn't speak. She made it quite obvious she didn't want to so I didn't even try.'

'Are you married yet?'

'No. And I'm not carrying a torch either, if that's what you're getting at.' The latter was a lie of course.

Gil called out and a man emerged from the back of the showroom. 'Harry, my partner,' he said in explanation.

A few minutes later Eddy and Gil left for the local pub, where they ensconced themselves in an out-of-the-way corner where they wouldn't be overheard. Eddy brought Gil up to date on his career. The first pub that had started it all, leading up to his now owing the Black Lion Brewery.

'I always knew you were a winner, Eddy,' Gil said. 'And it couldn't have happened to a nicer bloke.'

Eddy came to the nitty-gritty: why he'd travelled down from Glasgow to see his old employer. Lowering his voice a little, he said, 'You once mentioned to me you had high friends in nasty places.'

Gil's eyes narrowed. 'Yes,' he said slowly.

'To put it bluntly, I want someone killed. Do you have a contact?'

'Christ Almighty, Eddy, you're joking! What would you want to get mixed up in a thing like that for?'

'So you don't have a contact?'

'I didn't say that.'

'Then you do?'

Gil sipped his large G and T. 'Are you certain about this?'

'Yes.'

'Absolutely?'

439

'Absolutely.'

'He's expensive. But the best there is.'

'Then he's the one I want.'

Gil shook his head. 'Times change right enough. Who'd ever have thought you'd come asking me something like that.'

'Life's full of surprises,' Eddy said. 'I found that out early on. Now look, I want to make my visit to London as brief as possible, so can you put me on to this person this morning?'

'I can try. There's no guaranteeing he'll be there, though. He might be out on a job or tied up in some other way.' Gil finished his drink and stood up. 'I'm going out to make a phone call. You wait here.' He paused before leaving. 'I ask again, are you certain about this?'

'Make the call, Gil.'

While Gil was gone Eddy sat staring into his drink. He was seeing Norrie Smart at the high window and hearing Norrie's moan after he had come crashing to the ground. He also thought of Danny Porteous, whom he'd liked.

Ten minutes later Gil was back. 'You're in luck. He's available,' Gil said.

'What do I do? Do I meet him?'

'No. You speak to him on the telephone.'

Gil took Eddy round the corner to a public telephone box. There was somebody using it so they had to hang on for a few minutes. When the box was free Gil went inside and dialled, Eddy having to stay outside while he did so. When he made his connection he spoke briefly, then beckoned Eddy in. After Eddy had taken the phone Gil left the box to go back outside.

'Hello?' said Eddy.

'I don't know your name nor do I want to. Nor will you ask me mine. Okay?'

'Yes.'

'Now tell me all you know about the party in question.'

When Eddy had given all the information he had on Turk McGhie there was a fairly long pause.

Finally the man asked, 'Is there a time limit?'

'I'd prefer sooner rather than later.'

440

'Okay then. My fee is five hundred quid. Half in cash now, the other half when the job is done. Money to Crabtree on both occasions. He'll get it to me.'

'Fine,' said Eddy.

The man hung up.

Eddy stared into his now dead receiver. It had all been so cut and dried, formal almost. The man had been well spoken. He might well have been discussing some minor problem with his bank manager.

Ten days after Eddy's trip to London, two patrolling Glasgow policemen came across a figure slumped in a tenement close. As the pubs weren't long out they thought it must be a drunk.

They discovered their mistake when they saw what remained of where the man's face had been. There was a small, neat hole at the back of the neck where the bullet had gone in. On emerging, the bullet had taken the face with it.

The policeman searched the corpse's pockets but there was no identification.

Neither of the policemen were particularly disturbed about what they'd found. They'd seen it all before. Murders were an everyday occurrence in Glasgow. The only unusual thing about this one was that a gun had been used. Shooters were a bit uncommon.

'Whoever he was, he carried nice razors,' one of the policemen remarked.

'Ivory handled. Expensive,' his mate replied.

One stayed behind while the other went to call up the meat waggon.

It was a great day for Eddy. Black Lion beer was back on flow and this time there would be no Turk McGhie to play with matches or otherwise put a spanner in the works.

It was eight o'clock at night and he'd been at work since eight that morning. A twelve-hour day and he was shattered. He decided a drink was in order so he stopped outside the Renfrew Hotel and went into the back bar where he ordered up a large whisky and half-pint chaser. The hotel was one of the few outlets for his beer that he hadn't previously been to in person. He was in the process of lighting a cigarette when he saw her in the corner. He knew the face but for a moment or two couldn't place her.

Then he did. The woman drinking on her own was Susan, Kirk's wife. He wondered whether to ignore her or not. Then he thought about how upset she'd been the night of the big fire when he'd had the fight with Kirk. He felt he should at least attempt to apologise. After all, he had no quarrel with her. It was her man who was his enemy.

'Mrs Murray, isn't it?' he said, having walked over to her table.

She glanced up at him, her face puffed and swollen from crying. 'Yes, that's right. Who are you?'

She'd had a fair amount to drink, that was obvious. And Eddy recalled she'd been the same way last time he'd seen her.

'I'm Eddy King. I own Black Lion.'

'Oh yes,' she said.

'I thought I should apologise to you for the other night. It must have been very distressing for you.'

'Was it true? What you accused Kirk of?'

'Yes. But I can't prove it.'

An expression of indescribable sadness came into her eyes, eyes which seemed to be sunk like deep holes into her face.

Eddy was about to walk away again when on a sudden impulse he said, 'Can I join you?'

'Why?'

'No reason other than you're alone as am I.'

She regarded him thoughtfully. 'Why not?' she replied, and nodded to a vacant chair.

Once he'd sat he said, 'Look, I hope you don't think I'm sticking my nose in, but is there anything I can do to help?'

'In what way?'

'You, eh.. appear to have been crying.'

She ran a hand over her face. 'That noticeable? I hadn't realised. Well no, there isn't anything you can do, Mr King..'

442

'Call me Eddy.'

'All right, Eddy, there's nothing you can do. Unless you can tell me how to make my husband get rid of his mistress and start paying attention to me again?'

Another woman, Eddy thought. The same old Kirk.

'That stuff's never a solution,' he said, indicating her glass.

She smiled bitterly. 'Can't face the nights without it.' Then, 'I must be crazy. The first stranger to talk to me and here I am laying all my problems at his feet!'

'I'm hardly a stranger,' replied Eddy. 'Don't forget Kirk and I spent two years together in Germany. And I also sold the pair of you a used car once. You can't call a man a stranger who's sold you a used car.'

'I suppose not,' she grinned.

'And I was the one who was forward in asking if I could help.'

There was silence between them for a few seconds and then she said, 'You must have got to know him pretty well in Germany.'

'We were inseparable for a while but we fell out.'

'Over what?'

He thought of telling her and decided against it. 'It's not important now. Let's just say it was at the time.'

'He hates you for taking over Black Lion.'

'I'm sure.'

'You do know the Major's my father, don't you?'

'Yes. He mentioned.'

'He and I never got on all that well. He and my mother were abroad a lot when I was a child.'

'I like him,' said Eddy.

'He always wanted a boy. I was a disappointment to him.'

'I'm sure it wasn't as bad as that.'

'I'm still a disappointment to him because I haven't given him a grandchild. I guess I'm just a disappointment all round.'

Eddy finished his drink. 'Would you like another?'

'Please.'

He went to the bar and ordered for them both. In the mirror he watched her staring into space.

Not particularly a looker, he thought. But she wasn't unattractive.

An hour later they emerged together out into the night. He was a lot drunker than he'd intended, having forgotten he hadn't eaten all day. The alcohol was going straight to his head as a consequence.

Susan stumbled and might well have fallen had he not grabbed her. 'Whoops!' she exclaimed.

'I think we could both do with a cup of coffee to sober up,' he said.

She hiccuped in reply.

He racked his brains trying to think of somewhere that would be open but nothing came to mind. When it came to restaurants and coffee bars, not to mention pubs, Glasgow was notorious for its early closing hours.

'Look, I live not all that far away,' he said. 'Why don't I drive us there and then when we've had coffee I'll run you back to your car.'

'All right.'

He drove slowly and carefully, desperately concentrating on the road. He was lucky inasmuch as there wasn't much traffic about.

He shivered as he got out of the car. The cold night air was further compounding the effects of the alcohol on him.

'Lots of coffee, and black,' he said, leading her up the close stairs. Despite his ever-increasing affluence over the past few years he'd continued to live in the same house.

Once inside Susan gazed curiously around. What she saw was a typical bachelor's place. Mess and muddle everywhere.

'You live here alone?' she asked.

'That's right,' Eddy replied as he filled the kettle.

Susan collapsed into a chair. She'd been all right for the past half-hour but now she was suddenly morose and dejected again.

'He still loves me,' she said. 'It's just he's been sidetracked by that bitch.'

'I'm sure he does.'

'I know he does because I can feel it here.' And she placed her hand over her left breast.

Eddy concentrated on trying to spoon coffee into cups.

'Do you think I'm attractive?'

'Pardon?'

She repeated her question, a furrow in her brow as she spoke.

'Yes I do.'

'You wouldn't lie?'

He turned to stare at her. He'd found her attractive in the hotel and he still did. More so. 'No,' he replied.

He was pouring the milk when the idea presented itself to him. I'm more drunk than I'd thought, he told himself. He had to be to even consider it. To seduce Kirk's wife. God, what a blow that would be to him! And the ideal revenge for what had happened with Leoni. He knew how lonely she was. Her conversation had been full of it.

He almost laughed out loud. Seduce Kirk's wife and then make sure the bastard found out! It was the perfect riposte and would knock a hole as big as a fist in Kirk's ego.

Christ, he was pissed! he thought, holding his head. He should've eaten something.

She came to him, swaying across the room. 'Are you all right?'

He turned into her and took her in his arms. She gasped but that was stifled as his mouth joined with hers.

Her mind was numb with alcohol and awash with emotion. She so desperately wanted to be loved, to be cherished. Her body was crying out for release, after all this while. And if Kirk could have his damned Ciona Crammond, why couldn't she have someone?

Tears streamed down her face as she pressed herself close to Eddy.

Disentangling himself, he took her hand and led her through to the bedroom.

She walked with head bowed.

EDDY, SUSAN AND RACHEL

Kirk was in Ciona's flat mixing some Black Velvet, which had become their favourite drink, when the telephone rang. Both of them were naked underneath their robes, having just made love.

'Ciona Crammond speaking,' Ciona said into the receiver, at the same time winking and pouting a kiss at Kirk.

Kirk blew a kiss back. Then poured himself a glass of Black Velvet which he eagerly sampled. Smooth as a maiden's thigh, he thought. He chuckled, pleased with himself at having conjured up such a phrase.

'Oh!' said Ciona, sagging where she stood. Her hand clutched the wall for support.

Her face lost colour and became pinched, the rosy afterglow of love fading completely from her cheeks. It might have been an illusion but it seemed her very hair lost its sheen.

'Thank you for ringing. I'll be home as soon as I can get there,' she said, and hung up.

'What's happened?' Kirk asked. Obviously it was something dreadful.

Disregarding the Black Velvet, Ciona made her way across to where the drinks stood and poured herself a huge brandy. She shuddered after she'd taken a swallow. Her shoulders hunched and started to shake. Tears splashed from her eyes.

'Ciona?' Kirk said, putting his arms round her.

'Mummy and Daddy,' she sobbed. 'They were killed an hour ago in a road accident. Some drunk ran into their car killing them instantly.'

'Oh my angel,' said Kirk, pulling her to him and holding her close.

For a little while she cried and he made soothing noises, stroking her as she gave vent to her grief.

Finally she said through her sobs, 'I've got to drive down to Helensburgh.'

'I'll drive. You're not in a fit state to.'

'But you can't. It's Susan's birthday. She's expecting you home in an hour.'

'Then she'll just have to wait.'

Ciona broke away to light a cigarette with trembling hands. 'At least there was no pain,' she said.

'And they were both a good age with their lives behind them.'

'And they went together. They would have liked that,' Ciona said softly. 'They were very much in love you know. From the day they met neither looked at another person.' She paused before adding, 'I'm going to miss them dreadfully.'

He took her in his arms and kissed her. 'I love you,' he said.

She looked up at him through eyes still brimming with moisture. 'You ring Susan while I wash my face. Then we'd both better get dressed.'

'I'm ever so sorry. Truly I am,' he said.

She gave him a brave smile before heading for the bathroom.

Damn! he swore to himself when she was gone. Of all the days for this to happen. Susan's birthday! And he'd promised faithfully to be home early for the special supper she was laying on for the occasion.

He glanced at the clock and worked out how long it would take him to get to Helensburgh and back. He was going to be dreadfully late, probably past midnight.

But what else could he do? He couldn't allow Ciona to drive in the state she was in. Nor could he explain the real reason to Susan why he was going to let her down on this day of days.

Sighing, he picked up the telephone. There was going to have to be yet another invented crisis at KM.

'I understand, Kirk,' Susan said into the phone. 'There's no need to go on. You do what you have to and I'll see you when you get in. Yes .. yes all right .. 'Bye now.'

She hung up. Then exhaled, long and slowly.

'You chromium-plated, died-in-the-wool bastard,' she said.

She refreshed her drink and then carried it to the fire where she stood gazing into the flames. She was wearing a special dress she'd bought for the occasion and that morning she'd had her hair especially done. And all for what? Nothing. He didn't even care enough about her to leave his mistress for an hour or two on her birthday.

She felt wretched and lonely standing there. Abandoned. The way she'd done as a child of four when her parents had gone off leaving her at Miss Buchan's School For Young Ladies.

She swallowed her drink, enjoying the warmth it spread through her insides. She contemplated pouring herself another, but decided against it. She would make a phone call first.

Eddy was at home studying some papers when the phone rang.

'Hello?'

'It's me.'

'Happy birthday. I've got a present for you. When are you coming over to collect it?'

Susan smiled. She'd mentioned briefly some months back that today was her birthday. It was just like Eddy to take it in and not forget.

'How about now?' she suggested.

'What about Kirk?'

'He's off with his fancy woman somewhere. He won't be back for hours yet.'

'I'll be expecting you then.'

'I'm on my way,' she said and hung up.

Eddy returned to his papers. It was a Tuesday night.

451

Normally he saw her on Thursday nights and occasionally Mondays.

He never had told Kirk about their affair, as his alcohol-muddled brain had suggested that night they'd first gone to bed together all those months ago. It had been a stupid idea. The sort of thing Kirk might well do. But not him.

Anyway, he'd come to discover he actually liked Susan. Apart from the sex aspect, which they both enjoyed, he found her relaxing and an enormous pleasure to be with. If asked to describe their relationship, he'd have said they'd become good friends who were having an affair.

Kirk sat at his desk rereading the article in the paper spread before him.

Five police officers had been suspended from duty pending inquiries of corruption. The new Chief Constable had stated on his appointment some six weeks previously that he would scourge all corruption from his force. It would seem the scourging had begun.

Kirk dialled and asked to be put through to Superintendent McIlwham.

'It's Murray. Can we speak?' he asked, when McIlwham came on the line.

'Hold on a moment and I'll have this transferred through to my private office.'

A few seconds later McIlwham announced, 'It's safe now.'

'I've been reading about the suspensions.'

'Got a lot of people in a flap, that has. It would seem that bastard means what he says.'

'What about you?'

'I'll have to be doubly careful from now on in.'

'So they're not on to you yet?'

'Not as far as I know. But should they start asking questions I'm going to have a lot of trouble explaining away the house I live in and the car I drive. Both are way outside what I should be able to afford.'

Kirk chewed a nail. He didn't like this at all.

'Are you worried?' McIlwham asked.

'Frankly, yes.'

'To be truthful so am I.'

'So what happens if you get your collar felt?'

'From your point of view?'

'Precisely.'

McIlwham said slowly, 'I've been thinking about that. You see my problem is if I go down what happens to the wife and kids? What'll they live on? There won't be any money coming in apart from what she can get out of the parish. I'd certainly be a lot happier knowing they were being looked after.'

Kirk got the message loud and clear. 'Just supposing you do go down. What sort of amount would you have in mind?'

'Say fifteen a week arriving by post. That would make life an awful lot easier for them.'

'And what would I get in return?'

'My word that I'll keep my mouth shut. Your name will never ever be mentioned.'

Kirk sat back in his chair and thought about that. Fifteen pounds a week was nothing. McIlwham was being clever by not asking too much. As insurance went it was a small price to pay for the man's guaranteed silence.

'Consider that an agreement, should the worst come to the worst,' Kirk said.

'Let's just hope it doesn't,' replied McIlwham.

Eddy followed Mike Jardine into a pub called The Neuk. With Turk McGhie dead, and no other trouble of that sort having reared its ugly head in the meantime, Mike Jardine and Sandy Pettigrew had been upgraded to representatives with the special brief of trying to win back some of Black Lion's lost outlets.

The Neuk was one such outlet which had gone over to KM but which had now returned to the Black Lion fold.

Since McGhie's death KM's momentum had stopped and indeed was now beginning to fall back. Without the Damoclean threat of McGhie hanging over their heads, free houses were leaving KM, some returning to Black Lion while others were giving their business to the other surviving breweries.

Eddy was a pleased man as he strode up to The Neuk's bar. KM was on the retreat while Black Lion was expanding again. Expanding slowly, mind you, but expanding nonetheless. And that was the main thing.

It had been Eddy's own idea he visit every outlet that returned to Black Lion. It was the sort of gesture that went down big in Glasgow that he, the boss man, thought enough of the pub or outlet to put in a personal appearance.

'Mr King, I'd like you to meet Mr Hannigan, the publican,' Mike Jardine said.

'I'm Eddy and you're .. ?'

'Rab.'

'Welcome back to Black Lion, Rab. I know it's going to be a pleasure doing business with you again.'

Hannigan pumped Eddy's hand and then beamed round the pub.

'Anyone who'd like a drink on Mr King of Black Lion just step up to the bar,' announced Mike Jardine.

A grinning Eddy was nearly bowled over in the stampede.

Kirk was at home, sitting sunk in thought. Ever since Turk's death things had started to go wrong. The straight sweep to a Glasgow monopoly had been halted and there was nothing he could think to do about it. He had considered hiring another hard man but with the police situation the way it was at the moment he thought it best to lay off those sort of tactics for a while.

Another four police officers had been suspended and three of the originals had been committed to Barlinne Prison pending trial. So far McIlwham was safe, but according to him he had the feeling the net was closing in. From one or two hints McIlwham had dropped, it seemed he'd been up to a great deal more than merely looking after KM's interests.

Anyway, Kirk thought, no matter what happened to

McIlwham, he was in the clear. He had his arrangement with McIlwham to thank for that.

But the prime source of his moroseness was Eddy King and Black Lion Brewery. They were his main competitors and under Eddy's guidance regaining ground they'd lost when that old fart the Major had been running the place.

And thinking of the Major .. that was one thorn in his flesh who wasn't long for this world. According to Susan the old fart was so gone with cancer he'd have to be admitted to hospital as soon as he was proving too much for his wife Jean to look after at home.

Good riddance to bad rubbish, Kirk thought; then, fingering the scar on his cheek, and if you're in as much pain as Susan says you are don't go quickly, but rather linger on, drawing it out.

Susan entered the room to say she'd just had an emergency call. A horse in nearby stables had come down with some mysterious fever and her presence was required right away.

After she'd gone, Kirk thought of how she'd picked up of late. She wasn't drinking nearly as much and there was a new spring to her step and gleam to her eye. Opening up a practice had certainly made a world of difference to her, he thought. It had given her a new zest, a new sort of life about her. There were times when he definitely regretted not being able to have sexual relations with her. Of late she had been extremely fanciable.

Putting Susan from his mind, he went back to thinking about Eddy and Black Lion. If only he could get rid of them somehow the other smaller breweries, the few left that is, would soon fall to him.

But how? That was the question. How?

Hours passed and Kirk sank lower and lower in his chair as he cudgelled his brains to no avail.

'I don't understand why you don't move out of this place,' Susan said. She and Eddy were in Eddy's front room.

'I don't see any reason to, that's why,' he replied.

'But it's a slum!'

'Only outside these four walls, not inside,' he grinned.

And it was true. Inside his house he had the very best money could buy. He'd never forgotten his night at London's Ivy Restaurant with the actor knight. Since having started to make a great deal of money he hadn't stinted himself when it came to the luxuries in life. And always he insisted on the very best. Top quality.

'That's true,' Susan admitted grudgingly.

On her first visit to his house all she'd seen was bachelor muddle. But on subsequent visits when sober it had surprised her to see what was beneath that muddle, and it had surprised her even further to discover what unerring good taste Eddy had. Whether it was silver for the table, pictures for the wall or even material for curtains, Eddy had the knack of choosing whatever was just right. To begin with she'd thought there had to be another woman somewhere in the background. Even if only in an advisorial capacity. But no. Eddy chose and selected everything himself.

Eddy looked up from the novel he was reading – a Thomas Mann story he'd only recently come across – to say, 'Maybe someday, should I ever get married. But until then what's the point? I know and like the people roundabout, and what's more they know and like me. I feel at home in this area. If a wife and children come along sometime then I'm only too willing to review the situation. But until then I'm staying put.'

There was a basic honesty about Eddy which attracted Susan. So different to Kirk, who was completely the opposite – and yet Kirk had his qualities too. She sighed. Why was it women always fell for the bastards? It was a question she couldn't answer.

Eddy placed his book on his lap and put his clasped hands behind his head. He always felt so contented when he was with Susan, he reflected, her presence being enough to satisfy him.

'Do you mind us not going out and about more?' he asked.
'No.'
'We could if you wanted to. It's just . . . well I prefer being home, cosy with you.' Susan smiled as he went on, 'Listening to the radio, reading a book, even sitting doing nothing makes me feel so contented when you're there. Does that sound soft?'

'Terribly,' she mocked.

'No, be serious.'

'I enjoy just being with you too.'

'Do you, eh . . feel that way with Kirk?'

Her smile became wistful. 'Perhaps once. But that was before he met Ciona Crammon. Now he can be there but we're not together, if you know what I mean.'

'I know.'

She sat lost in her thoughts for a while and when she looked again in his direction it was to find he'd fallen asleep.

She took that as a compliment.

Kirk was aghast. 'What?' he exclaimed.

'I'm going to America. New York to be precise,' Ciona replied.

'But why?'

'You haven't been listening. I've been offered a job there in the office of one of London's top agencies. It's an enormous step up and an opportunity I'd be crazy to let slip by.'

'But I thought you wanted to stay in Glasgow?'

'Only when my parents were alive. But with them gone there's nothing to keep me here.' It was now four months since she'd buried her parents in the cemetery at Craigendoran, a small village just outside Helensburgh.

'Nothing to keep you here?' Kirk echoed. 'What about me?'

'We've had good times together . . .'

'I'd thought we'd get married one day.'

A look of feminine interest expressed itself on Ciona's face. 'You never mentioned it,' she replied. 'Anyway you already are married.'

457

'I could get a divorce. Scottish law being what it is, it would take a while mind you, but there's nothing to stop it happening and then you and I could wed.'

'I don't think so, Kirk,' Ciona said gently. 'You're a lovely man and we've had great times together. But I wouldn't marry you for all the tea in China.'

'Why not?'

'Various reasons, one being I could never trust you not to do to me what you've been doing to Susan. You're a born marital cheat. I doubt you could stay faithful if you tried.'

'That's just not true. It wouldn't be at all like that if you and I were married.'

'No?' she queried mockingly.

'For Heaven's sake Ciona, I love you!' he said imploringly.

'I think you probably do. For the time being, anyway. But how long would it last? Till the next piece of skirt came along that you fancied, I suspect.'

'You've got me all wrong!'

Ciona laughed. 'I doubt it.'

'Listen, I'll start divorce proceedings right away . . .'

'Do what you like. I'm still off to America. This is a chance in a lifetime and I'm grabbing it with both hands.'

'I just don't believe this!' Kirk said despairingly, running a hand through his hair. 'I thought you and I had something special going together. That we understood one another.'

'I understand you, all right. I always have.'

He pulled her into his arms. 'Please?' he pleaded. 'At least think it over. Consider marriage.'

'I already have and the answer is still that I'm going.'

Kirk sighed. 'God, I never realised how hard you are. I can see it now all right, though.'

Ciona laughed again. 'Me, hard? Isn't that a touch of the pot calling the kettle black?'

'Only in business. I've had to be.'

She shook her head. 'If you really believe that, then you've been kidding yourself all these years. Look at the way you've treated Susan. Well I'm certainly not going to put myself in

458

the position where you could treat me that way.'

'It would be different with you. I swear!'

'I don't believe you, Kirk. Oh, you might be faithful and loving for a little while but soon the old eye would begin to wander and before I knew where I was I'd be sitting home on my birthday while you were out gallivanting elsewhere with God knows who.'

'That's not fair. It was your parents that had died that night. You were in no fit state to drive yourself.'

'Yes, that was a little bit uncalled for,' Ciona admitted. 'Nonetheless, it's still true. But thank you all the same; I did need you desperately that night. You were a tower of strength.'

Kirk ground his teeth in frustration. He was going round and round in circles here and getting nowhere.

'Is it because I'm working-class and you're, well you're what you are?'

'That's got absolutely nothing to do with it.'

'You never introduced me to your parents when they were alive, nor have I ever met any of your friends from that background.'

'Kirk, you're a married man! What was I supposed to say? "Mummy and Daddy, I'd like you to meet Kirk, he's a married bloke I'm having an affair with"?'

'Well you wouldn't have had to put it like that.'

'What other way would I have put it? One minute after being introduced they would have started asking questions of you and me. And I was never in the habit of lying to my parents. By omission, yes. But not face to face. Besides, my father would have seen right through it. He would have known you were married. Don't ask me how. He would just have known. And as for my friends, the same thing applies. It never figured in my scheme of things that you and I would get married. You were just a nice man whom it was fun to be with, and that was that.'

'I see,' he said slowly.

'I'm genuinely sorry if you read more into it than that. I certainly never intended you to.'

They were in Ciona's flat. Kirk crossed to where the drinks were and poured himself a large one.

'Don't make it any more difficult than it has to be,' Ciona said.

'Is there someone else?'

'No.'

That mollified him a little.

'When do you go?' he asked.

'That hasn't been settled yet. But probably next month.'

'So soon?'

'They have a new campaign coming up they want me to work on.'

'Is it a permanent position or temporary?'

She shrugged. 'If things work out it could be permanent, should I want it that way. Then again I may decide after a while that I want to come back to Britain.'

'I'm going to miss you,' he said into his drink.

'You'll meet someone else. Or you could even start up again with your wife.'

'Do we continue seeing one another till you go?'

'Of course.'

'Are you sure I wouldn't be boring you?'

'You will do if you come out with nonsense like that.' Adding a few seconds later, 'Now how about some dinner? I'm starved.'

It was a cold bitter day with the wind howling off the sea.

Kirk shivered and pulled the collar of his coat up even higher. He wished he'd thought to wear a hat; he could certainly have used one.

A group of passengers emerged from the terminal to walk across to where a plane stood ready for flight. Even at this distance Ciona was easily discernible because of the distinctive fur coat she wore.

The coat had been his going-away present, albeit there was a side of him said she didn't deserve one.

The coat had cost him a small fortune. Perhaps he'd spent

that amount of money hoping it would cause her to change her mind and stay. But it hadn't and now she was on her way.

At the bottom of the steps leading up to the plane she stopped and turned to stare at the visitors' platform. She waved once. Then she mounted the steps and disappeared from view. And out of his life.

A few minutes later, the plane's propellers burst into life and shortly after that the plane itself was taxying down the runway. Once in the air it made a wide sweep round and over Prestwick. Then it headed out to sea, beyond which lay America.

Kirk stuffed his hands deep in his pockets and headed for the exit.

He felt terribly alone. And for some reason second-rate.

It was ten days since Ciona's departure and Kirk was randy in the extreme.

He let himself in through the front door and, having hung up his coat, went through to the drawing room where he found Susan reading a magazine.

Susan looked up in surprise. 'You're early again,' she said.

His reply was an indistinct mumble as he poured himself a drink.

'Like one?' he asked.

'Please. But make it small.'

Susan regarded him thoughtfully as he sank into his chair. He'd been positively melancholic for the past week, which was most unlike him. And that coupled with the fact he was coming home early night after night could only mean something was up. Ciona must be away on holiday, she thought. Or perhaps a business trip.

As though reading Susan's mind Kirk said suddenly, 'We've broken up, in case you've been wondering.'

'Pardon?'

'Ciona and I. I gave her the elbow.'

Susan didn't reply to that. Instead she dropped her gaze back to her magazine.

'Don't you want to know why?' he asked.

Susan didn't reply.

'Susan?'

'All right, why?'

'Because I'd come to realise what a bloody stupid fool I've been. She was an infatuation, that's all. In reality she meant nothing to me. Nothing at all.'

'It took you a long time to discover that.'

He pulled a face. 'So who's perfect? I certainly never claimed to be.'

'What's this leading up to, Kirk?'

'I want us . . . to be man and wife again.'

Susan smiled thinly. 'Do you think you can come to me and with one snap of your fingers have me running back to you again? God! What a low opinion you must have of me.'

'I have nothing but the highest opinion of you. Always had.'

'Well that wasn't the way it came over . . .'

'If you mean Ciona then I've explained that. It was an infatuation. It could've happened to anyone. But as I've just told you that's over now, for good. It's finished.'

'Bully for you.'

'If you're going to be unreasonable . . .'

'How do you expect me to be, after what I've been through? The lies, the deception, the degradation. Have you any idea at all what I felt like, knowing you were off sleeping with that . . . that woman? Night after night, sitting here with only the fire and a drink for company, knowing you were out with her, wining and dining her, taking her here, there and every bloody where, from all accounts? The laughter, the sniggers behind my back. That's Susan Murray, her husband Kirk is knocking off Ciona Crammond, you know, the beautiful advertising lady. Poor bitch. Yes, poor bloody bitch! And after all that, I'm supposed to forgive and forget all within the space of a few short seconds. Well I've got news for you. It isn't going to be like that. Now if you'll excuse me, good night.'

And throwing her magazine to one side she swept from the room.

Kirk gave her ten minutes and then followed her up to the bedroom where he found her sitting at her vanity table brushing her hair. She had already changed into her nightdress.

'I think I'll have a shower,' he said.

He stripped and went through to the shower where he spent a leisurely quarter of an hour under steaming hot water. When he finally towelled himself dry his entire body shone a healthy pink. He splashed talcum powder over himself and then liberally doused his face with after-shave, choosing a brand from amongst a number which he knew Susan was particularly fond of.

Returning to the bedroom he found her pretending to be asleep. Crossing to her side of the bed he sat. 'Susan?'

There was no reply.

'Susan?'

Again no reply.

He pulled the bedclothes down, then slipped his hand down the length of her back.

He smiled to himself when he heard her breathing change. He found her bottom and stroked it. Something she'd always liked in the past.

'Go away,' she hissed.

Languorously, he continued stroking, deeply sensual strokes that became wider and more probing.

'No Kirk,' she said, eyes still closed.

'Can't a man be allowed one mistake? It'll never happen again, I swear.'

'Go away.'

'I love you, Susan. Always have done. Always will do.'

'You're annoying me. And get your fingers out of there. That's private.'

'But I'm your husband.'

'You should have remembered that before you started screwing that tart.'

'Being with that tart, as you call her, has made me come to appreciate just how lucky I am to be married to you. She's fish and chips compared to your *filet mignon*.'

463

Fish and chips! he thought. Ciona would have loved that!

'Please Kirk. You're annoying me.'

'You still love me. I know you do.'

'Talk about ego! When it comes to that, you certainly take the cake.'

He brought his free hand down, through the covers she was clutching to her front, to a breast. He kneaded it gently, occasionally flicking her nipple with his pinky.

'I'm not going to tell you again to stop it,' said Susan.

'Come on, love.'

With an exclamation of annoyance she opened her eyes to stare at him. 'Take your hands off me this instant,' she said through gritted teeth.

His finger slipped inside causing her to suck in her breath. He lowered his mouth to kiss her neck.

He grunted with pain and astonishment as her nails raked his cheek. Her hooked hand flailed again but this time missed.

He pulled both hands free to hold his damaged face. Blood oozed through his fingers to fall to the covers.

'I mean what I say,' Susan hissed.

'Why you . . .'

Breath whooshed out of her as he forced her hands back into the bed. She brought her knee up but probably caused herself more pain than she inflicted on him when she came into contact with his thigh. Her eyes blazed with anger.

Letting go her hands he tore off the covers. Blood from his cheek splashed over her nightdress and one exposed breast.

'You won't . . . you won't . . .' she gasped as he tried to heave himself on top of her.

Her fists drummed against his chest. And when that proved to be no deterrent she lashed out again to rake his other cheek. Passion mingled with anger enveloped him then. Grasping her nightdress he ripped it, needing three goes before her naked length lay exposed beneath him.

She clawed his back, his neck, his sides, but it was no use. He was far too strong for her.

'You're my wife, damn you, and I love you,' he said, and,

forcing her arms back yet again, manoeuvred himself into such a position that he could go into her. This he did in a pile-driving, thrusting motion which instantly filled her to capacity.

For the first few seconds he was urgent, brutal, and then he got hold of himself and played her the way he had the very first time he'd made love to her. The fight melted from Susan in an overwhelming welter of sensations. For the truth was she still loved Kirk and had desperately wanted this to happen ever since he'd taken up again with Ciona Crammond.

Kirk was a master at lovemaking and he employed every nuance of technique and trick in his repertoire as he brought Susan thrilling to orgasm after orgasm after orgasm.

When, at long last, they finally fell into an exhausted sleep there was no doubt they were man and wife again.

'I see,' said Eddy.

Susan twisted her handbag in her hand as she stood facing him. 'I'm sorry, but that's the way it is.'

'And when did you two get back together then?'

'Last night.'

'Well, I suppose you know what you're doing.'

'I don't regret what happened between us. I'll always think of you kindly.'

'And I you. He's a lucky man. But then from what you've just told me it seems he's come to realise that.'

'I always knew that Ciona Crammond wasn't really for him. But he had to find that out for himself, I suppose.'

'And he gave her the push?'

'Yes,' smiled Susan.

I wonder? thought Eddy. I wonder?

'It was good of you to come and tell me like this. I appreciate that,' he said.

'What else could I do? Send you a note? That would have been absurd.'

Eddy came to her and took her in his arms. 'I'm pleased for you, Susan. I won't even pretend to like your husband. But if his being back with you makes you happy then I'm pleased that's the case.'

'I'll miss our evenings together. I enjoyed them.'

'Even if we didn't do all that much?'

'I seem to remember there were times we did quite a lot,' she teased.

Eddy laughed. 'If you put it that way, then yes we did.'

Suddenly he was excited and wanting her. He knew from the sudden startled look in her eyes she could tell.

'No, Eddy,' she said putting pressure on to break away.

'One last time, Susan?'

'It wouldn't be right.'

'One last time to remember you by. You won't deny me that, will you?'

One part of her was surprised that, under the circumstances, she wanted to go to bed with him. Another part wasn't.

Eddy's lovemaking was a completely different experience to Kirk's. Kirk's was mountains and troughs of wild, abandoned, ecstatic passion. Eddy's was cosy like the many nights they'd spent together.

'Come on, Susan, where's the harm?' he urged.

She was going to miss his safeness, she thought. The utter dependability that was him.

He saw she was weakening so drew her back close. Placing his mouth against hers he kissed her tenderly.

'All right,' she whispered. 'One last time.'

Hand in hand they made their way through to the bedroom.

'There's no doubt about it,' said Doctor Goldberg. 'You're thirteen weeks gone.'

There it was, the confirmation she'd so desperately been praying for.

Smiling, she nodded, a glint of moisture in her eyes. At long last, after all this time, they'd finally gone and done it.

Goldberg took out a stubby fountain pen and wrote on the

scrap pad in front of him. Tearing off the top sheet of paper he handed it across to her.

'Accordingly to the tests and the information you gave me, these are your dates.'

'Thank you,' she replied in an emotion-charged voice, accepting the sheet of paper.

'My receptionist will give you details of my ante-natal clinic and I shall expect to see you there regularly. In the meantime, if anything at all worries you, contact me and I shall be only too happy to answer any questions you might have.'

'You've been most kind, doctor.'

He smiled. 'That's what I'm here for.'

She rose, gathered herself together, thanked him again and then left the surgery.

After she was gone Goldberg's smile faded to become a hard look of speculation.

'Hmm!' he said, staring at the door. Then, 'Hmm!' again.

'No!' exclaimed Kirk.

'Yes!' she said.

'My God!' he roared, and catching her in his arms birled her round and round.

Suddenly he stopped, thinking what he was doing. This was stupid of him, dangerous. He set her down immediately.

'It's definite now?' he demanded.

'Thirteen weeks, according to Doctor Goldberg.'

'Which is more or less how long we've been back sleeping together. This calls for a drink! A celebration!' And capering on the spot, 'We're going to have a baby! We're going to have a baby!'

Susan stood rooted at the thought which had just struck her. Kirk was right. It was thirteen weeks since they'd been back together as man and wife. Thirteen weeks back, thirteen weeks pregnant. Could it possibly be that...? No, she told herself. No. And yet...

'A toast!' said Kirk, thrusting a glass into her hand and

disturbing her train of thought. 'To our child! My child!'

Smiling in a rather lopsided way, she drank.

A little later she made her excuses, saying she wanted a bath. Once upstairs she stripped and then sat on the bed in her dressing gown.

She racked her brains trying to remember the precise day she and Kirk had made up. And it had been the next one she'd slept with Eddy for the last time. So there was an overlap there. Then she recalled an engagement she'd had two days after Eddy, which meant she could be precise about both days in question. Hurrying to her vanity table, she opened a drawer and extracted the diary she kept there. Swiftly she leafed through its pages.

Her heart crowded into her mouth when she finally saw what she hadn't wanted to. According to her dates, the baby she was expecting could be either Kirk's or Eddy's.

'God!' she whispered, closing her eyes and hunching forward.

It was eleven o'clock that night and Susan had been asleep for well over an hour.

Kirk sat in his favourite chair with a bottle of whisky by his side. Three-quarters empty, the bottle had been full when he'd opened it.

His eyes were screwed up in concentration as he sipped his drink. Since Susan had gone to bed he'd had time to think properly, the initial euphoria having passed away.

A million to one chance, Goldberg had said. And now that one chance had come up. Or had it?

Of course the baby had to be his, he told himself. Susan just wasn't the type to have an affair. It wasn't in her. At least, so he'd always believed. But on the other hand, how well did he really know her? He would have said through and through, but was that really the case?

He shook his head. This endless speculation was getting him nowhere. He was looking a gift horse in the mouth. Against all odds he'd been given one more chance. He was going to have a family after all. And of course the child was his. Any other idea was ridiculous.

But no matter how hard he tried to convince himself there was still that worm of doubt wriggling at the back of his mind.

A million to one chance was awful long odds to come up. Awful long.

Keith beamed when Jean told him the news. 'A grandchild, a *grandson* at long last!' he said.

'There's no guarantee it'll be a boy,' said Jean hurriedly.

'Of course it'll be a boy. What else would it be? Boys run in the family, you know that. Our having Susan was a sheer fluke, the sort of thing that probably only happens every ten generations or so.'

Jean stared at her husband, thinking how ill he looked. He'd lost a great deal of weight and was now only a shadow of his former self. Bones showed clearly through his skin while his face had become so sunken it was like looking at a talking skull. She knew from having spoken to the doctor that he was being given whisky laced with morphine and cocaine twice daily. That was to deaden a little the terrible pain he was having to endure.

Keith's skeletal hand reached out to clasp hers. 'Six months to go, you say?'

She nodded.

'Then I'll have to see I hang on that length of time.' He gave a weak grin. 'For I'll be damned if I'll be pipped at the post now. I waited long enough for a son and then a grandson to be beaten by a few measly months.'

'That's the spirit, Keith.'

'A wee boy!' he said, his eyes lighting up. 'A wee boy at long last.'

Then suddenly, his grip digging into Jean's arm, he said, 'They wouldn't deny me seeing him, would they?'

'Not Susan. She'll bring him, I'm sure of it.'

'That's all right then,' Keith said, relaxing his head back on to his pillow.

469

Minutes later he was asleep, his mouth curled upwards in a smile. Jean knew he was dreaming about the grandchild that was on its way.

She left him to his slumber.

'The A.C.C. Crime wants to see you right away,' the voice on the phone said.

'Okay,' replied McIlwham and hung up.

He sat there for a moment or two staring straight ahead. There it was, the phone call he'd been dreading all this while. He'd been rumbled.

There was a leaden feeling in his stomach as he rose and made his way upstairs to the office of the Assistant Chief Constable, Crime. He took a deep breath before knocking.

'Come in,' the A.C.C.'s voice rapped out.

'You sent for me, sir?'

The A.C.C.'s face was a stone mask betraying not one flicker of emotion.

'Know what this about, Superintendent?' he asked.

'No sir,' McIlwham lied.

'You've been under investigation for some time now. And as a result of that investigation you are hereby suspended.' He paused. 'Any comment?'

'What am I supposed to have done, sir?'

'Accepting bribes from various parties.'

'May I know the names of these parties, sir?'

The A.C.C. rattled off three names and McIlwham knew he was sunk.

'I see, sir,' McIlwham replied.

'I'll need your warrant card, McIlwham, and have you any court appearances coming up?'

'Several, sir.'

'I'll arrange a replacement officer for those.'

McIlwham laid his warrant card on the desk in front of the A.C.C. 'Can I go now, sir?' he asked.

The A.C.C., his eyes never wavering from McIlwham's, nodded.

Without a further word McIlwham left the room.

The A.C.C.'s stone face cracked to display disgust and anger. Contemptuously he threw McIlwham's warrant card into a drawer.

On leaving the station, McIlwham went straight to a pub where he ordered himself a drink.

His thoughts were in a turmoil as he stared into his whisky. The good thing was the three names the A.C.C. had thrown at him were tiddlers. Sure, he'd accepted money from them but the amounts involved had been minimal. If he was charged on these three offences alone he couldn't possibly draw a heavy sentence. A year, eighteen months at the most, he figured. So it was to his advantage to keep his mouth shut about his dealings with Murray and the others he'd been helping. But they weren't to know that.

He'd already made an arrangement with Murray and one other. Now was the time to inform the remainder what was expected of them.

And who knew? Perhaps when he came out again one of them might be grateful enough to give him a job. Murray was his best bet there, he reckoned. He'd fancied running a pub on retirement, anyway.

Kirk threw the report he'd been studying down in anger. Another five outlets lost in the past month, three of them to Black Lion.

God damn you, Eddy King! he raged.

Rising abruptly, he strode to his window where he stood gazing out over Glasgow. Why in hell's teeth had McGhie gone and got himself killed? What a gut blow that had been to him. The mystery of Turk's death had never been solved. The police put it down to a revenge-motive gang killing.

Not that the police had tried all that hard to solve the mystery anyway, the truth being they didn't care who killed Turk. If they'd found the murderer they'd probably have given him a medal rather than charge him.

471

And, thinking of the police, he'd lost his contact there when McIlwham had been suspended. That was another bad loss; McIlwham had been useful in so many ways.

Well at least he didn't have anything to fear there. McIlwham was going to be charged on the three original counts, which meant, McIlwham having agreed to keep his trap shut, that Kirk's involvement with the bent Superintendent would be kept secret.

Eddy King, he thought bitterly. Everything had been going forward smoothly until that bastard had appeared to throw a spanner in the works. Staring out over Glasgow he saw nothing but Eddy's face. Despair and frustration welled in him. With the use of force currently ruled out, McIlwham's suspension being one of the main contributory factors to that, there just had to be another way to knock out Eddy and Black Lion. There just had to be.

Patience, he told himself. Patience, lad. The answer would come in time. Of that he had no doubt.

'Stop fussing!' exclaimed Susan. 'Honest to God, you're like an old mother hen.'

Kirk grinned. 'I just don't want you to be doing anything you shouldn't, that's all.'

'I'm pregnant, not an invalid, you know.'

'I just don't want you to take any chances.'

'I promise you, Kirk, I have absolutely no intention of doing anything that would cause harm to either myself or the baby. Give me credit for some sense.'

'I do.'

'You could have fooled me the way you've been carrying on these past few months. Honestly, you'd think I was the first woman ever to have a baby.'

He looked down at his hands and cleared his throat. The thing was he couldn't tell her just how precious this child was, not without explaining about Leoni von Kruppermann and the dose that bitch had given him, which he had no intention of doing.

472

This was his last chance to have a child. There would be no repeats.

'Just take it easy, that's all I ask,' he said.

Susan sighed and rolled her eyes to Heaven.

'How about a drink?' she asked a little later.

'Do you think that's a good idea so early in the evening?' he replied.

She sighed again.

'What I want is your confirmation this baby will be all right. That it won't be deformed in any way,' Kirk said.

'I take it you're worried because of what you contracted in the Army?' Doctor Goldberg asked.

Kirk nodded.

Goldberg made a pyramid with his hands and stared at Kirk. 'Providing you were cured out in Germany, as you say you were, then you've nothing to worry about. Damage to the baby can only come about if the male partner infects the female, who in turn passes it on to the unborn child.'

'Well that's a relief,' said Kirk smiling.

Goldberg went on, 'And as you're both still young the possibility of mongolism is extremely remote. So if I was you I'd put my mind at rest.'

At the door Kirk said, 'A chance in a million. Incredible that it came off, eh?'

'Yes, quite incredible,' replied Goldberg, smiling with his mouth, but not his eyes.

'Come on, Mr King, cheer up!' said Maisie, handing Eddy a drink. She was the barmaid he'd had a fling with before taking up with Susan. This was the first time he'd seen her since then.

The Christmas party was in full swing and it was obvious from the flushed faces and goings-on that the brewery employees were enjoying themselves. Eddy had decided to treat the staff, and some of the people from his pubs as well, because of all the hard work they'd put in over the year. He considered them a good, hard-working bunch and the party was a token of his appreciation.

'Here, put this on,' said Maisie. And before Eddy knew what was happening he was wearing a green pointed hat which had a gold star on its front.

'He looks like Noddy,' someone said, causing a roar of laughter to go up.

'Just you lot wait till Monday. I'll show you then who's Noddy!' Eddy said.

They all laughed again, knowing he didn't mean a word of it.

Patting his pockets, Eddy discovered he was out of cigarettes. Muttering excuses he made his way to his office where he knew he had a spare packet in his desk drawer.

He was about to light up when the door opened and Maisie slipped inside.

'It's getting a bit too much through there,' she said with a smile.

He lit two cigarettes and handed her one.

'Thank you,' she said throatily.

'Enjoying yourself?'

She nodded.

He suddenly felt ridiculous wearing the pointed hat so he removed it and sat it on the desk.

Maisie regarded him quizzically. 'Why did you stop seeing me, Eddy?' she asked, and when he didn't reply right away, 'Another woman?'

'Yes.'

'Serious?'

'We've broken up.'

'That doesn't answer the question.'

He blew smoke into the air, watching it spiral to the ceiling. 'I was very fond of her, if that's what you mean,' he replied.

Maisie came to him and put her arms round his neck. Drawing his head down to her she kissed him. The female in her didn't fail to note that part of him was holding back. It hadn't been like that the last time they'd kissed. But that had been before he'd met this other woman.

474

Breaking away, she made for the door, where she stopped. 'I think you should try and see her again,' she said. And smiling enigmatically, she left the room to rejoin the party.

After Maisie had gone, Eddy poured himself a whisky and then sat at his desk to drink it. He'd never imagined he'd miss Susan so much. But he did.

His relationship with her had been nothing like that with either Annie or Leoni. He'd loved both of them whereas with Susan he... he... he what?

As though a curtain in his mind had been suddenly drawn back the truth dawned on him. He'd come to *love* Susan. Perhaps he hadn't realised that was so because unlike the others, which had more or less hit him instantly, this had sort of sneaked up on him to catch him unawares.

He examined his feelings again. There was no doubt, and it only amazed him he hadn't realised before, he loved Susan Murray, Kirk's wife.

The biter bit, he thought ruefully. That drunken night he'd first slept with Susan, he'd intended using her as a card against Kirk. Instead of which the involvement had backfired in his face.

'What a balls-up!' he said into his drink. 'What a bloody balls-up!'

Every weekday afternoon a copy of the *Evening Times* was laid on Eddy's desk, which he'd glance through, providing he had the time, with his afternoon coffee.

That particular afternoon he had the time.

The news was unspectacular and sport was virtually non-existent. He read through the gossip section, called The Chit-Chat Column, which he rarely did.

The piece about Susan and Kirk was the fourth article. It stated that Mrs Susan Murray was expecting and that Mr Kirk Murray was overjoyed. There followed a brief story about Kirk and KM Brewery's meteoric rise and how Susan was the daughter of Major Keith Gibb, until recently the owner of Black Lion Brewery, KM's chief rival.

Eddy laid the paper down and pushed it away from him. Any thoughts he'd entertained, and he had given it quite a bit of consideration, of trying to win Susan back had just been blasted by that article. Now she was pregnant by Kirk she would want to stay with him. The baby would be the cement that would render whole again the cracks that had previously divided them.

Eddy shook his head. When it came to women it seemed the very Fates conspired against him. He wondered idly what he should do that night. He didn't want to go home to the house all on his own. Somehow since Susan had gone back to Kirk it had seemed a terribly lonely place to be. Prior to her coming into his life he hadn't minded being there on his own. Now he did.

He considered going to the pictures but there was nothing on he really fancied seeing. Nor did he want to go to a pub. He didn't want to fall into the same trap as Susan had for a while.

He would go to the theatre he decided, the Citizens'. It was a new season and Annie and Toby had gone, he'd previously checked on that.

He'd never seen Annie again after the night of the brewery fire. And he had the feeling he never would again.

He hoped she was happy. He just wished he could be.

'Mr Murray?'

Kirk looked up at the staff nurse who'd entered the waiting room where he'd been passing the time doing some paper work.

He came to his feet, papers clutched in his hand. 'Yes?' he demanded eagerly.

'You've got a wee girl.'

For a split second he was disappointed but he brushed that aside. 'Is she healthy? I mean, is everything as it should be?'

The staff nurse smiled. 'She's absolutely perfect, Mr Murray,' she replied.

Relief flashed through Kirk. Despite Goldberg's assurances

it had preyed at the back of his mind that something would be wrong with the baby.

'Your wife's also fine,' the staff nurse went on. 'Tired, of course, but that's only to be expected.'

'When can I see them?'

'They're cleaning the baby up now and also sorting your wife out. Fresh nightie, a bit of a wash, that sort of thing. I should think they'll let you in in about fifteen minutes.'

Kirk gave a combination nod and smile and sat. A wee girl. Well as long as she was healthy, that was the main thing.

In fact in a way he'd been hoping it would be a lassie. He knew via Susan just how much the Major was longing for a grandson.

Well, even at the last the old fart would be denied.

'A girl,' said Keith hollowly. He just couldn't believe it. He'd been so positive it would be a boy.

'A bonnie wee lassie,' said Jean encouragingly. 'I've seen her. And you know I think she's the spitting image of you.' That last was a lie, dreamed up as a consolation prize to try and take the edge off his disappointment. But it didn't work.

'Gerald had two boys and so had my father,' Keith said, his voice sounding as though it came from a long distance away. 'Boys run in the family.'

'Maybe they'll have a boy next time.'

'I won't be here to see it though.'

'Of course you will, Keith. You're tough as old boots. You've a lot of life left in you yet.'

He closed his eyes and sighed. The spark that had been keeping him going since learning of Susan's pregnancy died within him. Already shrivelled, he seemed to shrivel even more.

'I'd like to sleep now,' he said. 'So tired.'

Jean leant across to kiss him on the cheek. 'I'll be back tomorrow morning,' she said.

'Aye,' he breathed, the sound like a wind going out of him.

When she was gone he turned his head to the wall. In his mind he was young and back in India. Such good days, such marvellous times, he thought. And there was Jean just as he'd first seen her. Velvet nights, twinkling stars overhead, warm scented smells that belonged to India and India alone.

His one regret was he'd never had a son. If only ... if only ...

In the early pre-dawn hours of the morning when all human life is at its lowest ebb, he passed away.

The instant before he went he muttered one word. 'Gerald,' he whispered. Then he was gone.

Susan sat nursing the baby at her breast. Rachel, she'd decided to call the wee thing. It wasn't a name that had connections with either Kirk's family or her own. It was merely one she liked and which she thought suited her daughter.

Her daughter, yes – but certainly not Kirk's. For Rachel was the spitting image of Eddy.

She'd known the instant she'd clapped eyes on Rachel who her father was. The resemblance was remarkable. The same eyes, the same look about the face, the same shape of the head.

Rachel bawled lustily as Susan removed her from the now empty breast, and continued bawling while she did up the front of that bra cup and undid the other. The bawling only ceased when the tiny mouth fastened like a leach on to her other nipple.

Susan crooned as the baby fed. For the umpteenth time she told herself there was no reason for Kirk ever to find out he wasn't Rachel's father. After all it was quite common for children not to look like either parent. Her mother's side she would say, should it ever come up.

Yes, her mother's side of the family. That was the answer.

McIlwham felt as though he'd been struck by a sledge-hammer. He sagged a little as the judge's words echoed in his ears.

'... this terrible corruption in our police force ... must be stamped out ... intend to impose the maximum sentence I am

llowed under the circumstances ... officers must realise they
are not above the law ... betrayal of trust ... of colleagues and
the community at large ... hereby sentence you ... Ronald
Alan Forbes McIlwham to five years ... five years ... five
years ...

The number repeated itself over and over again in
McIlwham's head. Five years! When he'd been expecting no
more than a year, eighteen months at the very most.

In a daze, the court swimming before him, he was led away,
downstairs to the cells, from where he would be taken by Black
Maria to start his sentence.

'Strip!' shouted the warder. 'Put your clothes in the basket
provided and then queue up by the door here. And hurry up,
get a move on. I haven't got all day!'

There were six of them that had come in the Black Maria to
Barlinne Prison. From what McIlwham had gleaned during
the journey, he was the only first-time offender. He shivered
as he took off his clothes. It was freezing in the room. When he
was naked he walked to the door indicated, where he stood
clutching his basket.

When all six were ready, the warder opened the door and
shouted at them to go on through. They found themselves in
another room, this one divided by a counter behind which
stood several trusty prisoners. There were also two other
warders present to keep an eye on things.

'Baskets on the counter!' shouted the original warder.

The trusties went along the line, going through each basket
and writing what it contained on an official form. When each
item had been detailed the new prisoner was asked if he agreed
with the itemisation, and on saying he did the new prisoner
was asked to sign the form, after which the basket was taken
away.

The next part of the procedure was their being issued with
their prison outfits, moleskins as they were referred to.
McIlwham was handed a well-worn corduroy jacket and
trousers which didn't match in colour, being different shades

of brown. After these he was given a singlet, underpants and boots with no laces. There were no socks.

One of the new prisoners started to put the underpants on which proved to be a mistake as he soon found out.

'*Not yet*, you stupid man!' a warder screamed. 'We don' want your filthy bodies in our clean clothes. Wait until you've had your bath.'

The prisoner hastily removed the underpants, wilting unde the warder's fierce gaze.

Christ, what have I let myself in for? McIlwham thought He'd have given his eye-teeth to be back in his comfy hom with his equally comfy wife... Get a grip of yourself, h chided himself. You'll soon settle in and get used to it. But i was a grim prospect.

'This way!' shouted the original warder, when the six new prisoners had collected their new clothes. The trusties looke on unsympathetically.

McIlwham and his five companions were herded along corridor into a bathroom comprising many stalls. The wate had already been run in six of the baths. In each case it was n more than six inches in depth and smelled strongly o disinfectant. The soap they were issued was carbolic. The were allowed ten minutes in the bath and then they wer ordered to get out and dry themselves. The towels were lik sandpaper.

McIlwham climbed into his moleskins and then, sitting o the edge of the bath, tugged on his laceless boots. When th order came he shuffled off with the rest of them down to th cell block where he was put in a cell with two other men.

In the days to come he reached the conclusion that the wors thing of all about being inside was, when he and his cell mate were locked away for the night, the utter degradation of havin, to use the toilet situated in one corner of the cell in full view o the others.

The second worst thing was the smell. A fetid combinatio of stale sweat, urine, excrement, unhealthy bodies – an perhaps even unhealthy minds – mingled with the sauce of fea nd hopelessness. The stink was everywhere and indeed eemed to be impregnated into the very brickwork itself.

McIlwham was put to work sewing heavy canvas mailbags or the Royal Mail.

On her second day out of hospital Susan went to her father's uneral, which had been delayed so she could attend.

Kirk hadn't come, of course. Nor had she expected him to. nstead he'd taken a few hours off his work to stay at home and ook after the baby. She had suggested getting someone in for he short babysitting session but he'd insisted he do it ersonally. She'd been touched by that.

It was a small funeral, the Major not having had many riends. Susan stood with her mother, who right at the very eginning of the ceremony broke down and cried. In her heart he didn't think her mother would be long behind her father. They'd been that sort of couple.

While the minister droned on about the resurrection to ome, Eddy kept his eyes fastened on Susan. He knew she was ware he was watching her. She looked good, he thought. She vas carrying a bit more weight than normal but that was only atural under the circumstances. Her face still held the bloom f motherhood. He guessed correctly it had been a happy regnancy for her.

Jean Gibb threw a handful of earth on to the coffin, followed y Susan as second mourner.

The ceremony over, everyone started trooping towards heir cars parked outside the cemetery walls. Jean and Susan vere with several other people so Eddy didn't feel too guilty bout taking her away from her mother for a moment or two.

'Susan? Can you speak for a second?'

'It was good of you to come, Eddy,' she said, joining him.

'Not at all. I owed your father a lot, as you know.'

'You look well.'

'I was just thinking the same about you back there. And ongratulations, I believe they're in order. Rachel, isn't it?'

'That's right.'

'I read about the birth in the paper. I'm happy for you. Is Kirk pleased?'

She thought that might be some sort of dig or insinuation but searching his face she saw it wasn't so. It hadn't occurred to him Rachel might be his. That was a relief.

'Very. He thinks the world of her.'

'And what about you? Happy?' he asked softly.

'Extremely.'

'No regrets?'

'About what?'

He smiled. 'No regrets,' he said, answering his own question.

'Are *you* happy?' she asked.

'Oh yes,' he lied.

'That's good, then.'

Suddenly it was awkward between them. He smiled falsely while she played with her hands. Overhead, crows cawed forlornly.

'I'd better get back to Mother,' she said.

Eddy nodded. 'Good luck then.'

'And you.'

On a sudden impulse she kissed him on the cheek. 'Take care.'

He strode away from her in the direction of his car. A three time loser, he thought bitterly. It seemed he would never win where women were concerned.

Kirk had had very good reasons for volunteering to babysit while Susan went to her father's funeral.

The baby had been fed and was fast asleep in her crib. He sat reading a newspaper, patiently waiting. He rose the instant the doorbell went.

'Come in Doctor Aitken,' he said. 'You're nice and prompt.'

Aitken looked around, blinking. He carried a small black bag in his right hand.

'The child's upstairs,' said Kirk, and led the way to the baby's bedroom.

Aitken didn't ask questions. He just got on with what he'd come to do. From his black bag he extracted a syringe. 'Could you bare her arm, please?' he said.

Kirk gingerly picked up Rachel, who immediately awoke. She smiled up at him, eyes wide, trusting. He didn't find it easy but eventually he managed to roll up her sleeve. He thought how tiny her arm looked. No bigger than a doll's. He grimaced as the needle slid in. The moment it did, Rachel started squawling and trying to pull away. On Aitken's instruction he held her more tightly.

'There we are,' said Aitken, when the syringe was about half-full. He pulled the needle out and rubbed the spot with some impregnated cotton wool.

Rachel was really bawling now, so Kirk held her close and crooned a lullaby he remembered from his mother's knee.

'When can you let me know the results?' he asked.

'Usually takes about a week. But if you're in a hurry I can have it rushed through. That'll cost you a few pounds extra, though. Not for me but for the hospital.'

'Hurry it through.'

'Right. I'll probably have the results tomorrow afternoon then.'

'You know my number at work. Ring me there.'

While Kirk tried to settle Rachel again, Aitken let himself out.

True to his word, Aitken rang Kirk the following afternoon at KM Brewery.

'Your baby has B-type blood,' Aitken said.

'Thank you, doctor,' Kirk replied and hung up.

He stared at the phone for a few seconds before taking a book from his desk drawer which he opened at a marked place. He'd got the book from the library and had already read the relevant sections. He didn't have to read the page again to know what he'd feared was in fact reality. He read it nonetheless.

When he'd finished he ran his fingers through his hair and

stared off into space. His normally good complexion had gone pale and there was a small red anger spot on either cheek.

His intercom buzzed but he ignored it. His secretary popped her head round the door. When she saw the expression on his face she hurriedly closed it again.

Finally Kirk rose and crossed to the drinks cabinet where he poured himself a stiff whisky. He drank it neat, then poured himself another.

'Oh, you bitch!' he muttered.

Susan looked up as the outside door closed. Kirk was later than usual. An infrequent occurrence now that Ciona Crammond was out of his life.

He stumbled into the room. His face was flushed and hair awry. There was a terrible expression on his face and his eyes positively glittered with a combination of anger and other emotions. He made straight for the drinks and poured himself a whisky. He'd been drinking steadily since the afternoon, when Aitken had rung.

'What's all this about?' Susan asked.

He turned to face her, a vicious slash of a smile twisting his mouth upwards as he swayed on the spot.

'Look at the state of you,' she said.

'Who's the brat's father?' he demanded harshly, coming straight to the point.

Susan was taken aback. 'I beg your pardon?'

He lurched across to her and leered in her face. 'Who's the brat's father?' he repeated.

'Which brat?'

'The one, I presume, who's upstairs in bed.'

A cold wind washed over Susan. She decided to try and bluff it out. 'If you mean Rachel, you're her father,' she replied.

Kirk shook his head. 'No I'm not.'

'Of course you are. What makes you think otherwise?'

He slurped whisky into his mouth, spilling some of it in the process, which stained his shirt front.

'You see there's something you don't know about me,' he slurred. 'Something I only found out when I went to see, at your suggestion, Doctor Goldberg. Remember?'

Susan nodded.

'He took what's known as a sperm-count and it was found that my count was nine thousand which is one thousand less than fertility level. In his own words, it would be a chance in a million for me to father a child.'

'Why didn't you tell me this before?' Susan asked quietly.

'I had my reasons. Not least of which was pride, the pride of masculinity. After all, what man wouldn't find shame in the fact he was sterile?'

'But you said there was a million to one chance? That means you're not completely sterile, surely?'

'Precisely what I clung to. Especially when you announced you were pregnant. The long shot has come off, I thought. The one in a million chance has come up. Aren't I the lucky man!'

'So what's made you change your mind?'

He poured himself another drink. Everything was getting very fuzzy around the edges now. And although he didn't realise it he was swaying even more than he had been.

'I wanted that baby to be mine. I desperately wanted it. But being the naturally suspicious bugger I am, I decided to make absolutely certain I was the father. Well, not absolutely certain, I couldn't do that, but what I could establish was I *could* be the father.'

This was a nightmare, Susan thought. 'Go on,' she said.

'So I had a blood test done on Rachel and guess what?'

'What?'

'Well let me put it this way. I'm an A blood-group, I know that from the Army. And you're also A, I know that from looking at your chart at the hospital. There it was, quite distinct, A blood-group. Which brings us to Rachel, your daughter but certainly not mine. She's B, you see. And according to the medical books A plus A can never equal B. Therefore I cannot be her father.'

Susan bit her lip and lowered her gaze. Her heart was pumping nineteen to the dozen.

'So,' said Kirk, 'that brings me back to my original question. Who *is* the brat's father?'

Susan shook her head.

He grabbed her by the shoulder and shook her. 'Tell me, woman! I want to know.'

'It's unimportant.'

'Not to me it's not!'

She decided attack might be her best form of defence. 'Anyway, what right have you to go on like this? You, who had an affair with that advertising tart.'

'Shut up about her,' he snarled.

She continued vehemently, 'I'm supposed to turn a blind eye and keep my mouth shut while you go out whoring night after night, but let me give you back a little of your own medicine and look at you! Nearly beside yourself with righteous indignation.'

'You were trying to pass the brat off as mine. Can't you see that's different?'

'If you're as sterile as you say you are, then we'd probably never have had a child. Be thankful that we've got this one.'

'Thankful!' he barked. 'You just don't understand, do you!'

'I understand that we both wanted a baby and now we've got one.'

'But she isn't *mine*! What good's a child to me who isn't mine?'

'She *is* mine. Doesn't that mean anything to you?'

He dismissed that with a drunken wave of his hand. 'Are you still seeing the father?' he asked.

'No.'

'I don't believe you.'

'Don't judge others by yourself. I don't lie.'

'You did about her upstairs.'

Susan had no answer to that.

'A bloody cuckoo in the nest. Who would ever have thought

486

that would happen to me?' he slurred. Then suddenly, like a volcano erupting, '*Fuck!*'

Susan rocked back in her chair. And for the first time fear took hold of her. She stared mesmerised at his contorted face which seemed as though it must surely explode from within.

'Who?' he choked, stumbling to her and taking hold of her dress. 'Who?'

She shook her head.

'Who was it, damn you?'

Thank God Rachel's safe upstairs, she thought, a second later crying out as his hand cracked against her cheek.

A berserk rage swamped him then. His hand flashed again and again knocking her head left and right, left and right. Her lip burst and blood spurted over her chin and his hand. His watch caught her cheek, ripping it open.

'Tell me!' he screamed.

And when he still got no reply he threw her to the ground where he started putting the boot in.

Susan retched and was sick as his foot thudded into her stomach. The pain exploding inside her was unbelievable in its intensity. On her hands and knees she tried to crawl away through the sick but she collapsed again when his foot smashed into her ribcage, causing a cracking sound.

Falling to the floor Kirk grabbed her by the front of her dress and pulling her into a half-sitting position proceeded to shake her as a dog would a rat.

'Who? ... who? ... who? ...' he repeated over and over again.

He's going to kill me, she thought. And her only regret was Rachel. For the wee one's sake she must somehow survive this terrible beating. Please God! Please! she prayed. For the baby's sake.

She was still praying when unconsciousness suddenly took her into its bosom.

Kirk came to his senses kneeling over her prostrate figure. For a stunned moment or two he thought he'd killed her, but a quick feel in the appropriate place told him her heart was still beating. Although a long way from being sober the events of the past few minutes had burned a great deal of the alcohol from his system. Coming to his feet, he staggered to the telephone. Susan had to have medical treatment. That was obvious. And as he dialled 999 he made up his story. After being told the ambulance was on its way he stumbled upstairs to their bedroom from where he got a quilt which he used to cover her.

She looked dreadful, both eyes already discolouring and her cheeks puffing up like pastry. Her lip was still seeping blood but the blood on the torn cheek had coagulated to form a long lumpy maroon line.

Going through to the downstairs bathroom he doused his face with cold water after which he combed his hair. He was getting more sober and regaining his composure by the second.

Susan started to moan. Her hands clutching her stomach while she slowly writhed.

'Help's on its way,' he said, kneeling beside her. He was appalled at what he'd done. He'd intended giving her a beating but nothing like this.

'Can you hear me, Susan?' he asked. And when he got no reply he repeated himself. 'Can you hear me?'

When he still failed to get a reply he put his hand on her arm and shook her very gently. 'Susan?'

She stopped writhing and blinked her eyes open. They were like two currants sunk deep in still swelling blue-black dough.

'I'm sorry,' he said. 'Truly I am.'

She opened her mouth but no words came. Only some pink spittle which slowly meandered down to her chin.

'I didn't mean it. I didn't know what I was doing. Please, please believe that,' he pleaded.

'So sore,' she whispered.

'They'll give you something for the pain and then everything will be all right. But listen, love, you mustn't tell them I did this to you. They could put me inside for assault and battery. Do you understand?'

'Yes,' she croaked.

'I'll say you were upstairs with the baby and came downstairs to disturb an intruder. He panicked and beat you up before fleeing. When I came home I found you like this. Now is that clear?' And he went over it all again.

As he spoke her eyes were on him, probing him, staring at him as though she'd never really seen him before. He wilted under her gaze, unable to look her in the eye. It was a relief when the doorbell rang and he was able to come to his feet.

'Now don't forget the story,' he said, before hurrying to the door.

There were two ambulancemen, one of whom carried a stretcher. Kirk showed them straight through. One man prodded Susan gently all over and while he did Kirk told the lie about having come home and found her this way and how she'd muttered to him about coming down and surprising an intruder.

'A couple of broken ribs, I think,' said the ambulanceman who'd carried out the examination.

'If I ever catch the swine who did this to her, so help me God I'll murder him,' Kirk said.

Despite being as careful and gentle as they could, Susan cried out in pain as she was being lifted on to the stretcher.

'My baby,' she husked. 'I won't go without my baby. She mustn't stay here.'

The second ambulanceman looked strangely at Kirk then. 'Where is the baby, missus?' he asked.

'She's upstairs,' Kirk replied before Susan could. 'I'll get her.'

'Best wrap her up well. It's cold outside,' the first ambulanceman said.

'Won't go without her. Won't,' Susan repeated.

'Don't you worry, lass. We'll take the wean along,' the second ambulanceman said.

At the top of the stairs Kirk started shaking. He hurried through to the baby's room, picking Rachel up and wrapping her in the warm blankets that had been covering her. Rachel

489

awoke and started to cry. A thin, tremulous wailing sound that, to Kirk's ears anyway, seemed to say she was aware all wasn't well with her mother. Clutching Rachel to him he hurried back downstairs.

Susan insisted on taking the baby, whom she hugged tightly to her bosom. Tears oozed from her eyes to fall coursing down swollen cheeks.

The ambulancemen covered mother and daughter with a red blanket before lifting them and taking them outside to the ambulance.

'I'll follow in my car,' shouted Kirk, locking the front door.

He winced and his stomach turned over when the ambulance's siren started up.

Kirk sat with his head in his hands. He'd been in the hospital waiting room over an hour and a half now. All he'd been told so far was that Susan was being attended to and that a policeman was interviewing her about what had happened.

There were about twenty in the Accident and Emergency waiting room and nurses and doctors came and went constantly.

'Mr Murray?'

Kirk looked up to find a very young nurse smiling at him.

'If you'd like to come with me you can see your wife now.'

He followed her down a corridor and into a lift.

They rode the lift up to the private wing where, on his instructions, Susan had been installed in a room with bathroom attached. He found her alone staring at the ceiling. The colour surrounding her eyes had deepened to a rich purple. The rips on her cheek and lip had been neatly sutured. She was a ghastly sight.

'How are you?' he asked when the nurse had gone.

There was no reply.

Licking his lips he moved closer to the bed. 'I, eh ... was told a policeman had been to see you.'

Still no reply.

He'd started to sweat under the arms and down his back.

'Did you say anything?' he asked.

'They've taken Rachel away to check her over. I told them she was all right but they wanted to make sure.'

He nodded.

'She cried all the time they were stitching me up. It was just the strangeness of the place, I think.'

'How long before you ... you get home?'

'A week at least they say. Maybe ten days.'

'I really am truly sorry, Susan. But finding out about Rachel was such a shock. You see I've come to love her since you brought her home. And then to find out she wasn't mine at all ... it was one helluva blow. I just went out my mind.'

He paused before continuing. 'I've always thought of you as a far better, more worthwhile person than myself. I never ever conceived of you having an affair. You were too good a person for that in my mind. For you to cheat would be like finding out there was no God after all or something equally as shattering. I'm not denying I was initially attracted to Ciona Crammond but the fact I did something about it was because I'd just learned I was sterile. Can you imagine what it was like to be told that?'

'You should have confided in me.'

'I should have done but I didn't. What I did do was go out and prove to myself that I was still a man. Because that's all going to bed with Ciona was. A reaction against my sterility. And then when you told me you were pregnant I was over the moon. We were to have a family after all and that meant so much to me. The shock of learning Rachel wasn't mine was traumatic, to say the least. To be truthful, I came home intending to hurt you because you'd hurt me. But I never meant it to be as bad as this. Please ... please forgive me? Please?'

The hardness she felt towards him melted. She'd sinned as much as being sinned against. There was fault on both sides. Her hand crept out from beneath the covers to lie on top of them. She extended her hand palm upwards in a gesture of invitation. He sat on her bed and took her hand in his. There was moisture in his eyes when he said, 'We'll start again.'

'The three of us?'

'As you said, Rachel's part you and I'll continue loving her for that part.'

'Thank you,' Susan whispered.

'I have to ask, what did you tell the policeman?'

She smiled. 'What you told me to say. That I came downstairs and disturbed an intruder. He panicked and beat me up. I was asked for a description but I said it was all very hazy. All I remembered was there had been a man. Short, fat, tall or whatever I couldn't say. The next thing I really knew was waking up and finding you kneeling by my side.'

'You're marvellous,' Kirk said. And kissed her on the cheek that wasn't stitched.

'You'd better go now. I'm awfully tired.'

'I'll be back tomorrow morning,' he said, rising. 'And if there's anything you want, ask them to get it for you. Or if they can't, get word to me at the brewery and I'll get hold of it.'

'I feel a lot better already,' she said.

He blew her a kiss at the door.

Eddy had taken to frequenting a Black Lion pub just round the corner from Albion Street, where he was fond of talking to many of the journalists who used it as a watering hole cum second office.

He found the company of these men stimulating, learning a great deal about the world at large from what they had to say. In a way the journalists reminded him of the actor knight who'd impressed him so much when he'd been in London. They had the same spirit of adventure and excitement about them. The same surging life force.

Eddy was just ordering up a pint when a journalist called Dougie Mitchell, whom he'd become particularly friendly with, came through the door.

'Better make that two pints,' said Eddy to the barman as Mitchell joined him.

'So what's happening amongst Mungo's children tonight?' he asked.

Mitchell shook his head. 'Very quiet. A stabbing in Jamaica Street, a bird giving her boyfriend a sherricking outside the Dennistoun Palais, a couple of half-cut eejits trying to break into a bonded warehouse just off St Enoch Square, none of which is likely to make page two, far less page one.'

The pints came up and Eddy paid.

They talked for a few more minutes about this and that, then Mitchell said, 'Your big rival's wife got a right duffing-up the other night. She surprised an intruder, who gave her a proper going-over.'

Eddy frowned. 'You mean Kirk Murray's wife?'

'Aye, the same.'

'Is she badly hurt?'

'A couple of broken ribs. A face like she's just gone twelve rounds with Rocky Marciano. Myself and a few of the boys went to see her, thinking there might be a story in it, but according to her, her mind's a blank about what actually happened. The *Express* and the *Herald* gave it a couple of lines; my paper didn't.'

'When did you say this happened?'

'Three nights ago. We saw her the following day.'

Three nights ago meant it had happened the day after her father's funeral, Eddy thought. The day after he'd last seen her.

'Have they kept her in hospital, do you know?'

'Oh, I'd think so. She was in a pretty bad way.'

Eddy tried not to let too much interest show in either his face or voice. 'Poor woman,' he said. 'Knowing where Murray lives, I suppose they took her to the Western Infirmary?'

Mitchell nodded as he drank his pint.

'She'll be all right there. It's a good hospital that,' said Eddy. And promptly changed the subject.

Eddy sat on one of the several chairs provided with a newspaper held in front of him. He'd been there for half an hour waiting for Kirk to leave. He knew Kirk was with Susan, having seen him when he'd briefly glanced through the small glass panel on Susan's door.

Visiting time was almost up and he was beginning to think he'd have to go away and try again another time, when suddenly the door to Susan's room opened and Kirk emerged.

Immediately Eddy buried his head in the paper from which place of concealment he listened to Kirk's approaching footsteps. Stopping at the lift Kirk pressed the down button. When he glanced in Eddy's direction all he saw were feet and legs projecting from underneath a newspaper. When the lift arrived he stepped inside and seconds later was plunging downwards.

Eddy waited till the floor numbers above the lift confirmed that it had reached the ground floor before turning and making his way to Susan's room.

He tapped the door and entered.

'I hope you don't mind, Susan, but I ...' The rest of the sentence died in his mouth when she turned to face him. 'Jesus Christ!' he exclaimed.

She grinned ruefully. 'Not a pretty sight.'

'You can say that again.'

Susan was feeding Rachel, who was twisting both hands in the air while sucking lustily.

'Kirk's just gone,' she said.

'I know. I was lurking outside waiting for him to go. I wanted to see you but I didn't want to cause any friction. That's why I didn't bring you anything. I thought you might have trouble explaining away a bunch of flowers or a bowl of grapes that hadn't come from him.'

Eddy glanced around but there were no flowers in the room. Evidently Kirk wasn't the flower-buying type. At least not as far as his wife was concerned.

'An intruder, I was told,' he said.

'That's right.'

Eddy shook his head. 'Bastard to do that to you.'

Susan dropped her gaze to stare at the baby.

'So this is the young lady,' Eddy said, coming closer and peering at the suckling Rachel.

A few seconds later, Susan removed Rachel from her breast and adjusted her nightdress. She then put Rachel to her shoulder in order to wind her.

'I find this bit difficult because of my broken ribs,' she said.

'Here let me,' said Eddy and took the baby into his arms.

Rachel stuck out her tongue and smiled at him. She smelled very strongly of milk and powder. Eddy gathered her to his shoulder and gently patted her back.

'You look like you've been doing that all your life,' said Susan.

'Hidden talents,' he smiled back.

The smile died when the door opened and Kirk marched in.

'Forgot my brief-case ...' said Kirk, the last two words hanging suspended in the air when he caught sight of Eddy.

'What are *you* doing here?' he demanded.

Eddy's mind raced, trying to think up an explanation. Susan sat speechless.

'I think I know,' Kirk said slowly.

'Kirk ...' Susan started to say.

'Shut up!' he hissed.

Kirk looked at Rachel's face, then at Eddy's, then back again at Rachel's.

'So it was *you*,' he said in a choked tone of voice.

'What are you talking about?' Eddy said.

'You're the baby's father.'

Eddy was thunderstruck. That possibility had never even entered his head.

'It's obvious,' said Kirk. 'I don't know why I didn't see it before. Rachel's the spitting image of you.'

Eddy held the baby from him and stared hard at her face. Kirk was right. She did look like him. And in fact, now he'd been told, the more he looked at her the more he saw the resemblance.

'No wonder you wouldn't tell me who the father was,' Kirk

said to Susan. 'Of all people to choose, it had to be him. You bitch!'

Susan cowered away from his anger. 'Don't hit me again, please,' she pleaded.

Eddy sucked in a breath. 'What does that mean?' he demanded.

'No,' said Susan, shaking her head.

Eddy swung round on Kirk. 'Did you ... was it *you* did that to her?'

Kirk glared at Eddy.

'Oh, you bastard.'

'Give me that child,' said Kirk, a vicious smile on his face.

'You just said she's mine.'

'She is. But she carries my name and as such is my daughter.'

Eddy's grip on Rachel tightened. His mind was whirling. The revelations of the last few minutes had left him not knowing whether he was coming or going.

'Is the baby mine?' Eddy asked Susan.

'Yes,' she whispered.

There it was. Confirmation of the obvious.

'But you'll never have her,' taunted Kirk. 'I will. And by God, that's something that's going to eat your guts out for the rest of your life.'

Eddy wanted to put the baby down and go for Kirk. To hammer him. To do what he should have done years ago. But somehow, and the effort plainly showed on his face, he brought himself under control.

'Please go, Eddy, before matters get worse,' said Susan.

'Give me the baby,' said Kirk, extending his hands.

Eddy couldn't bear the thought of Kirk bringing up his child. If he could beat Susan up the way he had then what might he do to Rachel? The very thought caused Eddy to shudder.

'I'm waiting,' said Kirk.

Eddy felt then that his entire life had been in preparation for this moment. Annie Grimes, Leoni von Kruppermann, even Gloag.

'Divorce Susan so I can marry her,' he said.

Kirk's smile was that of the shark. 'Get stuffed,' he leered.

'You don't love Susan. The only person you've ever cared about in your entire life is yourself. And perhaps your mother, although she'd rank a poor second.'

'Watch your mouth, King.'

'I should have sorted you out in Germany.'

'Just because you couldn't hold your woman that's no reason to start whining now.'

'What woman?' asked Susan quietly.

'The Countess von Kruppermann,' said Eddy. 'She was my girlfriend until your husband took her away from me. He found the thought of screwing a title irresistible.'

'Kirk?'

Kirk swallowed, at the same time glaring hate at Eddy. 'She meant nothing to me,' he said.

'But you slept with her?'

'Yes.'

Susan sagged a little. 'And us only newly married. But knowing you now as I do I suppose I shouldn't be surprised. I was a fool to think you'd remain faithful for two years. Two weeks would be stretching it.'

Rachel pawed at Eddy's lapel. His heart went out to the wee lassie, this extension of himself. That thought brought a lump to his throat.

'Tell me,' said Susan to Kirk, 'how many other women are there that I don't know about?'

'None. I swear.'

She regarded him steadily, obviously thinking he was lying.

'There's only been Leoni and Ciona ...'

'Leoni?'

'The countess. No one else. You have my word on that.'

Susan lay back on her pillow, her expression still disbelieving. She'd had Kirk's word too many times before.

497

'And why did you choose my wife to have an affair with, King? Pure coincidence?'

'Are you thinking I was trying to get back at you because of Leoni?'

'The thought had crossed my mind.'

'Eddy?' said Susan when Eddy didn't reply straight away. The word came out a pitying plea.

Eddy knew he'd have to tell the truth. 'When I first ... when we first ... the night Susan and I ...'

'Oh my God!' she said, burying her face in the pillow.

Eddy moved close beside her, the baby between them. 'Susan, that was in my mind that first night. I was going to sleep with you and then see Kirk got to hear about it. But I couldn't do it. I liked you too much, and then later it became more than that.' He paused before adding, 'I fell in love with you.'

Kirk barked out a laugh. 'You're breaking my heart,' he said scornfully.

Susan cried into the pillow.

'Now give me that child and get out of here,' said Kirk.

It came to Eddy then what he must do. 'I'll make a deal with you,' he said.

Kirk frowned. 'What sort of deal?'

'Divorce Susan and relinquish all claims on Rachel and I'll sell you Black Lion.'

Kirk's eyes narrowed. 'You mean that?'

'I've never been more serious in my life.'

Susan looked up from her pillow, her expression one of incredulity. She couldn't believe that Kirk was even considering the offer.

Kirk was ice-cold inside. After all these years and a number of aborted attempts, Black Lion could be his for the taking. At long last. At long bloody last!

'We could have lawyers start to draw up the papers today,' Eddy went on, 'Black Lion becoming officially yours the day Susan is free and your hold over Rachel relinquished.'

'Kirk?' said Susan.

Kirk took a deep breath and then another. With Black Lion finally under his control it would only be a short time before he'd come to realise his dream and have a Glasgow monopoly. And after that major hurdle, surely nothing would be able to stop him extending his empire to include all Scotland.

And what was Susan to him after all? Not very much, if he was truthful. There were plenty more fish in the sea. And as for the brat? The sooner he saw the back of her the better.

'Kirk?' Susan said again.

He disregarded her. '*Give* me Black Lion and it's a deal,' he said.

'You mean for nothing?'

'Exactly.'

Eddy looked at Susan and then down at Rachel gurgling away, blissfully unaware of the drama going on around her.

'And that includes the pubs you used to own before you bought the brewery,' added Kirk.

'Eddy, you can't,' said Susan.

Kirk retorted quickly, 'If he doesn't I'll make sure you never get a divorce. I'll have my lawyers tie any attempt you make for one in so many knots, it'll take a lifetime to unravel. And in the meantime Rachel will be my daughter, subject to my wishes, under my jurisdiction.'

'You've got yourself a deal,' said Eddy. 'Providing it takes place from now. By that I mean you don't see Susan or the baby again.'

'And Black Lion?'

'Officially yours the day the divorce is absolute. I'll appoint you manager in the meantime.' Then Eddy went on to name a few more provisos to guard himself against a double-cross.

Somewhere during the last few minutes all the love Susan had felt for Kirk had melted like so much snow in a hot desert sun. She felt nothing for him now, except perhaps to despise him. How could she ever have loved a man like that? And yet despite all the pain and heartbreak he'd caused her in the past, she had done up until a few minutes previously. Somehow in her muddled, love-starved mind, she'd mistaken sex for love.

A mistake she saw, with hindsight, quite clearly now. What a gullible fool she'd been! But ever since her days at Miss Buchan's School For Young Ladies her need for love had been a desperate one.

She knew then Kirk had been using her all along. Why he'd married her, when it had been made quite clear to him he wouldn't get the brewery because of it, she didn't know. But he hadn't loved her, nor had he ever. Of that she was certain.

Eddy and Kirk had stopped talking, their arrangements complete.

Eddy, still holding Rachel tightly to him, gestured with his head towards the door. 'Now *you* get out of here,' he said.

Kirk flushed at being spoken to like that. He was about to make an angry retort when Susan said softly, 'If you don't go right now I'll change my statement to the police.'

Kirk's flush deepened. 'I'll expect your lawyer to be in touch with mine this afternoon,' he said to Eddy.

He then left the room without saying another word or looking back.

When he was gone Susan mutely held out her arms for her baby.

'You're well rid of him,' Eddy said, handing Rachel over.

Susan wept copiously.

McIlwham was humming to himself as he turned away from the urinal, his fingers fumbling with the buttons of his flies. His fingers froze when he saw the man confronting him.

'Hello Superintendent' said 'Baa Baa' Lamb.

McIlwham's frightened gaze dropped to the home-made knife 'Baa Baa' was holding pointed at him. The knife was a sharpened nail set in a piece of bamboo, lashed into place by mail-bag twine.

'Ten years you got me for a fit-up. You knew bloody well I never did yon burglary. Somebody planted evidence and that somebody was you,' hissed 'Baa Baa'.

McIlwham backed away as 'Baa Baa' advanced. 'You've got it all wrong,' he said.

'Like hell I have.'

'If there was a fit-up I had nothing to do with it.'

'Pull the other one, Superintendent. You were in charge of the case. It couldn't have been anyone else but you.'

'Baa Baa' was a small rat-faced man with bandy legs, the latter a legacy of childhood rickets. He had a name as a ferocious fighting man. The type who only stopped when they'd either won or were dead.

McIlwham decided on a change of tactics. 'If you weren't guilty of that job then you were of a dozen others. Caley Motors and Yoker Leather, to name but two. They screamed your handiwork.'

'But you couldn't prove anything otherwise you would have nicked me for them.'

'You were guilty as sin.'

'Aye, but you couldn't prove it so you fitted me up. You, Superintendent. You.'

McIlwham knew that if he didn't do something now he'd be a dead man within the minute. 'Baa Baa' couldn't allow this conversation to go on too long in case someone else came into the toilet.

'I couldn't believe my luck when I saw you in the cell block,' 'Baa Baa' went on. 'And talking about luck, yours just ran out, pal.'

'Baa Baa' tensed himself for a lunge. As he did so McIlwham threw himself at him, one hand going round 'Baa Baa's' neck, the other grabbing hold of the fist which grasped the knife.

'You would, would you!' 'Baa Baa' exclaimed as they struggled.

Fear lent McIlwham strength he didn't normally have. The hand clamped round the knife fist was a vice of iron.

'Help!' McIlwham shouted. 'Help!'

'Baa Baa's' foot snaked round McIlwham's leg. 'Baa Baa' pushed and then pulled, knocking McIlwham off balance. They both went tumbling to the toilet floor where they rolled over and over.

McIlwham screeched like a banshee. 'Help! Help!'

Suddenly he was on his back with the point of the knife edging towards his left eye. Sobbing, he exerted every ounce of his strength to push it away.

'Baa Baa's' rancid breath washed over McIlwham's face as the point of the makeshift knife inched closer to his eye. Even his superhuman strength lent him by fear wasn't enough to match that of 'Baa Baa', who was a man possessed.

McIlwham screeched again, a long drawn-out yodelling sound that sawed the eardrums. He was convinced a hideous death was only seconds away.

And then suddenly it was all over. Warders appeared as though out of the woodwork to disarm 'Baa Baa' and haul him off the prostrate McIlwham.

'Baa Baa' lashed out to send one of the warders hurtling back against a washstand. Retribution was instantaneous. Fist and boot went in, time after time. 'Baa Baa' writhed and choked but wouldn't give in. Snarling, he was hauled from the toilet face down and at waist level, a warder on each leg and arm.

'If I don't get you someone else will!' he shouted as he disappeared through the doorway. 'You can count on that!'

'You all right?' a warder asked McIlwham.

'Shaken, that's all.'

'Then get back to work.'

Trembling all over like a leaf in an autumn wind McIlwham returned to his mail-bags. Nor was he unaware that every eye he passed was on him.

Right on the dot the door clanged shut for the night. More than ever, McIlwham felt like a man who's just been buried alive.

There were three of them in the cell, one and three being the customary numbers – this an attempt to prevent homosexual pairing off.

'Well, well, well,' said Cooper. 'Imagine our friend McIlwham here turning out to be a bluebottle. You could have nocked me over with a feather when I heard that.'

'Aren't you the sly one?' added McNaughton, the third member. 'You sure kept quiet about that.'

McIlwham lay on his bunk, staring at the bottom of the bunk above him. He was still very much shaken from the accident in the toilet.

'I wondered when you never said what you were in for,' smiled Cooper. 'Now we know why.'

'What was it then?' asked McNaughton.

'Still not telling?' smirked Cooper.

McIlwham pulled out his makings and rolled himself a rout. The tobacco helped to calm him a little.

'Come on McIlwham you can tell us,' urged McNaughton.

McIlwham didn't reply. He wasn't afraid of these two. Neither of them were the physical type. Who he was afraid of were the others in the prison whom he'd either sent down himself or else helped send down. At a conservative estimate here must be at least a dozen in the various cell blocks, a number of whom, like 'Baa Baa' had been fit-ups.

Without warning the cell lights went out, plunging the small, curved-ceilinged cell into darkness. The only thing relieving the Stygian gloom was the cheery glow from McIlwham's cigarette.

'A bloody bluebottle!' said Cooper and laughed.

The previous night they had been a threesome in the cell. Now they were two and McIlwham, a fact McIlwham was only too painfully aware of.

At least a dozen other bastards out there, he thought. How many of them might take it into their heads to try for revenge Baa Baa' had done? Fear encompassed him like an ice-cold blanket. If he behaved himself, as he had every intention of doing, he would get full remission for good behaviour, which would mean he'd be out in three and a half years. But would he be alive then? That was the big question. He'd just never considered this turn of events. And how stupid of him not to have foreseen it would happen.

For the rest of the night he gazed into the darkness,

rethinking his position. When morning came he'd worked ou
what he'd do to try and protect himself.

When the door was unlocked, he was the first out headin
for the sinks. En route he fell into step alongside one of th
warders. 'I want an interview with the Assistant Governor i
charge of the wing,' he whispered.

The screw's eyes flicked sideways and he gave the slightes
of nods.

McIlwham strode ahead to turn off to where the sinks wer
situated. As he washed he felt incredibly vulnerable. Ever
few seconds his back rippled with gooseflesh.

Later, when breakfast came he couldn't eat it. He would'v
thrown up if he'd tried.

Eddy parked the car and then leapt out to help Susan who wa
holding Rachel. When she was safely on the pavement he too
her case out of the boot.

The area around Susan's eyes was still discoloured but th
swelling had gone. Her stitches had been taken out, leaving a
angry red line on her cheek and another small one on her lip
The doctor had assured her she wouldn't retain a scar in eithe
case.

The street was filthy, tin cans, garbage and other debr
littered everywhere. Several women were hanging out c
windows talking and calling to one another. The air was s
thick with chimney smoke you could taste it on your tongu

Eddy smiled reassuringly as they made for the close. Goin
up the stairs he said, 'We can move later on when I've g
myself sorted out. I'll find somewhere nice, I promise you

Susan thought of her mother, whom she was convince
wouldn't be long behind her father. When Jean went th
house would be hers. She'd mention it to Eddy later and se
what he thought.

Neighbours had washed down the stairs which smelle
strongly of disinfectant. Eddy had told them he was bringir
his future wife home. Sometime during the following wee
most of them would call by to be introduced and say hello

Once inside the house Susan put Rachel to bed in the cot ddy had bought. While she was doing this Eddy put the ettle on. He was making the tea when she came through to and by his side. Through the kitchen window she could see ore wee boys playing 'guns' on top of the brick and concrete ir-raid shelters. The guns consisted mainly of walking sticks nd carved pieces of wood.

'Any regrets?' he asked, handing her a cup.

'No, nor will I have.'

Eddy stared up at the bleak sky. En route from the hospital he'd asked him if he'd decided yet what he was going to do nd he'd replied that he'd go back into selling used cars. After ll, that and pubs – he included running Black Lion in the tter – were the only things he knew.

'I love you and the baby,' he said awkwardly.

'I know. I'm only sorry you had to give up everything to get s.'

Eddy smiled. 'You and Rachel are worth a hundred Black ion's. Kirk was the one who lost out on our deal. Not me.'

Susan's eyes brimmed over with tears when he said that.

'Welcome home,' he said, kissing her on the top of her nose.

She laid down her cup and came into his arms. Neither had ver felt so much at peace as they did at that moment.

The rightness of their being together was indisputable. hey were a couple.

was Kirk's first morning as manager of Black Lion Brewery. ntil such time as the divorce came through and Black Lion ecame officially his, he'd be splitting his working day etween it and KM. When it was his, as Keith Gibb had recast, he intended ending production of Black Lion beers nd turning its brewery into a subsidiary of KM.

At the moment his lawyers were working full out to push the ivorce through, but the Scottish divorce laws being what they ere it was going to take a little while for that to happen. A year inimum, possibly even two.

In the meantime with Black Lion now under his control he

could turn his full attention to those other breweries stil[l] surviving. Well, survive they might have done but not fo[r] long. He would see to that. And when they were gone, th[e] Glasgow monopoly he'd dreamed about for so long would b[e] his.

Smiling, he leaned back in his chair and put his feet up o[n] what had been Eddy's desk.

Nothing could stop him now.

Nothing.

McIlwham sat in the interview room drumming his fingers o[n] the wooden table in front of him. He was waiting for Chie[f] Superintendent Cairney, the Officer In Charge of his case.

The warder standing in front of the door opened it whe[n] there was a knock. Cairney entered.

'Well?' asked McIlwham eagerly, the moment Cairney ha[d] sat down.

Before replying, Cairney pushed a packet of cigarettes and [a] box of matches across to McIlwham, who muttered his thank[s]. Tobacco was like gold inside. He lit up, savouring the luxur[y] of a tailor-made.

'I've spoken with the Deputy Chief Constable and he take[s] your point about there not being a prison in Scotland in whic[h] you'd be safe. He's therefore authorised me to do a deal wit[h] you providing you come totally clean, names, dates, the fu[ll] thing, about everything you were up to and connected wit[h] before being sent down.'

'Reduction in sentence?' McIlwham asked.

Cairney shook his head. 'That's out. But you will b[e] transferred to an English open prison where no one will kno[w] you and where life should be an awful lot easier than in here[.]'

Relief surged through McIlwham. He was going to com[e] out alive, after all.

'When does the transfer take place?' he asked.

'As soon as you've given us everything you know. An[d] McIlwham . . . it had better be good.'

McIlwham thought of his wife and the money she w[as]

506

receiving every week. It was going to be tough on her when that stopped. But it would be tougher on him unless he got that transfer.

'I'm ready when you are,' he said.

Cairney nodded to the warder who left the room, returning less than a minute later with a stenographer. McIlwham puffed on his cigarette while sorting out his thoughts. He started to speak when he saw the stenographer was ready.

'I'll begin with a man named Kirk Murray who owns KM Brewery...'

And as the minutes rolled by, McIlwham spoke at length and in detail about Turk McGhie, Danny Porteous, the burning of the Black Lion pub, the burning of the Black Lion Brewery, intimidation, bribery... The list went on and on.